ABOUT THE AUTHOR

Chris Rose is an ecologist who founded the London Wildlife Trust and the British Association of Nature Conservationists. He has researched and conducted campaigns for WWF International, Friends of the Earth and Greenpeace, and is now Director of Media Natura, Britain's green media charity.

His previous books include *Crisis or Conservation* (Penguin 1984) with Charlie Pye-Smith and, most recently, *Acid Rain: It's Happening Here* (Greenpeace 1988).

THE DIRTY MAN OF EUROPE

CHRIS ROSE

The Dirty Man of Europe

The Great British
Pollution Scandal

SIMON & SCHUSTER

LONDON · SYDNEY · NEW YORK · TOKYO · SINGAPORE · TORONTO

First published in Great Britain by
Simon & Schuster Ltd in 1990

First published in paperback by
Simon & Schuster Ltd in 1991
A Paramount Communications Company

Simon & Schuster Ltd
West Garden Place
Kendal Street
London W2 2AQ

Simon & Schuster of Australia Pty Ltd
Sydney

A CIP catalogue record for this book is
available from the British Library
ISBN 0–671–71074–5

Typeset by Learning Curve of Watford
Printed and bound in Great Britain by
Richard Clay Ltd Bungay, Suffolk

Contents

For Sharron Rose

AUTHOR'S ACKNOWLEDGEMENTS

In 1980, as a research student at London University, I was trying to study competition between plants, by watching lichens. Unlike the more difficult plants such as grasses or primroses, lichens were flat, and, I wrongly thought, they did not change much, so making ideal subjects on which to test some theories. To my puzzlement, and the surprise of lichen experts, I found the plots near London were being populated with a confusing richness of lichens supposed to have been long-since banished to remoter regions by air pollution. This was due to the decline in one pollutant (sulphur dioxide) but it soon turned out that other closely allied pollutants – acid rain – were limiting the scope of the recovery.

Some years after that brief brush with pollution science, I went to work at Friends of the Earth to campaign for protection of countryside habitats but at Des Wilson's behest, quickly became embroiled in campaigns on pesticides and acid rain. Since then, I have never quite escaped the pollution issues, which now also occupy the time of our politicians, and are the focus of attention for much of the press.

I am not a 'pollution expert', indeed I'm not sure there are any 'pollution experts', only people who live and work with the science and the issues one at a time, building up such a store of arcane knowledge that we call them experts. My job has usually been on behalf of one environmental group or another, to try and disentangle genuine uncertainty from the fact-filled smoke-screens that are often laid down by government or industry to justify delay. My job has often been to try and help put the case for cleaning up the environment to help people and nature.

Despite the long term outlook which tends to range from the apocalyptic to the squalid, the day-to-day ins and outs of particular pollution issues are frequently very tedious. Yet it is in the handling of what seem to be the minutiae that political sleight of hand so often occurs. This should make us all grateful to the few 'experts' among the press, on Parliamentary Select Committees, in lobby groups working in the public interest, and places such as colleges and universities, who spend the long hours needed to comb through annexes of official reports, or follow up obscure tit-bits of information, in order to track down or unmask pollution problems. It is to these people who have made available the mass of advice and information I have used in writing this book, or whose work I have simply drawn on directly, that I owe a great debt. As to omissions or the errors that may have crept into it, I take responsibility for those.

I make no apology for the fact that it is written from the viewpoint of the public outside looking in, and has relied mainly on the work of groups such as the World Wide Fund for Nature, Greenpeace and Friends of the Earth, as well as Parliamentary inquiries and inter-governmental reports. The UK government is one of the most secretive in the democratic world, and it is habitually reluctant to give out any information other than its publicity leaflets or that which can, with determination, be purchased from HMSO. As to putting its own case, the government has an abundance of 'usual channels' through which its views are made to appear, often unattributed and unquestioned, in the press. It also spends £200m a year on publicity services such as advertising campaigns. This excludes the cost of the 600 or so government press officers, their press releases and so on.

In the year or so I have spent writing this book, my own view of Britain has usually included a twice-daily walk past Cardboard City near Waterloo Station, where litter and discarded packaging serve as bedding and housing for part of our growing wave of homeless people. Above Cardboard City, each morning, some commuters crawl across Waterloo Bridge in a queue of BMWs, while others sit in buses which are overtaken by pedestrians braving the traffic fumes. Below them, the Thames may contain a few salmon stocked by the water authority but it also carries more sewage pollution than it should, along with organo–chlorine pesticides, heavy metals and radioactivity. An extreme case of Britain in a mess? If it is, then it's an extreme example of government failing to clean up its own backyard.

As I write this, the government has announced a plan to remove the homeless to somewhere less visible but not to build them homes or to tackle the root causes of their plight. It bodes ill for the Prime Minister's televised 1989 declaration that by 1995 'we shall have got rid of' most of Britain's pollution problems.

*   *   *

I would specially like to acknowledge the help of the following people, and organisations: Gwynne Lyons, Andrew Lees, Simon Roberts and Friends of the Earth; Stewart Boyle and the Association for the Conservation of Energy; Steve Elsworth, Tracy Heslop, Tim Birch, Paul Horsman, Sue Adams, Peter Melchett, Andy Tilrite and Greenpeace; Christer Agren and the Swedish NGO Secretariat on Acid Rain; Bill Hamilton (whose idea it was), Susanne McDadd, Guy Pearson, Nicholas Brealey, Liz Paton, David Kinnersely, David Withrington, Peter Sand, Fred Pearce, Roger Milne; Stephen Joseph and Transport 2000; Keep Britain Tidy; Tessa Robertson and the World Wide Fund for Nature; Claire Holman and Earth Resources Research; Nigel Haigh, David Baldock, Jonathon Hewitt and the Institute for European Environmental Policy; the House of Commons Select Committee on the Environment; Thames Water Authority; the Paris Commission; Elsie Rose, Pauline Smith, Chris and Maggie Bligh, Una O'Donoghue, Mandy Duncan-Smith, Simon Bryceson, Rhonda Gregory, Charlotte Lester and the press office at the Ministry of Agriculture, Fisheries and Food.

INTRODUCTION

On 23 October 1989, Paul Brown of the *Guardian* newspaper reported that the inhabitants of the Yorkshire village of Drax were suffering from a strange new form of pollution.[1] Sewage bacteria were raining down on their homes in a fine dust. A community medicine expert from York warned that the silt might contaminate food. The immediate source of the pollution was steam from the giant cooling towers of the Central Electricity Generating Board's Drax power station, which took water from the River Ouse. The power station had fallen victim to one of Britain's sewage-laden rivers. Untreated sewage was being poured into the river upstream, with more swilling up from the Trent on the tide.

Neither fairytale nor joke, the airborne sewage of Drax was Britain[*], the 'Dirty Man of Europe' in miniature. Throughout the 1980s, rivers across the whole country had deteriorated as standards were allowed to slip. At Drax the Ouse is classed as 'biologically dead'.

For a long time few people had noticed what was going on, because the government systematically fiddled the pollution rule books by changing the 'consent conditions' for sewage works. As a result, a works might double or treble the amount of urine and faeces it pushed into a river, while still 'meeting its legal target'. This did not happen once, but was deliberately organised by the 'Department of the Environment', again and again. Only privatisation was to bring the full scale of the decay to light.

Drax power station is notorious for more than flying sewage spores, however. It produces 10 per cent of Britain's electricity and it burns coal. Drax epitomises what is known as the 'tall stack policy'. It has a very tall chimney – which wafts fumes beyond the immediate environment, usually out to sea towards Scandinavia. The Swedes and the Norwegians know about Drax because it produces more sulphur dioxide, the principal component of acid rain, than both of their countries together.[2] In the acidified areas of southern Norway, Britain is the largest single source of sulphur pollution.

Of course this is not just due to Drax. The UK boasts a whole network of giant power stations with 'tall stacks'. They were built to rid Britain of smog, but in so doing they created exports of acid rain. And unlike the power stations in countries such as Sweden, Norway or Germany, Britain's are prodigious sulphur producers. The land along the Trent has so many that it is known to pollution analysts as 'sulphur valley'. Throughout most of the 1970s and 1980s Britain fought off international pressure to fit pollution flue gas desulphurisa-

---

* Note: throughout 'Britain' and the 'UK' are used interchangeably, although legally 'Britain' excludes some parts of the UK such as Northern Ireland.

tion (FGD) equipment to its power stations, and even now, when a handful are to be fitted with the equipment, the UK will remain the largest sulphur polluter and exporter in Western Europe beyond 2000.

Power stations such as Drax also produce large amounts of NOx (oxides of nitrogen), another source of acid rain. Britain has a track record of obstructing controls over these too. As with sulphur, for large sources such as power stations the UK will remain the biggest NOx polluter in Western Europe well into the next century.

Pollution scrubbers will do nothing to reduce the carbon dioxide produced from the coal burned in power stations. This is another British contribution to the international atmosphere: with just 1 per cent of the world population, the UK produces 3 per cent of the world's carbon dioxide from fossil fuels. The CEGB[3] alone manages 1 per cent. The power station managers may hope that they will encounter fewer droughts in future (drought concentrated the sewage in the water), but if, as some predict, Britain becomes warmer and drier in a greenhouse climate, low water levels may become the norm. Carbon dioxide is of course a greenhouse gas, warming the earth's atmosphere. In 1990, two years into the debate over curbing such gases, Britain already opposed countries such as West Germany, the Netherlands, the Scandinavian states and Austria, which all wanted commitments to reductions, and sided more with the USA and Japan, two major polluters.

Of course, Britain would need fewer power stations if it did not waste so much energy. Power stations such as Drax simply evaporate much of it as steam (and, in this case, sewage), leading some to re-christen the CEGB the 'Central Atmospheric Heating Board'. After Margaret Thatcher's Road-to-Damascus conversion to the rhetoric of the greenhouse effect in 1988, Britain rang with cries from government ministers for more energy efficiency and electricity conservation. Yet talk was not matched with action. Indeed, in 1988 and 1989 ministers cut budgets for insulation schemes and the Energy Efficiency Office, and the government threw out a Lords amendment to the Electricity Bill which would have promoted conservation. At the time of writing, Britain is trying to back out of a commitment to fit a number of power stations with FGD equipment.

Before leaving Drax it is worth considering why so much pollution is allowed into the Ouse and the Trent at this point, even if the sewage works all operated correctly. The explanation is probably that the river is tidal, and shortly becomes the Humber Estuary. For many years Britain put almost no controls over what could be put into coastal waters. Indeed, Britain is still the only country actively pursuing a large-scale policy of pumping raw sewage into the North and Irish Seas, and dumping sewage sludge contaminated with industrial chemicals. It plans to continue, despite international protests, until 1998.

This policy of using the environment as a treatment works is known as 'dilute and disperse'. Almost every other developed country now seems to regard it as a nineteenth century anachronism which should be abandoned. Many instead employ principles such as best available technology (to control pollution), the precautionary principle (under which West Germany stopped all

North Sea dumping while Britain continued), and the polluter pays principle (under which the USA has imposed the multi-billion dollar Superfund and the Dutch impose swingeing pollution taxes, while British officials have repeatedly failed to prosecute and fine industry for breaking pollution laws).

Dilute and disperse means out of sight, out of mind. In general, we pollute, others receive. It is part of the story behind Britain's grimy reputation as 'Dirty Man of Europe'. Both acid rain from our power stations (and cars and factories), and sewage nutrients flushed into rivers such as the Thames tend to end up on the other side of the North Sea.

But dilute and disperse, much criticised by the House of Commons Environment Committee, has also been allowed to create massive problems within the UK. As with the sewage rain of Drax, pollutants let loose in the environment do not always behave as they are assumed to. From the 1950s onwards for example, British officials decided to pump staggering quantities of radiation into the Irish Sea at Sellafield (then called Windscale). By the mid 1980s the government changed its mind (emissions peaked in the mid 1970s), not least because long-lived radiation was turning up on the beaches, in fields and in seafood, and not 'dispersing harmlessly' as it was supposed to. But by then it was too late. Some of the plutonium now found along the Cumbrian coast and in the Irish Sea, will end up as neptunium, with a half-life of over 2 million years.

Even Britain's rubbish collection has relied on dilute and disperse. While throughout the 1970s and 1980s other developed countries opted for separation of toxic and less toxic waste, and put effort into recycling, re-use or waste minimisation, Britain simply threw 90 per cent of its waste away in holes known as 'landfill'. These holes are now viewed by toxic waste experts from other countries as 'an unexploded timebomb'. This is not least because Britain deliberately mixed domestic waste such as litter with hazardous products such as pesticides.

The European Community takes a different approach from the UK. It sets specific standards for emissions of pollutants and their concentration in the environment. From entering the Community in 1973 to the end of the 1980s, Britain was in increasingly frequent conflict with the European Commission and its European partners over the environment. At the time of writing, for example, Britain faces the possibility of legal action in the European Court over the contamination of groundwater by pesticides and of drinking water by nitrates.

Without pressure from Europe, it is difficult to see how Britain would have made any environmental progress (possibly with the exception of curbing radioactive emissions) in the 1980s. Britain had the legal and administrative machinery to require FGD on power stations but, before an EC Directive was drafted, showed no signs of using it; even small pilot schemes in the 1950s were shut down. Left to its own devices, Britain would probably still be setting standards for fumes from diesel engines by running lorries past people sitting in deckchairs (the EC will instead require specific, measurable emission limits). Without an EC Directive, it seems equally certain that Britain would not have adopted catalytic converters for cars (it argued against them until the very last minute).

Many of the standards set by the European Community have long been adopted in the UK (for example, limits on nitrates in water based on World Health Organisation limits): the difference is that the EC means business about enforcement. The British civil service was dismayed, for example, to discover that the Commission regarded a Maximum Admissible Concentration as a maximum not to be breached, and not a vague piece of gentlemanly guidance.

It is the vagueness of Britain's traditional approach to pollution control – sprinkled with concepts such as the Victorian principle of 'best practicable means', only now replaced by the equally antediluvian 'best available technique not entailing excessive cost' – which has proved a recipe for fudge and smudge, a quagmire of intellectual fuzziness and a licence for administrative laxity, which has allowed the progressive deterioration of the UK environment. Forests are dying, lakes have become acidified, city streets are filled with fumes, rivers are loaded with nitrogen and groundwater is polluted with pesticides, but few alarms are ringing and even less action is being taken.

Armed with policy instruments suitable for the Victorian era of choking, dust–ridden air within industrial towns, and rivers so grossly polluted that people ran from the banks, Britain triumphed over the London smogs and cleaned up the Thames, though not until the 1960s. Then in the 1970s and 1980s, the United States and Europe developed new policies and methods to match a whole new range of more insidious and more complex environmental problems. Britain, however, sank into the deep sleep of the just, or at least the self-satisfied.

When 1980s industrial recession and 'restructuring' caused some of Britain's most antique pollutants such as sulphur dioxide, to decline, the UK attracted quizzical international interest by claiming this as a tremendous step forward. Interest turned to irritation and anger as Britain began systematically blocking international cooperation to cut pollution.

At home, nothing was done about steadily increasing problems such as contamination of groundwater by nitrate. Nor was Britain planning for the future. While other countries were re-equipping and extending their public transport infrastructure, London traffic, its density encouraged by generous subsidies to company car drivers, choked back to the speeds of the First World War. British Rail trains achieved operating profits but later became dirtier, shorter, less frequent and more uncomfortable.

While California began 'forcing' the development of technology such as catalytic converters by setting future air pollution standards that existing technology could not meet, the UK set standards (such as for sewage on beaches and radiation in the sea) that 'could be achieved'. While Swedes and Norwegians searched for evidence of critical loads (the levels of acid deposition which cause long term changes to ecosystems), official British research was mainly concerned with demonstrating that its acidifying pollution dispersed with no discernible effect. The Germans and Dutch pressed for precautionary action to cut North Sea pollution on indicative evidence of ecosystem change. Britain instead demanded cause-and-effect proof of the type more appropriate for a school physics experiment.

Tourists visiting Britain in the 1980s were struck by a welter of pollutants. In London they noted with puzzlement the layers of litter and the taxi fumes. On a trip to Shakespeare's birthplace they might have found unleaded petrol almost unavailable, the fields ablaze with strawburning, and the Avon, swan-free (courtesy of lead fishing weights) and polluted with sewage and farm waste.

As the 1980s progressed, the British public became more and more alarmed at the state of the environment. The British government, however, showed no particular interest, and grew increasingly isolated from its European partners.

The discovery of the ozone hole in 1985 led to rapidly escalating international concern. Still the UK government saw no reason to examine its own policies. Following the ICI line, Britain actually lobbied against swift measures to reduce the chemicals that caused the depletion.

Finally, with HRH The Prince of Wales and HM The Queen making critical noises, seals dying prophetically in the North Sea, the press clamouring for action, and with other governments gripped by alarm at the news that the greenhouse effect had arrived, Margaret Thatcher, the Prime Minister, declared herself a 'Friend of the Earth' in September 1988.

Her about-turn came too late to salvage Britain's reputation abroad but it galvanised environmental politics at home. The environment, which had rested quietly under a heap of other priorities for a decade, was suddenly pulled out into the political limelight. Emerging from its sleeping quarters like a green Rip van Winkle, Her Majesty's Government now set about trying to convince the world that Britain was no longer 'The Dirty Man of Europe', with a cascade of policy initiatives, photo calls, conferences and seizing of other people's initiatives.

Richard North, environment correspondent of the *Independent*, wrote in March 1989: 'Britain's environment has been in safe hands for the past decade: that will be Nicholas Ridley's message this morning when he launches a series of pamphlets celebrating the government's green record.[4] Mr Ridley's speech is a determined attempt by the government to shrug off Britain's international reputation as the "dirty man of Europe" . . . . The Secretary of State for the Environment will be speaking at the Queen Elizabeth II conference centre where in November 1987 he astonished his continental colleagues by claiming that he had pulled off a coup by getting them to agree pollution control standards for the North Sea. Those colleagues thought *they* had changed *his* mind.'

Britain's Prime Minister hosted an international conference on saving the ozone layer. 'Politicians have a habit of jumping onto moving trains, then claiming to be driving them,' noted the magazine *New Scientist*.[5] 'Margaret Thatcher announced that she was leading the call to strengthen the ozone treaty. In reality, she was falling into line with international opinion. Scientists knew stronger measures were needed before the treaty was signed. It was Britain that had originally prevented them.'

Joe Farman, 'discoverer' of the ozone hole, was a member of the British Antarctic Survey. This enabled the Prime Minister to adopt ozone hole science as a patriotic venture, almost a British invention (appropriately, as ICI was one of the world's leading CFC manufacturers). Margaret Thatcher the scientist now came to the fore, displaying remarkable foresight in overriding her science advisers over funding for Antarctic research in 1982. 'I clashed quite vigorously with them,' she remembered in 1989. 'They didn't want to spend very much on Antarctica. Well, I've always been interested in Antarctica, I did actually over-ride them and say that the British Antarctic Survey must have more money and it was they who discovered the depletion of the ozone layer.'[6]

But as Roger Highfield, technology correspondent of the *Daily Telegraph*, had pointed out, when in 1988 the government had announced £23 million for the Survey, most of it was for facilities such as a landing strip and a base, while only £500,000 was destined for ozone research - 'far short of the £3 million which Mr Farman believes is needed.' [7]

Mrs Thatcher reinforced her message at the 1989 Conservative Party Conference, declaring that 'It is we Conservatives who are the true friends of the earth'. The real Friends of the Earth (FoE), however, had come to other conclusions. Jonathon Porritt and Charles Secrett of FoE detailed 55 specific environmental misdemeanours by the government, ranging from trying to weaken EC regulations on air pollution to taking nearly seven years to reply to a House of Lords report on hazardous waste. [8]

The growing debate over international action on the greenhouse effect provided Britain with another opportunity to claim leadership on an issue about which it had done little or nothing of any practical use. 'Britain takes lead in war on greenhouse effect', said a particularly obliging headline in *The Times* in May 1989. 'World greenhouse effect treaty already drafted', said another a few days later, as Britain's UN Ambassador, Sir Crispin Tickell (for once a genuine expert on the subject), put forward proposals for a global climate convention. It was in the usual mould of 'an umbrella' making general commitments supported by specific undertakings in protocols to be added later. It was not a British invention. Drafting a treaty is easy: getting political commitment to one that demands action is the difficult part, and here Britain would not even commit itself.

At an international meeting on reducing carbon dioxide emissions at Noordwijk, in the Netherlands in autumn 1989, *The Times* duly reported, 'UK plays key role in securing accord on "greenhouse" gas'. The British delegation made considerable play of their role in 'mediating' between Japan, the USSR and the USA which wanted to do little, and the Netherlands and France, which wanted a firm commitment to stabilise carbon dioxide emissions at 1989 levels, as of the year 2000. The UK declined to make the commitment.

This sort of posturing, however elegantly presented, cuts little ice with either Britain's neighbours or the environmental organisations. Environment Minister Chris Patten told environmental groups in November 1989 that he would rid Britain of its 'dirty man' stigma 'by playing a very active role on the key issues . . . at national, European and global levels'.[9]

The trouble is, Britain had for a long time played a 'very active role', but it has not been a very constructive one. Nor, when it has come to the crunch, has the UK delivered results or leadership by example.

Britain could rid itself of the 'Dirty Man of Europe' reputation by pulling itself up to the standards of the best countries in practices such as waste management, recycling, air and water pollution control, least-cost energy planning, use of renewables, integrated transport planning and waste minimisation. All these can be achieved without any technical or political revolutions. Britain must also show that it believes in environmental quality, which requires a change of attitude.

In the long term it is undeniable that society needs to put itself on an entirely new 'post-industrial' footing, but whether that is an evolution from the old model, through a combination of consensus planning and market forces, or whether it happens by electing people who offer a particular 'green' vision of the future, has little bearing on the central issue of this book. For what it is worth, of the five 'campaign issues' used by the British Green Party in its 'breakthrough' in the 1989 European elections, three were simple pollution issues. The Green Party has yet to excite anything more than a little criticism for other spiritual, social or economic ideas.

Similarly, readers looking to this book for a manifesto for nature, or a recipe for restructuring society with green consumerism, ecologically sound building societies or ethical trusts, will be disappointed. The responsibilities discussed here are primarily those of governments, and of individuals and companies in relation to government, for it is in this sphere that the 'Dirty Man of Europe' got its name.

To get Britain going on the road to a cleaner, greener future, the dirty old man of Europe will have to give up some ingrained habits. For one thing, it must give up looking for motes in the eyes of others. One of the first official responses to criticisms such as those in this book, is to quote places where pollution is much worse. Almost the whole of industrial Eastern Europe, for example, has air pollution on a scale that would make a Victorian cough. Photochemical smog is now a major problem in many industrialising tropical countries. Italy's Po Valley has pesticide contamination of its groundwater worse than anything found in Britain. New York has a waste problem so large that a 'landfill' site cannot go much higher for fear of threatening the flightpath to Newark Airport. The USA may shortly blow new holes in the ozone layer with the exhaust from more shuttle flights and high-flying supersonic aircraft. France has a chain of Pressurised Water Reactors with serious flaws (six of which threaten Britain) and 16 more reactors being built or on order.

So what? These problems all demand solutions, but Britain is in no way providing them. Any implication that resources used on Britain's problems will somehow detract from solving those of Eastern Europe or the Third World is not simply disingenuous but a lie. And protests from civil servants, industrialists or politicians that environmental groups should concentrate their attentions elsewhere are no more than the squeaks of those finally cornered.

Britain deserves to be compared not with the superpowers or with the developing world but with the countries of Western Europe, which it aspires to treat as its equals. The record is not good. There is a gulf between Britain's claims and the reality of its performance.

This book is not an attack on politicians in general or on Margaret Thatcher in particular. It just so happens that she has presided over a decade or more of ecological misrule in which Britain has acquired the name 'Dirty Man of

Europe'. Politicians cannot be blamed for creating pollution: they do not, after all, come to power with that in mind. But politicians must take the blame for not stopping or reducing pollution, when they, and only they, can provide the wherewithal to solve it.

Part I

INTRODUCTION

Water: Pollution in Our Seas, Rivers, Wells and Taps

'The sea,' said atomic scientist John Dunster in 1958, 'has always been regarded by coastal and seafaring people as the ideal place for dumping their waste and this is, of course, a very reasonable and proper attitude.' In the decades that followed, Dunster helped put his philosophy into practice at Windscale, discharging radiation into the Irish Sea. 'Almost everything put into the sea is either diluted . . . or broken down,' noted Dunster, 'or stored harmlessly on the seabed . . . Not the least of the attractions of the sea as a dumping ground has been the lack of administrative controls.'[1]

In the mid 1980s, radioactive house dust, leukaemia and contaminated divers finally caught up with Windscale, by then re-named Sellafield in the interests of public relations. Discharges were drastically reduced. In 1989 Sellafield won the Institute of Public Relation's 'Sword of Excellence' award for 'Restoring Confidence in Sellafield'. Fittingly, the newly constructed visitor complex at Sellafield also won the coveted 'Best Loo in the Country Award'.[2]

Fitting, because Britain's sewage authorities had long followed the same policy as Dunster and flushed faeces and urine into the sea. Indeed, throughout the 1980s Britain defended both large scale pumping of sewage into the sea and sludge dumping, which had been all but abandoned in other countries, on exactly the principle that it was diluted and 'broken down harmlessly'. This is a cornerstone of British pollution policy. It is called 'dilute and disperse'. It is not pollution treatment or prevention; it deals with pollutants by spreading them about.

In 1959, following anxiety over cases of poliomyelitis, an official British committee declared that sewage on bathing beaches was not a hazard, unless it was 'aesthetically revolting'. For 30 years, despite continuing reports of sick swimmers, paralysed children and food poisoning from contaminated shellfish, this remained the official view. Even now, 300 million gallons of sewage are disposed of in British coastal waters every day.[3] Meanwhile, fishermen off the Tyne complain they now land condoms, used sanitary towels and syringes, where 30 years ago there were abundant fish.

During the last ten years Britain has conducted a war of scientific propaganda with its continental neighbours over the state of the North Sea. Stanley Clinton-Davies, then Environment Commissioner of the European Community, explained to Granada Television's 'World in Action' in 1989: 'The fact of the matter is that virtually every other country in the community says the dumping of sewage sludge at sea is harmful. Britain denies it. Britain asserts that its scientists – or its scientific opinions available to the government – know best'.[4]

Clinton-Davies, a formidable friend of the environment, was sacked for his pains, almost certainly on the instructions of Britain's Prime Minister. Within a year the UK would concede the case, but it would still be in deep trouble over its water pollution policies.

For Britain's streams, lakes and rivers, the past fifteen years have been something of an environmental Dark Age. Pollution laws have been deliberately weakened in order to make it easier to privatise the water industry. Farm pollution incidents have soared and major companies such as ICI have been allowed repeatedly to break their pollution standards without prosecution.

Today, reservoirs and coastal seas suffer the sort of algal blooms caused by eutrophication (excess nutrients from sewage and fertiliser), although officials claim they do not exist. Groundwater is widely contaminated with nitrates and pesticides (these, with radioactive waste, are discussed in a later chapter), and a growing number of wells contain metals and industrial organics. At the European Court Britain is in the dock over tapwater contamination, having failed to out-manoeuvre Carlo Ripa di Meana, Clinton-Davies's successor.

The UK has a sordid record of deliberate attempts to disguise pollution by reorganising statistics and changing the meaning of definitions, as well as attempting to evade or neuter European initiatives, as over the Directives concerning 'Drins' and nitrates. It has been said that Britain's sewage facilities had become so run down in the 1980s that its rivers will not regain the purity of the 1970s until the twenty-first century.

CHAPTER 1

Out of Sight, Out of Mind

Acid rain is frightening, but most people believe it falls on foreign countries. The greenhouse effect is global, but it is thought to be gradual and remote. Pesticides and nitrates may already be in your water, but they are invisible. Sewage, however, is unambiguously nasty, and all too tangible. When the Green Party achieved 15 per cent of the popular vote in the 1989 European elections, it did so with a national press campaign which focused on sewage as a vote winner. 'To stop the flow of raw sewage, use your ballot paper,' said the Greens.

Unlike most of its neighbours, Britain has for years pumped a lot of sewage straight into the sea, defending the practice as the 'Best Practicable Environmental Option'. 'Sea outfalls' – pipes through which sewage is pumped out to sea – date back to the engineering of the Victorians. Some are miles long, many extend to only just below the low water mark. Overall more than one flush in ten ends up in the sea. In England and Wales about 6.5 million people (13 per cent) are connected to sea outfalls, out of a total population of 50 million. More than a million people's sewage goes straight into the sea raw.[1]

British sewage treatment is an inheritance of the industrial revolution. Before industrialisation, house and garden, town and country were linked in most things, including sewage. 'Night soil' was collected from latrines and taken at night to fertilise market gardens around towns. But cities grew (between 1807 to 1861 the population trebled to 30 million[2]) and became too large. Sewage got from cesspools into wells used for drinking water, and in 1832, 5,000 Londoners died from cholera as a result. In 1848 the City Sewers Act required all London houses to be connected to drains, and could also stipulate the use of flush water closets.

Within six years 30,000 cesspools were abolished and sewer refuse was put into the river, which was being used for drinking water.[3] Cholera returned in 1849 and 14,000 died.[4]

In July 1858 *The Times* reported that observers in the Houses of Parliament 'were suddenly surprised by the members of a committee rushing out of one of the rooms in the greatest haste and confusion . . . foremost among them being the Chancellor of the Exchequer, who, with a mass of papers in one hand and with his pocket handkerchief clutched in the other, and applied closely to his nose, with body half bent, hastened in dismay from the pestilential odour . . .

other members of the committee also precipitately quitted the pestilential apartment, the disordered state of their papers which they carried in their hands showing how imperatively they had received notice to quit.'[5]

The immediate stomach-wrenching cause was probably hydrogen sulphide bubbling up from the mud of the river bed, with its characteristic smell of 'bad eggs'. The sediments at the bottom of the Thames were an increasingly thick, sticky, black mess, more and more composed of the solids from human sewage. These solids, along with urine and other biodegradable garbage in the river, mopped up oxygen from the water.[6] The last salmon definitely known to have been caught upstream of Westminster had been landed nearly three decades before. Indeed almost every river fish was in decline.

When the 'Great Stink' got up the nose of Parliament in 1858, the government gave the Metropolitan Board of Works a fair wind to bring in a major new engineering scheme designed to solve London's sewage problems at a stroke. It was to be one of the greatest set pieces of Victorian sanitary engineering: the flows of sewage along tributaries and street sewers up to then entering the Thames from the north or the south were intercepted by several gigantic sewers running from the west, and taken to the east, finally being deposited in the river, well downstream of London at Barking and what is now Thamesmead.

A prohibition was introduced on taking drinking water from the Thames below Teddington Weir (then as now the upper limit of the tidal Thames). With filtration (and, later, chlorination), the Victorians began to supply piped water from upstream to townspeople downstream, while sewerage moved sewage further downstream. This has remained the basis of the system for London and many other cities until the present day.

The shortcomings of the new system became apparent when, on 3 September 1878, the London paddle steamer, the *Princess Alice,* was on its way back to London Bridge from a day trip to Sheerness and collided with another ship and sank. Among the 650 people who died were a number of strong swimmers, overcome by the fumes from the river, or poisoned by the water itself.[7]

The ensuing official inquiry heard that Barking, famous as a fishing port since 1320, had gone into rapid decline as huge banks of sewage silt built up in the river around the outfalls.[8] The engineering had relieved Westminster but only moved the problem downstream. Later, sewage would be dumped at sea.

So the strategy was to put sewage first in the river, then further downstream, and finally out to sea. In many ways the history of sewage pollution has been one of 'out of sight, out of mind', or, as one water scientist put it, 'flush-and-forget'. In terms of domestic sanitation, it brought Britain a century of success. In terms of environmental quality, it was at best a delayed problem and at worst a disaster moved from one place to another. Now there is growing concern about the degree of treatment and the need to deal with nitrogen, phosphorus and other chemicals which simple Victorian systems do not remove. But it was over the crass issue of beach sewage, the unfinished business of Victorian engineering, that the UK finally ran into trouble.

Sewer Politics: Britain Brought to
Book by the EC Bathing Water Directive

In 1959 Mr Tony Wakefield, whose daughter had died from poliomyelitis after swimming in the sea, failed in an attempt to persuade the UK to treat its sewage rather than tip it into the sea. Mr Wakefield started the Coastal Anti-Pollution League. The government would provide no information on which beaches were 'safe', so Wakefield circulated a questionnaire to coastal local authorities and, on the basis of their replies, found that 190 of 633 beaches were at risk from pollution. Officially, however, there was no problem and, had it not been for the European Community (EC), Britain's policy would remain unchanged today.

The EC Directive Concerning the Quality of Bathing Water (76/160/EEC) defines bathing water as 'fresh or sea water in which bathing is explicitly authorised, or is not prohibited and is traditionally practised by a large number of bathers'. Member states can either 'authorise' bathing only at a set number of beaches or identify 'traditional' beaches for swimming. Greece and Belgium have 'authorised' beaches; all other countries identify 'traditional' bathing beaches.

The Directive sets 19 standards to assess water quality on beaches. The main bacterial standard is a limit of 2,000 faecal coliform (gut-living) bacteria per 100 ml seawater, although it has been suggested that this could be halved, and that other bacteria such as streptococci should also be monitored. The amount of coliform bacteria in water has been used as a measure of its quality for assessing a public health risk since 1918, by authorities in the USA and most countries except Britain. Gut bacteria can cause diarrhoea and other stomach upsets – gastro-enteritis – and their presence may indicate more dangerous bacteria and viruses which are more difficult to detect. It is a far cry from the vague idea of declaring all water safe unless it looks 'aesthetically revolting'. It stipulates sampling frequencies and the number of samples that must pass before a beach is declared safe to swim from.

The UK's Department of the Environment (DoE) initially avoided the Directive's main force by circulating Water Authorities with an 'advice note' which pointed out that chilly Britain should have fewer swimmers than Mediterranean countries and so few of our beaches should qualify for inclusion. 'Evidence collected by Water Authorities for the purpose of this Directive', said the DoE, 'has shown a tendency for the British holidaymaker to sit on the beach but not to venture into the water.[9] As Nigel Haigh of the Institute for European Environmental Policy observes, 'the advice note also pointed out that the financial implications were potentially significant'.[10]

This sort of nudge-nudge, wink-wink advice is typical of the relationship that existed between the Department of the Environment and the Water Authorities. As 'advice notes' might become public there was no direct instruction to minimise the number of beaches found to 'qualify' for the Directive, but the implication was clear enough. Because action might have to be taken to clean up sewage if a beach failed, the DoE and Water Authorities tried to keep them out of the Directive.

It was even suggested that 'in the European context, there are no British bathing beaches used by a "large number" of people'.[11] As of 9 July 1979, the DoE decided that, unless more than 500 people were in the water together, a beach was not a 'bathing water'. More than 1,500 people per mile meant it was, and beaches with 750-1,500 per mile might or might not be included. Consequently, only 27 of the 600 beaches in England and Wales where people swim regularly, were 'identified' by the December 1979 deadline.[12] Notable omissions were Blackpool and Brighton. The UK's growing reputation for being reluctant to implement EC environment legislation was reinforced when tiny Luxembourg, with no coast, managed 34 beaches.

What was at the back of this rather extraordinary exercise? When the UK identified only 27 beaches, it received a Reasoned Opinion from the European Commission that it was acting illegally. The Commission picked on Blackpool as a sensitive test case. The UK contested the Commission's view but by 1986 a Cabinet paper (since leaked to Friends of the Earth) conceded that 'DoE and FCO lawyers have advised that if the case were pursued to the European Court of Justice we would very likely lose; there is no real scope for a purely technical/legal defence.'[13]

The Commission's Environment Directorate had also told the UK of complaints about beaches at Bude in Cornwall, Great Yarmouth in Norfolk and Southport/Formby in Lancashire. Under threat of legal action, the DoE officials sought 'a stay of the [Blackpool] action . . . its eventual withdrawal, and an understanding that similar cases would not be pursued, a deal, a bargain'.

Even now, presentation was clearly high on the civil servants' agenda: making government policy look like genuine and new anti-pollution action when in fact it was the bare minimum needed to conform with EC rules. One of 'the most difficult issues', said the memo, was, 'Can we have a "new policy" which does not call (Blackpool and possibly a few other special exceptions apart) for actual major new action and expenditure?' It concluded: 'We think this is possible but good presentation will be needed.'

So the UK was threatened with legal action by the European Commission because it had deliberately excluded beaches from the Directive with the motive of saving money. The same internal DoE civil servants acknowledged that, 'Our nomination for the purposes of the Directive of only 27 waters in 1979 was done by the government to hold down the pressures on expenditure.'

Ken Collins, Chairman of the European Parliament's Environment Committee, points out that West Germany also had some waters used for bathing which did not conform to the EC standards, but it followed clear and concise criteria. The Netherlands used what Collins calls 'relatively vague criteria' (10-100 people using a beach a day), but under Dutch law bathing is specifically prohibited in unauthorised areas. This, says Collins, 'is a more creditable approach than that originally adopted by the UK'.[14]

Britain managed to find another 364 traditional bathing beaches by ·1987. By 1989 it had increased the number to 403. However, a third of English and Welsh bathing beaches and nearly half of those in Scotland were too contaminated with sewage bacteria to meet the EC's standards.

In 1987 bacterial levels at the 27 UK resorts designated under the Bathing

Waters Directive were investigated by scientists from the Robens Institute of Industrial and Environmental Health and Safety.

The European standard was met on only 56 per cent of the beaches. During intensive ten-day periods of monitoring, only 37 per cent met European standards, while only 18 per cent met US Environmental Protection Agency (EPA) standards and just 11 per cent met Canada's exacting Toronto standards. All eight Fylde beaches failed (one had 40 times the bacterial limit), while Cornwall was cleanest.[15]

In 1988, famous names were still among those beaches failing to meet the EC Directive. For example, Grand Pier at Weston-super-Mare, Lyme Regis in southwest England, Southend in Essex, Hunstanton in Norfolk, Worthing, Broadstairs and Southsea on the south coast, Cleethorpes on Humberside, Whitley Bay in Yorkshire, Swansea Bay and Rhyl in Wales, and Blackpool in Lancashire were all too polluted to qualify.[16] At Seaton-Carew near Hartlepool, bacterial levels were 1,500 times higher than the specified limits.[17] In 1989, 109 British beaches failed, while only 8 passed the EC's stricter 'guideline' standards. This time Seaton-Carew had bacteria at 2,050 times the limit.

By 1989 the national press had taken up the story. The *Daily Telegraph* published the entire list of failing beaches on its front page on 22 May. 'Come on in, the water's DISGUSTING', screamed a full page article in *Today* newspaper on 29 May (adding, 'Sun, sand, and tide of filth as Bank Holiday Britain throws caution to the balmy wind'). The newspaper reported how raw sewage entered the sea near the Devon resort of Torbay, and that 'children played in the sea just 10 feet away from slicks of brown sludge at two packed holiday beaches'. 'Both beaches, at Watcombe and Maidencombe, are officially listed as safe by the Department of the Environment,' said the newspaper.[18] The *Daily Express,* a staunch political supporter of Mrs Thatcher, declared on the same day that Britain's beaches were 'filthy' and carried a photo of a man about to enter the sea, captioned, 'Polluted: Braving the sewage at Babbacombe, Devon'.[19]

Britain does not yet monitor for viruses under the Directive. When asked in 1989 by the BBC's 'Nature' programme why the UK was using 'only half the criteria' for beaches, Water Minister Michael Howard replied that Britain was using an 'achievable' criterion.

Blue flags

The government turned to the officially-funded Tidy Britain Group for some friendly PR. On World Environment Day 1989, Minister Michael Howard announced the 'Blue Flag Awards' for the 22 cleanest and most litter-free beaches in Britain. Begun in 1987, the Awards are run by the Water Authorities Association and are based on a combination of the requirements of the EC Bathing Waters Directive, provision of facilities and absence of litter.

In 1989 Blue flags could fly at Weymouth, Clacton and Porthmeor, but it was far from a comprehensive scheme. If there were red flags for failures, more than 100 beaches would have been signalled 'off limits'. Not a single beach in the whole of Wales, Yorkshire or Lancashire managed to pass the basic requirements to enter the competition.[20]

Visibly warning us where not to swim would hardly do wonders for the tourist trade, valued at £7,000 million from foreign tourists alone each year,[21] and a domestic industry employing over 1 million people.[22] Nor would it be popular with local authorities whose beaches failed, or with hoteliers, whose number includes such prominent Conservative supporters as Lord Forte.[23]

Water Minister Michael Howard announced moves to clean up 'un-acceptable' beaches, but added by way of reassurance that he was in any case 'advised' that all water was safe to swim in unless 'it looks so disgusting no-one would contemplate bathing'.[24] Press and public were disbelieving: 'He can't,' commented one TV report, 'be serious'.[25]

Mrs Thatcher fared no better. On 22 March 1989, in an interview with Michael Buerk on BBC 2, she declared that 'all sewage disposed of is treated – you will find it is treated'. In fact most sewage piped into the sea is *not* treated except for sieving, while sewage sludge dumped from boats is not treated to remove nutrients or contaminants like heavy metals.

Skirting round this problem, ministers and civil servants began referring not to 'marine disposal' but to 'marine treatment'. So on 23 March 1989, Environment Secretary Nicholas Ridley told a critical House of Commons that discharge of raw sewage into the sea was the 'best environmental option' in many areas because it was 'treated through the disinfecting actions of salt water, sunlight and waves, which together break down the bacteria as effectively as inland treatment'.[26] Mr Ridley, it seemed, saw the sea as a super sewage works whose function was to provide 'treatment'. So now there was no longer any such thing as disposal of sewage 'untreated'.

By 1989 the prospect of legal action in the European Court made it impossible to avoid the Bathing Water Directive, but impending privatisation created political pressure to hold down investment. The DoE calculated that 60 schemes costing £250 million, with another £250 million in prospect, would be needed if English beaches were to meet the Directive by the year 2000. After meeting the North West Water Authority, the DoE noted that, with privatisation, such schemes 'would mean higher charges and/or a lower sale price'.[27]

To ensure that Britain's 400 designated bathing beaches would be cleaner by 1995,the government planned that the Water Authorities should spend £100 million not on more treatment but on longer pipes. Plans were announced for 44 new long sea outfalls to replace short ones . Not everyone was impressed. At Blackpool, where levels of human gut bacteria have reached 20 times the EC limits, North West Water plans a £50 million outfall into Morecambe Bay at Fylde. Fishermen who make daily use of the Bay's shallow waters fear the discharge will ruin fishing grounds, and already blame sewage for sores, skin irritations and other illnesses.[28] More than 16,000 people had objected to the plan by April 1989. At Bude in Cornwall, the Water Authority wants a 1,000-metre pipe to push sewage further out to sea. Valerie Newman, a Bude Councillor, commented, 'Just because we have the sea handy, I don't see why we should pollute it.'

Is Sewage Bad for Health?

The doctrine that all mixtures of sea water and sewage are safe to swim in, so long as the suspension is a fine enough soup not to contain any 'disgusting' (i.e. recognisable) lumps, has been the official British line of thought since at least 1959. In that year the Medical Research Council reported a study based on 150 children which concluded that 'bathing in sewage-polluted sea water carries only a negligible risk to health', and there was no link between poliomyelitis and swimming in the sewage-contaminated water. The research was prompted by the case of Mr Tony Wakefield's daughter who died of poliomyelitis after swimming in the sea near a sewage outfall.

The British case for 'marine treatment' of sewage was reiterated in a 1987 lecture by Edmund Pike and Valerie Cooper from the Water Research Centre. 'When sewage is discharged to the sea,' they said, 'the same biological processes of purification occur as in a sewage works . . . For example the dilution measured at the sea surface about the outfall diffusers will be at least 50-fold and, after four hours' dispersion, the dilution will easily exceed the 5,000-fold necessary for compliance with the coliform standard in the Directive. By comparison, the decay of faecal bacteria and most pathogens during full treatment of sewage is usually no greater than 90-99.0%.'[29] Ultraviolet and salt will hasten the death of bacteria, say WRC scientists, the time for 90 per cent to die off being as little as 20 minutes in 'thin layers of sea water exposed to bright sunlight' but as much as 'about 100 hours in the dark'.

Thus, in theory, well-sited outfalls should solve the problem. Doubt, however, abounds. For one thing, bacteria and, in particular, viruses may not die off so conveniently, but may live for weeks. Professor Jay Grimes of the University of New Hampshire believes some can persist in sea water for up to 17 months; 100 hours is in any case long enough for bacteria to reach people or their food (as is 20 minutes).[30] For another, many outfalls are short, and active bacteria and viruses do come into contact with swimmers. Wildlife and food fish may be affected even by long outfalls, and the nutrients contained in sewage are delivered straight into the sea. At the University of Maryland, Professor R Colwell has also found that bacteria in sea water may survive unnoticed by standard techniques as viable but 'unculturable' spores.[31]

Whether or not the 'treatment' theory is right, the antique nature of Britain's sewage-disposal equipment, the failure to build new plants to cope with increasing populations and the impact of flash floods and storm surges have meant that sewage has been unequivocally present along the coast. 'The clear fact is that sewage is being washed back onto our beaches,' a dissatisfied Sir Anthony Meyer (Conservative) told Environment Minister Nicholas Ridley in 1989.

Fishermen and beachcombers have for decades been stumbling upon slimy brown lumps of turd, and unsuspecting swimmers still enjoy close encounters with pieces of rubber, paper and cardboard whose previous owners never intended, when they flushed them down the loo, that they should become sea-going. Moreover, swimmers have persisted in reporting sickness which they believe can be traced to sewage in the sea. In 1981, for example, Mr and Mrs

Winter developed bacterial infections after swimming in the sea at Lowestoft, where used contraceptives and lumps of sewage were visible on the beach.[32] In 1988 Dean and Alex Levy became paralysed after contracting a viral infection on a school canoeing trip at Southend. Their parents and many others believe sewage in the water was to blame.[33]

In 1984 the Royal Commission on Environmental Pollution reported studies outside the UK which linked children's 'viral illness of the digestive system' to swimming in the sea, adding, 'We believe it is now necessary to modify the reliance hitherto placed on a report published almost a quarter of a century ago which in any case concentrated on only a few serious diseases'. A 1983 US Environmental Protection Agency study found that 'the risk of gastro-enteritis associated with swimming in marine waters' was related to the amount of enterococcus bacteria present.

Similarly, epidemiological studies in Alexandria (1981), Tel Aviv (1983-4), Malaga and Tarragona in Spain (1979), and on five beaches in France (in 1983), all showed positive links between bacteria in sewage-infested water and the frequency of diseases ranging from skin, eye and ear infections to colds, abdominal discomfort, nausea and pruritis. Ducking the head into the water was also found to be a factor significantly increasing the likelihood of infection.

The World Health Organisation concluded there was 'strong evidence that . . . swimming activities in coastal areas where faecal pollution is present carry a real public health risk'. A 1990 United Nations Environment Programme study identified a 'particularly strong' link for children under 5.[34]

Britain has always argued that UK waters are too cold for sewage viruses or bacteria to be a real risk. In summer 1987, the Robens Institute of Industrial and Environmental Health and Safety interviewed 1,900 beach-goers in two southern England resorts, one clean and one with 44 times as many sewage bacteria on its beach. The study, reported in *Lancet*,[35] showed that swimmers who ducked their heads in the water at the polluted resort had significantly more stomach upsets, nausea, diarrhoea and 'general illness'. The scientists involved stress that this did not prove a 'causal link between bathing in sewage-polluted water and gastro-intestinal illness', but they criticised the official 1959 view that there was only a 'negligible' risk as 'increasingly difficult to sustain'.

Viruses are an increasing cause of concern, especially in shellfish that efficiently filter them from sea water. In 1986 the WHO stated: 'What is most alarming from the public health aspect is the incidence of bacterial and viral pathogens in molluscs from approved harvesting waters.' Viruses found in shellfish such as oysters or mussels destined for the table include echoviruses and cocksackie A viruses.

Seafood species that do not sieve huge volumes of water might seem to be safer but even this may not be the case. Crabs, for example, are highly mobile and may 'acquire viruses from polluted waters before being trapped in high-quality waters'. In 1987 the Medical Research Council told the Commons Environment Committee that 'the main risk associated with estuarine waters is from the consumption of shellfish which have been contaminated with human bacteria and viruses. Viral diseases, in particular hepatitis and gastro-enteritis, are the most important problem. There was some evidence to suggest that the number of cases resulting from the consumption of contaminated shellfish is increasing.'[37]

The Public Health Laboratory Service (PHLS) estimated that 'food poisoning' due to shellfish such as oysters, cockles and mussels had doubled between 1971 and 1986. There were three times the number of outbreaks of viral gastro-enteritis in the later part of the period compared with the earlier, while hepatitis outbreaks increased fourfold.[38]

The effects of viruses are difficult to detect as many have long incubation periods. In the case of AIDS it is years and in the case of hepatitis several weeks. Symptoms are often difficult to diagnose. Very little is known about the incidence of many viral diseases in Britain, perhaps because, as the Medical Research Council points out, compared with the United States, research into infectious diseases in this country is 'relatively weak'. Looking for any extra effect due to infection from sea water or a river is therefore difficult. However, it is relatively simple to trace people who have fallen ill after eating shellfish, and this gives some indication of the sewage contamination of our marine environment.

The PHLS explained the standard method of flushing out bugs to the Commons Environment Committee. Oysters, before being consumed raw, are retained in tanks of recirculated water, purified by chlorination or ultra-violet irradiation. The purpose is to enable the animals to rid themselves of contaminating micro-organisms. Other molluscan shellfish (cockles, mussels) are lightly cooked, so that the flesh can be removed from the shells. The traditional microbiological test applied to shellfish is to estimate the number of bacteria of faecal origin which they contain. In adequately prepared shellfish, risk from pathogenic *bacteria* will be low. But, the laboratory says, *viruses* such as those which cause hepatitis or gastro-enteritis may be present in the final product even when the test for faecal bacteria is satisfactory. 'It is extremely difficult,' the Lab warned, 'to demonstrate the presence of these viruses in shellfish by laboratory tests although people eating them may become ill.'[39]

The WHO says the flushing is 'questionable'.[40] *Salmonella* bacteria for example, have been known to survive in oysters for 49 days, and have persisted for two weeks despite methods designed to eliminate them within 48 hours. Viruses leading to serious diseases may be even more difficult to remove. The WHO says, 'virus carriage for hepatitis A in oysters has been reported to range from six to eight weeks.'

Human gut viruses have been found to survive in oysters for five months during the winter. This probably explains why virus outbreaks occur from raw shellfish consumption in winter, and why the simple presence or absence of viruses in sea water may not correlate with viruses present in the shellfish, whether or not they have been 'purified' in a tank.

The inadequacy of such cleaning methods may cause growing concern in future. In the early 1980s shellfisheries on the western side of the Wash had to be closed owing to pollution. During 1986 the shellfishery on the eastern side was also closed.[41] The Public Health Laboratory warns that 'it is certain that diseases from polluted shellfish are under-reported'. It discounts the idea that people are simply reporting more food poisoning, saying 'causes may include a growing density of population, inadequate sewage disposal, changing eating and recreational habits'. At present the UK has adopted no standards for viruses.

A more subtle risk is that viruses will help bacteria become more dangerous. In August 1989 marine scientists and virologists alike were surprised to learn from a report in *Nature* that viruses occur in sea water at densities of up to 100 million per millilitre.[42] Thus a typical 250 ml cup of water would hold 25,000 million viruses. These are very tiny viruses but may have some public health implications as 'bacteriophages', that is viruses which live on bacteria. Viruses can inject their genetic material into bacterial cells. Evelyn Scherr, of the University of Georgia's Marine Institute, says that 'the most fundamental implication of high viral abundance . . . is that routine bacteriophage infection of aquatic bacteria is likely to result in significant exchange of genetic material.'[43]

Such transfer of genes may mean that marine or freshwater bacteria can adapt rapidly to new factors in the environment: they may, for example, become resistant to new antibiotics reaching the sea or a river from sewers. As Scherr says, 'There is also the disturbing possibility that indigenous bacteria could acquire traits from pathogenic bacteria or artificially engineered bacteria released into lakes and coastal waters.' In other words, resistant bacteria flushed down a hospital or household toilet could pass on their resistance to those living in the seas around a sewage outfall.

Some antibiotic resistance already occurs among bacteria on beaches, presumably due to bacteria from sewage. In 1988, Dr L Barnard and Partners of Southend studied 50 strains of *E. coli* bacteria taken randomly from local sea water. They were tested for sensitivity to a number of antibiotics: 28 of the strains were resistant to one antibiotic, ampicillin; 8 were resistant to sulphonamides and ampicillin; and 1 was resistant to no fewer than nine antibiotics: ampicillin, sulphonamide, neomycin, carbopenicillin, nitrofurantoin, gentamicin, chloramphenicol, trimethoprim and nalidixic acid.

'It may be argued,' say Barnard and Partners, 'that the survival rate in sea water of these resistant organisms may be different from that of more usual strains of *E. coli* but it is clear that they survive at least long enough to be found. It is also clear that they can be found off beaches which have complied with the EEC bathing beach regulations. If such resistance became common, coupled, as it is, with resistance to other presently useful antibiotics, it would mean that many of today's run-of-the-mill, easily treated infections would become much more difficult to treat.'[44]

The EC Waste Water Directive now seems certain to force a British beach clean up. Of Britain's 590 significant marine sewage outfalls, 46 are long and have only 'primary' treatment. Of 253 of the larger outfalls, 48 are on estuaries, and for these the proposed Directive implies installing primary and secondary treatment; 87 coastal ones would need at least primary treatment, at a cost of £1.5 billion.[45]

Curbing Sewage Pollution

Sewage Treatment

'Treatment' of sewage is an enormous subject in itself. 'Treatment' can mean anything from a crude chopping and sieving prior to dumping into the environment to carefully organised biological and chemical processes carried out in lagoons, ditches, or chambers of concrete and steel, the latest using molecules – fine membranes.

The objectives are to contain and prevent hazards to human health (pathogenic bacteria or viruses, parasites), to remove and neutralise toxic industrial chemicals (such as pesticides, heavy metals, PCBs), and, in the most sophisticated systems, to remove the nutrients nitrogen and phosphorus.

Fish vary in the amount of oxygen they need but none can tolerate less than 5 per cent 'saturation'. So one of the principal objectives of sewage treatment is to reduce the biological oxygen demand (BOD) – the amount of oxygen it will take from water. Biological oxygen demand has been a key test since a Royal Commission on Sewage Disposal of 1898-1915. The standard is now the amount of oxygen used up chemically and biologically when a sample is 'incubated' at $20^{\circ}C$ for five days.

Conventional sewage treatment uses several steps to cut down BOD. The example below is for a Merseyside sewage works.[47]

(1) *Screening or Primary Treatment*. Removes floating cloth, rubbish and so on. Grit settles out in channels. This can reduce carbon and nitrogen loads by 5 per cent.

(2) *Settlement*. The sewage is moved slowly through tanks. Fine particles settle out as a 'primary sludge'. Carbon and nitrogen loads are reduced by up to 30 per cent (equivalent to 30 per cent reduction in BOD). The effluent now has a dissolved oxygen content of 2 mg/litre.

(3) *Biological filtration*. The sewage is passed over clinker or other materials with a very large surface area. Here microbes convert organic matter to carbon dioxide, water and nitrogen.

(4) *Activated sludge process*. Air is forced into the sludge to enable microbes to break it down, further.

(3) and (4) are alternatives. They are followed by:

(5) *Settlement*. Creates 'secondary sludge'. After this the effluent has an oxygen content of 5 mg/litre and BOD of 20 mg/litre. Nitrogen should by now have been reduced 90 per cent.

This is now normally discharged into a river. Steps 2-5 are 'secondary treatment'. Further ('tertiary') treatment, as is increasingly required in Europe, involves:

(6) *Stripping of phosphates*: by chemical and electrical means.

(7) *Denitrification (Nitrogen removal)*: by chemical and electrical means.

Nutrient Removal

Nutrient removal (6-7 above) is generally known as tertiary treatment or polishing of effluent.

To cut nitrate Britain favours 'denitrifying' ion exchange plants. By 1998 Anglian Water, the region worst affected by fertiliser, will be building at least 27. Such plants exchange nitrate for another ion formerly held in a resin, usually chlorine.

Biological systems usually involve growing bacteria which themselves 'denitrify' water. These are cultured in steel and concrete containers, using a chemical feedstuff such as methanol.

Phosphate is made insoluble by adding ferric sulphate, which converts it to insoluble ferric phosphate sludge, which is removed for use on agricultural land, provided it is not contaminated with heavy metals. This removes about 95 per cent of the phosphate. At the sewage treatment works in Stalham (Norfolk), which has a population of about 5,000, the cost of this method of phosphate removal is about £2.00 per head of population served.

Much greater use could be made of ecologically benign systems such as root zone treatment. This low-cost, low-maintenance method of sewage treatment was developed in West Germany. Its installation cost can be about half that of a conventional treatment plant and operating costs are about one-fifth.

A large bed of reeds is planted on a lined bed and sewage is broken down as it trickles through, helped by aeration and suction by the roots, and the bacteria that live among them. If all but the smallest works had nutrient removal by chemical methods, the cost would be around £300 million a year (capital costs negligible); using biological treatments capital costs would be £1,500 million but operating costs would be around half those of chemical treatment.

Many smaller UK towns could follow the example of Arcata in California, where a 15,000 population sport 'flush with pride' sweat shirts. Instead of a conventional treatment works, they have opted for a primary treatment plant and a series of marshes in a 154 acre wetland, which also serves as a park and wildfowling area. The ecological diversity of the lagoons overcomes the algal bloom problems of old-fashioned systems just using oxidation ponds, and they have attracted over 200 bird species. The town saved a US$50 million bill required for a conventional system to meet stringent state laws, and the ecological system is cheaper to run.[48]

Reed-bed and lagoon systems could be established on surplus farmland and have multiple ecological and land use benefits. At the time of writing 110,000 hectares have featured in the first two years of Britain's set-aside programme, to take land out of production.

Sewage can also be composted with straw, which at least in theory cannot now be burnt in the fields, to create mulches, peat substitutes and fertilisers. Large volumes of sludge are already sprayed directly on fields (42 per cent of Thames Water and 28 per cent of North West Water's sludge) but the UK policy of mixing industrial and domestic sewage creates a contamination problem. Although solubilisation and other methods may remove toxins, the engineers who dominate water companies are likely to advocate incineration of sludge instead, which creates its own potential air and ash pollution problems.

The Great Sludge Struggle

Sewage sludge results from treating raw sewage. According to the Oslo Commission (established under the Convention for the Prevention of Marine Pollution), sewage sludge has 'the consistency of milk'. Unlike milk, however, it concentrates organohalogens (organic molecules containing such elements as chlorine or bromine) and heavy metals, which may become adsorbed (stuck) on to the surface of organic or clay particles. This is particularly true of British sludge because it has been policy to mix human sewage with industrial waste.

From 1983 the UK has been almost alone among countries bordering the northeast Atlantic and the North Sea in dumping sewage sludge at sea. West Germany stopped altogether in 1983, after first shifting its dump site from the German Bight to the north Atlantic when research showed environmental damage. Of all the countries party to the Oslo Commission, only Ireland joins the UK in dumping sludge, and then only at a minimal level. In 1986, the UK dumped 97 per cent of the total, more than 7.9 million tonnes (Ireland contributed only 220,000 tonnes).[46]

In 1980, 30 per cent of Britain's sludge was dumped at sea by fleets of Water Authority 'gravyboats'. West Germany then dumped only 2 per cent of its sludge at sea, although it produced 2.1 million tonnes against Britain's 1.5 million tonnes. Since 1980, UK dumping has continued at the rate of 7-8 million tonnes, including raw sludge, activated sludge, digested sludge from heated anaerobic digestion and sludge from cold digestion.

UK sludge is dumped miles out to sea at 13 sites licensed by the Ministry of Agriculture, Fisheries and Food (MAFF), including Thames Estuary (over 4 million tonnes a year), the Mersey (1.5 million tonnes) and the Clyde (1.7 million tonnes). Some are close to international waters used for fishing, while tides and currents carry Britain's pollution towards the Netherlands, Belgium, Denmark and West Germany. The UK produces 27 kg sludge per inhabitant and dumping at sea is one of the cheaper disposal options (others include incineration and spreading on the land).

Sludge in the North Sea: Britain v. Europe

Throughout the 1980s Britain was locked in a 'scientific' dispute with its neighbours on the effects of sludge dumping. In a parallel to the policy of 'tall stack' chimneys without pollution controls that created acid rain, the UK's 'longer pipe' policy moves the problem out to sea but does not cure it. Dr Volkert Dethlefsen, a German fisheries toxicologist, calls such disposal of sewage the 'prolonged chimney approach'.[49] But the UK's practices of using long outfall pipes and dumping sludge go further, says Dethlefsen, and 'demonstrate the multiple chimney approach'. One coastal pollution input is laid on top of another in a common stream and no single output can be blamed for damage, nor can it be shown that removing that *particular* source of pollution will solve the problem. This does not mean that pollution is not causing damage. And long sea outfalls and sludge boats do nothing to prevent nutrient pollution.

Scientific concern grew from the 1970s when long-term eutrophication (see below) and build-up of toxic chemicals were detected in the Baltic. By the 1987 North Sea Conference, Britain was completely isolated over the sewage sludge issue. Not until the 1990 Conference did it fall into line with the European consensus, and even now will go on dumping until 1998.

West Germany dumped sludge from 1961 to 1981 in the German Bight. Studies found high levels of heavy metals partly from dumping and partly from the Elbe. From 1973, the normal animals were progressively displaced by one suction feeder which enjoyed 'optimal conditions' sucking in the organic sewage sludge. By 1976 even this species was dying out as oxygen was consumed by bacteria and chemicals. Eventually large numbers of the polychaete worms took over. Even 8-9 km from the dumping ground animals died off and summer oxygen became depleted.[50] In 1981 dumping was halted but investigations went on. After 12 months, oxygen and species diversity were still low. Two years further on many species had begun to recolonise.

From 1977 continental scientists found that in the German Bight, as well as in Danish and Dutch coastal waters and the Dogger Bank, 'certain diseases were quite frequent, especially those probably caused by bacteria. Infected species were cod, flounder, plaice and dab'.[51]

The German government concluded: 'A crucial ecological hazard is indicated by the high prevalence of diseased fishes in this region' and while there was no 'clear cause-effect relationship between sewage sludge dumping and effects on marine organisms . . . the combination of results . . . led to the conclusion that a negative environmental input of sewage sludge could not be ruled out.'

The German government now stated what has generally become known as the 'precautionary principle':

> Due to the fact that natural conditions in the German Bight are difficult to assess, that under those conditions harmful alterations cannot be recognised in due time and, taking into account that any damage might be irreversible, it is essential that prudent precaution is taken. Instead of furnishing clear proof of a cause-effect relation between sewage sludge dumping and environmental deterioration, the decision to terminate the dumping of sewage sludge was taken on the basis of precautionary considerations resulting from bioindication, coincidence of measurable stress factors, and analysis of continuing trends within the ecosystem.

The UK, on the other hand, maintained that dilution made effects at the dump sites negligible (or implied that local effects were acceptable), while it demanded evidence of 'chronic' damage such as heavy metal poisoning or fish diseases before it would agree to stop dumping on the Precautionary Principle.

Britain was already bound by the Declaration of the first North Sea Conference in 1987, which stated: 'Wastes including sewage sludge, containing such amounts of substances which are or could be harmful to the marine environment, will not be dumped in the North Sea.' To West Germany, the words 'could be harmful' meant that responsible authorities such as governments 'should not wait for undisputed evidence of harmful effects in the marine environment before taking action'. The UK, in contrast, interpreted this as a request to improve the quality of its sewage sludge. In the decade 1976-86 mercury was reduced from 4 tonnes a year to around 1 tonne, cadmium from 10 to 3.5, copper from over 220 to 150 and zinc from over 730 to around 490 tonnes by industrial controls. Chromium and nickel showed less marked declines and lead increased from 127 to 169 tonnes. Nevertheless, UK sludge still contains over 400 tonnes of heavy metals and PCBs (polychlorinated biphenyls), gamma-HCH (an isomer of the organochlorine pesticide lindane), aldrin, dieldrin and endrin because the UK mixes industrial and domestic waste. Thus the long-term problem will remain – whether the pollutants enter via rivers or directly – unless new technologies are used to remove toxics at the sewage works, industry converts to zero-discharge, or the domestic and industrial sewers are separated.

Britain made extensive use of scientific obfuscation in delaying action. In 1989 the UK's paper on sludge dumping in the Oslo Commission's *Review of Sewage Sludge Disposal at Sea*[52] ran to 13 pages but led to no firm conclusions. In five and a half pages, the German contributors set out why they had stopped dumping. In contrast, the UK report started by referring to 'gaps in knowledge' and emphasised that Britain's sludge-dumping sites are selected for currents which will dilute and disperse the sludge.

The report admitted that Thames Estuary and Liverpool Bay shrimps showed high levels of cadmium and that sludge 'may have contributed' to raised lead levels in fish 'and possibly to zinc and copper in some shellfish species in Liverpool Bay and off the River Humber'. Levels of mercury and organochlorines were also linked to sludge.

Heavy metals at UK sludge sites reached ten times background levels and at Garroch Head, in the Firth of Clyde, nutrient enrichment caused species to die off within 2–3 km from the centre. When dumping was moved away, the number of bottom-living species increased from 3 to 38. At Liverpool Bay, 'fauna in the immediate vicinity of the dump site was relatively impoverished'. In tests Dover sole developed fin rot after 13 months' exposure to sewage sludge and shrimp larvae were killed by sewage sludge at dilutions of one part in a thousand.

But the UK found no cause for alarm and 'no evidence' that sewage sludge was 'the cause of disease or mortality in marine fish populations'. While sludge caused 'minor, transient changes', these 'conformed with the familiar notion of successional change along a gradient of increasing organic enrichment', it said. The language, while purportedly being objective, is itself peculiar. Would a fireman say, 'The house burned by the familiar processes of combustion', and so take no action?

The DoE concluded that the Mersey dump site was under ecological stress and would be damaged by increased dumping. But there was to be no halt to dumping as a whole. In fact, North West Water anticipated an increase in dumping. In September 1989 the *Annual Report on the Disposal of Waste At Sea* reaffirmed the UK view. The government stated baldly that its studies were 'designed to detect at an early stage, any adverse environmental changes so that any remedial action can be taken'. During the two years 1986-7 there were 'no indications' of such changes. Thames Water commented in the Report that dumping was 'vital', while North West Water found it 'a clear economic solution' and was 'convinced of the scientific justification'.

As the March 1990 North Sea Conference approached, Britain tabled a draft resolution suggesting only 'monitoring' of dumping. Then extraordinarily, two days before the meeting, Environment Minister Chris Patten announced that the UK would end dumping by 1998 at a cost of £1.7 billion. 'I don't think anybody when they're swimming off our beaches is going to regard this as an excessive price,' said Patten.[53] Britain's scientific objections of just a few months before had suddenly disappeared. A pro-Patten leak later appeared in the *Independent on Sunday*.[54] The Prime Minister had 'personally investigated the scientific evidence' and Patten had to argue the case on the precautionary principle. In some ways this was just news management by Patten's office: the Prime Minister's scientific training was in glue and ice-cream. Accepting the precautionary principle depended not on the evidence but on policy, and this was a political U-turn.

Fish Diseases

In their 1985 *Review of the Mersey Clean Up Campaign*,[55] Greenpeace researchers catalogued a series of fish-disease pollution studies. They found aflatoxins causing liver cancer, deformities in larvae and hatchlings from pesticides and heavy metals, inducement of a bacterial disease by high copper levels, and hyperactivity caused by DDT. All were laboratory studies, but the potential obviously exists for these diseases to occur in wild populations.

In 1986, Dick Vethaak of the Netherlands Fishery Institute found North Sea fish with 'contamination [which] often approaches or even exceeds the levels which have sub-lethal effects according to laboratory experiments . . . The concentrations of cadmium, mercury, copper, lead and zinc generally appear to be above the "no effect" level, whereas the concentrations of iron and PCBs are even above levels that are considered to be sub-lethal.'[56] There was a 'high frequency of liver cancer observed in flounder and dab' which 'may be directly related to specific contaminants'. Pollution, it says, is 'most likely a contributing factor in at least three of the most common skin diseases in flounder . . . lymphocystis (a viral disease), ulcers and fin rot (bacteriological conditions). Dab and flounder over 3-4 years old in Dutch waters had liver cancer rates up to 40 per cent in some areas.

Dying from Excess: Eutrophication

Each year some 1.5 million tonnes of nitrogen and 100,000 tonnes of phosphorus enter the North Sea.

Nitrogen and phosphorus are essential for plant growth and in nature often limit the production of plants. However when an ecosystem receives abnormal amounts of nutrients (at sea it is usually nitrogen that is limiting), algae multiply to the point where they can outstrip the ability of zooplankton and other animals to graze them. This process is called eutrophication. In large enough numbers, algae can use up all the available oxygen as, although they produce it by photosynthesis in daylight, they respire and use it up at night. When the algae die, their rotting bodies use up more oxygen and may release toxins. The carpet of dead algae that may build up on the sea, lake or river bed can then smother other life. Some form 'red tides', releasing large amounts of toxins as they die. (A similar bloom caused closure of 200 miles of North East Coast shell-fisheries in May 1990.)

The Baltic, one of the shallowest and most polluted seas in the world, began to eutrophicate in the 1960s and today suffers the fate of an over-fertilised duck-pond. Its deeper waters contain little oxygen.

By the 1970s, scientists in Denmark began to think the same problems were arising in the North Sea. In the Kattegat off Denmark, fishery declines were linked to nutrient inputs from rivers. By 1987 the Danish parliament was debating heavy investment in engineering works to reinstate floodlands removed by canalisation schemes in the 1960s. The lost shallows were rich in plant growth and animal life which filtered out sediments and nutrients such as nitrates and phosphates.[57]

Sebastian Gerlach from the University of Kiel found a doubling of nitrogen and phosphorus between the 1950s and the 1980s in German and Danish waters.[58] In 1987 Denmark adopted a policy of reducing nitrogen and phosphorus entering the North Sea by 50 per cent and the first conference of North Sea states agreed to halve the overall input of nutrients to the North Sea via sewage effluent, with a target date of 1995. However, the North Sea Conference Agreement's phrase 'where those inputs are likely to cause pollution' was used by Britain to argue that, so long as there were no acute problems from nutrient pollution in its coastal waters, the pledge to reduce sewage effluent by 50 per cent need not apply.

Britain also holds that there is no overall eutrophication problem in the North Sea, and none in waters of other countries which required a cut in British pollution. 'The North Sea is rather well looked after,' said Nicholas Ridley. British rivers put 210,000 tonnes of nitrogen into the North Sea a year, less than West Germany and its upstream countries (255,700 tonnes) and the Netherlands and those up the Rhine (518,000 tonnes). However, the UK has also been estimated to contribute 13,200-250,000 tonnes from air pollution and in total it probably exceeds the 'German' air and water total for nitrogen pollution.[59]

In 1988, the West German Environment Ministry stated: 'The scope, frequency and seriousness of algal blooms has significantly increased in the past 25 years. It can be supposed that a high level of nutrients in coastal waters' has contributed.[60]

In May 1988 Charles Clover of the *Daily Telegraph* wrote that it seemed 'the North Sea, Britain's moody, often violent neighbour, was in danger of his life.' A Danish fish farmer reported that 'his entire stock of salmon, worth £1 million, had been suffocated by a colossal "bloom" of microscopic algae'. The immediate cause was a 'concentrated slick of algae, 30–100 feet deep and six-miles wide' composed of *Chrysochromulina polylepis*, stimulated by chemical fertilisers washed into the Skagerrak and Kattegat.' This maritime Chernobyl, said Clover, was 'the biggest ever recorded . . . Some resourceful fish farmers managed to tow their salmon cages out of the way. Others were not so lucky. By the end of the month, when the belt of algae began to die out, £120 million worth of damage had been done to the Norwegian fishing industry alone.'

Britain says long-term monitoring shows algal blooms have not been increasing.[61] Satellite imagery and cruises by research ships sampling water for nutrients and plankton may resolve the argument. But few if any scientists would argue that pollution-related blooms do not occur, and should the Precautionary Principle not apply here too? Andrew Lees from Friends of the Earth points out that the government's own Nitrate Coordination Group accepted in 1986 that, while in its view blooms off Norway, West Germany and Denmark were not 'initiated' by nitrate, its 'presence in coastal waters enhances the extent of the blooms and the consequent problems of deoxygenation or of the release of fish toxins'.[62]

One indication of an overall change in the North Sea may have come from studies at University College North Wales by Paul Tett. He has found a rise in small flagellates (algae with whip-like flagella which they use to swim), at the expense of diatoms, which he describes as the 'grass of the sea'. Tett points out that the increase in nitrogen and phosphorus pollution has not been matched by a rise in the supply of silicates. Whereas diatoms need silicates to grow, the flagellates do not.

As to British coastal waters, in 1986 the Nitrate Coordination Group acknowledged that, in Liverpool Bay, 'blooms have been more frequent since 1978 than between 1961 and 1977', and reported foam and organic solids from algal blooms washed up on the beaches of North Wales. 'The frequency of blooms is increasing in off-shore waters . . . and may be related to nitrate,' although there is 'no clear evidence that nitrate concentrations are increasing in British marine waters or causing any practical problems.'[63] In 1987 the Nature Conservancy Council said it was 'well known that Portsmouth and Langstone Harbours on the south coast suffer from excessive algal growth because of sewage pollution'. Government adviser Dr Brian Bayne of the Natural Environment Research Council's Plymouth Marine Laboratories has reportedly suggested that the Wash, an important fish nursery ground and the feeding place of hundreds of thousands of migrant birds, is poised for a large algal bloom.[64]

By midsummer 1989, Dutch researchers had come up with a list of four British estuaries – the Thames, Humber, Tyne and Forth – which they classed as 'at risk' from the damaging effects of algal blooms.[65] By September, the Dutch research team had identified a series of British estuaries and coastlines suffering four types of algal bloom. Their findings were presented at an inter-government Paris Commission seminar in Oslo. Leaked to FoE, the study showed the whole east coast of England and Scotland as 'vulnerable' to eutrophication, with raised levels of nitrate. Liverpool Bay, the Humber, the

Thames Estuary and Lyme Bay also had algal blooms.

The EC has drafted new standards for a Directive 'Concerning the Protection of Fresh, Coastal and Marine Waters against Pollution Caused by Nitrates from Diffuse Sources', which would curb nitrate from sewage or fertiliser affecting 'areas of land which drain directly or indirectly into . . . estuaries, coastal waters and seas which are found to be eutrophic or which in a short time may become eutrophic if protective action is not taken'.[66] All sewage works on rivers serving a population equivalent to 2,000 or more and all those on coasts and estuaries serving a population of 10,000 or more would require full secondary treatment to meet the standards, while in sensitive areas, nutrient removal would be required. Nitrogen levels might have to be cut as much as 7 times.

Evidence from Dutch studies suggests raised nitrate levels across the whole of the southern North Sea, which implies that 'sensitive areas' could turn out to be large, especially if the Precautionary Principle were applied. Under the Helsinki Convention, the Baltic Sea was accepted as a sensitive area in which dumping could not be risked, and it was stopped.

Officially, however, Britain has no 'sensitive areas'. In 1988 the UK government fended off enquiries by announcing that Water Authorities were conducting a survey. It has not been published. In a letter to the Authorities in December 1988, the DoE pointed out that 'Identification of such waters would call for corrective action. Alternatively, we must be in a position to demonstrate that we have no such waters in order to reject claims that nutrients from the British are causing problems further afield.' The letter did not quite instruct the Water Authorities not to find a problem but it signalled a strategy. First, find no problem at home. Second, make sure there is no clear evidence that our pollution is causing problems further afield.

Britain's industrialists echo the acid rain arguments: 'The strong currents off the British coasts mean that waste is dissolved, dispersed and degraded long before it reaches the other side of the North Sea. The North Sea is not a closed sea like the Baltic or the Mediterranean; it is flushed out by the waters of the Atlantic every two or three years,' says Dr Ted Thairs, head of the Confederation of British Industry's Committee on Environment, Health and Safety.[67]

However, computer models by Delft Hydraulic Laboratory show how nutrients from sewage sludge, dumped for example at the mouth of the Thames, make their way fairly directly towards the algae-rich problem areas off Holland, West Germany and Denmark and the National Environmental Research Council acknowledges that currents move British pollution in that direction.[68]

In June 1989, matters took a bizarre turn. A DoE civil servant, D. H. Roberts, sent a testy letter to the secretary of the Paris Commission, saying, 'I have already informed you that the UK has no problem areas where in the terms of the Convention "these inputs [of nutrients] are likely, directly or indirectly, to cause pollution". . . This has meant that the preparation of an action plan – in the terms of the Second North Sea Declaration to reduce nutrients – is not necessary.' However, for reasons not explained, the DoE added that some measures 'to reduce nutrient inputs are being taken'.

The matter now became highly controversial. 'As the Netherlands delegation is coordinating maps submitted by other delegations,' wrote D. H. Roberts, 'would you please inform them that there are no problem areas to be shown round the UK coastal and estuarine waters.' Too late. The *Observer* published two maps, one (blank) showing the official DoE view of eutrophication around Britain's coasts, the other showing the Dutch view.[69]

A 1993 conference in Denmark will determine if the UK has 'sensitive areas'. If so, European legislation may well demand strict nutrient removal to West German standards.[70]

Action in other North Sea countries

Britain's neighbours had begun to take action even before the algal blooms of 1988. In 1987 Denmark began curbing fertiliser applications and requiring the best available technology to reduce nitrogen and phosphorus at all larger coastal sewage works.[71] In 1988 Sweden announced plans to cut discharges of nutrients in sewage by 50 per cent by 1992 along sensitive coasts, and by 1995 in other areas.[72]

In June 1988, West Germany unveiled plans for all towns with over 5,000 inhabitants to limit nitrogenous waste from sewage works to 10 mg/litre by 1989 (one-third of the level commonly set in the UK).[73] The cost would be DM14 billion, adding £100 to the average householder's annual water bill.[74] Germany also plans to cut phosphates released in the effluent from sewage treatment plants to levels of 1 mg/litre or below for towns of 100,000 inhabitants or more. After 1991 German companies will also have to meet charges for nitrogen and phosphorus pollution they produce.

A 70–90 per cent cut in nitrogen and phosphate pollution is planned under the Dutch National Environmental Policy Plan, with a 50 per cent reduction by 1995.

The European Community also plans a Directive to reduce phosphate. Britain is the second largest single North Sea phosphate polluter.

Seas Heavy with Waste

Surrounded by countries grown rich on industry, the North Sea has received some of the heaviest loads of pollution in the world. During the seven years up to 1982, it is thought that some 140,000–230,000 tonnes of metals and poly-cyclic-aromatic-hydrocarbons (PAH) were entering the North Sea each year. Altogether from 1975 to 1982 the North Sea received an estimated 300–1,100 tonnes of cadmium a year, 7,400–19,500 tonnes of copper, 3,800–5,200 tonnes of chromium, up to 100,000 tonnes of mercury, 2,400–5,600 tonnes of nickel, 12,400–21,800 of lead, and 36,800–107,100 tonnes of zinc. In addition, there were 200 tonnes of arsenic and some 150–1,500 tonnes of PAH.[75] Over half the solvent load and 20–50 per cent of the metals came into the southernmost seven per cent section, an area of 37,500 km^2 between northern France, Belgium, Holland and the UK. Mercury was entering the North Sea at two and a half times the natural rate, while lead, copper and zinc inputs are 12 times the natural amount.[76]

Since the early 1980s some inputs of contaminants, particularly heavy metals and chlorinated organics, have been significantly reduced, following the 1987 agreement to cut inputs of the most hazardous pesticides, metals and solvents by 50 per cent. The quantities, however, are still enormous. The 1990 North Sea Quality Report records over 11,000 tonnes of heavy metals entering the North Sea from rivers, with a similar amount from air pollution and incineration.[77] Rivers also disgorge 100,000 tonnes of phosphorus and 1 million tonnes of nitrogen, both of which can trigger algal blooms. An estimated 300,000–600,000 tonnes of nitrogen fall from the air: a component of acid rain. More heavy metals flowed in from 1.6 million tonnes of liquid waste in 1988, and 55 million tonnes of dredgings yielded 1.3 tonnes of PCBs, 11 tonnes of PAH and some 13,000 tonnes of heavy metals.

Taking inputs from rivers, sludge dumping, dredging and industrial waste together, the UK is the worst polluter of the North Sea with lead, cadmium and copper. Indeed, once airborne contaminants are accounted for, and continental inputs separated by country rather than rivers, the UK may well be the heaviest polluter of the North Sea for all heavy metals.[78]

Many of these substances cause cancer, birth defects or pose other serious hazards. Low levels of mercury in the diet of birds may have adverse reproductive effects without being lethal. It is most dangerous in the organic 'methylated' form, a transformation which natural micro-organisms can make when the metal settles out on estuarine sediments. In birds, methyl mercury causes degeneration of the spinal cord.[79] In mammals such as man, the main toxic effects are disturbances of the central nervous system and brain lesions.[80] Lead is a potent neurotoxin and PCBs cause reproductive and immunological defects in mammals.

The Paris and Oslo Commissions, which respectively cover pollution from rivers or pipelines and ship-dumped pollution, monitor pollutants in the Irish Sea, English Channel, North Sea and northeast Atlantic in a Joint Monitoring Programme.

One of the most toxic heavy metals is cadmium. In 1986, monitoring showed the highest levels in fish or shellfish in the Severn, the Humber, the Gironde Estuary in France and the Orkdalsfjord in Norway. French oysters contained most cadmium, at 52.7 mg/kg, more than twice the 'higher level' threshold of the Paris and Oslo Commissions, while British mussels, at 6.05 mg/kg from the Humber and 19.21 mg/kg from the Severn, also exceeded the threshold, in the latter case by a factor of four.[81]

As to mercury, in 1986 the Oslo and Paris Commission scientists sampled shrimps, oysters, cod, haddock, blue mussels, flounder, plaice and pollack from 15 estuaries or coasts in Belgium, Ireland, the UK, Norway, France and West Germany.[82] The two highest concentrations in mussels were both from the UK. Mussels from the Firth of Forth had up to 0.51 mg/kg – 40 per cent above the 0.3 mg/kg Environmental Quality Standard taken as the lowest legal level among several European countries and the USA. Flounders from the Mersey and Liverpool Bay were also over the limit.

The Danes apply an 'alarm level', to show where action against mercury contamination should be taken, of 0.1 mg/kg. Cod, plaice and flounder from the Mersey/Liverpool Bay, flounder and mussels from the Firth of Forth, and flounder from the Thames Estuary would all raise an alarm in Denmark, although they do not in Britain. Of the other countries in the study, only fish from the Elbe and the Weser showed mercury levels as high.

One place, however, stands out as an example of continuing bad practice and a warning of the long-term consequences of pollution, and that is Britain's Mersey Estuary.

The Mersey: a marine blackspot

Described by Michael Heseltine as the 'open sewer of the northwest',[83] and by the Royal Commission as 'the worst example' of an 'estuarine blackspot', the Mersey receives more untreated domestic sewage, trade effluent and surface water runoff than any other area in the UK.

In 1980, the North West Water Authority (NWWA) announced a £90 million (to become £170 million), 15-year plan to clean up the Mersey.[84] It aimed to turn the estuary into a Grade 2 'fair' river, without 'solids' (sewage) on the banks, by 1995. Since then the 1995 objective has been downgraded to just 'preventing further deterioration', although £2,500 million of UK and EC funds are earmarked for pollution control.

Fish disappeared from the Mersey in 1948. Enormous petrochemical works brought new pollutants to the river, such as PCBs (widely used as plasticisers in paints, in resin and electrical insulation in transformers), and by 1970 the polluters included power stations, chemical industry, petroleum refineries, paper and board makers, iron and steel works, textiles, food processing, soap and detergent manufacturers, engineering works, rubber processors and glue makers.[85]

From 1979 NWWA focused its efforts on improving sewerage facilities. Its capital expenditure was the highest of any authority: £180 million on new and repaired sewers and other works in 1987/8.[86] Oxygen at Howley Weir, Warrington, increased eightfold between 1960 and 1981, a dramatic improvement attributed to improved sewage works but which may also have been due to a collapse of industry.[87] In 1963 a fifth of water samples in the estuary had no detectable oxygen; by 1988 only 1 per cent had no oxygen.

Fish and bird life has returned to the river, feeding on invertebrates. These changes resulted partly from the population's sewage receiving basic primary treatment for the very first time: Widnes for instance, got its works only in 1984. By 1995/6 the NWWA aims to treat the sewage of 700,000 people (currently put straight into the sea). By 1988 the NWWA believed the pollution load of the Mersey had been cut by 75 per cent and 'gross pollution' had declined 45 per cent. A third of sewage in the estuary is now treated and fish have increased from 7 to 36 species.[88]

The increased connection of industry to sewers earned NWWA £19.3 million in 1986/7 [89] but it creates more sludge – which NWWA has been disposing of in Liverpool Bay – and mixes toxic chemicals with domestic sewage. Greenpeace's survey ship the Beluga found no fewer than 250 substances, thought to be halogenated hydrocarbons and their breakdown products, in one effluent stream from a Mersey sewage works.[90] Up to 1988 NWWA planned to dump up to 2.6 million tonnes more sludge: this plan was subsequently abandoned following Welsh and Scottish objections.

But the Mersey is still intractably polluted with toxic substances such as PCBs and heavy metals. While the water may clear and species may return, they may be permanently stressed by invisible chemicals which can build up in their bodies.

As early as 1979, when many sick and dead birds were found on the estuary, heavy metal pollution was recognised as a major problem. In this case emissions of tri-alkyl lead from a plant making petrol additives was probably the cause. Mercury, mainly from chlor-alkali works, is a major Mersey pollutant: a study of people and fish in the estuary was used to set European standards for 'acceptable' mercury pollution. Mersey fish now have mercury levels just below the European standard. Between 1978 and 1988 NWWA believes mercury inputs decreased 90 per cent, but 80 per cent of that emitted from Runcorn and Ellesmere Port now lies in the sediments of the Manchester Ship Canal. There is a long-term problem of what to do with dredged silt, and the effect of 'remobilisation' on birds, fish and people.

The Ministry of Agriculture's Irish Sea Status Report even accepts that 'some members of the local fish-eating community are likely to exceed the FAO/World Health Organisation Provisional Tolerable Weekly Intake' for mercury.[91] In 1988 the Ministry's Marine Pollution Group recognised mercury as 'the most important single problem' in Liverpool Bay. Each day 7.8 kg still reaches the bay from industry, 1.1 from sewage sludge, 6.6 from dumped dredgings, 0.5 from the River Mersey and up to 0.5 from sewage discharges.

Worst of all, the Bay is shallow and currents return the mercury rather than taking it out to sea. There is, say the group, 'a flywheel effect whereby the accumulated mercury "reservoir" in sediments of the Bay represents a source of exposure to fish which would persist even if other inputs were stopped completely'.[92] Sediments are actually drawn into the estuary along the seabed, not washed away.

The Mersey also contains far higher levels of organochlorines such as PCBs than estuaries such as the Thames. A 1978 survey[93] found almost 1 kg of PCBs entering the Mersey every day (seven times the amount in the Thames). In 1987 the MAFF group estimated that up to 54 g of PCB, 48 g of DDT, 0.37 g of 'drin' insecticides and 128 g of lindane (HCH) were entering the area daily from trade effluent, rivers and sewage.[94] Mussels, shellfish and the livers of fish in the Mersey Estuary all showed 'significantly elevated' levels of these very persistent and fat-soluble chemicals.[95] It is officially admitted[96] that 'for several persistent substances the assimilative capacity of the Bay is being fully utilised or even exceeded'; that is, the estuary cannot cope.

Greenpeace points out that in 1984 MAFF acknowledged[97] that the Liverpool Bay dump site for sewage sludge, which was supposed to be 'dispersive', was overwhelmed and 'incapable of adequately dispersing sludge particles at the rate of dumping which has taken place since 1975'. A cycle of accumulation and 'resuspension' means the sludge has 'no permanent sink'. Yet, says Greenpeace, '13 years later the practice continues'. It is calculated that 12 per cent of the gut bacteria and 42 per cent of the nitrogen in the Mersey come from sludge, and ammonia levels are very high (e.g. 70 times that of the Forth).

The Mersey is as strong an argument for the precautionary principle as you are likely to find. As well as 1.2 million tonnes of sewage sludge, the Bay has to cope with 28,000 tonnes of industrial waste and 3.5 million tonnes of 'dredge spoil', which in 1984 included 1 tonne of cadmium, 113 tonnes of chromium, 103 tons of copper, 60 tons of nickel, 191 tons of lead, 560 tons of zinc and 3 tons of mercury. Its ecological capacity is exhausted, both at the dump site, where nickel is ten times and zinc 50 per cent higher than elsewhere, and in the estuary as a whole.

In 1972 a paper in the scientific journal *Nature*[98] tentatively linked fish disease – epidermal lesions, lymphocystis and fin damage – in dab and plaice of the northeast Irish Sea to PCBs. In 1983 a new survey of Liverpool Bay found an increase in fish rot in several species (but a decrease in other diseases). In 1986 another investigation showed a higher rate of disease. Greenpeace highlights the fact that dab were more diseased in Liverpool Bay than elsewhere in the Irish Sea.

An unpublished report to the Lancashire and Western Sea Fisheries Committee in 1972 on the decline of fishing in the area acknowledges that 'tainting of the taste of river-caught fish has been detectable for years but a greater danger is the accumulation in commercial fish of slowly degradable substances such as radioactive materials, heavy metals, pesticides and organochlorine compounds'.[99]

'Proving' a link between fish disease in Liverpool Bay and pollution is still, says the Greenpeace study, virtually impossible. And 'if proof is impossible, then available evidence must be weighed . . . It is difficult not to conclude that adverse anthropogenic effects in wild fish populations exist.'

Dumping and Burning

On 31 December 1989 Britain failed to meet a North Sea Conference deadline to cease dumping industrial waste. At one time in the 1980s the UK granted 100 licences for such activities. By 1987 there were 20 and by 1990 there should have been none. But exploiting a loophole which allowed continued dumping of waste where there was 'no practical land alternative' and where it was 'causing no harm', at the end of 1989 the UK planned to allow the dumping of 6,000 tonnes of drug waste by Fisons, 42,000 tonnes by Sterlings from paracetamol production, and 3,000 tonnes of salt by Orsynthetics. Objections were lodged by Sweden, the Netherlands, Denmark and West Germany, all of which had ceased dumping. As *ENDS* magazine noted, 'to MAFF's embarrassment . . . Fisons withdrew its application'.[100]

At an Oslo Convention meeting the UK now made a new promise; to stop dumping by 1995. Baroness Trumpington told the House of Lords, 'none of these wastes [those dumped at sea] will continue to be dumped at sea after the end of 1992'. But she added in the next sentence, 'In two cases it might not be technically feasible to meet this deadline.'

As of 1990, Britain's outstanding dumpers were ICI and Sterling Organics.

In the midst of a massive advertising campaign profiling itself as the company with 'World Solutions to World Problems', ICI announced it would end its annual dump in the River Tees of 60,000 tonnes of ammonium sulphate from making perspex for car lights, and of 165,000 tonnes in the North Sea. ICI vigorously denied that the dumping did any environmental damage, saying that only 'community concern' had prompted its decision. ICI's dumping will continue until the mid-1990s.

British Coal dumps waste at Seaforth in Northumberland. Coal dust and lumps of coal cover the entire beach, while, offshore, waste extends over 40 km^2 of sea bed, smothering marine life and ruining fishing. After a brief respite during the miners' strike of 1984, the UK's inputs rose from 0.7 to 2 million tonnes in 1985.[101]

Incineration is one environmental insult which cannot be laid mainly at the door of the UK. Burning waste at sea began in 1969 as 'an interim method of disposal of wastes pending development of environmentally better solutions'.-[102] The tonnage of hazardous waste incinerated at sea increased steadily in the 1980s, growing from 86,000 tonnes in 1983 to 94,000 tonnes in 1984, and to 101,000 tonnes in 1985,[103] with relatively little from Britain.

Much of the waste that has been burnt has been chlorinated hydrocarbons. Figures for 1986 show a cocktail of toxic substances ranging from dichlorotoluene, tolylchloride and benzaldehyde and xylenes used in making herbicides and softeners for PVC, to alcohols from adhesives and synthetic fibres, and the solvent 1,1,2 trichloroethane. At present, these wastes and others are burned in a defined zone 100 miles off Scarborough on the Yorkshire coast. Hamburg University researchers have found 'high levels' of highly toxic partially-burned chemicals hexachlorobenzene and octachlorostyrene in North Sea sediments at dump sites.[104]

Now countries must deal with the waste in new ways. The Netherlands aims to promote internal re-use so that 10,000 tonnes will be 'avoided' by 1990 and 25,000 tonnes by 1995. Recycling (which the Dutch take to mean re-use by other companies) is due to increase from 20,000 to 25,000 tonnes between 1990 and 1995, while another 10,000 tonnes will be dechlorinated. At the same time, land incineration will reduce from 51,100 tonnes in 1987 to 49,000 in 1990 and 19,000 in 1995.

The Dutch aim to enhance prevention and recycling. The British on the other hand, are official advocates of land incineration, hoping at the same time to earn foreign currency from importing waste to be burnt.

Oil

The conventional picture of oil pollution is of a huge tanker stranded on the rocks, with millions of gallons pouring into the sea. Birds struggle in the tarry black slick, TV crews fly over, environmentalists declare a disaster, and politicians and oil companies try to appear to swing into effective action. Booms are laid out, oil is sucked up, birds are caught and cleaned with detergent, action plans are announced and an 'emergency' is 'dealt with'.

Apart from periodic disasters, the North Sea receives over 400,000 tonnes of oil a year.[105] Some 70 per cent comes from land run-off, a quarter comes from sea transport – in leaks and routine use of the sea to dispose of bilge water and through illegal washing of tanks (Greenpeace calculates that 2 per cent of oil pollution arising from shipping can be ascribed to 'involuntary' operations and 72 per cent to deliberate ones), some 3 per cent is thought to come from the atmosphere, 1 per cent from natural seepage and 1 per cent from offshore oil rigs.

More than 2.78 million tonnes of oil have been produced from the North Sea since exploration began in 1959 and the size of spills may seem relatively small. Evidence collected by the Advisory Committee on Pollution of the Seas (ACOPS) shows that stronger regulations against routine discharges from shipping have worked. According to the ACOPS 1987 Report, 500–640 oil spills were recorded each year between 1975 and 1982, but from 1983 there was an improvement, with fewer than 400 a year.

Spills from ships continued to decline in 1987 but, owing to an increase in oil pollution from platforms, the total rose to 436 in 1986 and 500 in 1987. Offshore oil rig spills in the UK sector stood at 91 in 1985, rose to 165 in 1986 and increased to 254 in 1987.

In 1986, 3,799 tonnes were spilled, of which 3,540 came from British platforms, including 3,000 tonnes of oil from a single pipeline fracture. Britain therefore emerges as the main oil polluter of the North Sea so far as the oil industry is concerned. While some of this may be due to greater production in the British sector and on British platforms, there also seems to be evidence of lower British standards. British platforms discharge more than three times as much oil as Dutch platforms.

As *ENDS* had noted, the increase in reports of pollution from the UK sector 'followed an aerial surveillance programme by the Dutch authorities in 1985/6, which detected a larger than expected number of oil slicks originating from UK oil platforms'. It seems to have taken Dutch spies-in-the-sky to stimulate the British authorities to warn operators that they would have to smarten up their act, increase their own flights and find slicks. British fines for oil spills in 1987 totalled less than £12,000 while the value of oil extracted from the British sector was £4.7 billion.[106]

The Paris Convention countries have also set a limit for deliberate 'production water' oil discharges from oil rigs and other exploration structures of 40 mg/litre and will set a date to end them altogether in 1992.

Comparing oil platforms, in 1986 the average Dutch platform produced 20 tonnes of hydrocarbons in production water, while the average British platform produced over 70 tonnes: three and a half times as much. As to the 40 mg/litre limit, which is only a target standard, a total of 41 platforms exceeded this level in 1986 and between them discharged 975 tonnes of hydrocarbons, of which 80 per cent came from the UK sector. Almost half of this came from just two platforms, and here the oily water reached six times the target limit.

Another routine source of pollution from oil exploration is through 'cuttings' – the rock and sediment produced by drilling. In 1988 the Paris Commission decided that the oil content of cuttings disposed of into the sea should not exceed 100 g/kg of dry cuttings. But, as *ENDS* notes, the UK and Denmark rejected the decision, the UK unexpectedly lodging 'last-minute objections following lobbying by the oil companies, arguing for a looser standard of 150 g/kg for all but the largest drilling installations'. [107]

Overall, oil pollution from routine (deliberate) discharges from platforms increased from 8,315 tonnes in 1981 to 26,537 tonnes in 1986. In relative terms Britain's contribution declined from 90 per cent to 72 per cent although in absolute terms it more than doubled.[108]

Accidental Chemical Spillage at Sea

As many as 500 times a day, a ship passes through or across the Straits of Dover. In shipping terms, the North Sea is one of the busiest places in the world. Like a motorway or railway carrying cargoes of chemicals, toxic waste and oil, such traffic poses a risk to the environment.

Greenpeace has reported that 5–10 per cent of all the ships passing through the North Sea carry a hazardous cargo,[109] and that in the three years from 1980 to 1983 some US$30 million worth of containers were washed overboard from ships in storms. The risk of losing toxic substances overboard is probably also increased by the long-established practice of stowing hazardous cargoes on deck, where they can be most easily jettisoned.

In the ten years from 1976 to 1986 more than 100 people were advised to visit hospital as a result of exposure to chemicals washed up on the beaches of southern England.

On 13 January 1984, 250 drums of the toxic pesticide dinoseb were washed overboard from *Dana Optima* 200 kilometres east of Newcastle.[110] On 26 August 1985, the *Mont Louis* collided with a cross-Channel ferry and sank off Ostend. It carried uranium hexafluoride, which is highly toxic and turns into an acid gas on contact with water.[111] On 28 May 1988, 550 tonnes of cyanide-based acrylonitrile sank with the 1600-tonne tanker *Anna Broerre*, 70 miles from the Norfolk coast, after running into the 57,000-tonne *Atlantic Compass*.[112] Panic ensued in Great Yarmouth when a warning was given that a gas cloud could affect the area, causing vomiting, diarrhoea and eye or nose irritation.

On 6 July 1988, the gas rig Piper Alpha exploded and caught fire. Burning fiercely, and with the loss of 167 lives, it toppled into the sea, taking to the sea bed some 4 tonnes of PCBs.

On 13 March 1989, the MV *Perentis* sank 20 miles northwest of Guernsey in the Channel, carrying several tonnes of Rhone-Poulenc (formerly May and Baker) pesticides, lindane and permethrin.[113] Although built as a coastal ice-breaker, the ship was en route from the Netherlands to Indonesia. Paul Johnston, a Greenpeace research fellow, estimated that, to be diluted to 'safe' levels, the lindane would require mixing with all the water in the English Channel. The chemical company accused Greenpeace of wild exaggeration, claiming that, unlike other organochlorines, lindane posed 'no risk of accumulation in the food chain'. The Ministry of Agriculture disagreed, and the authorities closed 200 square miles of fishing grounds. Nevertheless, on 26 April, after several weeks' searching with minesweepers and a midget submarine, the French navy called off attempts to recover all the cargo. Four drums of permethrin were left on the seabed, and a container of lindane which was recovered and taken under tow sank again and was lost.

Radioactive Discharges

For decades Britain created more radioactive pollution of the seas than any other country in the world, mainly from the 'treatment' and the disposal of nuclear waste, although the use of radioactive isotopes in medicine, industry and research plays an additional role, as do nuclear power stations. This is discussed in more detail in Chapter 9. In 1990, Britain was left isolated at the North Sea Conference by insisting (though without plans to do so) on its right to dump radioactive waste on or under the sea bed.

Conclusions

Like a crowded high street with a major litter problem, the contaminated shoreline of Britain stretches embarrassingly right around the country, and our pollution is readily apparent to Continental neighbours. In the end, political claims to be 'green' or environmentally sound will wash up along with the tar balls and drift plastic if government action doesn't safeguard the quality and ecology of the seas.

Toxic substances – fewer than 1 per cent of the 50,000 estimated to be found in the seas are known – will remain a long-term hazard. In the medium term, eutrophication may be the greatest problem. All North Sea states face the challenge of a legal requirement to reduce cadmium, mercury, lead and dioxins from land, sea and air sources by 70 per cent on 1985 levels by 1995.

And what happens in the coastal seas may yet presage bigger problems in the oceans. The choking of the North Sea will be dwarfed by any major changes in the ecology of the pelagic or benthic ecology of the oceans – the webs of life in the sunlit waters at the top of the oceans, and the fish, worms and bacteria which recycle sediments in the abyssal depths.

In an era when the ecological limits to the earth are at last accepted, it may seem strange that Britain is arguing with its neighbours over whether or not the North Sea's dab and Dover sole are, or will become, sick as a result of pollution. The arguments between North Sea states may seem a backyard squabble in comparison to global climatic change, but in truth the village-pond politics of the North Sea are an important test of Britain's commitment to environmental policies. Here there is but a short step between conceding the need for action and having to spend real money to do something about it. Hence the continuing disputes over whether or not the North Sea is ultimately healthy or dying.

Britain has a few bright spots in its record. One metal compound over which

Britain has taken some welcome action is tin. The organic compound TBTO (tributyl tin oxide) makes a very effective 'anti-fouling paint' for ships. But, as well as killing barnacles attempting to establish themselves on the hull of a ship, TBTO dissolves into the sea, where it is extremely toxic to many forms of marine life (it causes dog whelks to change sex and deforms oyster shells).

Because of lobbying from the oyster industry, Britain successfully pressed the Paris Commission to restrict TBTO and other organotins for use on small boats and to curb discharges of organotins from dry docks in June 1988. Yet no action was agreed for the much larger volumes of TBTO used on sea-going ships. The Commission agreed that a ban here 'might not be achievable for economic reasons', and referred the issue to the International Maritime Organisation.[114] Human blood cells are also extremely sensitive to TBTO, which in the USA has been found entering the human diet.

New problems, such as organophosphorus pesticides and nutrients from fish farming in Scottish Lochs, are steadily worsening. Meanwhile, by the time Britain ceases sewage sludge dumping, if it does so, around 500 million tonnes more will have entered the seas. In May 1990 the House of Commons Environment Committee asked the DoE to arrange warning signs on the 97 beaches which failed to achieve the standards of the EC Bathing Water Directive. Mr Dennis Roberts of the DoE emphasised the 'administrative difficulties' involved in this great undertaking. Sir Hugh Rossi, chairman of the Committee told him: 'The great British public is very impatient with administrative difficulties being put to them as an excuse for no action.[115]

Perhaps they will not have much longer to wait, as within days of Sir Hugh's criticisms, the European Commission finally lost patience with the UK and began legal proceedings against it for breaches of the Bathing Water Directive, with a prosecution over the sewage contamination of Blackpool, Southport and Formby. Commissioner Carlo Ripa di Meana was said to be 'surprised, annoyed and very saddened' to learn how the UK had planned to evade the Directive as long ago as 1986.[116] Subsequently, the commission began proceedings against Britain over 130 beaches.

CHAPTER 2

Pollution of Rivers
and Fresh Water

Britain's writers, painters and poets have never been far from water when they have ventured out of doors. And, as befits a nation of hobbyists, rivers have provided a wealth of recreation. Isaac Walton wrote in *The Compleat Angler* about his experiences with the fish, mayflies and waterweeds along the then unpolluted water meadows of the middle Thames and launched the country's most popular pastime. The same stretch of river entered the hearts of people all over the world as the backdrop to Jerome K Jerome's story *Three Men in a Boat*.

So, perhaps not surprisingly, the nation always seems to have felt a twinge more shame about sullying rivers than it has, for example, about the air or the soil. The dirtying of the Thames was one of the most decried British acts of pollution, and the clean-up of the river was eagerly trumpeted by officialdom ranging from Prime Minister Margaret Thatcher to the minor officers of Thames Water Authority.

It should perhaps be equally unsurprising that, guilt-ridden but self-satisfied, we proved reluctant to admit that our rivers were once again in decline. Secretary of State for the Environment Nicholas Ridley mounted a spirited defence of Britain's water pollution record in November 1988, saying, 'It seems fashionable to denigrate ourselves as the "dirty man of Europe" but the facts do not support this.'[1] A few months later, the *Sunday Times* began its front-page lead on 26 February 1989 with the words: 'Britain's rivers are being polluted at a faster rate than at any time since national records began. In two years, 453 miles of top quality river have been spoilt by pollution, more than twice the length of the M1. Some successes,' said the paper, i.e. such as the clean-up of the Thames, or of the Tame in the Midlands, 'hide a real down-turn in river quality in many parts of the country. Fourteen per cent of Britain's rivers are getting worse.'[2]

The government's response was to take the bull by the horns and try to talk away the problem. 'I warmly welcome the campaign by the *Sunday Times* for cleaner rivers,' Michael Howard, the Minister for Water Planning, wrote in the same newspaper a week later. 'The government has already shown the high priority it attaches to achieving a cleaner water environment. We are now embarked on the most comprehensive campaign in this country's history to improve the quality of our rivers.'

'Let us be clear that we start from a position of respectability. 90 per cent of our rivers are in good or fair condition,' wrote the minister. Labour, he said, had slashed expenditure on sewage treatment by 50 per cent after the International Monetary Fund forced the Callaghan government to cut expenditure. Labour had not implemented the 1974 Control of Pollution Act and this had led to more pollution. The Conservatives, however, would now privatise the water industry and this would make it easier for the water industry to borrow and 'to spend the money necessary to bring almost all our sewage treatment works up to scratch by 1992'.

Unfortunately, the minister was not being clear at all. The government's own ecological agency, the Nature Conservancy Council (NCC), had been expressing concern at the progressive 'relaxation' of pollution controls for some years. True, the Labour government had cut expenditure, but this continued under the Thatcher government, and it was then that even the relatively crude river-grading system picked up a decline in water quality. True also that Section II of the Control of Pollution Act (dealing with water) had not been implemented by Labour as of 1979 (five years' delay), but then it had to wait until 1985 (another six years' delay) for the Conservative government to do so, and even then some aspects were not given force until 1989.

As to a shortage of money, while privatisation would permit water industries to borrow, who had refused the cash to them before, if not the governments, both Labour and Conservative? This, commented the *Financial Times* in August 1989 was 'one of the Thatcher government's oddest justifications for privatising the water services'.[3] For, when it became necessary, the government indeed imposed both price rises and a large injection of public cash to help purify drinking water supplies. 'These expenditures are necessary but it is not obvious why privatisation was necessary to achieve them,' said the *Financial Times* .[4] As to sewage works 'coming up to scratch' (which we shall discuss below), this was mainly to be achieved by lowering the targets they had to meet.

Village Rules

David Kinnersley is an ex Chief Executive of North West Water Authority and a one-time economic advisor to the National Water Council. In 1987 he advised the Rt Hon Nicholas Ridley, then Secretary of State for the Environment, about the privatisation of Britain's water industry. In his care at North West Water, he had the River Mersey. It could hardly be said that Mr Kinnersley didn't know a thing or two about pollution, and the organisation of rules and regulations governing water.

Yet, in his book *Troubled Water: Rivers, Politics and Pollution*, Kinnersley goes back to the Cambridgeshire village of Foxton in 1318 for an example of a pollution control system which really worked.[5]

The village kept detailed records of how it used the common stream which flowed through its centre. In the year 1318 it recorded:

'Nicholas Wherry allowed the brook to be unlawfully widened by neglect, to the extent of two feet: fined 6d. John Kersey fined 12d for diverting the brook which flows through the middle of the manor, to a width of half a foot, and causing a nuisance. Rosyia Kelle widened the stream by half a foot: fined 12d.'

The historian Rowland Parker asks: 'What were they trying to do, with their half a foot here and two feet there?' His answer is that, 'They were trying to gain a little personal advantage by making their own personal ponds in the course of the Brook, to facilitate their own drinking and that of their livestock. If they had been allowed to get away with half a foot, they would have taken half a yard, two yards, three yards. . .'

Those living downstream would have suffered. But in a village where everyone knew one another and it was obvious who was doing what with the river, where there was a well-run system for enforcing fines big enough to deter wrong-doers, the common property of the stream was kept in a good state, to everyone's advantage. The system lasted for over two hundred years. By 1492 the village also had anti-pollution rules:

'1492 John Everard, butcher, allowed his dunghill to drain into the common stream of this village, to the serious detriment of the tenants and residents; fined 4d; pain of 10s. 1547 [following similar entries for 1521 and 1541] All tenants and inhabitants shall attend diligently on a certain day fixed among themselves to clean and scour the public 'rivulus' from the manor of Mortimers as far as the Conyngerth, each on the frontage of his house and land, and from the Conyngerth as far as the village of Fulmer; pain of 12d.
1562 All inhabitants are ordered that henceforth they shall not let out their gutters and cess-pits at any time before eight o'clock at night; on pain of 12d.'

Parish pump politics could control the human pollution associated with village life. The industrial revolution emptied the countryside in favour of work in the towns. It upset the balance of social controls as much as it was to upset the balance of nature.

In 1876 the Rivers Pollution Prevention Act made it a criminal offence to pollute any British river. But, as Tim Birch of Greenpeace has commented, although the Act remained in force until 1951, and 'appeared to prohibit all forms of pollution, there was a severe restriction on the circumstances in which the prohibition could be enforced. It proved virtually impossible to enforce the Act in the industrial areas where the pollution was at its worst'.[6]

The Thames Clean-up

In *The Tidal Thames, A History of the River and its Fishes*,[7] zoologist Alwynne Wheeler records that at the turn of the century, more sewers were built to 'intercept' flows to London's river, and, coupled with treatment of effluent, the river improved enough for smelt and flounders to be caught upstream of Beckton between 1898 and 1900. Improvement continued up to the end of the

First World War, when the population of London increased and the suburbs growing up around London began to add their own effluent at small sewage works discharging into Thames tributaries. Improvements at Beckton, including sludge-making processes, were outweighed by the general worsening of water quality in the Thames basin until the 1950s. Anglers as far upstream as Kew and Richmond noticed a reduction in weeds, molluscs, leeches and fish between 1933 and 1955. At Gravesend the shrimp fishery dwindled, and from 1914 to 1950 it seems there were very few fish (if any) in the Thames between Chelsea and Gravesend.

By 1950 there was almost no life in the central London Thames except beds of tubifex worms. These worms, which can occur at up to 100,000 to the square metre, carpeted the river bed in some areas, making it appear red at low tide. This is because they take in oxygen through blood in their tails, when they are exposed to the air.

Not before time, Parliament passed the 1951 Rivers (Prevention of Pollution) Act. This set out to 'maintain and restore the wholesomeness of rivers and other inland and coastal waters' and made it illegal to discharge sewage, poisons, noxious matter or other pollutants into a river without the permission of the then River Boards. This permission was given (or withheld) in the form of a 'consent'; the system is still in use today.

But, says Tim Birch, the 1951 Act 'failed to adequately control ongoing industrial pollution'. Some pre-1951 discharges were 'held on file' until 1985. Most existing discharges were given 'deemed' consents (i.e. allowed to continue) and until 1960 there were no controls over discharges to estuaries and other tidal waters, which prompted a rush of industries keen to locate on the coast.[8]

On the Thames, an investigation showed that most of the pollution came from just five large sewage works, that a tenth of the effluent was industrial in origin, and that the practice of flue gas washing at two power stations further reduced oxygen. Some progress in improving effluent treatment began in the 1950s – Beckton outfall had equipment to treat half its full flow by 1959, while across the river at Crossness full secondary treatment was available for all sewage by 1964.

The investigators aimed to improve the river to the point where salmon could once again migrate up the Thames. Oxygen saturation of water would have to be at least 30 per cent for the two months of April and May when smolts (young salmon) are migrating down to the sea, in nine years out of ten.

At least four factors now contributed to improving the Thames. First, heavy public expenditure between 1956 and the 1970s in upgrading sewage works meant that effluent quality improved. A retrospective study identified the opening of the 500,000 m^3-a-day Crossness sewage treatment works in 1964 as the turning point.[9] Second, gas works which were situated throughout the capital closed down in the 1970s, as natural gas (methane) came on stream from pipelines connected to gas fields in the North Sea. Third, some industrial effluents were controlled or treated. Fourth, most of the small power stations along the Thames closed down, as the CEGB shifted generating capacity to its newer, larger stations in rural areas. Partly by design, and partly by good luck, a dramatic improvement took place in the quality of the River Thames.

In 1964, Mr Colman, an engineer working on the construction of the new West Thurrock power station, brought Alwynne Wheeler a strange fish that had become caught on the screens over the cooling water intakes. Any fish at all would have been of interest because Thurrock was upstream from Gravesend in the 'fishless zone', but Colman had brought a real curiosity, a 'tadpole fish', or lesser fork-beard, a marine species common in the North Sea from Scarborough to Norway but hardly known in the Thames.

Wheeler and Colman cooperated to investigate further finds on the screens as the new station was tested. In November 1964 he found a lampern, a relative of the blood-sucking lamprey, and once common in the Thames. Then a sand goby and a stickleback. In 1966 the station recorded the sea-going John Dory and smelt. Meanwhile, up at Fulham, power station workers were finding up to 30 lb of roach caught on the screens at each tide.

From 1967 to 1973 a total of 74 species were recorded at power stations up and down the river. These included 18 freshwater, 43 marine and 6 migratory species, which showed that the Thames had improved from the sea right through to its freshwater sections.

Finally, in November 1974, a salmon was caught on the screens at West Thurrock. The fish came from the small stock of salmon spawning in East Anglian rivers and which from time to time were caught in or near the Thames Estuary. Confirmation that salmon were not just around the Thames mouth but apparently trying to swim upstream to spawn came on 30 December 1976 when two anglers found a 600 mm male washed up dead at the mouth of the River Ember, a tributary of the River Mole.

By 1977, said M. J. Andrews of Thames Water, 'a population structure indicating freedom from pollution stress was first recorded for fish at West Thurrock Power Station'.[10] By 1980, over 100 species, representing 95 per cent of those native to the Thames and the North Sea, had been found.[11]

So far as the press were concerned, the problem of the polluted Thames was over. By association, the problem of Britain's dirty rivers was also over.

The House of Commons Environment Committee re-stated the accepted wisdom when it opened its 1987 Report *Pollution of Rivers and Estuaries* with these paragraphs: 'Unlike some developed countries, the UK has a strong tradition of tackling water pollution and a good record to prove it . . . Here at Westminster, we need only to glance out of our windows to appreciate the dramatic nature of these improvements . . . The Thames Estuary counts among our great post-war success stories in estuarial restoration but there are other industrial rivers and estuaries up and down the country, such as the Trent, the Tees and the Tyne, where recovery has been just as dramatic.'[12]

In one sense, this is absolutely true: these rivers were dead or close to it, and restored to life. In fact, the Thames recovered from a condition of total death to a fairly good state – the watery equivalent of the clean-up of the London smogs.

Yet, even before the Commons Environment Committee was writing its laudatory account of British pollution control in 1986/7, the old cycle of neglect and action had begun to repeat itself, as investment in sewage facilities was being progressively cut back.

The Failure to Sustain an Improvement

In February 1969 the Labour government set up a Working Party on Sewage Disposal under MP Lena Jeger. It found that although 'full biological treatment was already provided for areas where 80 per cent of the population live . . . on yearly average values for suspended solids and BOD [Biological Oxygen Demand] in final effluents, nearly 60 per cent of works were outside the conditions they were required to meet by their consents (the figures would have been even worse if based on individual sample results).' In other words, locally run and financed sewage treatment was poorly run and under-financed. The idea was that larger centrally controlled Authorities would solve the problem.

There were many shortcomings with the system: for one thing existing discharges and all those to sea or estuaries were missed out; for another, the discharges and the consents were kept confidential 'to safeguard commercial confidentiality', and there was no strong national body setting standards. Indeed, the main polluters were often the local authorities that ran sewage works, and they were represented on the River Boards which were responsible for enforcing the law and setting the standards. Prosecutions were rare.

A national body had been set up, in the shape of the Water Resources Board (WRB), in 1963, but it dealt with providing supply, not with treating sewage and preventing pollution. This imbalance had a long tradition. There had been no central government watchdog to make sure that the sort of progress going on in the Thames was repeated on the Mersey or the Tees.

The WRB was an enthusiastic adherent of what became known as 'supply-fix forecasting', in other words, planning for an expansion of supply based on past growth in demand. David Kinnersley records that 'the WRB persuaded themselves and others that demand for abstractions [i.e. supply from rivers or groundwater] would double over 30 years'. The WRB proposed barrages on the Wash, Morecambe Bay and the Dee, as new freshwater sources, and more upland reservoirs which were upstream of pollution problems. One 'unfortunate' effect of the overestimate of demand was the massive Kielder Reservoir in Northumberland, built for steel-making that never happened.

In practice the use of piped water supplies grew at 3 per cent a year in the 1960s but only 1.6 per cent in the 1970s and 1.2 per cent in the 1980s. Recession and industrial restructuring mean that the current forecasts for water use in the year 2000 are for an increase of no more than 50 per cent.[13]

The focus on water supply during the 1960s and 1970s had two important implications for the state of Britain's rivers in the 1980s. First, so long as you could build new reservoirs for supply, the quality of rivers and groundwater was not of crucial importance. Second, so long as there was a perceived need to expand supply, measures to improve sewage treatment would receive a low financial priority.

All water functions were reorganised by the 1973 Water Act, which in 1974 gave the 11 new Water Authorities in England and Wales combined water supply and waste treatment functions, as well as responsibility for issuing pollution consents and seeing that they were complied with. Kinnersley points out that 'the most serious problem inherited from the 1960s was poor performance of sewage works and little and patchy enforcement by River Authorities where consents were not complied with'.[14]

Environmentalists pointed out that the Authorities were being asked to act as both 'poacher and gamekeeper', a recipe for slack standards and corruption of principles. Nevertheless, in the euphoria of the times, with salmon returning to the Thames and the guarantee (not to be fulfilled for 11 years) that publicly available information would keep the Authorities up to standard, the Act became law. The Act also left some 28 Statutory Water Companies in place, serving specific geographical areas. These Companies only supply water, usually from artesian wells. Some local authorities continued to run sewage treatment works on a contract basis after 1974.[15]

With adequate funds the new Authorities might have proved effective and enthusiastic watchdogs for water pollution but they were now progressively starved of resources and, as a result, were unable to maintain the standards at their own sewage works. In such circumstances they were in a weak position to prosecute others.

The 1974 Control of Pollution Act and Onwards

The 1974 Control of Pollution Act (COPA) set out to control pollution of water, air and noise. Opposition spokeswoman Margaret Thatcher, MP, described it as 'the most comprehensive attempt for many years to bring pollution under control'.

COPA Part II consolidated and extended existing water pollution controls on the consents system. COPA's major new contribution was the introduction of a public register which would contain information on consents and the frequency with which they were met or broken. But, like the rest of the water provisions, this information clause remained inoperative until 1985. In 1976, despite a severe drought, the water supply did not fail and Kinnersley believes that, when the Labour government looked around for public expenditure cuts to help resolve its balance of payments crisis, the water industry presented 'a ready victim'.

In 1978 the 'consent standards' for sewage works were changed. The National Water Council (NWC) had proposed river quality objectives (RQOs) in 1977. Tim Birch of Greenpeace relates: '. . . many sewage works were regularly breaking the terms of their consents . . . [and now] instead of setting absolute limits it was argued that RQOs should be set for rivers and estuaries. Discharges from sewage works and industries could then be set to ensure that RQOs were met.' In theory this would avoid wasting money on over-lavish treatment plants. However, as Fred Pearce put it in *Watershed: The Water Crisis in Britain*, 'The new concepts were not in practice set to meet properly thought-out RQOs. They were based on nothing more sophisticated or scientific than the existing standard of works. A bad works got a loose consent, regardless of the conditions of the receiving river.'[16]

In 1979 Mrs Thatcher came to power with a new philosophy about public utilities: they should be made to pay. Her government imposed a ceiling on capital expenditure, borrowing limits, financial targets and performance aims.

'Consulting with industry' caused delays in 1975, 1978, 1982 and 1983 says Tim Birch, the delays being caused 'both by Labour and Conservative ministers'. Michael Heseltine and Tom King, Environment Ministers under the Conservative government, said the Act was to be re-examined as concern was mounting that it would cost a lot of money to implement. Civil servants then announced further 'slippages', blaming 'the complexities of subordinate legislation'.[17]

COPA's fate was sealed when, seizing the opportunity created by a political climate in which 'enterprise' values had been successfully pitted against 'social' expenditure, the Confederation for British Industry mounted a concerted effort to draw the Act's teeth. Part II of the Act, said the CBI in 1984, was 'a busybody's charter' and 'one of the worst bits of legislation on the statute book'.[18]

The Thatcher government's recipe of financial stringency, says Kinnersley, was a 'harness designed for a moderately athletic workhorse' but 'applied to an elderly and stiff-jointed camel'. There was 'little sign of improved performance'. To meet the purely financial targets imposed by Whitehall, Water Authorities now adopted a system known as current cost accounting.

The books looked better but there was a cutback in capital expenditure, the very thing that was required to update and improve ageing sewage works. At the same time the Authorities withdrew staff and many smaller works became unmanned. The result, as the Commons Environment Committee put it in 1987, was 'overloading of existing sewage works and operational failure'.[19]

The Water Authorities had set out to achieve spectacular improvements by improving pollution 'black spots' – rivers which, like the Thames in the 1950s, had been dead – but they were now overwhelmed by the wholesale failure of the main sewage system which faced rising demand for treatment at a time of reduced expenditure.

The annual investment in sewerage and sewage disposal in England and Wales had risen steadily throughout the 1960s, a golden age of good intents if not consents. Investment in real terms peaked, at over £800 million (at 1985/6 levels), in 1973/4. It then plunged to just over half that amount by 1982. By 1987 North West Water, the Authority with the greatest legacy of crumbling sewers, would tell the Commons Environment Committee that there were 2,000 overflows – i.e. sewers which leak in storms – in its region, of which 1,000 would soon need replacement. At least 5,000 such overflows needed replacing around the country as a whole.[20]

Government financial priorities and environmental quality had collided, and the environment lost. It was a deliberate programme of allowing more pollution in order to save money, unprecedented in modern times.

In 1985/6 the government tightened the financial targets again. Andrew Lees of Friends of the Earth points out that South West Water has to return 1.5 per cent on existing assets and 5 per cent on new assets.[21] At the same time, the government proposed to reduce the External Financing Limit so that by 1988 the Authority would be almost self-financing. As a result, the Authority increased its charges by 10 per cent and reduced expenditure on things such as pollution control. 'The Government's constraints,' concluded Lees, 'led to a serious deterioration in the standards of service in the period 1981/2 to 1986/7.'

The official river quality surveys for the South West area showed that from 1980 to 1985, 1,107 km of river deteriorated while only 96 km improved.[22] 'With resources limited by the Performance Aims Regime, response times [to incidents] are worse, but most significantly less effort has been put into pollution prevention,' wrote the Authority.[23]

Staff were cut by 25 per cent, the emergency callout rate went up almost 30 per cent (partly due to increased blockages of sewers and equipment breakdowns as a result of less maintenance), and 20 per cent of sewage treatment works failed to meet their standards – four times the target level.[24] All of these factors led to dirtier rivers.

Water pollution grew everywhere except in official statistics. Here it actually went down.

Fiddling the Books

'Moving the goalposts', once a schoolboy sporting phrase, has passed into common parlance and is much favoured by the civil service. It means changing the rules as you go along. While government departments may express themselves in other terms, such as 'introducing a new basis of comparison'; whatever the words used, the meaning is the same: fiddling the books.

When the Control of Pollution Act's provisions were implemented, over ten years late, in January 1985, the Department of the Environment (DoE) sanctioned a 'Review of Consent Conditions'. Of 6,000 sewage discharges in England and Wales, 1,600 were granted 'relaxed consents'. This means a licence to make more pollution. The reason was that Section 31 of the Act now gave the public an opportunity to bring private prosecutions against the Authorities, should they fail to meet standards. From August that year it also became possible to consult a public register giving details of consents and water samples, including effluent from sewage treatment works. To avoid the embarrassment of being prosecuted for failing to meet their own standards, the Water Authorities were encouraged by the government to apply for weaker standards ('relaxed consents'). By 1986, 1,800 sewage works became dirtier, legally.[25]

This wholesale increase in pollution was disguised with official language: 'Resources should be allocated so as to achieve the most beneficial overall impact on the river as a whole, rather than concentrating on the quality of individual discharges,' said the DoE. 'Pending the development of overall policy and procedures based on such objectives, the government will be willing to approve some limited and localised downgradings of effluent quality where it is clear that resources can be put to more effective use elsewhere'.[26] Fine in theory; it sounded as if overall quality might even go up.

In practice, standards of rivers got worse. Despite relaxation of consents, sewage works broke the new, weaker standards.

Sewage Levels in Rivers

Major sewage works have 'numerical' consents defined in terms of 'pollution factors': Biological Oxygen Demand (BOD), which removes oxygen and reduces fish and invertebrate life, Suspended Solids (SS), fine silt-like organic material which chokes fish and coats plant leaves, and ammonia, which can also deplete oxygen in the river. In alkaline water especially, ammonia can be toxic to fish.

In 1969 a government memorandum, 'Recommendation on Sewage Discharge' had set standard consent conditions of 20 mg/litre for BOD and 30 mg/litre for suspended solids (SS). The greater scale of pollution now sanctioned by government is indicated by the example of Mogden sewage works, which discharges into the Thames. In 1989 it was proposed to accept an effluent of 50 mg/litre BOD (i.e. more than twice the 1969 recommendation) and 55 mg/litre SS until 1992, and where the 95 per centile was already 41 mg/litre and 50 mg/litre.[27]

In the Mersey Basin, for example, the 31 largest sewage works were dirtier in 1988 than in 1978, with the allowed level of biological oxygen demand at Swinton trebled. Monitoring in the region fell fourfold and the length of rivers 'too dirty' for fish went up from 340 to 1224 km.[28]

The Commons Environment Committee pointed out that one Water Authority had breached 40 per cent of its discharge consents in 1985, and had still exceeded them in 20 per cent of cases a year later.[29] The Committee found the DoE strangely unable to give it key information about pollution trends. '1986 is the first year for which the DoE has sought comprehensive compliance statistics from water authorities and astonishingly the DoE could give little information on the full extent of non-compliance either now or in the past,' it said.

A New Meaning for 'Satisfactory'

The MPs discovered that in 1986 no fewer than 22 per cent of the total 4,355 sewage works were regarded as 'unsatisfactory' by the Water Authorities Association. But even this was not the full picture. Sewage works now had a special rule different from that for other industries. Instead of having to comply with discharge consents the whole time, the 'consent' would be deemed 'met' if 95 per cent of samples were satisfactory; that is, 1 offence in 20 was discounted. As Kinnersley notes, 'no offence could be proved or punished (unless the authority pleaded guilty) until the end of the year or the averaging period in which it occurred.'[30]

In July 1988 the Department of the Environment said the Water Authorities would meet their latest, relaxed consents 'in the shortest possible timescale – which is probably about three years or mid 1991'.[31] It was, commented the magazine *ENDS*, 'the first public evidence that the government was attempting belatedly to get to grips with this issue'. But the target was soon abandoned. In November 1988, ministers assured Parliament that 'all' or 'almost all' sewage works would be up to standard by March 1992.[32]

Environment Secretary Nicholas Ridley wrote to Conservative MP Cranley Onslow, a council member of the Anglers' Cooperative Association, promising that the government did 'not intend to relax consents on a general or long term basis'. Any consents which were 'relaxed' to allow more pollution would be 'temporary, will take account of the need to protect the receiving water, and will be limited to the period required to carry through the necessary improvement programmes'.[33]

On 21 November 1988 the DoE wrote to the Water Authorities to arrange a further reduction in required standards, this time to enable the water industry to be privatised. As *ENDS* pointed out, the Authorities would be unable to sign flotation prospectuses if their businesses were committing criminal pollution.[34]

Yet, despite government assurances of 'no general lowering of standards', at least 2,300 of 6,430 works were now eligible for relaxed consents. Andrew Lees and Gwynne Lyons at Friends of the Earth said these 'temporary relaxations' meant the government was 'bending the rules to suit the circumstances'. FoE pointed to another letter from the DoE to the Water Authorities, dated 1 February 1988, as conclusive proof of the government's motives: 'The prime purpose of the present exercise,' said the DoE, '. . . is to bring non-compliant works back into compliance as soon as possible.'[35] But works were to comply not by improving their performance, only by being granted a more generous licence to pollute.

The government did its best to disguise this fact. In a letter to a member of the public in June 1989,[36] the Department of the Environment stated that relaxed consents would in general 'regularise the current performance' but 'would not permit a deterioration in performance'. To anyone accustomed to normal use of English, this sounds like an assurance that pollution will not exceed today's levels, or certainly this year's levels. But that is not what the DoE meant.

The New Meaning of 'Current'

'Current' now turned out to mean anything up to three years old. Friends of the Earth obtained an obscure memorandum, 'Estimation of Relaxed Limits', produced by North West Water's Scientific Planning and Research Manager for its engineers in February 1989. This revealed that 'The assessment of current quality is to be made from "Register" samples only and this is to be based on the calendar year 1988 unless it can be shown that a longer period of either 1987 and 1988 or 1986, 1987 and 1988 give a more realistic assessment of "current" quality.'

Friends of the Earth saw this as the first part of a 'fiddle'. With up to three years' data to choose from, there was plainly scope for picking a 'current' level dirty enough to permit some increase in pollution without a measured 'deterioration in performance'.

The New Meaning of 95 per Cent

What the Water Authorities next did to set new pollution levels was mind-bending in its audacity. It is such a blatant fiddle that it is hard to credit, which is perhaps why nothing was done to prevent it.

Already a works was taken to meet its 'consent' if 95 per cent of samples were within the limit each year. Thus the limit is referred to as a 95 per centage limit, and compliance is '95 per centile compliance'. The Authorities did not abandon this terminology but they changed what it meant. To quote from the NWWA memo, 'the 95 per centile assessment is to be taken as the mean value of current quality (as defined above) times 2'. If that does not seem to make much sense, it is hardly surprising: it doesn't make sense. The new standard was calculated by taking the average of the sample results in a year (1985, 1987 or 1988), and then arbitrarily doubling it. This would almost always create a far higher value, sanctioning much lower performance than the original '95 per centile' even though it went by the same name.

'This procedure ignored the statistical basis of the term '95 per centile' and just used it as a label for the much greater pollution level the authorities wanted to allow' says Andrew Lee of FoE, 'It made it a racing certainty they could avoid prosecution.'[37]

Rounding Up

Incredible as it may seem, the official conjuring tricks did not end there. 'The figure thus arrived at,' instructed the memo, is 'to be rounded up to the nearest 5, e.g. 36 would be rounded up to 40, 44 to 45 etc., etc.' As FoE said, this builds in a further 'relaxation'. If, for example, the limit value was 31 and thus automatically became 35, it would mean an extra 13 per cent pollution without anyone noticing.

If there was any doubt as to where North West Water had got these Kafkaesque ideas about statistics, it was dispelled by the announcement in the same memorandum that the rules 'are now being applied nationally [by HMIP]'. HMIP is Her Majesty's Inspectorate on Pollution, under the direct control of central government.

It seems hard to believe that ministers, with their acute awareness of Mrs Thatcher's personal commitment to successful privatisation of the water industry, did not realise what was going on. Andrew Lees of Friends of the Earth points to a DoE press release issued in May 1989, quoting Nicholas Ridley: 'And let me put it clearly on the record: this approach is not a lowering of pollution standards in the run-up to privatisation. . . .' 'As you will see,' said Lees, 'that assertion is simply not true.'

A Licence to Pollute

By summer 1989 a bureaucratic safety net was provided to the privatised water companies in the form of the doubled average consents, the 95 per cent rule and the generous rounding up, all permitting much increased pollution without breaking the law. Nevertheless, the government evidently still feared that water privatisation might be affected by prosecutions, and in June it moved a last-minute amendment to the Water Bill, carried by 309 votes to 203, which granted the new water companies a year of immunity from prosecution for illegal pollution from sewage works resulting from actions by the old Authorities.[38] Immunity meant in effect a licence to pollute.

Fiddling With the 'Look-up Tables'

Even this, however, was not the end of the matter. As Friends of the Earth researcher Gwynne Lyons has pointed out,[39] since 1985 the Water Authorities had used 'look-up tables' to check whether or not effluent samples showed an offence. Under the Water Act of 1988 the records of these had been included on registers open for public inspection. For a member of the public or a body such as a fishing club to draw on samples for a prosecution, the sample has to be 'formed', that is split three ways, with one part delivered to the discharger, one tested, and one held in reserve in case of a dispute. This makes it more difficult and more costly to take samples, which naturally tends to reduce their number.

The system applies to discharges both from sewage treatment works and from industry as a whole, with one important difference. While a single tripartite sample above the consent level would be enough to land an industrial polluter in trouble, a sewage works is treated differently, and can be prosecuted only if a number of tripartite samples show breaches of the consent over a whole year. Naturally, this makes prosecution much more difficult.

When the look-up tables were introduced in 1985 it had been decided that an upper limit should be determined, which should never be exceeded, and any one breach of which would be an offence. It was not until 1989 that this 'upper tier' was set, but then only for works with an interim relaxed consent, and at three times the normal limit. (According to Gwynne Lyons, even the National Rivers Authority had wanted an upper tier set at only twice the normal limit.)

The effect of this became apparent in 1988 when the NWWA was prosecuted by Derbyshire County Council for pollution from Whaley Bridge sewage works. Although the prosecution was partly successful, two of the four charges were thrown out because the magistrates treated the 95 per cent compliance rule as applying to specific determinands (the different substances) tested and not the sample as a whole. Tim Birch of Greenpeace comments: 'Such an interpretation doubles the number of samples in breach of consent which are allowed to pollute rivers'.[40]

The Whaley Bridge prosecution was to throw up even more evidence of shortcomings in pollution control.[41] On 1 March 1989, the 30 mg/litre BOD and 45 mg/litre SS consent was breached by values of 640 and 860 mg/litre respectively. Tests for January to March showing a four-fold breach of consents were published in April, but the tests showing a massive twenty-fold excess of pollution were not released until 29 July. 'We only found these extra readings by accident,' a Derbyshire County Council source told the *Independent* newspaper. The significance of the delay is that, to have force, a legal action must take place within six months of the alleged incident. The law says the Water Authority has 28 days to put details of an incident on the register, but does not say when the updated register must be passed to the registrar. 'The law looks clear but it is not. Instead it provides a loophole authorities can walk through and escape prosecution,' said the chairman of Derbyshire County Council's planning committee.

From November 1988 to September 1989, at least 750 works were already breaching consents and more than 1,000 relaxations were applied for. Gwynne Lyons called it a 'wholesale dispensation'. Some of the applications for 'time-limited' consents were not for 1991 as originally envisaged or even 1992 but up to 1994. 'Standards,' says Lyons, 'are being relaxed despite the Secretary of State's duty to maintain and restore the wholesomeness of rivers under section 1 of the Water Act, and the government's obligations under European Law.'[42] More than 200 more or less unenforceable 'descriptive' consents, with no quantified levels, were also given or applied at smaller works.

Most of the long-term relaxations of 'numerical' consents serve populations of 250,000–1,000,000. In theory there should be a thousand-fold dilution of the sewage effluent by river water. In addition, the river is supposed to achieve certain River Quality Objectives according to specific river quality criteria, but these have had no legal force. Where the consents are descriptive (1,500 smaller works) there are no specific levels, only general urgings, and, as the House of Commons Environment Committee has noted, 'there is (on paper) no way of judging whether their effluent is satisfactory or not',[43] although first hand evidence suggests it frequently is not.

The River Surveys Show a Decline

Just as the public were getting used to the idea that the Thames was a cleaner river running with salmon, the first hard evidence began to emerge that environmental quality was diminishing. Since 1958 British rivers have been classified according to the National Water Council system into four grades, based on biological oxygen demand, suspended solids, ammonia and the river's suitability for fish. The system is as follows:

Class 1:   1A: supports trout and/or salmon (salmonid fish) and provides quality supplies of drinking water.

           1B: less high quality than 1A, but used for the same purpose.

Class 2:   supports 'coarse' fish such as roach and pike (cyprinid fish), but suitable for drinking water only after advanced treatment.

Class 3:   polluted to such an extent that fish are absent or only sporadically present.

Class 4:   grossly polluted and likely to cause a nuisance.

Although crude, the classification indicates river quality. From 1958 to 1980, five-yearly surveys of river quality showed a continuing improvement in the standard of rivers. From 1980 to 1985, of 37,911 km of rivers surveyed in England and Wales, 5,437 km became worse while only 4,489 km improved. Most notably, some 656 km of rivers dropped out of the top class of 'good'. The greatest problems were in the South West, where over 1,000 km of river worsened, largely owing to pollution from farms.[44]

The 1985 Survey showed a net deterioration in 903 km of river (2.5 per cent of the total length surveyed) when compared with 1980. A questionnaire circulated by the magazine *ENDS* showed that another 514 km had been downgraded by 1986. When the Survey was repeated in 1988 it showed a net improvement of 104.5 km.

What exactly do these improvements and deteriorations mean? FoE say, 'The NWC classification system is so crude that it masks ecologically significant increases in water pollution. Even though the levels of pollution may increase sufficiently to harm the wildlife living in the river, the river remains in the same class.'

FoE's concern is supported by evidence from the Nature Conservancy Council (NCC), which is charged with protecting Britain's natural and semi-natural ecosystems and wildlife. In 1987 the NCC wrote: 'Water pollution alongside land drainage is the main problem of wetland wildlife in Britain. It takes many forms such as enrichment by sewage and industrial effluent, toxic chemical pollution, acid deposition, siltation, herbicides, pesticides and industrial discharges. There has been insufficient consideration of the requirements of nature conservation in water quality management and the criteria used for judging "clean" rivers are not enough to guarantee that sensitive plant and invertebrate communities will flourish.'[45]

The NCC's view of what is 'clean' is more demanding than that of the Department of the Environment. The NCC aims to conserve ecosystems complete with the many species that are sensitive to pollution (indeed, in freshwaters this is the great majority of species, only so many of them have disappeared from so much of our environment that we have come to think of sensitive species as the exception rather than the norm). The river quality objectives (RQOs), on the other hand, are set in relation to use for drinking water, fisheries and amenity.[46] As FoE point out, the Authorities or the DoE can say that 'this river meets its objectives for water quality' even if it is almost dead, because the objectives may be set very low.

'There has been a tendency on the part of Water Authorities to allow water quality to slip to the bottom of class 1A or from 1A to 1B,' says the NCC. 'Meanwhile, considerable resources have been expended on reducing the total length of rivers in classes 2, 3 and 4. This present strategy heightens the mediocrity of our rivers in wildlife terms.'

In 1987 the Commons Committee called for 'clear national water quality objectives'[47] and the government announced that 'upon enactment of the new legislation' it would set up legally binding quality objectives for rivers, estuaries, coastal and underground waters. But, as FoE pointed out in 1989, 'There will be no legally binding RQOs, other than those set under EEC Directives, until autumn 1992. The government knows that the continued discharge of poor quality sewage effluents will cause further deterioration in river quality'.[48] (There is a large number of EC Directives relating to water – see Appendix at the end of this chapter.)

Monitoring and the *Torridge Report*

While public concern at the state of Britain's rivers has grown, during the

1980s the standard of information available probably declined significantly.

Financial cuts have reduced the usefulness of monitoring, as samples have become fewer and concentrated on a few chemical parameters that may say little or nothing about ecological changes. For instance, in its *Torridge Report*,[49] South West Water reduced its sampling of river quality by half between 1980 and 1985, from 7,000 samples a year to 3,500. At the same time, water pollution incidents (especially from farming but also from overloaded sewage treatment works) were increasing (from 1,100 in 1980/1 to 1,700 in 1985/6 and a predicted 2,200 in 1986/7).[50]

Because the objectives for rivers were based only on maintaining the status quo at sewage works, it was, in SWWA's words, 'considered that there was no need to collect information on these river waters'. But, from 1980 to 1984, 60 per cent of its sewage works broke their consents and even the Authority admitted this idea proved to be 'naive'. By 1984, 'no estimate of the effects of this non-compliance' could be made on the 'quality of the receiving water-courses', as in the majority of areas monitoring was no longer carried out.

The *Torridge Report* records that from 1966 to 1973 four samples were taken at 18 monitoring points on the river Torridge each year. In 1974 the number of monitoring points dropped to 10 with a frequency of six, which was 'rarely achieved' for the following six years. As a consequence, admits the Authority, 'The effect of [farm drainage] discharge into the Torridge Catchment was not always recorded in the chemical quality of the monitored lengths of the river Torridge, and the majority of pollution events were missed.'[51] Raised ammonia and reduced oxygen levels could be present at levels 'stressful' to aquatic life in the river for up to 60 days without being detected under the scheme of sampling in use in 1986.

Consents for Industrial Pollution

Industrial water pollution was effectively unregulated until the 1950s and then many polluting industries were granted 'deemed consents'. All trade discharges still without a formal consent in October 1987 were granted a deemed consent. 'Industries which complained that they could not afford the necessary improvements in effluent treatment were also granted deemed consents,' says Tim Birch of Greenpeace. Formal new consents with tougher conditions will not now apply until 1992.

No national figures have been published to show how far industry meets its legal pollution targets. Birch says there is a 'disturbingly high' rate of indus-trial pollution above the legal limit, and points to the 'very low prosecution rate'. In 1986/7 the Welsh Water Authority found 64 per cent of trade discharges were illegal. From March 1986 to December 1987 a quarter of trade effluents and private sewage works failed to stay within limits in Yorkshire, and from August 1985 to December 1987 Severn Trent found that 37 per cent of trade discharges were illegal.

However, in 1987 Yorkshire brought only 10 prosecutions as a result of 763 breaches, involving 150 companies. In Severn Trent, 789 breaches also led to just 10 prosecutions.

In his 1989 report *Poison in the System*,[52] Tim Birch details a case study of the Merseyside chemical company, Norsochem. By using the COPA consent register, Greenpeace calculated that Norsochem's factory in Widnes was discharging the following impressive array of pollutants each year: chemical oxygen demand (COD) – 4,259 tonnes; suspended solids – 102 tonnes; cadmium 29 kg; iron 14 kg; total heavy metals 2.9 tonnes; cyanide 1.4 tonnes; ammonia 508 tonnes; benzene 16.3 tonnes; toluene 17.3 tonnes; HCHs (chlorinated hydrocarbons) 108 tonnes; phenols 3.8 tonnes.[53] Benzene and toluene are carcinogens – cancer-causing chemicals – and are also known to cause birth defects. Benzene, toluene and phenols are treated as 'priority pollutants' in the USA.

At Norsochem's outfall 1, the COD consent value was a maximum 6,500 mg/litre; in other words, each litre of effluent must not use up more than 6,500 milligrammes (65 grammes) of dissolved oxygen in each litre of water. Yet on 8 July 1987, Norsochem discharged effluent with a COD of 33,300 mg/litre, five times the legal limit. But, says Greenpeace, 'They were not formally warned or prosecuted by NWWA despite the Authority's contention that companies with deemed consents are prosecuted if they are in gross violation of their consent terms.'[54]

This case was one of only two samples taken from Norsochem's pipe in the year July 1987–July 1988; the other was also above the consent level.

Not far from Widnes, ICI's plants at Rocksavage and Castner-Kellner on the Weaver Navigational Canal broke their consents 90 times between June 1987 and June 1988 but, says Greenpeace, 'ICI received only one warning letter from NWWA and were not prosecuted.'

ICI's pollution is now part of NWWA's target for the clean-up of the Mersey. However, their case illustrates a more general scarcity of prosecutions against industrial polluters in breach of their consents. During 1975–1986, for example, the NWWA made only 10 prosecutions for breaches of discharge consent conditions, despite 118 of 194 discharges by industry being 'unsatisfactory'. Like MAFF and DoE, the Authority preferred 'emphasis on discussion and persuasion' rather than prosecution.[55] It has proved equally ineffective.

In 1988, Environment Secretary Nicholas Ridley said, 'The Water Authorities incredibly have been given the role of gamekeeper and poacher. It never works and I think there has been some hesitation to prosecute the industrialists who have exceeded their discharge consents, for no other reason than that a lot of Water Authorities are also exceeding their discharge consents.'[56]

But industrialists were also heavily represented on the Authorities. From 1987/8 the Severn Trent Authority's 13 board members included a member of the CBI's Grand Council; a non-executive board member of British Gas; a director of the Central Electricity Generating Board; and the chairman of Industrial and Heating Services Ltd. Environmental interests were supposedly represented, but only by an appointee of the Ministry of Agriculture, namely the executive chairman of Birmingham Anglers Association Ltd.

The same year in the North West, the 10 board members had amongst their number the chairman of the CBI's North West Environmental Committee (who was also president of the Paper and Board Industry Federation, representing a major polluting industry), a senior former commercial adviser to Esso Europe, and a counsellor on the Department of Trade and Industry's Enterprise Initiative. The interests of the environment were represented by the chairman of the Regional Fisheries Advisory Committee.

Northumbrian Water boasted 11 board members, including one who was on the Board of Tioxide Group as well as being chief executive of the Cookson Group's Metals and Chemicals Division; and a former deputy group secretary of ICI Chemicals and Polymers at Billingham (on the Tees) in Cleveland. A member of the Northern Area and Regional Fisheries Committees was there to speak up for conservation.

Meanwhile, in Yorkshire, the board's 12 members included Gordon Jones, chairman of the Authority and a former managing director of steel and engineering companies, as well as manager of Industrial Sales at Esso Petroleum; the chairman of Rowntree Mackintosh Ltd; a former director of BP and a former managing director of BP Chemicals in Belgium. Yorkshire's environment was represented, again, by the chairman of the Regional Fisheries Advisory Committee.

Viewed with the rosiest spectacles available, and with the greatest possible faith in human nature, it is impossible to avoid the conclusion that these gentlemen, with such backgrounds and interests, would be likely to err in favour of acceding to industrial demands rather than upholding tighter environmental standards in the face of protests from the CBI and its members.

In addition, the meetings of Water Authorities which had originally been open to the public to ensure accountability, were allowed to become secret. The 1979/80 Report of the NWWA stated, 'In general industry supported the philosophy behind the review of conditions of consent for all industrial discharges and cooperated well in agreeing revised consent conditions.'[57] 'Hardly surprising,' says Tim Birch, since 'this meant that industry was allowed to legally discharge more pollution than before.'[58]

Meanwhile, Birch points out, deemed consents were awarded to outfall pipes leading into estuaries or tidal waters, bringing them within the COPA umbrella but not imposing any new standards. Lastly, the 95 per centile rule, meant to apply only to sewage discharges, was now also applied to some industrial pollution, in breach of S32 of COPA which made it an offence for any consent to be broken if it is not a Water Authority discharge.

The government has pursued a deliberate policy of connecting industry to the sewers and up to a fifth of sewage effluent is industrial. Water companies earn money from the service, but heavy metals and toxic organics can often poison, overload or pass straight through the UK's existing sewage works. As a result, rivers as well as sewage sludge are widely contaminated.

Heavy Metals In River Life

Levels of heavy metals in fish give one of the best indications of the degree of industrial contamination of rivers. In 1987, Dr Chris Mason of Essex University reported a survey of mercury, lead and cadmium in the muscle of 221 fish, principally eels and roach, but also gudgeon, brown trout, perch and pike, from 67 sites in Great Britain.[59] A significant number had 'concentrations of metals . . . above recommended standards for human consumption'. A quarter of the eels sampled by Mason exceeded the mercury level of 300 ug/kg, set in a proposed EC Directive, mainly those from East Anglia and northeast Scotland.

For lead, the World Health Organisation has proposed a tolerable maximum intake of 3,000 ug/person, with a tolerable concentration of lead in fish flesh of 2,000 ug/kg. At 15 per cent of the British sites, the average level of lead in fish exceeded this level;[60] 16.7 per cent of the eels sampled contained more than this, and over 25 per cent of the roach exceeded the limit, along with one in five of the trout.

'There are,' says Mason, 'apparently no quality standards relating to the amount of cadmium allowed in food stuffs,' but, assuming a similar relationship between the weekly intake and the standards in fish flesh to those for mercury, WHO standards would have been exceeded in 23.3 per cent of eels Mason studied, and in 6.7 per cent of roach.[61]

Pollution Incidents

Individual instances of pollution are recorded by Water Authorities as 'incidents'.

For 'incidents' to have been recorded we must rely on a Water Authority scientist or, more likely, a fisherman or member of the public being on hand to notice a sudden and obvious change in a river, most usually the presence of dead fish or the visible pouring of pollutants into the river. So, if a chemical company discharges an extra 10 tonnes of waste at its outfall pipe, it may not get noticed and recorded as an incident, whereas the same 10 tonnes spilt down a drain from a crashed road tanker probably would.

'Pollution incidents' are thus largely a record of pollution caused through equipment breakdowns or accidents, and through pollution of previously or usually unpolluted rivers. They are just the tip of the pollution iceberg. 'Incidents' do not take account of the chronic long-term deterioration of rivers, although they contribute to it, and they do hit the headlines. This makes it all the more worrying that pollution 'incidents' have been steeply on the rise since 1979.

In 1986/7 the House of Commons Environment Committee noted that 'published figures show that reported pollution incidents of all kinds rose by more than a half from 13,000 to around 20,000 in the five years 1980–1985'.[62] In 1987/8,[63] over 23,250 incidents were recorded, a rise of 2,000 on the year before. Incidents in Wales rose 53 per cent, in the North West 19 per cent and in Yorkshire 21 per cent.

Few offenders are prosecuted. Of the 23,250 incidents reported in 1987/8, Water Authority staff substantiated 13,696. Of these, 37 per cent were due to industry, 21 per cent to sewage pollution, 18.5 per cent to farming and 23.5 per cent to other causes.

Pollution Incidents Due to Farming

Pollution incidents due to agriculture grew from almost nothing in the early 1970s to become a major problem in the late 1980s. 'Hay ricks and duck ponds are rare sights on today's farm,' wrote the Commons Environment Committee in 1987. 'Silage stores and slurry pits seem to be their successors. Slurry can be 100 times and silage 200 times as polluting as domestic sewage.'[64]

In 1979, there were 1,500 reported incidents of farm pollution; by 1985 the number reached 3,500. 'Widespread alarm,' said the MPs, 'was expressed to us on this topic. For the most part, farm wastes pollute high quality rivers which were previously clean.' By 1985, said South West Water, farm pollution made up over 30 per cent (622) of the pollution incidents in their area. It was, said the Authority, 'a direct, unwelcome consequence of national agricultural policy which has concentrated on increasing production without adequate consideration of wider implications.'

Farming now produces mind-boggling quantities of pollution. On the once-unpolluted River Torridge in Devon, South West Water calculated that the average Devon dairy herd of 53 animals created potential pollution equivalent to that of a community of 465 inhabitants. 'If silage is made for winter storage, which is likely, then an average crop for a herd this size would be 650 tonnes. If this crop had been wilted then there would be 145,000 litres of silage effluent to be disposed of at a rate of 19,000 litres per day. The potential pollution load of this effluent is equivalent to that of a community of 10,800 inhabitants,' said SWWA.[65] For each tonne of silage, 100 gallons of silage liquor are produced. Severn Trent Water calculated that a 400-tonne clamp of unwilted silage would produce as much pollution as the town of Derby.[66]

The Commons Environment Committee took particular issue with the Ministry of Agriculture, a body which has always regarded itself as the guardian of the agricultural rather than the public interest. 'Our major concern,' they said, 'is the complacent attitude of MAFF. Their evidence to us barely conceded that agricultural pollution has been heavily implicated as one of two major threats to water quality. . . MAFF's failure to take farm pollution seriously is encapsulated in its ineffective approach of "positive encouragement" [rather than regulation]'.[67]

In 1988 the number of farm pollution incidents increased for the ninth time in ten years, to nearly three times the 1979 number.[68] Of the 4,141 farm pollution incidents, 815 involved silage liquor and 2,272 involved dairy or cattle wastes. A survey in the Severn Trent, South West and Yorkshire areas showed that 46 per cent or more of all dairy farms had pollution problems. Severn Trent Water pointed out that this dispelled the National Farmers' Union view that as few as 1 per cent of farms were responsible for the pollution.[69]

In 1987 the House of Commons Environment Committee had highlighted and criticised the agricultural escape clause in the 1974 Control of Pollution Act, which allowed farmers to plead 'Good Agricultural Practice' as an excuse to pollute. Under that Act, farmers enjoy a defence against prosecution if a river or stream is polluted through 'an act or an omission which is in accordance with good agricultural practice'.[70]

Whether or not the defence was used, the special legal treatment for farming creates a climate of opinion in which farm pollution is not taken seriously, and in which farmers get financial and moral help rather than face prosecution as would other small businessmen. Under the 1989 Privatisation of Water Bill, the special defence of 'good agricultural practice' was due to be abolished but, at the same time, the government is grant-aiding pollution measures for farmers, rather than making the polluter pay.

The immediate causes of pollution by slurry (liquid excrement produced by farm animals, usually living in sheds) and silage (decomposing grass sweetened with other vegetable substances and fed to animals in winter) are usually storage facilities that are inadequate, poorly constructed or completely absent. Both used to be rare problems. Animals were kept in fields and ate grass. Their manure was spread on the fields, either by the beasts themselves or, for those kept indoors over winter, by the farmer. But, since Britain joined the EC, more and more farms have gone over to 'zero grazing' systems. Animals are kept in sheds all the time, grass is cut and made into silage and fed to them in sheds, and slurry is a waste product because arable and dairy farms are now concentrated into different zones of the country.

Other countries have similar pollution problems but deal with them differently. From discussions with officials in the Netherlands, Switzerland and West Germany, the Commons Environment Committee concluded that it was 'perfectly feasible' to control farm slurry and silage. The Dutch, they pointed out, suffered enormous problems with excess production of manure and yet, despite an influential farming lobby, had introduced controls on the number of animals a farmer was allowed to keep and were to introduce regulations on the structure and construction of slurry pits and silage stores. In West Germany, the total volume of slurry that can be spread onto land can be restricted.

'In the UK,' the Committee noted, 'a farmer can double his holding of, say, pigs without having to demonstrate any increase at all in his ability to handle the extra waste. By contrast in Switzerland we learnt that storage capacity . . . has to be of sufficient size to outlast the winter months, when manure is not spread on the land.' Although the 1974 Control of Pollution Act gave powers for the government to stipulate how slurry lagoons and silage clamps should be constructed, the decision actually to use them was not taken until May 1989.[71]

Few farmers were prosecuted. The magazine *ENDS* reported in 1989: 'Despite the larger number of incidents, prosecutions declined from 225 in 1987 to 148 in 1988. South West Water, which accounted for 45 per cent of the serious incidents, prosecuted only 6 per cent of the offending farms.' Reported average fines remained minutely small: as little as £165 in Wales, and only up to £630 in Yorkshire.[72] In 1986 even a Ministry of Agriculture and Water Authorities Association report found that 'polluters find it cheaper to pay the fine than to undertake the work necessary to prevent pollution'.[73]

In Scotland, the picture was even worse. During 1987, agricultural incidents rose 49 per cent from 478 to 713. A quarter of recorded fish kills were due to farm pollution, principally silage effluent. A report found that poor construction and maintenance of silos accounted for 60 per cent of all leaks. The Scottish River Purification Boards increased their rate of prosecution, from 2 in 1982 and 7 in 1986 to 17 in 1987 (2.4 per cent).[74]

Pollution Incidents Due to Industry

Industry remains the single largest cause (over a third) of pollution incidents. Many industrial 'pollution incidents' are accidents which could be prevented if facilities were better, procedures safer, equipment more modern and operators better trained and more careful.

According to the *Sunday Times*, for example, widely available modern equipment to detect corrosion in pipelines was not used by Shell at its Stanlow Refinery, which released 150 tonnes of oil into the Mersey affecting 2,000 birds on Saturday 19 August 1989.[75] Pipes close to or connected to the one that broke had leaked in 1986 and 1988. The newspaper pointed out that the Department of Energy's Pipeline Inspectorate employs only one man to check 37,000 miles of onshore pipe and required a pressure test which, 'Safety experts say. . . does not provide an adequate check for internal and external corrosion on pipelines.'

Other reports suggest that Shell's monitoring equipment failed to identify the spill until 3 p.m. although it had been seen at 2.38 p.m.[76] In the interim, most of the oil entered the river. 'The subsequent clean up was a shambles,' said the *Sunday Telegraph*, quoting 'senior figures in the oil business'. Specialists from Southampton were not summoned until 29 hours after the incident, and local oil cleaning equipment was not used. Fire brigade sources told the *Sunday Telegraph*, 'Shell's major concern was with their fractured pipeline, not the slick. They more or less threw their hands in the air and said "Over to you".'

The new National Rivers Authority pressed the prosecution against Shell, and secured a £1 million fine. The judge highlighted Shell's 'good' environmental record as one reason why the fine was not higher, which makes the £120,000 Shell handed out to small conservation groups through its Better Britain Competition in 1989/90 look like a PR bargain. Shell spent £10 million on advertising in 1989.

Many incidents are 'small' but their effects can be serious. On 10 August 1989, for example, 5 miles of the River Lyd, at Lifton in Devon, and part of the Tamar were polluted by heavy fuel oil.[77] In May 1989 a similar incident occurred on the Lyme Brook, a tributary of the River Trent.[78] As in several other serious incidents, vandals were blamed for opening valves, this time on an oil tank at a textile factory owned by Coats Viyella. In what Severn Trent called 'one of the worst incidents of oil pollution we have had' 2,000 gallons of 'thick black oil' flooded down the river. Fairly prompt action was taken to place booms down the river and bring in 'skimmers'. But, one wonders, why cannot all companies with such potential hazards be required to have locks on the valves or containment such that it is a physical impossibility for spills to go downriver?

The Commons Committee were impressed by a visit to Shipley Europe Ltd, a chemical company on the Binley Industrial Estate near Coventry, where they were shown an extensive system of underground emergency tanks which would hold the large amounts of fire-fighting water that would inevitably become contaminated in the event of a fire.

On the Rhine, BASF and Sandoz have both now invested in large 'catch basins' for the same reason, as well as to trap spills before they reach water-courses or sewers.[79]

Water Privatisation

In political terms, neither right nor left shows any particular propensity for protecting the environment. Unfettered pursuit of short-term profit, with all the environmental costs borne by society at large and not by the industry concerned, is a guaranteed recipe for environmental destruction. On the other hand, you need only look at centrally planned countries such as the USSR, China or Poland to see that the same activities can be pursued with equal or even worse results in the name of the state or the people.

Privatising Britain's water supplies, its rivers, reservoirs, sewage works and drains, creates a potential conflict of interest between private profit and public access to clean and natural water. On the other hand, the state-run Water Authorities have shown themselves very insensitive to public concerns over pollution, for whatever reasons.

So, whereas the Labour Party has opposed water privatisation, and the Conservative government promoted it, on grounds of political theory, environment groups have voiced their concerns over the likely effects of the particular proposals, rather than the principle of privatisation.

As the Thatcher government's privatisation plans gathered steam, an extra economic factor soon emerged which linked the financial viability of the appropriately named 'flotation' with future water companies' ability to meet the EC's environmental standards. Once it was realised that a successful privatisation would depend on meeting pollution standards, this created major political difficulties for the government.

First, it became impossible to hide any longer the fact that Britain's sewerage system was creaking with age, blighted by crumbling sewers, over-loaded and failing to meet its own standards. Domestic law meant it would be illegal for the Secretary of State to authorise flotation of Authorities if they were breaking the law themselves: hence the books had to be fiddled to turn illegal levels of pollution into legal levels.

Second, Britain was lagging badly on implementation of several EC Directives related to water and had saved money by putting off the necessary action. The new standards were generally no higher than those of the 1970s in the UK but the EC would insist on enforcement. Nobody would want to invest in a company which would sooner or later face massive and unknown expenditure on treatment facilities, so the bill had to be met. Or be made public. This meant reversing government policy and allowing a massive write-off of Authority debt (i.e. giving away public money) in order to finance the investment before shares were offered to the stock market. £4,520 million was written off and £1,190 million extra cash injected.[80]

Third, in the year running up to the privatising of the Authorities in autumn 1989, pollution leapt up the scale of public concern, a move fuelled not least by the Prime Minister's own 'green conversion' in September 1988. This made it a political embarrassment for the government to have to argue that Britain's tap water, rivers and beaches were filthy enough to require enormous increases in public expenditure, while for years it had claimed that they were among the cleanest in the world.

The theory and history of water privatisation since it was mooted in 1985 is recounted by the economist John Bowers and his colleagues in the CPRE/RSPB 1988 report *Liquid Assets*.[81] In 1989, John Bowers and colleagues were back with a second report *Liquid Costs*,[82] commissioned by WWF and Tessa Tennant of Media Natura.

The government's estimates of the costs of meeting 'environmental standards' – including the Drinking Water Directive (see next chapter), renewing sewerage works and meeting the Bathing Water Directive – increased from £2,500 million in December 1988 to £18,630 million in August 1989. Ministers presented it as privatisation paying for higher standards but this was almost wholly untrue.

Liquid Costs points out that the identifiable environmental costs add up to only £5,660 million. The extra £13,000 million can only be accounted for by a wholesale renewal (amounting to a quarter of the total service assets of the industry over ten years) of neglected infrastructure, including mains, sewers and water treatment facilities. The costs, said the economists, 'are not the consequence of rising environmental standards. Indeed, for the most part, it is not true that industry faces a new tougher set of environmental regulations. Consent levels for discharges are easier than in the late 1970s and river water quality has declined. The investment programme over the next decade will do no more than arrest the decline. The river standards of the late 1970s are unlikely to be seen during the rest of the century.'

When privatisation was first mooted, the government proposed technical measures to ensure internal efficiency. Now, however, it brought in CPT or 'Cost Pass Through'. This would encourage large capital investment – which might help meet environmental standards – but would pass the cost straight to the water consumer. This might well cause consumer resistance, while water shareholders would not have to pay for improvements.

Bowers' team concluded that privatisation may well delay a recovery in river quality and encourage a deterioration in the early 1990s, lead to over-abstraction from rivers (also concentrating pollution) and postpone essential renewal of infrastructure until the late 1990s.

An optimistic view of privatisation was provided by Environment Secretary Nicholas Ridley. Interviewed by the BBC, he said: 'Privatisation has been a glorious example of helping quality because it has forced us to work out the difference between the role of providing water and the role of supervising quality, and we've got that right now. Now, I don't have any doubt that this will provide a huge improvement.'[83] As the *Financial Times* pointed out, while separating the clean and dirty functions was a good idea, it was difficult to see why you had to privatise an industry in order to do it. The new National Rivers Authority is, in any case, not a private but a public body.

Britain's Rivers Today

By 1989 it had become apparent to many that Britain's rivers had changed for the worse. In the words of the *Daily Telegraph*, 'For Britain's rivers, the 1980s has been an appalling decade. Starved of resources and the will necessary to keep it healthy, much of our river network has become a dumping ground for industrial waste and sewage. By 1987 ten per cent of our rivers had been classed as biologically dead.'[84]

But anyone trying to assess the true state of Britain's rivers is hamstrung by a lack of information: there is no comprehensive monitoring system using sensitive ecological indicators. Incidents data do not reflect deteriorations in the ecology of rivers. Figures for prosecutions tell very little of the overall story.

In 1987, for example, Southern Water brought only 8 prosecutions from 1,795 incidents and the Severn Trent brought only 37 from 4,435 incidents.[85] In 1989, the Severn Trent Authority was itself prosecuted by Derbyshire County Council for 17 alleged offences of exceeding the consent standards for its sewerage works, part of the Council's objection to the Authority's plans to relax conditions at seven works for up to three years[86] but prosecutions of Authorities were extremely rare.

Relating river quality to changes in pollution from sewerage works is made all the more difficult by the statistical devices of the DoE. The press, public and pressure groups have to rely on anecdotes, piecemeal observation of problems and records of individual incidents.

In February 1989, 5 million gallons of untreated sewage poured into the Stour near Kidderminster, which flows into the Severn. According to the *Sunday Times*, it was 12 hours before Water Authority officials were informed.

In June 1989, Thames Water found itself defending a decision to ask for a relaxed consent at Wargrave, Berkshire, three months after it was fined £4,500 (Thames made profits of £206 million in 1988/9) for exceeding its existing consent. The action was brought by Wargrave Residents' Association as a private prosecution. Despite the fact that the application was to increase the ammonia by 33 per cent and the BOD by 39 per cent, the Thames Water Director of Operations claimed to the *Sunday Times* that there would be no worse 'pollution load' and it would not lead to lower standards.[87]

In July, Devon trout farmer Claude Caple suffered pollution from farm slurry upstream for the third time. 'Dead wild fish were yesterday floating in the jet black waters of a Devon river poisoned by 50,000 gallons of pig slurry,' wrote the *Independent* on 31 July 1989.[88] Pig slurry first entered Caple's trout farm in 1981, killed 24,000 fish in 1983, and in 1989 he said, 'we have lost the business.' Kingfishers, said Caple, had just returned for the first time since 1981, when the original pollution took place.

Rivers are also the main recipients of an unknown number of sewer 'overflows', many no more sophisticated than a hole bashed in the side of a pipe at a convenient point. Raw sewage flushes from these into rivers when rain overcomes the dwindling capacity of Britain's crumbling sewers. One estimate is of at least 5,000 such inadequate 'overflows'.[89] At Newtown in Powys, for example, 'residents have complained of faeces, sanitary towels and condoms floating in the Severn'.[90]

The Rother

In 1989 a *Daily Telegraph* journalist, Graham Coster, visited the river Rother with Greenpeace pollution consultant Steve Simpson. The Rother, with a number of other Yorkshire rivers, was featured in the comprehensive Greenpeace report *Poison in the System*.[91] 'Even the ducks on the Rother,' wrote Coster after his visit, 'know better than to dive in, though no one has told them that this is officially the dirtiest river in Britain.'[92]

From its source at Pilsey in Derbyshire to where it joins the river Don, the Rother is heavily polluted by old and new industries and by sewage. In proportion to its 58 km it has more Grade 4 (biologically dead) lengths than any other river in the country.

Iron oxide run-off from a disused mine and the Clay Cross sewage works make the Rother Grade 3 even in its first 6 kilometres. At Hasland near Chesterfield, the National Smokeless Fuels factory turns coal into a cleaner fuel but at the same time creates heavy chemical pollution of the river. Coster describes 'a strong smell of ammonia, and khaki water streaking out to lie on the river like clots of cream'.

The YWA consents specify levels of nitrates, phenols, permanganates and suspended solids. Studying a print-out of the consent limits and the values monitored by YWA, Coster found that, whereas the permanganate value should not exceed 25 mg/litre, in 12 of 17 samples a greater value was recorded. 'On 4 November 1988 the permanganate value was 384' – 15 times the legal limit. Suspended solids, which were supposed to stay below 40 mg/litre, reached 580 mg/litre on 12 April 1988 – 14 times the legal limit. Ammonia breached the level on five occasions.

A little way downstream, at Old Whittington sewage works, the Rother becomes Grade 4 for the rest of its route. Downstream of that works is Staveley Chemicals, owned by Rio Tinto Zinc. Here, caustic soda and benzene are made. Coster writes, 'At an outflow pipe a strip of water the colour of Worcester sauce was coming out. The rat swimming across looked as if it was having to push its way through.' Staveley's ammonia consent is set at 100 mg/litre, five times the level of the upstream sewage works. 'The plant,' noted Coster, 'was allowed to put mercury in the river as well – one of only six licensed by the EEC – although in strictly limited concentration, and it had recently commissioned a £1m treatment unit to reduce its mercury emissions. Also coming in for the first time at this outflow was carbon tetrachloride.'

Staveley, observed Coster, 'was banal confirmation that people will do what they are able to. If you let industry put a lot of ammonia in the river, it will; if you make it clean up its mercury, it will.'[93]

Coster's walk down the Rother took him through Rother Valley Country Park, used by over 600,000 people a year, and where an artificial lake had been constructed on the site of an abandoned open-cast coal mine, which was 'thoroughly pleasant'. But although in 1974, the year of the ill-fated Control of Pollution Act, it had been planned that a clean-up of the Rother would mean its water could be used for the lake, it was now filled with water pumped in from a brook several miles away, and the Rother, too polluted to be used, 'flowed on right through the middle of the Park, focal and redundant, and out the other side'.

In 1990 the NRA promised that voluntary clean–ups by industry would put fish back in the Rother by 1993. But it plans to do so without prosecutions, allowing law-breaking to go on. 'If industry gives an indication of working towards an agreed programme, we will turn a blind eye to minor infringements,' said its local pollution manager.[94]

The Avon

There are several river Avons in England, which is perhaps unsurprising since the Celtic Afon, as in Welsh, means river. The river Avon that flows from Naseby Reservoir in Northamptonshire is an artery of middle England both ecologically and socially, traversing the centre of the country from east to west. By rights the Avon should be clean. For the most part it flows through a deeply rural landscape and through small market towns. Its course is lined with the sites of famous battles and houses, not to mention the home of the English-speaking world's most famous writer. Touching as it does on some of Britain's most famous tourist attractions, it should surely be conserved as an economic and a natural resource. Sadly it is neither clean nor conserved.

The Times launched an investigation of the Avon in May 1989 with help from Peter Riley of Friends of the Earth. Journalist Paul Vallely travelled the length of the river. 'A rural idyll?' he asked. 'Not so. For, like most English rivers, the Avon is significantly and increasingly polluted. The Avon is far from being the worst river in Britain: it is just a fairly typical one.'[95]

There are 829 km of waterways in the Avon catchment and 19 sewage works which failed to meet their consent conditions in 1989. Fifteen of these works, discovered Vallely, were having their consent conditions relaxed so as to accommodate the new pollution. Even at the source of the Avon, run-off from rape fields treated with heavy doses of chemical fertiliser and pesticides enters the waters.

The first large sewage works on the Avon is at Rugby. The works are now inadequate. 'Constructed for a far smaller population in the 1930s,' wrote Vallely, 'to save money, pumps were not installed and the system was gravity-fed. Pumps have been introduced since and the authority has, over the past few years, spent over £1.7m trying to update it. But such money is small beer for the scale of work required in modernising plants which are still largely based on Victorian technology. A tour of the ancient plant at Rugby is more like a visit to an industrial museum than to a modern system of waste disposal. When a part of the creaking equipment broke down recently, the system had to operate on half-capacity for weeks while an engineering firm manufactured the replacement which was so antique that it was no longer kept in stock.'

Discharging 19.5 million litres a day, Rugby 'consistently fails to meet the standards which the law demands'. From Rugby, the Avon is too polluted with sewage to be abstracted for drinking water.

Downstream comes Finham, which serves Coventry with a major and modern works including a £3.5 million tertiary treatment plant. Nevertheless it turns the river from Grade 2 to Grade 3. At Leamington Spa foul sewage and rainwater mix in sewers which overflow during storms, sending 'the contents of the city's lavatories . . . neat into the river'. At large and small plants Vallely found 'there was clear evidence of . . . toilet paper and used condoms caught in driftwood around the outflows or caked around the storm drains' owing to uncontrolled overflows.

On the river Arrow, a tributary of the Avon, the rapidly growing population of Redditch New Town is overwhelming the capacity of the small watercourse. Peter Riley told *The Times*, 'In dry weather about 75 per cent of it is sewage effluent. It is only a small river. It is just not big enough to take the additional flow.' Local anglers reported that, 'Yields of fish are down to a quarter of what they were. The big fish are surviving but the small ones don't seem to be able to grow.'

The swan population on the Avon has dropped from over 100 pairs to a few dozen. Canoeists have been warned not to practise submersing 'rolls', while fishermen have been warned against eating eels caught in the river because of pesticides. Peter Riley has demonstrated that high levels of both DDT and dieldrin are present in the Evesham stretch of the Avon, thanks to illicit use by market gardeners and farmers. And 'the quiet banks of Stratford and the frontage of the Royal Shakespeare Company's theatre,' said *The Times*, 'once famous for its swans,' is now 'lined with fast food detritus'. Which may be the least of the Avon's problems, but it is certainly an indication of how little Britain cares for its environment.

Lake Windermere

'Had Wordsworth been strolling along the banks of southern Windermere earlier this year,' wrote Francesca Turner in the *Guardian* in August 1989, 'his sensibilities might have been sorely miffed by the sight of raw sewage dangling from branches in a manner humbly described by North West Water as "aesthetically revolting" and "grossly offensive".'[96] Whereas many people are aware of the gradual eutrophication of the shallow, peaty Norfolk Broads with nutrients from farm waste and sewage works, the idea that deep, clear, cool Lake Windermere could be seriously polluted is somewhat shocking.

Nevertheless, eutrophication is taking place. In 1979, the Institute of Freshwater Ecology, which is based beside Lake Windermere, first alerted the North West Water Authority to a build-up of nutrients and a response from plankton. Farm nitrates, detergents and sewage from a growing tourist population have led to lower oxygen levels over the lake's southern basin. Here, two of the lake's four unique populations of char are found. The risk to the sensitive char led the NCC, Lake District National Parks Authority, Cumbria Wildlife Trust and South Lakeland District Council to object to a proposal by NWWA to relax the consent for Tower Wood sewage works on Bowness Bay. The works failed to meet its consent in 3 of 48 tests in 1988 – 9. A fault at the works led to the raw sewage decorating branches on the shorelines.

A £3 million improvement to the works starting in 1990 should give all the sewage good 'conventional treatment' but not nutrient stripping. At Esthwaite Water, a Site of Special Scientific Interest, phosphate from sewage was causing eutrophication until a stripping plant was built. 'As yet,' wrote Turner, 'NWWA is not prepared to pledge the extra cash required for this installation' at Windermere.

The Thames

A Thames Water Authority video states, 'On 23 August 1983, Mr Russel Dolg caught a Thames salmon by rod and line. It was the first time for 150 years. Today with the industrial revolution over and the current pollution strictly controlled, the river is clean.' If this were true, nowhere should be cleaner than the upstream tributaries where salmon spawn in cleanwater gravel river beds with a high oxygen supply to feed the eggs buried among the stones. But despite the salmon now found migrating up the Thames, the river may not be clean enough for a breeding population to establish there. Salmon are continually reintroduced to the river from hatcheries by Thames Water at a cost of £60,000 a year, but there are chemicals in the water which may affect the eggs' development.[97]

On the upper Thames tributary of the river Ray, Mike Walsh of Granada's 'World in Action' found fisherman Robin Pizzey. Holding up streamside vegetation he said, 'You should be able to see freshwater shrimps and aquatic life. . . There's nothing alive. . . it's just a mass of muck and it stinks.' The fisherman cited the freshwater crayfish as an indicator of pollution. He hadn't seen one for ten years. As a child he used to play under the bridges catching crayfish. 'We used to have buckets of them. You don't get them now.' Pizzey described nearby Hammington Brook, another Thames tributary: 'That was badly polluted by farm effluent earlier this year,' he said. 'It was said to be six times more toxic than raw sewage – the fine was £500.' How much damage was done? asked reporter Mike Walsh. 'It wiped the river out, it just wiped it out. There were fish dead everywhere,' said the fisherman.

Mr Pizzey wrote expressing his concern to Nicholas Ridley, his local MP. Mr Ridley replied, 'I think it is true that the quality of the Thames as a whole has improved enormously. I hope you will find this reassuring.'[98]

Downstream in Berkshire, 'World In Action' found a besuited and urbane local resident Mr Tom Berman less than reassured about the state of Wargrave sewage works. Here the growth of a local housing estate had overloaded an inadequate sewerage works, creating waves of murky brown scum up to 15 cm deep on the river. Wargrave village holds an annual regatta on the Thames but in 1988 it had to be cancelled. 'The poor old anglers. . . they were having to fish over bushes festooned with condoms and sanitary towels. I mean it really is unbelievable.'[99]

Berman and his fellow residents discovered that Wargrave sewage works had an ammonia limit of five mg/litre in 1982. In 1983 it was raised to 15 – a threefold increase – at the request of TWA.

'World In Action' asked Peter McIntosh of TWA how he felt about 20 per cent of his sewage works committing criminal offences by breaking consent standards (even though many of them had already been relaxed).

> McIntosh: 'Yes, that's a difficult situation and indeed we were prosecuted last year.'
> Walsh: 'Do you think that you could have expected more prosecutions?'
> McIntosh: 'No, I hope not. I don't see that it would help anyone if we were prosecuted frivolously many more times.'
> Walsh: 'Frivolously?'
> McIntosh: 'We have many very large expensive programmes to improve matters and I don't think further prosecutions could cause us to go any faster.'

Downstream, the London Wildlife Trust was objecting to proposals to more pollution from the two much larger sewage works at Mogden, and at Long Reach (Dartford). Thames Water proposed for itself a biological oxygen demand of 65 mg/litre, whereas the current average was 28.6 mg/litre (and the 95 percentile was 72.3).

The impact of such increased pollution on the Thames may be considerable, because, at times of low flow, the volume of sewage effluent entering the tidal part of the river is four times as great as the freshwater flow over Teddington Weir,[100] some of which is already sewage effluent from further upstream. Below the weir, there are more than twenty storm overflows in need of repair.

Conclusions

During the 1980s progress in curbing water pollution was reversed and Britain's rivers became generally dirtier. Once-pure waters lost their freshwater life as agricultural pollution spread and ageing sewerage works vomited their overload into them. The Nature Conservancy Council's plea for an ecologial component in setting river quality objectives was ignored and an array of statistical fiddles worthy of the Ministry of Truth were used to try and convince the press, public and water shareholders that standards had improved and not slipped.

The water industry has spent very large sums of public money to 'explain' itself to the public. Mr Gordon Jones, chairman of the Water Authorities and Yorkshire Water, defended a £9 million expenditure on a 'general awareness campaign' as a response to 'vilification and a lot of criticism'. It is really a compliment to the one or two campaigners, such as Andrew Lees of Friends of the Earth, who have worked to expose the pollution sanctioned by Water Authorities, that the chairman of the industry felt he had to spend millions on such a campaign. The financial purpose of the advertising, which amounts to publicly funded propaganda, is very clear. Simply adding 1 per cent to the share price of a £7,000 million privatised water industry could mean £70 million extra profit.

The privatised industry takes on many of the investment priorities of the old Authorities. The Victorian emphasis on prestige supply projects, for example, still dominates water industry thinking. When journalists queried Thames Water's ability to overcome the drought in 1989, chairman Roy Watts emphasised the capital's new £200 million ring main system.[101] At the time, 100,000 people were queuing at London standpipes, and a breakdown at Hampton filter beds had led to wriggling green worms coming out of taps (don't worry, said TWA, it proved the water was not actually polluted). Yet, as Friends of the Earth pointed out, even the government stockbrokers S. G. Warburg had determined that 15–30 per cent of all water in the supply system is lost through leakage (equivalent to a waste of £15–20 million a year). But neither the National Rivers Authority nor Secretaries of State have any duty to conserve water.

Whether the NRA can use prosecutions to enforce higher standards will be a major test of its effectiveness. During the 1980s the philosophy of not prosecuting offenders was shared by both Water Authorities and the Department of the Environment.

The *Daily Telegraph* has reported that the NRA's members 'privately believe that pollution could be worse than current figures show . . . [because] . . . the Water Authorities have been disingenuous in compiling water pollution statistics.'[102] If so, it would be no surprise. 'Any organisation that thinks it may happily go on polluting our rivers and seas, or thinks it is likely to get away with it scot free would be making a very great mistake,' said Lord Crickhowell, chairman of the NRA, on its first day of operation. Let us hope so, but it has to be remembered that similar things were said about the 1974 Control of Pollution Act.

By early 1990 the NRA reported beginning over 100 prosecutions. However, it also emerged that during the run-up to privatisation – from April 1987 to September 1989 – the HMIP had deliberately neglected to prosecute, lest it frighten off investors. 'The lack of prosecutions angered staff,' an official confided to *The Times*.[103] 'There were numerous valid cases which could have led to convictions but the political climate, that is privatisation, precluded any action.'

There are also practical doubts over the NRA's effectiveness. In September 1989, for example, it emerged that, because Water Authorities were running down the use of sand filtration to treat water supplies in favour of the cheaper chemical disinfectants, a major new health hazard was being transmitted from farm waste to human beings. A parasite, *cryptosporidium*, was passing from rural rivers, polluted with farm waste, into tapwater supplies. Sand filtration traps 99 per cent of the organisms but disinfectants do not. Cases of diarrhoea caused by the parasite grew from 1,900 in 1985 to 5,321 in 1989. David Wheeler of Surrey University's Robens Institute told the *Sunday Correspondent*: 'The health risk is mainly to children under five and other vulnerable groups. It is potentially lethal.' Friends of the Earth declared itself 'appalled' that the NRA had no powers to order farmers to take 'preventive measures' against the pollution leading to the problem.[104] Eighty per cent of sewage works were not being monitored at weekends because of NRA staff shortages.[105]

As of April 1990 the NRA had found itself too short-staffed to effect a significant clean-up of rivers, and was pressing the government for greater finance.[106]

APPENDIX

EC Directives on Water

There are more European Community Directives on water than on any other environmental topic. An authoritative study of EC Directives is Nigel Haigh's *EEC Environmental Policy and Britain*, now in its second edition.[107]

(a) Directives Relating to 'Dangerous Substances'

Several Directives relating to 'dangerous substances' set environmental quality objectives (EQOs) and apply to *all* waters.[108]

One is the Drinking Water Directive (80/778) discussed in Chapter 3. Another covers Dangerous Substances in Water (76/464). As a 'Framework' it creates two lists of toxic substances. The intention is to prevent any of them from getting into the environment. 'Daughter' Directives have then set limits for List I substances, which include mercury, organophosphorus pesticides and cancer-agents. The UK has to 'eliminate' List I substances and the Directive has resulted in a much more specific approach to setting standards for river, estuary and coastal water than otherwise planned. List II includes less dangerous but still hazardous substances such as cyanide, lead and ammonia[109] and is also known as the Grey List. The government has to draw up a plan for their reduction with deadlines.

The UK government firmly opposed the idea of fixed emission limits when the Directive was under negotiation from 1974 to 1975. After protracted wrangling, the result, adopted in order to get some agreement, was to have fixed limits for List I substances and no fixed limits for List II. As Nigel Haigh has pointed out, this was illogical on both sides.

In the case of sewerage works, it means much more specific terms ('consents') for pollution discharges. In the past, for example, most consents have been only crudely defined by a few parameters such as BOD, SS and ammonia. While this is a reasonable way of getting a general picture of the short-term gross biological effects of most sewage effluent, it tells you absolutely nothing about heavy metals, complex organics or other chemicals that may be present, or their long-term effects.

In 1982 the EC Commission identified 1,500 potential candidate chemicals for the Directive and investigated 500 for the risk they posed to water; 108 were selected for further investigation, to which they added 21 substances already investigated, making 129. These were then published in a

Communication.

As of 1988, limits were set or to be set for mercury, cadmium and its compounds, the organochlorine pesticides HCH (lindane), aldrin, endrin and dieldrin, carbon tetrachloride and chloroform, DDT, pentachlorophenol, chlordane and heptachlor. For List II, the priority chemicals are chromium, lead, zinc, copper, nickel and arsenic.

(b) Directives which make standards for 'designated' stretches of waters

Water Standards for Freshwater Fish. This Directive (78/659) allows member states to designate waters of their choosing as suitable for salmon and trout or other 'coarse' types of fish. Nigel Haigh has called it 'a prop against backsliding which is particularly important at a time of financial cutbacks'.[110]

(c) Directives principally relating to marine pollution

Shellfish Waters. This Directive (79/923) aims to ensure some coastal waters are suitable for shellfish growing, and is not in itself a directive to make the shellfish clean enough for eating.

Bathing Water. Mainly by ensuring that no significant amount of sewage is present, this directive (76/160) aims to improve or maintain the quality of bathing waters (which in the UK so far means beaches). The UK has been forced to make extensive changes to its sewage disposal practices as a result (see Chapter 1).

Titanium Dioxide. These Directives (76/176; 83/29; 82/883) set out to measure and reduce waste from the titanium dioxide industry .

Oil Pollution at Sea. This is not a Directive but a Resolution (OJ C 162 8 7 78) followed by a series of Commission decisions. It has led to a Community information system on control and reduction of oil pollution at sea, and was stimulated by the Ekofisk blow out in the Norwegian sector of the North Sea and the *Amoco Cadiz* disaster in Brittany. After the Sandoz fire at Basle which polluted the Rhine, the Commission proposed it should be extended to cover rivers as well.

The *Dangerous Substances* Directive seems likely to continue to be a sore point between the UK and the European Commission. In relation to a daughter Directive for chromium, for example, in an internal July 1986 memo a DoE civil servant wrote that the government considered 'Community-wide quality standards for List II substances to be unnecessary and inappropriate'.

The UK says an environmental quality objective encompasses the use of the water, while a standard applies only to a level or amount of a substance being put into it, and is set so that the objective can be achieved. Under the Dangerous Substances Directive, the European Commission asks member states to develop national programmes for reducing List II substances but retains the capacity to coordinate the production of these. The Commission proposed just two standards for chromium, one for fresh and one for seawater in 1986. The DoE rehearsed its objections thus: 'Although our firm policy is to maintain and improve the quality of our water, it would not be sensible to aim in the near future for very high standards everywhere. The proposal should allow for a number of standards set according to the attainable uses of different waters.' The EC suggested 5–50 ug/litre, depending on how hard the water was, for the limit of chromium present. 'This,' noted the DoE official, 'is much more stringent than the most stringent standard established by the UK (for the protection of salmonid fish) because the latter is expressed as an annual average. . .'

While only 500 km of British rivers would fail to meet the EC chromium standard (as a result of pollution from the tanning industry and industrial tips), the DoE discovered that the higher standard 'would have considerable financial implications for industry' and 'set a precedent for Community actions on List II substances' – a case of the UK setting targets to suit industry.

One particularly polluting chemical process was singled out for early attention by the Commission because it releases large amounts of mercury. 'Chloralkali' processes create industrial chlorine by putting an electric current through mercury 'cells' containing alkali chloride compounds. In the six years it took for the Dangerous Substances Directive to be agreed,[111] the UK had argued determinedly for quality objectives related to the receiving water. So, for instance, if a discharge was into an ocean with fast currents or a large estuary, a greater discharge should be allowed than for a small slow river. Continental countries had most of their factories along slower inland rivers and, from a mixture of economic self-interest and greater concern for the environment, they argued for fixed limits to discharges, which for all new plant would be based on the 'best technical means available' (BTMA).

The continental countries had two valid arguments on their side. First, if for whatever reason one member state could have lower standards requiring less money to be spent on pollution-control technology, then it would have an unfair commercial advantage. This would be a breach of the Treaty of Rome's commitment to free trade. Second, if the pollutant will effectively always remain a hazard, it is desirable to limit total emissions to the environment at least by the best available technology. The UK position has most logic if the pollutant decays or becomes harmless at low concentrations. This is not the case with List I-type substances.

Convoluted wording finally satisfied both parties. Limit values were set for two types of factory, and quality objectives were set for fish flesh and waters.

Haigh says that because major companies such as ICI were aware that mercury discharges were to be a focus of attention as early as 1974, new pollution controls were introduced. ICI spent £25 million at 1982 prices and £1.09 million a year in running costs on reducing mercury emissions, while BP installed a £1.3 million resin bed absorption unit at Sandbach. At Sandbach the quality objectives for the discharge into a canal could not be met, so the discharge is controlled by a limit value: the very principle the UK objected to.[112]

Several morals come out of this story. First, until the Dangerous Substances Directive came along, there was no real national attempt to control or even assess point sources of substances like mercury, even though in theory the powers existed under the Control of Pollution Act. Second, until the Directive hove into view, industry was not using the best available technology to limit emissions. Third, without the Directive, much higher levels of mercury emissions would have continued to be granted discharge consents by the Water Authorities (if they were monitored at all). Fourth, the doctrinaire argument over whether to limit emissions with limit values or quality objectives is not a question of simple right or wrong: both have their advantages and limitations.

CHAPTER 3

Tap Water: Nitrates, Lead and Aluminium

While seas and rivers may be dirty, British tapwater is supposed to be pure, and its pollution causes more concern than any other. In Stanley Kubrick's film *Dr Strangelove*, US Air Force General Jack Ripper sends his B52s to bomb the USSR because he fears the Russians have polluted the drinking water of the West. 'As human beings,' he tells his RAF liaison officer Group Captain Lionel Mandrake, 'you and I need fresh pure water to replace our precious bodily fluids.' While marines machine gun his East Anglian air base, the deranged commander observes that, 'You never see a Commie drink a glass of water – and with good reason.' The fictional General Ripper was obsessed with fluoridation. A crank in the 1960s, his worries over the wholesomeness of water would put him in much better company today.

Today it is not so much fluoridation as nitrates and pesticides which generate international conflict over water quality. In October 1989, after four years of dispute, the European Commission finally began its legal attack on the UK for allowing excess nitrate in the water supply of Norwich and Redbridge, and for illegal levels of bacteria and aluminium elsewhere.[1] As Geoffrey Lean and Fred Pearce wrote in a survey reported in the *Observer* in August 1989,

> 'Millions of Britons drink water contaminated above international safety limits with poisons. Well over two million people are at risk from excessive concentrations of lead, which damages children's brains. Two million people drink water containing more than the European Commission's Maximum Admissible Concentration (MAC) of aluminium, which is increasingly believed to cause Alzheimer's disease (incurable dementia). At least 1.7 million people consume water that breaks European limits for nitrate, suspected by some scientists as a cause of cancer. . .
> 'Friends of the Earth identified 298 water supplies exceeding MACs for dangerous pesticides. A tenth of Britain's groundwater supplies are thought to contain cancer-causing solvents above limits drawn up by the World Health Organisation. And nobody even knows the full extent of contamination by trihalomethanes – other suspected carcinogens – except that it is widespread.'[2]

Nitrates

In the sandy soils under General Ripper's airbase, as in aquifers throughout the agricultural Europe, the 'time bomb' of nitrate pollution has been ticking away since the 1950s. Nitrates take a decade or more to reach the level of boreholes. The source of nitrate pollution is now undisputed: changes in agricultural practices, including the ploughing up of permanent pasture but, most importantly, the enormous growth in the use of artificial fertilisers.

Pasture, especially natural or long established pasture, acts like a biological sponge, holding large amounts of nitrate. When pasture is ploughed up or overloaded by nitrogen input, organic nitrogen is oxidised and the highly soluble nitrate ion is washed quickly through the soil and into rivers or groundwater. When arable land replaced pasture over much of Britain between the 1950s and 1980s, there was little in the soil ecosystem to hold nitrate back (only rarely is it all used by the crops). So nitrate from the enormous growth in artificial fertiliser applications is rapidly leached away. British farmers now put 1.6 million tonnes of nitrate fertiliser on the land each year, an eightfold increase since the 1940s.[3]

The countries of the European Community used 1.7 million tonnes of fertiliser in 1953 but this grew to 8.9 million tonnes by 1982.[4] As a result, significant nitrate problems now exist in almost every European country. Six were surveyed by David Baldock of the Institute for European Environmental Policy (IEEP) in 1989 (see table).

Nitrate in Drinking Water in Six Countries

---

1. Denmark
The most affected areas are rural parts of areas in western Jutland. 6 per cent of the population (300,000 people) receive water with a nitrate content above 50 mg NO_3/l, mostly from private wells.

2. Federal Republic of Germany
Worst affected are areas of Schleswig-Holstein, the lower Rhine, western Westphalia, Lower Bavaria, and smaller areas under horticulture and vines, such as the Upper Rhine, the Palatinate, parts of Unster-Mittelfranken and Wurttemberg.

Approximately 5 per cent of all those consumers on public supplies receive water with nitrate above 50 mg/litre. About 25 per cent of the population receive drinking water with more than 25 mg NO_3/litre. In addition, there are some private supplies affected. As in France and the UK, the number of consumers affected by water supplies with high nitrate levels is falling, but not the number of contaminated sources which is still rising in some regions.

3. Spain
Most affected are Valencia, Murcia, Catalonia and the Mediterranean coast. An estimated 1 per cent of the population receives water above the limit (approximately 350,000 people). This number is increasing, due to fertiliser pollution.

4. France
Most affected areas: the regions of Brittany, Centre, Poitou – Charente, Champagne-Ardenne, Bourgogne, Picardie, Ile-de-France and Nord-Pas-de-Calais.

Some 860,000 people receive water with an average nitrate concentration above 50 mg/litre. Approximately 1,725,000 people receive water with a maximum concentration of above 50 mg/litre.

5. Netherlands

Worst affected areas are sandy soils in the eastern, central and southern parts of the country where intensive livestock units are concentrated. Over 99 per cent of the population is connected to the public water supply receiving water with less than 50 mg/litre nitrate. An estimated 100–200,000 use private wells, many with high nitrate levels.

6. United Kingdom

The most affected regions are in East Anglia, Lincolnshire, the East Midlands and West Midlands, especially in arable areas. Some 850,000 people are supplied with water with a nitrate concentration above 50 mg/litre. Nitrate concentrations are still rising in many groundwater sources.

Source: responses to IEEP questionnaire to national ministries in early 1989, preparatory to a meeting at Toulouse, April 1989, supplemented by other data.

Nitrogen and Health

Although the existence of nitrate pollution and its health implications had been known for decades, in the UK it was not thought to be much of a problem until 1984. High levels of nitrate can cause 'blue baby syndrome' (infantile methaemoglobinaemia), which is potentially fatal (see below: Government Advice), but there had only been 3,000 cases worldwide since 1945, and 14 in the UK since 1950.[5] Nigel Haigh of the IEEP points out that in 1979 the Royal Commission on Environmental Pollution reported that evidence for the other major health worry – the potential for nitrite, which is formed from nitrate in certain conditions, to create 'nitrosamines' and cause stomach cancer – was only 'weak and equivocal'.[6]

In 1970, the World Health Organisation (WHO) took the health threat seriously enough to recommend a European standard for drinking water of 50–100 mg/litre. US authorities adopted a 45–50 mg/litre standard as a precautionary measure.[7]

From 1973 the Health Protection and Environment Directorates of the European Commission had also been working on measures to control wastes and 'trace' substances in water: they adopted a 50mg/litre nitrate limit for the 1980 Directive Relating to the Quality of Water Intended For Human Consumption (80/778/EEC), which also controls pesticides and metals. Countries had to meet the standards, unless 'derogations' were allowed, by 17 July 1985. They were not met by the UK, which also granted itself invalid derogations, and the country ended up in the European Court (see below).

Despite the reassuring noises of the Royal Commission in 1979, by 1984 the UK's Standing Technical Advisory Committee on Water Quality (STACWQ) reported that, if present trends of fertiliser use were to continue, mean nitrogen levels in surface waters would increase by 2–3 mg/litre (as nitrogen) by 1994–2004 and this would cause widespread breaches of the 11.3 mg/litre nitrogen level (50 mg/litre nitrate). Supplies to millions of people would be affected.

The Department of the Environment (DoE) had foreseen difficulties with the Directive,[8] and now asked the Department of Health for advice on nitrate levels, most probably so that the UK could argue for laxer standards.

Unlike the US agencies and the EC, the DHSS/DoE Joint Committee on Medical Aspects of Water Quality proposed in 1984 that it would be acceptable to relax the EC standard by 60 per cent, from 50 to 80 mg/litre. The Department of Health issued a 'guidance note' to Chief Environmental Health Officers in 1985 which, in the words of David Wheeler of Surrey University's Robens Institute, 'dismissed the possibility of a link between nitrates in water and stomach cancer in the UK' [9].

This policy may have seemed 'reasonable' to the civil service, but it had two major flaws. First, it was illegal. The Commission took a far stricter view of what the Drinking Water Directive meant than what the UK felt it ought to mean. Second, raising the limit to 80 mg/litre was an administrative judgement not a medical one. In 1988, the government's Chief Medical Officer, Sir Donald Acheson, told the DoE that the level should remain at 50 mg/litre, mainly because, if a cancer risk existed, it would be a result of long-term exposure. He was apparently repeating old advice.

The Government Advice on Nitrates and Health

When the DoE asked the Chief Medical Officer and his Committee on Medical Aspects of the Contamination of Air, Soil and Water for an opinion of the health risks of nitrate, the chief points were:

- The concentration of nitrate in public water supply should not exceed 100 mg/litre;
- Water undertakings (now the companies and plcs) should 'nevertheless continue to make every effort to keep the concentrations below 50 mg/litre';
- Monitoring for infantile methaemoglobinaemia should be carried out where the values are 50-100 mg/litre and babies should get bottled water at or above 100 mg/litre.[10]

The UK government has since tried to use Acheson's opinion to argue for an upwards revision of the 50 mg/litre limit. However, the Medical Officer wrote: 'A preferred standard of 50 mg/litre is the result of a long established consensus amongst scientists in the United Kingdom and internationally,' although '*transient* excursions' above that level would have no importance 'in relation to the postulated role of nitrate in causation of cancer, since in this context the long-term average content is the significant figure.'

'I must emphasise,' said Acheson, 'that the present scientific evidence on the ill effects of nitrate on human health does not point unarguably to a precise standard. The consequences of permitting the distribution of water containing average nitrate concentrations in the range 50–100 mg/litre cannot be placed beyond doubt. Indeed, even the current standard for nitrate in water does not totally guarantee the absence of ill effects. One can only say that, with any increases in exposure, the likelihood of ill effects occurring and the extent of ill effects which might occur would be expected to increase. . .

'I must emphasise that the present nitrate standard of 50mg/litre remains, in our view, the appropriate preferred standard. Nothing of substance has emerged recently on which to question it.'

Acheson added: 'I would accept [using] the average concentration [rather than a maximum] in relation to methaemoglobinaemia,' which goes less than half way to the justification that the DoE was seeking for a relaxation of the 50 mg/litre standard. 'I could not agree,' he said, 'to any interpretation of this advice that meant accepting avoidable delay in taking appropriate action in the most affected areas.'

Cancer

Acheson's advice says: 'A variable proportion of ingested nitrate is converted to nitrite in the body. Nitrite can then react, mainly in the stomach, with a wide variety of compounds which are ubiquitous components of the diet, to form N-nitroso compounds. The evidence that such a reaction does actually occur in humans, most markedly in individuals with low stomach acidity, has strengthened in the past few years. Some dietary components, including vitamin C, tend to inhibit the reaction.'

'If nitrate does, indirectly, cause cancer, it will be the long-term average that matters and the effect of any increase in cancer rates would be expected to take many years to become apparent . . . The epidemiological evidence shows that nitrate cannot be having a major effect on cancer in the general population in the UK. Nevertheless, the inherent limitations of such evidence mean that we cannot absolutely exclude a small risk.' He adds: 'It should be noted that much of the evidence deals only with cancer of the stomach, because this was the subject of the original claims. Extrapolation from animal studies predicts that nitrosamines, and hence nitrates, would be as likely to cause other types of cancer in humans.'

'There is no proof,' said the medical advice, 'that nitrate leads to human cancer but, nevertheless, experts in the UK consider that the theoretical likelihood of an effect is sufficient for them to advise government to seek ways of restricting the total intake of nitrate.' They observed that for someone with an average British diet, although preserved meat and vegetables contain nitrates, it is water, once the level of nitrate reaches 50 mg/litre, that will be the main source. Since vegetables are an important source of vitamin C, the medical experts favour controlling nitrate intake via water rather than food. (The average daily intake of nitrate is about 60 mg a day, 75 per cent attributable to vegetables. Some people take in 110–120 mg, and water contributes 10 – 80 mg depending on pollution.)

Infantile Methaemoglobinaemia

The government's advisers say that this is a rare condition 'in which the ability of the blood to carry oxygen is decreased, characteristically causing a grey/blue tint to the skin'. Drugs aside, nitrate over 100 mg/litre is the principal cause. The last UK case was in 1972. Babies in high nitrate areas are given bottled water.

The EC Drinking Water Directive

This Directive has been a major source of conflict between the UK and the European Commission. It sets a guide value (maximum) for nitrate of 50 mg/litre but permits member states to apply for permission to grant 'derogations' (exemptions) where the levels arise from geological factors ('the nature and structure of the ground'), or 'exceptional meteorological conditions'.

The date by which all supplies should have met the Directive's standard was July 1985, but little was done in the UK as the government hoped to negotiate a laxer standard. Instead, in November 1985, with the backing of the farming lobby, which feared that controls or taxes would be imposed on nitrogen fertiliser, the DoE granted water suppliers no fewer than 57 derogations, 48 of them for contamination by nitrates.

At the same time the government took it upon itself to interpret 'Maximum Admissible Concentration' (MAC) as meaning an average over three months and not an absolute limit. Specifically, the DoE 'granted' derogations for supplies where nitrate exceeded 50 mg/litre but did not exceed a three monthly average of 80 mg/litre and a maximum of 100 mg/litre 'except in exceptional and transitory circumstances'.[11] The DoE's claimed justification for this last step was medical advice from the DHSS, although, as we have seen, this interpretation owes at least as much to administrative convenience as to scientific advice.

The nitrate derogations affected 2 per cent of the population. Aware that removing nitrate from water supplies could be a very expensive business, that curbs on the use of nitrogen would probably enrage the agricultural lobby, and with privatisation on the horizon, the issue became progressively more important for the DoE. As the STACWQ had made clear in 1984, the nitrate problem would go on getting worse for decades into the future. This was hardly a welcome dowry for the investors that the government wanted to attract into a newly privatised industry. Everything the government did from this date onwards had privatisation in mind.

In fact, as early as 1983 *ENDS* magazine had warned that the government was legally wrong about the Directive. Friends of the Earth and other environmental organisations now challenged the government's interpretation of the Directive on two grounds. First, they argued that a Maximum Admissible Concentration should be treated as an absolute limit not to be breached, and not the basis of an average. Second, FoE pointed out that Article 9 allowing derogations for nitrate levels arising from the 'nature and structure' of the ground was intended to cover exemptions for water from nitrate-bearing rocks and soils, whereas most of the nitrate found in UK groundwater stems from highly unnatural levels of fertiliser.

In 1985, the government set up a Nitrate Coordination Group (NCG) including DoE, the Ministry of Agriculture, Fisheries and Food (MAFF), the Fertiliser Manufacturers' Association and the National Farmers' Union, but excluding consumers, environment or health groups. After various delays it produced a report, *Nitrate in Water*, in December 1986. This showed that 1 million East Anglian and Midlands consumers regularly drank water above the 50 mg/litre standard, and another 3.8 million drank water almost as polluted during 1984/5. 'However,' says David Baldock of the Institute for European Environment Policy, which has advised several governments on the issue, 'in twenty years' time five million people could be drinking water well over the 50 mg/litre limit. In the long term seven people in ten will be drinking water with more nitrate than the European limit in the Anglian region and half those in Severn Trent.'[12]

Nitrate concentrations in groundwater, noted the report, are rising steadily and will reach equilibrium at over 100mg/litre. The NCG dismissed the use of slow release fertilisers, taxes or quotas, favouring education for farmers and avoiding 'unacceptable economic consequences' for the agricultural industry. To ensure that everyone's nitrate levels stayed under 50 mg/litre the NCG estimated that immediate capital spending of £50 million would be needed, and £150 million would be required within 20 years.

On 11 August 1987 the European Commission began its formal moves against the UK for unlawful levels of nitrate in drinking water in Tower Hamlets, in Bassetlaw District, Scotland, and at five supplies in Norfolk.[13]

Several months later, on 2 December, the government conceded that an average was not a maximum after all. The Secretary of State for the Environment told the House of Commons that 'after taking legal advice' he had decided that 'the term "maximum admissable concentration" in the European Community Drinking Water Directive should relate to individual samples and not to averages over a period'. In its reply to the Commission on 11 December, the UK said it would now withdraw the derogations (which happened on 10 April 1988).

The withdrawal of derogations was disclosed to Parliament by Junior Minister Colin Moynihan on 20 January the following year. A major row now blew up between the Ministry of Agriculture and the Department of the Environment. *ENDS* magazine wrote in January 1988, 'The government's retreat in its interpretation of the 1980 EEC Directive on drinking water quality in the face of legal challenges by the European Commission turned into a rout this month when it withdrew permission for 48 water supplies to exceed the EEC limit. But a decision whether nitrate contamination of water is to be reduced by curbs on land use or by treatment with untried technology is being held up by a conflict in Whitehall on whether farmers should be compensated for income losses resulting from land use controls'.[14]

The climbdown over averages was communicated to all chief executives of Water Authorities and Companies on 10 March and the derogations were formally rescinded in April. By now, almost eight years had elapsed since the birth of the Directive, and three years had gone by since the nitrate limits were supposed to have been complied with.

The Environment Commissioner Carlo Ripa di Meana later recalled:

'the UK . . . drew attention to the practical steps being taken to deal with the nitrate problem, such as the taking out of service of several sources, the development of experimental denitrification processes and advice and publicity to farmers . . . The UK nevertheless drew attention to the fact that denitrification processes are in an early stage of development and that further research is necessary and that the protection of water sources may take years to have the desired effect. . .'[15]

This set the new tone of the UK's argument: everything possible was being done and therefore any breaches of European law should be disregarded while 'things were brought up to scratch'. Many people found this a strange attitude from a government committed to law and order. Muggers who decided to phase out mugging by 1993 could hardly expect to be let off, yet the UK expected to go on breaking the law with impunity.

The Commission noted that another letter from the UK dated 5 January 1989 had tried to make the case that 'all supplies which presently exceed the nitrate admissible concentration will be brought into progressive compliance between now and 1995, all but two supplies complying by 1993'.[16] But a promise of jam tomorrow wasn't enough to satisfy the Commission, which issued a Reasoned Opinion against the UK's implementation of the Drinking Water Directive in April. The UK's measures, said the Commission, were 'not being achieved with sufficient rapidity'. Except where a delay or derogation was allowed under the Directive – and the UK had now also accepted that its grounds for derogation had all along been invalid – 'all supplies of drinking water in the United Kingdom were required to be in compliance with the Directive by 20 July'.

'In view of the long-standing nature of this infringement,' the Commission concluded that it could not 'accept that any further delay in remedying the infringement should be permitted.'

By now the British government was plunged headlong into preparations for selling off the water industry. Urgent talks began in London and Brussels as the UK tried yet again to negotiate a way round the EC rules. As the autumn flotation of the water industry neared, each additional future commitment to spend money on water treatment became a political liability. Shareholders, after all, were interested in a short term return on their money.

In June, the *Observer* Business pages warned that the Commission was 'poised' to prosecute Britain in the European Court early in 1990 and this could 'effectively wreck the Government's controversial water privatisation plans'.[17] Water Minister Michael Howard was to meet Commissioner Carlo Ripa di Meana 'to extend the framework by six years', while the government was preparing (successfully) to throw out a Lords amendment to the Water Bill which required compliance with EC rules by 1993.

In July, *The Times* reported that in Brussels talks had again broken down. Signor Ripa di Meana said, 'If Britain cannot meet our demands in two months, it shows a lack of goodwill, and we will definitely go to the courts.'[18]

At home the UK government launched a desperate news management campaign to 'frame the debate' along its own lines. An essential component of any pollution argument is backing from 'independent scientific' opinion to

undermine the views of opponents. On 20 July, the *Daily Telegraph* published
an article entitled 'Is our water really worse than theirs?' by Con Coughlin,
which purported to explain the 'science and politics behind the EEC's verdict'.
If this was not a government-inspired and briefed story, it must have warmed
the cockles of the Ministry's heart. 'Nitrate,' it informed readers, 'as most
gardeners know, is produced whenever there is intensive cultivation of the soil.
Thus in agricultural areas high levels of nitrate are produced which gradually
make their way into the water table and ultimately into our water supply.' Did
fertilisers play no role? Apparently not.

'Such worthy bodies as the World Health Organisation,' the article sneered
or just condescended, depending how you read it, had inspired the European
Commissioners to set nitrate limits, because of blue baby syndrome and a fear
of stomach cancer. The first factor, the newspaper explained, was not important
as no cases had occurred since 1972, while 'the claim that high levels of nitrate
cause cancer has yet to be proved.'

Having dismissed the basis of the EC Directive, the article now went on, as
the government itself would like to imply, that, while others had muddled
about wrongly trying to control nitrates, Britain had been engaged on work of
an altogether higher order, 'in the interests of good water'. This, it turned out,
was the elimination of bacteria. 'When it comes to the purity of our water, we
have virtually no traces of bacteria in the finished product, which is more than
can be said for some other Common Market countries,' Dr Derek Miller, assis-
tant director of the soon-to-be-privatised Water Research Centre told the newspaper. The bacterial breaches of the Directive (see below) and trihalomethanes
produced by chlorinating sewage contaminated supplies were not mentioned.

And then, the *Daily Telegraph* discovered 'the truth': 'privatisation of
Britain's water industry . . . runs against the grain of Mr Delors' social
strategy.' Here was a socialist plot that would have launched General Ripper
into a pre-emptive strike against Brussels. Almost apologetically, Mr Coughlin
conceded that 'Britain also has been less diligent than some of its neighbours
in setting out a timetable for reducing nitrate in water'.[19]

Elsewhere in the *Daily Telegraph* that day, Mr Michael Howard, Water
Minister, was in a bullish mood. 'Minister Warns EEC Not To Prosecute on
Water', declared the headline. 'Mr Howard: We will hear no more of the
matter', ran the caption under his photograph. Stout stuff. So perhaps Britain
was about to send a gunboat to shell the Perrier works after all? Employing one
of those supremely disingenuous somersaults of logic that only long training in
double-speak and the official brand of British arrogance can confer, Mr
Howard told a Westminster audience of backbenchers that 'If the Commission
were to take us to the European Court I can think of few things more calculated
to bring the Commission into disrepute.'[20]

While other European countries (not to mention the United States) were
struggling to comply with a 50 mg/litre nitrate limit, the minister revealed that
Britain had once again discovered unique drawbacks to the proposed solution
to pollution, which made the cure, as it were, worse than the disease.
Denitrification could create a risk to health. 'I'm very confident that when the
Commission learns at first hand that it is not technically possible, they will see

the overwhelming good sense of the British government and we will hear no more of the matter,' declared Mr Howard. So it was not after all, the pressure from the farmers, or the cost, or the private discussions with the fertiliser manufacturers which had motivated the UK to drag its feet over nitrates, but a uniquely shrewd insight into the better interests of public health.

On 24 July it was the turn of *The Times*. It reported that the difference of view between the government and other countries had now led the Royal Commission to announce an inquiry into the evidence of the health effects of nitrate in groundwater. The Commission's two-year inquiry, said *The Times*, 'may produce new evidence exonerating the water supply'. Quoting Lord Lewis of Cambridge University as being 'sceptical of claims made by Mr Di Meana about nitrate concentrations in British water', the newspaper ventured the opinion that 'Backing for Lord Lewis may emerge today when the Royal Society is due to hold an open seminar on scientific evidence about the purity of the water supply. The Royal Society note on the seminar indicates that "less fashionable" chemicals than nitrates might be worth attention.'

While the Royal Commission has never been accused of acting as an arm of government, its inquiries are not conducted with the same open-eyed approach to political manipulation as are those of the Select Committees of the House of Lords or House of Commons. *The Times* story is interesting because it links the report on the Commission's activities with the Royal Society, a body which had become embroiled in official political-scientific propaganda exercises before, such as the five-year study of acid rain financed by the Central Electricity Generating Board.

At the same time as backbench morale was being boosted and the government's view was being channelled to the voters, a lid was being kept on the facts about water privatisation and pollution cost. On 20 July, the generally anti-government *Guardian* reported that 'scientists at water authorities have been threatened with criminal proceedings if they talk about the costs of dealing with nitrate pollution.'[21] After the Water Bill was enacted, said the newspaper, 'all staff at the Anglian Water Authority were warned that statements about water quality must be cleared with the organisation's lawyers and merchant bankers. They were also told the penalty for non-compliance was up to seven years in prison and an unlimited fine under Section 77 of the Financial Services Act. Mr Ken Hipwood of Anglian Water said that the costs of dealing with the nitrate problem had been calculated but they were being kept secret.'

However, the UK failed in its attempt to head off the EC Commission, even though it made a last-minute offer to bring forward compliance of five water supplies contaminated with nitrate, from 1995 to 1991–4, 'a shift,' according to *ENDS*, 'which, until then, the UK had insisted would be impractical.'[22]

On 18 September, Environment Minister Chris Patten flew to Brussels for talks with Environment Commissioner Carlo Ripa di Meana, according to *The Times* still 'optimistic that he could head off threatened prosecution of Britain by the European Court' by showing that 'Britain was doing everything it could to comply with the European drinking water legislation.'[23]

But on 20 September the Commission announced that for the first time it would take Britain before the European Court of Justice. Proceedings were also begun against France and Belgium. The slow legal process of 'trans-posing' the Directive into national law, especially in Northern Ireland, was one of the Commission's grounds for prosecution. Another was the level of nitrates in water: up to 100 UK supplies may have breached the 50 mg/litre level between 1985 and 1989. The last cause was lead pollution (see below), which breached the Directive's rules in 17 Scottish supplies.

Toxic Algae in the Reservoirs

Just as the European Commission was preparing to issue its legal summonses, embarrassing evidence of a major new problem of eutrophication in the nation's water system was coming to light, as rivers and reservoirs used for drinking water fill up with nitrate and phosphate. On 17 August the public were warned to stay away from Kings Mill Reservoir near Mansfield, Nottingham, 'after it turned bright green'. Severn Trent blamed algae 'caused by hot weather and lack of rain'.[24]

Then, as Michael McCarthy reported in *The Times* on 9 September 1989, 'Europe's biggest reservoir was closed to people and animals after the discovery of a possibly poisonous bloom of algae in the water.'[25] Windsurfers, walkers and fishermen were banned from the 123 billion litre Rutland Water reservoir, which serves 700,000 people around Northampton, Milton Keynes, Peterborough and Daventry. The cause was *microcystis*, a type of blue-green alga which produces microcystin, a toxin to both people and animals. The closure order was prompted by the deaths of a dozen sheep and as many dogs. Nevertheless, the director of quality for the new Anglian Water plc, Peter Matthews, told the press, 'I can assure all our consumers that the water we are providing from the reservoir is absolutely safe to drink.'

By 15 September two Cornish reservoirs and one in Devon were also closed to the public owing to blue-green algae. By now a total of 26 reservoirs had been sealed off throughout the country mainly owing to blooms of blue-green algae.

The underlying reason, said Andrew Lees of FoE, was over-enrichment with nitrates and phosphates. Gwynne Lyons of FoE says that Anglian Water will in future have special equipment to remove phosphate from the 'raw' water entering some of their reservoirs. Brian Moss of Liverpool University has esti-mated that phosphate levels in rivers of lowland England are 100 times the natural background, and nitrogen levels are 10 times background.[26]

Altogether 63 waters containing toxic algal blooms were identified by the National Rivers Authority, 37 of them in Anglian Region and 10 in the South West. By the end of the century, the nitrate now seeping through soil and rocks will put rivers such as the Thames, Great Ouse and the Avon 'over the limit' of 50 mg/litre.

In April 1990, Anglian Water admitted that 1.25 million customers had drunk water probably contaminated with *microcystin*. Anglian Water and Water Research Centre scientists were accused by an Australian expert on *micro-cystin* and by US scientists of 'playing down' the findings.[27]

The Ecological Impact of Nitrates

Two rivers illustrate the impact of nitrate pollution. One is the river Tay in Scotland: a salmon river, still famous as the 'silvery Tay' and flowing unpolluted down from Ben Lawers, out of the Grampian Highlands. It has an abundant wildlife and a nitrate average of 2.8 mg/litre. The other is the river Great Eau in Lincolnshire, which has an average nitrate level over ten times as high: 37.6 mg/litre. No nitrate-sensitive plants or animals could survive here.[28]

The Nature Conservancy Council[29] has officially advised the DoE that nitrate levels in rivers 'of special interest' for conservation should not exceed 15 mg/litre and in lakes should not exceed 7.5 mg/litre. 'Of special interest' in effect means almost any unpolluted river. Low-nitrate rivers are now so rare, thanks to sewage discharges, fertilisers, slurry and silage, that each one is important for conservation in itself. A few, like the river Wye which flows from Plynlimon in mid Wales down to the Severn, are designated 'Sites of Special Scientific Interest' and support salmonid fish such as trout, otters, a wide range of invertebrates such as crayfish and dragonflies, along with many plants that are sensitive to high nitrate levels and which have disappeared over much of the country in recent years.

The NCC agrees that in nearly all British freshwaters it is phosphate rather than nitrate which is the limiting factor in controlling eutrophication and that a phosphate directive is required to deal more effectively with it. 'However,' the Council said in its evidence to the House of Lords Committee examining the EC's proposal for a Directive on nitrate in vulnerable waters, 'the nitrate pollution that occurs is caused by the application of chemical fertilisers and animal slurries, which contain a mixture of phosphate and nitrate. Control of these substances, albeit in zones designated for drinking water protection, will have an indirect benefit for wildlife.'

The NCC also identified more direct benefits to wildlife. Eutrophication is nitrate limited in the Norfolk Broads during the summer, as it is in Loch Leven and the lakes of Cumbria. Eutrophication of coastal waters is usually nitrate limited (see Chapter 1) and many species are adversely affected by nitrate long before eutrophication runs its full course (and thus the 'limiting factor' argument becomes significant). Although nitrate pollution of the Broads is well known, recent studies are reported to show that streams in areas such as the Cotswolds are now equally polluted.

The NCC says that the normal nitrogen:phosphorus ratio for many aquatic plants is around 10–20:1. In waters such as Hickling Broad and Hoveton Great Broad in Norfolk, and in Loch Leven, the supply of nitrogen becomes limiting in July and August when agricultural crops grow rapidly, rainfall is light and nitrate applications are low. 'A few blue-green algae can store nitrogen, others can use atmospheric nitrogen, so algal communities can change from the normally dominant green to blue-green algae at this time,' says the Council.

Fish-fry populations and reed swamp development are both damaged by nitrate. The NCC states that loadings of nitrate in rivers 'have been sufficiently high at biologically critical times of year (e.g. early spring) to cause environmental damage'.[30] Studies by the German researchers Sukopp and Schindler have shown that the stems of reed mace *Typha* are weakened and tend to break at even 11–20 mg/litre nitrate, while, in the Broads, an extensive dieback of the elegant Norfolk reed *Phragmites* is attributed to nitrate pollution.

The *Sunday Times* interviewed a Norfolk fisherman, Frank Wright, in 1989. Thirty-four years before, Mr Wright earned a paltry 20th position in a fishing competition on the River Ant with a 20lb catch of bream. Now the River Ant contains up to 60 mg/litre of nitrate and 'days could pass without a bite'. 'The truth is,' said Wright with slight exaggeration, 'the Broads are dead.'[31] The NCC's regional officer, Dr Martin George, was also reported as saying that 95 per cent of the Broads were affected by nitrate and phosphate pollution from fertilisers and sewage. To remove excess phosphate from all the Broads would cost an estimated £20 million.

The benefits of reducing nitrate applications have already become apparent in the 'environmentally sensitive area' (ESA) of the Brecks in Norfolk and Suffolk. Here, on highly permeable sandy soils, the ESA provides money to persuade farmers to return to more traditional methods and farm less inten-sively. As a result, some long-lost annual plants once characteristic of the area are starting to return .

In Denmark, the authorities encourage and finance the re-establishment of fringing plant communities and marshes alongside rivers which were once canalised. The plants provide shelter for animals, trap silt and draw nutrients from the water. Bacteria in mud and in the root mass naturally denitrify the water. The NCC proposes that farmers should now leave uncultivated strips of land alongside watercourses as 'soaks', acting as wildlife habitat and fitting in well with MAFF plans for set-aside of land to help curb over-production of food.

The Draft Directive on Nitrates in Ground and Surface Water

Directly linked to the tapwater issue is the EC's proposal to control nitrates entering water liable to suffer from eutrophication (see the discussion in Chapter 1).

The Draft Directive has adopted the same 50 mg/litre nitrate standard as the Drinking Water Directive and proposes the designation of 'zones' that are 'vulnerable' to being polluted with nitrate up to 50 mg/litre, either directly or indirectly. The UK government has opposed it.[32] The National Farmers' Union has attacked it as 'unreasonable, unworkable and far too sweeping'.[33]

Once all water which contains or could on present trends contain, 50 mg/litre nitrate is designated 'vulnerable', steps would have to be taken to reduce nitrate pollution. Limits might be set for the amount of animal manure put on the land, and for inorganic fertiliser application, based on crop and soil types. In some months fertiliser would probably be banned, and a range of optional measures such as training, use of catch crops and set-aside of land (for example to be used for forestry or nature conservation) would follow.

The draft also proposes that sewage treatment works serving a permanent population of 5,000 or more should have treatment facilities to cut nitrogen in effluent to 10 mg/litre (equivalent to 48 mg/litre nitrate) where the discharge is into a vulnerable zone. The NCC points out that this would not be enough to protect many waters, and nitrogen removal equipment would have to be operated to achieve a lower level.[34]

In a joint memorandum addressed to a House of Lords Select Committee,[35] the DoE and MAFF detailed a series of objections to the plan. The Parliamentary Under Secretary of State, Mrs Virginia Bottomley, reiterated the familiar British line that while the government was 'already considering the scope of agricultural restrictions,' it 'believes that wherever possible, they should in the first event be on a voluntary basis, with compulsory powers being retained as a fall-back.' The 'polluter pays' principle had also been abandoned. 'The government also believes,' said the Minister, that 'where farmers restrict their activities beyond the degree which could be regarded as good agricultural practice, they should be compensated.'[36]

Coming from an administration whose leader laid claim to effective action on global issues such as the hole in the ozone layer and the greenhouse effect (see Chapter 11), this revealed a remarkable weakness in the position of the DoE. Its attempt to make farmers pay for the pollution they caused had been overturned by the environmentally primitive MAFF. Not only that, but, unlike other industries, farmers would actually now have to be paid to stop polluting the environment. The final ignominy was that it was the Environment Department not MAFF that now had to provide public justification.

The UK's objection to the proposed Directive was that it was 'unreasonably restrictive' to designate large river catchments 'simply because, for a short period of time in the autumn, the water may temporarily exceed 50 mg/litre although throughout the rest of the year it will be well below that figure.' Such 'temporary exceedances', said DoE, could be dealt with by natural denitrification in storage reservoirs, by blending or by using other sources.

On the surface, there is something in the government's view. But once again it overlooks or rejects the underlying philosophy and purpose of a Commission's proposal. The UK view would be logical if nitrate pollution was not a problem at all below 50 mg/litre, and if it was in equilibrium. But that is not the situation. Nitrate levels are increasing, there is a large 'slug' of pollution working through the groundwater system and the ecological effects and cancer risk do not disappear below 50 mg/litre. In trying to protect sources of water for drinking, the EC proposal is a step towards environmental purity rather than a sticking-plaster solution which does the minimum needed to avoid the worst nitrate pollution. In many of the large catchments to which the DoE refers, impact of nitrate may now be over the limit for only a week each year, but in future it may be for two weeks, then three, then a month or more: when does the UK propose to take action?

And what does the UK mean by a 'large' catchment? The UK makes no proposals for a definition. Instead it proposes that the 50 mg/litre limit should be treated as an average not a fixed limit.

The MAFF-DoE memorandum also contains several contradictions which illustrate the confusion and conflict in government circles. 'It is important to note,' says the document, that 'the UK draws a higher proportion (70 per cent) of water from surface sources than any other member state except Eire.'[37] Thus (presumably unfairly) the UK 'would be more affected by this part of the

Directive than other states.' Why this should be an objection to the control of pollution from nitrates is not clear, and it also overlooks the government's own study commissioned from Sir William Halcrow and Partners.[38] The Halcrow report showed that,while overall some 30 per cent of UK drinking water comes from aquifers, this varies from 6 per cent in Wales to 74 per cent in Southern Water's region. Would this mean, then, that the government would accept curbs on nitrates in the rivers of Kent but not of Wales?

The UK memo claims to assess the 'scientific basis' of the Commission's proposals[39] and notes haughtily, 'There seems to be an underlying assumption that the nitrate problem is concerned with the quantity of fertiliser and manure applied, whereas studies in this country, and elsewhere, have established that the problem is much more complicated than this, reflecting, for example, other aspects of farming practices.' Although it fails to name them, these 'other aspects' include the ploughing-up of old pasture and the number of stock kept on grassland.

A study by the Water Research Centre (WRC) showed that nitrate losses of 30–40 kg per hectare often occur under winter cereals and are worse under potatoes, rape and other vegetables, while only 2–5 kg/ha are leached out under grass, even fertilised with 200 kg/ha. But, with heavier stocking, even grass leaches more nitrate. To meet the EC 50 mg/litre standard the WRC believes the leaching rate must be (at most) 20 kg/ha in eastern England and 30 kg/ha in the wetter west. [40] On this basis, nitrates might have to be cut by more than 25 per cent to achieve a real reduction in leaching.

The DoE and MAFF memorandum also claimed that, 'in common with current UK policy,' the Draft Directive shows 'a belief that measures must be taken to protect water sources from contamination by nitrate'. But it then goes on to criticise the Draft Directive because it 'fails to recognise that a different mix of measures including water treatment or blending may be required depending on local factors, such as geology, rainfall and farming practice.' In other words, the focus is again on treatment rather than prevention.[41]

The UK proposed to argue for more 'discretion' for individual governments, for example 'aiming' to reduce nitrate levels while being allowed to set its own rates of application of manure. From past experience with UK rules that allow 'discretion', it is not very hard to imagine that the practice might bear little resemblance to the 'aim' of the policy.

If the UK has its way, then the Directive should have little impact, for it notes, 'We do not believe that it will be necessary to apply measures in the UK to protect waters from eutrophication due to nitrate.'[42]

In May, the UK government produced counterproposals in the shape of a consultation paper from MAFF.[43] This proposed setting up 'nitrate sensitive areas' (NSAs) in which sources are at or over 50 mg/litre, to be identified by the National Rivers Authority. Proposals to reduce nitrate would then be put to MAFF, which would in turn consult interested parties. On the basis of the MAFF-DoE memo this would seem likely to include the farming and fertiliser industries, and would give the Ministry of Agriculture almost total control over the policy.

The NSAs, said MAFF, would be designated on a 'pilot basis'. According to the magazine *ENDS*, it seems likely that 'at least five years will elapse before further NSAs are [then] designated unless the government's hand is forced by EEC legislation.'

Controls on farmers' use of nitrates would just be voluntary to start with, and legal limits would be imposed only if the voluntary controls turned out to be ineffective. Conversion of cereals to grassland would probably involve compensation, although avoidance of autumn fertiliser applications would not. Farmers would be invited to enter into contracts for low nitrogen farming. Only if a legal system was eventually brought in would a breach of contract become a criminal breach of the law. Otherwise, as the NRA later pointed out, the only sanction against polluters would be the recovery of compensation. The National Farmers' Union welcomed the proposal while awaiting details of how much money farmers would get. FoE termed it 'pathetic'.

In August, the Agriculture Minister, John Selwyn Gummer, announced plans for 12 experimental water protection zones including: Branston Booth, Lincs; Sleaford, Lincs; Chalford, Oxford; Egford, Somerset; Millington Springs, Humberside; Ogbourne St George, Wilts; Boughton, Notts; Tom Hill, Staffs; Wildmoor, Hereford and Worcester; Wellings, Staffs and Shropshire; Milton, Derbyshire. In an area restricted to just 15,200 hectares farmers would be offered compensation to reduce fertiliser inputs. Farmers over another 22,400 hectares, would merely be given advice and asked to use less fertiliser; there would be no money for them, and no other sanctions (The Swells, Gloucestershire; Bircham and Fring, Norfolk; Sedgeford, Norfolk; Fowlmere, Cambs; Far Baulker, Notts; Dotton and Colaton, Devon; Cringle Brook, Lincs and Leics; and Bourne Brook, Warwicks).

It now emerged that the new National Rivers Authority had warned MAFF that the voluntary approach was 'an insufficiently secure base'.[44] 'A single ploughing may be all that is needed to negate five years of land use control, and the nitrate locked in the root system could be irretrievably lost,' said the Rivers Authority. Voluntary controls could, it warned, end up as a 'costly failure'.[45]

At the time of writing it is not clear what will happen to the Draft Directive. As has been seen above (Chapter 1), the same measure will call for controls to prevent eutrophication in coastal water and Britain has been fighting the battle-of-the-maps at the Paris Commission. As to inland waters, the UK apparently intends to argue that the controlling factor in eutrophication is not nitrate but phosphate. 'Where there is a danger of eutrophication in this country,' says the government, 'usually the limiting factor is phosphate, and not nitrate; if confirmed this would mean that zones would not therefore need to be designated to prevent eutrophication.'[46]

For scientific assessment of a subtle ecological issue such as the causes of eutrophication, it is important that the information used to decide policy is openly available for scientific debate. In this case, it seems that the DoE will decide behind closed doors. The DoE wrote to Water Authorities 'seeking from them assessments of the zones that would need to be designated' if the Directive came into being. It also has information on nitrate levels held as part of the Harmonised Monitoring Programme and 'separate information on farming practices'. It seems this will be used by the DoE to 'assess' the EC proposals although none of the facts will be available to the public.[47]

The UK also hopes that the need for unanimity in the Council under Article 130S will enable it to exercise a veto on the proposal. But should the UK fail to deflect the Commission and the Directive goes ahead, then its impact could be considerable. In the 'worst case scenario,' say MAFF and DoE, 'it is possible that most of the Anglian region would have to be declared a water protection zone as well as substantial parts of Severn Trent and other areas, accounting in total for the great bulk of the UK arable protection area.'[48] The Soil Survey and Land Research Centre at Silsoe has identified 15 per cent of soils in the Midlands, eastern and southern England as lying over chalk, limestone or sand-stone, and so vulnerable to nitrate leaching.[49]

Would this be the worst case scenario or the best case scenario? After all, almost the whole of industrial Britain became a controlled, smoke free area under the Clean Air Acts, of which the current government is so proud some 30 years later. It is a fact that the water supplies of the Anglian region, and others besides, are seriously polluted with nitrate and that on present trends this pollution will get much worse. There seems a *prima facie* case for prompt national action.

If the 'polluter pays' and preventative principles were genuinely applied, there would, as the memo fears, be 'major agricultural and related consequences'. But these would be for the general benefit, not for the worse. The government, it seems, is still thinking short term. Indeed it illustrates its 'worst case' scenario with the observation that the 'major changes' in farming would 'benefit water quality little if at all in the short to medium term'.

As an example it gives the 'extreme case' of chalk areas once downland but converted to cereals mainly in the 1960s and 1970s which, if returned to unfertilised grassland, would reduce nitrate to 50 mg/litre only after 2040. A return to downland would be popular with walkers, with Britain's 3 million paid-up members of nature conservation organisations, its 10 or 20 million 'green consumers', with local people who now suffer spraydrift, and with consumers of water.

A few hundred or a few thousand farmers might oppose a return to downland because it would mean lower profits. But it would save the country money in not producing surplus cereals. And much of the land in question is not naturally good for cereal growing. Without heavy use of fertilisers there would be no cereals on it. In the year 2040 our children and our descendants might think it was an 'extreme case' not to have begun to take action to reduce nitrate pollution half a century earlier.

Nitrate Solutions

According to the 'polluter pays' principle, the costs of dealing with pollution should be borne by the people who create it. But who is this in the case of nitrates: is it the farmers, the consumers who buy high nitrate-produced food, or the fertiliser manufacturers?

The consumer has had little or no choice in the matter: without organic food widely available it has not been possible to choose to avoid creating nitrate pollution by avoiding conventionally grown crops (in any case, organic farming can still create some nitrate pollution, see also below).

The blame must lie with the fertiliser manufacturers, who undoubtedly have done their best to encourage increased consumption by heavy advertising to farmers, and who in many cases also own farms themselves and supply seed of varieties specially bred to respond to high levels of nitrogen. The farmers who have undoubtedly profited from producing heavier crops of higher-yielding varieties that rely on nitrates also share the blame.

The government, too, has a responsibility, as through the Common Agricultural Policy of price support system it has guaranteed a market for cereals and encouraged intensive production. The Thatcher government has opposed planning controls over agriculture that could have stopped the spread of intensive arable farming. And at one time it was UK policy for fertiliser use to be encouraged by direct grants and subsidies.

A MORI Poll conducted in November 1988 showed that of a hypothetical £100 to be spent on cleaning up nitrates and pesticides in the public water supply, people felt industry should pay £39, farmers £19, the government £31 and the consumer £11.[50] (Asking if the 'government' should pay of course begs the question, where does the government get the cash from if not from the consumer? In practice, as we have seen, it is British policy to subsidise the polluting farmers rather than make them pay to clean up the pollution.)

The precautionary principle suggests that, as the future damage done by pollution is often more costly than the extra expense of avoiding it in the first place and in any case it is often unacceptable, even if a money cost can't be put on it, then prevention is better than cure. In the case of nitrates, it is increasingly evident that stopping the pollution at source is going to be far cheaper than trying to deal with the consequences afterwards.

Prevention can take several forms. Nitrate application can be banned or severely controlled in areas where bore-holes will be particularly affected in the short term. It can be limited across the whole country or across wide areas liable to suffer in the longer term (for example, on all permeable soils such as on chalk, limestone, sand or sandstone). Quotas can be introduced, which might or might not be tradeable between farmers (David Baldock of the IEEP suggests that within the National Farmers' Union a debate over quotas ended with victory for those in favour of no such regulation). Taxes can be imposed either to raise funds for pollution control or to discourage over-use of nitrates, or both.

Lastly you might choose to rely on advice to farmers and fertiliser manufacturers. This 'voluntary' approach, as we have seen, is the one traditionally favoured in the UK. Its success is almost invariably limited to the few cases where free advice enables a businessman to make immediate cost savings. According to the DoE,[51] since 1979 government advice to cereal farmers has reduced autumn applications of nitrate by 60 per cent . At the same time, more cereals have been sown in the autumn rather than the spring and sowing has been earlier (e.g. in September not October). Both factors have reduced nitrate loss from arable land and some 'fast responding' aquifers have shown slight decreases in nitrate pollution as a result, says the DoE. But there are other reasons for farmers switching to autumn cereals than a desire to curb nitrate pollution, and this is likely to be the limit of what the 'voluntary approach' can achieve.

The two water regions of Britain with the greatest nitrate problems are Anglian and Severn Trent. Following the government retreat over the terms of the Directive in 1988 it was estimated that Anglian would have to spend £60–£70 million over the following 10 years to clean up the water supplies of Bedford and Norwich, along with a total 25 supplies that had been subject to derogations. 'Remedial measures,' said the magazine *ENDS*, 'will be needed at 42 sites in the Anglian region. Ion exchange denitrification plants will be installed at 23 locations. Another four will employ denitrification technology. A combination of blending and source replacement will be used for the other 15 locations.' Within the next 20–25 years Anglian expects another nine supplies to go over the limit.[52]

In 1988, Severn Trent had already begun a £7 million capital programme to bring 17 'derogated' supplies below 50 mg/litre by 1991 by blending and taking sources out of commission. *ENDS* noted that around 6 per cent of Severn Trent's abstracted groundwater supplies exceeded 50 mg/litre of nitrate but 'with a continuation of present land use practices the figure will rise to 20–25 per cent by 2011'.[53]

This, said *ENDS*, was 'the issue causing the water industry most concern'. It could still be averted but only 'if action to reduce nitrogen leaching at source is taken immediately'. No such action has been taken: the pilot projects apply to just a handful of catchments.

Other countries are further advanced. Since 1985 the German Drinking Water Ordinance has specified 'protection zones' of 100–500 metres around bore-holes,[54] and the UK Nitrate Coordination Group noted in 1986 that the Germans were giving 'consideration . . . to stricter catchment area regulations laying down maximum nitrate fertiliser application rates, banning its use at certain times of the year and requiring changes in the land use'. In Lower Saxony, the spreading of manure and slurry was already controlled.

In Denmark, farms with more than 20 head of cattle must have access to stores for slurry and effluent with at least six months' capacity. Liquid manure cannot be spread on the fields from harvest until 1 November (unless it is onto growing vegetation or crops for the next winter). Nor can it be spread on frozen ground. Similarly, Danish farmers must comply with a limit of two head of cattle per hectare, equivalent to an input of about 170 kg of fertiliser nitrogen on each hectare each year. To keep more animals, the farmers must possess a written long-term agreement to deliver surplus manure to other farms, or to common storage plants or biogas plants. No such system is proposed for the UK.

Dutch manure and fertiliser rates are due to be reduced until a 50 mg/litre soil water concentration is achieved at 2m depth, later to be cut to 25 mg/litre. Under the National Environmental Policy Plan, the Netherlands aims to balance its national nitrogen and phosphorus budget by the year 2000. New pig and poultry farms are banned and grassland applications are limited.

In theory, Section 31 of the 1974 Control of Pollution Act gave Water Authorities powers to restrict farming activities in protection zones, but the powers were never used.[55] The question of introducing nitrate protection zones got serious consideration only through the Nitrate Coordination Group in 1987.[56]

In 1988, the DoE published a report *The Nitrate Issue: A Study of the Economic and Other Consequences of Various Local Options for Limiting Nitrate Concentration in Drinking Water*. This studied the economics of reducing groundwater pollution in ten catchments overlying chalk, sand or limestone aquifers. In five of them the nitrate level already exceeded 50 mg/litre and it was due to exceed that level in the others by 1991–2004. The study compared the costs of prevention through land use controls and of treatment by removing the nitrates from abstracted water.[57]

In eight out of ten catchments the report's authors calculated that the immediate cost of water treatment or blending was less than the 'local cost' of farming measures, but, once Exchequer savings from reduced agricultural production were included (i.e. savings in public grants and subsidies paid to farmers to produce crops), in most cases it was cheaper to establish protection zones with curbs on farming than to treat the polluted water.[58]

While changing agricultural prices and subsidies will have a marked effect on which options look most economic, as *ENDS* remarked, 'controls based on a combination of land use and water measures' are probably the best option. It is also significant that the DoE study did not consider the costs of several 'uncostable' factors such as the increased corrosion and organic contamination which denitrification can cause but which would not be incurred by preventative methods.[59]

Lead

Lead is a poison which impairs the development of the nerves and the brain, especially in children, and which will poison anyone if enough is ingested. These days acute lead poisoning is a rarity, but children are still at risk from chewing flakes of lead-based paints, which taste sweet.

As early as 1943 American researchers R. K. Byers and E. E. Lord had published a paper *Late effects of lead poisoning on mental development*.[60] Research in the 1970s and 1980s showed a link between lead entering the body and the state of health. Pollution consultant Brian Price, who campaigned with the pressure group CLEAR (Campaign for Lead Free Air), highlights a crucial study by Dr Robert Needham in Boston, USA. Needham examined the IQ of children and the quantity of lead found in their (shed) milk teeth. 'He found, after allowing for some 37 factors not related to lead,' says Price, 'that those children having high lead levels in their teeth did significantly less well in tests than did those with low levels.' As Price points out, the importance of his finding was that such 'high' lead levels were common in city children in Britain. Dr Robert Stephens of Birmingham University says Price concluded that 20 per cent of urban children in Britain could be suffering 'some form of lead-induced mental impairment'.[61]

Lead dissolves in acid water. In naturally acid areas, or where acid rain has made the water more acid, lead pipes are a serious hazard to health because the water strips the metal from the pipe walls and it ends up coming out of the tap. The Romans were fond of lead vessels for food and drink and used lead-based glazes on pottery: lead poisoning was common and has even been proposed as a cause of the madness among high-ranking Romans which contributed to the fall of the Roman Empire. The palliative for drinking water supplies is to dose the water supply with calcium carbonate (lime) to raise the pH (that is, reduce the acidity) and stop the lead dissolving. The only cure, however, is to remove lead from the water system altogether, by replacing old pipes and tanks.

Although lead in water would be an important factor in high blood and body lead in some areas, high levels were also observed in people living in areas with lime-rich 'hard' water with low lead levels. Campaigners and many scientists believed lead from the tetra-ethyl lead added as an anti-knock agent in petrol had to be the cause. The government, under pressure from companies such as Associated Octel, disagreed.

In 1980 the government published a report *Lead and Health* , which, says Price is 'now notorious'.[62] This report, also known as the Lawther Report after its chairman Professor Patrick Lawther, played down dust and airborne lead as sources of contamination. Robert Stephens showed in 1982 that a 2-year-old child in a high-density traffic area could ingest 54 per cent of its lead via the air (some directly, but most from dust picked up on fingers and food), while 46 per cent would be accounted for in food and drink. While nationally the proportion of lead taken in by people from water is 6 per cent, in areas with high lead levels in water this can rise to more than 50 per cent .[63]

In a vigorous and ultimately successful seven-year campaign, CLEAR forced the government to admit both the exposure to lead due to lead in petrol, and the health hazard posed by lead as such. The problem of lead in water, however, remained.

A 1975/6 random daytime survey for the Department of the Environment revealed that over 7 per cent of the tapwater in England exceeded the EC limit while in Scotland the figure was over 34 per cent.[64] In its ninth Report, *Lead in the Environment*, published in 1983, the Royal Commission on Environmental Pollution called for more vigorous action to reduce the hazard from lead in drinking water. Although a voluntary programme of treatment (water hardening) and replacement of lead plumbing was begun, it was not enough. Grant-aid was available, but only in houses with rates below a certain level. And these grants were later affected by cuts in government expenditure. The result is that many homes still have lead pipes.

As of 1982 more than 300,000 households still had water with more than 100ug/l lead in their tapwater. Studies in Glasgow showed that mothers with higher than normal levels of lead in their bodies had more stillbirths, and babies born small. Lead passes freely across the placenta into the unborn child from the mother's blood.[65] Dr Michael Moore of Glasgow University showed that mothers who drank water with a high lead level were twice as likely to have mentally retarded babies; 61 per cent of mothers involved in stillbirths or whose foetuses were abnormal had placental lead levels over 1.5 ppm whereas only 7 per cent of those with normal babies had such high lead levels.[66]

The most recent study in Scotland involved more than 800 6–9-year-old schoolchildren in Edinburgh. Children with higher blood lead levels did less well in IQ tests, number skills and reading ability. Dr Robin Russel-Jones, at one time chairman of CLEAR, stated in 1989 that 'A later stage of this study also showed a clear link between blood lead level and aggressive/anti-social and hyperactive behaviour in children. These effects occurred at what were previously considered very low levels of lead in blood. There was not only clear evidence of a dose-response relationship, but no indication of a threshold below which effects would cease to occur'.[67]

In 1989, it was estimated that over 2 million people in the UK still drank water contaminated with lead. Many of them (but not all – see below) were in Labour-controlled Scotland, and many of these were in old, poor tenement housing. It is hard to escape the feeling that this proven hazard would not have been allowed to continue, poisoning children and adults, if the victims had been residents of Weybridge or Sloane Square rather than the Gorbals.

In his book *Acid Rain*, Fred Pearce describes what happened to a report on the severe lead pollution in Scotland. 'The most devastating evidence about the scale of the problem was "presented to Parliament" in 1980. Actually, a report was placed in the House of Commons library late one afternoon just before Christmas. The study, by the Greater Glasgow Health Board, revealed that more than a tenth of all newborn babies in Glasgow entered the world with more lead in their blood than is considered safe for adults. . . Five percent of the mothers in the survey had more than the international limit of 350 micrograms of lead in every litre of blood in their bodies. Eleven percent of their newborn babies exceeded the limit.'[68]

The EC Drinking Water Directive set a Maximum Admissible Concentration (MAC) of 50 ug/litre of lead in tapwater. The formal date for compliance was July 1985 but, as Nigel Haigh notes in *EEC Environmental Policy and Britain*, in 1983 the UK government set itself a target of complying with the lead limit only by December 1989. By March 1987 the UK had applied to the Commission for a delay until 1989 for all areas where, on a random survey, more than 2.5 per cent of the properties showed the MAC was exceeded.[69] Between 38 per cent and 57 per cent of houses in the UK have lead pipework, while around 27 per cent are in areas with 'plumbosolvent' (lead dissolving) water, and half of these homes have lead in the connection pipe leading to the tap.[70]

In November 1988 the UK sent plans to the Commission, indicating the 'completion of necessary works' by 1992. In April 1989 the European Commission sent Britain its Reasoned Opinion alleging an infraction of the EC Drinking Water Directive and citing the UK's record on eliminating the hazard from lead. 'From the information submitted by the United Kingdom, the Commission is of the opinion that little had been done by way of systematic work on the problem of lead in drinking water in Scotland between the adoption of the Directive and 20 July 1985. The Commission indicated, by a letter of 9 August 1988, that it required a commitment that all Scottish water supplies would be in conformity with the lead parameter of the Directive by the end of 1989.' 1992 was better, but not good enough, said Brussels.

A striking example of the opposed thinking in Brussels and Westminster now emerged. The Commission said, 'In view of the long-standing and widespread nature of this infringement of a toxic parameter of the Directive, the Commission cannot accept any delay beyond 1989.'[71] Contrast this with the words of a House of Lords Select Committee considering exactly the same problem: 'because of the high proportion [of homes with polluted tapwater] and the long-standing nature of the problem, the Committee believe that the two years for compliance with the Directive is wholly unrealistic.'[72]

The Commission also focused on the way the UK was measuring lead in tapwater. Lead levels from a system with lead piping are much higher in the first few pints that come from a tap that has been left turned off than after the water has run for a few minutes, as this flushes out much of the dissolved lead. The UK government measures the lead in tapwater that has been running for several minutes, as it would be if you had a bath in it, and not the first few pints or cupfuls, as you would use for cooking or making a cup of tea. Quite understandably, the Commission objected to this procedure, which made UK tapwater appear to have less lead in it than the consumer experiences.

As of 1989, 70 water sources in Scotland had water which needed chemical treatment to make it safe for putting through lead pipes,[73] including supplies in Fort William, Edinburgh, Glasgow and Peterhead. Although the Scottish Office would not say how far supplies exceeded MACs for lead, at least 17 schemes were in progress to reduce lead in water that would not be completed until as late as 1992.

The government is now faced with the realisation that treatment alone will not get lead levels down to the 50 ug/litre required by the Directive.

When Friends of the Earth researched the tapwater survey of England and Wales run in the *Observer* in 1989,[74] they found that lead exceeded the legal limit in a far larger and more widely distributed number of supplies than had previously been supposed. Water suppliers' own records for 1987–9 showed that such surprising areas as Bath, Brighton, Huntingdon, Braintree and Waveney had lead pollution of drinking water above the MAC. A chunk of East Anglia from north Bedfordshire up to Hunstanton was affected, but the worst areas were in north Wales, Lancashire, Greater Manchester, Merseyside, Yorkshire and the southwest.

Reservoirs in the Lake District, for example, supply acid lead-stripping water to Greater Manchester. At Dilworth near Preston, a tapwater sample contained 3,600 ug/litre lead, that is, 72 times the 50 ug/litre limit. Another from Blackburn contained twice as much: 7,750 ug/litre lead or 155 times the EC limit and 77 times the action level. Even Hythe in Kent had 147 ug/litre while a sample in the area of Huntingdon went 9 times over the limit at 450 ug/litre. Altogether they found 122 supply areas with lead above the MAC.

Lead can also get into water from the solder in copper pipes. Research by the Water Research Centre in 1981 showed that long runs of copper piping with lead solder could produce high levels of lead in tapwater. The WRC suggested it should be banned, but the government has taken no action. Schools, of which no survey has been published, may have a particularly large number of lead pipes, despite the risk to children.

Dr Robin Russel-Jones pointed out in September 1989 that, although the UK planned to achieve the EC 50 ug/litre level, which conformed to the prevailing WHO level, the WHO itself was planning a revision downward to 25 ug/litre or below.[75] In February 1990, a MAFF study discovered that children and pregnant women were receiving more lead than had been thought, and recommended a level of 10 ug/litre, as applies in the USA. The cost of replacing all the pipework that poses a danger of lead contamination has been put at £1,000 million by the WRC and a committee apparently advised the DoE that the cost could be £405–£2,000 million.

Aluminium

Unlike lead, aluminium is a relatively recent arrival in the pollution debate. It gets into water supplies in two ways: either from acid soils, where it becomes soluble at low pH (there are huge amounts in the soil and these are washed out by acid rain where there is little organic matter to bind the aluminium), or by being deliberately added to peaty water to remove the suspended organic matter and make the water clear, by a similar chemical process. We also take in a considerable quantity of aluminium in certain foods, but this is normally in a 'non-bioavailable' form.

Since the 1960s there have been growing suspicions that Alzheimer's disease (a form of senile dementia) is associated with high levels of aluminium. The disease is growing in importance as the population of many western countries ages: it kills 120,000 a year in the USA. Scientists at the Medical Research Council (MRC) reported that a link might exist as long ago as 1968. People living in Guam and west New Guinea suffer unusually high rates of Alzheimer's disease and live in areas with high levels of aluminium in the soil. Since 1986 Norwegian research has also suggested that in the southern, most acidified parts of the country, there may be a link between high rates of Alzheimer's disease and aluminium in water.

The characteristic signs of Alzheimer's disease visible with a microscope are tangled clumps of nerve cell fibres in the brain and 'senile plaques, knobby patches of dying nerve fibres'. These are thought by researchers to be the result of low calcium and magnesium and high aluminium in the brain.

Kidney dialysis patients are particularly vulnerable to aluminium in water supplies as their bodies are continually 'flushed' with large volumes of water. In England Sheila Brayford from Staffordshire died from brain damage in 1981 when she absorbed about 100 times the normal level of aluminium in dialysis.[76]

An MRC group reported in January 1989 that people receiving drinking water with high levels of aluminium stand a 50 per cent greater chance of suffering from Alzheimer's disease. The study encompassed 1,203 dementia patients in 88 districts. For those with raised aluminium levels in the water supply (of 110 ug/litre), the risk was found to be 35–50 per cent higher in people under 70. The Council's research showed highest aluminium concentrations in Northumberland, Durham, Tyne and Wear, Devon and Cornwall. The lowest were in Suffolk, Cambridgeshire, Hampshire, Nottinghamshire, Derbyshire, and Norfolk.[77]

Camelford

Aluminium poisoning became famous in Britain when on Wednesday 6 July 1988 a 20-tonne lorry-load of aluminium sulphate was poured into the wrong tank at Lowermoor treatment works and polluted the water supply of Camelford in Cornwall. The water became acrid and bitter. It curdled milk in tea, was just drinkable in coffee, and, when people washed in it, the water turned blue.[78] The treatment plant, where the aluminium sulphate was routinely used to clear the water by removing organic matter, serves 7,000 homes and 20,000 people.

The lorry driver, a relief worker from ISC Chemicals in Bristol, came on the wrong day and found nobody at the plant. He put the chemical in what he thought was the storage tank but wasn't. Edward Pilkington writing in the *Guardian* later commented, 'What at first glance appears to be no more than a simple case of human error becomes, at closer examination, as much a story about bungling management and an inadequate safety system born of years of cuts. John Lewis, the district manager in charge of Lowermoor, had been voicing his concerns about the safety of the treatment works for some years before the accident. As early as August 1986 he wrote to South West Water's headquarters in Exeter complaining that 'we seem to move from one crisis to another. Proper pre-planning is becoming more and more a dream.'[79]

Staff cuts and reductions in overtime, both introduced as part of the Authority's attempts to increase book profits, were blamed by Lewis in more than one confidential memo for procedures which cut corners and increased the risk of accidents. He had asked for a new security system for Lowermoor but was refused on cost grounds. The number of safety advisers working in the field in SWWA's region was reduced from six to two after a visit from the government's 'flying accountants', brought in to see that the Authority met its 'performance aims' after financial cuts in 1980. The same accountants apparently proposed getting rid of river wardens and people in pollution control.[80]

Len Hill, South West Water chairman until 1987, was one of those who protested that government cuts meant a 'greater likelihood of disruptions and deteriorations in service to our customers and possible health and safety implications . . . Experienced operators on site are able to detect failures but these procedures are not followed due to decreased manpower.'[81] Mr Hill was replaced by Ken Court, from Blue Circle Cement.

The reaction of the SWWA to the incident was a mixture of panic and secrecy. The aluminium sulphate was added to the 'contact tank', a bad place because it was the last stage in the treatment process before the water left for the town. That was at 4.30 p.m. Not long after the lorry driver left, the water became more and more acid and alarms went off. By early evening, emergency staff reached the plant. But at first they didn't realise what had happened and, instead of stopping the supply and cleaning out the tank, they flushed out the system, which sent the acid down the mains into the homes of the area. The Authority's early explanations mentioned lime dosing equipment and spoke of 'a slight acidity problem'.[82] This was later altered on 14 July to 'high acidity'.

It was not until Friday morning, after a day and a half had elapsed, that the real fault was diagnosed. By this time the rivers Camel and Allen had been polluted with aluminium, killing 60,000 trout and salmon.[83] Pilkington talked to Dr Richard Newman, who was out on an early morning call, on the Thursday. He watched in disbelief as water gushed from the fire hydrants and flowed down the road into the river, where the fish were dying. The SWWA had opened the hydrants at night to try and clear out the system before the town woke up.

The attempt failed and no warning was given to the public. Pilkington recounts how when Winifred Harper turned on her tap, 'out came a yellowy, stinking acerbic fluid which curdled the milk'.[84] She, like others, telephoned the Water Authority and was reassured that the water was safe to drink. Still, it tasted so bad she had to make sugary coffee instead of tea. 'For the first few days,' wrote Pilkington, 'it was all quite humorous. People laughed about their pink towels turning blue, the result of copper leached from the hot water pipes by the acidic water. The press, slow to grasp the significance of what had happened, treated it as a light hearted story about bleached hair turning green.'

Postmaster and chairman of the Camelford Chamber of Commerce Walter Roberts noticed that his solar panels had become corroded. Clive and Anne Ahrens, who had a holiday cottage in Helstone village, found a white sludge at the bottom of a glass of water poured from the tap. The SWWA told them it was safe to drink. On one farm 1,300 chickens died, and on another 10 lambs out of 40 (the rest being made ill). The Ahrens' 40 ducklings also died within a fortnight.[85]

By Friday 8 July residents of Camelford were being supplied with water at up to 500 times the Maximum Admissible Concentration under the EC Drinking Water Directive of 200 ug/litre (0.2 mg/litre). Independent tests put the levels at up to 3,000 times the limit.[86] Considerable efforts were then made to clean out the system but not to inform the public. Indeed, the Authority orchestrated a positive attempt at secrecy. A SWWA document obtained by the *Guardian* stated that, 'If public reaction escalates to a major extent over the weekend the Department of the Environment should be informed.'

The emergency staff had realised at 5 a.m. on Thursday 7 July that dialysis patients were at special risk from the aluminium, but the house of Robert Hill, a local man with kidney failure and a dialysis machine, was not contacted until the next day. The Authority blamed Dr Grainger of the District Health Authority, who, 'since he had received no complaints', 'took no positive action'. Fortunately, Mr Hill was in Truro Hospital at the time, out of the area. Otherwise he might have suffered the same fate as Sheila Brayford.

John Lewis, the man who had complained about the effect of financial cuts on safety at Lowermoor, was the only person to be sacked as a result of the incident. He told the *Guardian* that he believed senior management took deliberate steps to hush up the dangers. As soon as the contamination was confirmed, he was told to treat the information as confidential. His views were later confirmed by SWWA's own non-executive director John Lawrence who commented in his own report: 'There seems to be a culture in which the public are told as little as possible and expected to trust the Authority to look after their interests.'[87] Even Ken Court admitted that, with hindsight, the secrecy was 'mistaken'.

But the health effects were only just beginning. People began to complain about feelings of sickness, vomiting, diarrhoea and headaches. It seems likely that these were connected not just with aluminium but with copper, lead and zinc stripped from the insides of pipes, solder and fittings by the acid. Similar problems occur in Sweden where many private supplies are highly acidified as a result of acid rain. People presented symptoms to Dr Newman such as skin rashes, lip blisters and, in particular, mouth ulcers. He estimated that there were more than 300 cases. According to Pilkington, 'One child he examined had such a lacerated tongue he compared it to sago pudding.'[88]

Other people suffered arthritis and aching joints and muscles. Dr Newman was seeing five or six people each surgery with the same symptoms, and 'the pharmacist reported a flood of people asking for remedies'.[89] A year later, some still had the symptoms. Flautist Tim Wheater, well known for playing with the group The Eurythmics, suffered an outbreak of lip blisters and ulcers which destroyed his ability to control the flute, and lost him a year's income. Winifred Harper was diagnosed as suffering from Parkinson's disease, which both she and Dr Newman suspected to be connected with the water poisoning. 'Anybody can make a mistake. To err, it's only human. I can forgive them for that. But I will never forgive them for covering it up,' she told Edward Pilkington.

Dr Grainger and some of the local doctors dismissed the ulcers and sore throats as 'common', saying they 'could well have occurred as a coincidence'. According to the *Sunday Times*, 'A Government Minister has implied that their [the people of the area] problems are imaginary or psychosomatic and a senior Whitehall official has suggested that the whole thing was a "hoax", devised to thwart the Government's privatisation plans.'

Many of the indigenous Cornish people of the area suffered symptoms but have accepted compensation from the Water Authority. 'It's too big for us to tackle,' said one, Keith Hill, his wife adding, 'We keep quiet because we see ourselves as second best – so we don't make demands when perhaps we should.' But the newcomers were more belligerent and less respectful of authorities of all kinds. A number were still pursuing court cases against SWWA at the time of writing.

If it had not been for an alliance of Dr Newman, consultant ecologist Doug Cross and Walter Roberts – three local residents who formed the Camelford Scientific Advisory Panel and conducted their own investigations – and for John Lewis, who lost his job, it is doubtful whether very much would ever have come out about the incident. On 11 July Cross had taken a sample of his own tapwater into the local North Cornwall District Council offices and asked for it to be analysed, but the Council refused. The *Sunday Times* reporter Peter

Gillman recounts how the Panel went to the Trading Standards Office at Bodmin but was told that there was nothing to be done because water was not covered by the Food Act. The Office referred them to the Office of Fair Trading. Here they were told to call the Water Research Centre. The WRC said not to worry as copper was not particularly toxic.

Eventually they learnt from Dr Grainger that there was some contamination with alum (aluminium sulphate) but that this was 'not particularly dangerous'. On 19 July Roberts and Cross wrote to Dr John Lawrence at SWWA suggesting that the public had been exposed to a more serious hazard than had been admitted: they were told that they could meet Lawrence but he would give them no information. Then on 22 July someone rang Roberts anonymously and told him that a lorry-load of aluminium sulphate had been tipped into the water supply.

Roberts called a meeting of the Town Council and he and Cross asked the police to start an investigation. The police were 'sympathetic' but according to Cross were 'even more in the dark than we were'.[90] On 3 August, Roberts and Cross met with Lawrence but he only said that the lorry story was 'hearsay'. Not until the anonymous informant had rung again on 4 August and there had been more calls to Lawrence, and they had finally made contact with John Lewis, did the Panel begin to find out what had really happened.

On 22 July, the Water Authority had admitted for the first time that aluminium had been involved by placing a small advertisement in the local press saying 'that the water was no more acidic than lemon juice'.[91]

From 14 August onwards the Water Authority 'went public' and issued numerous statements and explanations. On 18 August it met with the Health Authority's officials and asked them to conduct a public health survey which it would pay for, mainly to reassure the public that, although the EC limits for aluminium had been exceeded over 500 times, and those for sulphate, copper, zinc and lead had also been broken, there was no long-term harm.

A number of people who were previously healthy now reported difficulties with their memory, digestion, concentration and muscle control. Some said they were sensitive to the water, their symptoms leaving them when they drank bottled water. It was also discovered that the Poisons Unit at Guys Hospital and a DHSS toxicologist had wanted to visit the area to do tests but had been 'warned off'.[92] On 31 October 1988, Minister Colin Moynihan told the House of Commons that there would be 'no adverse or long-term effects'.

Peter Gillman suggests that it was not until TV South West made a film 'A Trust Betrayed', and consulted Dr Neil Ward of Surrey University, that a plausible explanation for the conflicting evidence of poisoning and the official view that it could not happen came to light.[93]

Ward believed that the Water and Health Authorities had misunderstood the chemistry of aluminium. Whereas there is a lot of aluminium in substances like antacid tablets and toothpaste, this remains insoluble because acidity is low. This makes it highly soluble and capable of being absorbed by the body. Mixed with water, aluminium sulphate becomes increasingly acid. The cocktail of metals that resulted from the high acidity 'fitted the textbook on metal poisoning,' said Ward.

The Health Authorities at this time maintained that the maximum aluminium level had been 109 mg/litre, but the Ahrenses still had their jar of water and when it was analysed at Somerset Council's laboratories it was found to contain 620 mg/litre, 3,000 times the EC limit. Government minister Robert Freeman now had a meeting with Roberts and promised a new inquiry. This time it was a team from Southampton University. At first they said it wouldn't be necessary to go to Camelford, then they said it would. The resulting Clayton Report said there would be no long-term health effects.

In June 1989, Neville Hodgkinson and Peter Gillman of the *Sunday Times* reported that Clive Ahrens had been found to have aluminium in his hip bone, laid down as a band (as is common in people living in areas of high lead in water). The discovery was made not by the local health officials or the DHSS but at Ahrens' own instigation, using the services of a London specialist and Manchester University's rheumatology department which studies aluminium uptake in dialysis patients.[94]

Dr Ward has spoken of the potential effects on children who were unborn at the time of the incident.[95] Mr John McGarry, a consultant obstetrician, is attempting to monitor all children from the area born after the 6 July incident. In November 1989, following police investigations, it was announced that SWWA would be prosecuted. In February 1990, Dr Tom McMillan, a clinical psychologist at Atkinson Morley Hospital in London, said most of his 11 Camelford patients still had their lives disrupted by the poisoning. French holidaymakers in the area at the time of the accident still had up to four times the normal level of aluminium in their bodies almost two years later.[96]

The 'not invented here' or 'not discovered by us' syndrome runs strongly in British official circles and official inquiries are more than capable of requiring standards of rigour and a quality of proof from external or 'independent' evidence which are never applied to the government's own sources. In the Camelford case, the muddled official response has done little to engender confidence in the abilities of the DoE, DHSS or their local networks to deal effectively with any similar incident in future. When in August 1988 the overstretched Health Authority belatedly sent out a questionnaire enquiring about symptoms that might have been suffered as a result of drinking the water, one went to 450 'occupants' of a graveyard in St Tudy, which happened to have a tap in one corner. According to the *Guardian*: 'the rector of St Tudy filled in the questionnaire for them. Under "symptoms experienced" he wrote: "General symptoms of claustrophobia and inability to walk. At times we feel as if everything is getting on top of us".'

Whether or not the Camelford aluminium case is ever proved to have led to long-term damage to the health of people living in the area, it was certainly a major pollution incident. The Authority reacted wrongly and secretively. The Health Authorities and the DoE were confused and ineffectual.

In May 1989 a similar accident occurred in SWWA's region, albeit on a much smaller scale. At Jennetts in Bideford, north Devon, on 15 May 2,300 litres of aluminium sulphate spilled when a hose came loose from a tank. A nearby stream was polluted for 1,000 metres and 20 fish died. And at Watercombe on 5 May the River Yealm was found to have two and a half times the permitted level of aluminium.[97] After the Jennetts incident, John Lawrence, who had written the critical report on the Authority's attitude, declared his disappointment that increased safety and greater openness had not been implemented since the Camelford incident. 'This is an unfortunate and extremely regrettable incident,' he told a newspaper. 'Obviously the message has not got through to some parts of the organisation.'[98]

In June 1989 aluminium sulphate also entered a water supply intended for tens of thousands of people at Fossany Bane Works near Newry in Northern Ireland. The works was unmanned at the weekend. Somehow the chemical got from a storage tank into water supplies. Under a third of the 23,000 litres stored was thought to have got into the supply system .[99]

In August 1989 it was reported that 13,600 people in Dumfries and Galloway had been supplied with water containing up to 1,000 times the EC limit for aluminium, starting in March 1989. 'After aluminium blocked filters at a treatment plant at Penwhirn Reservoir near Stranraer,' wrote the *Sunday Times*, 'the authority decided not to tell its customers and then issued safety advice that proved to be incorrect and inadequate.'

Friends of the Earth contacted the European Commission asking for legal action in relation to the Drinking Water Directive, because from 5 to 21 March the plant produced water with excess aluminium levels. After 8 April the aluminium returned to tapwater when a mains burst: sludge was found at the bottom of a glass of water but when it was sent to the authority for analysis it was discarded as 'too sludgy'. Strangely, another sample of water divided in two and analysed both independently at the Glasgow Institute of Biochemistry and at the Water Board's Dumfries laboratory showed two very different results. The Institute found 92 mg/litre and the Authority only 12.5 mg/litre. But 'there was no cover up,' the Director of Water and Sewage was reported as saying in the *Sunday Times*.[100]

People in Wigtown suffered diarrhoea, sickness and mouth ulcers. Local doctors were said to be sceptical because the water suppliers dosed the water with a large quantity of lime to prevent soluble forms of aluminium being formed as had happened at Camelford. However they were said to be 'furious' that the Scottish Office, the local community health specialist and the water suppliers had reassured people that there was no risk to health.

The 1987–9, FoE-*Observer* tapwater survey found 154 water supply areas with aluminium at above the EC level of 200 ug/litre (0.2 mg/litre). Most of the aluminium contamination is due to aluminium sulphate added to water to remove cloudiness. As a result of the 'evidence of a causal link' between high levels of dementia and raised aluminium (even at around half the EC limit), the Thames Water Authority has now decided to cease using aluminium in water treatment. Dr Paul Altmann of the Kidney Unit at the London Hospital in Whitechapel is reported as saying: 'It is when you are absorbing aluminium over many years that it is potentially damaging. The low-level, continuous exposure arising from aluminium sulphate in water purification is very worrying. The practice should be stopped.'[101]

Between 1987 and 1989 London aluminium levels broke EC limits in

Barnet, Merton, Sutton, Croydon, Enfield and Epsom and Ewell supply districts.[102] In the Calder Valley district, the Yorkshire Water Authority's data showed the EC limits were met less than half the time in 1988. Eccup water treatment works supplying Leeds failed 'regularly' and only 38 per cent of the works supplying Wales met the standard. In Hertfordshire, Hatfield was being supplied with aluminium at four times the EC limit (800 ug/litre) at one time in 1988. Egham reached 850, Bracknell 710 and Staines 642 ug/litre. On 20 November 1989, the same treatment works at Camelford again polluted water with twice the EC limit for aluminium.

Other Contaminants

There are many other 'trace' contaminants in our tapwater besides nitrate, lead and aluminium. Trihalomethanes, for example, are created by the reaction of chlorine, added to kill bacteria, and a wide range of organic matter, from sewage to peat. One such substance is chloroform. The EC has set a limit of 100 ug/litre but a US study suggests this should be significantly reduced because of a 'highly significant relationship' between chloroform and cancers of the bladder, colon and rectum. West Germany has already set a limit of 25 ug/litre. The FoE-*Observer* tapwater survey found that 84 areas had drinking water contaminated with trihalomethanes beyond the EC limit of 100 ug/litre, including Broxbourne, Enfield, Epping Forest and Haringey in north London, most of Devon and a large tract of the Midlands from Lincoln to Montgomery.[103]

In December 1989, in water supplied to 500,000 people on Tyneside, phenol pollution combined with chlorine to create foul-tasting chlorophenols. Chlorophenols are potential carcinogens. In a similar 1984 incident, phenol polluted 2 million peoples' water on Merseyside, and although the public were told it was safe, a subsequent study found 40 per cent of consumers had at least one symptom of poisoning.[104]

Antibiotics and hormones used in human drugs have been detected in drinking water and our rivers. Vinyl chloride, a known carcinogen, can leach from PVC pipes into water, as can epoxy resins, asbestos from asbestos cement and PAHs (poly aromatic hydrocarbons) from the bitumen used in lining old cast iron mains pipes.[105]

According to studies by the Water Research Centre, PAHs leached from the insides of old London water mains are present at up to five times the EC limit of 0.2 ug/litre. PAHs are some of the same group of cancer-causing substances that are found in cigarette smoke, oil and vehicle exhaust fumes. Replacing the old steel and iron pipes lined with coal tar would cost £1,000 million, David Wheeler of WRC told the Consultative Conference on Water Privatisation in October 1988.[106] Coal tar linings were banned from the 1970s onwards after advice from WRC but, said a TWA spokesman, someone would now have to foot the bill for replacing the old linings 'and it looks like the ratepayer'.

Trichlorethylene and tetrachlorethylene used in dry cleaning and degreasing also pose threats to health, especially through contamination of groundwater, and have been detected in tapwater. The Halcrow Report commissioned by the

DoE pointed out in 1988 that up to 8,000 people around Luton and Dunstable were drinking water with these solvents at four times the World Health Organisation's maximum recommended level, while about 80,000 drank water with trichlorethylene at 150 per cent of the limit.[107] In 1989, carbon tetrachloride and chloroform were found in a bore hole near the government Harwell Laboratory in Oxfordshire, affecting supplies to 3,500 homes.

Conclusions

Water privatisation, commented the *Observer* in August 1989, 'has crystallised public concern about the state of our drinking water. Most people cannot believe that private companies, with a primary duty to their shareholders, will put public health before their profits.'[108] The newspaper pointed out that, while Nicholas Ridley had created the National Rivers Authority to oversee the state of river water, he had refused to create a similar body to monitor tapwater and bring prosecution of polluters. 'The new private companies,' the *Observer* concluded, 'will, in effect, police themselves.'

The prospects are not encouraging. In 1989 Nicholas Ridley himself denounced European standards for water as 'ridiculous, extravagant and unnecessary'. And it soon emerged that the government had systematically arranged breaches of the Drinking Water Directive that would stretch into the next century.

During the switch from publicly owned Water Authorities to privately owned water companies, the government extracted 'pre-privatisation undertakings' from the Authorities. The details of these became apparent in October 1989 after the new Act became law. These included exemptions granted to the new water companies by the DoE, so that they did not have to comply with EC rules. Time-limited exemptions for high aluminium, iron and manganese were granted to Northumbrian and Southern Water under the 'nature and structure of the ground' clause. As these metals came from natural sources, such a move was perfectly legal.

However, it also emerged that the DoE had agreed similar exemptions for lead, trihalomethanes, coliform bacteria and pesticides.[109] These could well be illegal. The UK could find itself in greatest difficulty with exemptions granted for pesticides in Southern Water's area, namely for the herbicides Atrazine, Simazine and Propazine, where a treatment facility is not planned until 1997 or 1998. 'Under the Water Act 1989,' commented the magazine *ENDS*, 'the NRA's main powers to prevent the entry of these pesticides into water sources from diffuse discharges will only be exercisable if the Secretary of State chooses to designate water protection zones in the areas concerned. There is little sign that this ranks prominently among the DoE's present priorities.'[110]

A few weeks later, FoE obtained a government document showing that some water supplies would now be in breach of the Drinking Water Directive until 31 December 2000, and in some cases perhaps even longer. Again, agreements had been secretly made as 'undertakings' in the course of privatisation. Thames Water was allowed 'illegal' pesticide levels until the last day of 2000, while in Environment Minister Chris Patten's own constituency Wessex Water had the same plan. No date had been set for pesticides to meet the MACs in Severn Trent . Aluminium would be in breach of EC limits for an unknown number of years in Northumbrian Water's region.[111] The water supply areas where such 'undertakings' have sanctioned breaches of the EEC Directive are shown in the Appendix.

Previously, Chris Patten had promised EC Environment Minister Carlo Ripa di Meana that Britain would have almost all its supplies cleaned up by 1995. One of Minister Patten's officials was now quoted by the *Observer* as fearing that 'Ripa will hit the roof when he sees these documents. Britain's apparently gratuitous flouting of the law is a very serious matter indeed.' FoE planned to take the matter to the High Court. Interviewed on BBC Radio 4, Andrew Lees of Friends of the Earth declared, 'I have been given clearance by my Board to seek a judicial review . . . we are very serious about this issue and are going to go for it.'

So far the evidence for drinking water prosecutions has had to be wrung from the Water Authorities themselves. Data should still be available from the new privatised water companies, but whose responsibility will monitoring be?

It seems a fair bet that the water companies will be less than enthusiastic about providing the public with evidence that will provide for their own prosecution. Lean and Pearce wrote in August 1988, 'In theory Local Authorities could fill some of this gap by taking their own samples of drinking water. In practice, however, they are short of resources and manpower, squeezed by government curbs on spending. And the water privatisation legislation weakens them even further. It repeals a duty conferred on them by the existing regime to monitor the wholesomeness of water in their areas. And a little known provision may enable the Environment Secretary to prohibit them from checking water quality altogether.'[112]

To date it has been the keepers of the government's cheque books rather than those who conduct the nation's health checks who have dictated policy over drinking water. Whereas the government publicly estimated the cost of meeting EC water standards at £3–4 billion, City sources put it at £22–32 billion over 11 years.[113] City analysts UBS-Philips and Drew suggested in a report released in August 1989 that the cost of meeting just the lead levels in the Directive would be £2,500 million.[114]

It is the fear of frightening off investors that has stopped the government investing in water quality. As the *Financial Times* pointed out, there are rational arguments for the government to borrow the money, instead of trying to hold down investment in order to raise the funds from private investors and short term price rises for consumers of 7 per cent above inflation or more. 'It would be wrong for water users in the next five to ten years to be asked to finance the whole cost of projects which have been neglected in the past and which may be expected to last for 30, 50 or even 100 years. The cost to consumers should more appropriately be spread over future generations by borrowing,' commented the *FT*.[115]

In 1987 the House of Commons Environment Committee urged the creation of water protection zones and commented that there was 'no place for extended discussion' between the DoE and MAFF. Unfortunately it seems that it has been the agricultural ministry which has won the debate, and Britain is merely tinkering with the problem. John Mather, chief geochemist at the British Geological Survey, warns that a third of our tapwater could exceed nitrate levels within a few decades.[116] Nitrogen deposition from air pollution (which starts out as NOx or ammonia) is now also sufficient in parts of East Anglia to put groundwater over the EC limit.[117]

It has been pointed out by various 'consumer experts' and journalists, who feel they have stumbled on a minor scandal that deserves an exposé, that many mineral waters contain significant amounts of metals and salts. These are, after all, what gives the water its characteristic taste. Some are hazardous: for example, nitrates and radon, which is said to have been regarded as an invigorating tonic in some Italian mineral water. But at least the mineral waters are analysed and labelled. You can choose whether to buy them or not, and, coming from groundwater sources, their content is pretty constant.

Tapwater is not like that. Apart from the 1 per cent who have their own private supplies, the great majority of the UK population rely upon the decisions of the water suppliers to ensure that the great bulk of the water we drink and cook with is 'wholesome'. Yet, as we have seen, there are some very unwholesome things in our drinking water supplies, from pesticides to nitrates, metals and cancer-causing residues of plastic and bitumen. As tapwater comes with no warnings, and no analysis and varies from week to week, our reliance on the judgement of the suppliers is total.

Fortunately the vague concept of wholesomeness has been overtaken by internationally agreed standards set by experts, in our case drawn from the European Community countries. Unfortunately, the government is still taking the cheap option, not the best. Despite new evidence[118] that the brain damage caused by childhood exposure to lead as low as half the EC limit can affect people well into adulthood, in June 1990, the UK dropped plans to pull out old lead pipes, in favour of the cheaper but less reliable chemical dosing method.[119]

The UK has flouted the EC's Directive and disagreed with the standards it originally agreed to. Central government and the Water Authorities have deliberately hidden the truth from the water-consuming public by failing to conduct surveys (for example, not collating data on pesticides), using misleading types of measurement (for example, lead from tapwater running for several minutes), and simply withholding information (as at Camelford and in Dumfries and Galloway).

The result has been a loss of confidence in the purity of our tapwater. Like the air we breathe, water is a basic element: if you can't trust what comes out of the tap, then, most people feel, something is wrong.

APPENDIX

Areas where Future Breaches of the EC Drinking Water Directive were Sanctioned by the Government in 'Undertakings' to New Water companies in 1989.[120]

Thames Water

Pesticide levels will be allowed to exceed the EC limits until at least 31 December 2000. Even by then, Thames need only check the effectiveness of current water clean-up equipment, and not actually meet the EC pesticide targets.

Areas affected: Amwell, Ardley, Ashenden, Beacon Hill, Beckley, Bedwyn, Bladon, Boars Hill, Brasenose, Bromley, Cheshunt, Chessington, Cleeve, Croydon, Culham, Dartford, Datchet, East London, Edmonton, Enfield, Epping Forest, Eynsham, Frith Hill, Greenwich, Grimsbury, Guildford, Hampstead, Headington, Henley, Henley Knapp, High Wycombe, Horspath, Hounslow, Islington, Kensington, Knockholt, Lambeth, North Swindon, Over Norton, Reading, Richmond, Sheeplands, Shotover, Slough, Tower Hamlets, Upshire, Wash Common, Watlington, Windsor, Witney, Woodstock.

Wessex Water

Pesticide levels will be allowed to exceed EC limits until 31 December 1999. Water clean-up equipment must be installed at plants 'where appropriate' by that date.

Areas affected: Bath, Malmesbury, Colerne, Bowden, Devizes, Warminster, Poldens, Bridgwater, Weymouth, Purbeck, Blandford, Salisbury, Amesbury, Yeovil, Crewkerne, Chard, Wincanton, Sherborne.

Southern Water

Pesticide levels may exceed EC limits until clean-up equipment installed by 31 March 1998.

Areas affected: Andover, deadline 31 March 1996; Allhallows, Borstal, Colewood, Singlewell East, Westfield, Woolmans Wood, 31 March 1997; Testwood, 31 March 1998.

Severn Trent Water

'Occasional' breaches of pesticide levels allowed while improvements to clean-up equipment investigated. No date set for completing investigation or meeting EC limits.

Areas affected: Atherstone, Bedworth, Kenilworth, Leamington, Nottingham, Nuneaton, Polesworth, Stratford, Warwick .

In other parts of the region, equipment to combat high pesticide levels will be installed by 1997.

Areas affected: Blakeney, Cinderford, Drybrook, Lydney, Mitcheldean, Quedgeley, Ruardean, Stroud, parts of Wolverhampton.

Equipment is to be installed for the Loughborough and Leicester supply area by December 1996. At other works, water clean-up filters have to be installed by December 1997 or the works closed.

Areas affected: Allesborough, Dunchurch, Hillmorton, Kempsey, Napton and Priors Marston, Pershore, Pirton, Rugby, Stonehall, Worcester.

Northumbrian Water

Aluminium, iron and manganese levels exceed EC limits throughout Northumberland, including Durham, Darlington and Middleton, because of distribution system faults. A mains clean-up will be completed in unnamed priority areas by 1994, but no date is given for meeting EC limits throughout the region.

Part II

Air Pollution: Exhalations of Industry, Power and Transport

Just as Britain tried to 'deal with' water pollution with longer pipes and the principle of dilute and disperse, its reliance on exactly the same policy has drawn it into conflicts over air pollution.

Since the Middle Ages, British authorities have ordered chimneys to be raised in order to dilute ground-level pollution. London's long-standing reputation for 'fog' was based on smoke-filled fog, or 'smog', in which thousands of people choked to death. After 4,000 perished in 1952 the government introduced the Clean Air Acts, with 2,000 local Clean Air Zones. Low-level smoke and soot were banished, as households switched from burning coal to heating with coke and electricity (and, later, North Sea gas).

In the 1960s the Central Electricity Generating Board (CEGB) replaced urban power stations with short chimneys, which directly polluted the surrounding area, with a new generation of massive power stations with very tall chimneys. This 'tall stack' policy was intended to disperse pollution and dilute it to 'harmless levels', while smoke was to be trapped at source by simple electrostatic filters. Problems such as London smog would disappear. That was the theory, and it worked. Smog of the old London type vanished, but the result was acid rain[1].

For 20 years, from 1968 to 1988, Britain rejected Scandinavian claims that action should be taken to reduce the UK's upwind pollution. Britain, led by its electricity industry, waged an unprecedented war of scientific propaganda against researchers and politicians in first Norway and Sweden and later Germany and the rest of the European Community. Even today it is trying to back out of commitments to fit pollution controls.

From the early 1980s a new type of forest decline was discovered, first in West Germany and central Europe, then in the UK, Scandinavia, North America and Japan. Britain managed to isolate itself in international fora – such as the 35 Nation Convention on Long Range Transboundary Air Pollution convened by the United Nations Economic Commission for Europe (UN ECE) – by rejecting the scientific consensus that forest decline was linked to air pollution from industry, power stations and vehicles.

As the 1990s began, almost every western industrialised country was investing heavily in new rail links and traffic controls to combat growing levels of air pollution from traffic. Britain, however, had fought to impede European agreements requiring catalytic converters on cars and even as London's traffic slowed to pre-First World War speeds, planned to build vast new roads and to cut rail services.

Just as officialdom saw the legendary return of salmon to the Thames as evidence that Britain's water pollution was cured, so it gloried in the Clean Air Acts of the 1950s and turned a 'blind eye' to dying lakes, moribund trees and the links between car exhaust and human health that became apparent in the 1980s. On current plans, Britain will probably remain the largest exporter of air pollution in Western Europe.

CHAPTER 4

Acid Rain: Power Stations and Air Pollution

The First Acid Thursday

On the blustery, damp morning of Thursday 15 December 1983, a motley collection of protesters and student groups converged on Sudbury House, headquarters of the Central Electricity Generating Board (CEGB). There were Friends of the Earth, Greenpeace, the Ecology Party (now Green Party), and the Young Liberals. It was the first protest that the capital had seen about acid rain, an environmental issue which had stimulated political curiosity but very little action.

'Biggest Acid Rain Polluter in Western Europe' read one 60-foot message stretched across the CEGB's entrance. Baffled office workers opened their windows and leaned out to get a better view. 'Killer in the Sky' said a placard, held helpfully flat so that the Board's staff above could get a better look.

The CEGB was part of Harold Wilson's 'white heat' of British technology. For those times it was an environmentally sensitive organisation. Nature reserves were set up around new power stations to mollify local conservationists. The CEGB even had its own environmental department: 'We invented the term "environment",' CEGB employee John Clarke remembered some years later.

By the early 1980s air pollution had been a dead issue for more than a decade. Roses and conifers, long impossible to grow in London because of sulphur dioxide and soot, once again appeared in the capital's streets and gardens. Pollution 'experts' joked merrily that the only drawback of the clean air policy was that, with less sulphur pollution, mildew had also returned.

Agricultural students learnt that the dilute rain of sulphur from power stations was just useful extra fertiliser. Environmentalists paid it little heed: they spent the decade prior to 1983 worrying about issues such as the 1981 Wildlife and Countryside Act, the third London airport, motorways and nuclear power.

The CEGB had no pollution controls on its power stations, and produced most of the sulphur dioxide, a major component of acid rain, in Britain. Indeed, the Board's power stations produced more pollution than any in Austria, Bulgaria, Denmark, Finland, Greece, Hungary, Ireland, Holland, Norway, Portugal, Spain, Sweden or Switzerland.

Putting air pollution, especially invisible, smokeless pollution, back onto the political agenda, particularly in the teeth of determined opposition from the CEGB, was bound to be difficult. The people running the CEGB came from a generation who believed in the power of technology to solve problems, in motorways and in growth of consumption. Mrs Thatcher, a 1950s chemist, got on well with Sir Walter Marshall, a 1950s physicist and the CEGB chairman.[1] Both were devotees of nuclear power. There was an inbuilt resistance to the idea that a technical fix which had solved one pollution problem had actually created a bigger one.

Yet, seemingly from nowhere, acid rain had become the world's most dramatic environmental issue. On Environment Day 1983, Mostafa Tolba, executive director of the UN Environment Programme, declared:

> 'In northern Europe, Canada and the northeast of the United States, the rain is turning rivers, lakes and ponds acidic, killing fish and decimating other water life. It assaults buildings and . . . costs millions of dollars every year. It may even threaten human health, mainly by contaminating water. It is a particularly modern, post-industrial form of ruination and is as widespread and careless of its victims and of international boundaries as the wind that disperses it.'[2]

Despite its apocalyptic international profile, acid rain wasn't much of an issue in Britain. British environmental groups had only recently been roused by appeals from Sweden and Norway. Now, like a blindfolded child trying to pin the tail on a pretend fairground donkey, the environment movement was attempting to attach the blame to the CEGB.

The CEGB, however, had other ideas. Carrying the banner of the nuclear industry, it was well aware of what it meant to be a target for the new generation of environmentalists.

Walter Marshall had a natural flair for public relations. During the long-running Sizewell Inquiry on a Pressurised Water Reactor (PWR), he had upstaged Friends of the Earth by donating his tie to a campaign jumble sale. Later, when serious-minded Scandinavians handed in a dead salmon, Sir Walter would rise to the occasion by sending down his chef to collect it.

When the 1983 demonstration arrived outside the CEGB, it was witnessed by just a handful of press: foreign TV, the *Guardian*, the *Morning Star*, and local radio. Still uncertain of what tone to adopt, the campaigners brought six people dressed as Santa Claus, including, incognito behind his cottonwool whiskers, one Greenpeace Santa. 'Ring us when acid rain burns babies,' the *Daily Express* told activist Steve Elsworth.

Advice from the *Daily Telegraph*

In the mid-1980s the *Daily Telegraph* probably still spoke for the great bulk of Middle England, when, after Britain had yet again resisted international calls to reduce pollution, it announced:

> 'Good news . . . Britain is not going to let itself be rushed into any costly action, that would have little chance of success, to solve the problem of 'acid rain'. . . Indeed the whole theory of 'killer acid' from distant power

station chimneys falling in the rain where it damages trees and kills fish seems to us more like second-rate science fiction than a description of real events . . . Forest ecologists increasingly believe that the source of most acid is natural, not industrial.'

The *Telegraph* added, inadvertently creating a spectacular hostage-to-fortune:

It is vital to avoid any repetition of the 'ozone scare' of the seventies when many aerosol products were banned through mistaken fears that they would deplete the earth's protective ozone layer. This policy is said to have cost the United States economy 8,700 jobs and $1,520 m in lost profits. We must beware of hysterical solutions to complex problems urged by people whose real motive is often hatred of industry and capitalism.[3]

The *Telegraph*'s argument was wrong then and everyone knows it is wrong now. But the *Telegraph* was not taking its line from saloon bar advisers. Its editorial was almost certainly inspired by Sir Walter.

The CEGB versus Scandinavia

The CEGB was not just briefing the *Daily Telegraph*. Since the 1970s it had been fending off pressure from Scandinavia. The link between emissions of sulphur and nitrogen in industrial countries, its upwards transmission over great distances by the weather, and the consequent acidification of lakes and rivers, had first been made by a Swede, Svante Oden, in 1968.[4]

Oden found that Sweden imported far more pollution than it exported because of the prevailing winds. In 1972, the Swedish government hosted the United Nations Stockholm Conference on the Environment and called for international action to reduce transboundary movement of air pollution. Britain and West Germany rejected this in favour of more research.

The CEGB dealt with the early complaints by talking-down the problem and querying the evidence. Scandinavia was, after all, not a very important trading partner now Britain had joined the EC. The CEGB devoted its considerable resources to submitting the claims of any acid rain damage to the greatest possible scientific scrutiny. But this went much further than healthy scepticism. The CEGB drew no line between science and politics, and began to act as a lobby, using science as a political weapon. 'Scandinavians now accept that there is no evidence of damage to forests but they claim that fish lakes and rivers suffer from the additional acidity,' said its Annual Report for 1976/7.

In 1980 the Electricity Council anticipated forthcoming battles in its Medium Term Development Plan: 'We are aware that environmentalist pressure could lead to arbitrary restrictions on emissions.' As to laws to reduce pollution, the Council warned, 'The industry will strive to influence legislation before enactment.' It added: 'Long range drift from chimney emissions . . . is being studied in order to avoid arbitrary restrictions on atmospheric discharges . . . Initial research suggests that at best only a very marginal decrease in the long distance deposit of acid rain would result from a major reduction of sulphur emissions from the UK.'

By picking away at every factual link in the chain from furnace to fishless lake, Britain's electricity industry hoped to avoid any restrictions on atmospheric discharges, whether 'arbitrary' or not.

But having been once rebuffed, the Scandinavians set about collecting more evidence. A major Norwegian study was launched in 1972.[5] By 1975, Norwegian rivers such as the Tovdal, famous for salmon fishing within living memory, were turning acid and losing their fish and other life. By 1982, the Norwegians calculated that 2,000 trout fisheries had been lost, while 5,000 lakes across some 33,000 km^2 had turned acid, 1,750 of them losing all their fish.[6]

Throughout the 1980s Britain waged a war of scientific words with its neighbours. As Nigel Haigh of the Institute for European Environmental Policy (IEEP) later remarked of electricity privatisation, one of its 'great advantages . . . is that the CEGB will no longer be making not only British air pollution policy but also some of its foreign policy'.[7] As David Clarke MP put it, that policy had involved 'chemical warfare' in the form of dumping pollution on downwind countries.[8] It did much to establish Britain's reputation as the 'Dirty Man of Europe'.

With Sir Walter – soon to be Lord Marshall of Goring and known also to environmentalists as 'The Dark Lord' – leading the scientific battles of claim and counter-claim, at times the acid rain issue seemed to follow a pantomime script full of cries of 'oh yes you did' and 'oh no we didn't'. Unfortunately it was more serious than that.

What Is Acid Rain ?

The main gases contributing to 'acid rain', and which often end up in rain or fine dry particles, are sulphur dioxide (SO_2), nitric oxide (NO) and nitrogen dioxide (NO_2). Together NO and NO_2 are known as NOx. Ammonia, ozone and hydrocarbons also play important roles in creating 'acid rain' damage. SO_2 is formed when coal, oil or other sulphur bearing material is burnt. NO is formed from fuel and air at high temperatures, such as in furnaces, power stations and car engines. In air, NO is converted to NO_2. With sunlight and hydrocarbons, this forms ozone, part of photochemical smog. But at high NO concentrations, ozone levels are low as it reacts with NO to form NO_2. Because of this 'back reaction', photochemical pollution is worse away from the actual pollution source itself.

SO_2 in air mainly becomes sulphuric acid in raindrops, sulphate or ammonium sulphate (by reaction with ammonia). The longer it stays in the air, the more likely it is to be oxidised acid, the process speeded up by pollutants such as ozone and hydrogen peroxide. NOx can become nitric acid. The result is wet acid deposition (in rain), occult acid deposition (mist), and acid aerosols (the haze formed partly of ammonium sulphate particles). About half Britain's sulphur rains down as wet deposition and half is dry fallout.

Part of the 'acid rain' pollution nexus is photochemical smog, a dry chemical soup including hydrogen peroxide, hydroxyl radicals, ozone, PAN (peroxy acetyl nitrate) and acid sulphate.

Acid Rain: How Much Falls and Where

Since the 1950s a huge area of acid fallout has settled over Europe. Britain is part of this industrial shroud.

In 1870 the average pH of rural rain in Britain was about 5.0. (pH is a logarithmic measure of hydrogen ion acidity: below 7 is acid, above 7 is alkaline. Unpolluted rain is normally in the range pH 5.5 – 6.) By 1980 acidity had increased sixfold to pH 4.3. Nitrogen emissions had risen fourfold and sulphur three to sixfold. Today rain falling over Denmark, West Germany, Sweden and the East Midlands of the UK is often pH 4 or less: over 40 times the natural acidity.[9]

In terms of gas concentrations and what comes down in the rain, rural parts of central and eastern England are similar to northern Germany.[10] Rural parts of northern England, Scotland and Wales have similar conditions to Scandinavia. The southeast of England has moderate concentrations of SO_2 and NOx and relatively frequent episodes of ozone.

Average rainfall acidity of rain in west Britain is three times that of natural rain. In the east it is up to 16 times more acid. However, areas such as the Lake District and Wales receive the largest total acidity because of their high rainfall. The S. Pennines, the Lake District, Cumbria and Galloway receive as much acid in a year as the badly acidified parts of southern Norway.

The UK's highest sulphur pollution as dry deposition and gas is in the power station belts of the East Midlands, South Yorkshire and north Kent. Much of the Midlands has SO_2 above the 7 parts per billion (ppb) average identified by the UN ECE as critical in preventing harm to vegetation.

The equivalent NOx levels are exceeded throughout central and southeast England, with particularly high levels around London, Birmingham and Manchester.

Cloud and mist speed up conversion of SO_2, NOx or ammonia to acids. At Great Dun Fell in Cumbria, which is under cloud for part of 250 days a year, cloud is on average four times as acid as rain at the same spot, with more than twice the ammonium, nitrate and sulphur.[11]

The UK has 10 networks for monitoring air pollution.[12] SO_2 and soot are measured at 418 sites (the descendants of thousands set up for the Clean Air Acts) but, prior to criticism from the House of Commons Environment Committee in 1984, knowledge of other pollutants was threadbare. By 1990 the Department of the Environment had nine 'primary' sites (assessing a dozen ions, NO_2, SO_2, and particulate sulphate) and 50 'secondary' ones sampling acidity in rainfall. Ozone has been monitored at 17 places since 1985. A NOx and ammonia network covers 60 sites and 'rural' sulphur dioxide 27. Hydrocarbons are being checked in a 'pilot' scheme at one urban, one rural and one 'remote' site.[13]

Ground-level ozone, which has almost no contact with the 'ozone layer' of the stratosphere, forms in 'peaks' or 'episodes', strongly influenced by sunshine. Levels of 60 or more can affect plants. British ozone concentrations reflect traffic, industry (the source of NOx and hydrocarbons) and ozone clouds imported from the continent. Ozone formation is so influenced by sunshine that even the west of Ireland and northern Scotland experience summers with ozone damage. In most years, levels in southern England exceed the US National Ambient Quality Standard (120 ppb for one hour).[14] During 1976, when the weather was warm and dry, record-breaking ozone levels were detected, reaching over 200 ppb and exceeding 60 ppb on half the summer days. [15] Ozone occurs more frequently at higher altitudes, so uplands may be particularly at risk.

Despite the fall in low-level sulphur dioxide due to the Clean Air Acts, urban rain is still more acid than rural rain because fumes from traffic and oil-fired central heating add to pollution from more distant sources. For example, Norwich rain has been found to be twice as acid as rain at a rural site nearby. In February, 1985 SO_2 levels in London jumped spectacularly to over 1,000 ug/m^3 as the plume of a large power station crossed the city. On average a fifth of the sulphur in London and 45 per cent of that in Lincoln and York comes in from rural power stations.[16]

Trends in Emissions

Sulphur dioxide and smoke
Britain's SO_2 emissions peaked in 1970 at over 6 million tonnes a year. A downward trend after 1979 was caused by industrial recession and use of North Sea gas, reaching 3.8 million tonnes by 1987. Emissions from power stations, which account for about 80 per cent of the total, hardly fell at all. Whereas urban SO_2 concentrations fell fivefold from 1968 to 1988, rural concentrations fell by only half. By 1985, average urban concentrations were 38 ug/m^3 and rural concentrations were 28 ug/m^3. [17]

Without a major desulphurisation programme, any increase in industrial activity will stimulate demand for electricity and so increase SO_2 emissions from power stations. Today, emissions are again on the rise.

Oxides of nitrogen (NOx)
Each year the UK emits some 2.48 million tonnes of NOx (measured as NO_2). Power station NOx pollution (32 per cent of the total) fell from 859,000 to 792,000 tonnes between 1978 and 1988, while emissions by traffic increased from 886,000 tonnes in 1977 to 1.11 million in 1988 (45 per cent).

The Department of Energy estimates future NO_2 emissions at up to 2.1 million tonnes by 2000. If the targets of the EC Large Plant Directive are followed (see below), the UK will be Western Europe's largest NOx polluter in this category between 1993 and 1998.

Ammonia
Almost nobody studied ammonia emissions until recently, but estimates range from 370 kilotonnes for Great Britain to 405 kilotonnes for the UK.[18]

Dr Helen ApSimon of Imperial College estimates that British ammonia emissions have increased by 50 per cent since 1950, mainly owing to more intensive livestock production and use of agricultural fertilisers.

Hydrocarbons
In the UK, emissions of man-made hydrocarbons or VOCs (volatile organic compounds) increased 12 per cent in the ten years to 1985, largely owing to increased road traffic. The official Photochemical-Oxidant Review Group believes levels have doubled over the last 100 years, as a result of industrialisation.[19] It seems likely that with traffic growth and the possible warming of Britain's climate that they will increase.

The Pollution Export Business

On balance, Britain is a major pollution exporter. 'From the Scandinavian countries Britain is seen as the dirty man of the acid rain affair,' wrote the *Guardian*'s Anthony Tucker in September 1984. Not only was the UK the largest emitter of sulphur dioxide in Western Europe, it also exported 77 per cent of it, mainly on westerly winds to Europe.[20]

By the late 1980s, only 19 per cent of the sulphur falling in the UK was estimated to come from other countries, the lowest percentage in Western Europe. For example, 69 per cent of sulphur falling in Denmark, 53 per cent of that in Belgium and West Germany, 74 per cent of that in the Netherlands, and 89 per cent of that in Switzerland, came from abroad.

In 1988, EMEP (the UN ECE Convention's European Monitoring and Evaluation Programme) calculated that the UK contributed 7 – 11 per cent of sulphur deposited in Norway and 4 – 7 per cent of that deposited in Sweden. This, however, only accounts for pollution of a 'known origin'. In both countries, a significant fraction is of 'unknown' origin or 'background', in the air long enough to be difficult to assign to any one source. Of the pollution with a known origin, Britain contributes 17 per cent of the sulphur falling in Norway, around 18,500 tonnes a year.[21]

Moreover, Norway and Sweden are large countries running from south to north, with acidification problems only in the polluted south. In these problem areas, the UK contributed around 20 per cent of the sulphur,[22] over half as much again as any other country.

While sulphur pollution decreased throughout most of northern Europe in the period 1978–1988 and is expected to reduce by 25–50 per cent by 1995, nitrogen pollution is increasing. In the 1980s nitrate doubled in the lakes and rivers of southern Norway and ammonium increased. Dr Alan Apling of the DoE has estimated that the UK contribution to NOx pollution in southern Norway could be 'more than 50 per cent in some areas'.[23] By 1985, the UK was the largest exporter of NOx in northwestern Europe and the biggest contributor to NOx pollution at sites in Iceland, Ireland, Norway, Sweden, Belgium, the Netherlands and Denmark.[24]

The Origins of a Fine Mess: The Alkali Inspectorate

From the 1880s to the 1980s, Britain's thinking on air pollution developed hardly at all.

In 1862, *The Times* wrote: 'Whole tracts of country, once as fertile as the fields of Devonshire, have been swept by deadly blights till they are as barren as the Great Salt Lake.' At St Helen's in Lancashire the newspaper reported a 'scene of desolation. You might look around and not see a tree with any foliage on it whatever'. The cause was the 'alkali works' of the industrial revolution. These works made soda by the Leblanc process. The product was strongly alkaline but the by-product was acid. Moist air burned holes in people's vegetables and landowners complained of damage to trees.

This was 'acid rain' in the simplest sense. In due course, the government's response was to pass a law and appoint an Alkali Inspector named Angus Smith. Ten years later he coined the term 'acid rain'. It was the start of Britain's acid rain debate and the birth of its 'modern' air pollution policy.

The approved solution under the Alkali Acts was to build taller chimneys and to remove one of the acids (hydrochloric acid) from the flue gases. Smith advised the manufacturers on how to reduce emissions to better than the 5 per cent permitted under the new Act.[25]

At first everyone was happy. *The Times* noted 'fruit trees which had begun to blossom after having long ceased'.[26] But, within 15 years, air pollution was as bad as ever. The Act had failed to control smoke or sulphuric or nitric acid, and it set only a percentage reduction for the pollutant it did cover, without a total ceiling on pollution. Here were the seeds of the twentieth century problem of acid rain and other crises besides.

Smith's successor transferred the concept of 'best practicable means' used in local legislation into national policy. Manufacturers would be required to use these to reduce emissions, but it was never very clear how the 'best practicable means' would be defined. Discussions between the inspectors and manufacturers were a trade secret, but the Inspectorate tried to avoid placing 'an undue burden on manufacturing industry'.[27]

Lord Derby, who steered the Act through Parliament, would have felt quite at home with the parliamentary debate which took place after the 1952 smog some 90 years later. MPs demanded action but the government was not keen. It pointed to the 1936 Public Health Act which gave powers to local authorities, although these were patently ineffective. Industry lobbied against stringent restrictions. Prime Minister Harold Macmillan told cabinet colleagues, 'We cannot do very much, but we can seem to be very busy – and that is half the battle nowadays.'[28]

The impression of 'busyness' was achieved by setting up the 1953 Beaver Committee. Its Report was pre-empted by MP Gerald Nabarro, who proposed a Clean Air Bill. The government then produced its own, which became the 1956 Clean Air Act, forbidding 'dark smoke' as defined on an objective scale. The Beaver Committee defined 294 areas of England 'black', requiring smoke control, and by 1974 all but fourteen local authorities had taken some steps towards implementing the Act.

The Failure of 'Best Practicable Means'

The Act was a success, although the 'particulates' (mainly soot) raining down over Britain's cities had anyway been gradually decreasing since the 1920s. By 1980, soot had fallen 80 per cent.[29]

Unfortunately nothing was done about sulphur. In *Acid Rain* Fred Pearce records that the Beaver Report had also recommended the use of flue gas desulphurisation (FGD). It was not as if Britain was unaware of FGD – German engineers had visited a pilot scheme in Manchester in 1880.[30]

But the Alkali Inspectorate decided that FGD was not 'practicable'. Instead it opted to 'render SO_2 harmless' by 'dilution and dispersal' from 'tall stacks'. A few FGD schemes were installed: at North Wilford, Battersea, Bankside and Fulham. They were all later closed down.

Without FGD, rapid growth in electricity use led to an uncontrolled increase in emissions of sulphur dioxide. By 1960, power stations had become the largest single source.

'Dilution' did not 'render harmless' sulphur emissions. First, it was assumed that no long-range problems would occur; that is, that the acidifying or toxic power of the gases would be neutralised long before they got to Scandinavia or anywhere else. Second, it was assumed that the gas would be evenly mixed in the air, so that no dangerous concentrations would occur. Unfortunately, the Alkali Inspectorate was wrong on both counts.

Even official sources now accept that tall stacks tend to increase long-range transport of pollution.[31] In smoothly flowing medium speed winds, plumes from power stations can travel in a concentrated stream for hundreds of miles. Tall stacks (Drax is 259 metres tall[32]) can take emissions above a layer of air trapped near the ground into smooth air streams. On a steady southwesterly, a plume from Eggborough power station, 'labelled' with sodium hexafluoride, was tracked all the way across the North Sea to Denmark.[33] Such episodes are commoner than the planners of tall stacks assumed. Pollutants can also be actively deposited by local weather effects such as mist. Meteorological Office researchers followed Eggborough's plume crossing the Welsh mountains. In clear skies sulphur was being slowly oxidised and deposited. Once it entered low mountain cloud, production of acids increased 14-fold and fallout increased over 200 per cent. The total removal rate shot up to 27 per cent an hour, depositing the sulphur in a concentrated drizzle.[34]

Early Signs: Britain as Reluctant Witness

Acidified lakes and rivers were known to British scientists from the 1970s. The River Solway Purification Board and the Ministry of Agriculture conducted a ten-year study into Galloway's declining fish stocks in the 1970s. The North West Water Authority blamed acid rain for a fish kill on the River Esk in the Lake District. In Wales, the Cammdwr and Upper Twyi became acidified affecting salmon and trout fishing.[35] The Forestry Commission started to lime Galloway lakes in 1982.

At first, acid from rotting conifer needles was blamed, but the average acidity of rain in the Scottish Grampians had increased tenfold from 1962 to 1975,[36] and the suspicion grew that the strong acids of pollution were responsible. (The greater surface area presented by plantations means they may 'scrub' 60 per cent more pollution from the air than open ground.)

At the Pitlochry Freshwater Fisheries Laboratory, for example, researchers had measured rain of pH 2.4: more acid than vinegar. The CEGB, nevertheless, favoured the idea that land use and not pollution was the factor responsible for the increased acidity and low calcium of Scottish and Welsh lakes.

Britain Emerges as a Pollution Exporter: Stockholm 1982

By the time the Scandinavian countries invited Britain back to Stockholm for the 1982 Conference on Acidification, the sums had been done for exchange of acid pollution between Europe's nations, showing Britain to be the biggest producer and exporter of sulphur pollution in Western Europe. Armed with a decade of research results, Sweden and Norway proposed that the weight of sulphur falling in rain or dust on each square metre should be kept at less than half a gram ($0.5 \ g/S/m^2$ or 5 kg per hectare). Outside areas with such pollution, lakes were not dying. Within them, lakes and rivers had become acid. West Germany, prompted by the discovery of dying forests, now supported controls.

The CEGB said a $0.5 \ g/S/m^2$ target would imply 'an impossible' 80 per cent cut in sulphur emissions in the UK and 'require a capital investment exceeding £4,000m'.[37] Giles Shaw, Britain's junior minister, joined American calls for more research and played down acidification as 'a problem of great complexity' affecting 'certain limited areas of the world'.[38]

Britain now grew increasingly isolated from its European 'partners'. Clinging to the US axis might be good for morale but did nothing for Britain's environmental reputation. A German diplomat commented, 'It is very sad. The British have proved once more that the Channel is wider than the Atlantic.'[39]

Britain had four arguments to justify doing nothing. First, a lot had been achieved (other countries were only now catching up with the Clean Air Act). Second, a large reduction in UK emissions might not create a large reduction in the pollution deposited in foreign countries. Third, the increasing use of nuclear power would make expensive control technologies like FGD unnecessary. Fourth, it might be more effective to reduce other pollutants, for example those from West German cars.

The Conference ended with no apparent change. The new German position encouraged the European Community to ratify the UN ECE Convention on Long Range Transboundary Air Pollution.[40] Enough countries ratified the Convention to bring it into force. This achieved little, as it asked countries only to try 'so far as possible' to limit and 'gradually reduce and prevent air pollution using the 'best available technology which is economically feasible'.[41] Back in Britain, Shaw reassured the House of Commons that 'the acid rain problem' was 'not nearly as severe as the media make out'.[42]

Britain now opposed a European Community bloc which included West Germany, the Netherlands and Denmark, backing controls on motor exhausts and FGD for power stations.[43] The 'victims' of acid rain had also begun to form an alliance – the '30 per cent Club', a group committed to reducing 1980 sulphur emissions 30 per cent by 1993. It included Sweden, Norway, Denmark, Finland, West Germany, Austria, Switzerland, the Netherlands and Canada.

The 30 per cent Club: Britain Does Not Join

By 1983 Britain was effectively alone in Western Europe as a large unrepentant pollution exporter.

In June 1983, the Nordic countries proposed a 30 per cent Sulphur Protocol to the UN ECE Convention. The UK and the USA opposed it. In June 1984, when West Germany hosted an Environmental Conference, the '30 per cent Club' grew to 18.[44] Britain again declined to join. 'In a speech described as brusque and arrogant by West German sources,' reported Anna Tomforde in the *Guardian*, 'British representative Dr Martin Holdgate, the chief scientist at the Department of the Environment' said, 'We see no point in making heroic efforts at great cost, to control one out of many factors unless there is a reasonable expectation that such control will lead to real improvement in the environment.'[45]

At Helsinki in 1985, the '30 per cent Club' became official with a 30 per cent Sulphur Protocol to the Convention. Now Britain took issue with the base year of 1970. But, as Nigel Haigh of the IEEP has pointed out, even if 1970 (the year of peak emissions) was taken as a baseline, the UK would achieve only a 44 per cent reduction as against 80 per cent for the Netherlands, 56 per cent for West Germany and 50 per cent for Belgium.[46]

The Weakness of the Department of the Environment

Fred Pearce says that DoE scientists returned from Stockholm in 1982 'convinced that Norwegian claims about acid rain were largely right and the righteous warnings from the generating board about scientific uncertainties were largely prevarication.'[47] The civil servants determined to convince ministers 'that acid rain poses a real threat to forests and woodlands throughout Britain.'

In William Waldegrave the DoE had acquired an intelligent minister with a genuine sympathy for the environment. But the DoE found the Whitehall struggle more difficult than it had supposed. The CEGB could rely on the Treasury to oppose the expenditure to reduce pollution which did most damage in remote Welsh hills, Scottish lochs and other countries. The Department of Trade and Industry was lobbied by the Confederation of British Industry (CBI), which feared higher electricity prices and controls on factories. Although the Foreign Office was embarrassed at the offence caused to Britain's old ally Norway, it carried relatively little weight.

'A modest desulphurisation programme' was shelved owing to lobbying from the Treasury and the CEGB early in 1983.[48] A crucial meeting took place at Chequers on 26 and 27 May 1984. The DoE believed it had the decision to join the 30 per cent Club 'in the bag' and briefed journalists to that effect. The meeting pitched Martin Holdgate and Sir Hans Kornberg of the Royal

Commission on Environmental Pollution against Walter Marshall and Dr Peter Chester of the CEGB. The CEGB won.

Just prior to the 1985 Helsinki conference, the DoE was once again making some progress and, at the final meeting, it was the Foreign Office which enjoyed the casting vote. As Fred Pearce put it: 'The Foreign Secretary, Geoffrey Howe, had the deciding vote. His departmental brief was to assuage the diplomatic pressure from Norway and vote for joining the club. This he did not do. Sober mandarins from the environment department insist that the generating board engineered the debacle through Lord Marshall's "close contacts" with the prime minister.'[49] Others have it that Sir Geoffrey missed the crucial part of the meeting because he was playing golf. Foreign Office texts prepared for Scandinavia were hastily withdrawn.

The DoE's difficulty was made worse by its maladroit handling of the press and contacts with Britain's scientists and environmental groups. It failed to build the essential trust needed to form an effective lobby. Waldegrave had no seat at the cabinet table and his superiors were more interested in the privatisation of council houses.

The gentlemanly DoE lost its battles behind closed doors. Holdgate (now at the International Union for the Conservation of Nature) is a relatively cerebral individual, ill suited to match the vigorous propaganda of the CEGB.

The CEGB's Propaganda War

In 1983 the CEGB joined the National Coal Board (NCB) in a set piece attempt to 'frame the debate' and fix the timetable for any decision on acid rain by creating the Surface Water Acidification Project (SWAP). The NCB had a chairman, Mr Ian McGregor, of whom the Prime Minister approved. It produced the coal for 80 per cent of Britain's electricity, so, like the CEGB, it had a direct interest in denying the effects of acid rain, or at least delaying action as long as possible.

SWAP operated under the aegis of the Royal Society, giving it credibility in the eyes of the press and the collaborating Norwegian Academy of Science and Letters and the Royal Swedish Academy of Sciences. The Boards provided £5 million for research, which was not due to be completed until 1988. Environmentalists such as Steve Elsworth warned that the real purpose of the project was to muddy scientific waters and ensure delay. Marshall confirmed that 'it would be unwise to take any action on retrofitting desulphurisation equipment before the results of the scientific investigation have been published.'[50]

Compared with £1.5 billion for FGD to achieve a significant cut in Britain's sulphur emissions, it was a cheap way of buying time: a year's grace for each £1 million, about an hour's expenditure for the CEGB.

The ostensible objectives of SWAP were scientific but they also allowed for mischief. Quantifying 'other factors than acidity' enabled the CEGB to push its theories at SWAP's Royal Society launch, which even DoE officials described as a 'red herring'. 'It has all been carefully stage-managed,' said one disappointed Norwegian. 'It was a sham.'[51] The NCB was keen to play down existing evidence, calling it 'conjecture and speculation'. [52]

The CEGB extended its influence into the non-government sector, funding research by the Cathedral Advisory Commission and the Royal Society for the Protection of Birds. The Royal Society for Nature Conservation's junior branch 'WATCH' undertook an educational 'acid drops' project. The CEGB paid for advertisements in its magazine and funded WWF publications.

The CEGB used its scientific budget to 'shadow' work done by others, such as the Nature Conservancy Council (NCC). 'Every time we started doing a piece of research,' said an NCC officer, 'we'd find the CEGB then commissioned another research team to investigate the same thing.'

CEGB scientists became assiduous attenders of conferences. In 1984, at the Scottish Wildlife Trust's self-consciously neutral 'Acid Rain Inquiry' in Edinburgh, Board researcher Ron Scriven showed a series of misleading diagrams suggesting that hydrogen ion acidity at Eskdalemuir in Scotland came 'mostly from the Irish Sea'. The audience of conservation managers, journalists and the public found this puzzling. This must surely mean that acid rain was natural and the acidification of lochs had nothing to do with power stations.

This would have remained the impression if Scriven had not been followed by Dr David Fowler of the Institute of Terrestrial Ecology (ITE). Fowler had similar basic data but presented in a quite different way. Instead of a simple wind diagram, he had 'back-projections' of the actual path of the rain-bearing wind over the previous 48 hours. The 'acid rain' had passed over industrial areas of the UK, France or West Germany . Scriven had neglected to mention this in his presentation.

The CEGB was very concerned to block any suggestion of a direct link between power station emissions and acid fallout in rain. Such a link was made when on 20 February 1984 a heavy fall of black snow took place in the Cairngorms in Scotland. The winds that carried it there had passed directly over the power stations of South Yorkshire and the 'sulphur valley' area around the Trent, where there are 12 large power stations. On the same day, fish farmers in the West Highlands where rain fell, reported the death of trout. The black snow, full of oily soot, had a pH of 3, several hundred times more acid than normal.

News of the black snow did not leak out until Scots journalist George Rosie reported it in the *Sunday Times* on 19 September. [53] There were rumours that a team from the University of East Anglia who were researching the acidity of the Cairngorm snow pack had run into difficulty in getting their work published because CEGB staff were used as anonymous 'referees' to vet papers submitted to several scientific journals. Eventually it was published in *Nature*.[54] Trevor Davies of the UEA team estimated that at least 20 tonnes of soot fell on the Cairngorms that night, forming a layer of snow at least 5 cm thick and affecting an area of over 200 km^2.[55]

In 1985 the CEGB spent £200,000 to produce an 'educational' video on acid rain. It featured a Norwegian soil scientist Rosenqvist, who was almost alone in his belief that land use processes not air pollution were causing the acidification of lakes. It also included an interview with fisheries biologist Hans Hultberg, which had been edited to make it seem as if liming was a perfect answer to acidified salmon rivers. 'It is obvious that I have been exploited for propaganda purposes in a film in which I should never have allowed myself to appear,' he bitterly commented afterwards.

Mrs Brundtland, Norway's Prime Minister, complained about it to Mrs Thatcher and *New Scientist* reported that even the CEGB's own scientists 'discreetly let it be known that they were annoyed by the final version of the video.'[56] In the film, one of them, Dr Tony Kallend, appeared to explain that acid rain was nothing to be worried about as it was only as acid as Coca Cola. By Christmas 1985 the DoE publicly sought to distance itself from the CEGB video, acknowledging that 'the film attempts to minimise the British contribution to acid deposition in Norway when it is much the largest.' [57]

Confirmation Denied: CEGB Ignores Battarbee Research

In 1981 the CEGB had commissioned Dr Rick Battarbee, a geographer at University College London (UCL), to study diatom microfossils in acid lochs.[58] Silica-rich skeletons of these single-celled planktonic plants sink to form layers in the lake mud. As the diatom species differ in their sensitivity to pH, it is possible to 'read' the layers to reconstruct the lake's history.[59]

The CEGB's video did not not mention this study, which had effectively quashed any scientific doubt over what caused acidification. Batterbee and his team tested six hypotheses with unimpeachable rigour: the first was that Scotland's lakes were naturally acid and had not changed; the second was that acidification was slow and pre-industrial; the third blamed changes in burning or grazing; the fourth implicated just conifer planting, and the fifth, decreased agricultural liming; only the sixth implicated acid deposition from the combustion of fossil fuels.

In Galloway, Battarbee and his team found clear evidence of a recent and dramatic change in pH.[60] They studied six lakes, including some with afforested and some with treeless catchments, all lying on granite bedrock with little buffering capacity. Five had become significantly more acid in the previous 130 years (0.5 – 1.2 pH units). Round Loch of Glenhead showed an eightfold increase in acidity.

Scientifically, the evidence was devastatingly comprehensive. The diatom analysis was sensitive enough to pick up land use changes: lake records detected pollen change, showing variation in vegetation, but it was the coincidence of the onset of acidification with the industrial revolution, its rapid acceleration after the Second World War when the consumption of fossil fuels leapt up, and the appearance of industrial metals, which made the conclusive link. Finally, there were the microscopic soot spheres, produced by high temperature combustion, such as in the boilers of power stations.

Only Dr Peter Chester of the CEGB still seemed to find the evidence wanting. Interviewed by Central TV's documentary 'The Acid Test', Chester declared that 'You cannot possibly, by observing diatoms, be able to say it is definitely due to power stations or to any other cause. What you can say is that there's been acidification. Of course you'd expect to find fly ash at any period since people began burning coal in quantity. You cannot deduce from the fact that it was happening at the same time that it was a cause. That you cannot do!'[61]

In the CEGB's tangle of arguments, this was perhaps the most bizarre twist of all. When the CEGB agreed the hypotheses to be tested with the UCL geographers, every conceivable explanation had been included. Yet now here was the CEGB disregarding the logic of its own research plan.

Exaggerating the Costs of Action

Confronted with evidence of damage, the CEGB tried to frighten industrialists with visions of enormously inflated electricity bills as a result of FGD, and to impose a 'Judgement of Solomon' on environmentalists which meant 'accept either acid rain or nuclear power'.

The industry publication *Electricity Supply and the Environment* cited an 'undoubtedly huge expenditure'. The Board gave FGD costs as the increased cost of generating electricity at particular stations and not as that delivered to the consumer in electricity prices. The Electricity Council stated: 'the cost benefit ratio of installing FGD . . . would be very high as it is anticipated that the generating costs of a power station fitted would rise 25–30 per cent. . .'[62] In fact, electricity bills include many things other than actual generating costs – wages for example. And not all electricity comes from power stations requiring FGD. When these factors were accounted for, the increase in electricity prices shrank to 3–6 per cent over ten years (i.e. 0.3–0.6 per cent a year).

This the Board failed to make clear. So, for example, on 18 March 1984 *Sunday Times* journalist Brian Silcock unwittingly wrote: 'according to the CEGB, even a 50 per cent reduction in its own sulphur emissions would add 15 per cent to electricity prices.' Following correspondence with Steve Elsworth, Silcock wrote, 'I feel . . . that the CEGB was a bit disingenuous in giving increases in generating costs. It was all too easy, as I did, to equate those with electricity prices.'[63]

The CEGB did its best (for example in its 1984 *Acid Rain*) to promote nuclear power as 'the answer' to acid rain. It fully expected a massive expansion. A cabinet minute for Tuesday 22 October 1979 records how Mrs Thatcher approved a plan for 15 one giga watt (1 GW) nuclear power stations to be built from 1982. At a rate of more than one a year, Britain was to get 15 Pressurised Water Reactors. As it turned out, by 1989 Britain got only the half-built Sizewell B.

But work by Earth Resources Research for FoE showed that, as a means of reducing sulphur pollution, building a nuclear power station would be ten times as expensive as fitting FGD equipment to an existing coal-fired power station.[64] Furthermore, building enough to replace sufficient coal-fired stations to meet the draft EC Directive meant an impossible construction programme.

Nevertheless, the Board enjoyed a generally good press.

The Air Pollution Inspectorate and the CEGB

The evidence didn't fade away, and Britain's legacy of Victorian pollution controls came back to haunt it.

The Alkali and Clean Air Inspectorate spelt out its wobbly rationale for taking no action in its 1981 Report, saying that its powers were 'intended to protect the population and environment of England and Wales', so 'it is unlikely that action could be taken under the legislation solely to protect the environment of other countries.' However 'new fossil fuel generating plant' might warrant controls.[65]

When Marshall and his CEGB colleagues appeared before the 1984 Commons Environment Committee they were able to point to the vague Alkali Laws to justify their position.[66] 'The CEGB is required to use "the best practicable means",' he noted, but for power stations the Inspectorate specified no FGD technology.

'As drafted,' the law made no mention of cost. 'It implies only that if a control measure is deemed to be practicable' then it must be adopted. But it was 'well known' the Board said, that the 'financial impact' was considered in defining 'practicable'. What is less clear is the extent to which a demonstrable need must be proven before they insist on the adoption of otherwise practicable control measures. The Inspectorate is quite likely to take a precautionary attitude, where the cost/benefit ratio of a proposed control measure is still obscure but where the costs, in its estimation, 'do not represent an undue financial burden.' In other words, so long as it was cheap, the precautionary principle might be applied. But, if the measure was not cheap, the policy had nothing to say.

Here was a classic British fudge. The administration of vague rules and guidelines effectively removed control of pollution policy from the politicians who had framed the laws, and put a stop to any parliamentary scrutiny. The secretive negotiations between administrators and polluters meant there was no public accountability. The word 'practicable' was made of plasticine.

The CEGB revealed that 'all fossil fuelled stations built since the formation of the CEGB were subject to the condition that space must be left for the later provision of sulphur removal equipment should the Secretary of State require this to be fitted. In over thirty years, this condition had never been invoked.'[67] So, although either the Air Pollution Inspectorate or the Secretary of State for Energy could require FGD to be fitted, this had never happened. Leslie Reed, then Chief Inspector, told a House of Lords Select Committee in 1982 that the Inspectorate would 'almost certainly' require methods to reduce sulphur at new power stations but this had no immediate effect.

There could be no doubt that FGD was practical: it was widely employed in Japan, the USA had 88 units and 40 more under construction some two years earlier,[68] and West Germany had announced plans for a retrofit of 200 power plants and other large boilers in 1983 giving over 80 per cent FGD on power plants by 1988.[69] Altogether FGD was fitted in more than 1,000 power plants all over the world,[70] some with equipment made in Britain.

'Practicable', however, didn't just mean that it could be done. The DoE said 'best practicable means' meant 'both technical and economic feasibility'. The Inspectorate applied these principles in two steps, said the DoE. First it would try to prevent emissions, second to render them harmless if prevention was not practicable. 'In the case of SO_2 and NOx emissions from combustion processes,' said the Department, 'prevention, or partial abatement, has hitherto been regarded as impractical on grounds of cost, and operators are therefore required to render ground-level concentrations of the emissions harmless by dispersal from high stacks and dilution in the air.'[71] But acid rain and sulphur dioxide episodes both occurred. Emissions were not harmless.

The government could and should have required FGD on all its old power stations but it didn't. However, the EC soon had other ideas.

The EC Large Combustion Plants Directive

The EC's Draft Directive on Large Combustion Plant was first published in December 1983. The initial proposal was for a 60 per cent cut in sulphur dioxide and a 40 per cent cut in dust and NOx, on 1980 levels, by 1995. In the UK, the category was more than 80 per cent accounted for by power stations. The Draft Directive implied an active clean-up of 12 existing UK power stations, not just new ones. It was inspired by the FGD programme that West Germany had imposed on its own industry and power suppliers.

Nigel Haigh of IEEP notes that Britain soon became 'the most consistent opponent of significant early reductions'.[72] Environment and parliamentary groups pressed repeatedly for the UK to drop its opposition to the Directive. The 1984 Report of the Commons Environment Committee, chaired by Conservative Sir Hugh Rossi MP, prompted the first full-scale public and political debate on acid rain. Britain, said the MPs, should immediately join the 30 per cent Club and the CEGB should fit FGD to meet the Draft Directive on Large Plant. 'We firmly believe that the Government's present position pays too little heed to the weight of scientific evidence in Britain and in Europe that sulphur dioxide, nitrous [sic] oxides and hydrocarbon emissions are separately and in conjunction destructive to many natural and built environments.'[73] They were 'deeply disturbed' by Britain's position on acid rain as a whole. Small signs of a Conservative Party 'turquoise tendency' had emerged from the Bow Group which criticised the UK for 'trailing lamely along at the back of the international pack' and proposed a new Clean Air Act to halve the output of SO_2. It felt this would have 'electoral as well as environmental' advantages.[74]

The all-party House of Lords Select Committee on the European Communities issued a similar report to Rossi's. 'It would be foolish and dangerous for no action to be taken to combat air pollution,' said their Lordships, advocating that Britain should reduce sulphur dioxide emissions by 30 per cent.[75]

The government rejected all these advances. Instead, in December 1984 it announced that a 30 per cent cut was becoming 'an aim of policy'. What, many people wondered, was an 'aim of policy'? It was a wish or a hope but not a policy that would be implemented.

After much bitter debate, in March 1986 Britain quietly announced that it would be 'reviewing' policy following scientific advances made in the SWAP programme.[76] In July, the CEGB announced that it proposed to retrofit three 2000 MW power stations with FGD between 1988 and 1997. It would not be enough to join the 30 per cent Club, but it was a U-turn. In September, Marshall admitted that the CEGB was partly to blame for acidification of Scandinavia. He accepted that evidence of deep soil acidification and the discovery of a large soil reservoir of sulphate meant pollution had caused wholesale ecological change.

Unfortunately, the EC Directive negotiations were being separately conducted from the UN ECE negotiations and the UK's talks with Scandinavian countries. In 1986, the Dutch had the EC Presidency and proposed a cut of at least 50 per cent for West Germany and others, with 40 per cent for Italy and the UK. 'The Commission and West Germany thought this did not go far enough – others thought it went too far,' says Haigh.[77] Britain was one of those who thought it went too far. It was rejected.

In 1987, Denmark proposed even more favourable terms to the UK, but still no agreement was reached.

The Board was in no hurry to cut pollution despite the UK's U-turn. Marshall suggested that a quarter of all the acid rain which had fallen on Norway in the previous century had come from Britain. But even if all the power stations were shut down immediately, acid and sulphur would continue to bleed from the soil for years to come.[78]

The weary Norwegians rejoined that, even if the rate of deposition was falling, any extra sulphate entering soils already depleted in calcium would make acidification worse.

In 1988 West Germany proposed tighter limits for the EC directive. These, said the DoE, were 'a serious step backward'. The DoE claimed that the low sulphur coal (under 1 per cent) which would be needed was 'not readily available'.

Finally, in June 1988 there was yet another version of the Directive. By now, the negotiations had been a long and tedious process. The result, just as a camel is a horse designed by a committee, was a Directive with a separate emission programme for each country. After five years' argument, the UK agreed terms.

The Directive gave the UK something of a 'soft landing', with only a 20 per cent cut on 1980 emissions required by 1993, and just 60 per cent by 2003. The UK's intransigence had therefore won an eight-year delay. In 1982, well-informed observers had believed the CEGB's scientific propaganda was intended to win breathing space until more nuclear plants came on stream at the end of the century. Old coal stations would be pensioned off, and any new ones would have FGD put in more cheaply. So, despite seeming to lose every argument, the CEGB probably came close to achieving its original goal. In the end, the environmentalists had almost no impact on real action.

Spain aside (in second place), Britain's sulphur output from 'Large Plant' in the year 2000 will now dwarf that of the other Western European countries. It will be over a quarter of that for the entire EC, more than twice West Germany's and equivalent to those of France, Belgium, Denmark,

Luxembourg, Greece, Ireland and Portugal added together.[79]

Even though the Directive was agreed, Britain's policies have still caused controversy. Britain was granted a specially lenient deal because Environment Minister Lord Caithness argued that it could not fit FGD in the required timescale, and that it had domestic high sulphur coal which it 'had to use' whereas other countries relied mainly on imported low sulphur coal. At the same time, Caithness argued that the impact on the coal industry would be 'devastating' if low-sulphur coal had to be imported to meet the stricter emission limits being proposed by West Germany.[80]

Meanwhile West Germany, Denmark, the Netherlands, France and Belgium have to reach progressive reduction targets of 30 per cent, 60 per cent and 70 per cent, even though the UK's total emissions are already much higher and, unlike countries such as West Germany, it had invested in no controls to date.

As late as December 1989 Patten's junior Environment Minister David Trippier said that 'at least 12,000 MW' of power station capacity would receive FGD to meet the Directive. But as *ENDS* magazine pointed out, by February 1990 the electricity industry had committed itself to only one third of this: 4,000 MW of FGD.[81]

On 20 February, the Secretary of State for Energy, John Wakeham, downplayed the role of FGD in meeting the sulphur reductions, telling the House of Commons that FGD was 'an important means' of cutting SO_2 but 'there were other means too'.[82] He also said: 'The essence of the Directive is a commitment by member states to reduce their emissions of acid gases. It is not a commitment to any specific form of abatement technique.'

The government implied that it would allow the privatised electricity industry to meet the reductions in the Directive by importing low-sulphur coal and by building gas-fired power stations to replace coal capacity. Robert Malpas, chairman of the privatised power company Powergen, was quoted as saying that he would like to 'get away' with fitting FGD at just one of his power stations.[83]

This, however, was not the basis of the negotiations on which Britain was granted its special deal.

The government now denied that it was granted the terms it received under the Large Combustion Plant Directive on the basis that it would be fitting FGD so it could continue to burn high-sulphur coal. In a letter to Greenpeace acid rain campaigner Andy Tickle, D. Aspinwall of the Air Quality Division in the Department of the Environment wrote on 20 March 1990: 'You suggest that the Government has changed its plans for implementing the large combustion plants Directive. As you are probably aware the Directive does not specify how emissions from existing plants should be reduced. The Government has always envisaged that a range of measures would be needed.'[84] In other words, the plans had changed, but the government wanted to hide the fact.

Not only environment groups and analysts such as Nigel Haigh of IEEP are sceptical of the government's claims. The *Financial Times Survey of the Electricity Industry* noted: 'The British government and the generators are retreating from their commitment to the European Commission to put sulphur-scrubbing flue gas desulphurisation (FGD) equipment on 12,000MW of coal-fired plant in England and Wales at a cost of £2bn.'[85]

The *Financial Times* identified the government's desire to oil the progress of the electricity privatisation by reducing investment in pollution control. 'The Government is worried that privatisation proceeds would be severely reduced if the full FGD commitment were repeated in the prospectuses of National Power and PowerGen,' said the newspaper on 29 March 1990.[86]

National Power subsequently indicated that low-sulphur technology would be installed at Didcot, Tilbury and Ironbridge. West Thurrock and Ironbridge have already been converted by National Power. Powergen has converted Kingsnorth, but cancelled plans to install FGD at Fiddlers Ferry. It might fit FGD at Ferrybridge and Ratcliffe on Soar.

The use of low-sulphur coal reduces sulphur output by only about 50 per cent, compared with the 90 per cent removal that can be achieved with FGD. Using low-sulphur coal is therefore only a short-term economic palliative and will not reduce UK sulphur pollution to below critical levels.

Reneging on the sulphur agreement is likely to perpetuate Britain's bad environmental reputation in Europe. Nigel Haigh commented in a letter to the *Independent* on 20 February 1990:

> 'If Britain now decides to meet the legally binding percentage reductions by importing low sulphur coal, or by burning gas, it will be accused of having twisted the other member states.
>
> There are two courses open to the British government if it is to maintain its reputation, on which it prides itself, of honouring its commitments. Either it must achieve the reductions it agreed to by using technological means to remove the sulphur from domestic coal, or, if it chooses to see low-sulphur coal being imported, or gas burned in power stations, it must endure reductions in emissions closer to those agreed by West Germany, the Netherlands, France, Belgium and Denmark.'[87]

Following the announcement, the government began a news-management campaign designed to talk away the problem. The Prime Minister stated in March 1990 that it was privatisation that had enabled the sulphur cuts to be made in other ways. This comment would be bound to confuse, as the government was well aware of impending privatisation when she made her previous statement that the UK would fit FGD. She told an audience at the Royal Society, 'Let me confirm unequivocally . . . the United Kingdom will meet the commitments which it has solemnly accepted to reduce acid emissions.'[88] She did not mention the basis of the deal. Which was strange, as she had spelt it out very clearly less than a year before, in a BBC TV interview. Mrs Thatcher told the BBC's Michael Buerk:[89]

> 'Now the quickest way to diminish acid rain would be to say, 'Right, we will not use any British coal, we will use coal from overseas which has no sulphur.' Now I hardly think that would have been acceptable, either to the people of Britain, let alone to the mining areas, or to some of those

European Commissioners who are critical. So we didn't go about it in that way. We said we will try to extract that sulphur . . . so we are spending a fortune, well over a billion in the first instance, and then another £600 million after that, to try to take the sulphur out.'

Could it be that the Prime Minister didn't want to admit to a U-turn, to reneging on a commitment to European partners, 'some of those European Commissioners', 'the mining areas' and 'the people of Britain'?

Relying heavily on a low sulphur coal strategy in place of FGD, may create problems which could yet undermine even the short-term economic case for such a policy. It could create dependence on unreliable imports (as the world market for low sulphur coal is extremely susceptible to sharp increases in demand and expensive because of its popularity in the USA), adversely affect the balance of payments, be vulnerable to changes in the value of the pound, increase unemployment costs from the mining industry, and lead to the geological abandonment of UK mines, thus making it a difficult policy to reverse.

Reducing Sulphur and Nitrogen Emissions

Over 180 different systems of FGD exist worldwide, at least 30 of which are used commercially. Following privatisation it is probable that Powergen and National Power will fit the limestone/gypsum process to 12,000 MW of capacity (6 large stations). This mixes wet limestone with the hot gases. Calcium sulphate (gypsum) is formed, removing up to 90 per cent of sulphur. Other systems do not need large amounts of limestone and produce usable pure sulphur or acid rather than waste. Gypsum is widely used in the building trade as 'Plaster of Paris'. The UK market of about 3 million tonnes could be supplied by six FGD-fitted large power stations.

Power station NOx can be reduced with 'Low NOx' burners (now being fitted at 12 of the largest coal-fired power stations [90]), which have a different type of flame and can reduce NOx by 30–40 per cent. The cost is low.

For NOx reductions of 80 per cent or more, the USA, Japan and West Germany have opted for SCR (selective catalytic reduction), in which ammonia is injected into the superheated region of a boiler or outside it, in a catalyst bed at around half the cost of FGD. One process known as 'NOx Out' uses urea and achieves up to 80 per cent reduction at a quarter the cost of SCR. It is fitted in West Germany and the USA but not in the UK.

As of 1988 the UN ECE Convention included a NOx Protocol, under which UK emissions must not rise above 1987 levels: this will probably require power station controls as well as limits on traffic sources.

Pollution Targets and Critical Loads

Critical loads mark the limit of nature's ability to tolerate acid rain. Before they were defined, there were no ecological targets for pollution control, only political ones. The 30 per cent Club was an unashamedly political target, a 'first step' initiative. 'Critical loads' and 'critical levels' provide a rational basis for pollution control, if targets are set to meet them. The 0.5 g/S/m^2 Stockholm target was an early definition of a critical load.

Jan Nilsson, one of the originators of the concept, has defined a critical load as 'The highest load that will not cause chemical changes leading to long-term harmful effects on the most sensitive ecological systems.'[91] Critical loads have been calculated for nitrogen, sulphur and hydrogen ion acidity (taking into account rainfall and soil type) by international teams of scientists.

Soils high in carbonate (e.g. chalk, limestone) have high 'alkali production', so acids will be mostly neutralised and will have a high critical load. But, in Britain as in much of Europe, soils change markedly over a few miles or tens of miles, so targets must be set to protect the most sensitive soils, such as those based on sand or overlying hard, naturally 'base-poor' rocks.

The target reductions required to bring sulphur pollution below the critical loads will vary according to present pollution. In southwestern Scandinavia it will be 80–90 per cent, while in some parts of Europe the deposition is four times as great, indicating a reduction above 90 per cent. In the UK, sulphur and nitrogen will need to be reduced 90 per cent to safeguard all sensitive ecosystems.

For freshwater the key criterion is pH. Once it drops below 5.3, increased solubility of aluminium and other chemical effects lead progressively to the decline and loss of fish populations (see below). For the most delicate lake systems of Sweden and Norway even a 100 per cent reduction in deposition is not expected to return them to life; 3–7 per cent of the lakes in Norway's 1,000 lake study are in this super-sensitive category with a 'zero alkalinity' at 100 per cent reduction, and will require liming.[92]

High rainfall, coniferous vegetation, steep slopes, and coarse, sandy, free-drained, shallow soil with few chemical bases (e.g. calcium, magnesium) and a low capacity to adsorb sulphate all make soils more sensitive to acid and give a low critical load. Critical loads for forest soils agreed by the UN ECE's expert working group in 1989 range from 3kg/S/ha (0.3g/S/m^2) on granite, through 8–16 kg/S/ha for moderately easily weathered soils, to over 32kg/S/ha for limestone or chalk.

Large areas of the English Midlands receive several times the critical loads for even moderately sensitive soils. Only northeast Scotland, parts of the southern Uplands and a few areas in the southwest receive less than 10kg/S/ha a year, and in the 1970s deposition was higher. When soils receive more than the critical load, the natural capacity to neutralize acidity is overwhelmed, cations (e.g. calcium) are leached out, phosphorus is retained and aluminium and trace metals appear in the soil water. The result may be nutrient deficiencies, toxic levels of metals, and a long-term drop in pH.

For British lakes with limited alkalinity, critical loads of sulphur are put at 3–6 kg/S/ha, a level exceeded over most of the country. The load is set so as to maintain a pH of at least 5.3, the minimum for a bicarbonate rather than an aluminium buffering system, with aluminium levels of 30 ug/litre or less. In Wales, Plynlimon receives up to 16kg/S/ha and the Berwyns 31kg/S/ha, that is six times the critical load. The highest values have been recorded at Holme

Moss in the Pennines (43kg/S/ha, eight times the level) and at a site in Galloway with 31.4kg/S/ha.

Unpolluted ecosystems release only small quantities of nitrate in streams. At high deposition, nitrate is found leaching away because the soil processes and capacity of plants to take up nitrogen are exceeded. Low-productivity ecosystems such as heaths, peat bogs, chalk grasslands and many ancient woodlands have a lower critical load than productive systems such as commercial forests or reed swamps. (The acidifying effects of nitrogen and sulphur are additive, so high nitrogen and sulphur deposition should really be considered together.)

Previously unpolluted ecosystems begin to change almost as soon as extra nitrogen arrives because the plants and animals living there are adapted to low-nitrogen conditions. Most rare and threatened flowers and other plants cannot tolerate high nitrogen. Many of the biological effects involve direct toxicity, and are levels as much as loads.

Nitrogen pollution is now high enough to affect ecosystems throughout England and Wales. Only part of central northern Scotland may be below the critical load for sensitive plant communities such as those around some lakes and peat bogs. Unless nitrogen pollution is significantly reduced, many of the rare plants for which conservation sites were designated or nature reserves were set up will disappear. Research in the Netherlands, West Germany and Denmark has shown that at 20kg/N/ha heather gives way to grassland. Forest decline may be a similar process involving trees.

The southern Pennines has the highest calculated load of nitrogen at 25 – 55kg/N/ha. John Lee from Manchester University and Sarah Woodin of the NCC have shown that sphagnum peat bogs first killed off by sulphur dioxide now cannot recover because of high levels of nitrogen.[93] Tessa Robertson of WWF comments that critical loads present 'a stark picture for some of Britain's most valuable natural habitats'.[94]

Soil Acidification

Traditionally, soils were thought to have such enormous chemical reservoirs that they could buffer any realistic pollution impact but recent evidence shows they are much more vulnerable.

In 1984 90 soil profiles sampled by Professor C. O. Tamm in 1927 at Tonnersjoheden Forest in Sweden were re-examined by his son. Acidity had increased up to 0.9 pH units in the upper level and 0.7 units at a metre depth. In some places the pH dropped 1.5 units.[95] Goran Persson of the Swedish Environment Protection Board says such 'acidification . . . was not even considered conceivable' in the 1970s.[96]

Scientists from Aberdeen University have now found that sulphur pollution caused deep soil acidification between 1948 and 1988 at Balmoral, even though the area is remote from industrial centres. 'The same workers,' says the Nature Conservancy Council, 'have demonstrated that acid deposition has caused widespread acidification of upland peat.'[97]

An experiment near Bristol showed pollution downwind of a coking works could increase acidity tenfold in just 30 months.[98] Even soil with a 'fairly high clay content' became acidified at depth. Dry deposition of sulphur dioxide may, says a DoE review, also 'cause rapid surface soil acidification (over months rather than years)'.[99] Ammonium sulphate is also a powerful soil acidifier.

In the mid 1980s it was also discovered that the naturally leached soil of most of upland Britain is vulnerable to 'sulphate saturation'. Eventually this encourages displacement of neutralising substances and any further sulphate input, as in rain, causes calcium or other cations to flow out and, when these are exhausted, toxic aluminium.

A striking Norwegian experiment, in which a glass roof has been put over a whole catchment, shows the degree of such ecosystem damage. When polluted rain was substituted by clean rain, the 'bleeding' of sulphate from the soil reduced 50 per cent but after 36 months it still continued at up to seven times the rate of input.[100] In an unpolluted area, over 80 per cent of the added sulphate was retained in the soil.[101] In Britain, a DoE group has now estimated that to return Britain's soil and freshwaters to a pre-pollution state, a 90 per cent reduction in sulphur is required.

Damage to Freshwaters

The controlling factor of acidification is pH but the main toxic substance is aluminium. Its solubility and hence biological impact is strongly influenced by pH.

Permanently acid lakes have a pH below 5.6 and alkalinity close to zero because calcium and magnesium have been washed from the system. Many invertebrates, such as crayfish, cannot survive without a certain level of calcium, and are completely absent. High levels of aluminium – toxic to fish in several chemical forms – are often present.

Other vulnerable lakes endure episodes of acidity in which pH drops below 5.6 when a rainstorm or snowmelt flushes acid, sulphate or aluminium into the catchment. Such episodes kill fish. Aluminium hydroxide forms on their gills, mucus is secreted and the fish choke to death. Fish eggs and invertebrate larvae may be more affected by episodes of acidity than adult organisms. In particularly acid seasons, no young may be recruited. It may then take decades for a long-lived species like trout to die out completely.

The third category of river or lake is never acid because of high alkalinity. pH is usually above 6 and the catchment has well buffered soils.

Below pH 4.5 the main form of aluminium present is the Al^{3+} ion. At pH 3 – 4, aluminium combines strongly with organic matter – such as humus or peat – so that it is less of a hazard in peaty waters. Fish deaths in 'brown' (peaty) rivers are usually due to hydrogen ion acidity.

Fisheries' records show that 22 Welsh salmon rivers declined between the periods 1966–75 and 1976–85. Of these, 20 had become acid. Fish deaths resulting from acid surges have also been observed on the rivers Esk and Duddon in Cumbria, and Glaslyn in Snowdonia.

But a declining fish population may become increasingly dominated by young fish or, more often in lakes, a few large old fish. Anglers paying only occasional visits are unlikely to realise that anything is wrong until all the fish disappear. It seems likely that, if Prince Charles hadn't made it famous through his children's book *The Old Man of Lochnagar*, nobody might have known that, by 1984, only 13 trout survived in this highly acidified loch.

A surer way of assessing how far lakes have turned acid is 'diatom analysis' as used by Dr Rick Battarbee and his colleagues at UCL.

The UCL Studies

After showing how Galloway Lochs had become acidified, Battarbee has now produced similar evidence for 17 Scottish lochs, 5 English and 8 Welsh lakes.[102] Many show more than a tenfold increase in acidity since 1850.

The recent sediments contain soot characteristic of fuel-oil, which has been extensively used only since 1940, and magnetic particles which, says Battarbee, 'are predominantly spherical and can be identified as power station fly-ash.'

The fly-ash particles only appear in sediments after 1945, rising steeply in the 1970s. At Lochnagar, a nature reserve at 785 metres in the Cairngorms, fly–ash appears separately from fuel-oil soot from the 1960s onwards. This, says Battarbee, 'might, therefore, be an independent measure of the impact of large, tall-chimney, coal fired power stations built in the United Kingdom since 1960.'

Today, Lochnagar has a pH of 5. In 1800 the pH would have been 5.9. The nineteenth-century microfossil record shows a decline in plant plankton such as flourish in neutral conditions and an increase in acid-tolerant species.

At Loch Laidon, which lies in Rannoch Moor National Nature Reserve, the whole catchment is designated a Site of Special Scientific Interest. Here, contamination with metals, says Battarbee, occurs 'about ten years before the first evidence of acidification', which suggests that it took only ten years to exhaust the lake's capacity to buffer pollution.

Acidified lakes also occur throughout mid Wales and Snowdonia. Llyn y Bi is a small 3 metre deep lake which lies at 445 metres in the Rhinogs of Snowdonia National Park, the most acidified mountain range in Wales. Pre-war records show that this little lake held good stocks of the rare arctic char (a fish of the salmon family) and brown trout. The remains of an old boat house stand on the shore. But now, says Battarbee, it 'is virtually fishless'. The lean ecology here means the entire 150 years of diatom layers are just 5 cm deep. In this shallow bed of microfossils, Battarbee reads a progressive acidification from 1870. After 1900 acidity increased tenfold. As at other sites, the trace metal contamination – first lead, then zinc – predated the onset of acidification by a few decades. Fuel-oil traces and power station fly-ash appear in the late twentieth century.

Investigators are now focusing on ponds of 'decalcified' sandstones, including

Pinkworthy on Exmoor and Woolmer in Hampshire, where the acid-sensitive and rare natterjack toad has disappeared.

Only one part of the UK appears to have so far escaped: the northwest Highlands and Islands.

Disappearing Life: Acidification and Conservation

Diatoms are not the only plants affected by acid water. Certain species of sphagnum and the acid-loving bulbous rush may become abundant. Rare species such as awlwort, typical of the margins of delicate mountain lakes, the pipewort (restricted to Skye and western Ireland), Isoetes echinospora, the rare waterwort, and its relative Elatine hydropiper, and the various-leaved pondweed, are all likely to vanish.

As waters become acid, animal life too diminishes. Mayflies and several varieties of caddis disappear from acid streams, and the freshwater shrimp becomes scarce in soft water or below pH 5.7. In lakes, crustaceans, molluscs, leeches and mayflies dwindle, although predators remain more numerous, feeding on alternative prey. Dragonflies and stoneflies tend to be more common in acid water.[103]

Toads, frogs and newts are strongly affected. Exposure to water below pH 4 kills embryos in spawn. At slightly higher pH, embryos suffer spine deformities, and hatching enzymes are impaired. It seems that increased acidity has caused widespread deaths of tadpoles in southwest Scotland and the retreat of the common frog in northwest England. Toad tadpoles put into acid water develop severe leg abnormalities.

One of the few British birds studied in relation to acidification is the dipper, a small black and white bird which feeds on invertebrates along rivers. Stephen Ormerod, Stephanie Tyler and others from the RSPB and University of Wales have shown that dippers declined 80–90 per cent on the River Irfon at a time of acidification and afforestation. Along streams with high aluminium and low pH, dippers show a reduced ability to feed their young. Acid stress and calcium deficiency may both be significant. Of the apparently suitable streams in North Wales, 72 per cent are now without dippers.

Ospreys do not nest in the Galloway lochs, although they do 'prospect' the area regularly: it seems likely that it is the lack of fish that keeps them away. Unique varieties of the arctic char in Lochs Grannoch, Doon and Dungeon are threatened with extinction owing to a tenfold increase in acidity since the 1970s.[104] In Wales, the otter may not be recovering from declines caused by persecution and dieldrin, because of a lack of fish due to acidification.

In conservation terms, Britain is internationally significant for its peat bogs, both the lowland raised bogs and the blanket bogs and mires of the Flow Country and much of the upland Pennines and Welsh mountains. This heritage, together with its birdlife and scarce plants, is now threatened by acidification and nitrogen eutrophication. Lesser twayblade and heather have already declined on Peak District bogs, while the acid-tolerant cotton-grass and bilberry are now more common.[105]

Another British speciality in world conservation terms is the rich flora of mosses and lichens. More than 1,500 lichens, 680 mosses and 380 of the related liverworts occur in Britain (as opposed to only 1,700 flowering plants). Lichens were wiped out over large areas owing to sulphur dioxide emissions. Today, Britain has 70 per cent of the total number of mosses and liverworts in Europe and holds nearly one-third of its threatened lichens.[106]

From the nineteenth century onwards, biologists reported 'lichen deserts' around towns. A 1970s survey showed that much of England was devoid of all but one lichen *(Lecanora conizaoides)* which actually prospers in sulphurous conditions. Leicestershire for example, lost 89 per cent of the vulnerable species in its lichen flora and 47 per cent overall. The west of Ireland still enjoys rich 'mossy' and lichen-covered woods (and even a lichen-eating and spotted Kerry slug), not just because areas such as Kilarney have a moist climate but because they have so far escaped most of Europe's pollution.

In the early 1980s, lichens were observed 'reinvading' urban areas such as Greater London as SO_2 declined.[107] But close examination showed that species intolerant of acid conditions or high nitrogen levels were not reappearing. From remote rural areas came evidence of continuing decline because of increased acidity of rainfall. Lungwort *(Lobaria)* lichens became gradually extinct on 20 oaks studied at Monk Wood in Northumberland between 1969 and 1985. The oak bark had become acidified. Only a nearby ash tree, which had better buffered bark, retained the lichen.

One of the few lichens that are spreading is *Parmeliopsis ambigua*, known to lichenologists as the 'yellow peril'. Previously restricted to the acid substrate of debarked pine twigs, this lichen is now appearing on a variety of surfaces.[108]

Strangely, Britain's botanists have taken almost no interest in acidification, although plants such as cowslips, heather and many woodland flowers are also known to be affected by sulphur and nitrogen deposition. In Sweden, British species such as dog rose, cowslip and ladies' bedstraw are thought to have been lost from polluted woods, where the nitrogen-loving nettle and acid-tolerant wood sorrel now occur.[109]

Heathlands may be highly vulnerable. Dutch scientists have found that acid-loving rush and sphagnum species have taken over from *Lobelia* and Littorella (reduced from 500 to 30 sites) and 20 other rare plants of heathland pools. Changes in nitrification caused by ammonium and nitrate deposition are blamed, and heathland soils have become richer in nitrogen and more acid.[110]

Conclusions on Acid Rain

The acid rain problem may have disappeared from the headlines but it is far from being solved.

Britain remains a significant polluter of Scandinavia. In Sweden in 1988 it was estimated that some 15,000 lakes were acidified, just over 1,800 of which were 'seriously' acidified; 100,000 km of rivers and streams were also affected.

In Norway, a re-survey of 1,000 lakes studied in the 1970s showed that many lakes have actually lost more of their neutralising capacity in recent years, although sulphate levels are falling. The salmon has 'essentially disap-peared' from seven major rivers in southern Norway. Lakes across more than 13,000 km^2 are 'practically devoid of fish' and over another 20,000 km^2 the stocks are reduced.[111]

But Britain, too, has been quietly ravaged by acid rain. In the UK, lakes in Snowdonia National Park, most of mid Wales, the Lake District, Cairngorms, Pennines and even on the Surrey heaths, are dead or dying from acidity. Peatlands for which the UK is internationally important, and probably heaths, are being changed beyond recognition.

Britain remains the Dirty Man of Europe so far as SO_2 and NOx pollution is concerned, and will do so even when the EC Large Plant Directive is imple-mented by 2003. And Britain lags behind in taking action.

Britain still talks of anything more than a 15 per cent cut in the CEGB's emissions within ten years as being 'impracticable'. But the power industry in West Germany cut its sulphur emissions 75 per cent between 1983 and 1988.[112] The net emissions of Germany's power stations were reduced from 1.6 million tonnes to 0.5 million tonnes within five years, enabling it to go far beyond the 30 per cent Club target.

In Sweden, sulphur dioxide emissions will have been reduced 65 per cent between 1980 and 1995, 45 per cent by 1985. The UK's policies, note the Swedes, cause damage in other countries and are 'not in agreement with the principles of the Geneva Convention nor the Polluter Pays Principle'.[113]

Britain of course protests that 'no country is doing more' to reduce sulphur – but then no country in Western Europe creates so much pollution and has done so little (nothing) in the past. Yet even this calculated white lie will not be a particularly helpful excuse if the limited FGD programme agreed by the CEGB continues to lag behind schedule.

In December 1989 Greenpeace consultants suggested that by 1993 power station emissions would again reach 1980 levels and overall emissions would fall not 22 per cent as the government predicted, but only 10 per cent.[114]

Two years earlier the CEGB was vigorously rewriting history. 'Our approach then,' Derek Davis, a member of the Board, told the Commons Environment Committee as he sought to explained its role back in 1984, 'was 'agnosticism' rather than 'scepticism'. Peter Chester informed the same Committee that 'there certainly have been changes in knowledge. I think the word 'evolution' may be the more accurate word to use.'[115]

Chester was still trying to persuade the Committee that there was no urgency about reducing sulphur emissions. Given the CEGB's assertion that it might take 'decades or even centuries' for soils to recover, Robert Jones MP wanted to know, 'is that not all the more reason for getting on with it as quickly as possible and on as wide a scale as possible?' [116] 'Emissions will have essentially vanished' by the year 2020 when the CEGB had a completely new generation of plant in place, said Chester. Bringing down emissions faster might take £2 billion. If calcium recovery in soils was slow, we would have 'gained very little' by such pollution control.

Under the Environmental Protection Bill the DoE will control sulphur pollu-tion according to a national reduction plan administered by HMIP. This much is an advance, but whether they have the stomach to take on the power industry and the Department of Energy remains to be seen.

CHAPTER 5

Forest Decline

Waldsterben

In the higher reaches of the Black Forest near the spa resort of Baden-Baden there are some very stately forests managed under the system known as 'Plenderwald'. Here foresters maintain an irregular mixture of species, ages and sizes of trees, quite unlike the cabbage-field plantation methods employed in the UK . Many of the Plenderwald trees are massive silver firs, the species that was the original 'Christmas tree' even in England, before being replaced by the spruce.

These forests contain many species of trees (dominated by a mix of beech, spruce and fir), hundreds of wild flowers, deep carpets of moss and many lichens. They have their own bird fauna including the hazel hen.

At least until the 1970s, the Plenderwald forests were West Germany's traditional playground, more important to the citizens of the Federal Republic for weekending or walking holidays than Britain's New Forest or the South Downs, with a greater role in the national heritage of myth, folklore and literature than the Lake District to the English or the Great Glen to the Scots.

Until 1970 the foresters here say they could rely on a good sale of fir trimmings – used in Christmas decorations – to pay for the routine management of the rest of the forest.[1] Then in the 1970s (nobody can put an exact date to it) the foliage began to change, becoming sickly yellow or brown instead of shining grey and green. The needles began to fall and gradually families stopped coming.

Foresters had known of such things before. The fir is a native of the European alps and periodic declines or *Tannesterben* (fir-dying) had in the past been attributed to years of drought or warm winters.[2] This seemed to be an unusually severe *Tannesterben* . By autumn 1980 the decline started to affect spruce, concentrated in old trees on gravelly plains round Munich and in the central Bavarian forest.[3] This was put down to a '*Fichtesterben*', or progressive spruce death, but a year later it appeared in other species too, such as beech, oak and the mountain ash, and foresters grew alarmed. The decline was particularly marked in the Black Forest and in the Bavarian National Park in southern West Germany, an alpine region close to Austria and Switzerland, where fir decline may have slightly predated that in the Black Forest.

All the German-speaking foresters are in close touch with each other and by

1982 the decline had been identified in Switzerland and Austria, together with the Netherlands where Scots pine and beech were affected.

The decline was also unprecedented, affecting many species with no sign of a new disease organism (not that one was known which would sweep through many different types of tree at once), and no obvious climatic or soil factor involved. The blame fell on pollution; not the clouds of smoke and occasional waves of sulphur dioxide which were known to drift up from the industrial valleys of the Ruhr and kill off the sensitive firs, but the more insidious long-term changes implied by acid rain. Enormous political and scientific concern was stimulated by the realisation that such a decline had been predicted by Professor Bernard Ulrich of Gottingen University. Ulrich proposed that acid industrial emissions, principally the old enemy sulphur, were poisoning the forests through the release of aluminium in the soil. *Der Spiegel* magazine made *Waldsterben* a front-page issue in November 1981.

Bitter scientific disputes soon developed. By the mid-1980s well over a hundred hypotheses had been put forward to explain the forest decline. A recent one involves 'simple chlorinated solvents'. These halocarbons, such as tri-chlorethylene, are used as degreasants and in dry cleaning. As well as being a threat to the ozone layer and human health, it is now thought that they are especially attracted to the wax coatings on conifer needles, reaching 100 times the concentration in the air. In the presence of high ultraviolet light, they break down to release radicals which destroy photosynthetic pigments and may form TCA (trichloracetic acid), itself used as a herbicide.[4]

In 1986, one scientific reviewer noted: 'Sorting out the causal agents is among the most challenging scientific detective tasks of the century. Given the severity of the *Waldsterben* syndrome there is no time to lose in grappling with its causes and formulating effective control strategies'.[5] Inexplicable, unprecedented and catastrophic, *Waldsterben* took on the character of an apocalyptic plague. 'A specter is haunting Europe and North America - the specter of widespread forest decline,' wrote a respected US Institute as United States researchers reported that, in a survey of 17 states from Maine to Missouri, several species showed 'a systematic, regionally scaled and sustained decline in growth' over the previous 20 - 25 years. The political Greens took it as confirmation that industrial society was indeed not sustainable. Even highly conservative scientists became concerned that some large-scale change to ecosystems in industrialised countries seemed to be under way.

As experimenters came under pressure to test their laboratory theories in the forests themselves, it became increasingly clear that whatever was killing the forests, it was not a single known pollutant. Professor Peter Schutt of Munich University proposed a 'multiple stress' hypothesis.[6] He pointed out that a cubic metre of air over the affected forests had been found to contain 400 mainly unknown but man-made organic compounds. Trees were exposed to mixtures of heavy metals, acids, over-doses of nutrients and soil stresses including the leaching of important ions such as calcium and magnesium.

Supporters of Schutt's multiple-stresses hypothesis pointed to studies of tree rings in West Germany, Switzerland and other countries, which showed a long-term slowing in growth well before the year in which visible signs of decline had developed. They suggested that pollution stresses combined to weaken the trees so that, when a 'normal' stress such as frost or drought came along, the tree died or went into a rapid decline, before succumbing to competition from neighbours or invasion by fungal pests or other disease organisms.

The multiple-stress hypothesis explains the observed facts, although it does not confirm the exact pathways or relative importance of individual pollution factors. It is generally accepted by most researchers in the field (although there is now increasing concern over drought and climate change, see below), as is the three-step concept of forest damage, which distinguishes 'predisposing', 'inciting' and 'contributing' factors. The first, such as poor climate, dry conditions, the genetic make-up of the tree, the nutrient status of the soil, background pollution and the degree of competition from neighbours, will predispose a tree to succumb to stress. They are chronic weakening agents. The 'inciting' factors are triggering episodes and many include frost, insect attack, drought, mechanical injury or an episode of high pollution. The 'contributing' factors hasten death. They include bark beetles, fungi, viruses and competition.

While the complex of possible causes was being investigated, foresters began comparing notes on the common features of the forest decline, the 'symptoms' of *Waldsterben*. The visible signs are of two main sorts. The first involve loss of leaf area, through leaves and buds not developing fully, and leaves falling early. This is particularly noticeable in conifers such as yew, spruce or fir, where it makes the canopy increasingly lace-like or transparent. The second involve changes to the branching structure of the tree. In conifers this often involves 'fear shoots' or 'compensation shoots' sprouting from the upper sides of branches, and affected beech trees show a characteristic hooking of the short side-shoots in the top of the canopy, creating a 'fingered' rather than a fully-formed rounded tree outline.

Many other changes take place in the declining forests. The death of plants growing under the canopy, where rainfall drips onto them, is also quite widely reported. It is often difficult to disentangle cause and effect.

From 1985 the United Nations Economic Commission for Europe (UN ECE) began coordinating international surveys of forest decline, and has adapted the original German system to classify damage or health according to four categories, largely dependent on the loss of leaves and the density of the canopy. These are as follows:

Damage Categories Used in European Surveys[7]

Category	condition of trees	per cent crown thinning
0	healthy	0 - 10
1	slight damage or warning category	11 - 25
2	medium damage	26 - 60
3	severe damage; trees dying	61 - 99
4	dead	100

Damage is assessed visually, and many countries use the illustrated Swiss guide *Sanasilva* which shows the various stages of decline in all the commoner native British and European trees in colour photographs.

The first national West German survey took place in 1983 and included spruce, pine, fir, beech and oak. It showed 34 per cent of all trees were damaged to some degree. A year later damage had increased to 50 per cent and by 1985 it stood at 51 per cent. Some species were very severely affected: over three quarters of the silver fir were damaged, with 49 per cent in categories 2, 3 and 4 and 67 per cent in these groups by 1985. In many areas, by the late 1980s, up to 80 per cent of the mature silver fir had died.

While 66 per cent of fir trees in 27 plots established in 1980 had been considered healthy, by 1982 just 1 per cent remained so. In the same period, the number of 'moderately damaged' firs increased 12 per cent to 79 per cent.[8] The spruce decline was even faster: in autumn 1981, 94 per cent were still 'healthy' but a year later this had dropped to 6 per cent.

Preceding the national survey, regional studies in 1981 and 1982 had suggested that under 10 per cent of German trees were affected. The discovery of a national catastrophe led the forest-loving Germans into a maelstrom of surveys, scientific investigations and conferences. Besides a national flue–gas desulphurisation (FGD) programme on power stations, West Germany introduced its own laws to require catalytic converters on cars (devices containing a platinum-coated honeycomb which treat exhaust gases, transforming up to 90 per cent of the NOx, hydrocarbons and carbon monoxide).

By 1983 surveys had also begun in the Netherlands, France, Austria, Switzerland, Luxembourg and Italy, as well as in many Eastern European countries where short-range pollution involving sulphur dioxide and NOx was still a major problem. And not just the foresters and the ecologists but the public, and hence the politicians of Europe were galvanised by *Waldsterben* unlike any environmental issue that had gone before.

From Vienna, where the famous woods were now dying, came reports that 53 per cent of the country's population were more worried about the death of the nation's trees than any other factor, personal or economic. In Switzerland, too, forest decline became a national obsession, overwhelming concern at death from nuclear war, terrorism, drugs, gold smuggling or any of the other traditional Swiss worries. In areas such as the central swiss canton of Uri on the St Gothard pass, the death of protection-forests conserved to prevent avalanches, was soon threatening the homes of 150,000 people.

In Britain, things took a rather different turn.

The British Response

The Forestry Commission - A Recipe for Confusion

Just as the DoE lost its early struggles to get the Electricity Board to accept pollution controls, it fell to the Forestry Commission (FC) to pronounce on the state of the nation's forests, although environment scientists declared themselves convinced of the risk as early as 1982.

The Forestry Commission has two official roles in national life. It is the 'forest enterprise' which plants trees, and the 'forest authority' which does a little research, provides technical and policy advice to government and private foresters, and hands out grants to the private sector. By the early 1980s the Commission had been coming under increasingly severe criticism from conservationists and others.

Members of a House of Lords Select Committee on Science and Technology had criticised the quality of Commission research. Richard Grove of Cambridge University was one of many conservationists who attacked the Commission's policies of converting deciduous, often ancient, woods to conifers. The Royal Society for the Protection of Birds (RSPB) and the Nature Conservancy Council (NCC) assailed plans to afforest the unique peatlands of Caithness and Sutherland Flow Country, where the Commission was grant-aiding the private sector. Friends of the Earth found itself fighting alongside left and right-wing members of the House of Commons Public Accounts Committee to overturn the tax system which benefited investors in plantation forestry at the expense of wildlife and the taxpayer.[10]

The same critics pointed to the obsolete Victorian rationale of the Commission – which was established to plant trees for wooden ships and pit-props in a war in which timber would be a strategic material – and wondered aloud if the organisation as well as its activities should not be reformed or abolished. Free marketeers even talked of privatisation.

So, as the Germans put Britain under pressure to reduce air pollution to protect forests, all the ingredients were in place for conflict and confusion. The Commission – and the private foresters with which it was closely associated – was strongly disinclined to believe anything that environmentalists said. It had experienced air pollution as a problem solved, not a new one as did the rural foresters in West Germany and Sweden. It was ambivalent about acid rain because of its experiences with lakes. It managed very few semi-natural wood-lands and understood them very little, and had routinely fertilised, ploughed and drained its own forest soils so that long-term changes such as those feared on the continent would be masked by its own management. If long-term changes were taking place, the Commission's forests were not the place to look for them.

Even acknowledging these differences was an institutional difficulty. There were, for example, very few old Sitka spruce in the Commission's forests because the rotation of the plantation was only some 35–55 years. As its critic Richard Grove had pointed out, the original plan was for the trees to live much longer (and become more valuable timber), only the Commission had badly underestimated how windy it was in the British Isles, and the Sitka spruce suffered badly from 'wind-blow', which stressed the timber and made sure that the trees would never reach the grand dimensions they do in their native temperate rainforests of the Pacific Northwest. In Europe, it was the older trees – over 60 or even 100 years old – that were first and most severely affected by the new *Waldsterben*.

'An Element of Neurosis'

In 1982 the Forestry Commission's Head of Site Studies and Head of

Pathology paid a short trip to West Germany to see forest decline for themselves. They were unimpressed: 'There is undoubtedly an element of neurosis involved in the readiness of many foresters and some workers to attribute any decline without adequate critical investigation,' they wrote in a report published in 1983. 'German research,' they added, 'appears to suffer from lack of co-ordination . . . insufficient information is being paid to biological experimentation . . .'[11] It seemed, said the Commission, 'unlikely that the Sitka spruce, Lodgepole and Scots pine and larch forests in the uplands of Britain are in immediate danger.'

Utterances like these, which rubbished German claims and made reassuring noises about the UK, were no doubt music to the ears of government, which needed to justify no action over pollution from cars or power stations. Perhaps significantly, the Commission said nothing about more natural and lowland woodlands such as the New Forest or Epping Forest, where some pollution effects (on lichens) were already known.

Nor was anything said about unsolved mysteries such as the widespread dieback of ash trees, which the Commission itself had studied since 1960. Originally concentrated in the East Midlands, ash dieback is a term for a general thinning of foliage, and death of branches from the tree top down, often accompanied by massive production of 'keys' (ash seeds), very much the changes reported as *Waldsterben*. 'It is hard to turn a blind eye to something so obvious and widespread,' wrote the author of a forestry text in 1962.

In 1983, Dr R G Pawsey from the Commonwealth Forestry Institute reported an ash dieback survey[12] which showed that 80–90 per cent of the trees in areas such as north Buckinghamshire (near Milton Keynes) were now affected. No biological or physical cause could be found and the studies were abandoned. Dr J N Gibbs, a Forestry Commission pathologist, later pointed out that Pawsey's survey found no correlation with pollution, although Pawsey in any case had no detailed pollution data[13]. It was generally assumed that deep-ploughing, straw burning, fertilisers or sprays might be the cause of ash decline in arable areas, but no detailed chemical and ecological investigation was made. As ash trees are not 'forest trees' in its plantations, the Commission had little interest in them. (In 1989 a DoE/Forestry Commission survey of hedgerow trees found a correlation between ash dieback, acidity and sulphur, suggesting, says Andrew Tickle of Greenpeace, 'some synergism between air pollutants and agricultural factors'.[14])

It was also rumoured that in the late 1970s or early 1980s the Commission had sold Mark Wood and Latton Wood in Essex to the then Harlow New Town Corporation, because of slow growth and dieback attributed to air pollution.

By April 1984 international pressure on Britain was building and the Commission obliged government by supplying further arguments for inaction while taking part in 'more research'. Although the FC had yet to conduct a survey, it stated 'there is little evidence of damage to trees or forests in Britain from direct pollution and none from acid rain.'[15]

The Commission devoted 11 pages to a sceptical treatment of the chemistry of pollution and *Waldsterben* in Europe. Remarkably, its arguments began to sound like those of the Central Electricity Generating Board, as it sought to cast doubt on the very existence of an acid rain problem. 'It must also be noted that the Scandinavian interpretation of the water chemistry, in particular the role of acidity and the loss of fish, has been challenged,' noted the Commission. The challenge, of course, had come from the CEGB. The Commission's cited source for this information was Dr P F Chester of the CEGB, while those thanked for 'helpful suggestions during drafting' included Dr R A Skeffington, a researcher with the CEGB who at this time was also showing pictures of perfectly healthy trees from the Black Forest to British conferences.

Whether or not the Commission had now fallen under the influence of the CEGB, it seemed taken by surprise when the Scottish Friends of the Earth invited Dr Joachim Puhe from Professor Ulrich's team at Gottingen University to survey British sites 'likely' to show forest decline. Over a few days in May 1984 Puhe accompanied Andrew Kerr of FoE Scotland and other campaigners in a tour of Scotland, England and Wales which took in 47 sites, at 31 of which beech, Douglas fir and spruce were found with the same symptoms as those in West Germany. Trees outside the Commission's own Lake District Information Centre at Whinlatter Pass were among those listed as 'damaged'.

A few weeks later, Arnold Grayson, the Commission's research director, was before the House of Commons Select Committee on the Environment. He rejected the FoE Scotland study as 'alarmist', down-played damage to forests in West Germany as 'very small' and stated that 'no damage' had been seen in the UK. 'We have not seen anything of this kind in Britain,' added the Commission's Head of Site Studies.[16]

The Commons Committee made field visits to the areas highlighted by FoE, and reported that in Cumbria's Whinlatter Pass 'Forestry Commission officials have observed extensive dieback of shoots on Scots Pine, evidenced by browning of needles . . . Some damage was also observed on Norway Spruce and Sitka Spruce. A minority were badly enough damaged to be at risk of dying. Officials said similar damage had been observed in the past, but not on anything like a comparable scale.' Although the Commission found it 'disturbing', it asserted that the damage was not the same as that seen abroad and it blamed the winter of 1983/4.

Conflicting signals now began to emerge from the Commission. At the Scottish Wildlife Trust's Acid Rain Inquiry of September 1984, Dr Redfern of its Northern Research Station talked of the 'striking similarities'[17] between the damage which FoE Scotland had first discovered in Cumbria and northwest Scotland. This now affected Scots and Lodgepole pine, Douglas and grand fir, western hemlock and Norway spruce. Redfern said that 'typical damage is death of shoots below the leading part of the tree; we term that "sub top dying". Damage is most severe in older trees and at higher elevations.' In Cumbria, said Redfern, the 'height increment [growth] does appear to have fallen off markedly since about 1975/6 . . . down as much as a quarter in recent years.' To environmentalists – and an increasing number of foreign foresters and ecologists – it seemed that Britain too had all the signs of forest decline.

The Commission was in a difficult position. The overall government line was to stonewall international pressure for pollution curbs, pending more research. Much of the debate centred around evidence of damage. In summer 1984 a Commission scientist wrote in *Coal and Energy Quarterly*, [18] a journal funded by and used as a mouthpiece for the National Coal Board, that 'there is no damage [in British conifers] that can be defined as new' and 'the chances of similar damage [to that in West Germany] occurring here is considered low.' The article was vigorously publicised by the Coal Board's public relations section.

As the argument began to centre on what was or was not 'damage', the Commission pinned its definition to the yellowing of conifer needles. The 'crucial differences' between the British and German trees, said Redfern at the Edinburgh meeting, was that there was 'no needle yellowing' and especially no magnesium deficiency. Professor Peter Schutt from Munich was also in the audience. He disagreed, saying that yellowing was typical only of high altitude damage in foggy conditions, whereas green needles were falling off trees over wide areas at lower altitudes.

Whatever its internal opinions, in responding to the House of Commons Select Committee's report *Acid Rain*, the DoE peddled the Forestry Commission line that British tree damage bore only a 'superficial resemblance' to 'that associated with air pollution in West Germany'.[19]

However, prompted by the embarrassing visit of Puhe, in 1984 the Forestry Commission began its own 'Air Pollution and Tree Health Survey'.

1985: Attacks of Blindness

The results of the Commission's 1984 survey were announced in a press release on 5 March 1985. It announced that the survey had been stimulated by 'fears' that forest decline of the European type 'may be occurring in Britain'. While 'appreciable crown thinning' had been discovered in spruce and Scots pine, this was 'well within the usual range of our experience'. The results were 'very reassuring' with 'no sign whatever of the damage seen in West Germany or any unexpected abnormalities'. In particular, there was 'no sign whatever of the yellowing of needles which characterises the damage occurring in German forests'.

Given the discoveries of Puhe and its own observations, this was a strangely definitive denial. As it turned out, it seems to have been inspired by a desire to bolster government policy rather than to make an objective assessment of the state of trees. Conservation groups pointed out that the Commission was studying the wrong forests (its own and its younger plantations) and had delib- erately excluded the trees which, on the basis of continental experience, would be most at risk. Those at the edges of a stand or in an exposed position were excluded. It was, as it were, a survey designed not to find a problem, rather than one to check on the most vulnerable forests.

Even so, when the report was actually published in August 1985, the Commission's own figures proved to be remarkably similar to those reported from West Germany.

Like many scientists, campaigners at Friends of the Earth in London (including the author) had assumed that the absence of strong evidence for forest decline in Britain might be due to a combination of climate (moist conditions good for growing trees) coupled with the possibility that magnesium in rain coming in from the sea might counteract leaching by acid rain. However, by 1984 a stream of continental ecologists were visiting FoE's headquarters and appearing at conferences to remark that, so far as they were concerned, the trees looked much the same in Britain as they did in West Germany.

Following the Commission's strange response to FoE Scotland's survey, other British campaigners made visits to the Black Forest and the Netherlands. They returned convinced that Britain's trees – and especially its beech trees – were showing 'acid rain' or *Waldsterben* symptoms as bad as, if not worse than, those on the continent. On the Hornisgrinde, a mountain top half way along the spine of the Black Forest and littered with dying fir and spruce, the author and a colleague asked a German ecologist how something so dramatic had apparently started unnoticed. 'What,' they asked, 'had been the first sign that the forests were in decline?' The German scientist appeared to consider this carefully. Then with a sardonic smile he replied: 'I think the first sign, the very first symptom of *Waldsterben*, was an attack of blindness in foresters.'

With grant-aid from the World Wide Fund for Nature (WWF), FoE now involved over 500 volunteers in its own survey of yew and beech trees. These species were chosen as native, easily identifiable trees growing on a range of soils throughout most of Britain, which show clear symptoms. Declining yews lose needles and develop in the same pattern as other conifers, and affected beech show specific changes to their branching structure. The FoE study, published in October 1985 as *The Final Report: Tree Dieback Survey*, [20] was based on 1,638 beech trees and 1,546 yews at over 700 sites. The results showed that 69 per cent of all beech and 78 per cent of yew had some form of dieback.

FoE concluded: 'Typical symptoms of acid rain damage to trees are now widespread in Britain.' It discovered severely deformed and dying beech at Denny Wood in the New Forest, a major conservation site in an area run by the Forestry Commission, which objected to television filming of the dying trees. From Snowdonia, the National Park Officer wrote to say that, 'We see little point in completing the beech survey since so many beeches in North Wales are showing the exact symptoms you mention – i.e. small leaves, reduced leaf number (dieback) cluster twigs and leaf curl. In general many beeches, particularly those on the western edge of the Park show a general lack of vitality . . . We have also noted: 1. Unusual numbers of dead holly trees with sensecent branches or main trunks; 2. Ash trees with thin leaf canopies. Also ash and hornbeam showing very large numbers of keys (often apparently infertile) . . . 3. Sycamores with reduced leaf canopies and 10-15 year old saplings with yellowed necrotic leaves; 4. The odd Scots Pine with reduced needles; 5. Rowan showing reduced leaves and early leaf fall . . .'

Such symptoms – repeated at places up and down the country – were exactly those to be seen throughout northern and central Europe. Hollies were dying on the granite outcrop of Charnwood Forest in Leicestershire. At Llyn Brianne in mid Wales, Lodgepole pine showed extensive yellowing; on the acid sands of Surrey, beech were as deformed as those on the sandy soils of

Holland and in the worst affected areas of the Black Forest. And beech and lime showed dieback in Richmond Park. In Stoke Poges churchyard, whose large yew tree was immortalised in Thomas Gray's *Elegy Written in a Country Churchyard*, the 'yew tree's shade' was poorer than the poet had found it, as its needles were yellowing, branches drooping and canopy transparent.

Generally, said FoE, the growth scars of slow-growing beech twigs dated the onset of decline at 1965-70, while the 'fear twigs' on spruce trees had appeared from 1978 onwards. Damage was worst on exposed sites, on high ground and in rural rather than urban locations. Dieback was found on all soil types, but trees on acid sands were 'consistently bad'.

During the survey, FoE had also brought over Swedish ecologist and authority on beech trees, Professor Bengt Nilghard from Lund University in Sweden. British spruce, said Nilghard, were often 'in really bad condition', with symptoms of gas damage on older needles. Near Tintern, Sitka spruce growing on soil with a pH of 3.1 showed slight magnesium deficiency, while 'dead branches, early yellowing, brownish leaf-edges and early leaf-fall were also seen on many other tree species, eg ash, lime, chestnut and maple . . .'[21] 'Summing up,' said Nilghard, 'I must say that the only place where I have seen correspondingly bad situations in Central Europe before is around the biggest airports in West Germany.'

The British forestry establishment reacted with fury and not a little venom. After an article in *New Scientist* which summarised the findings of FoE and Nilghard, R G Pawsey wrote from the Department of Forestry in Aberdeen University that 'there is no evidence that acid rain or any other pollution factor is significantly affecting the general health of forest and other trees in this country. Dr Nilghard's proclamations,' declared Pawsey, were 'entirely spurious.'

The Forestry Commission's Director of Research, Arnold Grayson, wrote to *New Scientist*: 'To imply that we are deliberately trying to cover up evidence that trees do die back is obvious nonsense. Our concern is to see whether any new mechanism of decline is at work.'

Professor Hugh Miller, also from Aberdeen University and who had advised on the Commission's 1984 paper which questioned the link between acidity and fish losses, wrote that 'there is at present no evidence of damage' and 'When worried about the health of our trees it would seem preferable to heed qualified forest pathologists rather than respond to assorted ecologists and conservationists, no matter what their nationality.'[22]

Here, as in the pollution debates over the hazards of sewage or acidification of lakes, the Commission and its supporters were applying one line of reasoning whereas environmentalists and scientists in other countries were applying another. The view that almost everyone except the Commission subscribed to was summed up a few years later by the UN Economic Commission for Europe when it wrote in a report on damage surveys in many countries: 'Research results obtained so far indicate that air pollution is an essential, causal factor in the destabilisation of forests or even in the breakdown of some forest ecosystems.'

FoE argued that, lacking any other explanation and given abundant circumstantial evidence that pollution was bad for trees, a combination of natural and pollution stresses was the best explanation for the observed symptoms. The Commission seemed willing to call on practically any explanation except pollution.

Yet the Commission and its supporters were increasingly inconsistent. Sometimes there was no dieback or decline, at other times there was dieback but it was not connected to pollution, on occasions trees which had lost a third or more of their vegetation were normal. At Kew Gardens, an official-minded institution administered via the Ministry of Agriculture, a spokesperson neatly captured the illogical Commission view by telling a journalist who enquired about dieback of Kew's cedars, beech and yews, that 'there wasn't any dieback', and, if there was, 'it wasn't due to acid rain'.

Just like the CEGB and 'proof' of a link between pollution and damage to lakes, the Commission put up one condition after another as a 'test' of whether Britain's trees were showing decline, and then replaced it with a new argument if it was satisfied. This proved nothing in itself, but it made a mockery of the Commission's repeated claims to be particularly scientific in its approach.

1986: Britain's Trees Show Official Yellowing

In June 1986 the Commission released its own 1985 survey,[23] which now found a 'high degree of yellowing' in some Scots pine, as well as yellowing on Norway and Sitka spruce. But whereas the year before the absence of yellowing was proof that Britain did *not* have the same forest decline as in Europe, its discovery did not show that Britain *did* have the same forest decline.

Yellowing, said the Commission, was 'difficult to interpret' and might be connected to fungi or the weather. Not, this time, the 1975/6 droughts but now the coldest February in 40 years. The official press release explained that the survey showed that 'Britain's trees are in good health'. The report itself had no conclusions, so came to no conclusion about the yellowing.

In December the Commission reported on its 1986 survey. Now the Commission had changed the point of its survey. No longer was it to look for signs of forest decline, it was to investigate a link between pollution and forest decline. Although the survey found a 'worsening of tree condition' and conifer health was suddenly 'only moderate', there was, said Mr Grayson, 'No regional pattern of crown condition . . . and it is therefore difficult to ascribe the findings to a cause such as air pollution.'[24]

Yet the Commission's survey was a singularly unsuitable test of such a link. Its sites were on variable, disturbed and fertilised soils and mainly included only the less vulnerable trees. The survey was not detailed, comprehensive or controlled enough to investigate a geographical link to air pollution even if the right pollution data were available. In the rest of Europe, as Sally Power, Katy Ling and Mike Ashmore of Imperial College later pointed out, surveys 'have made little attempt to link tree health to variations in site factors, stand types or pollution climate. Instead emphasis has been placed on monitoring temporal and spatial changes in tree health. In Britain the Forestry Commission has attempted to relate variations in tree health to . . . slope, ruggedness of the site, altitude, and also to derived climatic and pollution data. No account has been taken of, amongst other things, the role of soil factors, of disturbance, or canopy density.'[25]

The body of the Commission's report, which was written by recently recruited geographer Dr John Innes, took a less bullish line than the press release. The report admitted that the survey 'does in fact show that in comparison with this year's results from West Germany, we have appreciably more trees in the slightly (11-25 per cent) and moderately (26-60 per cent) damaged categories.'[26]

While the report was acknowledging considerable dieback, the press release which accompanied it three days before Christmas (a traditional moment for government departments to 'bury' embarrassing statistics) spoke only of 'no sign . . . of the forest decline which is of such great concern in central Europe'.

At the same time as the Commission put out its 1986 study of conifers, it released its 1985 survey of beech trees. This study was organised by Commission pathologist David Lonsdale. Lonsdale found the results 'alarming', [27] but the official press release reassured the press and public that there was 'no sign' of forest decline among beech trees. Not surprisingly, many people found the whole issue thoroughly confusing.

In 1985, William Waldegrave, minister at the DoE, intervened to urge cooperation between the Commission and the Institute for Terrestrial Ecology (ITE). He didn't think FoE's study was a 'particularly good piece of scientific work' but 'didn't want to rubbish it'. In new surveys he said, a 'multi-stress' approach would be needed, while ITE's deputy director, Fred Last, commented, 'I don't agree with some of Friends of the Earth's conclusions. But many trees today have characteristics that are not healthy.' FoE's surveyors, said Last, were 'entitled to more rigorous answers' than they had been given.[28]

1987: Half a U-turn

By 1987 the European Commission had joined the UN ECE in the forest survey business and required all member states to undertake a standard grid survey, reporting on a set number of trees at regular 16 km intervals, using a common method. The Forestry Commission did the survey in Britain. When the results for beech trees were disclosed, they were almost identical to those of the much criticised FoE survey of 1985.

The grid survey showed that the majority of Britain's deciduous trees, and 60 per cent of all oaks, were in the 'moderately damaged' categories, having lost 26-60 per cent of their leaves. As to its own survey, which was now harmonized with those of 15 other countries contributing to the UN ECE study, the Commission's John Innes stated in its *Bulletin* 74 that: 'This report, together with those from previous years, indicates that both crown thinning and the yellowing of needles, the two symptoms most frequently associated with forest decline on the continent, are present in Britain. The extent of crown thinning and discolouration in Britain is similar to that in West Germany.'[29]

So forest decline had officially arrived in Britain? Well, not quite. Just as *Bulletin 74* was being published, a Forestry Commission booklet *Air Pollution and Forests* stated 'there is no sign of the type of damage seen in West Germany, occurring in Britain at the moment'. Although some of its own experiments were now showing that air pollution in southern England damaged leaves and made them fall early from trees, it could not bring itself to say as much. Instead, the Commission indulged in some verbal gymnastics with: 'This work is beginning to suggest that some types of tree grow better in air that has most of the pollution removed from it.'

Nevertheless, whichever way the statistics were presented, surveys showed that Britain's trees had as many deformations, lost leaves, stunted branches and thin and discoloured canopies as those in the supposedly worst-affected continental countries.

1988: A Faint Connection

In February 1988 the House of Commons Environment Committee returned to the topic of acid rain in its Air Pollution inquiry. By now, the Commission had retreated on the existence of symptoms, and adapted its surveys to include older and more exposed trees of a greater range of species. It had also begun open-top chamber experiments in which pollutants are filtered from the air so that tree growth can be compared in 'ambient' (polluted) and clean conditions.

The Committee chairman, Sir Hugh Rossi MP, asked the Forestry Commission's research director, Arnold Grayson, 'Are you coming to the conclusion that there may be some connection in the United Kingdom between the condition of trees and pollutants?' 'Very faintly,' replied Grayson, referring to experimental evidence that the fine roots of Scots pine grow less and the leaves of poplars fall earlier in ambient than in unpolluted air.[30]

As to other evidence, despite the fact that other countries and other scientists believe a more detailed approach is needed, the Commission persisted in using survey data to look for proof or a lack of proof that pollution was the cause of leaf-loss and canopy thinning. There was, said Grayson, 'no such indication'.

Rossi pointed out that the Commission's denial of a link between forest decline and pollution was 'quite contrary' to evidence from others and 'the Swedes, Norwegians and Germans who fear that there is a very, very direct connection'. Pointing to the Commission's admission that the key symptoms in Britain were now 'similar' to those in West Germany, Rossi expressed surprise that the Commission was 'apparently no further forward than in 1984'.

Why did the Commission's own publications catalogue the effects that NOx, SO_2 and ozone could have on trees, until 'one could scarcely but come to the conclusion that there is a strong connection between atmospheric pollution and damage,' yet 'we are still talking about not being satisfied.'

Grayson cited 'fungi, insects and so forth'. His colleague Dr Freer-Smith said, 'in many areas of West Germany there is evidence to link specific pollutants as a major causal factor; but I also think the Germans would accept that there are both natural and pollutant stresses interacting – the idea that has been referred to as the multiple stress hypothesis.' Not surprisingly the Germans would accept this, they had proposed it when the Commission had by turns been denying the existence of damage in West Germany and demanding proof based on a single pollutant (rather than multiple stress).

Freer-Smith added, 'The problem with surveys is that you cannot establish a causal relationship.' Unfortunately, in its public statements, the Commission had never shown such scientific rectitude, preferring such comments as 'these results give Britain's forests a clean bill of health'.

And only with extreme reluctance would the Commission agree that pollution should be reduced. FGD would bring only 'small' benefits in terms of forest growth said the Commission, 'in relation to the expenditure involved'. When, asked Henry Bellingham MP, 'did the Forestry Commission first urge the government to reduce emissions of both NOx and SO_2?' The answer: 'we have not done so.'[31]

Taking up evidence from Greenpeace which simply drew figures from the national forest surveys coordinated by the UN ECE and EC [32], Sir Hugh wanted to know if the Forestry Commission accepted that 'the beech forests of Britain are among the worst affected in Europe'. Mr Grayson replied: 'If we can assume that the same degree of care is taken in all countries showing – and I think it is true, certainly, of Switzerland and West Germany – beech observations, then you could certainly say that the health of beech trees reflected in crown condition must be borne out by observation.'

The Commission persisted in arguing that, as it was impossible to put a precise figure on what was a 'normal' and an 'abnormal' amount of leaf loss, it was impossible to conclude whether or not thin tree crowns were abnormal. 'It could be argued,' commented MP Andrew Hunter, 'that wherever there could be uncertainty, you are hiding behind it.'

In its 1988 survey, the Commission found that 'the condition of trees is poor' but 'no trend can be established', so it was 'not possible to determine . . . whether the trees in the United Kingdom are in a state of decline'. There was, however, 'increasing concern [in Europe] about the role of soil acidification' (it was not mentioned that this has been caused by air pollution). The report ended enigmatically: 'a potential problem exists . . . it is clear that air pollution, particularly in the form of acidic deposition, is affecting many aspects of forest ecosystems in Britain and there is an obvious need for continued detailed monitoring.'[33]

1989: The Imperial College Study

The Forestry Commission's 1989 survey showed a slight improvement in tree condition, attributed to recovery from 1987's storm damage and a wet, mild summer. Privately some Commission officials argued for an upbeat press statement saying that Britain's trees were recovering (or improving), whereas others, suspecting that 1989's autumn/winter drought would cause further leaf loss in 1990, were against it. Either way, the survey could do little to determine what really accounted for the state of Britain's trees. Over a third of the beech, for example, showed 11–60 per cent leaf loss.[34]

Also completed in 1989 was the first large-scale specialist study of beech and Scots pine growing not in Forestry Commission tree plantations but on natural or semi-natural soils. Funded jointly by the NCC and the FC, Sally Power, Katy Ling and Mike Ashmore from the Silwood Park research centre of Imperial College surveyed 72 beech woods and 26 heathlands with pine, recording details of soil pH, drainage and other site factors, as well as crown thinness, crown architecture (i.e. branching structure) and the discolouration of needles and leaves.[35]

The Imperial College survey avoided the ecological shortcomings of the Forestry Commission's census. The trees it examined were growing in soil conditions much closer to those of most European forests, and the woodlands and heaths studied were among the most important in lowland England for conservation. Among the 72 beech sites surveyed, 32 were designated Sites of Special Scientific Interest (SSSIs), National Nature Reserves or Local Nature Reserves. One was in an Area of Outstanding Natural Beauty, and only 14 were managed by the Forestry Commission. The sites included such famous names as Epping Forest, Burnham Beeches, Denny Inclosure in the New Forest, Oxfordshire's Wychwood and Selborne Hanger in Wiltshire.

To try and separate the effects of environmental variables from those of atmospheric pollution, the Imperial College researchers made a special study of the Chilterns, where there are a large number of beech woods on differing combinations of 'soil, slope and aspect within a more or less constant pollution climate'.

Overall, Ling and Power found approximately 25 per cent of beech in the worst two categories of deformity of branching. Clusters of beech woods with particularly reduced vitality were found in the Chilterns and Devon, while trees with very thin crowns were found in a band running from northeast of London through the Chilterns to the New Forest. Beech in the Cotswolds, Forest of Dean and south Wales had particularly thin crowns compared with trees in East Anglia and Kent.

With their more detailed study methods, Ling and Power found that growth deformation and the general thinning of the tree crown seemed to be responding to two different environmental influences. The soil's calcium content, rooting depth and texture showed no correlation with crown thinness, but the worst trees were growing on acid soils while those with the fullest canopy were found on soils with pH above 5.5. 'Crown architecture', or deformation of the branches, was also connected with acidity – trees doing best on soils of pH 7 or above – but not affected by calcium. Trees on sites liable to waterlogging showed particularly abnormal branching structure. In contrast, 'chlorosis' of the canopy – pale leaves – is connected to calcium, either through lime-induced chlorosis (as iron becomes unavailable at high pH) or on acid soils of low calcium content.

Having found that 'site factors' such as soil acidity had a major influence on the state of trees, the Imperial College team checked their results against the standard computer models of pollution – the same ones which are used (without accounting for soil and other site factors) in analysing the Forestry Commission's surveys. An immediately noticeable result was a strong connection between dry-deposited pollutants and sulphur compounds. On closer examination this turned out to be due to just one variable: sulphur dioxide. But, while woods exposed to high levels of the gas seemed to have thin canopies, unpicking the figures yet more showed the statistical relationship was due to just four of the most polluted sites. Not only did the correlation vanish when these were removed from the analysis, but the relationship also disappeared if the Warren Spring Laboratory model was replaced by the Harwell model.

So sulphur dioxide may or may not affect the density of the beech tree canopies. It would take more detailed research to discover what is going on, and Sally Power is now subjecting 16 beech sites to a closer analysis, studying soil conditions, root vitality and the nutrient content of leaves.

The moral of the sulphur dioxide correlation is that fitting statistical analyses to forestry data is not nearly as reliable as taking measurements on site. It indicates, perhaps, why the Forestry Commission's extensive pollution-census comparisons have yet to produce any results which seem to match experimental or indicative evidence.

However, the Imperial College study did come up with some firmer indications. Ammonia gas levels were negatively correlated with crown architecture in beech and needle browning in Scots pine. Crown chlorosis, thinness and architecture were all negatively linked to the local intensity of the 1976 drought, but only on acid and not on calcareous soils. All acidic sites showing correlations between pollution and tree health showed a negative impact at higher levels. In contrast, on the alkaline soils tree health was better at higher pollution levels.

So for some reason, perhaps directly connected with the underlying mechanism of damage, it seems that the soil pH determines the effect of an air pollutant. (Both Ulrich and Professor Ernst-Detlef Schulze of Bayreuth University propose that it is the chemistry of soils in drought conditions which drives a pulse of soil acidification, while the CEGB has recently proposed that drought slows litter decay, resulting in a shortage of available magnesium. The 1976 drought also coincided with record ozone levels.)

Another interesting aspect of the Imperial College study was the difference between sites of different categories. In the words of Ling, Power and Ashmore, 'trees at the fourteen Forestry Commission sites were found to be in substantially better health than those at the remaining 58 sites, as judged by all three major tree health parameters. One important reason for this may be that the mean tree age at the Forestry Commission sites was substantially lower (by 23 years) than the mean age for all the other sites' (which were SSSIs and nature reserves).[36]

'The critical factor', say the authors, 'seems to be that Forestry Commission sites are primarily on soils of intermediate pH.' No doubt this is good for growing trees, but it probably also goes some way to explain why the Forestry Commission's census work has failed to explain anything about the evident decline of many British trees.

The health of beech trees, indicated by crown thinness and crown architecture, was also significantly worse on the 32 sites designated nature reserves or SSSIs, probably due to the more sensitive soils of such woodlands. (Most nature reserves are on nitrogen-poor soils and many rare plant species are restricted to them, while most richer soils have been taken for farmland.) It seems there is a disaster in the making for conservation, or, more accurately, a disaster is under way, even though few if any of the nature conservation groups have shown much interest in it. 'It should be also noted,' say Ling, Power and Ashmore, 'that many of the sites in poorest health are of high conservation value. Thus of the 27 worst affected sites (as judged by a combination of crown thinness and architecture) twelve were SSSIs, including sites such as Denny Wood, Burnham Beeches, Epping Forest and the Cotswolds Commons and Beechwoods. . . the very poor health of trees at some sites of high national conservation value must be of particular concern.'

As Ling and her co-workers point out, the progressive defoliation of trees has considerable implications for the whole woodland ecosystem. At the time of writing, Katy Ling and Mike Ashmore have just finished another study which shows considerable changes in the ground flora of the Chiltern beech-woods. As the canopy becomes more transparent, some shade-tolerant species disappear and others become more common. But, significantly, many rare nitrogen-intolerant species found by botanist A S Watt in the woods in the 1930s are now nowhere to be seen, while nitrogen-loving and acid-tolerant species are found in their place.

In Epping Forest, purple moor grass now grows under dying beech where previously there was nothing but a complete cover of leaf litter. Here and in Burnham Beeches near Slough, the acid-tolerant 'hedgehog' moss *Leucobryum glaucum* is spreading over the forest floor. As the trees lose their leaves, the ground surface may also become wetter as their capacity to utilise water is reduced.

Unfortunately most of these changes are merely natural history observations. While the Forestry Commission spends 5 per cent of its research budget on chamber experiments and running statistics through computers, very little cash is available to look for effects in the field.

The Causes of Forest Decline

Nobody knows exactly what causes forest decline, but that does not mean that it does not exist. As late as 1988 the Forestry Commission was arguing that, because it lacked an 'objective idea of a standard' for a totally healthy tree canopy, it was not possible to be certain if a decline was taking place or not.[37] When pressed by Dr Derek Langslow of the Nature Conservancy Council at a 1988 DoE coordinating meeting to say what percentage of defoliation would indicate an unhealthy tree, Arnold Grayson referred the question to an official, who then, to the amusement of other civil servants and environment groups present, passed it back to him as a 'policy' matter.

In their 1988 monitoring report, the Commission rightly states that it is not possible to determine from comparing one or two years' British results with those from Europe whether 'the trees in the United Kingdom are in a state of decline'.[38] But that is a false question, because there are other ways of finding out whether or not forest *has declined*. One fairly obvious way is to look at the ground flora. No computer analysis is required to detect this phenomenon.

Something has certainly happened to the trees, and, measured in terms of defoliation or crown thinness, there has been a marked decline.

Andrew Tickle, another researcher from Mike Ashmore's stable at Imperial College and now a campaigner for Greenpeace, conducted a one-man survey of beech, oak and yew in nine southern English counties during two weeks in August and September 1988.[39] He found similar results to FoE and the Forestry Commission. Over a third of the beech, 45 per cent of the oak and 64 per cent of the yew were in the 26–60 per cent defoliation category.

In 1988, Tickle was fresh from his PhD research and writing in the careful language of academia. 'Local stress factors such as . . . particulate and gaseous vehicle emissions' were 'likely to have a strong adverse influence' on trees near large roads.

Tickle's carefully organised survey found little favour with Peter Freer-Smith of the Forestry Commission. 'We certainly consider it an unscientific leap straight through data on the state of Britain's trees to assumptions about one particular cause,' he said.[40] In contrast, Professor Mike Unsworth of Nottingham University described it as a 'very good piece of work', while the Earl of Caithness at the DoE similarly wanted to 'congratulate the author on the objective approach'. Caithness added: 'I am immediately struck by the broad similarity of the Greenpeace and Forestry Commission results for beech and oak.'

The Tree Council, an umbrella organisation which runs National Tree Week and whose members are dominated by forestry or silvicultural groups, many of whom had reacted with vitriol when forest decline in the British countryside had been first mentioned, now wrote of 'a consensus that high proportions of the trees at many [of the] sites surveyed showed serious symptoms of decline. Many factors affect tree health and rigorous scientific proof of the precise way in which they contribute, singly and in combination, to the problem is still some years away. But it already seems very probable that air pollution is an important factor and that its reduction would be beneficial. To wait for full proof before taking action would risk irreparable damage to the nation's trees.'[41]

The Tree Council also wrote to the Prime Minister. Its view was now much the same as that of governments throughout northern Europe. Mrs Thatcher now referred to progress on the NOx Protocol committing Britain to 'basing NOx control policies from the mid-1990s on the "critical loads" below which damage does not occur'. This may not be as encouraging as it sounds.

While most of Britain's 'partners' in Europe favour action now, Britain has been one of those dragging its feet over setting NOx targets, and 'from the mid-1990s' is hardly rapid action. Second, the DoE is helping coordinate work to set critical loads but will then propose action based on 'target loads'. These target loads may turn out to be far higher than the critical loads. They may be set so as to permit Britain to continue with 'business as usual'.

If, however, Britain does decide to adopt the precautionary principle, there will be no shortage of evidence to call on.

One of the more persuasive pieces of evidence that tree decline reflects a major long-term ecosystem change and not just the vagaries of weather conditions comes from studies of tree rings. A German white fir which died damaged in 1982 for example, showed normal growth from the 1890s before a sudden slowing of growth in 1958. The annual rings became very close together, and eventually, after two decades of very slow growth, the tree died.[42] Swiss forest studies showed that spruce trees visibly dying in the 1980s had become progressively more slow growing than their healthier contemporaries from the hard winter of 1962–3 onwards. The cold winter of 1948–9 caused a reduction in growth but there was a recovery. By the time of the 1976 drought, the sickening spruce were already lagging further and further behind. A similar pattern appeared in fir.[43]

In central Switzerland, some spruce trees which are now dying started growing slowly in the 1950s. Beech at 51 forest sites in the country showed slowing from the dry summers of 1983 and 1985 and in some cases from 1981, although detailed investigations by Dr Walter Fluckiger found no direct correlation between top shoot growth and the amount of soil water or rainfall.[44] In West Germany, Dr Andreas Roloff has shown that many declining beech forests undergo a prolonged period of very slow shoot growth.

Britain has few such studies, although the Forestry Commission has placed a contract with the Climate Research Unit at the University of East Anglia to research in this area.

Recently Dr David Lonsdale, the Commission's beech pathologist, has also conducted a survey of extension growth (i.e. twigs) in beech trees.[45] Lonsdale and his colleagues studied beech growth in 15 forests along a pollution gradient, from high pollution levels in East Anglia to low levels in southwest England. They looked at trees aged 70-150 years old, and examined their crowns and growth rings and shoot extension by cutting down five trees at each site. To detect decline as opposed to effects of age or site extreme factors, the study avoided very acid or alkaline soils (below pH 4 or above pH 7.5), and the analysis allowed for an automatic slowing in growth as trees get older. This done, the 'growth trajectories' of three age groups of tree were plotted back to 1955.

As would be expected, the analysis showed a clear effect of drought years. But when the post-drought seasons (when the worst damage is seen) of 1976, 1977, 1978, 1984 and 1985 were removed along with age, significant extra growth declines were found to have started at seven of the 15 plots, beginning in years from 1971 to 1979, continuing right up to the last year studied, which was 1986. At another two sites, significant reductions had occurred between 1961–9 and 1975–83. Although by 1986 no trees were showing significant growth increases, at three plots there was evidence for synchronous improvements in the years 1969–82, 1969–75 and 1962–73.

Nevertheless, the overall 'occurrence of sustained downward shifts before the 1975–6 drought is of particular interest,' he says,' and parallels the onset of "pre-drought" declines in West Germany.' Lonsdale and his colleagues discuss possible tree damage from ozone – a pollutant of the 1970s onwards – as a cause of the decline.

Greenpeace was aware of Lonsdale's work and drew it to the attention of the House of Commons Environment Committee. Peter Pike MP asked Arnold

Grayson, the Commission's director of research, about it. The work was still being analysed, said Grayson, but, 'We can say . . . that we do not think anything abnormal was happening before 1975.'[46] As we have seen, just the opposite conclusion was reached by Lonsdale in the version of his results sent for publication.

Scientists at Lancaster University and the Forestry Commission have been using open- top chambers to study the impact of air pollution mixtures on trees for more than ten years. In an experiment organised by P H Freer-Smith, from the Commission, and G Taylor and M Dobson, from Lancaster University, four groups of young beech trees were exposed to the summer air at Headley, Hampshire, while four others in similar chambers received air sucked in through a carbon filter to remove pollutants such as ozone.[47] Sitka spruce were given the same treatment.

The stomata (leaf pores for the gases and water vapour involved in photosynthesis and respiration) of trees grown in unfiltered air became progressively affected as the summer wore on, impairing the tree's ability to feed itself and control its water balance. The roots of beech exposed to normal air were noticeably smaller than those growing in the cleaned air. 'The most interesting discovery,' say the experimenters, was that 'reduced biomass of roots was increased by increased root length in the unfiltered treatment.' Beech trees in the polluted air produced longer, thinner roots which will be more vulnerable to drought stress since they will lose their strength and be prone to dehydration. The Imperial College researchers now concentrating on 16 beech sites in detail are also finding indications that the roots of declining beech trees are as affected as the parts above ground.

So, slowly and painfully, Britain's official scientists are confirming what continental and American scientists said some years before. Nevertheless, with the run-down of *Waldsterben* research in countries such as West Germany, Britain's painstaking entry into research on forest decline may yet leave it an expert latecomer.

Among those now uncovering the exact mechanisms of pollution processes and incidents are Dr David Fowler and his colleagues at the Institute of Terrestrial Ecology. At Bush research station near Edinburgh, Fowler has found 'substantial evidence' that the acid mists of mountain-tops and high altitudes which form in polluted conditions can damage the frost-hardening mechanisms in Norway spruce and beech. The result will be increased damage following frosty winters. Ozone also affects stomata, photosynthesis and frost tolerance.[48]

At a seminar organised by the Natural Environment Research Council in 1988 Fowler explained that the acidity of clouds formed along hills in the Pennines was often eight times more acid than rain in the same region, while the droplets deposited on vegetation at the top of the hill might be four times more polluted than those at the base of the hill.[49]

Such findings – together with the marked changes in soil properties over short distances – may well explain the localised severity of forest decline. In the Alps, for example, not only is ozone well known to occur at much higher concentrations on more days at higher altitudes, but long-lasting fog layers deposit thick coatings of polluted mist on trees at certain altitudes, while, just above the layer of cloud, there is severe exposure to winds which may bring long-range pollution.

In Britain, tree damage is often noticeably worst on hill tops. Trees here may be more often droughted (though not necessarily vulnerable to drought) and also receive most pollution. This is the case between London and Southampton, part of England's beech-belt of tree decline. As long ago as 1981, Dr Jean Emberlein was able to show (by putting a chemical tracer into the fuel of Fawley power station on the Solent) that on southwesterly winds the Downs even 25 km away received very high levels of sulphur dioxide pollution in the power station plume – at over 100 ug/m^3 – while a valley a mere 4 km further on received less than a sixth as much.[50]

Detecting such episodes as the wind moves round, as the influence of one source overtakes that of another and as air chemistry changes with the weather, requires continuous monitoring at each site. Sometimes, however, scientists happen to be in the right place at the right time, almost by accident. On 9 September 1989 David Fowler was doing fieldwork in Lincolnshire. He later told James Erlichman at the *Guardian* that there was 'a sudden change in the wind and a strong north-easterly with heavy mist droplets began to blow. We noticed, in a matter of hours, corrosion on brand new aluminium instruments we were using.'[51]

Fowler suspected very high levels of nitric and sulphuric acid. The mist turned thousands of hawthorn trees brown across a wide area of Lincolnshire between Ingoldmells and Theddlethorpe. The pollution was attributed to a build-up of emissions from cars and factories during warm stable weather over Europe, followed by exposure to the cold North Sea (creating mist). Later it was discovered that a region from Great Yarmouth to the Humber had been affected: more than 1,000 square miles.[52]

The pollution episode was over within a matter of hours. None of the official monitoring networks are equipped to detect mist rather than rain or dry deposition. If it had not been for luck, it would have gone unnoticed and the damage would probably have been put down to the weather.

The cause-and-effect mechanisms of forest decline will probably include such short-term pollution episodes, as well as long-term processes, which may be progressive and erosive (for example, leaching of calcium or magnesium from the forest system) or accumulative (such as build-up of nitrogen or sulphur). Weather will interact with them all.

In Ulrich's 'acidification pulses' during years of drought and warmth, higher temperatures increase the activity of soil organisms more than they do the metabolism of the trees. Rewetting dry soil has the same effect. The rate of formation of nitric acid exceeds the rate of uptake by the plant, leading to acidification. Nitrate rises and then falls, but when aluminium also rises it does not completely return to its former low levels, and the pH declines. Such studies have yet to be undertaken under beech woods in Britain. At Solling, Ulrich has also shown sulphate saturation: after 1977, soils which had been accumulating sulphate began to release it into groundwater as their capacity to hold more was exceeded.[53] This has been shown in the UK, although in unafforested soils.

In Switzerland, Walter Fluckiger has measured the interaction between afflicted beech trees and the soil, as polluted rains falls on them.[54] He found that potassium flowing down the trunk was present at up to 20 times the level in the incoming rain. 'The trees are exchanging potassium versus protons,' he says. In other words, to maintain a certain pH, the trees are moving metal ions from one place to another.

This does not explain tree damage symptoms, but it does show a response between pollution and the metabolism of the tree. When Fluckiger exposed the leaves of beech seedlings to acid mist, he found protons (hydrogen ion acidity) being pushed out from the roots, acidifying the rhizosphere (root zone), as the seedling sought to maintain its acid balance. It is here in the immediate root zone that the mycorrhizae or root fungi live, on which the tree depends for mineral nutrients. There is evidence that mycorrhizae don't like acidity or high nitrogen levels. The sudden 'disassociation' of mycorrhizae or death of root hairs may be one of the triggers that sends a tree into visible decline.

Many mycorrhizal fungi show themselves above ground as toadstools (their fruiting bodies). One is the well-known scarlet and white-spotted death cap. While poisonous to people, it helps provide birch trees with mineral nutrients. But evidence from the Netherlands shows that from 1912 to 1982, of 130 mycorrhizal fungi known from particular woodlands, 55 declined and not one species increased. The largest decline was among 29 species that live with coniferous trees: of these, 19 declined and none increased.[55]

It is at this level – the individual wood and the actual plant – that the mechanisms of forest decline are likely to be worked out. Statistical abstractions and averages may be very useful for deducing critical loads for soils or describing pollution climates but they are at too large a scale to disentangle the cause and effect by which one tree dies while its neighbour does not. At Wahgheningen University in the Netherlands, experiments have shown that mycorrhizal fungi conferred protection against copper and zinc toxicity, which may accompany acidification, as well as helping resist drought. A row of fir, pine, spruce or beech may look identical but below ground they could be associated with up to 20 different fungal partners. Their response to pollutants could well depend on which.[56]

The below-ground cooperation between fungi and trees is just one element of the ecosystem that is known to interact with pollution. Flowers, grasses, mosses and lichens can all respond more quickly than trees and it is known, for example, that nitrogen-loving species such as nettle, fireweed and raspberry have multiplied while others sensitive to acidification, such as cowslip and ladies bedstraw, have gone missing from polluted Swedish forests.[57]

The Swedes have also measured the progressive loss of needles from the canopy of declining forest, and shown a much reduced density of canopy-dwelling spiders in winter. These spiders form the main food for songbirds in winter, who in turn may be more vulnerable to predation by owls if they have to spend more time searching for food in thinner canopies.

Evidence of long-term tree decline has also come from North America, where the Appalachian Mountains, the New Jersey pine Barrens and the

Canadian maple sugar forests are all affected. Red spruce has grown 30-50 per cent slower during the past 10 years compared with the 30-year reference period 1932-61, and on areas such as Camels Hump mountain large areas are dead and dying.[58]

The UK Terrestrial Effects Review Group, convened by the DoE, notes that there is West German 'evidence of increased leaching [by acid rain in the narrow sense] from ozone pre-damaged trees'. [59] If substantiated, say the group, the ozone-acid rain link 'could have serious long-term consequences in nutrient deficient ecosystems'. As we have seen from the Imperial College survey, this could mean the loss of many of the most attractive and best-loved nature reserves or recreation woodlands. There seems little point buying land and putting a fence around it, if it then changes out of recognition as a result of air pollution.

The Critical Levels working group of the UN ECE has set a benchmark for damage by nitrogen dioxide in the presence of ozone and sulphur dioxide as an annual average of 30 ug/m^3 (16 ppb), and for exposure 95 per cent of the time of 95 ug/m^3 (50 ppb).[60] The 16 ppb value is exceeded in a wide area around London, in the East Midlands and near Manchester.[61] For ozone, the critical level depends on duration of exposure – for an eight-hour period, it is 60 ppb. Between April and September 1987, the 60 ppb level was exceeded more than 100 times in the southeast corner of England around Lullington Heath in Kent, over 50 times across much of central England and over 60 times in the Merseyside-Manchester region. Even as far north as Edinburgh and as far west as mid Wales, the level was breached more than 50 times, while land within miles of John O'Groats received doses over 60 ppb on up to 30 occasions.

Acting on its own, the critical level for sulphur dioxide is set at an annual mean value of 20 ug/m^3, or 7 ppb. Above 30 microgrammes (11.5 ppb), growth declines are detected in sensitive crop plants, but it is expected that forest decline will occur above this level. A daily critical level has been set at 70 ug/m^3 (27 ppb). The whole of the East Midlands and the Sheffield-Manchester region probably exceeds the 7 ppb level, together with part of north Kent. Many scattered locations will receive far high levels in episodes.

To set these levels, dozens of scientists from many countries scoured the literature to review the state of knowledge on everything from the impact of a seven-hour exposure of silver fir to sulphur dioxide, to a 60–week exposure of small-leaved lime to ozone. The levels are regularly exceeded at a large number of sites throughout the UK.

Critical loads for nitrogen and sulphur for forest ecosystems, soils and lakes are also exceeded across large parts of Britain (see Chapter 4).

Conclusions on Forest Decline

Although nobody yet has the whole picture, it seems clear that some of Britain's most ecologically important forests are in decline, even if some forestry plantations with young trees and rich soils are not. From denying the very existence of less than healthy trees, the Forestry Commission is now producing evidence which reveals a very similar history of decline to that found in West Germany.

The history of Britain's five-year U-turn over the existence of forest decline within its shores would be mildly amusing if it had not helped justify delays in government action to reduce pollution. The strange behaviour of the Forestry Commission, like the exact mechanisms of *Waldsterben*, remains a deep woodland mystery.

In an interview with Thames TV News in 1989, Sir Hugh Rossi said:

> 'We've come to the conclusion that there is no doubt that atmospheric pollution, whether you call it acid rain or something else, does contribute greatly to the damage that is now becoming more and more evident amongst trees right across the world. . . We've been to Sweden, we've been to West Germany, we've been to Norway. We've studied a great deal of literature produced all over the world, and we've come to the conclusion that the Forestry Commission is out of step with everybody else and I simply don't understand why.'

The best explanation seems to be a combination of climatic influences (mainly political) and site history (mainly institutional). The capacity of any such unaccountable public body to resist unwanted evidence presented from the outside and to obstruct investigation is not a phenomenon restricted to the Forestry Commission. It has, however, done nothing at all to help Britain's international environmental reputation.

In 1989, Greenpeace published a report, *Margaret's Favourite Places*, [62] which tracked the Prime Minister's move from the corner shop in Grantham, via Somerville College, Oxford, to a job in plastics in Manningtree, Essex, and on via Dartford, to Parliament, Finchley, Chequers and Dulwich, documenting dying trees at each location. 'Dear Prime Minister,' wrote Tickle in the introduction, 'You're probably far too busy to take much notice of the state of the trees in some of your favourite places. But . . . the great majority . . . are unlikely to outlive your children, let alone your grandchildren. . . Knowing your love of trees and the symbolism they hold for you, we hope you'll encourage your Government to act now to ensure the continuity of our heritage.'

On 30 October the Prime Minister replied.[63] She had read the report 'with interest', as did her 'colleagues in the Department of the Environment'. She welcomed Greenpeace's concern but had to point out that surveys such as those coordinated by the UN ECE (which indicated a high degree of damage in the UK) were misleading because 'standards tend to be applied more rigorously in some countries than others and because every species has its own natural geographical range, so its 'natural' health varies from country to country.' Nothing more was heard of the matter until on 22 March 1990, in a speech at the conclusion of the SWAP project at the Royal Society, Thatcher decided to pick on *Margaret's Favourite Places* 'as an example of hasty judgement' to illustrate pressure groups' urging government action 'without an adequate appreciation of the facts and underlying science'.

Greenpeace, said Thatcher, claimed that 'the damage . . . had been caused by acid rain'. The 'Forestry Commission's own scientists,' Thatcher told her audience, were 'intrigued' and 'they went out to see for themselves'. They found 'in all but one case, this was because of their age or changes to the condition of the site – *not* to air pollution as Greenpeace had claimed'.

On the face of it, the Royal Society had heard, as they might expect, another case of government scientists putting right outlandish claims from a pressure group. The truth was rather different. Greenpeace director, Lord Melchett, wrote to Thatcher pointing out that the report 'was not a scientific document; that was stated quite plainly within the text' and that it, like Thatcher's own initial reply, had identified air pollution as a possible 'contributing factor'. What is more, Greenpeace's own scientifically organised survey had been welcomed by the Environment Minister and Professor Unsworth.

Furthermore, Greenpeace had discovered from the DoE that, far from going to investigate itself, the Forestry Commission had been asked to look into *Margaret's Favourite Places* by 10 Downing Street. The Commission's own air pollution expert declined to do so, as he had previously been sent to spend several days checking a Greenpeace survey of trees in Cecil Parkinson's constituency, only to confirm their findings. Instead, the Commission sent an arboriculturalist specialising in disorders of amenity trees. 'You apparently based your remarks on a survey by someone with inadequate scientific expertise. We assume your attack on Greenpeace was designed to draw attention from the UK government's appalling record in reducing acid emissions,' said Melchett. At the time of writing, he had received no reply.

CHAPTER 6

Pollution from Traffic

Traffic smog is rising above cities and downwind of conurbations all over the world. But because cars and trucks are an international market, setting stricter technology standards demands international action, and here Britain's record has once again included delay and opposition.

In 1950, vehicle emissions were a minor problem. There were just over 2 million cars on Britain's roads. By 1988, there were 20 million and by 2025 there are predicted to be 50 million or more.[1] UK car sales rose to record levels in the late 1980s, topping 2.3 million by 1988, with over 5,000 new cars hitting the streets every day. Of course, it is not just Britain that is affected. There were 50 million cars in the world in 1950. Now there are almost 408 million, and there may be half a billion by the end of the century.[2]

In 1987, transport consumed 29 per cent of delivered energy consumed in the UK and 42 per cent of all 'end user' energy in terms of cost. Road traffic is by far the largest fuel user (76 per cent, only 3 per cent of which is public transport).

While other forms of transport also produce pollution (rail transport, for example, yields 1.5 per cent of NOx emissions), in terms of both sheer volume and per passenger-kilometre, road transport is overwhelmingly polluting. Air travel is also a significant and growing source of pollution which has received almost no attention. For every 100 passenger-km travelled, a typical commuter car or an aircraft uses 9 litres of fuel, a motor cycle 5, a bus 1.4 and a high speed train 0.9.

In 1989, Earth Resources Research (ERR) produced the first comprehensive study of transport pollution in Britain for the World Wide Fund for Nature (WWF). As of 1987, road transport produced 85 per cent of the UK's total emissions of carbon monoxide (4,470,000 tonnes), 45 per cent of the NOx (1,031,000 tonnes), 28 per cent of the hydrocarbons (664,000 tonnes) and 18 per cent of all carbon dioxide (98,000,000 tonnes).[3] The average car has been estimated to produce more than a quarter of a tonne of pollution every year,[4] and more than 10,000 separate chemicals have been found in car exhaust.[5] ERR's team – Malcolm Fergusson, Claire Holman and Mark Barrett – point out that 'a person commuting by car typically uses over six times as much fuel as they would travelling by bus'. Simply increasing the 'load factor' by filling up vehicles is an obvious way to increase efficiency and reduce pollution.

Schemes to encourage car sharing do exist and work well in other countries.

In Washington DC, for example, cars must be fully occupied to use the fast lane during the morning rush hour. In the UK, the average commuting car has only 1.2 passengers. If two car drivers shared a car, they would reduce their overall pollution by 60 per cent.[6] But the largest pollution reductions will clearly be made by use of public transport: a car driver switching to the train or bus may cut their pollution as much as 18-fold (95 per cent), and certainly 50 per cent. Cycling or walking, of course, create no pollution.

Because of the way fuel gets burnt in the engine, the speed of travel has a great influence on the quantity of pollution created. Above 30 kph (19 mph), the faster a vehicle goes, the more carbon dioxide and NOx it produces per kilometre travelled. (More carbon monoxide and hydrocarbons are emitted at lower than higher speeds.) The increase is especially great at higher speeds. 'In the UK,' says energy analyst Mark Barrett, 'the average motorway speed is 65 mph, yet, with a speed limit of 70 mph, 15 per cent of drivers average 80 mph. At this speed they produce over twice as much NOx per km as compared to an average car at an average speed.' [7]

Once a car runs into heavy traffic and begins to crawl along at lower than 15 kph (9 mph), it produces more NOx the slower it goes. (Emissions are measured as grams per kilometre. The slower you go, the 'higher' the emissions. But, as a result of increased fuel consumption and higher engine temperatures, at high speeds emissions also increase.) But, as we shall see, the best way (in fact, the only known way) to increase low traffic speeds within congested road networks is by increased use of public transport to create lower car density.

Petrol engines currently account for 85 per cent of pollution from road transport. The other 15 per cent comes from diesel, the vast bulk of which is accounted for by lorries (and in city centres, buses and taxis). Only 1 per cent of UK cars are diesel-engined (and 4 per cent of new cars).

Equivalent sized diesel engines produce little carbon monoxide and less hydrocarbons than petrol engine but heavy goods vehicles (HGVs) are large and produce much more. They produce about the same amount of NOx, more poly aromatic hydrocarbons (PAH) and, because of the sulphur content of diesel oil (which in the UK is 0.19 per cent [8]), a significant quantity of sulphur dioxide.[9]

Diesel exhaust is unpopular because its oily soot soils skin, clothes and buildings. The 'soiling capacity' of diesel has been estimated at 3 compared with 1 for coal smoke and 0.43 for petrol emissions, making diesel fumes about six times 'dirtier' than petrol. Diesel engines are also about 100 times smellier than petrol engines, owing to emissions of unburnt fuel, aldehydes and other compounds.

Diesel particulates are now the major source of black smoke in most urban areas (two-thirds of that in London). A study of stone decay at St Mary Le Strand, the church which stands on a road island at London's Aldwych, showed that smoke was seven times the urban background level. Thanks to the 3,000 buses, 13,000 taxis and 20,000 other vehicles which pass every day, the church is continually dusted with 'resuspended' particles that researchers believe to be old traffic emissions. Michael Schwar of London Scientific

Services says it is 'the dirtiest place in London where measurements have been made'.[10] The average sulphur dioxide level at the church was 60 per cent above nearby background. 'In London and similar cities, high sulphur at the kerbside is now due to diesel,' says Claire Holman. 'Generally high levels of sulphur are due to fuel oil in office heating systems and so on. Occasional very high episodes come from power stations outside the urban area.'

Standards and Technical Fixes

Catalysts

At present, the principal 'technical fix' to control vehicle pollution is the catalytic converter, a ceramic or metal honeycomb coated with rare metals, which fixes to the exhaust and has an internal area the size of a football pitch. The converter breaks down NOx, hydrocarbons and carbon monoxide to less harmful gases.

In keeping with its reputation, Britain was one of the countries most bitterly opposed to the introduction of catalytic converters in Europe. It opposed them at the Munich Conference on Acid Rain in 1984 and went on doing so until 1989.

This was despite the fact that a major manufacturer of the device was Johnson-Matthey, a Royston-based precious metals company. Britain even lost an order to supply landrovers to the Swiss army because Austin-Rover were incapable of supplying the vehicle with a catalyst to meet emission limits. In 1988 Johnson-Matthey announced plans to build a new factory, not in Britain where the government still opposed use of its product, but in Belgium.

As late as 1987, Friends of the Earth campaigner Adam Markham told a conference: 'Already more than a third of the world's cars are equipped with catalytic converters: that is about 130 million cars. In Britain you would find it virtually impossible to get a catalytic converter for your car. This is both because of the current government policy, which says that catalysts are not necessary, and because the availability of lead free petrol is not yet wide enough for one to be able to guarantee to get hold of it.' Tourists visiting Britain soon found this out to their cost, for, as Markham pointed out, 'Of course unleaded petrol is a prerequisite of running a catalytic converter-equipped car. The lead in petrol poisons the catalyst.'[11]

The first serious emission standards were required for all US cars in 1981 (following Californian standards in 1978). In the 1970s, the United States imposed standards that could be met with just an 'oxidative' catalytic converter breaking down hydrocarbons and carbon monoxide. The new standards set for NOx by the US Environmental Protection Agency (EPA) in 1981 forced the development of a new three-way catalyst technology which removed all three pollutants. Using a 'lambda-device' (an electronic oxygen sensor) to keep the air-fuel mixture at the 'stoichiometric' ratio of 14.7:1, three-way catalysts can remove 95 per cent of NOx, 90 per cent of hydrocarbons and 80 per cent of carbon monoxide. They have been mandatory on new US cars since 1983. They were introduced in West Germany in 1985, and were mandatory on new

Swiss cars from 1987.

Until May 1989 Britain opposed the introduction of three-way catalysts. Claire Holman has detailed the long and convoluted arguments between the UK and its European 'partners' over the issue.[12]

In June 1984 the European Commission proposed limits on car exhausts which would require US-style three-way catalysts. West Germany, which was already introducing the technology, backed the proposal, as did the Netherlands and Denmark. Britain strongly opposed such catalysts, arguing instead for lean burn engines.

Lean burn engines are more fuel efficient than normal petrol engines because they burn fuel with more air: in a mixture of around 22:1 (air:fuel). The problem was that nobody had succeeded in putting a lean burn engine on the market. And, while lean burn engines produce lower quantities of hydro-carbons and carbon monoxide, they reduce NOx by only about 50 per cent, as opposed to the 90 per cent possible with a three-way catalyst. The fuel economy of cars fitted with catalytic converters is almost identical to those without. Hertz quote tests showing 44 mpg as opposed to 45.5 mpg for a small car, 38.7 as opposed to 39.4 for a medium-sized car, and 29.7 as opposed to 30.4 for a larger car.[13] Other tests sometimes show greater fuel efficiency with a catalyst. In terms of pollution reduction, the catalyst-fitted car is certainly preferable. Performance, likewise, is not discernibly affected, taking for example, 0.4 seconds longer to get from 0 to 60 mph in a large car fitted with a catalyst while top speed in a small car was increased 0.1 second. Because three-way catalysts require a lambda sensor to operate effectively, the car needs to be fitted with electronic fuel management. Small cars which otherwise do not have this technology will become more fuel efficient.

In June 1985 the 'Luxembourg' compromise split cars into large and small engine sizes, and applied standards which would probably require catalysts but which did not need to be applied until 1988-93. Denmark stuck out for the right to apply stricter standards.

In 1986, Environment Minister William Waldegrave said the UK ruled out three-way catalysts but might require oxidation catalysts to cut hydrocarbons. Austin-Rover, trying to develop a lean burn engine, claimed a catalyst would add £1,000 to the price of a medium-sized car. By August 1987 all Volkswagens on sale in West Germany had catalysts. In December, the UK announced it would not meet the EC Directive date for emissions from large cars (1990/1) but would do so 'probably in the early 1990s'. *ENDS* magazine reported this was due to lobbying from a 'major manufacturer'.

In January 1988, Environment Minister David Trippier attacked catalysts saying that fitting them would 'entail additional costs that would not be justi-fied by the quality improvement likely to be achieved'. Strangely, even the government's own estimate now put the additional catalyst cost at £370. Britain's Society of Motor Manufacturers and Traders (SMMT) announced they would remain 'opposed to any form of catalytic converter'.

By February 1988 the EC proposed new stricter limits for small cars, at 8g of NOx plus HC per test (a standard test cycle), supported by Eire, Belgium and Luxembourg. Denmark, the Netherlands, Portugal, Greece and West

Germany wanted 5g/test which would require catalytic converters. The UK, France, Spain and Italy, wanting to protect their small but dirty cars against German or Japanese competition, pushed for more than twice as much pollution at 12g/test. By July, the Commission's proposal was adopted by majority voting, excepting France, reacting to pressure from Peugeot.

In August 1988 the UK announced it would be meeting the Directive dates for controls on small cars, but for large cars and vans catalysts would be required only three years later (1992 instead of 1989 and 1993 not 1990, respectively). The first catalyst-equipped cars went on sale in the UK in September 1988: a Toyota, followed by three Volkswagens. In 1988, 262 catalyst-equipped cars were sold in the UK. By now, however, the majority of Swedish cars, all new Austrian, Swiss, Canadian and US cars, 64 per cent of medium and large German cars and over a third of Dutch cars, had catalysts.

In September 1988, Mrs Thatcher gave her 'green speech' and the European Parliament voted for the 5g/test proposal. In November, the Council of Ministers adopted the 8g/test, with France, the UK and Spain all opposing fiscal incentives to encourage catalysts (such as tax breaks), which are used or supported by West Germany and the Netherlands.

By March 1989, 70 per cent of the public wanted government action on catalysts. The SMMT remained opposed but Vauxhall and, following a vigorous campaign by Greenpeace, Ford announced they would market catalyst-equipped cars. Using new powers to amend decisions made in the Council of Ministers, the European Parliament now reinstated the 5g/test.

In the end, the UK faced a political *fait accompli*. On 24 May 1989 Nicholas Ridley announced that the UK backed catalysts. In January 1990 a Consolidated Directive was published with US standards mandatory for all petrol cars. It also set legal limits to petrol evaporation.

Just why Britain spent years promoting lean burn engines so keenly is difficult to discover. Austin-Rover and Ford UK both promoted lean burn and suggested all sorts of problems with catalytic converters. Austin-Rover, the only remaining large-scale British car maker, had not invested in the equipment necessary to redesign its engines for unleaded petrol and to fit catalytic converters, even though its sister company Jaguar had for years been exporting catalyst-equipped cars to the USA, even to California, which had yet stricter standards. Ford UK held out the eventual prospect of a new engine plant to build lean burn engines in south Wales. Both companies had an incentive in avoiding strict standards which could be easily met by Japanese companies already pressing for greater import quotas to Europe's protected car market.

The present Directive will require all new cars under 1.4 litres to meet standards equivalent to those used in the USA since 1983 by 1 January 1993. The addition of a high-speed section to the standard 'test cycle' required by the European Commission means standards may become even tighter.

So all Britain's cars will eventually have catalytic converters. If left to itself the UK's cars would have been three to four times dirtier.

Lead in Petrol

To use catalytic converters, lead free petrol had to be widely available. This became inevitable after a 1985 Directive (85/210/EEC) which stated that each member state had to 'ensure the availability and balanced distribution within their territories of unleaded petrol from 1 October 1989', but in Britain the process was agonisingly slow. The 1985 Directive was initiated with West German support to allow the introduction of catalytic converters, which Britain opposed. Britain wanted to amend a different Directive to take lead out of petrol, following pressure from the Royal Commission on Environmental Pollution and others, as a result of Des Wilson's successful campaign at CLEAR.[14]

British environment ministers have since laid claim to having led Europe on lead. When unleaded petrol was introduced to the UK it was initially more expensive than leaded. It was only after considerable criticism from groups such as FoE that the UK government accepted the lessons of other countries and provided a price incentive of 10 pence. Yet even this was done not in the most environmentally beneficial way by increasing the price of leaded petrol (to encourage fuel conservation) but by cutting tax on unleaded (which will encourage waste). While in 1989 80 per cent of German garages sold unleaded petrol and unleaded petrol made up 56 per cent of the market, in Britain it still accounted for only 25 per cent.[15]

Diesel

For a time, sales of diesel-powered cars increased rapidly in environmentally aware countries such as West Germany, with consumers buying a 'cleaner option'. Sales are now dropping as it is realised that a petrol engine with a catalytic converter is much cleaner.

The particulate emissions from diesel are a serious health hazard (see below), and present catalyst technology will not work with diesels. 'No action has been taken to reduce emissions of particulates,' says Claire Holman, 'although it is understood that in 1985 Britain proposed to the EEC that there should be approximately a 30 per cent improvement in the smoke emission limits.'[16] Today Britain controls diesel pollution by its visible blackness. The standard is based on a quaint 1963 test in which 48 observers were paid by the Ministry of Transport to sit by the roadside as a lorry drove past, and, having been told to ignore the smell, assessed smoke exhaust as 'clear, light, medium or dark'.

In 1987 the European Community agreed standards for particulate emissions from cars, but, says Holman, these 'merely legislated on the status quo and require little cleaning up of engines'. They were three times weaker than those in force in the United States, which are met by electronically controlled fuel management. New cars with direct injection diesel engines would not need to meet them until 1996.[17]

The bulk of diesel emissions comes from heavy vehicles, mainly lorries. Under US regulations, the particulates from American trucks are to be cut sixfold between 1988 and 1994 but, apart from smoke, no European standard yet exists. Despite the black fumes visible behind many of Britain's trucks, taxis and buses, the UK's Motor Vehicles Construction and Use Regulation 22 states that 'every vehicle shall be so constructed that no avoidable smoke or visible vapour is emitted'. In theory, it is an offence to use a vehicle that has not passed a smoke emission test, but in practice, as Holman points out, 'it is used mainly as the basis for a smoke check in the annual MOT test' or other occasional checks. Every year, 13 per cent of the 200,000 vehicles tested fail these purely visual tests.

US diesel standards are now forcing the development of new technology. Johnson-Matthey is trying to develop a catalytic trap oxidiser to curb diesel emissions. One of the problems with this technology is that it oxidises sulphur in the fuel to acidic sulphate particles, which in one respect can make emissions worse not better. To overcome such problems, the USA is to reduce the sulphur content of diesel oil to 0.05 per cent, around a quarter of the British level. With new refining processes, the toxic aromatic chemicals in diesel could also be reduced by 50 per cent. [18]

Britain's two major diesel manufacturers, Perkins and Cummins, both believe they can meet the 1991 US standard. The UK, the Netherlands and West Germany all support such a standard in Europe. West Germany wants to see this by the early 1990s, the UK by the mid 1990s.

Traffic Growth and Road Building: The Engine of Destruction

Europe, with no help from Britain, has finally required state-of-the-art technology to control car pollution. Such technical fixes are necessary, but they are not enough. Lead-free petrol, catalytic converters, lean burn engines and cleaner diesels are now side-issues compared with the growth in traffic. Britain presently plans on a huge increase.

In 1989, the Department of Transport (DTp) produced estimates of traffic growth for the next 40 years showing an 83–142 per cent increase overall, comprising 82–134 per cent cars, 101–215 per cent light goods vehicles, and 67–141 per cent HGVs (with no growth in buses or coaches).[19]

In 1988, said the DTp, traffic comprised 328 billion vehicle kilometres, of which cars were 82 per cent, vans ('light goods vehicles') about 9 per cent, heavy goods vehicles 8 per cent and buses and coaches around 1 per cent.

The DTp works out its estimates on assumptions about growth in the economy, and past growth in traffic. 'Traffic on roads has increased 35 per cent since 1980,' notes the Department, 'with particularly high growth on motorways (where traffic has nearly doubled) and on trunk roads (where traffic has increased by half).' As to the future, it claims: 'As people become more prosperous they choose to acquire cars and to use them. There are still significantly fewer cars per head in this country than in the United States, France and the Federal Republic of Germany.'

The Department writes about increasing traffic as if it is an Act of God or fundamental law of the Universe about which nothing can be done. Yet traffic growth is encouraged by building new roads, and these are financed and planned by the Department itself. The fact that its own forecasts show no increase in bus traffic gives the lie to the idea that it is an inevitable process. Plainly, restraint on cars and investment in public transport would break the trend of ever-increasing car use, even if people still bought more cars. Other countries now plan on such 'trend breaching scenarios', but the UK still aims for 'saturation' and plans new roads.

Earth Resources Research created a computer model based on DTp forecasts and the known capacity of vehicles to pollute in order to predict what will happen to traffic pollution if, as the DTp plans, traffic more than doubles by the first quarter of the next century.[20] The model shows rising NOx, carbon monoxide and hydrocarbon pollution to 1992 and then a reduction until 2004 as new cars use catalytic converters. But, from then onwards, the effect of traffic growth takes over and emissions start to rise again. On the Department of Transport's own high forecast, NOx pollution will return to current levels by 2015 and increase by almost 30 per cent to around 1.4 million tonnes by 2020. On the Department's 'low' traffic forecast, car emissions on their own could fall 80 per cent by 2006, by which time all cars should have catalytic converters (assuming only 14 per cent of cars and 5 per cent of vans survive more than 14 years). But even in this optimistic scenario car emissions begin to increase after 2006, and the total NOx climbs back to 1 million tonnes, mainly owing to a massive increase from heavy goods vehicles.

'In the absence of stringent legislation HGVs will progressively dominate the total emissions from this sector,' say the modellers. They add: 'In the near future, NOx emissions seem set to rise at a higher rate than vehicle use, owing to the increasing adoption of turbocharging. This increases engine power, but approximately doubles the rate of NOx production.' Similarly, present technologies to reduce NOx from large diesel engines could increase particulates, 'a highly undesirable trade off . . . as particulates can directly impair human health.'

Although manufacturers are confident of meeting new US 1991 standards, 'There remains serious doubt whether it will be possible to meet far more stringent US legislation which is intended to come into force in 1994.' ERR concludes: 'there seems little prospect of a major improvement in the UK until new proposals can be agreed by the European Commission.'

Carbon monoxide and hydrocarbon emissions show similar patterns, although the former are reduced more effectively. However, catalytic converters do nothing to reduce emissions of carbon dioxide which, like the other pollutants, is a contributor to the greenhouse effect. The ERR/WWF study forecasts a 60–110 per cent growth in carbon dioxide from the UK transport sector by 2020.

The study's lowest estimates optimistically assume a 1 per cent annual increase in fuel efficiency from the early 1990s. While technically possible, the likelihood of this being achieved with current government policies seems remote. Present policy does not even encourage the sale of the smaller cars. Britain's 3.8 million company cars, sales of which rose from 40 per cent to over 50 per cent in the 1980s, and cars bought by self-employed people (both of which attract tax relief) now make up 60 per cent of new cars registered. Research by the group TEST (Transport and Environmental Studies) shows this taxpayer's subsidy has two effects. First, company cars tend to be 200–300cc larger than private cars. Second, they are driven further and faster. Both mean higher fuel use and more pollution. Four-fifths of cars entering London at peak times are company cars and they create almost a third of the NOx pollution in London.

In the 15 years to 1989 technical developments meant that a 50 per cent improvement in fuel consumption was possible on many car designs. The overall fuel efficiency of cars driven in Italy increased 40 per cent, in Belgium and France 25 per cent, in the USA 15 per cent. But the UK managed only a miserable 7 per cent. Britons lost the benefits of increased efficiency in car design by buying bigger, thirstier cars (by 1989 the 1500–2000 cc sizes outnumbered all other registrations). So to make real gains from fuel efficiency would mean a vigorous U-turn in Britain's present policy. Even then, traffic growth would soon need to be reduced. 'Even if the fuel efficiency of cars increased by over 30 per cent by 2020, carbon dioxide from vehicles would still increase by 20 per cent,' says EER. Enforcing the 70 mph speed limit would create a 2.5 per cent fuel saving, and a 60 mph limit would mean a 5 per cent saving.

Air traffic is also predicted to become a major source of carbon dioxide emissions. The Civil Aviation Authority anticipates a 6-7 per cent annual growth in air traffic until 2005. By 2020, CO_2 pollution from aircraft may make up 30 per cent of transport's contribution of this greenhouse gas.

Health Impacts of Pollution from Traffic

In Friends of the Earth's 1989 report *Air Pollution and Health*, Holman cites one of the last papers submitted to the Clean Air Council shortly before its abolition by the new Conservative administration of 1979. In it the Ministry of Transport claimed: 'There is no evidence that this type of pollution by motor vehicles has any adverse effect on health.'[21]

This view no longer prevails, but Britain has been much slower than other comparable countries in setting standards, limiting pollution and informing the public of hazards.

From studies of 28 air pollutants, the World Health Organisation (WHO) has set standards for ozone, sulphur dioxide, particulates, carbon monoxide and nitrogen dioxide in terms of human health. The WHO identifies the most sensitive groups as infants under 2 years of age, the elderly, pregnant women and sufferers from asthma, bronchitis, emphysema, chronic airway obstruction, angina, acute myocardial infection or other coronary heart disease. The number of people in these vulnerable categories in the USA is conservatively put at 20 per cent of the population. From the number of cases seen by British general practitioners, the report suggests that one person in five is at risk.

All these pollutants have additional sources, but road traffic is increasingly significant because it creates high concentrations where people walk, creates a cocktail of pollutants ideal for the formation of 'secondary pollutants' such as ozone, and is growing in both real and relative terms.

Particulates

Particulates are mainly elemental carbon (like charcoal) but have chemical 'nasties' such as PAH and heavy metals adsorbed onto the particle surface. With unhurried breathing through the nose, the 'larger' particles (over one-hundredth of a millimetre in diameter) are mostly deposited in the upper lung. Particles half this size will reach the fine airways themselves. If a person is exercising – such as jogging or cycling – breathing by the mouth means that even smaller particles get deposited in the lung.

Chemicals such as PAH are potential causes of cancer. Although there is an excess 2–4 per cent urban mortality from cancers, studies generally find no extra deaths among urban non-smokers. This suggests that the cancer-causing effects of tobacco smoke and vehicle particulates are somehow combined.[22]

Particulate pollution lowers visibility in winter and summer smogs. In Britain, particulates are measured together with sulphur dioxide. In 1985/6 concentrations exceeded WHO guidelines at 34 sites, [23] while 10 broke Limit Values of the EC Directive. The causes of these breaches were mainly smoke from domestic coal burning.

Sulphur Dioxide

SO_2 gas causes bronchitis and constriction of the airways. Sulphate particles formed from the gas are a serious threat, particularly to asthmatics and children. Once inhaled, they form sulphuric acid in the lungs. The WHO standard designed to guard against an increase in bronchitis is 250 ug/m^3, but US research suggests that a level of 30–100 ug/m^3 may be enough to cause higher rates of illness than in cleaner areas.

Despite the historic fall in levels of SO_2, Britain's urban and rural areas still regularly exceed the WHO guideline value of 350 ug/m^3. Three of London Scientific Services' four monitoring stations showed breaches in 1988, the central London roadside and east London sites breaking the limit seven times. These episodes are the result of pollution blown into London from surrounding power stations, and similar effects occur in other cities.

The European Community's binding Limit Values are complex, as they depend on smoke levels. The Guide Values, which are not binding, are 100–150 ug/m^3 for a 24-hour mean and 40–60 ug/m^3 as a year-long average. They are exceeded in many areas. Natural levels are around 5 ug/m^3.

Ozone

Ozone is a powerful oxidising agent (like the bleach hydrogen peroxide, which also occurs in photochemical smog). In the human lung it damages tissues and impairs defences against viruses and bacteria. 'At lower concentrations,' says Claire Holman, 'ozone and other photochemical oxidants irritate the mucous membrane of the respiratory system, causing coughing, choking and impaired lung function, particularly in people who exercise.' Controlled experiments show that levels as low as 80 ppb cause breathing difficulties, and exposure to the US National Air Quality Standard of 120 ppb while exercising led to a 7-hour delay before lung function recovered.

The UK government's Photochemical Oxidants Review Group [24] admits that, to date, 'There have been no systematic studies on the health effects of ozone conducted in the United Kingdom.' The WHO guideline of 50-60 ppb for an 8–hour period is frequently exceeded in rural Britain – for up to 37 days and 235 hours a year – while the 100 ppb limit (the WHO guideline limit for 1 hour's exposure) has been exceeded on as many as 16 days a year and for 154 hours. In 1989, monitors at Yarner Wood in Devon recorded levels exceeding 100 ppb for over 20 hours on one weekend alone.

Traffic concentrations – such as the crowded arteries of the South East, the Midlands, Bristol and South Wales and the Northwest – add their ozone-making hydrocarbons and NOx to industrial sources. While ozone levels in central London are generally low because the high NO concentrations break down ozone, as the 'plume' drifts away photochemical reactions can create a massive cloud of ozone some hours later. On 8 July 1983, for example, 165 ppb ozone was measured at a site 7 hours downwind of London, 65 per cent higher than the WHO's 1-hour limit. Comparison with air entering London showed that 72 ppb of this 165 ppb was the enhancement effect of London. Similarly, on 19 August 1984 a level of 134 ppb was recorded at a rural site 6 hours downwind, showing 33 ppb enhancement.

Aircraft flights to monitor pollutants have also detected ozone clouds entering Britain from the continent (where most of the sources are motor vehicle emissions), British ozone heading across the North Sea, and the effect of NOx and hydrocarbons from Merseyside, Humberside and the London area.

Carbon Monoxide

Carbon monoxide is 200 times more active in combining with bloodstream haemoglobin (the body's oxygen-carrier) than oxygen. The result, when carbon monoxide is inhaled, is respiratory distress. At high concentrations it is fatal, hence car exhaust suicides. At lower levels it causes drowsiness, slower thinking and reflexes, and headaches. Those at particular risk include heart patients, pregnant women, babies, the elderly and people suffering from emphysema or bronchitis.

The WHO sets guidelines of 100 mg/m^3 for 10 minutes' exposure, 60 for half an hour, 30 for 1 hour and 10 for 8 hours. (Natural background levels may be only a thousandth of the lowest of these guidelines.) In work for the London boroughs, London Scientific Services (LSS) has calculated that roadside carbon monoxide levels exceeded WHO guidelines for an 8-hour exposure on 24 days (one in four) between 1 October and 31 December 1988.

The highest emissions are from vehicles waiting at junctions or in traffic jams. London levels are thought to have been considerably higher in the early 1970s when they reached 60 mg/m^3 in pollution episodes, but they still reach double the 8-hour guideline.

Nitrogen Oxides

Oxides of nitrogen combine with hydrocarbons to form ozone but they are also a health risk in themselves. Acute exposure to nitrogen dioxide can cause hyperactivity or tightening of the airways in asthmatics, while tests on animals showed long-term changes to lung structure.

Average London levels of nitrogen dioxide rose about 25 per cent in the five years to 1985, in line with increasingly heavy traffic. The average roadside levels of NOx now reach 90 ug/m^3, and results from the Warren Spring Laboratory's monitor which stands by the kerb of Cromwell Road showed an annual average of 120 ug/m^3 in 1983, higher than that in Los Angeles. Other London and Manchester sites reach 45-65 ug/m^3. One day in 1982, levels on the Cromwell Road reached 3,000 ug/m^3.

The European Community has set a Directive limiting nitrogen dioxide. The Limit Value means that 98 per cent of 1-hour samples must be under 200 ug/m^3, half the samples over a year must not exceed 50 ug/m^3 and 98 per cent of the samples over a year must be below 135 ug/m^3.

In 1989, an analysis for Friends of the Earth by Harwell Laboratory and London Scientific Services[25] suggested breaches of the legally binding limit at Royal Free Hospital in north London, in Whitehall, and at the Norman Shaw Building (which houses MPs) in Westminster, while the guide value was broken at the Great Ormond Street Children's Hospital, in several other cities and outside the Department of Transport itself. However, the results from the official monitoring station do not breach the limit value. This is, says Holman, 'because it is situated in an alley around the side of a building.' It is also 10 metres up in the air. The Directive states that, in order to assess the 'individual risk of exposure in excess of the limit value as closely as possible', monitoring stations should include 'canyon streets carrying heavy traffic and major intersections'. At the time of writing, FoE is challenging the DoE's monitoring practice with the European Commission.

Monitoring

The picture which emerges is that Britain's traffic pollutants regularly breach European limits and international guidelines, sometimes illegally and on occasions by massive amounts. If a standard is now set for particulates, which may pose the greatest health threat of all, Britain could be in considerable difficulty unless it cleans up its lorries, taxis and buses.

As traffic grows, both winter and summer smogs are likely to increase. If, as a result of climatic change, periods of dry high pressure weather become more frequent, the position will become worse. One such episode occurred in November and December 1988. It created an atmospheric inversion over London, causing the 8-hour average carbon monoxide levels to rise to 16.2 mg/m^3 at the LSS central London monitoring site by 15 November and 19.8 mg/m^3 (almost double the guideline) in a west London school on the following day.

Heavily trafficked routes, such as the Old Kent Road, show even higher levels. Roland Woodbridge, a member of the Southwark Borough Pollution Group, told the *Observer* in 1989: 'The DoE says guidelines [for carbon monoxide] are only breached in exceptional conditions. But we don't find it takes exceptional conditions for that to happen. When weather conditions are exceptional, the guidelines are breached by a fairly enormous amount.'[26]

In 1988/9 in the London boroughs of Hillingdon, Ealing, Hounslow, Brent, Kingston, Newham and Southwark, nitrogen dioxide levels broke the EC Guide Value. In Hammersmith and Fulham, Westminster, Camden, Islington, the City, Tower Hamlets, Lewisham and Greenwich, this value and the legal Limit Value were exceeded. In Haringey, Southwark, Lambeth, Bexley and Hounslow, carbon monoxide topped the WHO levels and, in Bexley, ozone was detected at above the WHO limits.

This is the picture that emerges, but it is surprising that anything emerges at all. The heavy emphasis on London is not just because of its pollution problems – traffic is as heavy in parts of Bristol and Birmingham – but because a number of the London boroughs pay for the services of London Scientific Services, a high-tech independent consultancy which grew out of the old GLC Scientific Services division. In other parts of the country, monitoring equipment is simply unavailable.

The UK is obliged to monitor NO_2 because of an EC Directive. It has established a network of just six sites to do so (including the off-street London site). Holman contrasts this with Japan, where 'there are over 1,500 monitoring stations in 568 municipalities. Of these nearly 300 have been specifically located to measure air pollution resulting from motor vehicles with sampling inlets placed at the outside of vehicle lanes.'[27]

The UK ozone network set up in 1988 consists of 16 sites. In West Germany there are 200 provincial monitoring stations and 15 federal ones, with 10 more planned. Austria has one site per square kilometre in areas of high pollution (which would mean much of England), while in the Netherlands 89 NOx monitors, 29 ozone monitors and 207 SO_2 stations are linked to a system which can produce accurate maps of pollution as it moves across the country.

If the UK's local authorities had better information about the air pollution in their area, people might start wanting something done about it. Britain might find itself in the European Court over air quality as well as water quality.

How much longer the British will be kept in the dark about the threat to their health and environment may now be open to doubt. Fiona Weir, air pollution campaigner at Friends of the Earth, has been pressing hard for Britain to have public smog alerts of the sort used in other countries. In July 1989, 'one of the worst weeks for photochemical smog since 1976,' she mobilised medical support to press for DoE monitoring to be made public. 'The UK government currently has no intention of introducing air quality standards and refuses to make data available to FoE,' said Weir. 'Patients with heart disease are particularly sensitive to air pollution, and the risk of death undoubtedly increases when there is an increase in the level of pollutants,' said Professor Julian of the British Heart Foundation.

In West Germany smog alerts can be called by the *Lander* (states – equivalent to UK county councils but with much more power) based on sulphur dioxide, carbon monoxide and nitrogen dioxide. During alerts, factories can be closed and traffic restricted. In one such alert in Munich in 1987, the use of cars was restricted to alternate days by odd and even number plates.

The sulphur pollution necessary to trigger an alarm in Denmark is quite frequently reached in parts of the UK, while in Stockholm and Goteborg in Sweden pollution reports are given daily on the radio and in newspapers, together with the following day's forecast. Similar reports are routine in Canada and the United States. Warnings are also given in Melbourne, Australia, and in Switzerland, while an extensive system of alerts and controls is triggered by smog in Japan.

In the United States, the Environmental Protection Agency has stated that 'American people, especially those who suffer illnesses . . . need accurate, timely and easily understandable information about daily levels of air pollution. This information would allow them to modify their activities to protect themselves.' (Pollution alerts began in California in 1969.) The DoE apparently did not believe the British people needed such information.

Until 1989, the DoE published its monitoring results only in an obscure technical summary obtainable once a year from Warren Spring Laboratory in Hertfordshire. Only London Scientific Services, Greenpeace and Friends of the Earth had provided information on pollution episodes as they happened. As of summer 1989, the DoE agreed to make ozone data available, but only if a journalist telephoned during, for example, an ozone episode (over 76 ppb). 'It's ridiculous, a totally inadequate system, 'says Holman. 'How are journalists supposed to know when to phone up to get levels confirmed? Information should be sent out automatically every day, like the weather forecast, as it is in other countries.'

Roads To Congestion

In a 1989 White Paper entitled *Roads for Prosperity*, the government unveiled plans for a massive £12 billion, 2,700 mile expansion of the road network to accommodate its projections of traffic growth, with £5.7 billion due to be spent by 1992.[28] The road programme involved four new stretches of motorway and 492 miles of motorway-widening at a cost of over £4 billion, with more than 2,000 miles of other new roads and expansions, some effectively motorways in themselves. Many were on routes – such as the £434 million to be spent on widening the A1 and converting it to motorway – in direct competition to long distance rail for passenger and freight. Almost every route would damage wildlife, green spaces and countryside.

The Department of Transport claimed that one of the objectives of the plan was to 'improve the environment by removing through traffic from unsuitable roads in towns and villages'. Nothing was said about acid rain, human health or the greenhouse effect. The Department of Transport had moved one civil servant from other duties to keep track of pollution issues and what officials referred to as 'this environment thing'.

When asked by Malcolm Bruce MP what steps he was taking to cut emissions of carbon dioxide from traffic, Transport Minister Robert Atkins replied that 'new construction and improvement of motorways and other trunk roads over the next three years' would reduce congestion and this would reduce pollution.[29] In other words, the DTp was doing nothing. But research by Martin Mogridge strongly suggests that the Department's programme of building new roads will not reduce congestion: it will merely create bigger traffic jams.[30]

Mogridge has studied traffic in London. Here congestion in the days of horse-drawn traffic led the Post Office to consider building its own underground railway between mainline termini as early as 1846. 'Whether it will ever be possible to obtain an average reliable speed of over 8 miles an hour during ordinary business hours in Central London even with motor vans,' said the Post Office in 1911, 'is a matter of extreme doubt.'

The Post Office was largely right. It built its railway. Pressed by the road lobby, successive Transport Departments built bigger roads. Yet traffic speeds in central London have remained approximately constant at around 12 mph for many decades. From repeated tests of car and public transport routes, Mogridge argues that this is because road speeds 'are in equilibrium with door-to-door speeds delivered by the public transport systems'. In other words, people are using whichever is the quickest way of getting from A to B. Although not everyone has a car and not everyone would use it if they had, there are enough people who will switch from one type of transport to another to create the equilibrium. If public transport slows or its capacity is reduced, some take to their cars and (as on the day of a strike), congestion increases. If more road space appears, more people take to their cars until congestion increases to the point where car travel again becomes slower. People then go back (perhaps reluctantly, if it is now slow and if it is dirty and overcrowded) to public transport.

Thus, building new roads does not necessarily improve matters. In fact, so long as there are lots of potential extra car drivers waiting to fill new road space, it makes things worse, including more pollution. 'Only by speeding up bus and rail will it be possible to speed up cars and lorries,' says Mogridge.

The Mogridge principles do not depend on being in London. They will apply anywhere with a road network within which many drivers choose between the same roads, where there is a choice between private road transport and public transport, and where there is a 'suppressed demand' for road space caused by car ownership. As trunk roads and motorways expand, road commuting is encouraged, as public transport is cut and standards fall or prices rise (all of which are UK trends), more and more areas will be subject to the same choking process.

Mogridge sums it up: 'in conditions of suppressed demand the speed of the road network is determined by the speed of the high-capacity network (rail, bus etc).'

Nine environmental organisations attacked the *Roads to Prosperity* in a counter-document, *Roads to Ruin*, saying 'These new roads – and the extra traffic they are supposed to cater for – will cause serious environmental damage and will undermine other government measures to protect the environment. The forecast traffic increase will only be generated if the roads are built.'[31] In 1989, the Treasury admitted that the M25 had unexpectedly created traffic by encouraging a lot of new short-distance journeys (on some stretches 130,000 vehicles rather than 80,000, as had been planned). Forecasting, it explained, was 'not a perfect science'.

In 1988, the Department of Transport had commissioned a £5.5 million study of major new roads in London. These routes affected 10,000 homes and dozens of wildlife sites and nature reserves. Conservative backbench MPs threatened a suburban revolt. In December 1989, the minister reappeared with a smaller package. In March 1990, following a vigorous public campaign of opposition, Cecil Parkinson was forced to retreat and drop almost the entire £2 billion scheme, although £250 million 'improvements' still threaten 1,000 homes.

Costs and Benefits Justifying Roads

During Friends of the Earth's 1984 campaign to save Otmoor from the M40 it became clear that the trunk roads and motorways planned by the DTp were routed through a disproportionate number of wildlife sites and other land 'protected' against other forms of development. FoE located more than 110 roads damaging Sites of Special Scientific Interest such as Oxleas Wood in southeast London.

Because you can't develop nature reserves, the DTp says they have a low market value in cash terms. It therefore puts them into its cost-benefit analysis as completely worthless. Indeed, as Dr John Adams of University College London pointed out in the London Wildlife Trust/FoE report *London's Green Spaces: What Are They Worth?*,[32] the DTp sometimes gives such land a 'market value of less than zero' because, while impossible to develop, the land has costly obligations such as maintaining fences and looking after trees.

Many road schemes go from one wildlife site to the next. A proposed new road in north London (dropped in 1990) took an enormous detour to route itself down Parkland Walk, an old railway line and now a wooded nature reserve protected from building by the DoE, and therefore given a 'zero', negative or low value in the DTp's cost-benefit analysis. If such land was given a true or social market value, most of Britain might be off limits to road builders altogether.

The Department also fiddles the other side of the equation. For instance, it gives a higher value to the time of car drivers (whose time will be saved by a stretch of new road), than to pedestrians who may have to take a long walk to a footbridge to cross it. The cost-benefit system for roads is also treated as an Official Secret. At the East London River Crossing Inquiry, Rosie Barnes MP asked what value had been placed on the ancient Oxleas Wood with its 200 varieties of mushrooms, bird life and rare wild service trees. 'This information is not available,' said the DTp.

Another reason for the secrecy emerged at the same inquiry. If road pricing were applied (a bridge toll for the East London River Crossing), so few motorists would use the new road that it would be 'uneconomic' even by DTp assumptions.

The DTp's road economics are simply statistical fiddling to justify a massive hidden subsidy to road construction, very similar to the way the Ministry of Agriculture used to justify subsidies to intensive farming.

The details of the DTp's secret cost-benefit analyses may have long been a nonsensical sham. *Roads for Prosperity* provides an automatic stamp of approval to all 2,700 miles of the new road schemes it proposes. It forecast an 83–142 per cent traffic increase and then stated: 'The above forecasts will be used in appraising motorway and trunk road schemes. They will play an important role in the assessment of whether the benefits from a scheme over its lifetime justify the initial cost and the standard of provision.' This is a completely circular argument. The road schemes in the same document were only justified by the forecast. The forecast made the road schemes economic. In February 1990, Cecil Parkinson tried to disown the policy, saying, 'We never felt the country could afford or that we should attempt the outer forecasts.'

The Road Policy Juggernaut

At the time of writing, Britain's transport policy is clearly in crisis. In 1979 junior Transport Minister Kenneth Clarke predicted that the last link in the motorway network would be built by the end of the 1980s. Two years later, the government announced an increase in road building. In 1985 it announced 80 new roads and in 1986 opened the M25. Nicholas Ridley proudly announced that 'since 1979 we have increased spending on national roads by 30 per cent in real terms.' Road expenditure rose from £312 million in 1979 to £927 million in 1989.[33] Rail investment was run down. Commuter villages were created, out-of-town shopping centres gained planning permission, and factories were built without rail links. Rail lines were threatened with closure, services were run down, buses were deregulated and passenger-miles dropped 10 per cent.

Easter 1989 saw the M4 clogged up from London to Bristol in a 125-mile traffic jam. The Severn Bridge, pounded by the unplanned-for juggernaut traffic, was under almost constant repair. Large chunks of the M5 and M6 began to fall to pieces, as did the M1. Each lorry did as much damage as 250,000 cars. Quite soon plans were announced to expand the M25 to eight lanes. The CBI estimates that London road congestion costs £10 billion a year. Public transport investment would yield benefits exceeding costs by an estimated 60 per cent, but the road programme has enormous political momentum.

For one thing it is a long-cherished 'truth' that more roads must be built, and that the national limit to car ownership is 'saturation'. Bizarre as it may sound, growth until congestion had been the Department of Transport's official policy for decades. Dr John Adams identifies the origins of the policy as a 1962 paper by Mr J C Tanner, in the ominously named journal *Roads and Road Construction*, entitled 'Forecasts of future numbers of vehicles in Britain.'[34] The idea was to build roads in order to allow car ownership to increase to a 'saturation point'. At saturation point, which has officially been taken to be one car per household and two or more cars in 85 per cent of households, there would be no further increase in car ownership, no increase in car use and no need to build more roads.[35]

When this extraordinary policy was conceived and 'saturation' was far away, it may have seemed like an elegant laissez-faire solution. But by the late 1980s, even with fewer than half of Britain's households having regular use of a car (1985 figures[36]) and fewer than a fifth having two or more cars, the symptoms of saturation were already making themselves painfully felt. Even in the South East, the richest part of the country, more than a quarter of households had no car at all.

Such thinking is institutionalised in the Department of Transport. Stephen Joseph, director of the pressure group Transport 2000, puts it like this:

> 'We don't have a Department of Transport: we have a Department of Roads. There are over ten thousand civil servants employed to plan and build roads, and cater for cars. There are just 700 responsible for railways, canals, bicycles and the rest. Not only is there a massive imbalance, the two parts don't talk to one another and don't plan together. The result is not a transport policy but a road building policy.'[37]

For some politicians, the idea of no more motorways and restraint on cars may simply be too much to bear. In 1990, Margaret Thatcher referred to Britain's 'great car economy'. In the *Sunday Times* Robert Harris noted the Prime Minister's 'visceral dislike' of public transport. 'British Rail,' he added, 'encapsulates everything Margaret Thatcher hates. It is a nationalised monopoly. It is subsidised by the tax payer. In the Thatcherite ideal, families whiz up and down motorways in their own cars, responsible for their own actions.'[38]

'If people want to commute into London, who am I to say they shouldn't? If we believe in consumer choice, in individual freedom, why pillory drivers on the dreadful offence of congestion? . . . I make no apologies for being pro-motorist,' said Nicholas Ridley when Secretary of State for Transport in 1984. With Cecil Parkinson at the helm, the Department's 1989 plan for London's roads stated: 'It is a fundamental part of the Government's approach that people's aspirations to own and use a car should not be artificially constrained. The Government therefore regards restraint as very much a policy of last resort.'[39]

Britain also has a formidable pro-road lobby, first described in Mick Hamer's book *Wheels Within Wheels*.[40] It consists principally of those who profit from building roads (the construction, gravel, quarrying and concrete companies, some of whom are major contributors to Conservative Party funds), the commercial users, in particular the British Road Federation (the truckers), and, at least until recently, the car owners' associations, the AA and the RAC (in 1990, following the establishment of the Environmental Transport Association, the RAC announced plans to lobby for better public transport). Of lesser importance, but still pushing for more motorways, are the motor manufacturers, the CBI and the coach owners. When, in 1989, the government published its plans for massive new road schemes, the man from the British Road Federation was heard to remark, 'Well, I think we got most of what we wanted.'[41] Lastly there is the Treasury, aware that the government receives £16 billion a year from vehicle taxes, only a fraction of which returns to transport.

Transport Solutions

The government underpins its claim for new roads with forecasts of economic growth. But other countries achieve more growth with quite different policies.

The solutions to Britain's transport crisis are well known. They are just not implemented.

• They start with planning. An editorial in the *Sunday Times* aptly described the existing policy as 'patch, infill and fudge'.[43] 'Decades of ad hoc decisions,' said the newspaper, 'and un-coordinated development have produced the present mess and this government has done no better. Its instinctive mistrust of planning on a grand scale is misplaced with transport. The explosive growth in traffic, particularly in the southeast of England, is fast becoming unsustainable, while rebuilding roads only adds to the problem.'

• They include investing in public transport, because of the public benefits it brings, and can also include policies such as road pricing (charging for road use) as well as constraint. Up to now, as the *Guardian* has put it, 'the Government – alone in Europe – has been pursuing the potty policy of removing all subsidies from public transport while encouraging private cars. Indeed, the cumulative past neglect of public infrastructure is now so devastating that London's underground could barely accommodate extra passengers forced off the roads by economic pricing policies.'

• They include the realisation that although people may want to own a car, they can't all use them at once. Of course, continental Europeans too like their cars: the French, Belgians, West Germans and Italians all own more cars per head than the British.[44] Yet there is no longer any thought of a transport strategy based just on cars, lorries and public transport by free market mechanisms. Private car use may mean freedom of choice, but governments (national and local) see that individual choice would create too much pollution, danger, noise and discomfort for everyone else to be worthwhile. The congestion would damage the economy. The quality of life would obviously suffer. Pollution would become intolerable. Every government seems to have come to this conclusion, except Britain.

Together, such measures would help create an integrated transport system in which all forms of transport worked together instead of against each other. This is the object of transport policy in most of Britain's competitor countries. The Chartered Institute of Transport has warned that Britain's economic interests will suffer after 1992 unless the car is controlled, for example by road pricing.[45] Stanhope, a major property development company, has criticised the government for an 'uncoordinated transport programme', commenting 'what is needed is an integrated planned transport system for London, encompassing roads, rail, ferries and air'.[46]

Walking

Mrs Thatcher is said to have 'surprised colleagues' in 1989 by proposing that 'people should walk to work'. Fair enough perhaps if you live as close to work as Mrs Thatcher does to the House of Commons. The Swiss Prime Minister does indeed walk to work. In practice Mrs Thatcher makes the journey in a motor cavalcade. Her 'travel time to work's about 90 seconds,' said Tony Banks MP in 1990.

And it would be fair also if, like the Dutch, your country had pursued an active policy of living close to work, and had built homes and offices close together, linked by foot and bike paths. But for most of Britain there is no choice: if cars and lorries are to be controlled, then people and goods will have to go by public transport.

If the Prime Minister manages to reverse her personal policies, other obstacles to an integrated transport system could be swept away or, at least, negotiated around. Perhaps, said Banks, 'if just once in her life' the Prime Minister went by public transport, 'something would change'.

Transport 2000[47] points out that a third of all travel time is spent on foot and 80 per cent of all journeys are under 5 miles, with 33 per cent less than 1 mile. Journeys under 1 mile, however, do not appear in the transport statistics. The government effectively has no policy to help or encourage walking as transport. Local authorities whose rates were first capped then removed to be replaced with the poll tax are left to maintain pavements, which now are noticeably dirtier, more cracked and uneven than those of many other European countries – 200 people a year die from pavement falls in Britain. In 1986, over 60,000 pedestrians were killed or injured on Britain's roads: 170 a day. In 1987, road accidents cost Britain £4 billion and put 95,000 people in hospital.

Railways

Britain's railways are almost entirely Victorian. After the Second World War successive governments cut rail and built roads. Unfortunately, that was almost all they did. There was no attempt to integrate rail, bus and private transport. An ex-Transport Permanent Secretary, Peter Baldwin, told the *Sunday Times* that it was only when James Callaghan came to power in the mid 1970s that integration became a priority. 'By the time it occurred to anyone that an effective and integrated transport system is vital to the economic health of the nation, it was too late. There were already too many cars on the roads. The railways had already been slashed to pieces and of course there was no money.'[48].

After the 1976 sterling crisis, said Baldwin, the IMF said 'no more' and 'there we were sitting in our new offices in Marsham Street, knowing there would be the most almighty crisis, but knowing also that there was nothing we could do about it.'

Throughout the 1980s Britain's railways attracted growing numbers of passengers, but the quality of service deteriorated and overcrowding increased. From 1981 to 1984 less money was put into Britain's rail system than at any time since 1950. Although funds increased 75 per cent by 1989, they were still

5 per cent below the level when Thatcher came to power in 1979. In real terms, public spending on rail, bus and tubes was cut by a third between 1985 and 1988.[49] Train travel in Britain is now also more expensive than in most continental countries. The cause is the massive difference in public investment and subsidy (see table). Overall, Britain's investment in rail represents 0.23 per cent of GDP as against a European average of 0.67 per cent.[50]

Costs and Support to Rail Travel in Europe
(Figures per passenger-mile)

Country	Price of travel	Investment	Subsidy
UK	8.4	2.5	2.6
France	6.0	2.5	4.0
West Germany	6.0	7.0	17.0
Netherlands	5.8	3.6	6.5
Belgium	4.5	3.0	13.3

Writing in the *Independent*, Michael Harrison highlighted the 'vast gulf' of policies between Britain and other European countries.[51] Belgium encourages rail commuting by subsidising season tickets. A season ticket in the Netherlands covers the whole network for £900: some British commuters pay more just to travel to work. West Germany makes £3 billion from rail freight and uses it to subsidise passenger transport costs. Two-thirds of Belgium's rail network is electrified: it will take until 1991 to complete that for Britain's East Coast mainline alone.

Britain's trains run later as well as more expensively: 11 per cent failed to arrive within 5 minutes of the scheduled time in 1988. The figure was 3.4 per cent in the Netherlands and 5 per cent in Belgium. As of July 1989, Dutch railmen received £638–£1,246 a month. BR drivers got £660 and railmen £460.

In 1988/9, London commuters suffered trains routinely carrying at least 30 per cent of passengers standing up for 20 minutes or more. 'The reason for overcrowding is not inefficiency on the part of BR staff,' says Stephen Joseph. 'It is under-investment. In 1988 BR carried as many passengers as any time since 1960. The same number of people are travelling through Clapham Junction each day but in only two–thirds the number of carriages.'[52] But, while 85 per cent of those working in the capital went by public transport, it was still government policy to subsidise private travel by road.

With no cash for more trains, BR is actually trying to price customers off the railway and onto the roads, for example on the inter-City services between London and Scotland. Clearly, with lower prices (or just more seats), rail passengers could increase and road traffic could be reduced. When the Snow Hill Tunnel was reopened under the City of London and services from Brighton to Bedford were connected, London commuters using Bedford station increased from 7,000 to 17,000.

By March 1990 the only new London rail scheme announced was the one shown to be least cost-effective in the Central London Rail Study's options,[53] namely the extension of the Jubilee Line into Docklands, to be funded by developers Olympia-York. Private funds for the other more cost-effective and more important links – such as from Paddington to Liverpool Street – were not forthcoming. David Black, transport correspondent of the Independent newspaper, commented of the extension of the Jubilee Line that, 'It is the one line that if built on its own without the benefit of another cross-London link, will add to congestion at Waterloo, London Bridge and Liverpool Street, yet because it has the promise of private backing, it has government approval.'[54]

Even in this case the private sector contribution is small. Originally put at £400 million or 40 per cent of the £1 billion required to complete the scheme, by March 1990 London Regional Transport officials disclosed that Olympia-York's share of the financing would be only £120–150 million, or some 10–12 per cent of the costs.[55]

Outside London, the scale of the road programme illustrates what Colin Speakman of *Environment Now* has called Britain's 'bias for roads and against other forms of transport'. Speakman highlighted the case of Sheffield: 'Britain's fourth largest city, served by both the M1 and the Midland main line. £960m is to be spent on widening the M1, yet a mere £160m is required to electrify the Midland line from St Pancras to Derby, Sheffield and Nottingham. The Department is reported to be 'unenthusiastic'. 'This,' he concluded, 'is the politics of the madhouse.'[56]

Cycling

More bicycles are sold in Britain than cars, which ought to be good news as they are healthy, do not cause acid rain or greenhouse gas pollution and don't crush pedestrians. Yet cycling to work remains an unpopular and hazardous business. In 1988, an international survey showed that Britain was one of the worst countries in Europe for cyclists.[57]

The Netherlands has the highest bicycle use at 29 per cent of all journeys. But, contrary to popular belief, this is not just because much of the Netherlands is flat and the Dutch like bikes. The Dutch use of bikes is partly a result of a deliberate government policy of building separate bike paths and giving them priority at junctions.

The next highest bike users are in Denmark (18 per cent) and West Germany (11 per cent). Britain trails along at 4 per cent. Cities with high cycling levels include Delft (40 per cent), Vasteras in Sweden (33 per cent), Munich and Erlangen in West Germany (29 per cent), and, in England, Cambridge (27 per cent). London is below 3 per cent.

The same survey showed that, in Denmark and the Netherlands, cyclists feel safe and respected, facilities are good and there are widespread traffic restraint schemes to control and separate cars from cycle lanes. In Italy and Sweden, such schemes were being introduced and some cities had high levels of cycling. In Austria, Switzerland and West Germany, public transport was generally preferred to cycling because facilities were not so good, but local experiments were under way.

In the last group of countries – Britain, Belgium, France and Spain – there were few cyclists, speeding cars were a dominant factor, cyclists felt threatened or not respected by other road users and cycle lanes were rare. Cyclists were also frequently obstructed by other traffic.

Buses

The unromantic bus is one of the most energy-efficient means of transport. Provision of physically segregated bus lanes is probably the single most cost-effective short-term measure to overcome the transport crisis. At present, London has only 42 miles of segregated bus lane. A report by the London Regional Passengers' Committee recommends electronic control of traffic lights to give priorities to buses, more wheel-clamping of illegal parking, rail extensions and tax concessions for season tickets in place of company cars.[58]

A spokesman for London Buses, which supported the Committee's demands, stated that when extra policing was applied to prevent parking in bus lanes in the central south London area, bus services began running 15 minutes early. In other parts of London, average bus speeds are down to 3.5 mph, slower than walking.[59]

Other measures to simply reorganise traffic could bring almost immediate benefits at extremely low cost. Compared with building either roads or rail-ways, the reorganisation of roads to cut congestion caused by private vehicles, and to favour buses instead, would yield large short-term benefits at a low price. A system of continuous electronic bus lanes in London for example, in which the approach of a bus would change red traffic lights to green, would cost an estimated £10 million.[60] However, privatisation and deregulation of bus services is easier than privatisation of rail, where fixed track makes competition difficult to arrange. In Birmingham, such measures have led to a decrease in passengers.

Controls and Pricing

Paris bans all lorries over a certain size from the centre and goods are trans-shipped to smaller vehicles at the outskirts. Switzerland requires lorries to be shipped through a central Alpine area by rail, to reduce emissions causing damage to forests. Drivers crossing the Golden Gate Bridge in San Francisco are charged according to the number of passengers they carry. Bordeaux is to ban or restrict cars on 75 per cent of its roads. In Bologna, public transport is now free.

John Roberts and Nicholas James of the Transport and Environmental Studies (TEST) group have surveyed positive transport policies adopted elsewhere. In Freiburg in West Germany, for example, an 18 per cent change to public transport from car use was achieved by subsidised season tickets for bus and tram travel, while in the Netherlands the use of public transport is due to be doubled by 2010. In Stockholm, the toll-card allowing cars access to the city centre also serves as a season ticket for public transport. 200,000 car parking spaces are being removed from Paris. Los Angeles has car-sharing and mini-bus subsidy schemes, and the OECD suggests that car ownership would have been 80 per cent higher with £420 million more roads built in Singapore than now exist, if it had not been for the Area Licensing Scheme operating there.[61]

In Britain, taxpayers subsidise company cars. According to Michael Durham of the *Observer* : [in 1988] 'the government wrote off £2.4 billion in company car tax *perks*. That was £500m more than its entire subsidy of road and rail transport.'[62] TEST has calculated that if the amount of company car traffic in London were cut 75 per cent (an overall 10 per cent reduction) and the miles saved were allocated one-third to public transport and two-thirds to other cars (by sharing), bus speeds would increase 3.4 per cent, bus loads would rise 8.5 per cent and the number of underground travellers would increase by 9 per cent.[63] Since 1988, parking benefits have been tax free, encouraging more car commuting. Charles Clover, environment editor of the *Daily Telegraph*, has pointed out that, if free market mechanisms were used to deter traffic by including 'externalities' (such as car pollution) in pricing 'with full force tomorrow, few of us could afford to use cars, or to heat our homes as we do today. The most environmentally damaging things we do are to burn petrol in our cars and to turn the central heating on.' The government's proposed 'vast increase in road-building,' he added, 'would be exposed as an irrational short-term political move'.[64]

Road pricing has been proposed by all 33 London boroughs, and the Chartered Institute of Transport has estimated that electronic road pricing in London (within the M25) would cost £80 million but generate £1 billion.[65]

In 1990 it was reported that Parkinson argued in cabinet for road pricing, but the idea was rejected.[66]

Conclusions

Commuting and travel are still dominant forces in our lives. Between 7 a.m. and 10 a.m. every day, 1.15 million people commute into London reputedly some from as far afield as Doncaster. Transport and mobility have become dominant factors in our everyday lives. After a home, buying a car is likely to be the largest single purchase most people make. Much of the cost of a holiday is travel. In 1985/6 the average household spent more of its weekly expenditure on transport or vehicles than any other category. At 27 per cent of the total expenditure, travel costs four times as much as household durables, fuel, light and power or clothing, a quarter more than food, and more than housing itself.

Transport demonstrates the unavoidable limitations of technical fixes, and the links between the way we live and the pollution we create.

Electric or hydrogen-fuelled cars may be marketed in the medium term, but even they will be able to cause congestion and may create pollution from power generation. Transport shows the need for government action to produce public benefits where unplanned use of technology and the unfettered pursuit of individual interest will produce chaos, great public cost and congestion. As with sewerage, in the 1980s there was massive under-investment and poor planning. The result is pollution and inefficiency. If Britain maintains its present course of building more roads and encouraging more traffic, large areas of the country will become pollution sources on the scale of Los Angeles. In April 1990, the *Guardian* reported on a leaked minute from a DTp Transport Policy Unit meeting, at which civil servants Tim Faircloth, David Rowlands and Julie Osborne briefed the CBI. It made depressing reading. Fuel efficiency would not reduce carbon dioxide emissions as people were buying bigger cars. Government policy had ruled out boosting public transport and road pricing. The government supported the road programme and would do little internationally that would hurt British companies.

Britain's transport policy shambles will make it impossible effectively to reduce greenhouse gases or acid rain pollutants. Cecil Parkinson admitted to a WWF conference in May 1990 that traffic growth would preclude substantial CO_2 cuts 'in the short term . . . the year 2000, the year 2010, that type of thing'. If official forecasts come true then, even with catalytic converters, NOx emissions will return to today's levels by 2015.

Britain's present policy is not even a transport policy for the nation as a whole: 35 per cent of households have no car and 60 per cent of people do not have the main use of a car. Only half the population have driving licences, and only 41 per cent of women do. It is a transport policy for an affluent minority (even though many of them would still prefer to commute by a decent public transport system), for road construction companies and for the road freight lobby.

Part III

Land of Waste

Toxic and Radioactive Waste, Litter, Recycling , The Land and Pesticides

Britain, said the Commons Environment Committee during its 1988/9 inquiry into Toxic Waste, is the 'champion' of co-disposal. The DoE agreed with the MPs. Like tall stacks and long sea outfalls in the fields of air and water pollution, co-disposal is Britain's special contribution to the problem of waste. 'Co-disposal' is the practice of mixing the highly toxic with 'normal' rotting refuse. It is cheap but Britain is almost alone in thinking that it is a safe and effective way to dispose of chemicals.

As of 1989, 83 per cent of the 2,500 tonnes of waste got rid of in the UK went into holes in the ground (landfill); 8 per cent was dumped at sea; 7 per cent chemically or physically treated and less than 2 per cent was burnt. The Environment Committee noted: 'This contrasts with the situation we found in the US, where, of the disposal options available, waste minimisation is the most highly regarded, followed by recycling, incineration and other techniques such as stabilisation/solidification – while direct landfill is the least preferable option. Co-disposal is not legally permissible.'[5]

Because of its geology – with lots of clayey holes in the ground – landfill in Britain has been cheap. It has been assumed that it would cause no ground-water problems. It now emerges that this form of 'dilute and disperse' has left the country with a dense patchwork of contaminated land, spiked with chemicals from asbestos to dioxins and heavy metals. Many tips have gone unrecorded. Continental experts call it a 'timebomb'. Eventually much of it may need digging up, and cleaning up at great expense.

An easy-going attitude to landfill also attracted foreign waste imports. In 1989 some 40,000 tonnes of waste were imported to the UK.

The UK also holds the dubious first place among importers of radioactive waste, worldwide. The Sellafield plant, originally to help make nuclear bombs, now exists to make a business out of reprocessing radioactive waste. Sellafield is Britain's biggest yen earner. As well as Japan, it imports waste from Switzerland, Germany, Belgium, Spain and Italy. But even in the UK, not all radioactive waste is reprocessed, and Britain is now running out of places to store it.

Growing drought conditions may soon bring the problem of groundwater contaminated with pesticides, nitrates and industrial solvents to a head in those parts of Britain – such as the South – heavily reliant on groundwater. Britain faces EC legal action on the subject.

CHAPTER 7

Burying Toxic Waste

Britain enjoys a rich legacy of buried waste, much of it toxic. Geoffrey Lean and Polly Ghazi of the *Observer* revealed the true scope of the problem when, with Friends of the Earth in February 1990, they detailed a network of 4,800 current and disused 'toxic tips' throughout the country.[1] Some of these are strictly industrial (and there were essentially no controls until 1972), but many of them are mixtures of domestic or municipal waste, with the generally more hazardous chemicals from factories and commerce.

Today more than half the land being used for new building in Britain suffers contamination by industrial pollution.[2] The soil is poisoned by chemicals from asbestos to heavy metals, chlorinated solvents or complex organics, left behind when industry closed down, carried there by air or water, spilt in day-to-day manufacturing, or deliberately dumped.

The main sources of such toxic waste have been listed as:[3] waste disposal sites themselves, oil refineries, power stations, gas works, iron and steel works, petroleum refineries, metal products fabrication and finishing works, chemical works, textile plants, leather tanning works, timber treatment works, non-ferrous metals processing, manufacture of integrated circuits and semi-conductors, sewage works, asbestos works, docks and railway land, paper and printing works, heavy engineering installations, and installations processing radioactive materials.

Consultants Clayton, Bostock, Hill and Rigby estimate that 'most of the land within the areas covered by the London Docklands Development Corporation and the other Urban Development Corporations will be contaminated to a greater or lesser extent'. In urban areas, 'most land' is affected by 'aerial deposition and the disposal of ashes, soot and other domestic wastes'.[4] Surveys by CLEAR and the London Chief Environmental Health Officers[5] showed that 'the probability of finding land uncontaminated by lead' was negligible within 10 km of Marble Arch or near main roads, due to the legacy of car exhaust. It is inadvisable to grow and eat lettuces or blackberries in gardens there.

A West Midlands survey found that 'only 15 per cent of the land could be classified with confidence as uncontaminated and 16 per cent of the land was both suspect and already in use for some sensitive purpose (eg housing or schools)'.

Diffuse Contamination

In 1990 the Commons Environment Committee (chaired by Sir Hugh Rossi MP) reported specifically on contaminated land.[6] It heard from the Soil Survey and Cranfield Institute of Science and Technology that 'Diffuse contamination is, if anything, more important at the national level than the grossly contaminated sites which are normally thought of. . . .' This 'consequence of past policies of dilute and disperse' meant that dioxins were 'ubiquitous in the UK,' especially in urban areas, and even in non-urban soils. Almost 1 per cent of samples broke the EC and DoE limits for copper, nickel and chromium. This, said the scientists, 'represents a considerable land area which may be of great significance locally.'

Sewage sludge, 50 per cent of which is disposed of on land in the UK, creates another long-term threat to soil, especially because Britain mixes industrial and domestic wastes in the same sewage system. In 1985, the UK described proposals from West Germany, Luxembourg and Brussels for a Directive limiting metals in sewage sludge disposed of in this way as 'unnecessarily stringent'.

The MPs drew a sharp contrast between official attitudes in Britain and in other countries to contaminated land. The UK relied, sometimes ineffectively, on the planning system to protect people from the effects of poisons in polluted soil. (In 1987 planning permission was granted by one council for housing on a waste tip, and until 1985 planners received no clear guidance on whether to consider contaminated soil in granting permission.) This meant there was 'little pressure to encourage the decontamination of affected land' if it was not going to be developed. Moreover, 'the guidance from the DoE makes it quite clear that if contamination is discovered on a site, a different use should be considered as an alternative to remedial action.' One local authority, noted the Committee, 'was apparently of the opinion that it was DoE policy to discourage remedial action'!

The MPs discovered that the Department of the Environment's way of 'dealing with' the problem of contaminated land had been partly a verbal conjuring trick, which 'defined it away'. The 'DoE definition of contaminated land was criticised by a number of witnesses,' noted the Committee, 'who pointed out that land which contained toxic chemicals would not be classed as contaminated if no use were proposed.'[7] 'It is not surprising that the Department would wish to limit the definition,' consultant Mike Smith told the Committee, 'because the acceptance of the broader definition would mean that substantial parts of some urban areas would have to be classified as contaminated – as indeed they are.'

The Welsh Office found 746 sites covering 4,079 ha and Her Majesty's Inspectorate of Pollution (HMIP) estimated that there were 1,400 sites emitting large quantities of methane, but, apart from that, the government had little idea of how much contaminated land there was. Although the DoE's definition of 'derelict' relates to usability not pollution, it estimates that there is 10,000–27,000 ha of contaminated land in the UK. Environmental Resources Limited surveyed Cheshire and estimated 50,000–100,000 ha in the UK, while

Clayton, Bostock, Hill and Rugby suggested there might be 50,000 'suspect sites' with 50,000 ha of contamination.

In Avon, Woodspring District Council told the Committee of land surrounded by housing 'heavily contaminated with phosphorus wastes and radioactivity; the wastes spontaneously ignite when exposed to the atmosphere'. In the severely polluted Black Country, a typical site might contain '15–20 mine shafts to the acre, overlain variously with metal, chemical or sewage contaminants and in all probability concealing a deep marl pit holding methane-generating domestic and industrial refuse'. In Derbyshire's Amber Valley, the council reported lead contamination from mining; acid leachate from an old factory, threatening the River Erewash; dioxin disposed of at a 1970s tip; leachate from an old gasworks, and methane from the Loscoe landfill, which in 1986 caused a fatal explosion.

At Tameside in Manchester, residents were still concerned at the effects on wildlife and the 'high numbers of deaths, deformities and illnesses among pets' kept near the site of the old Stalybridge Chemstar works which blew up in 1981 leaving 400 chemicals, including asbestos, dioxins and benzene (a potent cancer-causing chemical).[8]

In the London borough of Greenwich, 'funny blue stones' in the back gardens of new houses turned out to be toxic chemicals. In Ilford, soil contaminated with 'mildly radioactive thorium and radium' had to be carted off to Harwell and Bedfordshire, when the British Nuclear Fuels site at Drigg was unable to accept it.[9]

The official UK response to such problems has been to cover them up and restrict the use that can be made of the land. The Dutch, in contrast, try to clean up the soil so that it can be used for any purpose. Dutch policy also aims to prevent 'problem-shifting'. The Dutch increasingly clean soil and expect to spend £15 billion on such work over 10 years. At Utrecht, for example, a former asphalt works left tar deposits to 50 metres depth, which was dealt with by controlled incineration of the soil before replacing it. Other methods used in the Netherlands include 'land farming', in which contaminated soil is treated microbiologically between layers of sand in controlled conditions, and wet extraction of contaminants. In the USA, contaminated soil is removed immediately (where there is a perceived threat to public health or the environment), or on a planned basis, or treated on the spot according to the National Priorities List, drawn up by the Environmental Protection Agency (EPA).

'There is very little true clean-up, in the Dutch or American sense, in the UK,' said the Committee in 1990. 'By far the most common treatment is the practice of covering up contaminants.' This was criticised as 'cosmetic', hazarding groundwater, and raising the possibility of 'serious problems in future'.

Britain is now moving large amounts of poisoned soil – the DoE was unable to say how much, but estimated 1–5 million tonnes – to landfill sites. This, pointed out the MPs, 'may be simply shifting the problem elsewhere'. Organised treatment is in its infancy in Britain (biological methods are, for example, being used at a 10 ha gas works site in Blackburn, but are less sophisticated than the Dutch systems).

The £149 million spent in DoE grants since 1979 (1989 prices) to improve 'derelict land' had not made decontamination of land 'an explicit priority'. DoE advice had since 1976 been devised by the important-sounding Inter-departmental Committee on the Redevelopment of Contaminated Land (ICRCL), but for six years it had only one member of staff and for the rest of the time only two. 'ICRCL guidance,' said Luton Borough Council, 'makes only passing reference to water quality problems. Indeed the DoE guidance which encourages the leaving of contaminants in the ground and covering them up virtually ignores the possibility of migration into groundwater. It is short-sighted and cosmetic.'

Diffuse contaminants, of course, do not confine themselves to the soil. The gradual percolation of chemicals through soil, and their carriage through air or water, has led to a very large number of 'toxics' being found worldwide. PCBs (poly chlorinated biphenyls) were first found to be globally distributed in the tissues of seals, whales and other marine life in the late 1960s. PCBs are suspected of causing cancer. After a five-year campaign involving environmentalists such as Graham Searle, their production was stopped in the 1970s.[10] They continue to appear at high levels in marine mammals because they are long lived and accumulate in fatty tissue. Old stores of PCBs continue to be suddenly dumped into the environment.

So, for example, Greenpeace reported in 1988 that quantities of Aroclor 1262, a highly chlorinated mixture used in resin and paint applications (rather than the frequent PCB use in transformers), were found in grey seals and a pilot whale that died in Liverpool Bay.[11] The presence of this 'rare' chemical, said Paul Johnston and R L Stringer of Queen Mary College, implied a recent release 'in considerable quantity'. The levels were approaching those found in the highly polluted Dutch Waddensee, and might be expected to interfere with reproduction. Indeed, Paul Horsman of Greenpeace adds that seals from the Mersey have since been found with occluded uterine ducts, a symptom consistent with PCB toxicity.

At the edge of the Bay, the mud of Weston Canal is highly contaminated with deposits of other often long-lived chlorinated hydrocarbons, the sort which at high concentrations qualify as 'special wastes'. Those present at high levels include chloroform, carbon tetrachloride, tetrachloroethane, hexachlorobutadiene and the stable hexachlorobenzene. The silt, say Greenpeace researchers, ranges from 'fine black anoxic mud with relatively low water content' to 'fluid blue and yellow deposits smelling strongly of hydrogen sulphide.'[12] The Weston canal silt is partly dredged into a lagoon, where it constitutes a toxic waste problem. Some of the chemicals are carried into the sea. Others may evaporate. Once in the environment, toxic chemicals live out their chemical and biological lives, whether viewed as toxic waste or another source of water pollution.

It seems likely that many developed countries are heading the way of the Great Lakes ecosystem of Canada and the USA. Here, after rivers caught fire and swimming was banned in some areas, heroic efforts were made to stop pollution from pipes and dumping, while legislation banned cancer-causing chemicals. But studies in the 1980s,[13] showed that levels of banned chemicals were still high or rising owing to concentration in the food chain. A mass of other chemicals had slipped through the legislative net because they were not known to cause cancer. Some of these also accumulate in fatty tissue.

Thus after the banning of DDT, bald eagles (at the top of the food chain) have shown some recovery in terrestrial parts of the eastern USA, while around the Lakes they are still suffering poor reproductive success. The reason is that chemicals such as DDT and toxaphene are being transported by air in a diffuse form all the way from Central America. 90 per cent of the PCBs reaching the Lakes now come from such long-range diffuse pollution. Similarly, run-off from farms and countless small sources in streams, through soil and local dust, contributes to an uncontrolled input of contaminants.

In 1981, a Lake Michigan study showed that mothers who had eaten a significant quantity of lake fish throughout their lives had significantly smaller and more premature babies, with disproportionately smaller heads. PCB concentrations in a mother's breast milk, and serum in the infant's umbilical cord, were 'associated with infant's decreased visual recognition memory (a measure of neurological development)'.[14]

In other words, like lead, PCBs were affecting the brains of children and passing our toxic legacy from one generation to the next. Perhaps unsurprisingly, the researchers have found a wide range of birth defects and growth abnormalities in wildlife at the top of the Great Lakes food chain.

At the 1990 North Sea Conference, Britain successfully pressed European partners to call in remaining stocks of PCBs by 1999. The UK wants to incinerate them; West Germany wants long-term underground storage.

The Tips 'Timebomb'

Waste tips are supposed to be a solution to the toxic waste problem; instead, they often pose some of the greatest threats. Dr Robert Holmes and Dr Alistair Clark of the consultants Dames and Moore[15] told the Commons inquiry that it was the mixing of complex hazardous chemicals, such as pesticides, with fairly harmless domestic waste – anything from cardboard to garden clippings – that led experts in other countries to believe 'the United Kingdom has a timebomb' in the shape of waste tips that might leak toxins into groundwater or air or need digging up for treatment ('remediation') at a later date. Because of such problems, West Germany was to restrict all organic solvent disposal into landfills. In the USA, co-disposal was banned.

Consultants Clayton, Bostock, Hill and Rigby told the MPs that given the long-lived nature of many chemical hazards, secure 'protective measures' such as impermeable membranes would be needed for 'as long as 200 years'. These should be able to withstand natural events such as once-in-a-hundred-years rainfall, low atmospheric pressure, bad workmanship, sewer repairs, and so on.

But Britain is already littered with leaking sites that do not contain their waste, and many dumps fall far below the standards set in other countries. The Hazardous Waste Inspectorate has admitted that 'If we have avoided major problems with co-disposal landfill in the UK, this is in some cases more due to luck than judgement.'[16]

Following disasters such as Love Canal (where housing and a school were built on a 22,000-tonne chemical waste tip), the United States established a US$8.5 billion 'Superfund' to clean up old waste tips, principally to protect groundwater. Strict legislation implemented by the EPA (Environmental Protection Agency) requires the polluter to pay for clean-up of its toxic waste. In May 1989, Bofors Nobel was forced into liquidation in Michigan, in order to finance a US$60 million cleaning up of just 68 acres polluted with paint pigment. There are an estimated 425,000 hazardous waste sites in the USA, and the cost of cleaning them up has been put at US$100 billion, more than the profits of the top 'Fortune 500' companies.[17] Almost 1,000 sites were identified as needing 'urgent attention'.

Denmark, West Germany and the Netherlands have identified serious problems (at Lekkerek the Dutch found 1,600 drums of illegally dumped toxic waste, including toluene, in 1980), but for decades the official British line has been that the UK has no significant problem. In May 1988, the Department of the Environment's Chief Scientist, Dr David Fisk, told the Commons Environment Committee that he 'remained confident' that co-disposal was 'environmentally quite satisfactory', on the basis of the findings of an early 1970s study (conducted for the government by the Institute of Geological Sciences) of the geology and chemistry of 3,000 UK waste sites. 'Of those,' said Fisk, 'about 50 were viewed as. . . some hazard or possible risk to groundwater.' [18]

Of these 50, 19 were examined closely and it was concluded that, with 'good engineering practice', there would be no threat to groundwater if chemical waste was mixed with domestic waste. The idea was that the biological activity of the rotting rubbish would break some poisons down (cyanide, said Fisk, was 'a good example'), while 'the research also found that the mineral substrate that surrounds the landfill sites very often acted as an attenuant by tying up some of the heavy metals which would have otherwise leached through to the groundwater supply'.

In other words, by letting the waste leak some way into the surrounding soil it would be sufficiently combined with other chemicals or broken down by bugs that there was no real hazard, so long as a small number of 'special wastes' (such as low flashpoint solvents and chlorinated organics) were excluded. This remained the DoE view throughout the 1970s and 1980s.

In 1989 the Commons Committee was more forthright: 'the consequences of the UK's failure properly to implement co-disposal at all landfill sites has been serious. It has damaged our reputation in Europe, with possible serious implications for future policy initiatives.'[19] 'We are not convinced that dilute and disperse is an acceptable principle upon which to base waste management,' said the Committee, 'both from the standpoint of implicit groundwater contamination and subsequent contaminated land development.'[20]

Holmes and Clark pointed out that co-disposal is 'absolutely at variance with the objectives of the EC Groundwater Directive,' which aims to prevent substances getting into soil water, not to encourage it as a means of 'treatment'. The UK has, indeed, been threatened with prosecution by the EC over the issue.[21]

'We understand,' said the MPs, 'that it is possible for someone to purchase an old landfill or other contaminated site without being aware of the fact. This is clearly unacceptable.' Clayton, Bostock, Hill and Rigby referred to the 'striking difference . . . between the UK and, for example, the Netherlands, FRG, Denmark and the USA'. The UK had 'failed to carry out more than a number of very limited programmes to "identify" or "discover" polluted sites that are currently, or have the potential to be, immediate hazards to health or threats to the environment.'

'While these countries publish lists of suspect sites and openly debate what should be done about them,' noted the consulting firm, 'the general UK approach, if we cannot avoid identifying them, is to try to keep things as quiet as possible and certainly not consider them as incidents requiring urgent action.'[22]

In 1989, however, a different sort of leak occurred when the 1970s geological survey was passed to Friends of the Earth. This revealed that, far from there being 'about 50' sites posing 'some hazard or possible risk to groundwater,' as Fisk had claimed the year before, the geologists had identified 59 sites as posing a 'serious' threat to groundwater with another 1,300 judged to pose some risk. In other words, from the 3,055 in the survey – which had remained unpublished for 16 years – 42 per cent posed some hazard to groundwater, and not, as Fisk had suggested, under 2 per cent.[23] Of the 59 sites identified as a serious risk, 20 were still in use in 1990. Two places, Ewelme in Oxfordshire and Halesowen in Staffordshire, had two 'serious risk' sites.

The National Rivers Authority told the Commons Committee that groundwater contamination was a 'serious problem' which would require increasing attention. For example, redevelopment of a gas works site in the Thames region had forced the closure of a bore-hole, chlorinated solvents had found their way into public supply sources in the chalk of Dunstable and Luton, while aquifers under Birmingham and Coventry were seriously polluted. The only way to deal with the contamination was to treat the water abstracted.

How large Britain's 'timebomb' may be, nobody knows. A 1988 DoE report *Assessment Of Groundwater Quality In England and Wales* [24] revealed that pollution from waste tips was 'the most significant threat' to groundwater in some regions. Bore–holes had already been closed because of contamination. Regions like Southern Water rely as heavily on groundwater as do continental countries and contamination will be made worse by the already severe problem of over-abstraction.

As of 1990, the DoE still seemed confused. Dr David Fisk told the Commons Committee that the 1988 groundwater review 'indicated that to date it had not been seen as a problem', and Minister David Trippier said 'the possible effects of contaminated groundwater are not significant on a national scale'. This, noted the MPs, was 'scarcely justified' by the groundwater review's own finding that 'groundwater is a national resource threatened by deterioration in quality due to contamination'.

The list of dumps disclosed by FoE may be only a small indication of Britain's waste inheritance. In the years since it was drawn up, Britain has enthusiastically dumped all sorts of waste into holes. FoE contacted 149 local authorities that count as 'waste disposal authorities' (WDAs) to obtain details of Britain's 1,891 currently operating waste sites, of which 1,147 were licensed to accept toxic wastes in 1989. Another 744 took only municipal waste, although this might contain toxic substances such as oil, pesticides or lead. In addition, they located 1,631 sites in England and Wales which had been closed since 1974. Few authorities have detailed records.

A Policy of Cheapness

Britain's relaxed waste policy has made it such a bargain to use this country as a dump that one company wanted to ship 1.5 million tonnes of domestic waste from the eastern USA to Cheshire, with a similar scheme in Cornwall. Under the headline 'Why Britain Plays Dustbin to Europe's Poisons', Steve Connor of the *Daily Telegraph* commented in 1989: 'The world is awash with hazardous waste, and Britain, like it or not, has become the 'dustbin of Europe. Most industrialised countries now produce more waste than they can dispose of. And most countries have tightened up their disposal regulations. Britain has not.' [25] In March 1990 the Welsh Affairs Select Committee called for a ban on import of waste for landfill.[26]

The Commons Committee attributed the 'pre-eminence' of landfill in the UK to its cheapness. The National Association of Waste Disposal Contractors estimated that it cost £5.40 a tonne to landfill a 'known special dry waste'; £10.60 for 'difficult' wastes; £16.16 for special wastes; and £21.80 for special liquids. In contrast incineration of PCBs cost up to £2,000 per tonne, difficult special wastes £100–1,000, and simple waste, £100–200 per tonne.

Moreover, in the UK, landfilling a tonne of standard industrial waste (zinc hydroxide) cost about £5 in 1988; in Belgium £15; and in West Germany and France £25. This was partly because of lower engineering standards imposed on sites in the UK. Even the DoE admitted that landfill was too cheap, saying that, if prices included methane and leachate control systems, restoration and aftercare (often not done in the UK), the cost of tipping municipal waste would be around £9. Actual prices ranged from £2 – less than a quarter of the 'ideal' price – to £5. The Sheffield waste recovery and recycling scheme only works because the City pays a rebate of £10 per tonne on what is collected, reflecting savings on landfill costs.[27]

Holmes and Clark point out that legislation in the US now places a 'cradle to grave' responsibility on waste producers. High-tech containment sites are favoured, they say, in order to meet 'strong regulations and standards' which 'may prove expensive in the short term but are considerably cheaper than having to perform a large number of contaminated land or groundwater remediation projects at a later stage.' [28]

Perhaps the greatest criticism of British policy is that it perpetuates the problem. It is not preventive. The Commons Report contrasted it with West German policy where Bodenschutz (soil protection) starts from 'the underlying premise that soil is a scarce and valuable resource which needs to be conserved . . . British policy should move closer to this concept'.

A Catalogue of Neglect

In February 1989 the Commons Committee opened its *Toxic Waste* report with the words: 'Never, in any of our inquiries into environmental problems, have we experienced such consistent and universal criticism of existing legislation and of central and local government as we have during the course of this inquiry.'[29]

The UK's annual production of waste of 2,505.15 million tonnes is made up as follows: liquid industrial effluent, 2,000 mt; agricultural, 250 mt; mines and quarries, 130 mt; industrial (hazardous and special), 3.9 mt; special, 1.5 mt; domestic and trade, 28 mt; sewage sludge, 24 mt; power station ash, 14 mt; blast furnace slag, 6 mt; building, 3 mt; medical wastes, 0.15 mt.[30]

Co-disposal mixes 'controlled wastes' (governed by Part 1 of the Control of Pollution Act and excluding explosives, farm wastes and mine or quarry waste) with other more ordinary rubbish. Within this, waste is classified according to where it comes from so that waste from a prison is 'household' while if the same waste emerges from a railway station it is 'commercial'. Then there are 'special wastes', including medicines, many poisons and highly inflammable chemicals. These get extra controls over their movement and disposal. Unfortunately these do not include clinical waste or many environmentally damaging substances.

The UK has reliable statistics only for the category known as 'special waste' (less than 1 per cent of the estimated total). From 1982 to 1988, 'special waste' imports to the UK increased twenty fold from 3,800 to 80,000 tonnes a year.[31] HMIP estimated in 1989 that total non-special waste imports in 1986/7 had been 183,000 tonnes, of which 130,000 were for landfill but only 10,000 would be in 1987/8.

'Hazardous waste' is a term used by an EC Directive (84/63/EEC) on the control and supervision of shipments across boundaries. Britain mainly says these are the 'special wastes' – but other countries use different definitions.

The UK also uses the term 'difficult wastes', meaning those 'harmful in either the short or the long term to the environment'. In Britain, 'toxic waste' as such is not a bureaucratic definition. The Commons Committee pointed out that, 'Just as, paradoxically, "acid rain" can be neither acid nor rain, so some substances normally benign may have toxic effects in the wrong place at the wrong time or if wrongly handled.' Toxic waste, they say, is simply a 'graphic and comprehensive' term.

Richard Marsh from Aspinwall & Co complained to the Committee, 'We have over 6,000 descriptions of waste, we have over 50 ways of describing asbestos, 30 ways of calling something inert. . . .'[32] The control, monitoring and inspection system was so understaffed, antediluvian and confused that many local authority officers responsible for enforcement were unable to crack down on 'cowboys', and concentrated on 'the responsible sector of the industry where they were more concerned to see that the forms rather than the land sites were correctly filled.'[33]

Except for the London Waste Regulation Authority (LWRA, a descendant of the abolished GLC), the UK's 199 WDAs are local authorities, legally charged with controlling waste by issuing and enforcing licences for dump sites. All except the LWRA are 'poacher and gamekeeper', both running their own dump sites and imposing controls on those that are privately run.

Above the WDAs is the Department of the Environment. It had not, however, shown much interest in waste since receiving powers under the 1974 Control of Pollution Act. 'DoE inaction on waste management has been a catalogue of neglect since 1974,' wrote the Commons Committee.

Following criticism by a Lords Committee under Lord Gregson in 1981, a Hazardous Waste Inspectorate was set up under the DoE in 1983. It was amalgamated into HMIP in 1987 as the Controlled Waste Inspectorate in the Air, Water and Wastes arm.[34] In 1988 the Environment Committee were 'surprised to discover' that 'the Inspectorate still had only six field Inspectors to cover England and Wales, comprising 5,000 sites in 117 Waste Disposal Authorities.'

Dr Harvey Yakowitz has made a comparison of waste control in West Germany, Japan, the UK and other countries, for the Organisation of Economic Cooperation and Development (OECD). 'In Bavaria alone you have 50 or 60 waste inspectors,' he says, 'whereas the whole of the UK has only a handful. In Japan there are a couple of thousand inspectors.' [35]

As the Environment Committee began its toxic waste inquiry, the government suddenly announced 13 new posts for HMIP, of which six would be field Inspectors. This 'upsurge of activity, too marked to be a coincidence,' said the MPs, included the appearance of two Waste Management Papers in ten months (the previous six years saw only four), four new items of legislation (the previous six years saw one) and four major consultation documents or draft legislation (previous score: one). The HMIP could not provide Rossi's Committee with an overall assessment of British waste disposal standards because it had no reliable figures. It declined to identify particularly bad offenders, suggesting that those responsible knew who they were. 'We are disturbed by this complacent attitude,' said the MPs.

The Hazardous Waste Inspectorate regarded 35 per cent of tips as 'poor' and noted in 1985 that, under the current licensing scheme, 'Hazardous waste disposal in particular is treated cursorily with the licence too often requiring disposals to be carried out "to the satisfaction of the Waste Disposal Authority" rather than specifying how disposals are to be made.'

The beleaguered waste disposal staff often have difficulty persuading their council solicitors to prosecute offenders such as fly-tippers. When they do, magistrates frequently impose pathetically small fines. In one case a farmer fly-tipped factory waste after being paid £150. After considerable effort he was tracked down, caught and prosecuted. He was fined just £100, showing that, if you're a fly-tipper, crime can pay. The LWRA found in a survey that Tower Hamlets alone contained 1 million tonnes of fly-tipped waste, and estimates that 15–20 per cent 'contains some toxic element, maybe asbestos or cyanides from gaswork wastes'.

The Environmental Protection Bill, introduced at the end of 1989 brought in the concept of 'Integrated Pollution Control' and reorganised WDAs in England and Wales, into companies formally distinct from the local authorities. The government had recently suffered the double embarrassment of a Canadian cargo containing PCBs en route to Rechem's high-temperature incinerator in

South Wales being turned back by dockers, and the Karin B, which had homed in on Britain as a likely destination for its homeless shipment of toxic waste. In October 1989, the government announced British backing for the Basel Convention under which 34 countries limit international waste movements.[36] In November the same year, it announced that Local Authorities would be required to keep a register of contaminated land and that each might have to nominate a Recycling Officer.[37] Toxic waste might also be excluded from co-disposal.[38]

Alternatives to Landfill

While Britain extended landfills, Europe was burning its municipal waste. Evidence received by the Commons Committee showed that 12 million tonnes of municipal waste a year were being incinerated in each of West Germany, Denmark, Sweden and Switzerland. Heat from most European incinerators is recovered to generate steam for district heating or electricity. Babcock Energy told the MPs that these countries were each saving the equivalent of 4 million tonnes of coal as a result. Britain incinerates only one-sixth of this (650,000 tonnes) in systems with recovery facilities.

Swedish systems firing heat and power schemes are said to recover all their costs or even to make a profit. At Goteborg, a 1,000 tonne-a-day waste incinerator supplies 100 MW of useful heat to the city and 14 MW of power. In summer it meets all the city's hot water requirements and in winter 25 per cent. [39] A Sheffield incinerator is due to provide heat to 7,000 homes. One in Coventry provides heat to industry. At Edmonton in north London it makes electricity. A refuse-fired district heating and power station proposed for New Cross in south London is planned to generate 30 MW of electricity and 75 MW of heat from a yearly burn of 400,000 tonnes of waste[40]. (Every 3 kg of household waste holds the equivalent heat value of 1 kg of coal.[41]) Secondary Resources, a Birmingham-based company, estimates it will save the city £3 on every tonne of refuse converted to saleable fuel pellets or humus at its plant, which coverts 92 per cent of the rubbish it takes in.

But incinerators have their problems. Unless carefully controlled and equipped with filters, they can produce a fallout of heavy metals, dioxins and furans. Many of Britain's 39 municipal incinerators were built in the 1960s or 1970s. According to the Association of Metropolitan Authorities, to retrofit them with controls needed to meet the pollution limits set under a draft EC Directive would mean spending £1m per plant, forcing the closure of half of them. 'This,' said the Commons Committee, 'is an expenditure many local authorities will seek to avoid, especially if they feel they will be able to get away with cheap landfill.'

Decomposing waste creates 'biogas', which is half methane (around a quarter of the biodegradable waste decomposes in the first 15 years). Waste gas specialist Keith Richards says that in 1986 the Department of Energy identified 300 dumps in England and Wales where the gas could be piped away and used to generate electricity. Three years later there were only 26 in operation, with 20 under study. West Germany has 50 and the USA 70.[42]

In 1988/9, a £5 million DoE fund was made available to local authorities for emergency works to deal with some of the 1,400 major landfill sites thought to be emitting methane. But the money was not available if *any part* of the council's capital programme was not contractually committed. So, for example, the council would have to check budgets from playground equipment to house repairs, and divert as yet unused funds to the gas project first, before it could ask the DoE to consider its request. Given such extraordinary bureaucratic hurdles, it seems unlikely that in practice much of the fund will be accessible to local authorities.[43]

Switzerland demonstrates the effect of high landfill prices. In the Canton of Zurich, there has been a dramatic increase in the composting of domestic waste, both by individuals (where it is used on the garden) and by local authorities. Researcher Andreas Grunig, says 'composting is prompted by the rising price of landfill and incineration: each householder is charged for garbage disposal and so saves money by doing it. And the price of landfill is high because of a shortage of sites.'[44] Similar composting schemes exist in an experimental form in Britain, but are severely hampered by the mixing of heavy metals (such as cadmium from ordinary batteries) and glass with compostable waste.

Amazingly, Rossi's Committee discovered that many councils keep the price of their own landfill sites artificially low 'in order to attract contractors' waste which might otherwise be fly-tipped'. This, said the MPs, 'is a very short sighted policy and confuses the proper operation of a well-managed site with law enforcement against illegal activities.'[45] Because publicly owned landfill has been kept artificially cheap, private sector firms claim their prices are forced down to compete, and money is not available for the sort of higher engineering standards that apply in other countries.

However, municipal waste is a small fraction of the total. Industrial waste is the biggest problem.

Waste from industry can be 'treated' with chemicals but this usually increases its volume, and has so far proved controversial. One particularly prominent company is Leigh Interests of Walsall in the West Midlands. One of Leigh's processes is known as 'Sealosafe' and involves mixing concrete with chemicals such as sulphuric and nitric acid, cyanide salts, organic acids, mercury, arsenic and lead, to form a stable 'polymer'.

Local people, some of whom live within 200 yards of the perimeter, have complained about smells and fumes from the site, saying that it causes sore throats, headaches, stinging eyes and vomiting. Journalist Sarah Boseley relates how 'Walsall Metropolitan Borough council, responsible for licensing waste disposal since 1986, became worried when one of their scientists went to take samples from a pit of chemical waste that should have solidified. "One of our chaps put his foot on it and his foot went in" said Environmental Director Mr Jeff Kirkham'. [46]

The Commons Committee visited the Leigh site and wrote: 'we were pleased to note the improvements made, apparently in honour of our visit, in comparison with photographic evidence of the site just a couple of months previously. The Company was convicted for 12 infringements of the Control of

Pollution Act in respect of this site in January 1989.'

In June 1989 the government Harwell Laboratory reported on the site for Walsall Council. Boseley writes: 'They confirmed that 1.3 million tons of hazardous waste was far from the rock-like substance promised in Leigh's promotional material for the Sealosafe process. In only one of three clay holes was the material fairly hard, and even then there was liquid present.' The council refused to renew the licence for the Sealosafe process. (It turned out that the reason for its failure was a form of co-disposal: organic waste added to the inorganic industrial chemicals had prevented the polymers from hardening.)

Waste Minimisation

Where treatment and landfill are discounted, more and more companies are turning to waste reduction and waste recovery. The European Council of Chemical Manufacturers' Federations set two 'Principles of Industrial Waste Management': '1. Waste reduction: take all economically and technically justifiable measures to minimise generation of waste through process optimisation or re-design; 2. Waste recovery: seek every opportunity for the economic recovery of residues as feedstock, for energy production, or any other purpose.' [47].

Waste minimisation, noted the Environment Committee, was now 'perhaps the highest priority' of the US EPA. A survey by the US Office of Technology Assessment found 'Most European Governments, including France, the Federal Republic of West Germany, Sweden, Norway, Denmark, the Netherlands and Austria, have placed a high priority on waste minimisation. Japan has concentrated on recycling technologies . . . the UK has taken little or no action'. [48]

The financial benefits, said the MPs, were 'impressive'. Both 3M and Du Pont had profitably achieved a 50 per cent or greater waste reduction in particular processes, reducing the costs of waste disposal, energy and raw materials. In the UK, ICI was 'only beginning' to discover the opportunities, although one process modification had saved £400,000 in 18 months. According to the OECD, waste reduction was the only tactic of environmental protection which directly benefited industry.

It is also interesting that prevention at source – avoiding making waste in the first place – is the long-held position of groups such as Greenpeace, which were for many years lambasted from many quarters as hopelessly idealistic.

CHAPTER 8

Litter

'Britain,' complained Mr Michael Medlicott, Chief Executive of the British Tourist Authority in 1988, 'is in danger of pricing and dirtying itself out of its place among the world's top five tourist countries. . . litter turns off people visiting our shores and we have a bad reputation and a bad image. London is one of the dirtiest cities in the world.' [1]

He was right. A year later, the Authority's own survey found 56 per cent of overseas visitors agreed the capital was a dirty and unpleasant city. 'London is so dirty it depresses me and makes me sad for you,' said Mayor Giampaolo Mercati from Borgi San Sepolcro in Italy, visiting the National Gallery in Trafalgar Square.[2] 'Britain's image abroad as "the dirty man of Europe",' wrote the Tidy Britain Group 'is hardly conducive to a healthy tourist industry.' [3]

Tourist chief Medlicott pointed out that foreign visitors to Britain experienced decrepit public services as well as a squalid environment. 'Many trains on the routes from seaports are inferior, and there is often no co-ordination between ferry and rail services.'

The Prime Minister, recalled Simon Jenkins in the *Sunday Times* in 1989, was 'so appalled' by litter between Heathrow and central London in 1986 that she 'rushed improbably into the arms of Richard Branson and established UK 2000 to "clean up Britain". It did not work.'[4]

In March 1988, Margaret Thatcher made a brief appearance in St James's Park to show the nation how to pick up litter. Her normally well-oiled press machine suffered a glitch when the TV crews arrived early enough to record park staff dutifully scattering specially approved items of litter, ready for Prime Ministerial attention. The futility of the gesture was not lost on the rest of the country: it was Thatcher's first unsteady foray into environmental care.

A year later she pondered 'how much further we can get by exhortation . . . in some areas it plainly is not working'.[5] In the 1990 Environmental Protection Bill, the government's answer was to increase litter fines from £400 to £1,000. But any fine is useless if it is not imposed. In 1987 only 1,888 people were prosecuted under the 1983 Litter Act, 18 of them in London, 23 in the West Midlands and 9 in Cambridgeshire and unless the law is respected, it will not work.

And what sort of example did the government set? It officially sanctioned the use of the environment as a rubbish dump, so could it be surprised when, after a decade or more, the nation's citizens started to behave in the same way as their leaders did with the European Commission?

Taking her cue from Mrs Thatcher's litter pick, Westminster Council leader, Lady Porter, hired advertising agency Lowe-Bell and introduced ZIP squads: Zone Improvement Patrols. At £88,000 a year, the squads, promoted with badges and fluffy toys, were supposed to check on shops leaving rubbish on the pavement where Westminster's 23 million foreign visitors might see it. Collecting more in rates than any other UK council (£570 million in 1989), Westminster had money in reserve (£40 million). But, according to the *Sunday Times*, since Lady Porter had been in power, 'the public relations budget had risen 400 per cent' while the waste budget increased only 20 per cent.

Conservative councillor Patricia Kirwen resigned partly in protest at Westminster's ineffective litter antics. 'Lancaster Gate which I have represented since 1982, has never been so dirty or shabby. . . . My postbag is full of letters fed up with the general shoddiness of the area,' she told the *Sunday Times*. [6]

As to 'dog dirt' – which, with cracked pavements, Britain's pedestrians put top of their environmental concerns[7] – Kirwen commented: 'Lady Porter's way of dealing with the problem of dogs fouling the pavements was to set up the Responsible Dog Owners Club. I don't think I've seen a proper pooper scooper on the streets since the launch.' The council had privatised cleaning services at a saving of £1.1 million but less than half this sum had been put back into cleaning.

Litter is a practical problem, not a party political one. Labour Sheffield runs one of the largest cleansing departments in Britain, with 2,500 staff and a £15 million budget for a population of 546,000 (£27.47 per head). 'City centre streets,' noted the *Sunday Times* in 1989, 'are cleaned up to five times a day.' Conservative-controlled Lichfield allocates £925,000 on collecting rubbish and cleansing for 96,000 people (£9.63 per head). The Tidy Britain Group says Tamworth and Fazeley - the responsibility of Lichfield Council – have a bigger litter problem than Sheffield.[8] *Sunday Times* readers voted left-wing Camden one of the dirtiest boroughs in Britain.[9] Other particularly littered areas were Manchester's main shopping centre, Brighton, where a reader complained the town was 'fast becoming a cess pit', and Leamington Spa.

Keep Britain Tidy?

It seems that one reason for Britain's dirtier streets is that it pays less for cleaning and uses old-fashioned and inadequate measures. *The Sunday Times* spent a day with street sweeper Dave Tidman, one of Westminster's road sweepers contracted from MRS Environmental Services. Paid just £150 a week, Tidman shovelled litter at Piccadilly Circus from 6 a.m. until 3 p.m. His beat, which included a Wimpy providing 6,000 customers a day with an average six potential items of litter,[10] remained rubbish–strewn most of the day. 'London is still in the grip of a Victorian, labour-intensive, cleaning system – with the human factor under heavy pressure,' concluded journalist Richard Caseby.

'The Champs Elysees is just as dirty as Leicester Square at one in the morning,' said Tidman's boss at MRS, Robert Seear. 'But it's clean at 6 a.m. because there's a full 24–hour sweeping service.' Similarly, Milan has a mechanised street-cleaning force which finishes the job before Britain's cleaners are sent to work. In Madrid, refuse is collected from businesses and houses daily. In Westminster, it is once a week.

Apart from Prime Ministerial exhortations, litter pick photo-calls and raising the fines, the government's main contribution is to provide £1.24 million (1988/9) to the Tidy Britain Group. With sponsorship from companies including Coca-Cola, Cadbury-Schweppes and Sainsbury's, the Group's emphasis is firmly on putting litter in bins, not on reducing packaging (60 per cent of all litter).

Most of the Group's funds go on administration and promotional events or publicity campaigns. In one year these include the Tidy Beach and Blue Flag scheme used by ministers to put a brave face on the state of Britain's beaches, along with 'Tidy the Derby' (featuring Sport Minister Colin Moynihan), 'Tower Hill Project' (featuring Environment Under Secretary Virginia Bottomley), 'Verge Purge' (featuring Roads Minister Peter Bottomley), and 'Britain in Bloom' (Mrs Bottomley again).

With a preface including no fewer than three separate messages of support from ministers Chris Patten, Malcolm Rifkind and Peter Walker, the Tidy Britain Group's report[11] reads like output of the government's PR machine. And that, perhaps in spite of the intentions of its founders and staff, is how the organisation is used. As a campaign it is so far a failure. As Simon Jenkins pointed out, the organisation even 'wisely changed its name to the Tidy Britain Group' as it had become painfully clear that the word 'Keep' was obsolete.[12]

Heavy promotion of the 'Tidy Britain Group' focuses press interest on litter. But publicity in itself has not solved the problem, even if it has given the impression that ministers are busy purging, blooming, picking or tidying.

Recycling

A survey by German consultants Tuebingen found that Britain was the second biggest producer of waste in Western Europe after the Federal Republic of Germany.[13] While the Germans recycled half their waste, of the small quantity Britain did re-use, only 5 per cent was sorted and composted. The best country for recycling was Denmark where only 12 per cent of household waste went to a landfill; in the UK it is 90 per cent.

In 1989, Friends of the Earth (FoE) estimated that the average four-person British family throw out 100lb of food, 350lb of glass, over 3,000 cans and the equivalent of six trees in waste paper each year.[14] Jonathon Porritt declared: 'recycling is treated as one of those archetypal motherhood and apple pie issues . . . everyone is unthinkingly in favour of it but they never think of doing anything about it.'[15] Recycling, he concluded, 'may indeed be a lowly and humdrum issue in the eyes of some, but Mrs Thatcher knows full well that many people care as much about recycling, litter and dog nuisance as they do about acid rain, nuclear waste and the greenhouse effect. Litter may indeed make better copy, but recycling is the way to get to the root of the problem.'

Britain's lowly performance is relieved only by isolated examples of progress made mainly through the efforts of local councils. Take glass: in 1989 Leeds City became the first council to recycle 15,000 tonnes of glass.[16] Yet the British Glass Federation estimates that Britain's ratepayers spend £23 million in disposing of glass each year, at the same time losing £43 million in its value if recycled.[17] Britain has one of the worst records in Europe for recycling glass: only Portugal and Ireland do less. A 1989 survey for designers Michael Peters found that only 16 per cent of Britain's glass jars and bottles were recycled, against a European average of 30 per cent. Denmark, Switzerland, West Germany and the Netherlands managed almost 50 per cent.[18] When in 1990 Perrier wanted to recycle 20 million bottles dumped because of benzene contamination, they found the UK recycling industry lacked the capacity.

As to aluminium, which requires an enormous amount of energy to be refined from raw ore, the European average for recycling is 13 per cent and Japan manages 42 per cent, the USA 55 per cent and Canada 65 per cent. The UK recycles just 5 per cent.[19]

Only 24 local authorities in the UK possess magnets for sorting steel cans from other waste and there are a mere 196 Save A Can sites in the whole of the UK. The UK achieves 8 per cent recycling of steel cans, whereas the European average is 20 per cent, with West Germany and Holland again reaching 50 per cent.[20]

A discarded Japanese newspaper, says Charles Clover of the *Telegraph*, 'has a 90 per cent probability' of ending up in another newspaper. In Britain, it is much more likely to end up in a hole in the ground.[21]

Denmark and Germany recycle about 30 per cent of their plastic, and the USA has a seven category coding system to make recycling feasible, but Britain recycles at most 5 per cent. Of the estimated 20 million tonnes of British domestic waste thrown away each year, 2.5 million tonnes is plastic.[22] Britain's first full-time plastics recycling officer was appointed in 1989 in Sheffield, profiled as Recycling City. Here 10,000 homes are encouraged by Sheffield City and FoE to pre-sort their waste in special bins so that it can be effectively recycled, and an experimental plastic recovery plant has been set up, paid for mainly by the British Plastics Federation.[23]

In 1989, FoE and the *Daily Telegraph* produced Britain's first comprehensive directories of recycling facilities.[24] Their researches showed that the best counties for bottle banks were the Scottish Borders (1 per 3,636 people) and Norfolk (1 per 4,043); the best for paper 'igloos' included Somerset (1 per 5,542); and the best can recovery was in Richmond, Surrey, where there was one Save A Can site for every 20,250 people. In Kent, by contrast, each Save A Can site was shared between a quarter of a million people, and, if everyone in Camden had decided to save cans, there would have been one collecting point between every 183,300.

FoE's campaign prompted Minister David Heathcote-Amory to declare an official target of recycling 'at least half the potentially recyclable domestic waste by the year 2000'.[25] If it were achieved, this would be a considerable step forward, even though Britain would still lag behind European neighbours.

Sheffield (Labour) and Sutton (Conservative) emerged from FoE's surveys as among Britain's best-performing local authorities, while Kensington and Chelsea (Conservative) and Lambeth (Labour) are among the worst, showing that, like litter, the problem has little or nothing to do with party politics. Sheffield estimates it is recovering enough newsprint to save 2,000 trees a month.[26]

It has been estimated that domestic waste disposal costs Britain £720 million a year, while, if recycled, the same waste would be worth £750 million.[27] Many of the obstacles on the road to a less wasteful Britain can only be removed by government action, however.

Take the example of paper. Tariffs and government buying policies could be used to stabilise the market for recycled paper (at present, the widely fluctuating price and availability of cheap virgin pulp severely hamper its widespread use). In the United States, federal government departments (using about 5 per cent of all paper) are now required by law to give preference to recycled paper. In February 1990, after advocating that products should include the environmental costs of their production, use and disposal,[28] the government's enthusiasm for using recycled paper diminished when it discovered that it might be a third more expensive. Officials compiling a report to Nicholas Ridley, Secretary of State for Trade and Industry, told the *Independent on Sunday* newspaper that progress was unlikely 'until the mid 1990s'. The government might produce new standards for recycled paper but it would be urging private industry to take action, rather than leading the way.[29]

If waste escapes recycling, it heads for disposal, which in Britain usually means a hole in the ground.

Product Design

Designer Anne Chick calls it 'Anticipatory Design': the simple idea that, like nature, human designers should build in re-use or natural decomposition when they create a product.[30] She quotes design guru Victor Papanek: 'the largest quick-food restaurant chain proudly proclaiming on its sign "31 billion hamburgers sold so far" is also one of the worst chemical polluters in the world. Each hamburger, fish sandwich, egg burger or what-have-you comes wrapped in its own styrofoam sarcophagus, is further wrapped in plastic foil and accompanied by numerous condiments each in its own plastic foil pouch. The beverages also come in styrofoam cups with polystyrene lids and plastic cup straws. . . .'

Disposability has even been built in to the 'houseware' once known as consumer 'durables'. Presenter and writer of the TV series 'The Secret Life of Household Machines', Tim Hunkin, found that a quarter of TV sets, washing machines and fridges abandoned to the rubbish tip had 'no obvious fault'.[31] Another quarter could 'have been repaired for less than £10 and an hour's work'. A tenth of the machines consigned to the garbage were 'current models still on display in showrooms'.

Behind the decision to dump, says Hunkin, lurks the ghost of Henry Ford. He is said to have 'dispatched a team of investigators to find out the most common faults in the then best-selling car in the world, the Model T. Ford discovered that abandoned Model Ts suffered a wide variety of problems, and it was only the crankshaft that was almost invariably left intact. On hearing this, he is said to have ordered his designers to make the crankshaft weaker by using thinner metal, and so the concept of built-in obsolescence was born.'

Hunkin estimated in 1988 that domestic machines such as fridges were, in real terms, half the price that they had been in the 1950s. Machines had become weaker and more difficult to repair. Screws, for instance, had disappeared in favour of difficult-to-repair glued plastic welds.

To date, the British environmental movement has made little impact on the market forces which – encouraged by industry – encourage resource profligacy. In 1971, Friends of the Earth staged one of its best-known 'actions'. It returned hundreds of non-returnable bottles, then only recently introduced, to the doorstep of Schweppes. As a stunt it was a resounding success: the photo went round the world as a graphic image of man's waste of resources. Unfortunately, the success of the image belied the failure of the campaign: the trend for more disposability and greater packaging has increased ever since.

As new materials have been introduced, the potential for re-use and recycling has declined. Between 1980 and 1987 the percentage of soft drinks sold in glass bottles (which are easy to recycle and could be re-used) fell from over 60 per cent to under 30 per cent, while the proportion of plastic bottles grew from under 10 per cent to almost 40 per cent.

In Friends of the Earth's recycling policy, *Once Is Not Enough*, [32] Alastair Hey and Geoff Wright argue that the trend could still be reversed. They point to Denmark, which in 1981 passed a governmental decree prohibiting non-refillable containers for beer and soft drinks, and permitting sale only in approved bottles. Despite complaints about impediments to free trade under the Treaty of Rome, the controls were upheld by the EC in 1985 on the grounds that the right to free trade only existed within the context of environmental protection. Britain, however, shows no inclination to reduce waste in this way.

As well as the physical resources contained in a disposable product, increasing attention is likely to be given to the amount of energy (with obvious pollution implications) consumed in its manufacture. The ecologist H. T. Odum remarked in the 1960s that potatoes were no longer made just from solar energy, but partly from oil – his point being that, although farming was becoming more productive, this was at the cost of growing inputs of fossil fuel. The net energy input to British agriculture probably exceeded its output (in food calories) some time in the 1950s.

Batteries are a clear case in point. Although their very purpose is to yield energy, it takes so much to make them, especially to weld together their metal components, that Simon Roberts of FoE says a disposable battery requires more than 50 times as much to make as it will give out.[33] All batteries contain lead, low-energy ones also contain zinc chloride or zinc with carbon, and higher-energy types usually contain mercury or cadmium. Manufacturers are trying to remove these last two heavy metals, but huge quantities of old batteries are now land-filled, gradually leaking into soil or groundwater. Very high energy sources such as the small button batteries of cameras, hearing aids and watches often contain high levels of mercury.

Rechargeable batteries can be used 1,000 times, but so far all contain cadmium. In Switzerland, Italy, Denmark, West Germany and Austria, batteries are collected for special disposal or recycling. Hazard labelling of batteries is standard in Sweden and Switzerland and proposed in Norway and Denmark. Britain, apart from voluntary pilot schemes begun by Varta and Memorex, is waiting for the EC to require action.[34]

CHAPTER 9

The Hottest Dustbin in the World

There can be little doubt that emissions from Sellafield Nuclear Reprocessing Plant (Windscale until 1981) have created the worst case of deliberate pollution not only in the UK but probably anywhere in Western Europe. In 1986 the House of Commons Environment Committee wrote: 'The UK discharges more radioactivity to the sea than any other nation. As the Ministry of Agriculture confirmed to us, Sellafield is the largest recorded source of radioactive discharge in the world and as a result the Irish Sea is the most radioactive sea in the world.'[1]

'Until 1969,' said the Ministry of Agriculture (MAFF) in its *Atlas of the Seas Around the British Isles,*[2] radioactive caesium-137 found in the North Sea 'originated almost entirely from the testing of nuclear weapons in the early 1960s. With the increase in the reprocessing of irradiated nuclear fuel in both the UK and France an increase above the fallout background was detected in the southern North Sea in 1970 and in the northwestern North Sea in 1971. . . .' That is putting it mildly. Between 1971 and 1978 MAFF data show a sixteen-fold increase in radioactivity along the east coast of Britain, and levels 4,000 times background around Sellafield on the west coast.

Radioactive water was pumped into the Irish Sea down the now notorious 2 mile pipe from Sellafield. Currents carried much of it northwards, round Scotland, down the east coast of England into the southern North Sea and then up towards Norway. In 1978 as it passed the Isle of Man it was 200 times background, and as it passed Northern Ireland it was 40 times background, as it was when it flowed through the Hebridean Minches. Even when it reached the waters off Sweden, the radioactivity was such that it created more contamination of Swedish fish than did Sweden's own nuclear power stations. Within six years, radioactive caesium emitted from Sellafield is detected in the waters of Greenland.

The UK National Radiological Protection Board (NRPB) calculated in 1978 that three-quarters of the total radiation dose delivered to people throughout the European Community from nuclear industry effluents came from Sellafield.[3] Many of the radioactive substances released from Sellafield are mistaken by biological systems for natural elements – for example, radioactive caesium can replace potassium in flesh – and they end up in fish, shellfish and wildlife throughout the Irish and North Seas. And they reach people: everyone in the British Isles.

In *Britain's Nuclear Nightmare*, [4] film-maker James Cutler and journalist Rob Edwards record the case of a Japanese family who moved for 18 months to England. They happened to be part of a medical study at Tokyo University. When they returned to Japan, the researchers were 'astonished to discover relatively high levels of caesium–137 in their bodies', the result of Sellafield's pollution.

Radioactive caesium carries some increased risk of developing cancer if consumed. But it is other much more radioactive chemicals such as plutonium, which cause most concern. Plutonium–239 is 20,000 times more toxic than potassium cyanide, and, if inhaled, one-millionth of a gramme can cause cancer in 7 to 30 years.[5]

Since 1952, fuel reprocessing at Sellafield has led to more than a quarter of a tonne of plutonium being released into the Irish Sea. Five per cent of it is in a mobile form and disperses far and wide like caesium. The rest was supposed to be dispersed in the Irish Sea and then bound 'harmlessly' onto sediments, entombed at the bottom of the sea.

That was the theory. In practice, perhaps through bubbles carrying particles to the surface, the sediments end up on salt-marshes where they dry out, and dust is blown onto land. Plutonium is found in the air, in house dust and in sand on the beaches around Windscale.

During the early 1980s, MAFF found that areas of silt along the shore at Seascale near Sellafield contained up to 500 times the background radiation, and anyone exposed to them for 1 hour would, in the words of Cutler and Edwards, 'get more than a year's "safe" dose from beta and gamma radiation alone'. (Gamma radiation is similar to X-rays.) If the particles were breathed in, the victim would be exposed to risk from alpha particles, which cannot penetrate barriers such as paper or skin but can cause severe tissue damage if ingested or inhaled.

A 1989 survey by Friends of the Earth showed radioactive contamination of 4 miles of the River Esk in Cumbria, south of Sellafield. FoE argued that particles of plutonium brought ashore from the sea bed during violent storms could pose a hazard to health. Similar contamination had been found by the Scottish Universities Reactor Centre at East Kilbride in the Conwy Valley in Wales, and on the banks of the rivers in Dumfries and Galloway.[6]

High levels also exist on the Ravenglass estuary. All the plutonium does not stay at the bottom of the Irish Sea. It is carried towards the shore by currents and then dumped at the mouth of estuaries, where a reaction between fresh and saltwater deposits large quantities of organic silt. Of Ravenglass estuary, which is a nature reserve, Cutler and Edwards say: 'an extraordinary state of affairs has been allowed to develop. The whole area is so poisoned by Windscale's radioactivity that only the sites of some atom-bomb tests and the area around Chernobyl are worse. If the estuary were within the boundaries of the Sellafield complex, employees would be forbidden from working anywhere near it. . . . It is a bizarre fact that anyone crazy enough to dig up a bucketful of Ravenglass mud and put it in a dustbin at home would be breaking the law.' [7]

Indeed, the mud would be classed as low-level radioactive waste. It would have to be removed to Britain's only official dump for such waste, at Drigg. But Drigg is itself on the edge of the Ravenglass estuary. The Institute of Terrestrial Ecology has measured plutonium in the estuary at 26,500 times the level to be found (due to bomb tests) in English woodland soil.

The grass around the Ravenglass estuary contains up to 200 times background radiation, while the NRPB has found levels 1,800 times normal in the livers of local sheep. In 1990, milk from around Sellafield was found to be the most contaminated of 6,000 samples taken near nuclear installations countrywide.[8]

The radioactive pollution around Sellafield will be with us, and with generations to come, for a very long time. Radioactive caesium has been emitted from Sellafield in large amounts, and emits penetrating radiation (gamma rays), but it has a half-life of 'only' 30 years and so little will remain in 300 years. Others last far longer: plutonium-239 has a half-life (that is, half of it decays in that time) of 24,400 years; amercium-241 has a half-life of 400 years, decaying to neptunium-239 which has a half–life of 2.5 million years. These three are alpha-emitters, throwing out alpha particles.

A Day out at Sellafield

Today, British Nuclear Fuels Ltd (BNFL) is trying to pretend that everything is cleaned up, that the problem has disappeared and Sellafield is a jolly place for a fascinating day out. By 1988, BNFL had spent £3.5 million in nearby Whitehaven on restoration work such as rebuilding the town centre, sponsored three rugby clubs, given £1 million to a running track and worthy local events from roller skating to rare natterjack toads. When a new railway had to be built, six pigeon fanciers got new lofts at £20,000 each. BNFL offers local doctors medical facilities. In 1987, the Cumbria County Council Education Chairman was BNFL's senior information officer, Les Tuley. BNFL worker Tony Hildrop served as chairman of the Cumbrian Tourist Board.

In 1986, BNFL's chairman launched a £2 million advertising campaign with the claim 'no industry provides as much information about itself. . . . our advertising is saying to the public in effect that our door is open. We have nothing to hide.' This open-minded approach did not stop the BNFL from detaining Grimsby schoolchildren on a visit to the plant – because they took pictures. And while BNFL was allowed to advertise on television, when Greenpeace wished to put its side of the case it was prevented from doing so by the IBA on the grounds that this would be 'political'. BNFL has spent £5.7 million on a visitor centre at Sellafield, and by 1989 its advertising bill had reached £8 million.[9]

All this activity and expenditure are designed to make the public forget Sellafield's past and not think the wrong things about its future. Cutler and Edwards recall the case of Dr Barry Matthews of the Soil Survey, who in 1980 happened to meet and talked to the Toms family from Newcastle on a Cumbrian beach. Matthews' boss, Dr Peter Cawse, had told him that he would not like to live near the shore at Sellafield. Their organisation, as part of MAFF and in touch with Harwell, was aware of the degree of contamination. The

Toms wrote to their MP. He wrote to Labour's Jack Cunningham, Sellafield's local MP, Labour's environment spokesman and a supporter of the nuclear industry. He contacted BNFL. They contacted MAFF, who contacted the Soil Survey. Matthews was sacked.[10]

A Policy Discharged

Since 1952, MAFF had played an essential role in approving Sellafield's discharges as 'safe'. The discharges had begun as a naive and arrogant experiment. The emissions from the pipe (which had been built in secret) were 'part of an organised and deliberate scientific experiment,' said John Dunster, whose aims 'would have been defeated if the level of radioactivity discharged was kept to a minimum'.[11] As with other British pollution policy, radioactive discharge to the sea was based on the principle of dilute and disperse. Reprocessing plants were also built at this time in the USSR and the USA and by France at Marcoule and Cap La Hague. The American and Russian sites used 'virtual zero discharge' technology. These methods were available to the British when the Windscale facility was rebuilt in 1964, but were not adopted. Peter Taylor of the Oxford-based Political Ecology Research Group cites 1978 evidence from the United Kingdom Atomic Energy Authority (UKAEA) to the Norwegian Royal Commission, showing that it would have cost Britain only 10 per cent more in capital and running costs to put the plant on a 'virtual zero emissions' basis from the outset.[12]

Instead, the UK used a loose chain of concepts that rationalised more or less whatever discharges the plant's operators wanted to make. One of these was the open-ended idea of ALARA: As Low As Reasonably Achievable. At the time of the 1977 Windscale Inquiry, objectors pointed out that the Radiochemical Inspector of the Department of the Environment (DoE) left the definition of what was reasonably achievable largely in the hands of BNFL, who would estimate what they could achieve and 'limits' were then set to meet this. 'It is clear that DoE has not in the past set specifications based on its own assessment of what has been achieved elsewhere or on what technology is available,' said Taylor.[13]

MAFF used the excuse that Sellafield was on the coast to justify discharges. It argued on that the 'assimilative capacity', expressed as the limiting environmental capacity (LEC), of the sea and the coastal ecosystem was such that the limits applied to inland sites were not needed. On this basis, for example, 4,000 Curies of the long lived alpha-emitting wastes were allowed to be pumped into the sea per year in the mid 1960s. But in 1970 more waste was being created in making the radioactive parts of nuclear weapons, and the UKAEA wanted to discharge more. The limit was simply increased to 6,000 Curies.

Taylor notes that by 1970 other countries were severely restricting the emissions of plutonium and its relatives because of their extremely long life times. Between 1972 and 1975 the US Environmental Protection Agency (EPA) told the Hanford facility to cut emissions from just 4 Curies to 0.13 Ci a year. At Marcoule in France, where the same amount of Magnox fuel was reprocessed as at Sellafield, a total discharge of 0.4 Ci was allowed: one ten-thousandth of the British level.

Another 'principle' by which Britain justified emissions was a 'net benefit' to society. The functions of Sellafield were to dispose of waste (which otherwise would have to be stored) by reprocessing, to create plutonium for a fast breeder reactor and (the original purpose and the one for which the on-site Chapel Cross and Calder Hall reactors were built) to generate plutonium to make atomic weapons.

In *Going Critical*[14] Walt Patterson describes how Britain got into reprocessing more or less by accident. The reactors built at Sellafield created electricity as a by-product. They were there to generate plutonium from uranium, by putting it through a short controlled chain reaction in the reactors. Being chemically distinct, it was easier to separate plutonium from uranium than it was to separate the 0.7 per cent of the uranium-235 which makes 'good' atomic bombs from the 99.3 per cent of the denser uranium-238 which does not. The by-products of irradiating uranium were highly radioactive 'fission products' such as strontium-90, caesium-137 and plutonium-240, 241 and 242. The separation process involved acids and was termed 'reprocessing'.

When Britain started a civil nuclear power programme, it first plumped for a design of reactor called Magnox, which was explicitly designed to produce fuel to be reprocessed rather than stored dry. Patterson points out that it was partly this build up of 'spent fuel', which, having been longer in civil reactors than the specifically bomb-making uranium, was much more radioactive with lots of fission products, that subsequently created the massive problems with reprocessing. Sellafield has also become the reprocessing centre for ceramic uranium oxide fuel from Britain's Advanced Gas Cooled Reactors and others abroad.

The idea was to separate and re-use some of the uranium and the plutonium, while holding the other radionuclides in storage until they had decayed enough to be disposed of in the sea. Unfortunately, this policy has turned out to have been ill-judged from the start, and the plant has been beset with accidents, from reactor fires to large-scale unauthorised discharges of 'hot' waste into the Irish Sea.

Most other countries have opted for dry storage rather than reprocessing. In the USA, the Ford Mitre Study group established by President Carter determined that far from curing a waste problem, reprocessing increased it.[15] Indeed it increases the volume of radioactive waste 160 times, which is one reason why environmental groups favour storage of existing waste rather than reprocessing. As other nations are keen to avoid the storage problem, Sellafield does a 'profitable' trade in radioactive waste imports (oxide fuel) for reprocessing. Other countries have not progressed with plans for reprocessing. (A proposed plant at Wackersdorf in West Germany for example, was abandoned in 1989.) In 1988, BNFL made a profit of £275 million with export sales rising 26 per cent.

At the 1977 Windscale Inquiry, says Taylor, 'Justice Parker [the Chairman] agreed . . . that reprocessing produced no overall economic benefits and was related to strategic considerations of fuel supply (future breeder programmes)'.[16] In theory such reactors use plutonium to bombard uranium from spent fuel from conventional reactors, so generating more plutonium. Sellafield could supply both plutonium and depleted uranium. But Britain's 'breeder' programme has now effectively been abandoned, presumably removing this 'strategic' justification.

As well as the dubious claim that emissions were 'as low as reasonably achievable' and of 'net benefit', Taylor says that the third major plank of UK policy was to stay within dose limits recommended by the International Commission on Radiological Protection (ICRP). The problems with these limits are several-fold. While masquerading as scientific, they are in fact intensely political. What is more, as used by MAFF, dose-limits are specific to certain groups and they depend, in the case of long-lived hazards such as plutonium, on guesses made at the beginning about what level of risk is acceptable, about how much of a particular food people eat and about where the hazard behaves in the environment all being correct and remaining constant in the future. In practice, models have turned out to be wrong, standards and diets have changed and people's perceptions of acceptable risk have altered.

For example, instead of it being 'safely' dispersed as theory dictated, some of the discharged radiation was found to get concentrated as much as 1,000 times in certain places. Ruthenium–106 built up in local seaweed collected and sent to south Wales for use in making laverbread. MAFF was employed to approve the discharges, which by 1962 were increased 6–50 times for various types of radiation. In 1967, MAFF discovered they had underestimated the amount of laverbread someone might eat by up to five times. MAFF, say Cutler and Edwards, announced that the collectors of seaweed had retired. In fact, they were told that their seaweed was no longer required.

In 1969, the authorities wanted more bombs and recycling, so discharges had to be increased. MAFF, as Cutler and Edwards put it, 'agreed to move the goalposts'. Plutonium discharges were allowed to go up over three times. In 1970, MAFF commented that, 'in the marine context', plutonium was a 'not particularly important type of radioactivity'. By the early 1970s, several hundred kilograms of plutonium were on the bed of the Irish Sea.

In 1974, the three-day week caused delays in reprocessing and emissions went up. Caesium and plutonium began to be detected in local fish. One local man ate so much of this fish that he would have exceeded the ICRP limit. By now emissions were 100 times those of the 1950s. MAFF had begun to get worried and wanted new standards to take account of build-up in fish and shellfish, but its requests got nowhere. Dr Tony Hetherington of MAFF wrote in an internal memo in 1974 , 'Conditions have deteriorated alarmingly.' In 1975, he stated at a US Conference that it was 'what sort of legacy one is entitled to leave in the environment to future generations which troubles me perhaps more than anything else.' He left MAFF. Later he met Cutler and Edwards and told them: 'I can remember night after night writing reports on these discharges . . . for all the good [they have] done I might as well have thrown them in the bin.'

Sellafield (then Windscale) emissions were greatest in the early 1970s. Yet, for unknown ecological reasons, the amount of radiation found in local shellfish continued to increase until 1982, although emissions declined. Taylor points out that doses received by local shellfish-eaters were greater in 1981 than when emissions were ten times higher, at their peak in 1974.[17] Moreover, rather than the gamma emitting caesium as had been expected, the exposure was mainly due to alpha-emitters such as plutonium.

As marine life became more contaminated, MAFF's estimates of the quantities eaten by local people conveniently went down. By 1978 they had been cut to a third of the 1973 figure. Strangely, their surveys showed that people in nearby Lancashire were eating more fish.

By 1980, when Matthews was sacked for being honest about the Cumbrian shoreline, MAFF had to accept fresh scientific findings showing that much more plutonium might be absorbed by the body than had been thought. As a result, MAFF's 'critical group' of fish eaters were now consuming ten times the quantity of radioactivity that would be permitted in America or Germany and three times background. Research by Peter Day of Manchester University then found that MAFF might have underestimated intake by 100 per cent.[18]

In October 1983, Yorkshire Television broadcast its programme 'The Nuclear Laundry' produced by James Cutler, which revealed that house dust in Ravenglass, the Scottish tourist town of Kippford and Seascale all contained plutonium, together with radioactive americum, caesium and ruthenium. In the worst-affected house, the kitchen floor was more contaminated than land at Rocky Flats nuclear weapons plant near Denver, which had been made off-limits for house building.

In November 1983, Greenpeace divers were collecting mud samples near the Sellafield discharge pipe when they were contaminated with very high levels of radioactivity. The cause was an oily slick of effluent (containing 6,000 curies of ruthenium 106 with a three-year half-life), which had been wrongly discharged from a holding pond for radioactive waste. The beach reached 100–1,000 times its normal radioactivity, and 25 miles of beach was closed for nine months. Eventually, BNFL was prosecuted by the government and fined £10,000. Greenpeace was also prosecuted and fined £50,000.

Following the 1983 spill, MAFF surveys indicated that consumption of molluscs such as cockles and mussels in a local 'critical group' of the population had fallen almost 50 per cent. As Peter Taylor pointed out in a Greenpeace submission to the Paris Commission, 'this is fortunate for BNFL, in that by 1985 the NRPB had recommended a principal dose of 1 mSv [milliSievert]. Had the 1983 consumption levels prevailed, MAFF estimate that the dose would have been 1.2 mSv.'[19] In Germany, he pointed out, the permitted public dose was 0.3 mSv and in the USA it was 0.25 mSv, a quarter of the British limit. (A milliSievert is a thousandth of a Sievert, which is 100 rems – a unit of radiation dose equivalent used by the ICRP in setting health limits. It takes into account the differing impacts of types of radiation on the body. UK 1987 limits were 50 mSv for workers, 5 mSv for the public, with a 1 mSv recommendation.)

Human Concerns

Walt Patterson notes that public attention was first drawn to Windscale by the death of two workers within 24 hours of each other – one from leukaemia, one from myeloma – in January 1975. A press visit followed, the first since 1962. It was then disclosed that BNFL planned a major expansion of its import-export trade, including to countries which had not signed the nuclear Non-Proliferation Treaty. BNFL would take their old uranium and turn some of it into plutonium, suitable for making weapons. This was the function of the massive new THORP (Thermal Oxide Reprocessing Plant), which BNFL planned as a replacement for its old 'Head end Plant' which had embarrassingly exploded in 1973.

Major public concern at Windscale emissions was stimulated by studies by V. T. Bowen, an American marine biologist from Woods Hole Oceanographic Institute who in 1975 warned of the potential results of plutonium discharges, which became widely known through the 1977 inquiry into the THORP proposal.[20] From then on, BNFL was under growing pressure to reduce emissions to zero, and this intensified – involving the Isle of Man government, Eire, the European Parliament, Nordic Council and local authorities in England and Wales – after the 1983 spill and the critical Commons Inquiry of 1986.

Taylor points out that, while BNFL emphasise the sums recently spent to clean up emissions, a tenfold reduction had been achieved by 1983, before any of the 'new' technology was in place, and a 70 per cent reduction on 1983 levels by 1985. These reductions, however, could have been achieved far earlier. 'The 1983–1985 levels,' says Taylor, 'are comparable to the normal operating levels of the French Cap La Hague plant in the decade 1964–1974'. [21]

While radioactivity had been spreading up and (mainly) down the coast, a horrifying series of accidents had been going on inside the plant. Workers contaminated with substances from plutonium itself to uranium and polonium (so radioactive it literally glows in the dark) had their tongues scrubbed with brushes and flesh cut away in desperate and often futile attempts to prevent them becoming radioactive. Many suffer horrible wasting diseases.

Sellafield is now most notorious for the discovery, made by the researchers of Cutler's programme, that the five nearest parishes showed five times the number of deaths from childhood leukaemia – a relatively rare condition – than could be expected by chance. This 'leukaemia cluster', as it became known, was investigated by an official committee under Sir Douglas Black. The 1984 Black Report – Investigation of the possible increased incidence of cancer in West Cumbria – accepted the existence of cancers near Sellafield but not any link to the plant itself.

Cutler and Edwards detail a series of statistical fiddles that officialdom employed in trying to deny their findings of high cancer rates (which they felt implicated the inhalation of seashore particles and exposure to fallout from a major fire in 1957). Cases were omitted and time periods carefully restricted. Later, after it was disclosed that far higher emissions of radiation had actually occurred than had been told to the Black inquiry, and once Professor Martin Gardiner of Southampton University and Dr John Terrell, the West Cumbria district medical officer, had reported in the *British Medical Journal* that children born in Seascale were ten times more likely than normal to die of leukaemia and three times more likely to die of other cancers, Black changed his mind. Some areas near Sellafield had a 'high likelihood' of increased leukaemia risk, he said in 1987, and there was 'quite a likelihood that here is a genuine link' between the childhood leukaemias and nuclear plants.[22]

Cancer clusters have been investigated at a series of other installations such as Dounreay[23] and Aldermaston[24]. The eminent epidemiologist Richard Doll and other researchers concluded in 1989 in the *British Journal of Cancer,* after reviewing data from around 15 nuclear installations, that there were 'significant excess mortalities in persons under 25 years of age from leukaemia and especially lymphoid leukaemia.'[25]

In 1988, researchers at the Manchester children's tumour registry and Christie Hospital in Manchester reported that the number of children suffering rare forms of cancer in northwest England had more than doubled since the 1950s.[26]

With the scientific verdict apparently in against Sellafield, 30 leukaemia families began what might be a two-year court battle to sue BNFL. In 1990, Gardiner published again in the *BMJ*, this time linking the at-work exposure of fathers at Sellafield, to the subsequent development of leukaemia in children.[27] The paper stated: 'The raised incidence of leukaemia, particularly, and non-Hodgkin's lymphoma among children near Sellafield was associated with paternal employment and recorded doses of whole body penetrating radiation during work at the plant before conception. . . . This result suggests an effect of ionising radiation on fathers that may be leukaemogenic [give the child leukaemia]. Fathers exposed to total doses of more than 100 milliSieverts, around 200 times natural background, were six to eight times more likely than normal to have a child with the disease.'

'This report is the first time scientific evidence has shown a link between nuclear processing and cancer,' said the trade magazine *PR Week*.[28] 'What has happened here will not enhance our image,' BNFL Chief Press Officer told the magazine, but he was 'adamant' that BNFL still deserved its PR award. 'It is how an organisation gets the message across and not what the message is,' he said.

Accumulating Waste

In April 1990, BNFL announced that it had won a £750 million order to reprocess German waste in the THORP plant, due to open in 1992. 7,000 tonnes had been booked in to the new plant, from Japan, the UK and Europe.[29] With Britain's nuclear programme running down and the 'fast breeder' effectively abandoned, the case for reprocessing now relies increasingly on BNFL's commercial interests. BNFL is reported to have sought waste contracts with 30 countries.

The House of Commons Energy Committee joined environmental groups in questioning why Britain needs to encourage such a hazardous trade: 'In the wake of the Lockerbie disaster, the consequences of a similar air accident or terrorist outrage involving plutonium are too horrific to contemplate,' said the group in 1989. Britain, it warned, had become a 'dumping ground' for other people's waste as a result of BNFL's activities.[30]

As well as reprocessing high-level waste, BNFL is storing it on site. (High-level waste consists of spent fuel and some reprocessing waste; intermediate and low-level waste range from less active reprocessing liquids and gases to contaminated medical equipment.) Indeed, nearby Drigg and Dounreay in Scotland now look likely to be Britain's only sites for storing all types of radioactive waste. Reactors from submarines, for example, no longer to be dumped at sea, will probably go to a BNFL compound. By 2000 there will be eight defunct submarine reactors.

Researchers from Sussex University's Science Policy Research Unit record that low- and intermediate-level waste has been dumped at Drigg (first in shallow trenches, now in concrete vaults) from the 1950s, while high-level wastes were reprocessed or dumped at sea.[31] Amidst growing concern at the volume of waste, in 1976 the Flowers Report of the Royal Commission on Environmental Pollution proposed the 'Flowers Criterion', that there should be no further expansion of nuclear power until 'final disposal routes' were established. In 1976, the DoE took over waste planning from the UKAEA, which had already identified 14 possible sites for 'repositories' for high-level waste.

'NIMBY' protests then intervened. The Sussex researchers note that, in 1981, 'political pressures within the ruling Conservative Party, and the fear of major local resistance, led to the abandonment of the programme.' The next year a government company – NIREX – was set up to find sites for all but high-level waste, which would be stored at Sellafield for 50 years. This breached the 'Flowers Criterion'. Then 'just before the 1987 general election . . . the government asked NIREX to abandon its investigations at four potential sites, all of which were in the constituencies of Conservative Ministers and MPs.'

This left just Drigg, as Greenpeace and the National Union of Seamen had precipitated a government decision to accept a London Dumping Convention call to ban deep sea rad-waste dumping.

The problems with the growing volumes of waste generated by the entire nuclear industry, and through reprocessing itself, have thoroughly undermined its economics. Gordon McKerron of Sussex University notes that waste management costs, once thought to be only a 'minor part' of reactor decommissioning, are now estimated to be 45 per cent of the total.[32] The Radioactive Waste Management Advisory Council estimated that NIREX needs a repository for 1.63 million cubic metres of low-level and 250,000 cubic metres of high-level waste by 2030. Existing site capacity will be exhausted at least by 2020, if not much earlier. In 1990, FoE found from a 13-country survey that the UK was alone in not having a timetable for dealing with high-level waste. 1,000 cubic metres were already stored at Sellafield, destined to be turned into 'glass' blocks.

FoE and Greenpeace question understanding of groundwater movement, gas migration and long-term seismological activity at possible deep-drilled sites under Sellafield or Dounreay. They want the waste surface-stored where it can be recovered and treated as technologies improve.[33] Chris Frizelle, a geological consultant to waste disposal companies, pointed out in 1988 that waste sites would need to 'be safe for a million years and to survive 10 ice ages', as well as being monitored for 300 years.[34] It seems unlikely that BNFL will be around to see its obligations through.

Shifting Standards

As of 1989 John Dunster, the man who designed Windscale's discharges, still sat on the ICRP, having recently left the NRPB. His career had spanned decades of changing radiation standards.

In her book *Multiple Exposures*,[35] Catherine Caufield points out that in 1934 it was acceptable to absorb 30 rems* of radiation a year (the first standard). In 1950 it became 15 rems a year, in 1956 5 rems, in 1977 the ICRP decided worker exposure should be 'as low as reasonably achievable', and in 1987 1.5 rems a year: a reduction of 95 per cent. The one constant was the public had been assured by government experts that all the standards were safe.

The 1987 revision was prompted by re-analysis of illness caused by the Nagasaki and Hiroshima bombings, which showed that risk estimates were a factor of five to ten times too low. The ICRP awaits the results of a UN Scientific Committee and US Academy of Sciences study due to be published in 1990, before revising its limits downwards again (the UK government will accept this).

The 1977, ICRP decided that, after studying other industries, an acceptable risk of death from working in the nuclear industry should be 1 in 10,000. Caufield quotes ex Scientific Secretary of the ICRP David Sowby as saying, 'It appears that industries with a death rate of 1 in 10,000 are about as dangerous as the public will accept.' Yet, whether by accident or design, Sowby and the ICRP seem to miss the point. It is not so much the risks run by a worker in the industry that worry people – especially if the risks are run knowingly and by choice – but the imposition, especially unknowingly, on others outside the industry.

The ICRP left the 1977 standard for annual exposure to radiation at the 1956 level of 5 rems per worker. However, this would not achieve a 1 in 10,000 risk. The ICRP calculated that a 5 rem exposure meant a 6 in 10,000 risk of dying from cancer, a 4 in 10,000 chance of suffering genetic damage, and a 10 in 10,000 risk of non-fatal cancer. To get as low as a 1 in 10,000 risk, it was calculated that exposure should be ten times less, i.e. 0.5 rem.

The limit was left at 5 rems because it would be too expensive for the nuclear industry to achieve 0.5 rem for all its workers. The US Atomic Industry Forum ('since Chernobyl,' notes Caufield, 'renamed the US Council on Energy Awareness') stated that 'a reduction in the exposure limit from 5 to 0.5 rems per year would cost the average nuclear power plant more than US$6m extra annually.' Following the link made between worker exposure and leukaemia in their children in 1990, trade unions represented at Sellafield called on the government to reduce worker dose limits.

---

*A 'rem' - Rontgen Equivalent Man - is a measurement of radiation absorbed by human tissue. It is the product of the dose in rads (now replaced by the Gray: 100 rads) and the quality factor. It is now superseded by the Sievert, which is 100 rems.

As to the public, the ICRP concluded in 1977 that it would be 'acceptable to any individual member of the public' to run an additional 1 in 100,000 to 1 in 1 million risk of premature death due to radiation. Caufield states that this implies that exposure of any member of the public should not exceed 100 millirems a year.*

Nobody has asked the public whether this is acceptable. BNFL claims that emissions at Sellafield will fall to five-hundredths of 1987 levels in future. But, by discharging huge quantities of radioactive substances to date, including a quarter tonne of plutonium, Britain has ensured that the risk will be run, not just in this generation but in many to come.

'During the next 100 years', Greenpeace points out, most of the remaining plutonium will decay to the more mobile Americium 241. 'Even if alpha emissions from Sellafield ceased immediately, the threat from Am 241 will continue to increase.' [36]

It is possible, of course, to avoid Sellafield, although difficult to avoid eating any fish from the seas around Britain. But even that will not keep you clear of Britain's other radiation sources, as a team from the Ministry of Agriculture and St Bartholomew's Hospital discovered in 1987 when they were searching for an uncontaminated population to compare against the people living near Sellafield. They thought that people living in Weybridge, Surrey, might be a good 'control' population, until they found high levels of iodine-125 in their bodies. In fact, they had twice the level of radioactive iodine of people near Sellafield. It was concluded that research establishments and hospitals must have contaminated the town's drinking water, which is taken from the Thames. Local cows and swans were also highly contaminated. [37]

Nor can some avoid fallout from Chernobyl. The Secretary of State for the Environment stated shortly after it fell: 'the incident may be regarded as over for this country by the end of the week.' But 'three years later,' said David Clark MP in 1989, 'we still have restrictions on 758 farms, 465,000 sheep and 413,612 acres as a result of radioactive contamination.' Indeed, in 1990 it was found that 400,000 acres of upland grassland will be affected for 150 years.[38]

Radon – a radioactive gas emitted from granitic rocks – is a serious hazard in significant areas of Britain. It may kill 2,500 people a year. The problem could be cured by relatively simple ventilation measures, at a cost of just £150 million a year. The government puts up 65 per cent of the cost. Radon controls in the USA are stricter by 25 per cent and no federal building may exceed the limits.

Emissions

Radioactive pollution ending up in the sea is reported to the Paris Commission. The latest figures (for 1986) record that Sellafield discharged 2,150 Tera-

---

*A millirem is one-thousandth of a rem, so 100 millirems is one-tenth of a rem, that is, one-fifth of the risk deemed acceptable for workers and one-fiftieth of the legal limit.

Becquerels of tritium (heavy water) and 161 TBq[†] of other nuclides, including a total 4.4 TBq of alpha-emitters (such as plutonium) and 118 TBq of beta-emitters.

The French reprocessing plant at Cap La Hague emitted a total 2,320 TBq of tritium and 1,120 TBq of other other nuclides. Throughout the 1970s its emissions were dwarfed by those from Sellafield, although now they will be comparable. From 1972 to 1976 Sellafield released 902,000 Curies[*], that is 33,407 TBq. Cap La Hague released 102,000 Curies, or 3778 TBq.[39] In 1986, emissions from the reprocessing plant at Sellafield equalled all the other discharges in the world.

As to power stations, Britain's standards appear laxer than those in other countries. Britain and West Germany have almost the same number of stations. Germany's 17 reactors have an installed capacity of 14,799 MWe, Britain's 16 reactors' capacity adds up to 11,124 MWe – less but not very different.

Both countries set discharge limits in Becquerels and file them with the Paris Commission.[40] In 1986, Germany's tritium limit for its 17 stations totalled 545.2 TBq. Britain's tritium limit for its 16 reactors was set at 7,215.5 TBq: more than 13 times as much. In terms of emissions per unit of power, German limits for tritium were 17 times stricter than the British ones.

As to the other more dangerous substances, Britain allowed itself a discharge of 96.49 TBq, 56 times more than the Germans, and, on a per unit of electricity basis, the British planned to release up to 72 times more radioactive substances.

Those were the limits. According to the Paris Commission, in practice Germany released 21 per cent of the tritium discharge limit, and 0.46 per cent of the limit for the more hazardous substances. In the same year, British figures show that our 16 nuclear power stations released only 11 per cent of Britain's limit, but this was nearly seven times Germany's total, and, on a unit of electricity basis, nine times as much. As to the more hazardous substances, in 1986 Britain emitted more than 1,000 times that released by Germany.

Whatever the cause, Britain's reactors seem remarkably dirty. In 1986 Dungeness A alone managed to release 38 times as much of the 'more hazardous' radioactive pollution as all Germany's reactors put together, while Hinkley Point B released twice as much radioactive tritium, and Hunterston B more than three times as much, as the entire German system.

[†]A Bq is a Becquerel, a measure of radioactivity: one disintegration per second. A Tera-Becquerel is 1 million million disintegrations.
[*]Curies named after Madame Curie who discovered much about radiation and died from radiation-induced disease, are no longer used by most authorities to measure radioactive disintegration. One Curie is 37,000 million disintegrations per second. One Becquerel is one disintegration per second. One Tera-Becquerel equivalent to 27 Curies.

CHAPTER 10

Pesticides

Weeds, it is sometimes said, are plants in the wrong place. If a pollutant is a chemical in the wrong place, then pesticides are classic examples. Many pollutants are unwanted by-products or waste: sewage, acid rain, heavy metal compounds. Most pesticide pollution, however, results as much from use of the product itself.

In theory, most of the problems laid at the door of pesticides should never arise. If the instructions for use are carefully followed, human and ecological hazards should not result from the 'normal use' of pesticides. This has long been the basis of the agrochemical industry's argument in favour of pesticides. However, normal practice is often wasteful and creates large-scale environmental contamination.

Sometimes it is simply not possible to follow the instructions. John Home-Robertson, a farming MP, told the House of Commons Advisory Committee on Pesticides in 1979: 'I doubt whether any of the Committee has had the practical problem of, for example, having to mix a supposedly soluble chemical in precise quantities into cold water while balancing on a ladder leaning against a sprayer in the corner of a muddy field. Have they ever had to eat a sandwich meal in a tractor cab with their hands covered in DDT and miles from the nearest tap, let alone proper washing facilities?'[1] On many other occasions, users do not appreciate the risks or show due care and attention.

At one time the agrochemical industry used to imply that pesticides posed little risk in themselves. In recent years a succession of controversies – such as those over 2,4,5-T and, more recently, dinoseb and ioxynil – have led the industry to admit that many pesticides pose genuine risks should they get into contact with human beings, wildlife or into the ecosystem at large. A growing list of pesticides once defended as 'safe' have now been banned, withdrawn or severely restricted. At the same time, the public has shown a willingness to pay more for food produced organically or by low-chemical methods. The chemical industry has fought back, alleging 'chemophobia' whipped up by pressure groups.

This book can only touch on the effects of pesticides themselves. Their number has grown rapidly. In 1961 there were 127 pesticide products in use in Britain, based on 14 chemicals. In 1973 there were 461 products based on 78 chemicals.[2] By 1985 there were over 3,000 products based on 420 active pesticide ingredients.[3] More than 200 are described in Andrew Watterson's

Pesticide User's Health and Safety Handbook . [4] A number pose short-term hazards as acute poisons. Some have the potential for causing cancer, birth defects or other serious health impacts. Yet others, such as organophosphorus insecticides, may cause long-term changes in the nervous system.

It is the long-term consequences of many pesticides which are of particular concern. As the House of Commons Agriculture Committee's Second Special Report in 1987 (also known as the Body Report after its chairman Sir Richard Body MP) put it in relation to freedom of information, 'the public should have knowledge about the potential long-term, as well as acute, effects of the pesticides it intends to use. At present there is an exclusive concentration on short-term or acute hazards and little information exists on chronic risks associated with use over many years.' [5]

Reliance on pesticides in agriculture has meant that pesticide pollution has become a regular feature of the rural scene. 'Pesticide flu' has become an almost accepted hazard of life in many villages surrounded by arable land. A school in north Hertfordshire has sent children home with a note warning that, 'as it is now the spraying season' pets and children should be kept off foot-paths. Oil seed rape, potatoes and cereals, often very heavily sprayed, are now bad neighbours. Aerial spraying makes up less than 2 per cent of applications but gives rise to many complaints.

Spray drift often takes the form of a fine suspension of droplets and parti-cles, creating a pollution haze across huge areas. In 1985 a consultant surgeon told Friends of the Earth, 'I would rather live in the smogs of Los Angeles than in the chemical soup of rural East Anglia.'[6] At least two-thirds of pesticide incidents do not seem to be reported to the Health and Safety Executive, and the true figure may be nearer 90 per cent.

The very purpose of pesticides – which are chemicals made to be sprayed around the environment, not confined to the insides of a factory – makes it likely they will get into general circulation. In the case of organochlorines, long lifetimes make this almost a certainty. An equally widespread and rather similar group of chemicals are the polychlorinated biphenyls (PCBs), and, although they are not made as pesticides, they are mentioned in passing in this chapter because their chemistry is similar.

The Growth in Use: Pesticides Everywhere

Whereas in the 1950s and 1960s the use of pesticides was limited to relatively few crops and the product range was restricted, if rather hazardous, an enor-mous increase in the volume of pesticides used took place in the 1970s and 1980s. For example, in 1982 pesticide sales grew 21 per cent taking the value of the home market to £329 million.[7] In the three years 1974-77, after Britain joined the EC and its Common Agricultural Policy, the cereal area sprayed with aphicides increased 19-fold; from 1979 to 1982 the area of crops treated with insecticides doubled, and that treated with fungicides more than doubled. The British Agrochemical Association's own figures show that from 1979 to 1982 the sprayed area of the five main crops – cereals, potatoes, sugar beet, oil seed rape and peas – increased 29 per cent for herbicides, 106 per cent for fungicides and 37 per cent for insecticides. In contrast, the cropped area increased only 4 per cent in this time.

Research by John Watts and Maurice Frankel,[8] used to launch Friends of the Earth's campaign on pesticides in 1984, drew on official sources to show that by the early 1980s crops such as hops were getting an average 23 sprayings a season, while one crop of lettuce benefited from 46 sprays with four different chemicals; 97-99 per cent of all main crops, cereals and vegetables were sprayed at least once. In the orchard, the average was 17 sprayings a season, for soft fruit and glasshouse vegetables it was over eight sprayings and for peas or potatoes at least five.

With around 4,546 million litres of pesticide being sprayed onto crops in the UK each year,[9] and with 23,484 tonnes of active ingredient being used in 1987, [10] a major chemical hazard had come to exist in simply moving around and storing pesticides. So, for example, when on 2 April 1985 a lorry with over 16,000 litres of Dursban 4 crashed on the M11 motorway in Essex, 24 km of the River Roding was severely polluted. Dursban 4 contains chlorpyrifos, an organophosphorus insecticide highly toxic to fish. All aquatic life downstream died.[11] Similarly, on 11 February 1985 the *Grimsby Evening Telegraph* reported that '10 workers were rushed to hospital after a 30 gallon spillage of poisonous chemical' at agricultural merchants Kenneth Wilson Ltd. According to Friends of the Earth's *Second Incident Report*, [12] 'The chemical involved was Ceresol (phenylmercury acetate) a fungicide used to treat wheat and barley seed. Mr Peter Hall, a director of the company, reportedly confirmed that the mercury in the Ceresol was very dangerous. If you drop it on your skin in a concentrated form it can get into your bloodstream.'

Meanwhile, little of the pesticide applied to fields is actually getting to its target. A conventional sprayer known as a 'hydraulic nozzle' produces a wide range of different droplet sizes. The bigger droplets, often making up the vast majority of the total spray volume, are heavy and tend to run off onto the soil or fall straight onto it. Around 20 per cent of the spray is in very fine droplets, of 100 microns diameter or less. These are so small that they tend to drift away. This leaves only 5 per cent – and often as little as 1 per cent – of the pesticide actually getting to the pest. 'The rest,' say Vic Thorpe and Nigel Dudley of the Soil Association, 'is simply pollutant.'[13]

Technology could significantly reduce the amount used. In 'controlled droplet application' (CDA), various mechanisms such as rotating discs or mesh cages produce droplets of a certain size, designed to cut out drift or run-off. This can achieve a 95 per cent 'stick rate' as opposed to the maximum 20 per cent achieved by most conventional spraying. Droplets can also be given an electrostatic charge (as in ICI's 'Electrodyn' system), making them 'home in' on the parts of crop plants where they are most needed.

Thorpe and Dudley pointed out in 1984 that CDA could save farmers four-fifths of their pesticide purchases. Since 1979, they say, 'CDA machines have been subject to a sustained propaganda campaign by industry and some official quarters to show that they do not work efficiently . . . While development has gone ahead abroad, it has come to a virtual halt in Britain . . .'[14]

Pesticides on Food

In 1983, a survey by the Association of Public Analysts (science laboratories working with county councils) detected pesticide residues in one third of all shop-bought fruit and vegetables. The same survey showed DDT (which was not supposed to be cleared for such a use) on ten per cent of apples including Cox's Orange Pippins, Bramleys and Russets.[15]

In 1984, Members of the House of Lords were surprised to learn that the lemon in their gin and tonic might be carrying an extra kick in the form of biphenyl fungicides. Dr Bob Poller of London's Queen Elizabeth College found up to 20 times the maximum recommended limit, carried in a cosmetic beeswax glaze added to the fruit. The lemons needed scrubbing to get rid of the huge doses of insecticide applied by growers and this made them less attractive, hence the need for the wax glaze.[16]

The Ministry of Agriculture's *Report of the Working Party on Pesticide Residues (1982–1985)*[17] stressed that residues of organochlorine pesticides (such as DDT) had declined in meat and milk, while it highlighted high levels in pork from China. But the independent London Food Commission noted that the incidence of others – carbamates and organophosphates – was increasing.[18] Such pesticides are substitutes for the organochlorine insecticides like dieldrin and DDT. However, many of the monitoring systems in use by public analysts would not even pick up the newer carbamates or pyrethroid insecticides.

The Commission noted that '42% of fruit and vegetables' contained detectable residues. This figure, the highest ever reported from a British survey, 'would undoubtedly have been higher still if all residues had been detected'. Even though 25 herbicides had been implicated as causing cancer, birth defects or genetic mutations, said the Commission, many herbicides were not detectable by the survey methods, nor were 'many fungicides, other than dithiocarbamates, even though many are designed to be long lasting'.[19]

Relatively little effort is put into pesticide analysis. In 1981, 87,000 food samples were tested for bacterial contamination but only 338 were given pesticide tests.[20] '1p is spent on public analysis for every £1 spent on food advertising,' said the Commission. 'Spending constraints mean that some Local Authority testing programmes would identify only 1/40th of the possible residues present.'

Mr R S Nicholson told the Commons Agriculture Committee: 'Last year I coordinated the work for the Association of Public Analysts and there were only 500 samples that came through the system. That is a very small proportion of the foods on sale . . . Pesticides change with the years. It was the organochlorides, now we are into organophosphorus, there is an increasing use of permethrin at the present time. I do not think there is any laboratory in the public service looking at permethrin, so there could be levels of that we do not know about.'[21]

The UK does not carry out routine spot checks to monitor food for pesticide residues as do countries such as West Germany or the USA. To do so, says the Ministry of Agriculture (MAFF), would not be 'cost-effective use of analytical resources'.[22] Between 1977 and 1979 US spot checks of imported agricultural commodities found that 5 per cent of shipments tested had residues of pesticides for which no US tolerance levels existed. These included chemicals not permitted in the US.

The British Commons Committee noted in 1987: 'The problem of residues in imported food may be more serious than generally realised. . . . The Association of Port Health Officers is very concerned about the situation but feels powerless to do anything about it. . . . We are told that some ports on the south coast never take any residue analysis samples.' [23]

Friends of the Earth, the Food Commission, the Public Analysts and the Nature Conservancy Council (NCC) all urged routine, random surveys, so that users applying too much pesticide could be tracked down.[24] A proper record-keeping system is also needed to check on levels of use. Ministers could have set up such a system through the 1985 Food and Environment Protection Act but opted instead for a voluntary Code of Practice.

In the UK there are still no comprehensive specific legal limits for pesticide residues in food. The UK uses the 'Codex limits' agreed by the United Nations Food and Agriculture Organisation (FAO)/World Health Organisation (WHO). They are also known as Maximum Recommended Limits (MRLs), or Codex Alimentarius Commission (CAC) limits. The European Community has set Minimum Reporting Limits and, under Section 16(2)(k) of the Food and Environment Protection Act (FEPA) of 1985, the government has powers to 'specify how much' of a pesticide residue can be left in a crop or foodstuff, in other words to set maximum residue limits. Confusingly, all these can be referred to as MRLs.

'When we asked MAFF why they had so far avoided setting maximum residue limits,' said the Body Committee in 1987, 'they discounted the very existence of a pesticide residue problem.' But, as the Committee also noted, 'Before the introduction of FEPA, the UK was almost the only developed country without statutory residue limits. Most of our EC partner countries tend to enforce more stringent standards than those recommended by the Codex Alimentarius.' [25] As to the consumer who might eat food with more than the MRL, the Ministry suggested that, 'In most cases, occasional exposure to higher-than-average levels of a pesticide in foodstuff has no public health significance.' [26] 'In our opinion,' commented Friends of the Earth, 'the Working Party's assurance is difficult to justify in the absence of epidemiological data from the supposed consumers.' Until April 1988 the government relied mainly on 'total diet studies' based on the average diet. Critics said they take no account of people suffering food allergies and chemical sensitivities, or the unusual diet of special and ethnic groups such as the Chinese.[27]

In 1984 a significant number of the food samples tested by the Public Analysts showed residues above the EC MRLs and the Codex CAC limits. Azinphos-ethyl was found on apples at up to six times the EC limit. Demeton-S-methyl, an insecticide and a possible mutagen, was found on gooseberries at twice the EC limit. Dithiocarbamate fungicide residues on lettuce exceeded the EC limit by eleven times, and mushrooms had more than twice the Codex limit and ten times the EC limit for the insecticide dichlorvos. This is ranked 'highly hazardous' by the WHO and a potential cause of cancer, birth defects and cell mutations, as well as being an allergen. [28]

Concern at the pesticide contamination of food is threefold. First, some pesticides are thought to cause birth defects, cancers or cell mutations and these probably have no 'safe lower level'. Chronic effects may take decades to become apparent. The Ministry even used dinoseb's 40-year history of use (before US authorities announced that it might cause birth defects) as a reason why it had not swiftly suspended its use in the UK. Equally, it shows for how long a hazard can go undetected. Second, some people seem to be, or become, 'hypersensitive' to pesticides even at low levels, close to the limits of detection. For them, normal toxicological assumptions do not apply. Third, high residues usually indicate abuse of pesticides on the farm. 'Although exceeding an MRL does not necessarily indicate a possible health hazard,' said the Body Committee, 'it does show failure to comply with the cornerstone of safe use – good agricultural practice . . . where MRLs are exceeded the Ministry should attempt to identify the cause and take steps . . . there is no indication that this is done.'

The Ministry argued against a spot check statutory system because it would impair its ability to track down sources of contamination. But it also opposed a record-keeping system on the farm needed to provide a real incentive not to over-apply pesticides.

In April 1988 the Ministry of Agriculture finally released its long-awaited proposals for regulations on pesticides in food.[29] Legally binding MRLs were to be set after all, but only for the 'most important fruit and vegetable components of the average national diet', not for all foods. Some limits were to be Codex limits, a few EC limits and many would be new ones defined by the UK itself (it implemented all EC Directives on MRLs).

However, when the regulations for cereals and animal products actually appeared in July 1988, many limits had been dropped and others had been relaxed. For example, the proposed MRL for carbaryl in celery was trebled and limits for dimethoate on turnips, onions and peas were all doubled, while the quantity of lindane allowed on cabbages, cauliflowers and sprouts was increased four-fold.

Among the MRLs proposed but not set was one for dimethoate on lettuce. Friends of the Earth pointed out that the United States Environmental Protection Agency (EPA) had reported that dimethoate posed 'risks of mutagenic, reproductive and fetotoxic effects and that the risk of oncogenic effects warrants further study'.[30] A Ministry of Agriculture Report of the previous year had also found that dimethoate applied to some British lettuces 'tended to exceed the CAC of 2 mg/kg and especially the European Community limit fixed at 1 mg/kg'.

In August 1988 Friends of the Earth was leaked the minutes of the government's Crop Protection Research Consultative Committee. It revealed that, in spite of official pronouncements to the contrary, the government's own advisers were worried about pesticide residues in food. 'Consumers' acknowledged the Committee documents, 'may be exposed to higher dosages' of some pesticides 'than has hitherto been suspected'. An 'important concern' was the sprout-suppressant tecnazene, residues of which were 'generally higher in UK-grown potatoes than in those produced and stored in other countries'.[31] The April 1988 government proposal had been for a 1 mg/kg limit to tecnazene residues in potatoes (although delayed for five years): in the event no MRL appeared in the regulations. This prompted Marks and Spencer to take matters into its own hands and impose the Codex MRL of 1 mg/kg for the potatoes it put on sale. In 1989 tecnazene was even found on 'organically' grown potatoes!

Farmers, scientists and retailers, the Committee said, now showed a 'high degree of concern' about 'major dependence on post-harvest chemical treatments, especially the wide range of fungicides used to control storage rots' – 80 per cent of crops in long-term storage were now chemically treated. Crude 'bucket and shovel' techniques were sometimes being used to treat stored food, said the Committee. 'Some 30% of wholemeal flour sampled' contained residues, as did half the brown bread tested.

And, despite the belief that pesticide stays in the skin of fruit, it was found that 'pesticides penetrate the flesh of the fruit' and 'the total amount . . . could be significantly more than that previously thought to be confined to the peel tissues.' One chemical which is taken up by the plant itself is the highly toxic insecticide phosphamidon. Although not approved for use in the UK, it may occur on imported fruit. Nineteen MRLs for this pesticide were proposed and then not set.

When the Ministry of Agriculture's Pesticide Residues Report was finally published, like FoE, it now expressed concern about consumers with 'extreme intakes of certain foods'.[32] Infants, young children and people with a limited diet were particularly vulnerable groups. Children were likely to be eating multiple residues of organophosphorus compounds in their rusks; 18 of 31 rusks contained primiphos methyl.[33]

'Eels with high residue levels (especially of dieldrin),' said the Report, 'may present a potential threat to the long-term health of people who consume them in large quantities, to fish-eating birds and to wild mammals such as otters.' As little as 5 grams a day could exceed the ADI (Acceptable Daily Intake - set by government).

The Ministry, the Industry and Secrecy

It is impossible to do more than scratch the surface of any issue concerned with pesticides and not recognise the enormous influence that the agrochemical and agribusiness industries have enjoyed with the UK government. The Ministry of Agriculture helped the industry to avoid a total 'ban' on DDT for 20 years. As early as 1945, Dr V B Wrigglesworth, a scientist with the British Agricultural Research Council's Insect Physiology Unit, warned that early reports of DDT's capacities seemed 'too good to be true' and cautioned that it might act like 'a blunderbuss discharging shot in a manner so haphazard that friend and foe alike are killed'. [34]

Unfortunately, Wrigglesworth was proved right. But, despite evidence of DDT building up through the food chain, DDT remained 'cleared' under the Pesticide Safety Precaution Scheme (PSPS) until October 1984.

The PSPS was a 'gentlemen's agreement' between the agrochemical industry and government. It would still be in place today if the EC had not forced the government to replace it with the statutory Pesticide Control Regulations (1986) under the Food and Environment Protection Act 1985. Under the PSPS, key committees which evaluated and 'cleared' pesticides met and considered evidence on health or ecological effects, bound by the Official Secrets Act. Experts who were invited onto the Pesticides Advisory Committee to discuss the impact of a new insecticide on the eggs of frogs were muzzled, just as if they were discussing a new type of nuclear submarine. The industry was well represented on the PSPS (indeed it was the source of almost all the data), as were civil service departments, whereas workers' organisations were relegated to relatively powerless advisory panels. Even expert non-government groups such as the Royal Society for the Protection of Birds (RSPB), which employed leading researchers, were excluded.

It was hardly surprising if industry got the benefit of the doubt, and it took longer to restrict or ban a pesticide in the UK than in many more openly governed countries. As of 1986, there were 41 pesticides (i.e. active ingredients, which would be found in many more branded products) on sale and in use in the UK but which were banned or severely restricted in other countries.[35]

The British obsession with secrecy – 'this stupidly secret society', as the *Sunday Times* put it in 1989 [36] – led the Ministry of Agriculture's Pesticides Branch into increasingly bizarre contortions when trying to 'defend' commercial secrets. In 1985, Friends of the Earth were able to obtain huge microfiche volumes of pesticide safety data from the United States on chemicals under suspicion of warranting further restriction, when the same information was subject to the Official Secrets Act in the UK. Dr David Clark MP, the Labour spokesman, was able to wave them under the noses of agriculture ministers during debates on the FEPA.

Today the ministry releases summaries of the data used by companies to seek registration for pesticides, but the meetings where 'reviews' take place and the thinking behind the decisions still remain secret for 30 years. In 1985, Freedom of Information campaigner Maurice Frankel obtained some papers from the Kew Public Records Office which threw some alarming light on the relationship between the pesticide industry and government 'regulators'.[37]

The Zuckerman Committee – an early and influential attempt to create rules for the safe use of pesticides – wanted the suspension of 'spraying operations in windy weather, particularly on land adjacent to public roads or footpaths', 'warning notices . . . placed on gates giving access to fields that are being, or have been sprayed' and 'statutory powers' to register chemicals.

The Infestation Control Division of the civil service responded to the Zuckerman Committee's draft report. In an internal memo which has a remarkably contemporary ring to it, the Division noted: 'Statutory control in one form or another is in force in some countries, including the United States, Canada, Belgium, Netherlands, Denmark, France and Switzerland . . . the Industrial Pest Control Association would be opposed to the licensing of rodenticides and insecticides but would support a voluntary approval scheme.' 'Local Authorities', the civil service noted, wanted 'the registration of pest control firms and operators', but this would be an 'unwarranted interference with the freedom of commercial concerns'.[38]

When the final Zuckerman Report *Toxic Chemicals in Agriculture* was published in 1951, notices on farm gates and the suspension of spraying in windy weather were not ideas to be publicised. 'There seems to be too much emphasis on administrative control in the Report,' noted Mr Sutherland-Harris, a civil servant. He suggested the key word should be 'precautions'. The result was the Pesticides Safety Precaution Scheme. In the third revision, the Zuckerman Committee merely suggested an 'Advisory Committee' to 'guide Departments on the scope of the initial investigations which should be undertaken by manufacturers and about the evidence which should accompany proposals to introduce new substances'. No statutory scheme was forthcoming.

These decades-old papers show remarkable consistency in ministry thinking on pesticides. Commercial users' interests and industry's desire for sales define the 'need'. The public interest, even local authorities' wishes, are secondary and not represented in decision-making.

The risks of secrecy were dramatically illustrated by the American Industrial Biotest Laboratories (IBT) scandal in 1984. Over 140 pesticides were 'cleared' for use using data later found to have been falsified from 800 IBT tests; 75 per cent were so badly done as to be useless. Frankel noted in 1986: 'In Britain, as elsewhere, IBT data had been accepted and regarded as reliable. Unlike other countries, however, Britain responded to news of the scandal in total secrecy. In the USA, the EPA has published a complete list of the pesticides which had in whole or part been tested by IBT. In Britain, this information has always been withheld, despite requests for it in the House of Commons.' [39]

Canada and Sweden banned pesticides after the IBT disclosure. Britain did not. The Ministry of Agriculture claimed that no IBT data had been crucial in any decision it took to clear a pesticide for use, but, says Frankel, it 'has refused to produce any specific evidence to substantiate this assessment'. The Canadians put new warnings on some pesticides, while IBT-tested chemicals were checked. No such warning was given out in the UK.

The voluntary PSPS was finally replaced as a result of the 1985 Food and Environment Protection Act, Part II of which gave ministers power to make regulations to control pesticide registration, approval and use. The crucial influence was a 1983 letter from the European Commission saying that the 'code of practice' of the PSPS infringed Article 85 of the Treaty of Rome, concerning competition.[40]

The Body Report summarised the position like this in 1987:

'There are two points of principle relating to public anxiety about pesticide use which were argued by the Campaign for Freedom of Information. The first is that 'opening up' the system will result in more knowledge about ill effects of pesticide use (and indeed their safety); the other is that the public as consumers, will have more choice, based on a better informed decision, over which products to use.'

The Report added:

'We accept both of these principles: clearly the release of health and safety
data will enhance our understanding of the possible effects pesticides may
have on human health and at the same time individual users will be able to
exercise some discrimination about the particular pesticides they use when
they know more about their potential effects or safety record.'[41]

Despite vigorous government statements in favour of freedom of information, the Ministry of Agriculture's attitude has remained less than enthusiastic.
The Body Committee noted: 'nothing in MAFF's original written evidence to
suggest that officials believed that public access to health data was either
necessary or desirable. . .' [42]

The Committee found quite a different attitude among officials when it
visited Canada and the United States. The US Federal Insecticide and
Rodenticide Act (FIRA) of 1947 had been amended in 1972 so that a pesticide's 'adverse effects' on the environment would need to be considered as
well as those on human health. All pesticides were also to be reviewed every
five years and, most significant, the public was given access to health and
safety data.

The result of the amended FIRA – or the pressures which it reflected – was
a sea change in the attitude of government and industry towards 'the pesticide
problem' in the United States. When Body's Committee visited the EPA in
Washington, they found that the officials 'were disarmingly direct about free
access to information on the possible health effects of pesticide products,
unaware of any valid reason why there should not be full disclosure of safety
data. Their main concern, as indeed we found with almost everyone we spoke
to in the USA, was with the poverty of data, particularly of an epidemiological
nature, on the chronic or long-term effects of pesticide use.'[43]

Dow Chemicals told the MPs that the need to provide public data made it
considerably more expensive to register pesticides in the USA than in the UK
or other parts of the EC. Nevertheless, the company was sure that public
anxiety would be reduced by full disclosure of health and safety data.

'We conclude from our extensive discussions in North America,' said the
Committee, 'that an opening up of access to health and safety data is perfectly
feasible.' The Committee felt it was the UK government itself, rather than
industry, that seemed reluctant to allow greater public access to information. [44]

The limited disclosure of pesticide information in Britain now applies to
new chemicals and to old ones coming up for review, which in the main is only
likely to happen where another country raises doubts over the safety of a
product. All existing information submitted under the old scheme – the great
bulk of it – will remain a secret.

Many older pesticides were approved when toxicology, chemistry and
ecology were rudimentary compared with today (especially with respect to the
pesticides' potential for causing cancer). More than 100 were last tested in
1965 or before. As a result, the tests applied were equally rudimentary and the
data often poor. But industry is naturally opposed to taking pesticides off the
market while they are tested at today's standards. The Ministry of Agriculture
voiced hopes of a ten-yearly review of chemicals, but only three pesticides

were reviewed in 1984. On the basis of testing 300 active ingredients on a ten-year cycle, it would take up to 20 years to review all the existing pesticides. In April 1990 an increase in pesticide examination staff from 54 to 86 was announced, enabling 25 pesticides to be tested a year, where eight could be before. The number of old chemicals to be tested, from a backlog of 250, was due to increase from 12 to 37 a year by 1993.

As to the basis of decision-making, the Body Committee found that changes in the US regulatory system 'amounted to a significant shift in the cost/benefit analysis toward scrutinizing more severely, and in a wider context, exactly what disadvantages the use of certain pesticides might entail'. [45] Britain still tends to assume that pesticides are 'innocent until proved guilty'. This may be reflected in the UK's slowness to curb the use of pesticides known to pose a hazard. For example, the 'severe restriction' of the organochlorine aldrin in Sweden dates from 1962, the ban in Norway dates from 1965, that in Hungary from 1968 and that in Finland from 1972. But the UK withdrew final clearance for aldrin only in 1989. Dieldrin was in use in the UK until 1988, whereas Norway banned it in 1965, Hungary in 1968, Sweden in 1970, and Japan in 1971. 2,4,5-T was banned in Norway in 1973, in Sweden in 1977, in Finland in 1978, and in the USA in 1979, but it is still used in the UK. In 1947 the Zuckerman Committee were given graphic accounts of workers dropping dead in the fields from the use of the dinitro insecticide DNOC. In the 1980s, as similar compounds were eventually shown to cause birth defects, the Advisory Committee on Pesticides asked for more data on DNOC for a review. No further data were provided and approvals for sale, supply and advertisement were revoked as of 31 December 1988. However, a year was allowed, until 31 December 1989, for existing stocks to be used up. 'Seven workers died in 1949,' observed the Pesticides Trust. 'Its [DNOC's] withdrawal comes a mere 41 years later.' [46]

The recent cases of dinoseb and ioxynil are discussed below.

The Case of Ioxynil

On 20 February 1984 pesticide manufacturers May and Baker Ltd (now renamed Rhône Poulenc) received a report from consultant toxicologist Dr F J C Roe, *Brief Opinion on the Likely Safety/Hazard of Ioxynil and Bromoxynil for Persons involved in their Manufacture and/or Use as Herbicides*. [47] The essence of Dr Roe's report was that tests with rats showed that high doses of ioxynil, used as a lawn weedkiller by gardeners and as an agricultural herbicide by farmers and growers, interfered with the metabolism of iodine and could lead to abnormal growth of the thyroid gland and an increase in tumours of the thyroid. 'Huge doses' could also produce birth defects.

James Erlichman, a *Guardian* journalist who has made extensive studies of chemical hazards faced by consumers, first made the ioxynil issue public on 25 June 1985 with an article entitled 'Six Weedkillers May Be Health Hazards'. [48] Erlichman revealed that, as of 13 June 1985, the Ministry of Agriculture had 'ordered' a 'voluntary' freeze on sales of existing stocks of six garden weed-killers containing ioxynil, made by May and Baker, Fisons, ICI, PBI and

Synchemicals. The order excluded sale of ioxynil products to farmers and other non-domestic users. Erlichman disclosed that the hazards of ioxynil were discovered only because new safety data had been needed to sell the chemical into a new foreign market, although it had been used in the UK for 20 years.

'It has yet to be explained why there was an interval of more than a year between May and Baker's being informed of the results of the toxicological study and the Ministry's request for a voluntary freeze on retail supplies,' said Friends of the Earth in their evidence to the House of Commons Agriculture Committee a year later.[49] 'Why was there no immediate warning to users of herbicides containing ioxynil, no withdrawal of existing stocks or of stocks supplied for agricultural and horticultural use. Should the manufacture have been halted pending a review?' asked FoE.

A review of the clearances of ioxynil-containing products was begun by the Advisory Committee on Pesticides in 1986.

The Case of Dinoseb

On 7 October 1986 the US EPA issued an emergency order suspending all registrations of pesticide products containing dinoseb, a herbicide which had been used for 40 years in Britain.[50] Research by the Swiss firm Research and Consulting showed that pregnant rats and rabbits exposed to dinoseb had produced deformed offspring. At the time, 25 dinoseb products were approved for use in the UK. The Americans were concerned that anyone using dinoseb could get a dose equivalent to that causing deformities in test animals if they weren't wearing protective clothing.

On 6 November, the clerk of the House of Commons Agriculture Committee inquiry into the health effects of pesticides wrote to the Ministry of Agriculture asking for reports on dinoseb 'in the hands of your officials'. Replying on 18 November, the ministry sent the public announcement by the US agency but no data, as they were 'covered by the promise of commercial confidentiality given to manufacturers'.[51]

The ministry emphasised that, 'In practice, in the UK at least, such levels of exposure [to dinoseb] ought never to occur . . . operators have to wear comprehensive protective clothing including gumboots, gloves, coverall, faceshield and hood.' While this may be fine in theory, it was not true in practice. In August 1984, for example, a leaking tractor splashed dinoseb onto a roadside worker who was taken to Bassetlaw Hospital, along with a fireman. Residents were told to stay indoors.

Sir Richard Body rejoined that the ministry's own consultative document had stated that 'the public should have the "fullest and most up to date evaluation" on the health implications of pesticides, indeed "the same information that the ACP has in making its recommendations to Ministers".' Body said that dinoseb was a test case for freedom of information.

On 8 December, the minister wrote back with some carefully worded qualifications. It now turned out that the proposal on disclosing safety data had only been 'a basis for discussion' and, although some access to information would be given, copies would not be provided and it would be on a 'reading room basis' only. Furthermore, the 'raw data' would not be available (that had been an 'inaccuracy'), only 'study reports'.

Lastly, it now emerged that, under the new Control of Pesticide Regulations (1986), the enquirer would have to write to Mr J A R. Bates, Head of the Pesticide Registration and Surveillance Department, Harpenden Laboratory, Hatching Green, Harpenden, Herts AL5 2BD, and give the following details: personal background, name, 'scientific qualifications and current employment, including name of employer', details of any commercial interests, product or active ingredient of interest, 'nature of data requested, e.g. which study report?', a justification for the request including 'enquiry or research project being followed and its aim', 'statement of data sources already explored', 'explanation of why the summary evaluation is insufficient and what the enquirer hopes to achieve by reading a study report', and 'whether the enquirer has approached the company, or has any objection to his or her request being made known to them'.

Far from being a mechanism for freedom of information, such arrangements are the means of suppressing it. The requirement to have to ask for a *particular* study report could easily be used to withhold information. If you don't know what information exists, then you cannot ask for it. Catch 22. It is a familiar Whitehall device for keeping things hidden from public view.

Four months after the first enquiry, Sir Richard Body finally won an invitation for his adviser, Professor J W Bridges of the Robens Institute at Surrey University, to submit his details, his reasons, who else he had asked about dinoseb, and so on, so that he could visit the reading room. It is no use asking Professor Bridges what he discovered. Anyone reaching the reading room has to sign a declaration not to disclose the information found there.

If it took four months for a knighted Conservative MP who was also the chairman of a Select Committee conducting a study into the health effects of pesticides to obtain permission for a Professor to gain access to information about acknowledged heath hazards of a pesticide, then the average member of the public must have little chance.

On 4 December 1986, after Body had begun his correspondence with the minister, MAFF acted to suspend all sales of dinoseb (and its related compounds) pending its scientific review. On 22 January 1987 a ban was imposed on the use of dinoseb, later to be revoked.

Incidents

When Friends of the Earth launched their pesticides campaign in 1984 it focused on legal controls and freedom of information. The organisation was surprised to be contacted by many people who had suffered 'incidental' exposure to pesticides. Many complained of immediate or long-term illness, others were just distressed or outraged by the obstructive and dismissive treatment they had received from the authorities once they tried to complain.

The prevailing view of the industry, summed up by R F Norman, the chairman of the British Agrochemical Association, was that 'we have a proud record of 27 years without any fatalities from pesticides and no unreasonable incidents'. Criticism, he said, came only from 'Lord Melchett and some other ecofreaks'. The incidents reported to FoE soon showed that, far from being a collection of ecofreaks, the people suffering from pesticide 'incidents', which they certainly felt were far from 'reasonable', included policemen, firemen, parents, children, farmworkers, teachers, farm secretaries, farmers, vets, ex-soldiers and drivers.

Friends of the Earth began to keep a record of 'pesticide incidents' and released details of more than 100 in *The First Incidents Report* in February 1985; [52] 55 per cent of the cases referred to problems with spray drift, and of these 53 per cent were associated with aerial spraying. FoE were now convinced, as others had been before them, that pesticide incidents were heavily under-recorded. The Body Committee noted that in 1983, for example, Open University researcher Joyce Tait found that 'of 24 farmers who claimed to have felt ill after working with pesticides, only one had made a report to the Health and Safety Executive'. [53]

Many people living in rural areas are reluctant to report incidents for fear of being branded 'trouble-makers' and losing the goodwill of farmers on whom they may depend, or who may be local magistrates. The symptoms reported included 'flu-like' feelings, skin rashes, burns, irritation, sore eyes and mouth, breathing problems and dizziness. In many cases there was absolutely no doubt that pesticide had reached the victim, though in hardly any was there an imme-diate medical investigation of the sort that might produce 'hard evidence' of pesticide poisoning (such as blood tests) that could stand up in court or find its way through the processes of the Health and Safety Executive (HSE) to be recorded as a 'case of poisoning'. The Body Committee concluded: 'While it is true that many such mild symptoms may be wrongfully assigned to pesticide use, it is at least as likely that sickness caused by pesticide exposure may be ascribed to other causes.' [54]

In 1985 the HSE identified 103 incidents involving 175 people, of whom about half were farmers, self-employed people and farm workers. The rest were members of the public exposed – by skin or inhalation – to chemicals on farm land.[55] Just 23 were exposed as a result of ground spraying, while 104 were exposed owing to aerial spraying.[56] FoE have argued that the risks and nuisance from aerial spraying far outweigh the benefits (which are mainly to a few very large farmers who call up air support when a sudden aphid outbreak strikes their 'prairie' farms).

In 1987, FoE published a *Second Incidents Report*.[57] This contained 71 inci-dents where human health was directly affected, of which only 23 seemed to have been investigated by the HSE. 'Such under-reporting is perhaps not surprising,' said FoE's researchers Dave Buffin, Blake Lee-Harwood and Andrew Lees, 'because of the HSE's limited resources. The Agricultural Inspectorate lost 28 inspectors between 1977 and 1986.' The active ingredients of the pesticides involved in incidents reported to FoE are listed in Appendix 1.

Examples of Pesticide Incidents Reported to Friends of the Earth [58]

Avon

In August and September of 1984, a farm labourer and at least two other local people from Farleigh, Hungerford, near Bath, were severely affected by Gramoxone (paraquat) and (unspecified) insecticides, used to spray potatoes.

The symptoms included conjunctivitis, cystitis, burning throats, headaches and sickness, and high concentrations of paraquat caused one person to black out, lose his power of speech and become numb in the mouth.

The worst-affected person could tolerate going into her garden only for a few weeks of the year, and has to drive 15 miles to find a spray-free area to walk in. The people in the village were afraid to make complaints as they did not want to get into trouble with their landlords or local farmers.

Cambridgeshire

Heather Cameron of Old Weston, near Huntingdon, was planting daffodils in October 1979 when a helicopter sprayed her with a pre-emergence weedkiller. As she was in the middle of planting thousands of bulbs she did not bother to protect herself and was exposed for 3 hours. Shortly afterwards, she and her four sons suffered severe respiratory problems.

Additionally, she and her youngest son lost their hearing and she also suffered loss of voice and a rash. She later had to go to hospital to have ovarian cysts removed, and spent the next two years there for various conditions. She was left with severe allergies and food intolerance, having to live on a very restricted diet.

On 23 July 1986, Heather was again a victim of pesticides when aerial spraying took place near her garden and drifting occurred. Extensive damage to her garden plants resulted and she also developed a rash on exposed skin and asthma-like symptoms. The spray was believed to contain the fungicide Rovoral (iprodione).

She had no success in her attempt to claim compensation, going so far as to take the HSE to the Parliamentary Ombudsman for neglecting to help her. He found in her favour and she was offered an apology, which in the circumstances she found 'insulting'.

Since this time she has again been accidentally sprayed, with severe effects including temporary paralysis.

Cambridgeshire

The *Eastern Daily Press* (12 June 1985) reported that 'a dose of farm spray wiped out a Brundall beekeeper's swarm. He lost more than 10,000 bees after a nearby raspberry field was sprayed with an unspecified insecticide'. The farmer concerned said that they 'mistimed the job' and that the raspberry canes should have been sprayed before the blossom came out. A spokesman for the Norfolk Beekeepers' Association said, 'most farmers are careful but this kind of thing still happens despite all the advice and help on offer'.

Cambridgeshire

A report in the *Fenland Advertiser* of 14 May 1986 gives details of the concerns of beekeeper Leonard Young from Walsoken, Cambridgeshire. He has stopped selling his honey out of his concern that it may be contaminated by pesticides. 'I've stopped eating and selling honey from hives that I know have had access to oil seed rape that's been sprayed in bloom. I won't be responsible for anyone getting poisoned. We don't know what these residues can do to us,' he added.

Derbyshire

The *Morning Telegraph* (17 January 1986) reported an 'Alarming Saga of the Derby Droop'. It told of 'a group of Derbyshire farmworkers who found that moves to improve the land had the opposite effect on their sex lives. The men are now part of the lore of medicine because of their complaint – Derby Droop.'

The cases emerged when four farmworkers on the same farm sought help from their doctor for impotence. Surmising that there may have been a common cause, the doctor suggested a combination of stopping exposure to farm chemicals and hormone treatment and the men were successfully cured.

The farmworkers' main exposures had been to a mixture of various insecticides, including dieldrin and mancozeb, and nine different herbicides, including 2,4-D and paraquat. Dieldrin, a highly toxic organochlorine insecticide, was banned for agricultural use in 1966.

Essex

Mrs Allshorn, of Upminster, phoned FoE on 14 June 1985 about an incident the previous day when 'spray drifted through the open window of the Bulpham Primary School assembly hall. Afterwards the children complained of runny noses, severe coughs, headaches, sore throats, and their attitude was weepy and irritable.' The pesticide, Metasystox R (oxydemeton-methyl), an organophosphorus insecticide, was being sprayed by a tractor on land belonging to Childerditch Hall Farm. Mrs Allshorn told FoE that 'the authorities treat you like a hysterical mother' and added that 'some parents did not even know that their children had been sprayed'.

The story was reported by the *Thurrock Gazette* (11 June 1985): 'Education chiefs, who are " very concerned" at the incident, have ordered a full probe into the cloud of pesticide which covered Bulpham Primary School.' Blood tests were ordered by Essex County Council, and the same paper ran a further story on 2 August 1985: county councillor George Miles told members of the County Education Committee that 'three years ago, parents at the same school thought that there was something wrong when the insecticide was used at nearby Childerditch Hall Farm.' He added: 'Last year the same thing happened again when the farmer treated parents in a very cavalier fashion.'

Essex

Mr David Jones, the Tendring District Footpath Secretary, informed the Ramblers' Association of an incident occurring on 5 July 1985. A party of schoolchildren were covered in the spray of an unknown pesticide while walking along a public footpath on the sea wall at Alresford Creek. An aircraft made several runs over them and, while they were waving at it, they were suddenly sprayed. The person in charge instructed them to cover themselves with their coats and stand at the bottom of the sea wall, but they were still affected by the spray drift. The police were informed but no further action resulted.

Kent

Mrs Clarke wrote to FoE on 18 April 1985 from the Birchington area of Kent after inhaling an unknown pesticide spray from neighbouring fields. Problems of 'swollen glands, wheezy chests, sore eyes, aching limbs, dizziness, sweating' which developed afterwards were corroborated by her neighbour. She continued, 'Until three years ago I had never had asthma, but since a large dose of Metasystox, I have not been free of it.' (The insecticide Metasystox contains demeton-S-methyl, an organophosphate.)

She subsequently contacted the local NFU and the HSE. She informed us that the HSE 'did reprimand the farmer for spraying on a windy day, and more or less denied that it could affect me'.

Lincolnshire

Thomas Sirr of Saltfleet, Lincolnshire, informed FoE that, on 11 June 1985, at about noon, a low-flying plane 'came over my land as I was outside working and spray continued to fall as it passed overhead, it did about 6 passes'. He suffered 'tingling in mouth and tongue, dry throat, headache, coughing bouts, gritty eyes, irritability and uncoordinated actions'. The plane was spraying fungicides – Cosmic (carbendazim, tridemorph and maneb) and Mistral (fenpropimorph) against red rust on barley.

Norfolk

A woman (who wishes to remain anonymous) working in horticulture in Diss, Norfolk, reported that in 1986 and previous years she has been experiencing 'general weakness, giddiness, numbness and shudderings' after working in a field fumigated with methyl bromide.

This highly toxic substance is on the Pesticide Action Network 'Dirty Dozen' list of dangerous pesticides.

Northamptonshire

Frances Boulton of Gretton, Northamptonshire, wrote to FoE in June 1986 after the herbicide MCPA, which was being sprayed close to her house, drifted onto her garden and killed all her plants. She was extremely distressed and regarded the offer of £100 compensation by the NFU as an 'insult'.

Three weeks later, a nearby corn field was sprayed while she was in her garden, and she inhaled some spray. She was ill for two days, with chest pains, dizzy spells, burning skin, sore eyes, nausea, ear pains, swelling thyroid and convulsions.

Effects on Wildlife

Other largely unsung victims of pesticide pollution include many wild plants, animals and birds.

Graham Martin from Birmingham University has suggested that the decline of the wild rose in hedgerows of the Vale of Evesham may be the result of herbicide pollution. Funded partly by the World Wide Fund for Nature (WWF), research by Dr Nick Sotherton of the Game Conservancy has shown a reduction in both the diversity and abundance of butterfly species in sprayed Hampshire field 'headlands', compared with unsprayed headlands. One unsprayed area held 800 butterflies while a sprayed area produced only 300. But it was the decline of the grey partridge rather than butterflies which motivated the Game Conservancy to look into pesticides. On a farm where spraying was curbed, the same researchers found that increased availability of insect food caused the partridge population to increase from 60 to 140 in two years, even though the now unsprayed headland area involved only 2 per cent of the farm. The 30 per cent loss in crop that was sustained here translated into a loss of only 0.7 per cent on the farm as a whole. [59]

An unexpected discovery of the Game Conservancy research was that a fungicide containing pyrazophos was also a powerful if unintended insecticide. The fungicide killed ground beetles, which not only are food for partridges but also eat aphids which damage the crop. The result was more insecticide spraying to 'control' the aphids.

Evidence is now emerging that there are other subtle effects of pesticides. Research at Monks Wood Institute of Terrestrial Ecology and the University of Reading suggested in 1989 that cocktails of pesticides are acting on birds not singly but together.[60] In studies with partridges, Colin Walker and other researchers have shown 'potentiation' of one pesticide by another even at low levels. The researchers found that the fungicide prochloraz, when given at levels to which the birds are likely to be exposed in the countryside, increased the level of enzymes known as cytochrome P450s. These enzymes activate organophosphate insecticides, which depress acetyl choline, acting as nerve poisons. So, for example, malathion (an organophosphate) was fatal when given after a typical dose of the fungicide, while without the fungicide no sign of damage was observed.

Work by Gail Johnston in the same team shows that organophosphates may also 'potentiate' the effect of carbamates, a second type of insecticide. In this case the organophosphates are believed to reduce the activity of enzymes which neutralise the carbamates. 'If these studies are confirmed in the field,' Colin Walker was reported as saying in the *New Scientist*, 'it may be necessary to rethink the way farmers apply their pesticides in the future.'[61]

In the early 1980s, without proper clearance under the then voluntary PSPS, two rodenticides began to be used in place of warfarin, to which rats were increasingly resistant. These are brodifacoum and difenacoum. Barn owls, already very rare as a result of habitat change, began to disappear on the farms where the pesticides were introduced. There was a 10 per cent further decline in barn owls on British farmland during the 1980s. According to the Pesticides Trust, although these two chemicals are now technically unavailable, they are probably still in fairly wide use.[62]

Organochlorines in Otters

In the 1950s, when organochlorine chemicals were first widely used in Britain, the otter was still widespread. Habitat destruction, disturbance and hunting all played a part in the otter's decline, but otters have also disappeared from places where habitat is still in good supply and there are no hunters.

A study of data collected by hunts has shown that the decline of the British otter started in the mid 1950s. Researchers Chanin and Jeffries attributed this to the introduction of dieldrin in agriculture.[63] When 31 otters were examined for organochlorines in the ten years up to 1973 it was found that 80 per cent of them contained a measurable amount of dieldrin.

When biologists examined the organochlorine contamination of otters between 1982 and 1985, 15 of 23 showed detectable levels of PCBs. In five the level exceeded that at which reproductive failure may occur.[64] Three of these otters came from East Anglia, which, as the authors point out, 'is downwind of several industrial areas of England and which now holds only a fragmentary population of otters'. One came from the southwest of England. Of the seven otters from Orkney, six had no detectable levels of PCBs.

Lindane was present in the tissues of 18 of the animals, but generally at a low level. Dieldrin was detected in 16, including otters found in eastern Scotland and England, Wales and southwest England. The Scottish site, say the researchers, 'was known to have received dieldrin in recent years from an industrial source upstream'. Otter 22 came from an area of Devon with several known dieldrin sources including a leaking chemical dump.

The results, said the research team, 'clearly show that residues of organochlorines in otters are still widespread and that elevated levels in some regions should give cause for concern.'

They suggest that otters' considerable appetite for fish (1 kg per day) puts them at risk from concentrations of PCBs in eels averaging 1.4–5.2 mg/kg fat (in Dorset), enough to 'eventually curtail the reproductive life of females'.[65]

Birds, Fish and 'Drins'

In May 1987 the RSPB detailed the story of the notorious chemicals known as 'Drins' (aldrin, dieldrin and endrin) in the UK, in evidence to a Lords Committee studying a proposal to amend the European Commission directive on these chemicals.[66]

Drins were first widely used in UK agriculture from 1955, principally against soil pests, while dieldrin was popular as a sheep dip. The deaths of large numbers of seed-eating birds soon followed (the chemicals have relatively high acute oral toxicity) in flocks which had fed on dressed seed. Not long after that, birds of prey such as sparrowhawks began to die, as organochlorines concentrated in their bodies after they had fed on small birds. Then, it was discovered that the physiology of egg shell formation was impaired by DDT and its metabolites and this was causing reproductive failure in peregrine falcons, as eggs broke in the nest.

From 1962, voluntary restrictions on Drins were introduced under the Pesticides Safety Precaution Scheme. Restrictions were placed on the use of Drins on spring-sown cereals in 1962. These were extended to sheep dips in 1965 and to autumn-sown cereals in 1975. 'These restrictions did not lead to a sudden reduction in use but a steady decline over a period of years,' commented the RSPB.

The declines in some birds of prey such as the sparrowhawk had been reversed, but other wildlife continued to suffer. The RSPB pointed to the decline in residues of HEOD (aldrin/dieldrin) in the kingfisher during the 1970s following the voluntary bans on use, but commented that by 1981, 'these residues had risen to levels similar to those recorded in the early 1970s'. Dieldrin was still being used in industry (mostly in wood preservation), aldrin was still used in farming and dieldrin was widely, if illicitly, used as a sheep dip, being detected on the fleece of British-reared sheep in 1980.[67] The PSPS proved repeatedly ineffective at preventing such abuse.

The RSPB cited continuing serious problems due to organochlorines. In 1983 on the river Mole in Devon, South West Water were alerted to the abnormal behaviour of rainbow trout fry at its hatchery at North Molton. After some months, the cause was traced to organochlorines. The Authority had been using the hatchery to stock its reservoirs and, when these reservoir fish were now checked, 30 per cent were found to carry 40–150 mg/kg wet weight dieldrin and aldrin in their muscle, while a fifth of them had over 150 mg/kg. 'Consequently,' noted the RSPB, 'SWWA advised the public against eating trout pending restocking.' What it did to encourage birds not to eat the fish is not known. An old sheep dip site eventually proved to be the source of pollution. In 1984, an activated carbon plant was installed to intercept the discharge (activated carbon causes most organic substances to bind to its surface and is the basis of many filters).

In 1985–6, 14 herons were found dead on the river Avon where it passes through the market gardens near Evesham. Of seven corpses analysed by the RSPB, 'five were found to contain potentially lethal levels of HEOD of 6–42 mg/kg wet weight in liver'. Four also had high levels of DDE (the metabolite of DDT). High levels of HEOD were also detected in eels, river sediment and water. On 30 July 1986, the Severn Trent Water Authority advised people not to eat eels caught downstream of Coventry. In summer that year the source was traced to a company repacking chemicals in Coventry. 'No prosecution was taken,' said the RSPB, 'in part because of the lack of EC quality standards for dieldrin.' In addition, Peter Riley of FoE was able to purchase a new 20 lb drum of DDT from Craven Chemical Company Ltd, a local farm supplier, for £32.20 and another from Velmark for £26.04, despite a theoretical prohibition which MAFF maintained was total. With the author, Riley photographed a drum in use on market gardens.

In the same year, eels downstream of Stroud in the river Frome were found to contain high levels of HEOD. STWA advised people not to eat them. Investigators believe the dieldrin came from factories washing imported sheep fleece.

In October 1985, the Newmill Channel, a tributary of the river Rother in Sussex, was polluted by a leak of dieldrin and tributyl tin oxide from a timber treatment works. Some 2,000 litres of the highly toxic timber-treating fluid seeped into the ground and got into the river via land drains. 'The incident.' added the RSPB, 'caused a total fish mortality along a 4.8 km length of the Newmill Channel between Rolvenden and Potmans Heath, Wittersham.' At least three herons, a kingfisher, a mallard and a cormorant were found dead. This time the company responsible was successfully prosecuted by the Water Authority.

On 10 May 1986, 225 litres of Protim 80, a wood preservative containing pentachlorophenol, dieldrin and tributyl tin oxide, entered Uddens Water tributary of the Moors River Site of Special Scientific Interest in Dorset, via a drain from a timber works. Wessex Water successfully prosecuted the company concerned, but not before 700 fish, two herons and a kingfisher had been killed and a major die-off of invertebrates had occurred. Farmers in the area were advised not to let their animals drink the water.

On 2 February 1989, 680 litres of lindane and tributyl tin oxide poured into the river Wey navigation in Surrey from a timber treatment company. Booms were placed across the river but they were not in time to contain a thick yellow slick of wood preservative which accumulated in backwaters and coated vegetation as far downriver as the centre of Guildford, some 6 km away. 'We know the stuff is very nasty and we are sorry,' an employee of the company concerned told the *Observer* newspaper.[68] Thames Water closed water intakes downstream of the incident. Ironically the leak was only discovered when detectives went to investigate a separate incident in which vandals had opened taps on an oil tank, allowing 13,700 litres of oil to flow into the same water. 'It's always the same, this is nothing unusual,' said an angler continuing to fish in the river a few days after the incident. 'The creosote is worst, it coats the surface of the river just when all the mayflies are trying to hatch.'

Following suspected arson, 25,000 litres of wood preservative containing lindane and TBT entered the Bourne, a Surrey tributary of the Thames, in March 1990. A supply serving 90,000 homes was closed. Thousands of fish died.

Such incidents, said the RSPB, illustrate the continuing problems with the Drins and the products they are still used in. Many of the inputs are now from particular 'point sources', but, as these are often large and the chemicals are long-lasting, they can be a significant source of pollution over wide areas. The similarity of the incidents – with timber yards and the wood preservative industry a significant and repeated source – shows that much tighter control over storage (for example, requiring all drainage to pass through an activated carbon filter) might be a technical solution to at least part of the problem.

The Drins Directive

Wherever such chemicals are used, some will inevitably reach the environment. Many other countries have imposed bans or more severe restrictions than apply in the UK, and in October 1986 the EC proposed to control Drins under the Dangerous Substances Directive. Britain's response was to try and weaken the Directive to the point where it allowed the status quo to be maintained.

In 1987, the Department of the Environment set up a Consultative Group to discuss the EC proposal for the Drins. Given the human health threat of the Drins and their notoriety for impacts on birds and fish, one might have expected the Consultative Group to include bodies such as the RSPB, the NCC (the government's official advisers on conservation), Friends of the Earth, the British Medical Association, the Consumers' Association and anglers. But, apart from two Water Authorities and eight civil service departments, the Consultative Group consisted of the CBI, British Insulated Callender Cables, the International Wool Secretariat Technical Centre, Prospect Dyeing Co Ltd, the British Wool Preserving Association and the British Carpet Manufacturers' Association. A less environmentally concerned group it would be hard to gather together.

Not surprisingly, perhaps, the DoE line was to push for far laxer standards than those proposed by the EC's Environment Directorate. In fact, while the EC proposed a water limit of 5 ng/litre (nanogramme = one-millionth of a gramme), the UK had wanted 200 ng/litre, although this was later downgraded to a more modest 50 ng/litre – a mere ten times as much pollution as the standard proposed by Europe. Annual mean concentrations of dieldrin alone reached 36ng/l in Yorkshire, where historic uses in mothproofing were thought to be the main cause of the pollution. As to the proposed fish flesh standard of 0.15 mg/kg, DoE told the Water Authorities it would be pressing for just a 'standstill provision' or, better still, the deletion of the standard altogether. The Consultative Group felt it would have 'considerable practical problems' with compliance if 0.15 mg/kg were adopted as the fish flesh limit, because it already knew that eels in the Severn Trent area had 0.46 mg/kg 'and even if sampling were to be confined to certain species and age of fish [a ploy to avoid sampling contaminated fish!] there would still be difficulties in some Yorkshire rivers including the Humber'.

It was the DoE's intention to negotiate a Directive which could be met by existing practices. As Andrew Lees of Friends of the Earth pointed out,[69] this was in direct conflict with a claim by government minister Lord Skelmersdale in 1985 in relation to the Dangerous Substances Directive that, 'Quality standards should not be set on the basis of existing levels; they must follow from a scientific determination of the levels needed to protect the environment.'

Lees also pointed out that the value for fish flesh had been set at half the US limit of 300 ug/kg because the EC limit would be an average not a maximum, and the object was to protect human health by limiting the input of Drins. 'In health matters,' Minister of State William Waldegrave had told Parliament in July 1985, 'it is essential to ensure that safety margins are sufficiently wide and that expenditure constraints are not the principal factors.' It was therefore strange to read in the leaked minutes of the DoE Consultative Group that, although the 0.15 mg/kg level adopted by the EC had originally been put forward by the UK itself, and although the Department of Health had recently advised a limit of 0.07–0.1 mg/kg for a critical group eating 100 g/fish/day, the UK now proposed to argue that the standard for dieldrin in fish flesh should be dropped altogether.

The UK's pressure, suggested Lees, was presumably what had led to the fish flesh standard disappearing from the Directive when it was adopted at the Council of Ministers on 21 May 1987. In May 1989 the government decided to ban aldrin, three years before the due date set by the PSPS. This was apparently prompted by marine contamination of the Cornish River Newlyn and its catchment, where it had been applied by horticulturalists. Shell, the manufacturers of aldrin, refused a FoE call to finance the clean up of the soil over 5,000 acres, saying to the *Independent on Sunday*, 'modern life doesn't work that way.' [70]

PCP, Lindane and Bats

Bats are exquisitely sensitive to lindane, an organochlorine pesticide which has been used in wood treatment since the 1930s. The 1981 Wildlife and Countryside Act gave special protection to all bats, making it an offence to disturb or harm them at their roost, and in theory this should have stopped anyone with bats in their loft from treating timbers with bat-harming pesticides. To help them, the Nature Conservancy Council has also produced a list of 40 bat-friendly pesticides.

Unfortunately over 500,000 buildings receive wood treatment every year in Britain, and many are still subjected to one of the 300 lindane-based products sold by some 80 companies.[71] Similarly, dieldrin, which is also toxic to bats, is probably still used illegally and for many years it was the active ingredient of wood treatment fluids.

Both lindane and dieldrin are persistent. One building was still found to have high lindane levels 29 years after treatment.

The fungicide pentachlorophenol (PCP) is also toxic to bats and is frequently found in products also containing lindane. PCP, says the Pesticides Trust, 'has been shown to kill pipistrelles, Britain's commonest bat, a year after treatment, by both contact and inhalation.'[72]

Pesticides in Drinking Water

Since July 1985 the European Community has laid down limits – Maximum Admissible Concentrations (MACs) – for many substances, including pesticides, under the Drinking Water Directive.

In November 1988, after combing through the detailed Water Authority records, from reservoirs, river intakes and ground water sources, Andrew Lees and Karen McVeigh of Friends of the Earth published a report, *An Investigation of Pesticide Pollution in Drinking Water in England and Wales*,[73] which set out pesticide data from 10 Water Authorities and the 28 Statutory

Water Companies (the private companies that supply certain limited regions with drinking water, principally from aquifers and mainly in southeast England, for example, the Colne Valley & Rickmansworth Water Companies west of London).

FoE found that between July 1985 and June 1987 the legal MAC of 0.1 ug/litre (i.e. 1 part per billion or ppb) for any single pesticide had been exceeded in 298 water supplies or sources. The MAC of 0.5 ug/litre for all pesticides taken together was breached over 70 times.

Not surprisingly, areas of Britain dominated by arable farming were worst affected. Nevertheless, the two most widely detected pesticides – atrazine and simazine – are herbicides employed by many local authorities and British Rail as 'total weed killers'. The regional breakdown is shown in the table; by far the worst areas were Thames and Anglian (no levels exceeding the MAC were recorded in Wales, South West, Southern or Northumbrian Water Authorities). The properties of some of the pesticides found in water are listed in Appendix 2.

Regional Distribution of Pesticide Contamination
of Drinking Water Supplies[74]

	Anglian West	North Trent	Severn	Thames	Wessex	Yorkshire
No. of breaches of a single MAC	113	2	34	122	26	1
No. of breaches of total MAC	58	5	5	9	2	0

The most frequently detected pesticides were atrazine (166 breaches), simazine (96 breaches), mecoprop (47 breaches) and MCPA (11 times). In one case, atrazine was present at 45 times the MAC for a single pesticide. Surface water was significantly worse affected than groundwater.

Twelve pesticides – atrazine, simazine, mecoprop, MCPA, 2,4-D/MCPA, propazine, dimethoate, 2,4-D, dichlorprop, bromoxynil, linuron, chlortoluron and dieldrin – were all detected above the MAC in surface waters. Atrazine was found in 32 sources and was detected at up to 18 times the MAC. Simazine was found in 26 sources, at up to 13 times the MAC. Groundwater was polluted by nine pesticides: atrazine, simazine, mecoprop, MCPA, MCBP, propazine, 2,4-D, 2,4,5-T and dichlorprop. Atrazine was found at almost five times the MAC and simazine, which was found at up to four times the MAC, occurred in 14 sources.

In reservoirs and 'impounding' water sources, eight pesticides were located: atrazine, simazine, mecoprop, MCPA, 2,3,6-TBA, dimethoate, dicamba and propazine, all above the MAC. Simazine was found at up to nine times the MAC. Seven pesticides exceeded the MACs in blended water sources: atrazine, simazine, mecoprop, MCPA, MCPB, dimethoate and dicamba – even though cleaner water can be mixed in these supplies. Mecoprop was detected at up to 10 times the MAC.

The worst-affected region overall was East Anglia. Here pesticides were detected at or above the MAC in supplies of the Anglian Water Authority, East Anglian Water Company, Essex Water Company and Tendring Hundreds Waterworks Water Company. 'The East Anglian Water Company's detection of the herbicide 2,4,5-T, in ground water sources at up to five times the MAC,' said McVeigh and Lees, 'merits special attention.'[75] They found the widespread contamination of surface and groundwater by atrazine difficult to explain purely from its known use by British Rail and local authorities. This suggests that more must be used in farming than was previously believed. Nobody knows because there is no record of use of pesticides in farming. Overall, within the AWA region, atrazine was detected in supplies above the MAC on 71 occasions, at up to 18 times the limit; simazine was found on 51 occasions at up to nearly 20 times the limit; and mecoprop was detected on 42 occasions.

The next worst hit region was Thames. Atrazine was detected at levels above the MAC on 71 occasions, at up to 45 times the limit, and simazine on 32 occasions.

Pesticides found in such supplies are very likely to end up in your tapwater. Many pesticides break down slowly, if at all, once they get into water. Brian Croll of Anglian Water has stated: '2,4-D, which has a persistence in soil of only a few days, has been recorded as undergoing no degradation in stream water after six months,'[76] and at the Como Seminar of the European Institute of Water he said that Atrazine 'very slowly degrades, if at all'. [77]

As FoE point out, with thousands of pesticide brands containing 350 active ingredients in use in the UK, and most of them soluble to greater concentrations than 0.1 ug/litre (the MAC for a single pesticide), 'it is hardly surprising that there is widespread water pollution by certain pesticides'. The tests done on pesticides before they are registered for use are also partly to blame. Pesticides are tested to see how they move through soil, but research stations have tended to enjoy clay-rich organic loams. In these soils, pesticide molecules can bind to both the clay platelets, which carry an electric charge, and to the organic substances in the humus. But there are few if any such substances in chalk or sands, and the rate of pesticide movement through soils such as these is far higher than was once realised. These types of soil overlie many aquifers used for drinking water.

According to the British Geological Survey, 'The most widespread threat [to ground water] is likely to be associated with certain herbicides, especially of the carboxyacid (e.g. MCPP, TCA, MCPA, 2,4-D) and phenylurea (e.g. Chlortoluron, Isoproturon) groups, which are very widely and regularly applied for weed control in cereal production on the permeable soils of aquifer outcrops.'[78]

Clearly, many pesticides sprayed onto fields become widespread water pollutants. In southern and eastern England, seven out of every ten glasses of drinking water are likely to come from groundwater. Elsewhere, the ratio is reversed and, nationally, 70 per cent of our supply is from surface water. In drought conditions, however, the 'base flow' of rivers, which is composed of groundwater rather than surface run-off, makes up 40–50 per cent of the entire flow. So the two problems are heavily interlinked. In the case of rivers such as the Thames, the dry weather flow is almost pure groundwater and sewage effluent.

Standards

In 1974 the UK joined a meeting of experts and was party to an EC decision to set an MAC of 0.1 ug/litre for any pesticide.[79] The interpretation placed on the very low MACs – close to limits of detection – set by the EC and by most countries is that they are 'surrogate zeros'. In other words, as Mr G Vincent of the Water Protection Division of the European Community put it, 'pesticides should not be present in drinking water'. Dr Fawell of the Water Research Centre agreed that the aim of introducing the MACs was to eliminate pesticides from drinking water. Even B. G. Johen of ICI, who is also the chairman of the key working group in the agrochemical lobby GIFAP (International Group of National Associations of Manufacturers of Agrochemical Products), stated: 'The contamination of water, particularly drinking water, by chemicals is basically undesirable and should be avoided if at all possible.'[80]

In practice, however, the UK government has used WHO's 1984 pesticide 'guideline values', and advice from the Department of Health, to generate its own 'guide concentrations' and these values are not set close to zero.

The WHO guideline value for MCPA, for example, is 0.5 ug/litre, whereas the UK guide concentration is 10 ug/litre. The WHO value for simazine is 17 ug/litre, whereas the UK guide concentration is 30 ug/litre.

According to the DoE, the WHO values are 'the maxima to which average concentrations may rise without an expectation of ill effect in the population in general'. Thus their function is not to lead to the elimination of pesticides from drinking water, as the EC MACs are intended to do, only to act as a 'red light' warning of imminent health problems. The DoE asks Water Authorities to 'report immediately' 'any occasion where a guideline concentration' or a WHO value is exceeded 'and to consider what remedial action is necessary'.[81]

The DoE had played down the whole question of pesticides in water supplies, telling the water industry, 'there is no need . . . to approach pesticide manufacturers for toxicological information on particular products.' [82]

FoE learnt that the DoE had also effectively discouraged the Water Authorities and companies from reporting breaches of the Drinking Water Directive. In July 1985, the DoE wrote to water suppliers saying that it was 'asking the European Commission to review the pesticides parameter so that limits more closely related to health risks of specific groups of pesticides can be used'.[83] A year later, it was back with an almost identical letter, which also went on to say that, in the government's view, the MACs were 'inappropriate'. Its reasons were:

(a) it is not possible to assess whether the MAC for total or individual pesticides has been exceeded because the current analytical methods are unable to detect any pesticides at concentrations above the MAC;

(b) no account is taken of the widely different toxicities of individual pesticides in applying the same value to each pesticide irrespective of its toxicity.[84]

Here again, the UK government seems to have been trying to circumvent an internationally agreed environmental law, rather than to put it into practice. The time to raise arguments over the technical merits of the Directive is during negotiation and development – which had taken ten years or so – not once it is in place. Environment Commissioner Mr Stanley Clinton-Davies wrote angrily: 'It is a disgrace that member states should fail to respect the laws which they themselves adopted. Water quality is a matter of wide public concern and we have an obligation to see that the law is respected.' [85]

The government's strategy for dealing with the MACs for pesticides seems to have been to try to renegotiate the Directive while failing to implement it, and to tell the Water Authorities not to worry about collecting or at least sending in the data. If it had not been for Andrew Lees and Karen McVeigh at Friends of the Earth, it seems unlikely that anyone would ever have known about the multiple breaching of the MACs. If the DoE was sent no data, then it could 'honestly' claim that it had no evidence of any breaches, should, for example, it be asked by an MP.

Nevertheless, we are left with the DoE's two arguments why the MACs are 'inappropriate'. The first, that analytical techniques are inadequate, can be only partly valid. As we have seen, Severn Trent was measuring concentrations of atrazine 30 times smaller than those measured by Thames Water: if the DoE's concern was one of scientific efficacy, would it not have been better to raise standards to those of the best? The second objection, that pesticides are of varying toxicity (and therefore a single MAC is inappropriate), has some scientific logic but conveniently overlooks the accepted logic of the MACs: they are set close to zero to encourage moves to eliminate pesticide pollution.

The DoE says that WHO guidelines are designed to protect 'the population in general'. But this means that the standards are not set to protect vulnerable groups. These, according to the Water Research Council (WRC), include bottle-fed babies, patients on dialysis machines, people with liver or kidney disease and anyone with a large intake of water in relation to their body weight.

The government also seems to have been breaking its own laws. Under the 1945 Water Act, the government imposes a duty on water suppliers to supply 'wholesome' water. Because all EC Directives must be 'transposed' into national law, this vague concept of 'wholesomeness' has to accommodate all EC Directives, which rely on specific limits, when they relate to drinking water quality. Although 'wholesomeness' has never been specifically defined, Andrew Lees and Karen McVeigh point out that the government's 1982 advice to water suppliers was that WHO guideline values 'have been accepted as giving guidance on criteria for wholesomeness'. [86] In May 1986 a consultation document, 'Proposed Legal Framework for Drinking Water Quality Standards', added: 'Water would not necessarily be wholesome if it met all the standards [i.e. MACs] but it would be unwholesome if it failed to meet one or more of the standards or any authorised departures from them.' [87]

As there are no 'authorised departures' (derogations under the Directive) for pesticides, this means that any water exceeding MACs is not wholesome and is thus illegal. Water companies might therefore be open to prosecution for supplying such water.

Treatment to Remove Pesticides From Water

Conventional treatment plants – mainly using filtration through sand – do not significantly reduce pesticides. 'Coagulation' involving flocculation with iron compounds, removes some (for example, organophosphorus compounds) but not all, and not completely.

The only more advanced water treatment process presently in use in this country is an activated carbon filter, which, in the words of Mr Hobson, a DoE official, removes 'some pesticides to some extent'.[88] In ideal circumstances a carbon filter can deal with 99 per cent of pesticide contamination. Nevertheless, even carbon filters need upkeep and some pesticides may displace others on their surface, making them an imperfect technical fix.

A resin exchange system and/or oxidation using ozone has also been used in conjunction with carbon filters, in French systems designed to eliminate pesticides. However, these are difficult and expensive processes. While the Dutch and French suppliers make wide use of filters, few suppliers do so in the UK. 'Thus,' say FoE, 'in most instances, the levels of pesticides entering the water supply system are virtually unchanged.'

The cost of treating and detecting pesticides is relatively high: Anglian Water spends £200,000 on detection and, where it has carbon filters for surface waters, they cost £0.03 a cubic metre to run.

Unfortunately the water treatment can itself cause additional problems. After chlorination, water contaminated with herbicides can become tainted, so that the customer notices an unpleasant taste. Some taints result from just a few ug/litre. In the case of 2,4-D,for example, chlorination can produce chlorophenols, which are human cancer-agents.[89] Even ozone-treatment has undesirable side effects. A French study reports that parathion reacts with ozone to create a more, not a less toxic chemical. Simazine in charcoal treatment has been known to create N-nitroso compounds, themselves carcinogens.[90]

Thus, on grounds of costs and practicality, most countries – but not yet Britain – have established water protection zones, catchments where the use of pesticides is banned. At a seminar in Como, Dr S C Warren of the WRC reported that statutory water protection zones exist in West Germany, Switzerland, the Netherlands and Norway.[91] In the Federal Republic, 33 pesticides are banned, 9 are partially banned and another 23 are banned in all protection zones, while 54 more must not be used in inner protection zones. Atrazine may be prohibited outside the zone where the concentration in supplies already exceeds the MAC.

In Italy, possibly the European country whose groundwater supplies are most heavily contaminated, atrazine has been banned on farmland where it exceeds 1.0 ug/litre. Molinate and atrazine were banned in Lombardy in 1986 and Bentazone was banned in 1987. But Italy is also the only EC state to have exempted supplies from MACs.

France anticipated implementation of the Drinking Water Directive by October 1989, having found atrazine in water 'almost everywhere' and detected large increases in early spring when spraying takes place. On vulnerable soils, mechanical weed control rather than herbicides is being used to protect supplies. Water is being treated with granulated or powdered activated carbon treatment to remove pesticides.[92]

In West Germany the Directive was endorsed in 1986 and the MACs are applied to breakdown products as well as to the pesticides themselves. Nine pesticides have been found at 0.5 ug/litre or more in drinking water. The Federal Association of German Gas and Water Industry believe pesticide pollution cannot be solved by treatment but only by a reduction in the use of pesticides. Supported by the senior Water Authorities' Working Group, the Industry Association has demanded a ban on the use of all pesticides that endanger groundwater. As of 1988, 33 pesticides had been banned, with a restriction on 86 further substances on certain crops in water protection zones.

The Netherlands have detected 19 pesticides above the MAC in water supplies. The MAC standards are supported by the water suppliers and the government has endorsed the Directive without exemptions. Aldicarb and 1,2 dichloropropane have been detected at up to 130–160 ug/litre. Carbon treatment is used to strip pesticides from tapwater supplies in Amsterdam. Where supplies have been contaminated with bromacil, the supply has been abandoned.

In Spain the government has endorsed the Directive without exemption. There is little information but in one case atrazine and simazine reached 2 ug/litre. Activated charcoal is used to treat water polluted by pesticides.

In Denmark the Directive has been adopted without exemptions. Pesticide levels are reported at below 0.01 ug/litre in surface waters.

Outside the EC, Norway and Switzerland, both with water protection zones, have adopted MACs.

Solutions to Pesticide Contamination

In the report by Lees and McVeigh, Friends of the Earth put forward one of their many lists of recommendations for government action. FoE's 'wish lists' are often an attempt to shift the UK government slowly towards the position of the most aware countries, and FoE tend to ask for the best in the hope of getting part of the way there.

However, when it comes to controlling pesticides in drinking water, FoE's recommendations are echoed or even overshadowed by the opinions of governments in other countries, water researchers in Britain and the water industry across Europe. With the apparent exception of the UK government, almost everyone agrees that radical changes in agriculture are the way to control pesticide pollution. FoE's recipe is as follows:

> There should be a five-year programme to reduce the usage of agricultural, industrial and other pesticides. This would involve:
>
> a. The introduction of sustainable farming systems (including organic

methods) which require less use of pesticides (including limits on the number of applications per year, specified timing of treatments and geographical restrictions).

   b.   Improved monitoring of pests and diseases, more precise targeting of pesticides (including Integrated Pest Management), lower application rates and more refined application methods.

   c.   Stringent controls, including bans, on the use of certain pesticides, including 'total weedkillers' used by local authorities, British Rail and spraying contractors.[93]

In January 1989 the European Commission began legal action against the UK over pesticide contamination of drinking water. The Commission's action was prompted by FoE's complaint that over 300 supplies exceeded the MACs and that the government had effectively advised suppliers not to report breaches.[94]

In April 1989, FoE again complained to the Commission after data extracted from Southern Water showed a further 19 sources or supplies had breached the MAC. In total, contamination of water with pesticides in the Southern area had led to 74 breaches between August 1987 and December 1988 (70 per cent of the drinking water supply of the SWA region comes from groundwater). Boreholes affected included Luddesdown, Throwley and Selling in Kent. Reservoirs affected included Allhallows on the Isle of Grain, Westfield near Hastings, Cobham near Rochester and Singlewell near Gravesend. [95]

Conclusions

According to a survey prepared by the European Water Institute for its Como Seminar,[96] the only countries with systematic groundwater monitoring are the Netherlands and the UK, although across Europe some 40 pesticides have been detected in groundwater.

After considerable criticism from the Royal Commission on Environmental Pollution in its Seventh Report in 1983, the UK government adopted the fine-sounding 'more specific policy on pesticide usage' to 'reduce the use of pesticides to a minimum consistent with efficient food production'.[97] 'Efficient' is a weasel word but, with food containing residues above recommended limits, pesticides running off into soil and water at what many consider alarming rates, and very little support for organic farming, Britain hardly seems to be meeting that worthy objective.

Together with the Agricultural Research Council, the Ministry of Agriculture does sponsor research into 'alternatives' to pesticides. As a result of such work, 70 per cent of the area of cucumbers and 40 per cent of tomatoes grown in Britain in 1986 were subject to Integrated Pest Management,[98] a system in which carefully calculated amounts of pesticide are used when necessary, in conjunction with biological control and other methods.

Such projects remain honourable exceptions, however. Free market pressures have encouraged a growing number of farmers to 'vote with their feet' and try to escape what the Royal Commission termed the 'pesticide treadmill' of more applications, more pest resistance and more problems, which can only be solved with more and newer chemicals. But the government system remains one geared to the sort of chemical farming promoted by the agrochemical industry and which became conventional in the 1960s and 1970s. Support services, grants and official standards for organic farming remain few and far between.

Under-resourcing of the whole pesticide control system remains a serious problem. Whereas, for example, the California Department of Food and Agriculture took over 13,400 samples to look for pesticide residues in 1987, in many cases analysing for over 100 active ingredients, the UK Working Party on Pesticide Residues sampled fewer than 3,000 and the number of multi-residue tests was limited.[99]

MAFF's inadequacies have even brought together old adversaries. In August 1989 the British Agrochemical Association, Friends of the Earth, the Green Alliance, the National Federation of Women's Institutes, the Pesticide Trust and the Transport and General Workers Union published a joint letter to Ministers responsible for pesticides, calling for: a completion of safety reviews of older pesticides by 1992; speeding up the introduction of new chemicals by reducing waiting time for approval to one year; recruiting an extra 100 Health and Safety Inspectors to enforce regulations properly; more frequent testing for pesticide residues over a broader range of foodstuffs, and a National Pesticide Incident Monitoring Scheme to replace the four different systems now in use.[100] Professor Gordon Conway of the International Institute for Environment and Development added his voice to the criticisms of the poisons reporting system, dubbing it 'a shambles'. [101]

As for 'freedom of information', the bureaucracy has used the poky reading room compromise to stifle public interest groups, which have not even been allowed access to the 'evaluations' of test data.[102] Friends of the Earth formally applied to see an evaluation of the insecticide aldicarb following a review of its immunotoxicity in 1987. They were told that no review had taken place and it had only been an 'ad hoc assessment'. In Wisconsin, USA, the pesticide had been banned, following research suggesting it caused AIDS-like suppression of the immune system. When FoE asked to see the evaluation for dinoseb, after the government granted its use following a temporary ban, the request was refused. No evaluation had been prepared, said the civil servant, 'because the new approval was a renewed approval'.[103] Again, there had been no review, only an ad hoc assessment. The new policy of openness, it seems, is the old policy of secrecy.

APPENDIX 1

Pesticide active ingredients involved in incidents reported to Friends of the Earth [104]

Active Ingredient	Type	WHO Rating	Possible Risks
Aminotriazole	Herbicide	UL	CARC, TERA, MUTA
Atrazine	Herbicide	UL	MUTA
Bromacil	Herbicide	UL	
Captafol	Fungicide	UL	CARC, TERA, MUTA, ALLERG
Captan	Fungicide	UL	CARC, TERA, MUTA, ALLERG
Carbendazim	Fungicide	UL	CARC, MUTA
Chlormequat	Herbicide	SH	
Chlorpyrifos	Insecticide	MH	
Chlorthalonil	Fungicide	UL	
Coumatetralyl	Rodenticide	SH	
Cypermethrin	Insecticide	UL	
2,4-D	Herbicide	MH	CARC, TERA
DDT	Insecticide	MH	
Demeton-S-methyl	Insecticide	HH	MUTA
Dicamba	Herbicide	UL	MUTA, ALLERG
Dichlorvos	Insecticide	HH	CARC, TERA, MUTA, ALLERG
Dieldrin	Insecticide	EH	CARC, TERA, MUTA, ALLERG
Dimethoate	Insecticide	MH	MUTA
Diquat	Herbicide	MH	TERA, ALLERG
Diuron	Herbicide	UL	ALLERG
Fenitrothion	Insecticide	MH	MUTA
Fenpropimorph	Fungicide	UL	ALLERG
Fenthion	Insecticide	HH	
Fenvalerate	Insecticide	UL	
Flutriafol	Fungicide	SH	
Glyphosphate	Herbicide	UL	ALLERG
Iodofenphos	Insecticide	UL	
Ioxynil	Herbicide	MH	TERA
Iprodione	Fungicide	UL	
Lindane	Insecticide	MH	CARC, TERA, ALLERG
Maleic hydrazide	Herbicide	UL	CARC, MUTA
Mancozeb	Fungicide	UL	ALLERG
Maneb	Fungicide	UL	CARC, TERA, ALLERG
MCPA	Herbicide	SH	TERA
Mecoprop	Fungicide	SH	
Metalaxyl	Fungicide	SH	ALLERG
Metaldehyde	Insecticide	SH	
Methyl bromide	Fumigant	NC	CARC, MUTA
Nuarimol	Fungicide	SH	ALLERG
Oxydemeton-methyl	Insecticide	HH	
Paraquat	Herbicide	MH	TERA, MUTA, ALLERG
Pentachlorophenol	Fungicide	HH	TERA, ALLERG

Active Ingredient	Type	WHO Rating	Possible Risks
Phenyl mercury-acetate	Fungicide	EH	
Phosalone	Insecticide	MH	
Phosphine	Rodenticide	NC	
Pirimicarb	Insecticide	MH	
Prochloraz	Fungicide	SH	
Propiconazole	Fungicide	MH	ALLERG
Propyzamide	Herbicide	UL	ALLERG
Simazine	Herbicide	UL	MUTA
Sodium chlorate	Herbicide	SH	MUTA, ALLERG
Sodium pentachlorophenate	Fungicide	NC	MUTA
Sulphuric acid	Herbicide	NC	
2,4,5-T	Herbicide	MH	CARC, TERA, MUTA
TBT	Fungicide	HH	
Thiophanate methyl	Fungicide	UL	
Triadimefon	Fungicide	SH	
Triazophos	Insecticide	HH	
Triclopyr	Herbicide	SH	
Tridemorph	Fungicide	MH	
Vinclozolin	Fungicide	UL	
Zineb	Fungicide	UL	CARC, TERA, ALLERG

The pesticides involved in the incidents reported to FoE were classified according to short-term (acute) and long-term (chronic) hazards/risks.

Short-term hazards

The acute hazards are rated according to the World Health Organisation's *Recommended Classification of Pesticides by Hazard*. This classification distinguishes between the more and the less hazardous forms of each pesticide, in that it is based on the toxicity of the technical compound and on its formulations. The WHO classification has been abbreviated as follows:

EH = extremely hazardous; HH = highly hazardous; MH = moderately hazardous; SH = slightly hazardous; UL = unlikely to be acutely hazardous in normal use; NC = not classified.

Possible long-term risks

Data on pesticides' properties were taken from Table 10, 'The toxicity of active ingredients cleared under the Pesticides Safety Precautions Scheme for use in Britain in 1985', pp. 29-48, *Pesticide Residues and Food. The case for real control* by Pete Snell and Kirsty Nicol, The London Food Commission, 1986.

CARC = possible carcinogen; TERA = possible teratogen; MUTA = possible mutagen; ALLERG = possible allergen/irritant.

APPENDIX 2

Properties of Pesticides Found in Water[105]

Atrazine
A widely used non-selective herbicide. Banned in all West German water catchment areas and nature reserves, and restricted in Swiss forests and water catchment zones. Implicated in causing tumours in animals and rated an 'equivocal' tumorogenic agent by the US National Institute of Health and Safety (NIOHS). Moderately toxic to humans. Animal tests show decreased body weight, anaemia and disturbed glucose mechanism in subjects dosed with it. Used in the UK since 1975.

Bromoxynil
An active post-emergence herbicide used against a wide range of broadleaved weeds, often mixed with other chemicals. It is one of a group of 'hydrobenzini-triles' used on 1.2–1.6 million hectares in the UK each year. As of 1988 it was due to be banned in the UK following US revelations that it caused birth defects in laboratory animals.

Chlortoluron
A pre- and post-emergence herbicide targeted on grasses and broadleaved weeds in winter cereals, which works by inhibiting photosynthesis.

2,4-D
Probably one of the most widely used herbicides, utilised in weed control on turf, in plantations and in nurseries. Many local authorities use 2,4-D. In the USA it is marketed with a warning not to permit grazing on treated fields for two weeks after application. 2,4-D is classified by the WHO as 'moderately hazardous' to people, and, as with all chlorophenoxy herbicides of which it is one, it is a skin irritant. The IARC (International Agency for Registration of Carcinogens) states, 'There is limited evidence that occupational exposure to chlorophenoxy herbicides is carcinogenic to humans.' 'Limited evidence,' say Lees and McVeigh, 'indicates that a causal interpretation is credible but that alternative explanations could not be adequately excluded.' 2,4-D has been implicated in a rare cancer called non-Hodgkins lymphoma in Kansas, USA. Exposure can cause fatigue, headache, liver pains and loss of appetite, as well as high blood pressure and liver dysfunction. The US Environmental Protection Agency says there is a risk that such chlorophenoxy herbicides become contaminated with the dioxin TCDD (an embryotoxic suspect carcinogen) during manufacture. Used in the UK since 1967.

Dieldrin
Most recently used in the UK in wood treatment, though formerly in wide agri-cultural and livestock husbandry use. At least one local authority in every nine

was still using it in 1979. Dieldrin has a high acute oral toxicity and is rated by the WHO as 'extremely hazardous'. The US EPA regards it as a hazard on the grounds that it causes cancer, attacks foetuses and causes birth defects, kills wildlife and can be absorbed and cause poisoning via the skin. Due to have been withdrawn from all remaining UK uses on 31 March 1989.

Dimethoate
A widely-used broad range organophosphate insecticide found in farming, gardening and their uses. Ranked moderately hazardous by WHO but not banned or restricted. The US EPA believed as of 1981 that it warranted further study as a cancer agent posing a risk of birth defects, fetotoxic effects and reproductive disorders, and withdrew its registration for dust formulations. Like other organophosphates, short-term exposure can cause disorientation (with sub-clinical effects) and 'flu'-type symptoms such as sweating, dizziness, nausea and vomiting. Long–term effects include brain damage. Used in the UK since 1971.

Linuron
A post-emergence herbicide used against broadleaved weeds and often mixed with other chemicals. It is rated only 'slightly hazardous' by WHO and is not banned or restricted. The IARC states that, as with 2,4-D, 'There is limited evidence that occupational exposure to chlorophenoxy herbicides is carcinogenic to humans.' Similarly, it too may become contaminated with TCDD. It has been in use in the UK since 1986.

MCPB
A post-emergence herbicide which is converted to MCPA by sensitive plants. It, too, is a chlorophenoxy herbicide.

Mecoprop
Another chlorophenoxy herbicide. Ranked by the WHO as 'slightly hazardous'. Used against broadleaved weeds.

Propazine
A triazine herbicide like simazine and atrazine. Not banned or restricted and not particularly toxic. Inhibits photosynthesis, and is used against grasses and broadleaved weeds.

Simazine
Used to control broadleaved weeds and grasses and in 'total weed control' (i.e. to kill everything) on non-cropped land. Lees and McVeigh note that it has 'a tendency to reach water sources after application'. Simazine is not particularly hazardous, but it is a slight skin and eye irritant and can cause disturbances to the central nervous system, liver and kidneys, and shows mutagenic effects (disrupts DNA) in laboratory animals. It causes workers exposed to it to complain of dizziness, nausea and 'olfactory deviations'. The WHO Second Consultation of Herbicides in Drinking Water noted that if simazine is treated

with granulated activated carbon it may give rise to N-nitroso compounds, which are known to cause cancer.

2,4,5-T

A brushwood killer still in use despite a vigorous campaign to persuade local authorities not to use it (a TGWU campaign led to more than 100 ceasing to do so by 1984). 2,4,5-T or its contaminant dioxin TCDD is a suspect carcinogen and teratogen and is embryotoxic. Used in the UK since 1980.

CHAPTER 11

The Global Atmosphere: The Greenhouse Effect and Ozone Depletion

A Silver Lining?

Of all the environmental crises facing the planet, contamination of the global atmosphere may be the one to give Britain a chance to shine by taking a lead in pollution control. In September 1988, Prime Minister Margaret Thatcher was able to hoist a Union Jack on the issue of global warming because, unlike acid rain, sewage or water pollution, Britain's emissions of greenhouse gases had not yet got it into serious trouble with its neighbours or the rest of the world.[*]

It is true that CFCs (chlorofluorocarbons) are greenhouse gases as well as attackers of the ozone layer, and ICI was responsible for a tenth of the world production,[1] but Britain had attracted no particular blame for that. Indeed, in 1989 Thatcher made a virtue out of necessity and hosted an international conference on how to improve the Vienna Convention on the Protection of the Ozone Layer.

Now the world faces the unprecedented challenge of cooperating to clean up global atmospheric pollution. International gatherings of scientists, diplomats and civil servants have been convened by the United Nations as the Intergovernmental Panel on Climate Change (IPCC). They reported to the 1990 Second World Climate Conference, and in 1992 when, two decades after the Stockholm meeting, the UN holds a Conference on Sustainable Development in Brazil, the world's nations will try to agree on a convention to protect atmosphere and climate.

What will Britain's role be: Dirty Man of the Planet, procrastinator or leader, internationalist or isolationist? At the time of writing, Britain has sided more with the biggest polluters who favour delay (Japan, USSR and the USA) rather than with more progressively minded European nations such as West Germany, the Netherlands, Norway, Austria and France.

If Britain is to show a genuine lead in dealing with the greenhouse effect, it must come from the back of the pack to the front of the field. Britain has to reverse its presumption against the precautionary principle, and adopt best

---

[*]'Greenhouse gases', which include carbon dioxide, CFCs, nitrous oxide, ozone and methane, act rather like a greenhouse by absorbing heat that radiates from the earth's surface, while being relatively transparent to incoming sunlight. Some of the heat they absorb is re-emitted downwards, warming the earth.

available techniques to cut down pollution rather than doing the bare minimum. Greenhouse gas pollution arises through transport, energy, intensive farming and many industries. Solving the problems of greenhouse gas pollution means considerable restructuring of these industries, and that could solve many other environmental problems at the same time.

North, South, East and West

Humanity's attack on the planet's air supply has some interesting political consequences. It puts all nations 'in the same boat'. Countries may argue over which is most to blame, but in the end an international bargain has to be struck. We all share the same atmosphere: there is nowhere to run from global climatic change.

It is generally assumed that the richer countries will be willing or able to finance 'adaptation' to shifts in climate. Whereas farmers in poor countries are already at the mercy of the weather and lack the infrastructure of investment, machinery, seeds, and advice to switch crops or locations, it is argued that farmers in Europe or North America may up sticks and move, or switch from cabbages to vines.

On the other hand, voters in the rich countries will be the least tolerant of change such as rising seas or the drought and storms expected to strike new areas and with greater severity. While the governments of Sahelian Africa are used to rebuilding their countries after 'natural' disaster such as a drought, in a country such as the UK or USA, even the loss of a tenth of the wealth could bring down a government. In West Germany, for instance, the outcry over forest decline owed much to the small but influential community of rural forest owners. With climate change the problem will not just be dying forests.

The wealth of Japan and the EC nations is based on trade. Even 'aid' programmes are designed to sell the products of the North to the South (leading, perversely, to a net transfer of wealth from the South). International trade may be especially vulnerable to climate change.

The developed countries have 'pollution guilt': a mass of historical pollution which hangs in the air, yet to exert its full power to erode the ozone layer and warm the atmosphere. The developing countries will want these 'previous offences' taken into account.

The developing world could industrialise in an equally polluting way, or it could choose a different route: utilising solar power and wind energy, keeping coal in the ground, and conserving, not destroying, forests. But why should it? New technologies are often expensive: the 'North' puts a high price on them. Old polluting ones tend to be cheap. To create a global greenhouse bargain the South will need to be paid for clean development. The North has most to lose, so it may yet have to transfer some of its wealth back to the South in technology and in aid to stem climatic change, or see its wealth blown away in climatic chaos.

Centrally planned economies of the East are the third political factor. The West decoupled economic growth from energy use after the 1973 oil crisis, but the East still uses mind-boggling amounts of energy to manufacture. The West must help pay if it wants these industrial dinosaurs to be cleaned up. Energy pricing and fiscal (tax) measures could achieve a massive reduction in the West's greenhouse gas pollution. But that will not yet work in Poland, Czechoslovakia or China.

Newly industrialising countries – such as India and Turkey – are somewhere between the centrally planned pollution puffers, the 'West' and countries still dominated by agriculture. Primitive and advanced technologies exist side by side. Laws for environmental protection often exist unenforced.

Thus the problem of global air pollution sets a new agenda for international development politics. The rich North must help other countries avoid going through a phase of energy-intensive development as they did, and instead move straight to an efficient future. If they do not, any control measures (whether measurable or painful) taken in the North could be wiped out by pollution from the South. The problem is unlike any other which the planet has faced. It promises to turn the world order upside down, or at least on its side.

The Ten-Year Warning on Ozone Depletion

News that the planetary roof had developed a hole came in May 1985.[2] The result was akin to scientific and political panic. Overnight, science fiction had become science fact. The destruction of the planet's ultraviolet (UV) sunshield was life threatening to pale-skinned people who went out in the sun. Once exposed to more UV, they stood a higher chance of contracting skin cancer. Every 1 per cent depletion in stratospheric ozone implies a 1–3 per cent increase in skin cancers.[3] Wealthy Australians and Californians – like Ronald Reagan who had a cancer on his nose – were suddenly in the front line of environmental hazard. But most of the politicians who were now stung into action had sat out a decade of warning and debate.

In *The Hole in the Sky*, [4] John Gribbin relates how in 1971 maverick scientist James Lovelock used an 'electron capture device' he had invented to track tiny quantities of man-made CFCs from the North Atlantic to the South Pole. Lovelock was interested in how life might regulate the physics of the planet. He called it the 'Gaia Hypothesis' after Gaia, a Greek earth goddess.

Lovelock discussed CFCs with a scientist from Dupont, a major manufacturer. They calculated that more or less all the CFCs ever produced were still in the atmosphere since they float around in the air, reacting with nothing. Some would last unchanged for over 300 years. Being 'inert', CFCs were a safe replacement for the dangerous refrigerant, ammonia. CFC use escalated in the 1950s when novelty aerosols were invented using CFCs as propellants.

In 1973 Lovelock published his results in *Nature*, saying the long-lived CFCs constituted 'no conceivable hazard'. But already others were mulling over his discussions with Dupont. Sherry Rowland from California University realised that CFCs would eventually percolate the 20 km up into the stratosphere. Here they would meet intense ultraviolet light, which would break them down. With Mexican Mario Molina he worked out that, at 1972 rates, CFCs would put half a million tonnes of chlorine in the upper atmosphere within 30 years, destroying 20 – 40 per cent of the ozone shield.

Fears that NOx pollution from high-flying supersonic aircraft would deplete stratospheric ozone prompted research which established that less ozone would mean more ultraviolet light reaching ground level. This implied an increase in skin cancers, damage to crop plants and large scale impacts on sunlit ocean waters where many commercial fish larvae and plankton live.

In 1974 Rowland and Molina also published in *Nature*,[5] prompting immediate calls to ban CFCs. A fierce debate erupted between US industry, which produced 1 billion spray cans filled with CFCs each year, and environmentalists, backed by Sherry Rowland.

In 1975 NASA took the lead on ozone research. The US National Academy of Sciences noted that CFCs were also strong greenhouse gases. If production grew at 10 per cent a year, by 2000 they might be more important causes of global warming than carbon dioxide. Dutch researcher Paul Crutzen realised that, because ozone too is a greenhouse gas, reducing ozone in the stratosphere means more UV reaching the lower atmosphere, increasing photochemical smog (and acid rain) near the ground. It would get hotter near the ground and cooler high up. This had unknown implications for the great divide in the atmosphere: the lid-like tropopause between the cold, dry stratosphere, and the lower 'troposphere', the warmer, wetter region which contains our weather. Disturb this and the jet streams, the major plumbing of the atmosphere, might be changed, with enormous implications for the weather.[6]

In 1977, the USA started a ban on non-essential uses of CFCs in aerosols. Even before a ban was brought in, cans had to carry a warning label. 'The bottom dropped out of the market,'[7] recalls an industry spokesman. A year later the Environmental Protection Agency (EPA) initiated regulations and by 1978 the USA had banned CFCs as aerosol propellants. That year, too, NASA put the Nimbus 7 satellite into orbit, carrying 'TOMS' (ozone monitoring) equipment for checking on the ozone layer from above. The 'Toronto Group' of countries – Sweden, Norway, Finland, Switzerland and Canada – also banned non-essential uses.

Britain did not. In 1976, with other European Community countries, it just backed a 'Resolution' to limit use of CFCs in aerosols and encourage substitutes. The Council of Ministers decided in 1980 to reduce production relative to 1976, by 30 per cent by 1981, setting a target of 480,000 tons a year in the EC. It was Britain's first ever overall pollution target for a particular chemical. It was not hard to meet, as substitutes and alternative technologies were available: 'the figure of 30 per cent was chosen because it was known that it could be achieved without creating too much difficulty for the industry, says Nigel Haigh of the Institute for European Environmental Policy (IEEP).[8]

The use of CFCs in aerosols fell dramatically in the Toronto Group countries and in parts of Europe. EC industry stayed within its target. But CFC uses in refrigeration, computer cleaning and foam blowing were on the increase worldwide. Global atmospheric concentrations from western Ireland to Tasmania showed a steady and rapid march upwards at 5 per cent a year.[9]

In 1981, the United Nations Environment Programme (UNEP) started drafting what was to become the 1985 Vienna Convention on the Protection of the Ozone Layer. The legal and political machinery moved slowly. Ozone depletion was still theoretical: scientists believed it had to happen and the Toronto Group had acted on the 'precautionary principle'.

The ozone warning was in the mind of President Carter, who began his 1977 Environmental Message to the Congress with the words: 'Environmental problems do not stop at national boundaries. In the past decade, we and other nations have come to recognize the urgency of international efforts to protect our common environment.' Carter directed the US Council on Environmental Quality to report on long term environmental trends. The result was the 1980 *Global 2000 Report to the President*. It noted: 'Atmospheric concentrations of carbon dioxide and ozone-depleting chemicals are expected to increase at rates that could alter the world's climate and upper atmosphere significantly by 2050.' [10]

However, by the time the massive Global 2000 study was complete, Carter's place in the White House had been taken by Ronald Reagan, an ex–actor who liked battleships and nuclear power and who opined that, once you had seen one Redwood, you had seen them all. He noted that 80 per cent of pollution (meaning hydrocarbons) came from trees. The warnings of Global 2000 fell on deaf ears.

Britain had no Global 2000 to sound a warning. In Margaret Thatcher's early years of power she was more concerned to bury environmental problems than to raise them. ICI, Britain's major CFC producer, suspended research on substitutes 'at a time in which concerns on the likely ozone depletion potential of CFCs was waning'.[11] It seems likely that Dupont did not suspend its research, which left it in an advantageous position later on.

By 1984, Britain's official sources were using the 'ozone scare' as a moral tale to illustrate the folly of rushing into action based on the precautionary principle. The *Daily Telegraph's faux pas* derided the 'ozone scare' as a mistake (see Chapter 4). Yet even as the *Telegraph* published, British scientist Joe Farman was investigating ozone depletion several thousand miles south of Fleet Street in Antarctica. He was about to ignite the issue once again, and this time it would not fizzle out.

Lighting the Blue Touchpaper

In 1982, Farman's ageing 'Dobson Spectrophotometer' began to show 'strange depletions' in the amount of ozone above Halley Bay in the Antarctic. By October 1984 Farman had confirmed enormous ozone losses with newer equipment. By Christmas Eve his paper was with the London office of *Nature*.

Meanwhile the lawyers had got UNEP's Convention on the table and it was signed without fanfare in March 1985. The Convention itself asked for no specific reduction in CFCs, even though Sweden, Norway and Finland had set such targets in 1983. The USA, Switzerland and Canada wanted a Protocol to ban all non-essential uses. The European Community wanted production limits: no agreement seemed possible.

The touchpaper of the issue finally caught alight on 16 May 1985 with the publication of Farman's report in *Nature*.[12] It showed there had been a 30 per cent loss of ozone over Antarctica since the mid 1970s. US scientists found their satellite had recorded the ozone hole all along, but the computer had been programmed to disregard such large losses as 'impossible'.

By August 1986 an Antarctic US team had found high levels of stratospheric chlorine and low levels of nitrogen compounds, consistent with the processes Rowland and Molina had predicted a decade before.

As the Vienna Convention talks took on new urgency, the US position shifted to proposing a freeze on total production, followed by reductions. In March 1987 the Europeans suggested a freeze (on 1986 levels) with a 20 per cent reduction. At Geneva in April, the USA and the Scandinavians stuck out for at least a 50 per cent cut.

Friends of the Earth researcher Kathy Johnston records that Britain now emerged as 'the main block to a unanimous EC position in favour of strict CFC controls'. The UK attitude was 'why worry when there's no conclusive proof?'[13] John Gribbin recalls: 'Britain was still dragging its feet, and dragging the EC (which has 12 votes but tries to present a united front) with it.'[14] 'The UK,' commented Nigel Haigh 'possibly under pressure from ICI – thought to be the largest producer in the community – was believed by many to be an opponent of significant reductions.'[15]

ICI admitted 'some lobbying efforts'. According to Johnston, 'even after the final negotiating session with Tolba [executive director of UNEP], the British position reflected ICI's: a freeze followed by a 20 per cent cutback would be sufficient.'[16] Richard Benedick, the chief US negotiator, accused Britain and ICI of being 'more interested in short-term profits than in the protection of the environment for future generations'. Behind the US position stood Dupont, the world's largest CFC manufacturer, whose less damaging HCFC 22 was ready to be marketed as a substitute. ICI's HFC 134a was still some years from the marketplace.

The UK was still the 'Dirty Man' of the ozone issue as late as August 1987 when the Department of the Environment (DoE) released the *First Report of the Stratospheric Ozone Review Group* (SORG). FoE pointed out that it was out of date. The DoE's press release claimed that the report showed that 'the present rate of CFC production' was 'unlikely to lead to a reduction of the stratospheric ozone layer'. 'Sprays not so damaging to ozone layer,' concluded one newspaper.[17] It was a clear case of the government trying to put a 'spin' on scientific research. This might have satisfied ICI (given observer status at the SORG meetings), but it didn't please Joe Farman. Breaking with civil service practice, Farman went public.

As Johnston notes in FoE's *Into The Void?*, the DoE then retreated. 'Barely a fortnight later,' she recalls, 'the DoE held a non-attributable briefing session for journalists which represented a climb-down, calling for an immediate update of the ozone review report and admitting that Britain would now support a 40–50 per cent CFC cutback at the Montreal protocol meeting, but with a longer timetable than other nations agreed upon, a timetable "considered more favourable to ICI's development of CFC alternatives",[18] 'We have to make an 85 per cent cut pretty sharply,' Farman told the *Guardian*.[19]

In the southern spring of 1987 (autumn in the north), a US$20 million NASA-led experiment, using a high-flying U-2 spy plane re-equipped with gas sniffing analysers and a DC-8 carrying computers, showed that as you entered the 'hole', chlorine monoxide went up and ozone went down. The hole was the size of the United States and as deep as Everest. More than 95 per cent of ozone was lost at some altitudes. Researchers saw chlorine monoxide, a key breakdown product of CFCs, as the 'smoking gun'. One now commented 'this was not so much a smoking gun as a signed confession'.[20]

The researchers rushed back to Washington. Bob Watson of NASA told a press conference, 'Things are much worse than we thought'.[21] It was the first week of October 1987. They were too late: politics had left science behind and 63 governments had just met in Montreal to agree a Protocol to the Convention (not all signed). This stipulated a freeze on consumption at 1986 levels by 1989, a 20 per cent reduction by 1994 and 50 per cent by 1999, with a 10 per cent increase in production followed by a 10 per cent cut by 1994 and 35 per cent by 1999.

The Protocol was a complicated compromise. It limited halons (used in fire extinguishers and in 1989 increasing 25 per cent a year over Antarctica[22]) only to 1986 levels after 1992, and omitted other ozone-depleting substances such as methyl chloroform. Even for CFCs it was woefully inadequate. Farman stated in November 1987 that 'a 50 per cent cut in the world's consumption of CFCs will not be enough. . . for every 6 tonnes of CFC that we allow into the atmosphere, 5 tonnes will still be there at the end of the year'.[23]

In March 1988, Watson was back with the results of the Ozone Trends Review Panel, an international group of scientists convened by UNEP and NASA.[24] This studied a host of historical measurements to check levels around the world. Ozone depletion was found in the north too. From Nottingham northwards, winter levels had been dipping 6 per cent since 1969. Further south, the reduction was 4.7 per cent, and in summer over most of Europe and North America it was 2 per cent. Until now, nobody had noticed.

Late in 1988, a US EPA report, *Future Concentrations of Stratospheric Chlorine and Bromine*,[25] showed that, just to keep chlorine pollution of the upper atmosphere to current levels needed not an 85 per cent but a 100 per cent cut, and all the countries in the world would have to join in. The UK's Second Ozone Review Group Report acknowledged that to close the Antarctic ozone hole 'even if no more man-made chlorine were to be released into the atmosphere . . . would take centuries'.

For the first time, human beings had very definitely fractured a major component of the planet. Nobody argued that the Montreal Protocol shouldn't be renegotiated.

In Britain, Friends of the Earth ran a successful campaign to force the aerosol manufacturers to introduce labelling. The aerosol trade association at first said pathetically, that there was insufficient room on an 'already crowded' label to permit this. After the appropriately-titled TV programme 'What on Earth Is Going On?' invented the label 'ozone friendly', manufacturers fell over themselves to promote CFC-free sprays. Prince Charles made headlines in the *Sun* when he 'banned' CFC hair sprays from his home. To the public it was confusing: was Britain a leader in CFC control, or a laggard?

'Britain has been able to meet the Montreal Protocol targets ten years ahead of schedule because 62 per cent of UK CFCs were tied up in this one sector,' said Fiona Weir of FoE, 'an unlikely eventuality had this usage been cleared up several years ago.'[26] In other words, Britain was making a lot of fuss about doing not very much.

In 1989, polar stratospheric clouds of the sort found over Antarctica and which play a central role in the depletion chemistry, were detected during the Arctic spring. Scientists said the Arctic stratosphere was 'poised' for loss of ozone. But renegotiation of the Protocol was still pegged to industry's timetable for bringing in commercial substitutes.[27]

The ozone issue, however, was only a curtain call for full-scale atmospheric disruption.

Greenhouse History: A Mad Frenchman and a Sensible Swede

An eccentric Frenchman called Baron Jean Baptiste Fourier deservedly features in most books about the greenhouse effect. He was a mathematician who became an artillery officer, Napoleon's governor in Egypt, and, while there, invented a theory which he called the 'hothouse effect'. Fred Pearce describes how: 'in his later life, the Baron's interest in heat became obsessive. He heated his home to absurd temperatures and swathed himself in layer upon layer of clothing, before one day he fell to his death down a staircase.'[28] The first person, perhaps, to die from the greenhouse effect.

In the 1890s, Svente Arrhenius worked out that doubling carbon dioxide in the air might raise the earth's temperature $5^{\circ}C$. He also predicted that the greatest warming would occur near the poles.

The industrial revolution, deforestation and agricultural intensification released increasing amounts of carbon dioxide, methane and nitrous oxide (laughing gas): all greenhouse gases. In 1958, at the end of International Geophysical Year, atmospheric monitoring stations were set up in locations far from industry – including Halley Bay for stratospheric ozone and on the mountaintop astronomical observatory at Mauna Loa in the Pacific for carbon dioxide.

It was soon clear that the greenhouse gases could become a global problem. A report on CO_2 was made to the White House in 1964. By 1974 levels had risen to 330 parts per million (ppm) from 315 ppm in 1957. By 1979 the World Meteorological Organisation's (WMO) First World Climate Conference noted that carbon dioxide levels had increased 15 per cent in the previous 100 years and they were rising rapidly at 0.4 per cent a year.

In 1985 a WMO-ICSU (International Council of Scientific Unions)-UNEP Conference brought together scientists from 29 industrialised and developing countries to agree that: 'Many important economic and social decisions being made today on long-term projects . . . such as irrigation and hydro-power; drought relief; agricultural land use; structural designs and coastal engineering projects; and energy planning – all based on the assumption that past climatic data . . . are a reliable guide to the future. This is no longer a good assumption.'[29]

Importantly, while doubling CO_2 had seemed a distant prospect, when other greenhouse gases were taken into account a significant increase in temperature looked inevitable early in the twenty-first century. The world was changing.

The Greenhouse Effect

If any politician thought she or he might still find a way to accommodate the 'ozone problem' like acid rain or North Sea pollution, the idea was soon banished by the 'arrival' of the greenhouse effect.

In autumn 1987, as attention focused on the high-tech drama of the ozone hole, the World Health Organisation (WHO), UNEP and ICSU met quietly at Villach in Austria and Bellagio in Italy. The 50 experts who met to discuss *'Developing Policies for Responding to Climate Change'*[30] treated global warming as a certainty. A rise of earth temperature 'larger than any experienced in human history' was expected within the next 100 years. By the middle of the next century it would probably mean a 30 cm to 1.5 m sea level rise. The effects would include erosion, wetland loss, bigger and more floods, and damage to port facilities.

The temperature increase could reach 0.8°C per decade up to 2050. With such rapid change there would be extensive forest dieback, species extinction, and further release of carbon and methane from forest soils, and urban- industrial pollution would be made worse. Tropical semi-arid areas already suffering drought and starvation might get drier as they got 0.3–5.0°C hotter. In the wet tropics, storms might spread and get stronger, flooding low-   lying regions. In the North, the tundra might melt, ice retreat, summers get cloudier and temperatures rise 0.8–5.0°C by 2050. Even if global average temperature rose only 1°C, climate systems meant that the rise at the poles might be as much as 2.4° C.

'These changes can be expected to affect marine transportation, energy development, agriculture, human settlement, northern ecosystems, carbon emissions, air pollution and security,' said the conference, concluding: 'major effects on ecosystems and society' were in prospect. A 'coordinated international response will become inevitable'.

One of those present was Sir Peter Marshall of the Commonwealth Secretariat. The Commonwealth began its own inquiry into the greenhouse effect. It soon discovered that 21 of its 48 states were low-lying developing countries. Some, like Kiribati and Tuvalu, lay only a few metres above sea level. Another expert present was G McKay, a representative of the Canadian government's agency Environment Canada. That country now invited the world to Toronto in June 1988 to a conference entitled 'The Changing Atmosphere: Implications for Global Security'. Also present was William H Mansfield, Tolba's deputy at UNEP. The UN agencies were now hatching a plan for a World Climate Convention to limit greenhouse gases, to be launched at the Second World Climate Conference in 1990 and confirmed by 1992 in Brazil, 20 years on from the original Stockholm Environment Conference.

Some governments – Canada, the Netherlands, the Nordic countries and agencies in the United States – had begun to take the greenhouse effect very seriously indeed. One of the very few Britons to take a governmental interest was the UK ambassador to the United Nations, Sir Crispin Tickell, who had written a book on climate. Tickell now watched as the intergovernment machinery began to move into action.

Before the machinery had a chance to move very far, events took an unexpectedly rapid turn. In March 1988, Richard Gammon from Seattle's Pacific Marine Environmental Laboratory declared that, 'Since the mid 1970s, we have been in a period of very, very rapid warming.'[31] In May 1988, Mick Kelly and Jackie Karas of the University of East Anglia's Climatic Research Unit noted: 'Temperatures are now higher than they have been at any time during the period of instrumental observations and the four warmest years in the global temperature record have occurred during the 1980s.'[32]

It turned out that 1987 had been the warmest year ever. (By the end of 1989 it was found that six of the ten warmest years in the 134 for which there were records were in the 1980s, 1988 being hottest of all.) When Jim Hansen from NASA's Goddard Space Flight Centre gave evidence to the US Senate on 23 June 1988, the cat was finally shaken from the bag.

Hansen produced a 30-year 'climatology' from 1951 to 1981.[33] 'The present observed global warming is close to 0.4°C,' he said. 'A warming of 0.4°C is three times larger than the standard deviation of annual mean temperatures in the 30 year climatology. The standard deviation of 0.13°C is a typical amount by which the global temperature fluctuates annually about its 30 year mean; the probability of a chance warming of three standard deviations is about 1 per cent.'

'Thus,' said Hansen, announcing the political arrival of the world's biggest environmental problem, 'we can state with about 99 per cent confidence that current temperatures represent a real warming trend rather than a chance fluctuation over the 30 year period.'

For politicians, 99 per cent confidence is good enough to treat as fact. But in case they still didn't get the point, Jim Hansen spelt it out in the sort of plain language unheard of in the British civil service. It was time, said Hansen, 'to stop waffling so much and say the evidence is pretty strong that the greenhouse effect is here.'

What excited more attention among the Congressmen was Hansen's model of temperature change at mid-latitudes over the next few decades. It predicted both unusually hot and cold Julys in the 1980s but, in the 1990s, the areas with a hotter July became larger and hotter weather became the norm – this meant the United States, within political lifetimes.

'It is not possible to blame a specific heatwave/drought on the greenhouse effect,' warned Hansen. 'However, there is evidence that the greenhouse effect increases the likelihood of such events; our climate model simulations for the late 1980s and 1990s indicate a tendency for an increase of heatwave/drought situations in the Southeast and Midwest United States.'

As he spoke, the USA was gripped by a record drought. The Mississippi dried up to the point that barges became stranded and the US-Canadian dispute over water from the Great Lakes became even more heated than normal when it was proposed to send water south to help out the ailing river. Washington sweltered. So far as the press were concerned, the greenhouse effect had arrived. Presidential candidate Bush stated that, if he was elected, 'the White House Effect' would deal with the greenhouse effect.

Observing all this, Sir Crispin Tickell sent Prime Minister Thatcher a four-page memo, followed by the Congressional testimony of US biologist George Woodwell, one of the authors of the Villach-Bellagio report.

As the story of Hansen's speech broke, scientists, politicians and environmentalists were already packing their bags and heading for Toronto, Canada. Here the Canadian government planned to take the world stage and propose a Law of the Atmosphere. Others, remembering problems with the Law of the Sea, favoured a simpler Climate Convention-with-Protocols, like those aimed at acid rain and ozone depletion.

A few grand speeches were made at Toronto, but its principal finding, brilliantly steered to by Canada's former UN ambassador, Stephen Lewis, was an agreement that CO_2 emissions should be cut 20 per cent by 2005, with a longer-term cut needed of at least 50 per cent. It was not an inter-government conference, so the conclusion had no legal weight, but it was remarkable none the less and has since become a benchmark.

The huge US delegation demonstrated the rivalry between NASA and the EPA as well as the significance of the issue. The small European delegations were visibly shaken by the scale and speed of events. Britain sent a message from junior minister the Earl of Caithness proposing more research.

Before Hansen and Toronto, the greenhouse effect was not at the top of the political agenda. Shortly before the atmosphere conference, Canada had hosted the 'G7' summit; the club of the world's seven richest industrial nations. The Canadians let it be known that Thatcher had shown no enthusiasm to discuss the greenhouse effect or the environment (other leaders had insisted on it). Now it became a political inevitability.

The Missing Magic Bullet

There are three principal responses to the global atmospheric crisis.

Adaptation – a Limited Potential

The first strategy is adaptation: societies can try to plan to live in a hotter, more hazardous and less predictable world by a mixture of techno-fix and laissez-faire. Until a few years ago this was a popular option. The engineering industry welcomed higher sea levels. They would encourage a boom in construction. Ronald Reagan's Interior Secretary Donald Hodel suggested 'personal protection' against increased ultraviolet caused by ozone depletion: sun cream and sunglasses.[34]

As politicians and planners took a closer look, however, it became clear to even the biggest enthusiasts of technology that the scope for adaptation was extremely limited. A 1 metre rise in sea levels could affect 300 million people worldwide and protecting them would cost £13 billion a year.[35] In the North, where taller sea walls are built, salt marshes, fish nursery areas in estuaries and nature reserves will be lost owing to increased erosion on the seaward side. (A

1 metre sea level rise will eliminate up to 80 per cent of US wetlands.)

While the cost of new sea walls would be one-tenth of the economic value of the resources they would protect in the USA, in Bangladesh they would cost ten times the economic value of the protected land. The world could not afford such adaptation.

If sea levels rise 90 cms Egypt will lose 15 per cent of its arable land and the homes of 8 million people. Forty per cent of Indonesia is vulnerable to sea level rise. On current estimates, the countries of Tuvalu and the Marshall Islands will cease to exist by the end of next century. A 2°C temperature rise would rob Papua New Guinea of 20 per cent of its farmland as crops had to be grown higher up mountainsides. Similar upheavals are promised in every continent, threatening the already precarious global food supply.

Another policy, already adopted on the east coast of America, is 'retreat from the sea'.[36] But in smaller, poorer and more crowded countries this is not an option: they will need help or go under. The world, and particularly the rich, cannot afford to do nothing in the face of such political tensions and the massive movements of refugees they will create.

No technological fix can protect forests, croplands or cities against storms, drought or rainfall with new and unwelcome tracks. In January 1990, Britain was hit by a 100 mph storm (below the strength of a hurricane) which did £1 billion of damage. Tropical reefs, the centre of enormous biological diversity, can take 20 years to recover after a serious storm (1988 saw the strongest hurricane ever in the western hemisphere), and huge areas will die out as seas deepen and temperatures rise too fast for the corals to adapt. Thousands of nature reserves will become 'prisons rather than sanctuaries'. World Wide Fund for Nature (WWF) scientist Rob Peters estimates that (even without the barriers of farms, roads and so on) some forest trees can migrate at only 20 km per century but may have to move at 15 times this speed if they are to adapt to a potential warming.[37] Like the Kirtland warbler, which now seems scheduled for extinction around 2070 as a warmer climate alters its habitat, vast numbers of species will die out and ecosystems collapse.

'Adaptation' may be a wise precaution but it is not a magic bullet with which to slay the greenhouse effect.

Juggling with the Atmosphere

The second option is to try and rebalance the atmosphere. Aircraft spraying ozone into the stratosphere have been suggested.[38] It might work, but in the past such apparently simple 'fixes' have often proved disastrously misjudged. Many politicians are keen on reforestation to 'scrub' CO_2 or 'sponge it' from the atmosphere by photosynthesis. The industrial forestry lobby is already pushing hard for this option.

Unfortunately, plantation forestry has an ecological record as poor in the developing world as it does in Britain, and conventional forest practices are unsuited to creating carbon-storage. Coal keeps carbon out of circulation for millions of years, peat for hundreds of thousands, but wood for only decades or centuries.

On the optimistic assumption that plantations could take as much carbon (a net 7.5 tonnes carbon per hectare a year) from the atmosphere as sycamore in plantations of the Southeast United States, Greg Marland[39] has suggested that reforestation of 7 million km^2 could remove and 'sequester' 5 Gt (Gigatonnes = 1,000 million tonnes) of carbon, approximately man's input from fossil fuels (estimated at 5.5 Gt with a further 0.4–2.6 Gt from 'biotic' sources such as burning forest, grass and oxidising peat).[40] This would require replacing the entire area of tropical forest lost to date. At present, forest is still being cleared. It means improving the creation:destruction ratio up to 26 times.

According to the Energy Technology Support Unit,[41] if the UK doubled its current forest area to 20 per cent of land surface it would absorb a total 3 million tonnes of carbon a year, or just 1.75 per cent of the UK's emissions of 171 million tonnes carbon (627 million tonnes carbon dioxide).[42]

Thus, converting the entire 80 per cent of the UK land surface not used for urban purposes to forestry plantations would absorb – not necessarily store – only 7 per cent of the UK carbon emissions. Even at Marland's assumed rates of growth, it would need a plantation the size of England, Scotland and Wales to its absorb the UK's CO_2 output. At 2.1 t/C/ha, the Forestry Commission's estimated rate,[43] an area three and a half times the UK would be needed.

Jimmy Goldsmith, the businessman brother of ecological philosopher Edward Goldsmith has, among others, suggested that the North should provide some US$20 billion to rent the ecosystem services represented by the forests and other ecosystems of the South. It is a good idea in principle: after all, at present the North simply abuses them.[44]

'Offsets', which allow the North to go on burning fossil fuels if trees are planted in the South, are a superficially attractive option. A US firm, Applied Energy Services of Connecticut has already been granted permission to construct a coal-fired plant on the condition that it plants 52 million trees in Guatemala, 'equivalent' to the 15 million tonnes of carbon it will release over 40 years. (Applied Energy is believed to have turned down an offer to use its funds to save tropical forest that faced destruction, and has amortized the US$1 million it spent on trees in the costs of the power plant.)

Such 'offsets' draw attention away from the real problem, which is fossil fuel use in the developed countries and continued deforestation. They are extremely attractive to politicians in the North, which as Adam Markham of WWF International points out, 'is responsible for more than 60 per cent of the greenhouse gases pumped into the atmosphere'.[45] There are considerable doubts about how effective 'offset' plantations would be as carbon stores. The only sure solution is to reduce fossil fuel use.

Expanded plantations for fuelwood have an inherent advantage because they substitute for coal or oil. Fuelwood and biofuel-use could help head off further reliance on fossil fuels in developing countries, and help wean developed countries off fossil fuels. One example is Los Angeles' plan to require all cars from 2007 to run on methanol (made from sugar cane or other crops) rather than oil (fossil fuel).

In any case, carbon dioxide creates only half the warming power of the greenhouse effect. There are no known ways of removing large amounts of other greenhouse gases such as methane or nitrous oxide, and there are no natural sinks for CFCs or halons (except the stratosphere). There is no magic bullet to shoot the pollution out of the atmosphere and allow us to pollute on a 'business as usual' basis. Which brings us to the third and most vital option: stopping pollution.

The Need to Halt Greenhouse Pollution

Politicians have never had to deal with an environmental problem like the greenhouse effect before. The workings of nature mean there are considerable time-lags before atmospheric pollution reaches its full impact. Unfortunately, like generals planning to fight the next war with the weapons that won the last one, politicians are loathe to believe that their old policies will not overcome every new difficulty.

In the business of curbing greenhouse gases and ozone depleters, everything depends on timing. Every year of delay increases the size of the future problem. Worse still, the penalty for a year's delay gets bigger with every one that passes. There are few signs that governments have grasped this essential and frightening aspect of the problem.

The existing atmospheric burden of CFCs, CO_2, methane and nitrous oxide has not yet exerted its full impact on warming the planet because of climate feedbacks such as ocean eddies, ice and water dynamics, the effect of clouds and the interactions between gases. Some clouds, for example, warm the earth like a blanket. Others are thought to cool it like a heat screen. What effect will global warming have on both types? We don't know.

The most important unknown is thought to be the rate at which the ocean transfers heat. It takes a longer time to warm up than the land, which delays greenhouse warming. Climatologists refer to the upshot of all these response variables as the earth's sensitivity. A highly sensitive model world is one where the ocean is assumed to equilibriate quickly with warmer air. An insensitive one takes longer to warm up.

The often-quoted prediction is an average world temperature rise of 1.5–4.5°C for a doubling of CO_2 or the equivalent mix of gases. The range of estimates derives from high and low assumptions of sensitivity. So far the earth has warmed 0.4 – 0.7°C since 1850: as might be expected on past pollution, if the equilibrium is 1.5 and the response is fast. But the equilibrium could be 4.5 or 5.5 and the response slow, in which case more is to come. As computer models become more complex and, it is hoped, more realistic, as more feedbacks are needed, the picture tends to look worse (for example 6.3 – 8.0°C), but we will not know for certain until the earth responds and the change happens.

The fact that we do not know how sensitive the planet is has more than academic significance.

In his 1987 report *A Matter of Degrees*,[46] Irving Mintzer of the World Resources Institute called this phenomenon of yet-to-be-felt pollution, 'global warming commitment'. It means that, even if all pollution stopped immediately, the earth would still go on getting warmer for decades to come. By 1987, the earth was estimated to be already committed to a 0.5 – 1.5°C rise above the pre-industrial average. A 1 degree C change is as great as anything experienced in the 8,000-year history of Western civilisation. Simply to hold warming there, we would have to stop all emissions immediately, which is clearly impossible. We are committed to such a rise, but what more are we committing ourselves to?

Mintzer assessed alternative 'futures', depending on the policies adopted by governments. The 'base case' was roughly what countries such as the UK are planning to do at the moment: 'No new policies are implemented to slow the rate of greenhouse gas emissions. No major effort is made to retard tropical deforestation or to make energy use more efficient.' The base case assumed lower than historical releases of CFCs, yet by 2000 the planet had reached 0.9 – 2.6°C and by 2030 1.6 – 4.7°C above pre-industrial temperatures.

But if, as many predict, fossil fuel use actually goes up, and 'if tropical deforestation is allowed to increase and if energy prices continue to ignore the environmental costs of energy supply and use', and if CFCs grow at historical rates, said Mintzer, things would get a lot hotter. Then 'the commitment would reach 1 – 3°C over pre-industrial levels by 2000' and, 'if allowed to continue, such a scenario would commit the planet to an increase in 2.3 – 7.0°C over the pre-industrial climate by 2030'. By the end of the next century the high emissions future commits the earth to temperatures 5.0 – 15°C higher than at present: hotter than for 1 million years.

As Mintzer pointed out, the planet is not locked in to either of these 'hot house futures', but it is getting more locked in with every day that passes. Mintzer's most optimistic 'slow build up' scenario limited commitment to 1.4 –4.2°C as late as 2075, but assumed that from 1980 there had been radical improvements in efficiency, 'greater use of solar energy systems, less reliance on solid fuels over the long term, and slowed tropical deforestation'. In reality, none of this had happened by 1990.

Similarly, Bob Watson of NASA says: 'for every year that fully halogenated CFCs are emitted into the atmosphere it will take an additional decade or more for the abundance of atmospheric chlorine to be reduced below 2 ppb' (the self-repairing level for the ozone layer).[47]

'If 30 years of delay is allowed for removing scientific uncertainties, identifying options, establishing international consensus, and implementing appropriate policies,' said Mintzer, the earth will be committed to an extra warming of 0.25–0.8°C. 'This increase – though a mere fraction of one degree,' warns Mintzer, 'equals nearly 50 per cent of the total emissions deposited in the atmospheric 'bank' through human activities and biotic processes [burning forests, cutting peat, etc] since the Industrial Revolution.'

In the time that has passed since Mintzer's study, the possible consequences of the global climatic change look worse but the uncertainties remain. A 1989 US EPA report to Congress, *Policy Options for Stabilising Global Climate* (which went on to be discussed by the IPCC) noted that recent studies 'suggest that a warming of 5.5°C as a result of doubling carbon dioxide may be at least as likely as a warming of 1.5°C'.[48] (The IPCC has three working groups:

Science, chaired by the UK; impacts, chaired by the USSR, and responses, chaired by the USA.)

The EPA emphasised the importance of the planetary 'sensitivity'. With low sensitivity, it said, 'early application of existing and emerging technologies to limit greenhouse gases could prevent an equilibrium warming commitment of greater than 2°C within a century'. 'If, on the other hand, the true temperature sensitivity of the Earth to doubling CO_2 is 5.5°C or even greater, then without very rapid application of existing and emerging technologies and development of new technologies, the earth could be committed to a global warming of more than 3°C by as early as 2010 even with application of many existing technologies to limit greenhouse gases.' One implies disasters, the other calamities. Both make immediate precautionary action a necessity.

Further uncertainties of potentially enormous significance include the ability of forests and sea life to take up carbon as the atmosphere changes, and the nature of the response. Small extra temperature increases such as that caused by the wait-and-see policy envisaged by Mintzer, could trigger catastrophic 'flips' in non-linear natural systems. The Arctic ice for example, may be part of a global thermostat that controls a large part of carbon cycling and heat transfer through the principal deep sea current which plunges to the depths of the North Atlantic south of the ice boundary and re-emerges in the Pacific. If the Arctic ice melts, it might cause sudden changes to the current, with global consequences for ocean ecology and hence for the atmosphere. Similarly, melting Arctic tundra may release vast quantities of methane, itself a green-house gas, causing a 'runaway' positive feedback of warming and more release. We do not know. But, as for a blindfolded person sawing into the branch they are sitting on, when change comes it may be unpredicted, consid-erable, unwelcome and irreversible.

In addition, for ecosystems, it is not just the total warming which is impor-tant but the rate of change. Since the last ice age, the average rate of tempera-ture change has been no more than 0.01–0.02°C per decade. Temperate forest trees are believed to be able to tolerate temperature change by migrating, but only to a maximum of 0.1°C per decade .

'This rate,' say American analyst Florentin Krause and German Professor Wilfrid Bach, 'is about ten times faster than the natural average rate of temper-ature change seen from the end of the last ice age to the present, but is signifi-cantly less than what current trends in greenhouse gas emissions are calculated to produce.'[49] They point out that humankind and 70 per cent of the flora and fauna on earth today have evolved during the last 850,000 years, in which time the average global temperature has never been more than 2.5°C warmer than the contemporary earth average of 13°C. Bach and Krause use the 0.1°C/decade and 2.5°C total increase to define targets for stabilising global climate: the closest anyone has yet come to defining ecological limits to green-house pollution. Exceed such limits and we may expect ecological collapse on a huge scale.

The key question for politicians – and for us all – is what we risk by waiting to resolve uncertainties, and what we gain.

To try and help politicians make up their minds, Stephen Schneider of the

US National Center for Atmospheric Research in Boulder, Colorado, has produced 'best estimates' of how long it will take to resolve the key uncertainties in the General Circulation Models that are used to estimate where and when it will get warmer in future, and thus how the planet will change.[50]

Schneider estimates that it may take only 0–5 years to resolve uncertainties about the impact of a doubling CO_2 or equivalent on temperature. That doesn't seem long. But to resolve the uncertainties over sea level rise he says, may take 5–20 years. And it will probably be 10–50 years before we can be 'certain' of the effects on rainfall, the sunlight reaching the earth's surface, evapotranspiration (by which forests give up moisture to the air to help form rain), soil moisture, run-off and severe storms.

Such changes could be vast. Rainfall may be 20 per cent up or down: enough to move deserts and destroy forests, as well as creating both drought and flood. It may be 30 per cent sunnier or cloudier: enough to disrupt almost any agricultural system. Soils may be 50 per cent more or less moist: if less, enough to turn the grain-growing regions to dust. Severe storms will change significantly, but these are most unpredictable of all.

If we agree that such changes are unacceptable, we must take action to avert them, hopefully before it is too late to do so, and in the knowledge that we will probably not know when it has become too late. These are arguments for action, but politicians, and especially British governments, have used just such uncertainties in the past as arguments for doing nothing.

With global climatic change, the need to take action now is increased by the decreasing effectiveness of action taken later. The greenhouse effect requires implementation of the polluter pays principle, otherwise the developing countries will not cooperate. And it requires the precautionary principle, otherwise not only do future generations bear the costs (and probably ourselves) but the costs get larger the longer the action is delayed.

Several scientists have likened a wait-and-see policy to a game of Russian Roulette. But rather than using a revolver, it is more like playing the game with a Gatling gun. And, at each spin of the chamber, the number of live rounds is increasing by an unknown amount.

Making 'greenhouse policy' requires changed political understanding of time, uncertainty and responsibility. So far, Britain's politicians – among others – seem incapable of comprehending what needs to be done, or perhaps they understand it too well. 'The IPCC,' said Richard Mott of the Environmental Law Institute in Washington in 1989, 'is dominated by the countries chairing the Working Groups: USA, USSR and UK. They have bought delay while giving the appearance of vigorous activity, by capturing the process of international negotiation.'[51]

Britain: Living in a Dirty Greenhouse?

Britain shows signs of playing a leading role in the production of greenhouse rhetoric, while joining other major polluters in vigorously applying the brakes to progress behind the scenes.

Britain's rhetorical passage into the issue began in 1988. At Toronto in June, the Norwegian Prime Minister Mrs Brundtland had spoken of a global 'heat trap'. In 1987, US scientist Wally Broecker had warned, 'The inhabitants of planet earth are quietly conducting a gigantic environmental experiment.'[52] The Toronto Conference Statement began: 'humanity is conducting an uncontrolled, globally pervasive experiment whose ultimate consequences could be second only to nuclear war.' A few months later, at the Royal Society, Margaret Thatcher also spoke of a 'heat trap', adding, 'we have unwittingly begun a massive experiment with the system of this planet itself'.[53]

Thatcher achieved headlines for her revelations, not because of their originality but because they implied that Britain would take action. But Thatcher's speech was carefully laced with references to the global nature of the problem. The world population had risen to 5 billion; there were 'implications for . . . energy production, for fuel efficiency, for reforestation'. 'In the past when we have identified forms of pollution,' said Thatcher, 'we have shown our capacity to act.' The Toronto Conference had concluded, 'It is imperative to act now.' Yet Britain now produced no plan of action for curbing global warming.

In a message sent to the Toronto Conference, the Earl of Caithness had anticipated more research 'in the next few years', with a 'timetable of response' based on the 'development of understanding over the next 10–15 years'. He noted that energy efficiency measures could be started (although in the following 12 months the government was to do the opposite).

In May 1989, David Fisk, DoE Chief Scientist who had been at the Toronto Conference, spelt out the official policy to a House of Lords inquiry.[54] 'Preventative' action could still be 10–15 years away. Measures which could be taken sooner included: 'good management of the world's forest resources' , 'implementation of cost-effective energy efficiency measures and development of economic alternative energy methodologies including nuclear power', wide ratification of the Montreal Protocol and 'full cost energy pricing (including environmental cost)'. Of these measures, the first is principally someone else's responsibility, the second is hardly implemented in Britain (efficiency is the highest priority but nuclear is now known to make no economic sense and even government forecasts show it falling in importance by 2020[55]), while the Montreal Protocol itself was grossly inadequate. The last could mean energy prices many times their current level, but would have a significant impact on reducing the UK's disproportionate greenhouse contribution.

In its response to the Commons Energy Select Committee's report on the greenhouse effect in 1989, the UK government attacked the Toronto target of a 20 per cent cut as 'arbitrary' and 'without scientific rationale'.[56] In so doing it merely aped Britain's most feeble excuses for not joining the 30 per cent Club on acid rain. Such a response could scarcely be less appropriate. The only CO_2 target with a scientific rationale was 50 per cent. Britain showed no sign of embracing that. The reply, drafted by the Department of Energy, dusted down another argument used to justify inaction on acid rain, saying that to take any action beyond current commitments 'at significant cost to the UK in the absence of agreed international action, might be economically punitive and unlikely to have any global impact'.[57] There were no international commitments in being.

In a speech to the United Nations on the greenhouse effect in November 1989, Prime Minister Thatcher announced £100 million 'for tropical forests'. It turned out to be over three years and funding the Tropical Forest Action Plan, a much criticised Food and Agriculture Organisation scheme that favours industrial plantations rather than forest conservation. She called for an 'international cooperative effort' but made no specific commitment to reducing Britain's own greenhouse gas emissions, merely producing £5.5 million for research.

Just prior to her UN speech, the UK met with other countries at Njoordwijk in the Netherlands. Tracy Heslop of Greenpeace recalls that the UK sided with the other big carbon dioxide polluters Japan, USA and the USSR (representing 48.7 per cent of world CO_2 output) and 'effectively stifled plans to cut CO_2 emissions. The UK wanted to wait for the IPCC science. This was the week before Mrs T's United Nations speech'.[58] UNEP, one of the organisers of the IPCC, commented that waiting for the IPCC to finalise its deliberations could delay action 'for the best part of a decade'. Peter Usher, UNEP's deputy general secretary commented, 'action is needed now'.[59]

The old 'wait-and-see' attitudes may well prove catastrophic. John Collier of the Atomic Energy Authority told the Lords in 1989 that, although energy efficiency measures could be put in hand now (though nobody in government was doing so), we 'had not yet reached the point where massive changes in energy policy are called for'.[60] This point, he said, might be at least five years away.

On the contrary, it may be that we are past the point where even massive changes will be sufficient to stop disastrous changes to the climate.

At the time of writing, the UK has yet to commit itself to a cut in carbon dioxide. After deriding the idea of targets, and insisting that it was essential to wait for the IPCC report at the Second World Climate Conference in November 1990, the government did do a sudden U-turn in May 1990, when Mrs Thatcher announced that 'Britain is prepared to set itself the very demanding target of a reduction of up to 30 per cent in presently–projected levels of carbon dioxide by the year 2005.'[61]

This, however, was not a cut but a licence to pollute at the same level in 2005 as in 1990.

Britain and CFCs

CFC production figures are collected but kept secret under the Montreal Protocol (Sweden and Denmark do release consumption figures). Using French government sources, Greenpeace has calculated that Britain's ICI is the world's second largest CFC producer and the biggest exporter of CFCs in Europe. In 1988, the UK exported 45,000 tonnes of CFC to 117 countries, 81 of which had not signed the Montreal Protocol.[62]

Britain probably consumed 66,000 tonnes of CFCs in 1988 – around 6 per cent of world consumption – and is a major contributor to ozone depletion and global warming by CFCs. CFC pollution is a problem created by the developed world: the USA, Japan and Western Europe used 70 per cent of the world's CFCs in 1985. Add in Eastern Europe and the figure is 84 per cent.

One million tonnes are manufactured worldwide, worth £1 billion.[63] In 1989, Britain was calling for an 85 per cent cut in CFC production but, as Tracy Heslop of Greenpeace points out, 'Other countries have moved faster: Sweden will phase out all its CFCs by the end of 1994 and Norway will manage 90 per cent by 1995.'

British ministers are fond of referring to the 'alarming' prospect of every Chinese or Indian buying a CFC-filled fridge. Yet Britain with 60 million people, already consumes three times as much CFC as China and India, with 1,800 million. On a per capita basis, each Briton is picking a hole in the ozone layer 90 times bigger than each Indian or Chinese. 'Even after the UK meets the terms of the Montreal Protocol,' commented Greenpeace, 'in 1989 it will be a larger user of CFCs than China and India combined.'[64] The UK's production of 105,000 tonnes compares with 444,000 tonnes in Western Europe as a whole. On a per capita basis, the UK produces double the European average, and six times the global average.

Including supermarket freezer cabinets and butchers' cold stores, there are an estimated 30,000 tonnes of CFCs in British refrigerator systems. Up to 75 per cent of these CFCs are lost through leaks and spillage. In 1989, West Germany set up a comprehensive national scheme to recover and recycle CFCs (this could supply the domestic sector almost indefinitely). In January 1990, ICI and refrigeration companies announced Britain's first scheme, after the Environment Minister David Trippier disclosed that he had been 'deluged' with letters from worried fridge owners.[65]

'The disadvantages of voluntary restrictions', says Greenpeace, are illustrated by the behaviour of industry. A survey in December 1988 showed that, despite the fuss made about aerosols by 'green consumers', over two- thirds of the electronics industry planned to continue using CFCs. In Sweden, the law has forced the use of other options. So far almost nothing has been done about halons: even the fire extinguishers in the London Ecology Centre are halon-filled.

The government has allowed CFC production to continue while ICI gets round to marketing substitutes. The cost of not doing so would be the short-term financial loss of refrigerator manufacturers, and people might have to wait a few years before getting a new fridge (though recycling could meet 10 years of CFC needs for refrigeration). Given the disproportionate delay in healing the ozone layer with every year of continued production, the cost of allowing this extra release may be the future death of the krill and plankton that sustain the food web of the South Seas, and those beyond, as well as greenhouse warming.

At the end of 1989, Britain was blocking moves by several countries – including the USA, USSR, West Germany and the Netherlands – to cut levels of methyl chloroform, a solvent used in dry cleaning and typing fluid, which causes an estimated 16 per cent of the present damage to the ozone layer. Unlike CFCs, it lasts only six years in the air and could be eliminated within 15 years of a prohibition. If it is not banned, it may not be possible to stop an Arctic hole forming. 'ICI . . . has been lobbying its customers to write to the government,' noted Richard Palmer of the *Sunday Times*. 'The firm's attitude mirrors the stance it took for a decade until a change of policy last year, against phasing out the most harmful CFCs.'[66] (see p.354)

Britain and CO_2

The Bellagio and Toronto conferences concluded, from current understanding of the global carbon cycle, that, if worldwide emissions were reduced 50 per cent, the biosphere and oceans might absorb the rest, stabilising concentrations. (More recent studies suggest that less CO_2 may be taken up by the oceans than was then thought.)

However, in 1987 Britain produced some 3 per cent of the world's CO_2 emissions, with around 1 per cent of the world population. So, to reach the global average (the amount produced by the typical Latin American), Britain needs to cut its emissions by two-thirds. To treat the atmosphere as kindly as the average inhabitant of Southeast Asia, the average person in the UK should reduce their use of the things that cause CO_2 emissions – transport, electricity, manufactured goods and so on – by over 40 times.[67]

If the world is to reach an overall 50 per cent reduction in present emissions, and to equalise carbon emissions on a per capita basis, British CO_2 pollution should be cut 80 per cent, to around one-sixth of present levels. Forecasts of future global CO_2 emissions (from fuel burning and forest loss) in the year 2040 range up to 20 Gt/C/year – three times the present level. Even the modest Toronto objective has met with little enthusiasm from the industrial countries: at the 1989 Hague Conference, the UK, Japan and USA rejected proposals from countries such as the Netherlands to achieve a commitment to the Toronto target or even a freeze at current levels.

Dramatic reductions could and must be achieved. In 1987, 21 per cent of CO_2 was produced by liquid fuels burned in transport, and the amount is increasing (Chapter 6) Catalytic converters do not curb CO_2, so the only practical solution is greater investment in public transport, traffic control and improved vehicle efficiency (prototypes could improve efficiency at least 50 per cent).

The immediate test of the government's commitment to reducing British CO_2 emissions lies in the energy sector. Over 38 per cent of our CO_2 comes from electrical generation, even though it produces only 15 per cent of energy used.[68] Switching from coal to natural gas yields a 40 per cent CO_2 saving. But the UK has only 50 years' supply of gas at present rates of use.

The Commons Energy Committee noted in 1989 that energy efficiency and conservation are 'almost universally seen as the most obvious and most effective response to the problems of global warming'.[69] Everyone agrees in principle and the reason is not hard to find. It takes 3 units of coal energy to produce just 1 unit of electrical energy, so saving 1 unit of electricity (e.g. from space heating, the most inappropriate use of this high-grade form of energy) will save 3 units of pollution.

Since the 1973 'oil shock', Britain has done much less well in terms of increasing energy efficiency than many of its competitors. By 1985, for example, Japan had increased GDP 46 per cent while its final energy use went down 6 per cent. The UK managed only an 11 per cent increase in GDP while energy use fell 12 per cent. The USA achieved a 17 per cent increase in GDP on the same fall in energy. And while the amount of business done per unit of energy in the UK improved over 20 per cent from 1973 to 1983, it improved only 5 per cent from 1983 to 1987. 'It is clear from the Japanese example,' said the Energy Committee, 'that it is possible to do much better.'

After reviewing dozens of studies, the Association for the Conservation of Energy (ACE) estimated in 1989 that if Britain pursues a 'business as usual' approach, CO_2 emissions will increase up to 20 per cent by 2005, while just applying existing energy efficiency measures and new supply technologies could achieve a 23 per cent reduction and a 2.3 per cent growth in GDP.[70] To achieve such efficiency gains requires government action. Market forces alone are not enough. ACE highlights three reasons why. First, there is a failure to provide consumer information, which economists call 'market transparency'; in fact it is supposed to be a condition for the free market to operate properly. Australia, the USA and West Germany all have energy-use labelling on domestic appliances: Britain has nothing. Efficient fridges on the European market use 80 per cent less electricity than some British models. Even some Polish fridges are more efficient than some British ones. David Olivier of Energy Advisory Services found in 1989 that a Danish Gram refrigerator cost £40 more than UK models but saved 70 per cent of the electricity. 'A large Woods chest freezer was only £5 more and produced a 60 per cent saving.'[71] Second, tenants are often paying bills while landlords are responsible for capital investment such as insulation. Third, industry plans a 20-year pay back while individuals will invest on a 2/3-year timescale. Consequently, a 'disproportionate amount of investment is going into expanding supply (to meet inefficient demand) rather than into improving the efficiency of energy use'.

In some American states, if increased efficiency is more economic than building extra power stations, the company must sell an efficiency service. In Stockholm the city council provides vouchers to householders so that they can buy energy-efficient light bulbs. Edinburgh University installed 740 efficient light bulbs in its halls of residence: £17,000 savings were made (more than the cost) and Britain produced 283 tonnes less CO_2 pollution as a result, just in the first year. The US Rocky Mountain Institute calculates that simply changing one 75W conventional 'incandescent' (i.e. hot) light bulb for one 18W energy - efficient bulb (the same brightness) will save 400 lbs of coal at the power station.[72] Using one energy efficient bulb can avoid releasing half a tonne of carbon dioxide. Says Stewart Boyle at ACE: 'If every household and office in Britain just changed one such a bulb, it would save enough electricity to shut down an entire 2000 MW power station.'

Until energy prices increase significantly, government-imposed standards and incentives are the overriding influence on energy efficiency. Unfortunately, in the late 1980s Britain was heading in the wrong direction. The *Financial Times* surveyed the energy conservation and efficiency market and found cavity wall insulation sales down nearly 17 per cent in the first half of 1989, draughtproofing down 15 per cent, double glazing down 20 per cent and 'a continuing market decline' forecast in each sector.[73]

Energy Secretary Peter Walker had given priority to energy efficiency and by 1986 Britain's performance had improved to fifth best in the EC, behind countries such as France, the Netherlands and Denmark. Cecil Parkinson replaced Walker and cut the resources for the Energy Efficiency Office over 50 per cent. At the time of writing, further cuts in real terms are planned in 1990/1 and 1991/2.[74]

Although the National Audit Office calculates a £2–6 return for each £1 invested under the Home Insulation Grant, 1989 was the first winter since 1979 when grants for loft insulation were unavailable. In the same year, energy survey schemes and the Energy Efficiency Demonstration Scheme were abandoned, while the number of people employed draught-proofing homes fell 90 per cent in two years.[75] Also in 1989, the Department of Energy (DoEn) dropped its 'Monergy' television advertising campaign encouraging efficiency. Yet the Electricity Boards advertised on TV encouraging people to heat their homes with electricity: an extraordinarily wasteful and polluting practice.

In 1990 Britain is moving to adopt new standards for the insulation of homes. Good news perhaps, except they are only as strong as those introduced in Sweden in 1935. British homes built (in one day) by a Finnish company to its national standards were so efficient that in their first year the heating only needed to be switched on for a few hours a day when temperatures reached the unusually low -15°C.

One of the policies which the government did promote as an 'answer' to the greenhouse effect was nuclear power. 'We have to look at having a much heavier nuclear programme,' said Thatcher in an interview with *The Times* on the greenhouse effect in October 1988.[76] 'If we want to arrest the greenhouse effect we should concentrate on a massive increase in nuclear generating capacity,' said Environment Secretary Ridley a month later.[77] In April 1989, and to the shock of independent scientists who had attended, Cecil Parkinson told reporters waiting outside the Downing Street seminar on the greenhouse effect that it had 'endorsed' nuclear power as a greenhouse solution.

All were soon proved wrong. At a global level, Bill Keepin and Greg Kats showed that even an enormous 11–27-fold increase in nuclear capacity would not hold down CO_2 emissions, because of increased pollution from non- electrical sectors such as transport. They also showed that energy conservation is a seven times more cost-efficient way of cutting CO_2 than building new nuclear capacity.[78]

Perhaps unsurprisingly, the DoE vigorously disputed their figures because Britain was still officially planning to expand nuclear power. Officials still promoted nuclear power, even when Dr Tim Jackson and Simon Roberts of FoE painstakingly analysed all the options for cutting CO_2 from coal-fired electricity generation and showed that nuclear capacity came 16th, various efficiency options occupied second, third, fourth and seventh place, and fuel switching came first in terms of cost-effectiveness.[79]

In summer 1989, Mrs Thatcher's government had thrown out a Lords Amendment to the Bill privatising electricity which would have required suppliers to promote efficiency. But privatisation now proved to have other more beneficial side-effects. Where decades of environmentalist delving had failed, the prospect of being taken to the European Court for unfairly subsidising nuclear power finally forced the Central Electricity Generating Board (CEGB) to 'come clean' about the true cost of nuclear power.

The CEGB had claimed that nuclear power cost 2.97p/kWh, compared with more than 3p/kWh for coal. Energy campaigners such as FoE's Simon Roberts had suspected that the true nuclear cost was much greater. In 1989, figures leaked from the Cabinet Office showed it to be a staggering 8–9p/kWh, three times that of coal. As an economic proposition, nuclear power had clearly been dead from the neck up since birth. Now, as Thatcher proved more committed to privatisation than to nuclear power, it was withdrawn from privatisation and Walter Marshall resigned. Nuclear was out of the running as a greenhouse panacea.

In 1990 FoE estimated that technologies such as Combined Heat and Power (CHP), flue-gas decarbonisation (currently energy inefficient) and renewables such as wave and wind power could provide a 5.5 GW contribution saving 17 million tonnes of CO_2.[80] A 90 MW CHP coal-fired station planned for Slough, for example, will employ a 'circulating fluidised bed' and utilise its 'waste' heat to achieve twice the efficiency of a normal station and use half the coal. But renewables may be able to do much more than this. In April 1990, the Department of Energy's Energy Technology Support Unit (ETSU), admitted to a remarkable past mistake. The 'Salter's Duck', a nodding-duck wave machine that generates electricity, had been consigned to the scrapheap of departmental priorities in the 1980s because it appeared 'uneconomic'. ETSU scientists put the cost of Salter's Duck electricity at 9.8 p/kWh. Professor Salter of Edinburgh University never accepted their calculations, but protested in vain. It now emerged that, ETSU had grossly over-estimated the likelihood of cable failure and the costs of materials, and the true cost would be only 5.2 pence![81] Clearly, on economic grounds, nuclear reactors should be shut down, Sizewell should be cancelled and money put into non-polluting renewables and energy conservation.

At present, however, UK emissions are slowly rising, owing to increased fuel use in transport. Between 1984 and 1987, CO_2 emissions rose 11 million tonnes to 158 million tonnes as carbon. The peak year, 1979, was 180 mtC.

'Biogenic' emissions should not be forgotten. While smaller (about 20 per cent) than fossil fuel emissions, the potential global release from forests and soils is large enough to wreck any negotiated plan to reduce carbon emissions from fossil fuels.

Most deforestation is now in the tropics. Britain affects it through trade and aid policies. Deforestation could release an estimated 6 Gt of carbon a year in future and, if linked to population increase, in the next 120 years deforestation could yield 334 Gt carbon, more than the sum of historic releases of biogenic carbon (150 Gt) and fossil fuel (183 Gt).[82] Britain's aid to the Third World could help fund more forest conservation, but from 1979 (when Britain was the most generous of the world's seven richest countries) to 1988 it fell 50 per cent in real terms, shifting the UK from 6th to 15th position among 18 Western aid donors.[83] At 0.3 per cent of GNP, Britain's aid contribution is still one of the lowest and less than half the target of 0.7 per cent set by the UN.

Dying forests – such as those affected by *Waldsterben* – also release carbon. Indeed, while *Waldsterben* itself may be caused by climatic change and pollution, it may now be adding to it as well. Changes to peat and soil can also put carbon in the air. Digging peat causes it to dry out (as does drainage for forestry) and carbon is released as CO_2: if Britain lost all its peat, it might release some 6 million tonnes, or 3.5 per cent of the UK annual carbon release from fossil fuels.

Britain's peatlands may store a small amount of global carbon but, as with tropical forests, it will be difficult for the UK to argue with other countries that they should conserve their resources for the common good if Britain is seen not to conserve its own. In 1990, the Highlands and Islands Development Board revealed plans for a major horticultural peat industry in the world-famous Caithness Flow Country, already 25 per cent lost to forestry.

Britain and Methane

Methane is 27 times stronger than CO_2 as a greenhouse gas. In the stratosphere it degrades to create water: another greenhouse gas. This water is thought to cause the beautiful 'noctilucent' clouds that glow in the twilit sky of the Arctic. These were unknown before 1885. The 'polar stratospheric clouds' that play a central part in ozone breakdown in the Antarctic may be formed in a similar way.[84]

Vast reserves of methane may exist loosely held in 'clathrates' – soft lattice-like submarine rocks – which some scientists fear might be released by higher sea levels and temperatures. Oil exploration – a major activity of British firms – may also release large quantities. Clathrates may contain more carbon than coal reserves[85].

Other major sources of methane are the microbes that live in the guts of cows (less intensive agriculture and less meat eating would significantly reduce emissions), wetlands, coal-mining, combustion (including car engines and forest fires), the guts of tropical termites and, possibly, natural gas in pipelines (it has been suggested that up to 12 per cent leaks into the atmosphere).[86] The UK's 3.5 million tonne emissions have been estimated to come 32 per cent from livestock, 29 per cent from coal mines, 20 per cent from landfill gas and 10 per cent from the natural gas grid.[87]

The logical first source to tackle is landfill sites. According to Her Majesty's Inspectorate of Pollution (HMIP) more than 700 'waste disposal sites' contain so much methane from rotting rubbish that they are an explosive hazard. Another 1,300 are a potential hazard. In 1986, the Department of Energy identified 300 as suitable for biogas production for energy but by 1989 there were schemes to collect the gas and use it to generate electricity at only 26 sites.[88] Another 20 schemes were under consideration. The USA has 70 and West Germany 50.

Less rubbish would mean less methane. Warren Spring Laboratory estimates that British tips produce 3 million tonnes of methane a year and this figure will double within ten years. Keith Richards of the Energy Technology Support Unit says biological decomposition can change 1 tonne of rubbish into 400 cubic metres of 'landfill gas' (approximately half methane, half CO_2 with other traces), capable of generating 7500 megajoules of heat.[89] Refuse gas saved Britain 250,000 tonnes of coal or £12 million in 1989 and could double by 1992.

Richards calculates that Britain's rotting waste creates the equivalent of 54 million tonnes of CO_2 a year, but, if it was recovered and burnt, its impact would be reduced to the equivalent of 16 million tonnes. Extracting gas from British rubbish tips could prevent the equivalent of 38 million tonnes of CO_2 reaching the atmosphere.

Methane could be the 'sleeping giant' of the greenhouse effect. Its lifetime is short (8–10 years) but it is increasing at 1 per cent a year and reductions may be technically difficult to achieve.

One of the most effective control measures may be to curb CO (carbon monoxide) emissions, which come very largely from traffic. CO is a very efficient 'scavenger' of hydroxyl radicals (OH) from the air. Its increase may have reduced a natural sink for methane, allowing levels to rise.

Britain and Nitrous Oxide

Nitrous oxide (N_2O) should not be confused with NOx (NO_2 and NO). It may be laughing gas but it is no laughing matter. It receives far less attention than it deserves. Sources are poorly known but include natural and disturbed soils, the oceanic nitrogen cycle, combustion and artificial fertilisers.

Nitrous oxide rivals CFCs as a long-lived gas (170 years) and is 200 times more powerful than CO_2 in its warming capacity. It is increasing at 0.3 per cent a year.

Fossil fuel use probably contributes 2–30 per cent of the total, so energy conservation and traffic reduction will reduce N_2O as well as other pollutants. Lowering fertiliser use will probably discourage soil microbes from producing N_2O on farmland as well as cutting nitrate pollution.

Talking Targets Down and Advocating Delay

The greenhouse dilemma posed for the UK government is not so much choosing between different strategies to restructure its industry or aid or science, for it shows, so far, no sign of doing any of those things. The problem is how to maintain a credible domestic and international profile on the biggest of 'green' issues, while continuing with policies which are established by virtue of suiting vested interests (such as massive car manufacture, sale, use and road building), or are central to political doctrine.

In the case of the latter, Mrs Thatcher's Conservative government has deliberately sacrificed the environment for the short-term financial interests of share-buyers in water privatisation and (at the time of writing) electricity privatisation, where the area boards will sell waste, not conservation. There is by no means a guarantee that a British labour government would not prove to be equally much hobbled by its own weight of political commitments to outdated and polluting industries and practices.

Thus Britain's greenhouse role has so far been one of doing business-as-usual while saying the opposite. All the old excuses and manoeuvres learnt in 10 years or more of being the Dirty Man of Europe, are being rolled out for use in the UK's greenhouse policy.

There are frequent calls for more research. When the Department of Energy rejected the call of the Select Committee on Energy for a UK commitment to a target to reduce carbon dioxide, it also announced that it would wait until research into market mechanisms in the energy sector had been completed before intervening, like the Americans, Japanese, Dutch or West Germans, to create market mechanisms to deliver energy efficiency. Bigger roads, it said, would help reduce congestion. Professor Ian Fells of Newcastle University, who was to undertake the research, pointed out that the contract had only just been signed. The government was, he said, 'always finding excuses for not meeting injunctions concerning pollution. It seems to me quite extraordinary that the Prime Minister says we lead in this area. Instead of leading, we are trying to find excuses for not meeting deadlines.' As to the government's claim that more road building would help reduce greenhouse gas emissions through greater efficiency, Fells said 'we have to reduce the amount of energy used by investing in public transport: building more roads is not the slightest help.'[90]

Mrs Thatcher's May 1990 announcement sounded like a cut in CO_2 emissions, but, in practice, it meant only a qualified commitment to a freeze at 1990 levels. It was also a freeze that would take place 5 years after the date of 2000 proposed by the European Commission. The European Commission Environment Commissioner commented that it would 'cause problems since the date proposed by the UK conflicts with the stricter date which the Commission has already put forward'.[91]

Mrs Thatcher's speech drew on the government's accumulation of reasons for not making cuts, to qualify the commitment it did make. Britain wanted to know 'what is happening in the regions'. The IPCC Report would provide 'the agenda' for the next 15 years. Significantly, there was an open-ended requirement that the UK would only achieve the freeze 'provided others are ready to take their full share'. This, it was said by government sources, was aimed at the United States. But as an excuse for not abiding by the commitment it could apply to any country.

The UK had been under increasing European pressure to at least agree the freeze at current levels as of 2000, for some months, and in February 1990, officials, such as David Fisk of the DoE, had gone out of their way to criticise the USA position at a Washington IPCC meeting. But the UK had taken up an immobile 'transatlantic' position, distancing itself from the USA administration, which, under Whitehouse Chief of Staff John Sunnunu, was blatantly opposed to action on CO_2, while not supporting European moves to agree a freeze.

Journalists were told that John Houghton of the Met Office had briefed Ministers as to the content of the IPCC paper, which concluded that emissions of the long-lived greenhouse gases (CO_2, nitrous oxide and CFCs) needed to be reduced 60–80 per cent if their atmospheric concentrations were to be stabilised at present levels. A 'business-as-usual' strategy implied a 1.4–2.8° C rise by 2030 and 2.6 – 5.8° C by 2090.[92]

Scientifically, the IPCC report presented little which previous reports by the EPA and others had not. The UK's sudden conversion to the idea of the freeze at 1990 levels was most probably attributable to Mrs Thatcher's personal concern that the forthcoming Montreal Protocol renegotiations, to be held in London, should be perceived as a success. The USA administration had let it be known that it would oppose a European plan to provide more funds to developing countries party to the Montreal Protocol, to help them switch from CFCs to substitutes and substitute technologies, thus making it less likely that countries such as China would become parties. The UK could not afford to be seen to be closely allied with such a USA position.

'The very demanding target of a reduction of up to 30 per cent in presently-projected levels of carbon dioxide by the year 2005', on which Mrs Thatcher built her case in May 1990, was a hurriedly-prepared Department of Energy estimate of future CO_2 emissions, which very few energy analysts agreed with.[93]

Stewart Boyle of the Association for the Conservation of Energy has anal-ysed the Department of Energy's past record of producing estimates of future energy use, and, hence, CO_2 emissions.[94] He points out that, in 1976, the Department estimated a UK energy demand for the year 2000 of up to 650 million tonnes of coal equivalent (mtce),whereas, the actual was just over 300. Since that time actual energy demand has remained more-or-less static, and official estimates of energy demand have progressively fallen, but still remained significantly inflated in comparison to reality.

The latest estimate for the year 2000, submitted by the UK government to the Inter-Governmental Panel on Climate Change,[95] shows energy demand climbing from the current level of under 350 mtce to as much as 500 mtce or more. This implies a 73 per cent increase within 30 years. Boyle points out that this estimate is far higher than six others produced for the UK, by the Stockholm Environmental Institute, the US Environmental Protection Agency, the Royal Institute for International Affairs, the Association for the Conservation of Energy, and the government's own Energy Technology Support Unit.

The DoEn estimates that energy-related CO_2 emissions in 2005 will reach 204–212 million tonnes (as carbon), 174–206 mtC in 2000, and 188–316 mtC in 2020.[96] It achieves such a high figure by making some extremely unrealistic assumptions about how energy will be used in the year 2000. Boyle points out that it assumes a use of electricity 'comparable only with the historically high growth period between 1955 and 1970'. It assumes a very high 'income elas-ticity' for electricity, meaning that consumers and companies will use large amounts of electricity in their economic activity. This is not only out of line with the factors assumed by other forecasters, it is contradicted by real life (there has been a trend in the opposite direction, though as we have seen, not as much in Britain as in competitor countries), and would represent a massive failure of the government's own energy efficiency policy.

Other models of energy use in the residential sector utilise the detailed database of the Building Research Establishment and conclude that on a business-as-usual basis, there will be a reduction in energy use in housing or no growth. The Department manages to forecast up to 26 per cent increase by 2005 and 31 per cent by 2020. 'To achieve the levels of energy consumption suggested by the DoEn model,' says Boyle, 'householders would literally have to leave windows open longer and run their central heating systems for up to 50 per cent longer than they currently do, not an impossible scenario but not a very plausible one.'

The Department of Energy forecast also assumes a substantial increase in the amount of traffic, and hence the carbon dioxide pollution it produces. This is estimated to rise 47–55 per cent by 2005, and 71–87 per cent by 2020, close to levels implied by the Department of Transport's 1989 estimates of traffic growth in the 1988 *Roads to Prosperity* (83–142 per cent by 2025).

The reason for the Department of Energy's extraordinarily high forecast was suspected to be a manoeuvre to build up UK forecasts so that 'negotiations' could start from a comfortable cushion of UK emissions. Even the CBI, in its unpublished 'preliminary comments' on the DoEn forecasts, noted that the projections of CO_2 were 'excessively high'.[97] 'These energy assumption forecasts,' noted the CBI, 'are not consistent with trends since 1970 (even after allowing for energy pricing effects). The forecast for industrial energy consumption in particular, appears to assume that the shakeout of the 1970s and the early 1980s will be reversed and that economic growth will be strongly associated with energy intensive industries. This has not been the experience in the 1980s.'

The DoEn paper was significant in being Britain's official forecast of major greenhouse gas emissions submitted to the Intergovernmental Panel on Climate Change, due to report to the Second World Climate Conference and to provide the database for negotiations on reductions in greenhouse gases. Hence the submission to the IPCC is the UK government view, rather than an academic exercise by the Department of Energy. This suspicion was confirmed by Mrs Thatcher's May 25 speech.

A striking insight into the development of government policy on CO_2 emissions came shortly after Mrs Thatcher's Bracknell speech, from a leaked minute obtained by the Labour Party, recording details of a meeting between the Department of Energy and the Confederation of British Industry (CBI) held on 10 January 1990.[98]

The CBI minute-taker recorded that the Department of Energy civil servant 'candidly admitted' that UK 'commitment to the IPCC may have been inspired initially by a desire to give the appearance of activity while postponing substantive action'. Things, however, had 'now moved on'. Mr Patten did 'not want the UK to appear laggardly on the international stage'.

The DoEn, noted the CBI, 'had been alert to the potential dangers of entering into commitments to cut emissions'. This was 'particularly in relation to its other policies – e.g. electricity privatisation, prospective privatisation of coal.' But this 'business-as-usual' perspective had now been tempered somewhat by a realisation that the rising tide of 'greendom' is likely to make some sort of international agreement a political imperative.

The UK was, nevertheless, active in the international effort, emphasising the costs of taking action. 'Of crucial importance,' noted the minutes, 'is the need to concentrate the minds of participants [at the IPCC] on the cost implications of cleaning up.' 'Cost,' the DoEn told the CBI opaquely, 'will be a much better base for the measure of sacrifice than the emissions targets themselves.'

Although the Noordwijk declaration had called for stabilisation in the year 2000, 'what this was to mean in practice was left vague, with actual targets being left to IPCC to decide. Thus, firm targets are likely to be a few years off.'

The Energy official noted that 'if Mr Patten's will prevails, we could expect to see proposals for increased VAT on fuel or possibly a fiscally neutral carbon tax'. There was a 'great deal of concern' in non-Environment Departments at such proposals. The DoEn was 'feeding in' its assessment study to the DoE to make sure 'any adverse consequences are, at the very least, fully anticipated'. The Treasury were 'extremely worried about the cost implications of cleaning up, for UK competitiveness and for the future of economic growth itself'. Transport, noted the man from Energy, 'appeared not so much hostile to greendom as ostrich-like. Arguments for greater public investment in rail, for example, were ruled out of court. Claims that new road building merely encourages further traffic growth (and hence emissions, *ceterius paribus*) were dismissed out of hand'.

The picture of UK policy-making is thus one of squabbling government departments fighting to defend traditional interests of their own industrial sectors, with no overall planning, and regarding the environment as a threat to the economy. This is in stark contrast to countries such as the Netherlands, where each industrial sector and each government department has taken part in drawing up energy and CO_2 emission targets in the National Environmental Policy Plan, and West Germany, where an equally detailed exercise has been carried out. In both countries, the need to protect the environment and to be efficient with resources is taken as a *sine qua non*, whereas UK industry and government still regards it as an external nuisance factor, which only has to be accommodated so far as the 'tide of greendom' makes it politically expedient to do so.

UK policy is far from beginning to address the problem of the man-made greenhouse effect itself. Mick Kelly of the University of East Anglia has detailed a strategy to stabilise the effective concentration of CO_2 in the atmosphere (i.e. accounting also for other gases) during the first half of the 21st century.[99] It requires very significant global action over the next 30 years.

Kelly finds that the rise in global temperature could be limited to 1.8+/-0.7°C above pre-industrial levels and 0.7+/-0.2°C above the 1990 level, while the rate of warming would be less than 0.1°C per decade, with temperature eventually stabilising at 2.1+/-1.0° C if: CFC production were eliminated in 1995 and greenhouse gases were avoided as CFC substitutes; deforestation was halted by 2000 (and reforestation to offset emissions of 1.65 billion tonnes C a year was established by 2020), CO_2 emissions from fossil fuel were cut to 30 per cent of today's levels by 2020, and the rate of increase in methane and nitrous oxide concentrations was cut to 20 per cent of its present value by 2030.

The IPCC's science report, which was greeted by Mrs Thatcher with a UK commitment to do nothing to reduce this country's carbon dioxide emissions by 2005, itself noted that an immediate 60 – 80 per cent cut in emissions of the long-lived greenhouse gases such as CO_2, CFCs and nitrous oxide was needed just to stabilise them at current pollution levels, with a 15–20 per cent reduction needed in methane.[100]

Gerry Leach, an energy consultant who advises several governments and attended Mrs Thatcher's Downing Street seminar on global warming, has calculated that Britain could readily cut its emissions by 20 per cent by 2005 (close to the 25 per cent which West Germany will probably adopt), while maintaining economic growth. Leach shows how a 20 per cent CO_2 saving would cost £20 billion at most, while yielding financial benefits of £119 billion: a net profit for Britain of £110bn. In a detailed six-sector study (industrial buildings, two types of gas boilers, fridges, light bulbs, housing insulation), he demonstrates how for just 'one-quarter of the UK consumer's annual energy bill', notes Leach (£8.1 billion), the UK could cut emissions by 10.5 per cent.[101]

Amory Lovins, Research Director of the Rocky Mountain Institute, has produced even more dramatic evidence of potential savings. He calculates that re-equipping buildings and industries with the best lighting commercially available, could save 92 per cent of the energy used for that purpose (and give better lighting). The cost is negative: a net internal cost of -1.4 C/kWh. 'Evidence is emerging', notes Lovins, 'that the corresponding efficiency potential in Europe . . . is probably not much smaller'. Lovins calculates that, overall, half the electricity currently used in the USA could be saved at no net cost. Due to technical improvements, the cost-effective potential for energy saving is 30 times today what it was 10 years ago.[102]

Steps to realise such potential are not technically difficult. David Olivier of Energy Advisory Associates in Milton Keynes estimates that if Britain's inefficient stock of domestic fridges were replaced with Europe's best mass produced models, 1500 MW of power generation would not be needed, saving an equivalent of 10 million tonnes of carbon dioxide pollution. The Americans have a law that requires energy labelling so you can see the cost of running an appliance like a fridge. But electricity is still relatively cheap and consumers demand a much quicker payback than commerce, so standards are needed too. The US law, the National Appliance Energy Conservation Act – sets standards that outlaw 90 per cent of fridges on sale in 1987, and would do the same here. It will avoid the need to build 25 power stations and save consumers US$28 billion in electricity bills by 2000. In the UK, meanwhile, it seems to be the political will and organising ability that is lacking.[103]

CHAPTER 12

Conclusions

Britain has become known as the 'Dirty Man of Europe' for many reasons. These concern the UK's pollution, its attitudes, its policies and how they are presented, made and conducted. Elements of Britain's unenviable reputation include its roles as:

• *a pollution exporter*: for example, on North Sea currents and airstreams. Britain has exploited its 'natural advantages' to the disadvantage of others downwind and downstream

• *a uniquely bad polluter*: for example, the UK is the largest producer of sulphur dioxide in Western Europe, the largest producer and exporter of CFCs in Europe and quite probably the biggest importer of radioactive waste in the world

• *a disproportionately significant polluter*: for example, on a per capita basis, Britain produces six times the global average of CFCs (and around twice the Western Europe average) and produces three times the global average for sulphur dioxide

• *a procrastinator*: for example, calling for research rather than action on acid rain, delaying an EC Directive by five years

• *a treater of symptoms not causes*: employing the 'dilute and disperse' philosophy across a whole range of problems from landfills to oil pollution and sewage outfalls

• *'Perfidious Albion'*, using disingenuous arguments and misleading statistics to delay or shirk responsibility: for example, drawing attention to Chinese coal reserves and tropical forest destruction as a hazard in the global warming debate, rather than taking action on its own carbon dioxide emissions

• *a tolerator of public squalor*: for example, failing to invest in modern litter cleaning, and allowing public transport to deteriorate

• *a law impeder and breaker*: for example, delaying and trying to undermine or evade Directives or proposed rules on nitrates, pesticides and eutrophication

• *an abuser of science*: for example, wanting to test the environment to destruction by demanding cause–and–effect pollution evidence that can be furnished only once damage (often irreversible) is done, and systematically accumulating volumes of small doubts while ignoring larger and more robust indications of ecological change, as in forest decline.

Some aspects of the 'Dirty Man' reputation could be wiped away fairly quickly. Others require changes in policies and in official attitudes that run very deep. At the time of writing, the government is preparing a White Paper on the environment, which it claims will set Britain's policy agenda for the next decade. During its preparation, a leaked Whitehall minute described it as only 'rather general and wide ranging'.[1] To revitalise Britain's environmental image, the government must deliver positive, practical action rather than words, whether in a White Paper or not. The Dutch National Environmental Policy Plan is a good model. Action should include:

• *Policy and institutional reform*: politicians must abandon some of their old gods, such as nuclear power and economic growth defined solely in financial terms, and they must clear away the institutions which sustain them. For instance, R&D funds must be withdrawn from nuclear power and road planning, and directed to other uses, while civil servants and technicians need to be reassigned and trained for useful jobs elsewhere.

• *Setting environmental quality standards and organising policies to achieve them*: for example, air pollution limits should achieve critical loads and levels set on the basis of human and ecological health.

• *Planning, locally and centrally*, to coordinate public investment, economic and legal instruments to achieve environmental results. This means intervention, not a laissez-faire attitude. Government should use both 'command and control' methods, as are being employed to reduce air pollution across many sectors in Los Angeles, as well as taxes and subsidies targeted to encourage the market to work for the environment, as is being done in the Netherlands and West Germany. Why not put a light railway round the centre of the M25?

• *Strict enforcement of laws*: for example, water pollution consents, littering laws and vehicle emission standards. Industrialists and others should be prosecuted and jailed for major offences, as has been done for breaches of pollution rules in the USA.

• *Education of the public* and interest groups to back up and help achieve environmental standards. In the Netherlands, a major public information exercise was conducted in 1985 to explain why considerable investment in acid-reducing controls on industry and power plant was needed. The UK needs to put pressure on industry to make its managers environmentally literate, and government should finance schools, colleges and the higher education system to achieve this.

If Britain undertook such a programme, it might deserve the environmental leadership which it presently annoys its neighbours by falsely laying claim to. The UK is not a world power, but if its environmental performance significantly improved it could take its place among the 'first division' of environmental achievers. These 'medium-sized' countries regularly start and help achieve international environmental reform. They include Sweden, Norway, West Germany, the Netherlands, Denmark, Switzerland, Austria and Canada.

Signs of Progress or Signs of the Times?

In the time since this book was begun, Britain has declared that it will ban strawburning (it has yet to do so) and put an end to sewage sludge dumping (in 1998). Progress perhaps, but does it signal a true change of heart? Are politicians embracing a new ethic which recognises the spiritual and social value of nature and the importance of a high-quality environment? Is it a start to wholesale policy reform, or is it Britain simply adjusting to the politically inevitable?

The fate of the Large Combustion Plant Directive, where the UK agreed to make sulphur reductions on one basis in 1988 and then moved to renege on the agreement in spring 1990, is not an encouraging sign.

Lectures and Excuses

In a move reminiscent of environmental *bête noire* Nicholas Ridley, in May 1990 Environment Minister Chris Patten did not show up at a Bergen environmental conference but instead sent his deputy, David Trippier. He refused to ally Britain to countries which wanted to pledge a carbon dioxide freeze at 1990 levels from the end of the century. Trippier invoked the diplomatic niceties of the yet-to-be-completed Intergovernmental Panel on Climate Change (IPCC) process as an excuse, even though the policy part of the IPCC was being emasculated by the United States, and even though all the countries pressing for action at Bergen were also part of the IPCC process. It confirms the UK's reputation.

'The UK drags its feet,' wrote the even-handedly sceptical *Independent* environment correspondent, Richard North, in a 1990 article 'Delaying tactics earn Britain its "dirty" Tag'[2] North heard from Peter Steif-Tauch of the European Commission how the British were 'brilliant at delaying tactics' but, in the end, 'industries which drag their feet gain nothing. They lose to other firms who gain markets in pollution technology'. North also found that 'again and again officials said the British claimed to need conclusive scientific evidence before making a commitment to spending money'. The UK spoke its mind and published good information, but 'often defends poor positions with a sort of superiority which reminds continentals of a colonial grandeur they resent'.

The protracted international negotiations over acid rain that took place throughout the 1980s gave repeated examples of a breath-taking British arrogance, as the UK chose to lecture other nations about the science and on Britain's past achievements (mainly the well-worn story of the Clean Air Act). It was depressing to see the British delegation departing to the airport with every appearance of smug self-satisfaction at having bamboozled the foreigners, wrongly interpreting the silence of other delegations as a sign of admiration rather than weary disbelief.

Xenophobia and remnants of the Empire mentality still pervade Britain's international relations, perhaps more among its scientific establishment than at the Foreign Office. Secrecy and the narrow base of Britain's civil service seal off Whitehall and Westminster from non-governmental organisations, academics, journalists and others in a way not found in most of Europe or in North America. While the integrity of those involved is normally beyond doubt, within official cloisters attitudes feed upon and reinforce themselves, initiative is discouraged at the expense of continuity, and prejudice festers. As Eisenhower put it, 'the uninspected inevitably deteriorates'.

It is from the slit trenches of Whitehall's scientific civil service, with its closed committees and byzantine systems for keeping matters of public interest secret (such as the 'Chatham House Rules' under which civil servants occasionally swap thoughts with normal human beings on a purely non- attributable basis), that Britain informs its policy views on matters of worldwide significance.

Not surprisingly, the official cast of players in Britain's environmental policy establishment is rather limited. Sir John Mason, for example, served as director of the SWAP acid rain project organised by the Royal Society for the Central Electricity Generating Board and the National Coal Board. It was described as a 'fund for independent research' on the basis that the Royal Society was independent of government, but how independent was it? Until then Mason had been the director-general of the government's Meteorological Office, which bizarrely was still part of the Ministry of Defence. Scandinavian scientists could not have been very encouraged when, at the start of the study, the *Financial Times* reported his opinion that: 'there was already a voluminous literature on acid rain but he considered it "not very impressive" scientifically and short on analysis'.[3]

Mason must have had plenty of opportunity to hear the views of Walter Marshall at the Royal Society itself, because, like Thatcher, Marshall was one of its Fellows. During his 18 years at the Met Office, Sir John would also have come across the substantial contract placed with the weather researchers by the CEGB, which hired a Met Office Hercules aircraft to fly up and down the North Sea analysing the air for the plumes from tall stacks.

More recently, in 1989 Mason appeared before the House of Lords Select Committee on Science and Technology to inform them of the Royal Society's views on the greenhouse effect, and particularly research.[4] Presumably drawing on his experience with the acid rain issue, he told their Lordships that 'our reputation for having this hard-headed critical, practical approach to problems is very well recognized abroad, and I am sure there are many countries who are looking to the UK for a lead'. Britain certainly has a reputation, but it is not perhaps quite the one that Sir John imagined.

Mason also went out of his way to highlight Britain's Met Office model of the world climate, the only non-American 'General Circulation Model', saying 'it is terribly important that there is a sane and critical voice outside the United States where we can make this strong independent judgement'. David Fisk from the Department of the Environment (DoE) spoke of the Committee of UK greenhouse research teams being smaller than the US ones but 'of the highest quality'. As a result, he said, the UK 'scores very highly'. The National Environmental Research Council (NERC) referred to a 'British breakthrough' in greenhouse ocean modelling.

Harmless enough perhaps, but very reminiscent of Britain's attempts to keep pace with the 'big science' of the US-USSR space race in the 1960s. Britain's efforts in that race eventually yielded teflon-coated frying pans. The language is also fiercely nationalistic, justifying an expensive computer model with arguments similar to those used for an independent nuclear deterrent.

The official greenhouse witnesses had noticeably little to say about the mundane matters of actually reducing greenhouse gases. Mason referred to the future menace of foreign emissions: 'The world population is still growing enormously. Nobody seems to want to tackle that problem.' The DoE referred to the need to protect tropical forests. But it seems that practical steps such as organising a public transport system that works, or getting garbage turned into compost, are not the output of Britain's best brains. Unfortunately such attitudes still flavour British environmental policy, and all too often mean that it is only when Brussels picks up some scientific finding or technological improvement that it gets translated into a programme of action.

Enforcement

If little has changed in terms of Britain's 'scientific' attitudes, what of the letter of the law? It is British accepted wisdom that, once a European Directive or other international agreement is in place, the UK is scrupulous in honouring its commitments in both the spirit and the letter. Foreigners, it is implied, are less reliable.

The European Commission's 'league table' of legal proceedings against member states[5] gives a crude indication of how countries are viewed by the enforcement officers of the Environment Directorate. In 1990, the UK lay in the middle, with 31 'crimes' as against 57 for the worst (Spain) and 5 for the best (Denmark). Also worse than the UK were Belgium, Greece, France and Italy. Better were West Germany, the Netherlands, Ireland, Portugal and Luxembourg. If nature conservation cases are excluded, leaving only pollution issues, the UK scored 27 while Denmark was subject to 3 legal actions, and Spain 28. Italy (28) and Belgium (39) had a worse record, but all other countries enjoyed a lower score. UK officials claim that the UK's figure should be 22 or 24. If water and air pollution are considered, the UK tops both lists of offences. UK claims to have a good record are misleadingly based only on the final stages of the drawn-out European legal process.

The British idea that our enforcement is excellent is something of an illusion. The DoE must be well aware of how it has manipulated statistics, not just for European Directives but for domestic laws (such as the 'relaxation' of pollution consents). In 1990 cross-checking on the figures used for the EC Bathing Water Directive by the Marine Conservation Society uncovered a peculiar DoE use of statistics. Heacham beach in Norfolk counted as a 'pass' even though two of 22 samples failed on two bacteriological criteria, making a 91 per cent total pass rate, not 95 per cent as the Directive requires. DoE, however said 22 tests with two criteria were 44 tests, so two failures meant a 95 per cent pass. Norfolk FoE and Great Yarmouth Environmental Health Officers also found from their own tests for viruses and bacteria that eight of the nine beaches should have failed, whereas the DoE had passed six of them. [6]

Will Britain now move to a regime of strict law enforcement, like the toxic waste police of New Jersey, USA? This would mean abandoning the 'gentlemanly' voluntary approach, which has been repeatedly shown to be ineffective. During the 1980s Britain let environmental standards deteriorate so badly that a tide of pollution has risen to well past legal limits. A huge number of polluters would now need immediate prosecution. British officials claim that strict enforcement would be 'unrealistic', but this is because their past enforcement has all too often been non-existent.

Impractical Means

Britain needs to switch from a negative approach to environmental quality to a positive one. Since Victorian times Britain's underlying environmental philosophy has been one of laissez-faire, in which technologies and standards are not specified, in which industry and individuals are left to regulate themselves through voluntary agreements, and in which the minimum possible commitment is made to putting things right. While this has agreeable connotations of liberty and progress equably made through a spirit of cooperation, it has turned out to be a system so slack that, wherever public funding has slowed, environmental decay has set in.

'Best practicable means' (BPM) was intended to be 'an ever tightening elastic band' leading to higher standards, but it turned out to be a shoelace that kept coming untied. In its latest manifestation, BPM becomes BATNEEC – best available technique not entailing excessive cost – which is still not a commitment to use best available technology or techniques.

It remains unclear how Britain will avoid accepting the claims of vested interests that an environmental standard involves 'excessive' costs. Britain will still be far from achieving the technology-forcing stance of California, which led to catalytic converters and other pollution control systems. Left to the vagaries of best practicable means, Britain's cars would have remained far dirtier.

Best available technology (BAT) is an accepted concept in other countries. Under the Rhine Action Plan agreed by West Germany, France, the Netherlands, Luxembourg and Switzerland, since 1987 chemical firms along the river have had to use BAT. West Germany has simultaneously imposed a pollution tax bringing in £7 million a year.[7]

Dilute and Disperse

Britain has yet to abandon the philosophy of 'dilute and disperse'. Co-disposal of waste continues. When a 1,000 tonne oil spill hit the ecologically sensitive south coast of Devon in late spring 1990, an official explained that, unlike West Germany and the USA which had equipment to remove oil, Britain's approach was to disperse it. It was, he agreed, not the best way but it was a 'question of resources'.

'Dilute and disperse' has once again got Britain into trouble with the European Commission. Pesticide contamination threatens to breach the Groundwater Directive because UK farmers are officially advised to tip used sheep dip fluid into the ground. In 1989 over 18,000 sheep were being dipped in Britain using organophosphorus pesticides, each consignment then presumably disposed of according to the official instructions, which break EC law. Moreover, farmers are themselves increasingly concerned at damage caused to the nervous system by even low-level exposure to these chemicals. This risk of enzyme damage has been known about for many years, but, while a study on the hazard was finally begun, it is limited to 22 individuals.[8]

Market Intervention – Market Mechanisms

For ten years the UK saved billions of pounds by neglecting environmental technology, monitoring and research, and by letting its environmental quality standards go unenforced or fall behind those of other countries. Now, in theory, British politicians of the right have been attracted by the idea of delivering environmental results through market mechanisms, on the grounds that it will not mean higher public expenditure. In practice, they have yet to take action.

One way of achieving this is to 'improve' the functioning of the free market by building all the costs of production, including externalities such as pollution, into the cost of a product.

Prompted by the International Institute for Environment and Development (IIED), the Central Policy Unit of the DoE commissioned Professor David Pearce of the London Environmental Economics Centre, in a joint venture with IEED and University College London, to write a 'think paper' on environmental pricing called *Sustainable Development*. This later appeared under the title *Blueprint for a Green Economy* by David Pearce, Anil Markandya and Edward Barbier, and is widely known as the Pearce Report.[9]

When Chris Patten took over the Environment Secretary's chair from the much-criticised Nicholas Ridley, he and his officials seized on the *Pearce Report* as evidence of fresh government thinking. It was also a useful stick with which to beat the polluting departments such as Energy and Transport, whose policies were undoing much the DoE tried to achieve. 'We are going to have to put our wallets where our mouths have been on issues like environmental quality,' Patten said after the launch of the Report.

Pearce's principle is simple enough. The damage done to forests and cathedrals by acid rain from cars or power stations, for example, ought to be taken into account in the price of electricity or cars. Costs with a market value are relatively easy to track down, to attribute and to add in, either directly or by imposing a tax on the product in order to pay the bill elsewhere. Costs with money values include hospital bills for radiation victims or the price of stonework repairs.

Indeed, around the world there are many examples of just such an approach in action. The US Superfund is one rather inelegant version, where companies creating toxic waste have had to pay for its clean-up. Because it came after the fact, it did not stop the pollution at source, but it has forced the pace in corporate thinking so that some US practice is far ahead of that in Britain.

A 1989 review by the Organisation for Economic Cooperation and Development (OECD) found 85 economic instruments in operation in 1987 in France, West Germany, Italy, the Netherlands, Switzerland and the USA, with 68 more in a further eight OECD countries, making a total of 153 instruments, 81 being charges and 41 being subsidies.[10] In 1988, the parliament of Sweden decided that in future, the costs of environmental damage and accidents should be included in the road tax levied on cars and lorries. Even after discounting a large amount on the basis that car drivers willingly put themselves at risk by driving, road traffic was found to be subsidised by 11 billion kroner above the tax income of kr25 billion.[11] This implies that, in Sweden, road users should be paying at least 50 per cent more in taxes. No such calculation has been made in Britain.

The Netherlands has used subsidies and taxes as direct instruments of policy. It has, for example, introduced a pesticide levy and uses the income to pay for pollution reduction on farms. In Sweden, an existing 5 per cent tax on fertilisers and pesticides was doubled in 1989. Italy has what *ENDS* magazine calls 'the most far-reaching eco taxes', which cover 'industrial emissions of smoke and sulphur dioxide, products made from a variety of plastics, pesticides, pig farming, aircraft noise' and other areas.[12]

Environmental pricing helps make the free market fairer in environmental terms: it removes a positive incentive to pollute because the air, sea, soil or water is no longer a free rubbish tip. A shortcoming of environmental pricing, and one common to any free market mechanism, is the difficulty in accounting for the many important victims of pollution or development which have 'social' or ecological values but no market value. The simplistic approach to dealing with this conundrum is to give them a surrogate or arbitrary value. But all this may do, if the thing is really important for spiritual, emotional, cultural or any other 'intangible' reasons, is to substitute a price for value.

The true value of the New Forest for example, has to do with its beauty, inspirational properties, history, value to future generations and a host of things not connected with its timber value and not at all well described by the turnover of the local tourist industry or even special tests of 'willingness to pay'. It may be that we have to decide to protect such a habitat from acid rain by controlling cars or power stations at a known cost, without ever being able to put a monetary value on it (see below).

However, by the 1990 budget it seemed that Patten's attempts to 'green' government economics had run into the sand. Greenpeace had proposed taxes on company cars. FoE had put forward a scheme to allow a higher ceiling on mortgage relief to better-insulated houses, encouraging home owners to improve energy efficiency.[13] VAT could have been removed from energy-saving products such as double glazing. Without increasing inflation, taxes on large-engined cars consuming large amounts of fuel could have been increased, while taxes on small-engined efficient cars could have been reduced. Others pointed out that comparable countries give significant incentives to reduce pollution. For example, the West German government provided tax refunds of up to £390 for motorists buying cars with catalysts, or who retrofit catalysts to older cars.[14] In the event, Chancellor John Major did none of these things.

There was no tax break to encourage energy efficient investment in homes. There was no carbon tax or duty increase on fossil fuels. Britain remained the only country in the EC with no purchase tax on gas or electricity.[15] There was no significant change in taxation of company cars – the tax scale was increased 20 per cent but this was 'no real discouragement' to the company car system, said Ian Morton, motoring correspondent of the *Evening Standard*.[16] The environment correspondent of *The Times* noted that there was 'little evidence of a greening of the economy'.[17]

At a Coopers and Lybrand Deloitte conference held with *The Times* newspaper on the same day,[18] Patten announced that the White Paper would contain no special incentives for the City to 'support British industry in its attempts to clean up and protect the environment'. 'I think clarification of where we think industry and government should be moving is as much an incentive as banks and investment managers should look for,' he said. This could only mean that the government was to provide no subsidies, tax breaks or other financial incentives to induce the country's dominant investors to think longer term and environmentally, rather than short term. In other words, no environmental pricing, no environmental economics, Patten's failure.

Environmental Standards

Britain has yet to seriously set and enforce standards to restore or safeguard environmental values. This will not be achieved by sticking artificial price tabs on them, although pricing pollution may help achieve the standards. In the Netherlands, for example, pollution charges were set high enough to induce polluters to reduce emissions. In 1985 they raised £330 million. ENDS magazine says, 'the scheme was largely responsible for a 50 per cent reduction in 14 industrial sectors between 1969–75, another 20 per cent by 1980, and an estimated further 10 per cent between 1980–6.'[19]

It is so long since Britain set out to achieve a major environmental improvement (such as the 1950s plan to restore the Thames to a standard fit for salmon) that government may have forgotten how to do it. One thing that government must do is to put some things above price, outside the market system. It should recognise that they are off-limits to development, and as Professor Tim O'Riordan has said of supposedly protected nature reserves and national parks, they should be made 'Minister proof'.[20] These absolutes should include environmental benchmarks as well as areas of natural heritage. They should be inalienable ecological cornerstones within which all policies would have to fit, and which would help define and conserve national identity. They would be untouchable except in time of grave national threat.

John Adams is a fellow academic of Pearce's at University College London, but a long-standing critic of analyses that rely on 'placing of money values on the environment'.[21] If government embraces pricing without setting standards, it could be worse for the environment and our quality of life, not better. Putting surrogate prices on the environment can easily become a way of knowing the price of everything and the value of nothing. As Adams says, it is 'an ethic that debases that which is important and disregards entirely that which is supremely important'.

During the Roskill Inquiry into the siting of the Third London Airport, 38 per cent of people interviewed by cost-benefit analysts said no amount of money would compensate them for the loss of their homes should they lie in the chosen site. Adams points out that, in his book *Cost-Benefit Analysis*, David Pearce writes of these responses: 'The replies [of those who could not be compensated by money] would seems to be inconsistent with the general view that "each man has his price". If the response is ascribed to some element of irrationality in the respondent, the problem arises of how to treat this element in the cost benefit analysis. The procedure of the [Roskill] study was to truncate the distribution at some arbitrary level.'[22] The arbitrary cut-off chosen by the Roskill Commission was twice the market price. This somehow assumes that the problem has been solved but in fact it has just been avoided.

Britain's road planners are particularly fond of cost-benefit analysis, but it has proved no more successful for roads than for airports. It seems likely that, far from being 'irrational', the people who refused to agree a price to surrender their homes or woodlands were sending a signal that they rejected the process of decision-making. People at Cublington were not being asked whether they accepted a new airport. Their community was just being measured for size. Similarly, as we have seen, the need for a new road such as the East London River Crossing is justified only by using a bizarrely loaded form of cost-benefit analysis concocted in secret at the Department of Transport. Yet there is no rational inquiry into whether a road or a railway is needed, nor a proper consideration of the environmental costs. Transport planning in Britain, like energy supply, is still based on the headlong and mindless projection of past trends into the future.

It is a problem of democracy, not just economics. Britain has what other Europeans call a 'democratic deficit': decisions are made privately by unaccountable cliques of Whitehall bureaucrats, the vested interests which their departments service, and rubber-stamped by ministers who show little signs of understanding the alternatives.

In Switzerland, the principle of building any new motorway through any conservation site has been the subject of a national referendum. The motorway lobby lost. It seems likely that, if such a referendum were held in Britain, the result would be the same, and few major new roads would be built. So far Britain has no mechanism for genuine public participation in deciding environmental standards. As Robin Grove-White, a senior research fellow at Lancaster University, and a former director of the Council for the Protection of Rural England, has noted: 'The time has come for Westminster and Whitehall to stop being so myopic. Employing economics and market forces for environmental ends will only help if they go with the grain of public feeling. That means listening, not imposing.'[23]

One reason is that, left to its own devices, the free market may not offer up environmentally sound choices. Economist Fred Hirsch cites the example of the progressive loss of an amenity through a 'tyranny of small decisions'. He uses the example of a bookshop, but it could apply to an unpolluted lake or an unlittered street. Hirsch points out that people may move to an area with an amenity such as a bookshop, only to see it disappear once general discount stores begin selling some of the most popular titles. 'Purchase of books at discount stores eventually removes the local bookshop. Yet bookbuyers can never exercise a choice between cheaper books with no bookshop and dearer books with one. The choice they are offered is between books at cut price and books at full price: naturally they take the former.'[24]

Mrs Thatcher's government implied that privatisation would mean that consumer pressure would force higher environmental standards from the water industry, but when challenged to say how privatisation could raise environmental standards if water consumers could not actively choose an unpolluting supplier rather than a more polluting one (they obviously could not because water supply is a regional monopoly), Secretary of State Nicholas Ridley retorted only that they could always buy Perrier water. So there is no real free market in water supply. And the Perrier company does not run the local sewage works. There is no free market in sewage disposal.

Further shortcomings of the free market are illustrated by the sale, or rather non-sale, of energy-efficient light bulbs. These 'green' bulbs are much more expensive than inefficient ones, and few householders buy them (although institutions do so where changing bulbs is a major labour cost) even though the savings in electricity made on each bulb, plus the length of its life, make it a more economic purchase.

One reason is that there is a flaw in the market: it lacks 'transparency' because Britain does not have energy labelling (i.e. the consumer doesn't realise how much money she or he will save). In theory this might be overcome by consumer demand coupled with enterprising manufacturers offering the information as a selling point. In practice, advertisers have been reluctant to invest in 'educational' campaigns to change the selling point of a product. It needs regulation to stimulate movement.

Another obstacle is that manufacturers have been unwilling to invest heavily in retooling plant to make more high-efficiency bulbs (and perhaps bring down the cost) and to sell fewer of the old bulbs. The first manufacturer to enter the market in a big way could bear a lot of costs in raising public awareness which others will then be able to cash in on. Technology-forcing regulations of the type found in the USA could overcome this (i.e. outlaw the inefficient bulbs) by making all manufacturers move at once.

A third factor is that the price of the electricity itself is too low because it takes no account of the pollution created in generation, so there is little incentive to buy the better bulb to save electricity. This too requires regulation.

Once all this regulation is in place, free market mechanisms would encourage a switch to better bulbs. Even then it might not work if there are psychological barriers which prevent consumers investing in the energy- efficient bulb even though it saves money. To get people used to the idea of buying the more expensive bulbs, Stockholm city council issued vouchers which householders could cash in when making their first 'green bulb' purchase –

intervention to help the market get going.

The official British mentality is usually against anything so obviously constructive. The liberal attitude of the Victorians, as Peter Brimblecombe has pointed out, was that 'the real solution lay in common sense'. This notion, as he says, 'has universally characterized almost all the ensuing environmental legislation of the United Kingdom'. Such laws assumed that, 'given time, people would obviously take the necessary steps that would so clearly lead to better conditions for all. In the case of smoky chimneys, it was thought to be self-evident that there would be great benefits from smoke abatement for both management and public alike.' [25]

Unfortunately, self-evident or not, left to themselves people and businesses do not always behave in a 'rational' economic way. This will always limit the effectiveness of free market mechanisms.

Setting standards for pollution also means accepting that, as more is discovered about the impacts of even low levels of pollution, the levels acceptable for public health and ecological integrity are steadily falling. The logical place for many of them to end up is at zero: that is at pre-industrial levels. This is already the trend for many toxic pollutants and the philosophy behind standards such as the EC Maximum Admissible Concentrations for pesticides.

Greenhouse gases are already present at levels so far beyond the capacity of natural systems to absorb or assimilate them that it may effectively become the norm for those too: elimination of CFCs and halons is already widely accepted. For developed countries a future without fossil fuels, unthinkable a few years ago, is beginning to appear essential.

As Grove-White has remarked, 'Today's "emotional" and "prejudiced" green critique has a way of becoming tomorrow's blunt reality.'[26] There is, after all, no reason why industrial processes and products should pollute. Biological systems perform many of the same chemical transformations using enzymes with far less 'pollution' or none, and in some industries zero emissions for certain processes are already standard. Waste from one process can become the feedstock of another. Ciba-Geigy say their conversion of raw material into product rose from 30 per cent in 1970 to around 60 per cent in 1988,[27] but in future industry will have to do better than this.

Standards must also be set high in the fields of basic technology, such as in energy use and supply, and will make sense only if operating in a planning system with an end in view, such as an integrated public transport system or a least-cost energy plan. For example, the 'Non-Fossil Fuel Obligation' (NFFO) set up under privatisation requires Electricity Boards to buy 20 per cent of their power from non-fossil sources such as nuclear or renewables. The government says it wants 600 MW or 2 per cent of the country's energy needs met from renewables such as wind, waste or water, by the year 2000.[28] The Department of Energy estimates that 20 per cent of the country's electricity demand could be met from wind alone by 2020. Engineering consortia and supporters of big-fix solutions are focusing on barrages proposed for the Severn and the Mersey, which could supply 6 per cent of Britain's current yearly electricity demand.

However, large tidal schemes are not the best approach to energy planning. Britain's estuaries are beautiful, important for fisheries and internationally vital for wildfowl and wading birds. Large tidal schemes could create environmental conflict. The first steps should be not more supply, but cutting back on what is generated needlessly.

FoE estimated in November 1989 that if the cost of two Pressurised Water Reactors (PWRs) (£3.8 billion) were invested in energy conservation, fuel consumption could be cut 20 per cent, saving £12 billion a year or £220 per head of population, and cutting CO_2 emissions 30 per cent.[29] A report quietly submitted by the Department of Energy to the IPCC revealed shortly afterwards that the potential for conservation to reduce UK energy use was not, as had been claimed, 20 per cent, but 60 per cent within 15 years, once measures such as 'good housekeeping', energy management, 'retrofits' on two and five-year paybacks, and improvements to buildings and machines were accounted for.[30]

'The study marks the beginning of a new era in the UK's energy policy,' said the magazine *ENDS*. But, to achieve such improvements, British standards from machinery to insulation must be raised to equal the best abroad.

The first sources of renewables to be developed should be the least environmentally damaging. But most require development to secure their full potential. Geothermal or 'hot rock' energy technically has the potential to provide five-sixths of UK electrical needs, but it requires deep drilling. Renewables expert Mike Flood said in 1989: 'For the past few years annual R&D expenditure on renewables has been around £15 million, compared with more than £200 million for nuclear.'[31] Perhaps geothermal should now receive some of the backing previously lavished on nuclear power? In the short term, land-based wind energy which costs a mere 2.26p/kWh, should be promoted, and Salter's Ducks rescued from their backwater.

Continuing Waste

The government has yet to take a lead on recycling or re-use, or even anticipatory design standards. The DoE may berate Marks and Spencer for its 'appalling' lack of recycling facilities[32] and require local authorities to appoint recycling officers, but the government itself falls down on recycling paper and does little or nothing to tax packaging or give grants and tax breaks to firms setting up recycling schemes. Simple regulation could force the worst firms to perform to the level of the best. Reedpak uses 100 per cent recycled paper in producing newsprint, whereas Bridgwater uses only 70 per cent and Shotton just 30 per cent. West Germany uses less virgin pulp in cardboard boxes, and Britain's tissue manufacturers use hardly any waste material at all.[33] A biodegradable plastic made by an ICI subsidiary without oil will be launched in 1990, but in West Germany not in Britain.[34]

In other countries, industry and government are heading towards higher environmental quality through setting and anticipating technology-forcing standards. In West Germany, for example, car manufacturers have been preparing to make it possible to recycle the growing level of plastic used in cars since 1982. According to the magazine *ENDS*, the European Commission is now expected to introduce a law requiring 'extremely demanding recycling targets' for plastic from cars.[35] Audi's chairman was giving speeches on recycling in 1985. Recently BMW chairman Eberhard von Kuenheim described the environment as 'the greatest single challenge' for the industry. The German Environment Ministry is proposing a £60 levy on the price of a new car to help pay for the cost of scrapping it. But a spokesman for the British Scrap Federation told *ENDS* in 1990, 'the view in the British car industry is that if you develop a recyclable car which costs 10 per cent more, you may soon be out of business'.

Who, however, is most likely to go out of business? Germany's car industry has been prospering while it is Britain's that has been shrinking. Once again, the British reluctance to invest in quality and environmental planning seems short-sighted, complacent and counter-productive. As to the challenge of meeting EC rules on recycling plastic from cars, 'whether German or British businessmen will be better prepared,' says *ENDS*, 'is a question which at present appears not too difficult to answer.'

Public Investment

Britain has yet to show active acceptance that the environment deserves major public investment. The most obvious example is public transport.

At the time of writing, the government shows no sign of a major investment in rail and a policy to reduce traffic, although just such policies are being undertaken in the Netherlands. It is not even providing public funds for rail links to the Channel Tunnel from regions beyond London. Ministers are still imposing a requirement for an 8 per cent return on rail investment, which prevents electrification of key lines, despite taking no account of the social and environmental benefits of rail, which for freight is eight times less polluting than road transport.[36] Demand for rail commuting has rapidly increased in areas such as the Leeds conurbation, where rail journeys have risen sevenfold in five years.[37] Government policies simply consign people to journeys of expensive misery, as subsidies have been more than halved in real terms and BR lacks the trains to move the passengers. Today's rise in Britain's overall energy consumption comes principally from one sector: liquid fuels used in private road transport. The greenhouse gases they release will, if unchecked by promotion of alternatives such as rail and bus transport, make it impossible for the UK to achieve significant reductions in such pollution.

Company car financing means that, with free fuel and petrol, driving is cheaper than public transport. 'The taxpayer is subsidising pollution by £320,000 an hour,' said Steve Elsworth of Greenpeace.[38]

The UK claims to want to lead on the greenhouse effect and is flirting with environmental pricing, yet with its company car subsidies the UK shoots itself in both feet. It is not as if Britain is pursuing other equivalently effective policies. It has yet to be heard in Europe's Council of Ministers proposing a switch to biofuels (like Los Angeles and Brazil) in order to reduce fossil fuel use. And, while Peugeot, Fiat, Saab and General Motors are all developing commercial electric cars, and the Swiss government is backing four small

Swiss companies, in Britain it is left to battery-makers Chloride and Clive Sinclair (who developed the C5). The UK government told *Greengauge* magazine in January 1990 that it did no research on electric cars and had 'no plans' to do so in future. [39]

Perhaps this is because Britain still intends to burn as much as possible of its coal and oil reserves, while research into the greenhouse effect continues. The lack of a UK electric car industry will mean, of course, that should there be proposals to make city centres all-electric, the British motor industry will be lobbying against them.

When it comes to raising funds for public expenditure on the environment, Britain could do as the Netherlands does, and raise and spend cash in the same sector at no overall cost. However, defence cuts could yield enormous sums – the so-called 'peace dividend'. A trident submarine costs £500 million. Developing 50 EH-101 helicopters will cost £1.11 billion.[40] In 1990, Alan Clark, British Minister of State for Defence, proposed cuts worth some £17 billion in UK arms expenditure over ten years. In the USA, it has been calculated that, for every US$1 billion spent on military procurement, 28,000 jobs are created. The same money spent on public transport would create 32,000 jobs. If spent on education, 71,000.[41] Similar studies are long overdue in Britain.

Globally, the Worldwatch Institute has calculated that three weeks of military spending could pay for primary health care for all children in the Third World, saving 5 million lives. For the price of a single nuclear weapon, 80,000 hand pumps for clean water could be installed.

Educating Business?

For the great part, Britain's decision makers show little sign of really believing that change must come, and that they should be leading it. Until very recently, most British politicians and the majority of the scientific establishment did not take pollution or environmental science very seriously. Biographer Hugo Young was told in an interview by Mrs Thatcher, herself once a chemist in plastics and ice-cream, that she felt 'the best researchers' would end up in the 'hard sciences . . . definitely not the Social Science Research Council or the Environmental Research Council, which she regarded as pseudo-sciences'.[42]

There has been an unhealthy and deep-rooted bias among many British scientists to discount or downplay evidence of chronic, subtle or as yet inexplicable pollution effects. Though buried more deeply since the Thatcher greening, this still leads narrowly trained scientists who may have little more understanding of environmental problems than a school student (often less) to pronounce on them as if they were drawing on years of relevant study and research.

And taking their cue from government, the trainers of British management have resisted the efforts of groups like the International Chamber of Commerce, which according to *Greengauge* magazine has been 'trying to get environmental issues on to the curricula of more than 35 universities, business schools and colleges of higher education for some time'. In Britain, there are no equivalents of the 'corporate responsibility' courses attended by 2,000 managers a year in the USA.[43]

There is even a feeling that the British have fallen in love with pollution. A Victorian referred to smoke as an Englishman's 'birthright'. Jolly jack tars below decks are supposed to have talked about a 'good fug' of tobacco smoke and stale air. In winter, British commuters are noticeably loathe to open a train window, preferring to cough and splutter over each other in a stuffy, over-crowded carriage. Some Britons still hanker after Sherlock Holmes-style smogs. Like the little people in a Lowry painting of Industrial England, memories of smoke from factory chimneys speak to the British of a time when industrialism worked, and everything knew its place, the wheels of industry kept turning, towns were for man, the country for nature and for milkmaids, and overseas was mainly the Empire, which produced rubber and coconut matting. It was all neatly divided into separate containers and governed by simple truths. Smoke was a bit of it. It is pollution nostalgia.

The politics of chronic and insidious pollution were external to this world of simple certainties. It remained so until after the Second World War. When today's politicians were at school, environmental pollution was not shown in the textbook diagrams of the economy or the British Constitution.

In the mind's eye of the average Westminster politician, little had changed by the time Mrs Thatcher came to power in 1979. As Charles Clover has put it, 'it would be fair to say of the early years of Mrs Thatcher's administration, preoccupied as they were with fighting inflation and the unions, that the Tories then still had a soft spot for pollution – on the age-old principle that "where there's muck there's brass".'[44]

Environment Minister Chris Patten wrote to environment groups in 1989 saying: 'I am tired of seeing the UK pilloried as "the dirty man of Europe". That tag is simply not accurate. I intend to nail the lie not by words but by actions.' But in reality Britain still is the Dirty Man of Europe. As a nation Britain acts dirty. Worse, it thinks dirty too. Our tolerance of pollution has become ingrained – part of the national way of life.

The Process of Change

As this book is written, the government is in a state of confusion over how to deliver environmental results, or whether it really has to. A 'Green Bill' is in Parliament (to be the Environmental Protection Act) which will among other things create government powers over the release of genetically modified organisms, introduce a more comprehensive licensing system for factories and Integrated Pollution Control (a unified assessment of pollution, whether it goes by land, air or water, applying to 3,500 processes), create waste disposal companies at arm's length from local authorities, establish a 'duty of care' on waste producers, set up public registers detailing (to some degree) radioactive waste and air pollution, and raise fines for littering.

It is the first major environmental legislation for 16 years and some of the proposals, notably Integrated Pollution Control, are a real step forward. During the passage of the Bill the government has also announced a ban on strawburning from 1992, potentially saving the equivalent of 4 million tonnes of coal for productive use in the soil, as an energy source or in paper and board making.

The Bill's critics describe it as a rag bag, although its contents are so threadbare that it might be better described as a string bag. They also point out, that with parts of the 1974 Control of Pollution Act still dormant after 15 years, it must also be doubtful whether government needs additional powers or more commitment to using them.

The government emphasises that the Bill is not its long term environmental action plan. This will take the form of the White Paper, which follows a promise made at the 1989 Conservative Party Conference. That came a year after Prime Minister Thatcher's 'green speech' of 27 September 1988 was greeted by a rash of headlines showing that at least some of the press saw it as an event of historic significance. 'Maggie: Friend of the Earth', said the *Daily Mail*. 'Tories "going for the green vote": Thatcher fears for future of the planet' was the front-page headline in the *Daily Telegraph*. 'Blimey. I'm amazed. I think of clichés about the Road to Damascus but it's of that scale,' Jonathon Porritt of Friends of the Earth told the *Telegraph*. 'This speech is impressive, a milestone for the environment,' he added. 'It is important that she is concentrating on climate change because it implies wide-ranging policy changes.'[45]

Others also announced a green dawn. Only Greenpeace remained churlishly unimpressed, saying that the Prime Minister's statements meant nothing when she was actively cutting budgets for NERC to work on climate change, and holding back EC measures to combat environmental damage.

The speech caught everyone by surprise, particularly some of the government's staunchest supporters. With uncannily bad timing, Peregrine Worsthorne, editor of the *Sunday Telegraph*, decided to launch an attack on environmentalism under the heading 'Green is for Danger' just days before. 'Terrible things are predicted for the year 2000,' wrote Worsthorne, 'now it is the "greenhouse effect" – a few years ago it would have been the "nuclear winter".' Worsthorne singled out Greenpeace as the principal target, but much of his attack could have applied to the Prime Minister. Environmental problems, he said, were too important 'to be left to the interplay of party politics, particularly ideological party politics. Neither capitalism nor socialism has any answer to the ecological problems which transcend the understanding of all the political isms.'[46]

Over a year later, the Conservative Party was doing its best to lay claim to the environment and Tories of the Worsthorne school of thought were keeping their heads well below the battlements. But the government had yet to turn its new green rhetoric into the 'wide-ranging policy changes' Porritt had pointed to. A Media Natura analysis, *Ground Truth: A Report on The Prime Minister's First Green Year*,[47] noted that, on the contrary, she had cut energy efficiency budgets, announced plans for a massive new road system, anticipated a 142 per cent increase in traffic levels and systematically lowered water pollution standards.

Throughout 1988 and 1989 Britain was gripped by green media hype, focused primarily on a wave of green consumerism and the introduction of green labelling of the sort already seen in the mid 1970s in the United States in relation to CFC-free aerosols, and in countries such as West Germany and Switzerland on a whole range of products in the 1980s. It is in the nature of the media to be more fascinated by the idea of green consumerism than the substance of industrial behaviour, just as it was more interested in the ideas in Thatcher's speech than her subsequent failure to put them into effect.

Easy to report, visible and easy to understand, Britain's first wave of green consumerism achieved little in itself, but it speeded the uptake of environmental sensibilities in areas – such as advertising agencies, market research companies and board rooms – which had traditionally kept their doors bolted and barred against criticisms of growth.

By autumn 1989 media interest in the green consumer had begun to wane, and advertising pundits had started casting around for signs of a 'green backlash' or 'green fatigue'. But before the cameras could focus on the first disenchanted purchaser of a phosphate-free washing powder which had never contained phosphate, or Peregrine Worsthorne had uncovered the first cadres of anti-greens mobilising in the Home Counties, the news media got a story on an altogether bigger scale. Amidst calls for democracy, freedom and a better environment, the communist regimes of Eastern Europe were collapsing, domino-like.

From then on, Thatcher's interest in the environment waned. George Bush's 1988 election rhetoric 'Whitehouse Effect' proved to be more a recipe for delay than for action as the State Department tried to draw the teeth of the IPCC process. But what had Thatcher and Bush reacted to, and how will change now step from rhetoric to reality?

Those who got most excited about Thatcher's speech included the 'green' educators, the alternative economists and philosophers who for years had taken on the uphill task of selling alternative futures wholesale. At one extreme they embraced entire prescriptions for living, from healing the inner self to saving the ozone layer. Most often they had been told that their demands or requests would be 'too expensive' or, less precisely, 'uneconomic'. Only rarely had this debate progressed very far at the intellectual level, for only rarely is politics dominated by ideas rather than events.

One of Thatcher's great accomplishments as a populist politician was to sell a 'commonsense' view of money, rather than some baffling economic notion. She made economic policy instantly tangible at the level of the supermarket checkout or the purse in the handbag. Political biographer Hugo Young has summed up the Thatcher prescription as 'good housekeeping'. For Britain in the early 1980s it was, he says, 'impossible to exaggerate the power of this image, with its connotations of thrift, prudence and balanced budgets, as the guiding star of the Thatcher economic programme. . . . these messages – the homilies of housekeeping, the parables of the parlour – were axiomatic laws of sound economic management.'[48] Environmental policy needs similar treatment.

Unfortunately, the Thatcher world view seemed to feature the environment as an ornamental garden, an extra for mountain holidays, the setting of golf courses or bracing clifftop walks, but not part of the real household economy. The environment was an add-on, its services counted as free, with no market value and thus no entry in the balance sheet, and not a serious political concern. 'It is exciting to have a real crisis on your hands,' she remarked during the Falklands campaign of 1982, 'when you have spent half your political life dealing with humdrum issues like the environment.' She probably spoke for 95 per cent of Westminster politicians.

By the time Mrs Thatcher came to power, environmental ideas might have been making headway among teachers and the media, but they had yet to take root in the stonier ground of political minds. The truth is that, for all the posturing over policy and any pretensions politicians may have regarding the power of ideas, in democracies they spend most of their time reacting to circumstance. As John Kenneth Galbraith has pointed out:

> decisions . . . are subject to the tyranny of circumstance. . . . In daily political discussion we think it greatly important whether an individual is to the right or the left, liberal or conservative, an exponent of free enterprise or of socialism. We do not see that, very often, circumstances close in and force the same action on all − or on all who are concerned to survive. If one must stop air pollution in order to breathe . . . there isn't much difference between what conservatives, liberals or social democrats will be forced to do. The choices are regrettably few.' [49]

Galbraith was criticising fellow economist John Maynard Keynes, who, writing in 1935 before Britain acquired its hugely powerful postwar government ministries and nationalised industries, pronounced that 'the power of vested interests is vastly exaggerated compared with the gradual encroachment of ideas'.

Keynes hadn't reckoned with the power of institutions to protect ideas. These have proved very effective at preventing the encroachment of ideas they don't like. And Galbraith was writing in 1977 before a decade of politics dominated by Reaganism and Thatcherism, a more dogmatic era than western politics had seen for a long time. Nevertheless, in their way both have been proved right.

When change came, it was through not the power of ideas so much as a few 'extreme events' which opened up cracks in the conventional wisdom and let the new 'green' ideas through rather faster than by the normal process of deadman's-shoes.

While a few politicians in Scandinavia and North America were reading the warning signs well before, it was not until 1982 that politicians in Britain and most other developed countries had to come to terms with the environment as a serious political hazard. They looked on with astonishment as dying forests forced the government of West Germany, the strongest economy in Europe, suddenly to introduce draconian pollution controls to prevent voters defecting to the fledgling Greens. After that, environmental problems could never be treated so lightly again.

For a few years the ecological nightmare of 'acid rain' spread, but it remained a neighbour dispute between rich countries, still apparently manageable by technological fix or by writing off forests and lakes as the price worth paying for motor cars and central heating. And, in most countries, the greens proved easier to marginalise than they had in West Germany.

By the mid 1980s it seemed that although the world was heading for serious economic and social breakdown through abuse of ecological systems – from the destruction of coastal seas to air pollution – real influence for environmentalism was still a long way off. Lobby groups still picked at the system from outside, and 'green' politicians were generally confined to the fringe. Most environmentalists were resigned to a war of attrition that might last decades before environmental catastrophes or the process of gradual encroachment would give their ideas currency. None foresaw that the late 1980s would see the almost complete collapse of opposition to 'green ideas', at least on the surface.

It started in 1985 with the hole in the ozone layer. This issue was different: it forced the environment into the economic reckoning process, because it provided incontrovertible proof that human beings had finally hit the planetary limits, with potentially disastrous results for individuals.

A year later came Chernobyl. It prompted Italy and Sweden to call for an end to nuclear power, and fatally wounded political confidence in the industry in many other countries. Chernobyl's fallout tracked over Europe and North America, convincing people who had never cared about acid rain that environmental hazards in one country really could threaten people in others.

The final straw came, of course, in 1988, with the greenhouse effect. On 'Green Thursday' in June 1989, the Greens took 15 per cent of the vote in Britain's European Parliament elections.

This was not the gradual encroachment of environmental ideas into British politics. It followed a series of seismic shocks to the established political landscape. But once the political heat went out of the issue (with no visible disasters or voter demands), and once the wheels of political accommodation had begun to grind, the environment once again receded from the forefront of the UK political agenda.

Some institutional change took place. Political parties recruited more environment researchers. All the media recruited environment correspondents. But, at the time of writing, Britain has now entered an environmental 'phoney war' in which major institutional change has yet to take place. It has to be a temporary phase, but it could last months or years. Most probably it is tied to the timetable of the global warming negotiations.

One factor makes change much easier to achieve. Not the Prime Minister's rhetoric but by far the most significant recent development in the politics of the British environment: the demise of nuclear power.

Nuclear Power Begins to Die but the Lights Do Not Go Out

Just as holes were being made in the Berlin Wall, the UK government pronounced a financial death sentence on nuclear power. The execution was not immediate, it was to be more a case of withdrawal of life-support mechanisms – a family with no heirs. It came in the form of the withdrawal of nuclear power from electricity privatisation. It attracted only limited press analysis.

'Nuclear power in Britain collapsed last week – an historic event of Berlin Wall proportions,' wrote Robin Grove-White on 25 November 1989.[50] While the reason given for the withdrawal of nuclear power from privatisation was economic, Grove-White commented, 'the reality the Government now has to accept is that the nuclear industry has had to be withdrawn from privatisation for *environmental* reasons.'

The massive 'back-end' costs of nuclear power which the City would not buy (such as decommissioning), noted Grove-White, had been 'relatively easy to put numbers to' for 30 years. Successive governments had chosen to ignore them. But now it was the threat of risks and 'externalities' such as the impact of future accidents and the economic, ecological, human health and other costs of dealing with nuclear waste, which had forced the Thatcher government reluctantly to re-route the industry from the energy mainline into a government-controlled siding, where it would live out its days on public subsidies levied from buyers of other electrical power.

As Grove-White pointed out, government had known about the problems with nuclear power for decades. When he shunted the industry into its siding, Energy Secretary John Wakeham claimed 'only on October 11 [1989] did I get the figures to make the decision', but few could believe that. Environmental critics who for 20 years had consistently argued that nuclear power was hazardous and uneconomic had been proved right.

It was not economic rationality or a need to supply electricity which had sustained the government commitment to nuclear power but something much deeper, and that is what made its down-grading so significant. It may have had something to do with maintaining the nuclear fuel cycle to create nuclear weapons. But it probably had more to do with the central role of nuclear power as the holy grail and church of growth-oriented technology. Generations had been brought up on the idea that nuclear energy would power the society of the future. Unlimited power would create material prosperity, happiness and a better quality of life.

Why did it take so long to reach the U-turn? In 1956, Britain's young Queen Elizabeth opened Calder Hall power station, next door to Windscale, with the words: 'Future generations will judge us above all else by the way in which we use these limitless opportunities which providence has given us . . . it may well prove to have been among the greatest of our contributions to human welfare that we led the way in demonstrating the peaceful uses of this new source of nuclear power.'[51] After 30 years, a major fire, hundreds of accidents, illnesses, cancers, and half a tonne of plutonium spread over the bed of the Irish Sea, the official speechwriters had begun to water down their praises, but a generation of British politicians still found it difficult to give up the nuclear faith.

On 18 March 1986, in the wake of a highly critical official report on the management of reprocessing at Sellafield, Energy Secretary Peter Walker declared: 'Nuclear power is the safest form of energy yet known to man.'[52] This was a fairly definitive statement, considering that other methods of generating electricity included solar, wind, wave, geothermal and hydro. It said a lot for the power of the idea of nuclear power.

Few such statements, about either nuclear power's safety or economics, have been heard since, for, less than a month later, a large explosion wrecked reactor 4 at Chernobyl in the Ukraine. Prior to it happening, the nuclear industry had always said such an accident was impossible. A graphite fire and partial meltdown followed, and within weeks there was significant fallout in the USA, Canada, throughout most of Europe and in Britain. It has been estimated that over the next 60 years some 50,000 people will die from cancers and other illnesses caused by the fallout.

As CEGB chairman, Walter Marshall was fond of saying, without nuclear power, the lights would go off and we would freeze in the dark. Now in 1989 Mrs Thatcher effectively signed the death warrant of the industry.

The short story of how the fortunes of nuclear power changed is an object lesson in how institutions can fix the future if they can write their own economic rules. If Britain is to reform other policies, similar changes will have to be delivered.

Before privatisation forced Mrs Thatcher's hand and stripped away the industry's shield against the economic democracy of the market, the government's set rate of return for investment in nuclear power was 5 per cent. Although this was later increased to 8 per cent, when analysts came to prepare the industry for sale, they wanted to set a rate of 10 per cent to make it saleable.[53] But, once they began pulling the economic skeleton of nuclear power from the CEGB's cupboard, the privatisers found that it relied purely on props which would be removed in the free market.

For example, the CEGB had allowed itself 40 years to pay off the bill for the high capital costs of building nuclear stations. For privatisation, the payback period would have had to be reduced to 20 years. The government had imposed strikingly different conditions on public investment in energy-saving such as loft insulation: here public money had to be recovered in just two years.

When the costs of decommissioning a worn-out nuclear reactor were taken into account (the costs of cutting it up, entombing some of it in concrete for 100 years, guarding the site, and removing other 'hot' parts to storage), and of dealing with the reactor's 'spent fuel' either by storing it as radioactive waste or by reprocessing it, then the economics of nuclear became even less attractive. Little thought had been given to such 'back-end' costs when the stations were built. For a long time it was assumed that the early stages of decommissioning would be cheap, for example that the Berkeley Magnox reactor on the River Severn (already closed) would cost only about US$30 million to decommission. But by 1989 official estimates reached £200 million per station, and the journal *Power in Europe* estimated the cost of closing down and decommissioning all Britain's ageing Magnox reactors as £3.5 billion within the first five years after shutdown.[54]

While the privatisation debate went on, stockbrokers Phillips and Drew estimated what the cost would be if decommissioning were carried out over 25 years rather than 100. After all, many people might not want to live next to a radioactive hulk and almost all Britain's reactors are only just above sea level (the generator room at Hinkley has already been flooded by a high tide): rising sea level owing to the greenhouse effect is something else that the builders didn't take into account. A 25-year decommission, said the stockbrokers, would cost some £12–30 billion.

With latest official decommissioning costs running at an estimated £500 million per station (a UK bill of £4.5 billion), giving each Magnox a negative value of £1 billion, in autumn 1989 the Magnoxes were pulled out of the privatisation. This means the taxpayer will have to go on paying another gigantic subsidy to nuclear power.[55]

But it was not the only subsidy. In November 1989 Britain's Advanced Gas Cooled nuclear reactors, somewhat younger than the Magnoxes, were also removed from the sale. And, by 31 December, the decommissioning costs of a Magnox had risen to £600 million. Nuclear power was proving to be, as Steve Elsworth of Greenpeace had once put it, 'a very expensive way of boiling a kettle'.

By now, the CEGB admitted that 'back-end' costs such as decommissioning would total more than £13 billion. Energy Secretary John Wakeham was told by advisers that the financial liabilities of nuclear stations might be greater than the £20 billion sale value of the electricity industry. These costs do not include such externalities as the bill for monitoring radioactive waste swilling about the Irish and North Seas, or any court settlement for the leukaemia victims of the dozen or more families from Cumbria currently suing British Nuclear Fuels Ltd.

The significance of the demise of nuclear power cannot be overstated. The government's continuing championship of nuclear power had kept alive a host of attitudes and policies characterised by the ideas of the 1950s. For example, because technologies exist, they should be used. That it is almost a moral duty to provide people with ever-increasing amounts of power. That it is acceptable to impose deaths on future generations so long as these are at a certain statistical level. That a minority of scientists and engineers know better than the public what is good for them. That it is all right to run an industry which could become a hostage to terrorists and which requires draconian constraints on public information, denies the right to know and creates its own armed police force.

These are not insubstantial assumptions to make in nuclear's favour when you consider that most of the alternatives involve only such things as lagging the loft, making equipment more efficient, being careful with resources and putting up windmills. If the struggle between the nuclear institutions and environmental concerns is now won, it should be possible to bring about genuine change across a whole range of government policies, and to unite wings of the 'environmental movement' previously divided by the issue as a political litmus test. Most Conservatives for example, could be relied on to support nuclear as an act of faith, just as socialists had to be in favour of coal. From the 1950s to 1989, government featherbedded the nuclear adolescent, and Thatcher was no exception. 'Mrs Thatcher's government has been pragmatic . . . it has been prepared to hand out public money in pursuit of what it believes in, whether roads or nuclear power,' wrote the *Telegraph's* environment correspondent

Charles Clover before the industry's collapse.[56]

Institutional problems remain, even though nuclear power may be a spent force ideologically. The UK is setting up a new company, Nuclear Electric, to press on with the Pressurised Water Reactor at Sizewell B. It is a tribute to institutional momentum, for Sizewell is the apotheosis of an uneconomic project. The Science Policy Research Unit calculates that at a 10 per cent rate of return, even though £700 million has already been spent on Sizewell B, it would still be cheaper to abandon it and build the equivalent capacity in combined gas cycle power stations. Nevertheless, Nuclear Electric's chairman John Collier said at the launch of the company, 'Make no mistake about it, it is my ambition to build more nuclear stations.' And although Wylfa B on Anglesey and Sizewell C have been shelved, the inquiry for Hinkley C continues at the time of writing.

BNFL also already runs a chain of reactors and is reported to be investigating building a PWR at Chapelcross or Calder Hall. Just as the Department of Transport will surely go on trying to build roads until its 12,500 road planners are assigned to other work, retrained or sacked, so too will a generation of nuclear engineers and companies such as Westinghouse go on trying to build and sell nuclear reactors unless regulations and restructuring finally decommission the industry as well as its reactors.

The Green and Pleasant Land

It is undoubtedly true that Britain's poor environmental performance has had something to do with the weakness of the Department of the Environment and its satellite organisations. That constructive but mostly ignored government critic, the House of Commons Environment Committee, has called for the establishment of an Environmental Protection Commission to combine the pollution control functions currently shared among Her Majesty's Inspectorate of Pollution, the National Rivers Authority and others.

As chairman Sir Hugh Rossi points out,[57] it should have control over such pollution sectors as marine pollution and farm waste and over waste minimisation, which have, respectively, been left with Agriculture and Trade and Industry since the DoE was set up in 1970. At the same time, the Ministry or Agency should shed the functions which currently preoccupy the DoE, namely housing policy, local government and urban development.

A new large agency would probably be an improvement. Confidence in the Pollution Inspectorate dropped so low in 1989 that the National Audit Office was asked by the Public Accounts Committee to launch an inquiry into the organisation. The under-resourced DoE's policy making and analytical capacity is often far smaller than that of non governmental organisations.

But which is cause and which is effect? It is no wonder that the structures are ineffective when the environmental attitudes and policies of government are so obstructive, niggardly and inadequate.

What has happened since the 'greening' of British politics – which is plenty of promise but little else – shows that 'greens' and environmentalists will still have their hands full in the 1990s and beyond. They should bear in mind that changing institutions and changing minds are two distinct problems. Where these aims have become confused, environmental campaigns have misfired or disappointed their backers. Tom Burke, director of the parliamentary lobby group the Green Alliance, is fond of quoting T B Macaulay: 'We must remember that argument is constructed in one way, and government in entirely another.' He is right. Now that environmental ideas have encroached on government, the challenge is to convert them into institutional change, and then into change on the ground.

Burke is an ex-director of FoE, a realist who is still remembered at one radio station for turning up in a taxi to do an interview to promote cycling. Ten years later, the Prime Minister had started talking about the greenhouse effect, but the government still hadn't done anything to encourage car drivers to switch to bicycles. Tom Burke summed up the position in *The Times* in 1989:

> 'The environment problems that will be prominent in the 1990s are just the same as those at the beginning of the 1980s. Climate change, acid rain, tropical deforestation, toxic waste management, ozone depletion, the loss of species and all the rest will still be with us as we go into the next millenium and beyond. All that we have done in this last decade is to recognize that they require political solutions. But that is simply to arrive at the starting gate. We have yet to get going.'[58]

There is, of course, some progress, but most of it is promissory and much is piecemeal, while the problems remain systematic. This is the balance that Britain must redress if it is to convert itself from Dirty Man of Europe to an environmental leader.

In April 1990, Sir William Wilkinson, chairman of the Nature Conservancy Council and a banker, spoke to the Royal Society for Nature Conservation's annual conference, and asked the simple question: 'What should we expect governments to do on our behalf?'[59] His answer any politician could understand.

> First, they should ensure that the policies they pursue with our money do not harm the environment . . . Second, should we not expect Government to spend our money on protecting our environment? Every man, woman and child in this country hands over, on average, nearly £4,000 each year to the Government to spend on those things we consider important to the life of this nation.

> . . . Is this green and pleasant land not important too? The Government spends more than £20 billion on defence of the nation. It spends less than one per cent of that on all its environmental programmes put together. Should we not expect Government to defend our environment with the same commitment it shows for the maintenance of our armed forces? Would there be much point in a strong army, navy and airforce if they were left defending an island from which nature had been banished, a foul and polluted rock in a sea of filth? It would be a country whose soul has gone.'

Afterword

A few weeks before the first edition of this book was published in late October 1990, the Government released its White Paper, *This Common Inheritance*. Few White Papers can have attracted such interest and such universal criticism. Appealingly designed and lavishly illustrated, the Environment White Paper had the appearance of an intermediate-level geography textbook. However, any student reading it would have been both misled and confused.

There are no proper references in *This Common Inheritance*, which is disappointing, as some of its 'facts' are decidedly suspect. For example, in its section on transport as a source of carbon dioxide contributing to the greenhouse effect, the White Paper hugely underestimates the potential for public transport to reduce emissions. A diagram based (though this is not stated) on present low occupancy rates for public transport shows only 17 people in a London bus, compared with what would be achieved if public transport were fully used.

Even more noticeable is what it does not say: in the section on acid rain for instance, there is no mention of the controversial use of low sulphur coal. Throughout, the document has lengthy and bland descriptions of environmental problems, outlining almost no specific commitments to take action. As Dave Gee, Director of Friends of the Earth points out, the distinguishing feature of the document was its choice of verbs: it was full of objectives that could be discussed or researched but there was very little that would actually be done. The Labour Party provided the most telling 'sound bite', summarising it as 'long on waffle, short on action'.

Environment groups were disappointed by the White Paper, although perhaps not as dismayed as the Conservative supporters who had hoped that it would be a convincing 'green' policy package to confound environmental critics at home and abroad. By spring 1990, the main environmental lobby groups had reluctantly come to the conclusion that Environment Secretary Chris Patten, who seemed committed to environmental reform, was losing all the key environmental disputes with other Ministries. Patten's failure to win crucial battles with the Departments of Transport and Energy was reflected in both the 1990 Budget and the White Paper: there were no 'eco-taxes', no targets to reduce NOx, no support for a carbon-tax, no targets to reduce CO_2 from transport.

Environment groups were very largely excluded from influencing what went into the White Paper; indeed, the DoE was itself trying to influence policies controlled by other Government Departments, rather than creating a document within its own limited sphere of influence. By early spring 1990, when it had become clear that Mr Patten would probably lose his struggle to reform UK policy, environmental lobby groups were determined to try and limit the damage which an inadequate White Paper would cause. Patten had invested considerable personal political capital in producing something significant on 'green' issues, and following his commitment at the 1989 Conservative Party Conference to launch a White Paper within a year, the Party's expectations were high. Environmentalists therefore feared that although the White Paper might be an empty vessel, it could be presented with enough gloss, promotional gimmicks and rhetorical flourish, to create the impression that something very significant had really happened.

Indeed, by the summer of 1990, Parliamentary 'friends' of Mr Patten were profiling the White Paper not, as it had originally been portrayed, as an epoch-making 'environmental Beveridge Report' but simply as a 'very substantial first word on the environment'. It was an achievement in itself, they told journalists with as much conviction as could be mustered, just to get all the Ministries even to think about green issues. It was the doing of the thing that was important, rather than the detail of what might or might not be in the document.

Environment groups, therefore, set out to make sure that the novelty of the White Paper (the first significant environmental policy for over two decades) would not of itself convince the press and public that a great step forward had been taken - even if the commitments were missing. While they were unable to dictate or even influence the content of the White Paper, environment groups could repeatedly draw attention back to the agenda of unsolved problems which already demanded urgent action.

Greenpeace decided to use Chris Patten's own 1989 pledge that he would 'nail the lie' that Britain was the Dirty Man of Europe - and apply it as a test of Britain's current policy performance, and of the forthcoming White Paper. Through a commission to Media Natura, the author was involved in preparing three Greenpeace products released before the Environment White Paper. A Report, *The Great Car Economy Versus The Quality of Life*, tracked the rise and fall of Patten's hopes for a green policy package, and was circulated in a pre-publication form to politicians, political commentators, press and researchers. It took as its central thesis the idea that the Government's dominant policies, such as Mrs Thatcher's commitment to ever increasing car ownership and use, were incompatible with Mr Patten's desire to see environmentally sound policies. It concluded, (rightly, as it turned out), that Patten's policies would lose. A second report, *Why Britain Remains The Dirty Man of Europe*, was published (the exact timing being fortuitous) the day before the White Paper, and provided a lengthy factual analysis of Britain's pollution policy, concentrating on Greenpeace campaign areas such as atmosphere and marine pollution. It was distributed to the environmental press and summarised the logic of its title in 17 points, which also appeared on thousands of specially-printed toilet rolls, hand-delivered and mailed to the image builders and advisers of the government, as well as their friends, colleagues and relatives.

The result of this, and other activities by environment groups, was the establishment of a wide public consensus that the White Paper went neither far enough, nor solved many pressing environmental problems. At all levels, and from almost every section of the press, informed coverage was pointedly critical. Most significant of all perhaps, was *The Times* leader entitled 'Not Green Enough', which led to furious lobbying of the newspaper by Ministers. Both *The Times* and The *Independent* noted that although the Prime Minister had been asked by Mr Patten to launch the White Paper, she had declined to do so. The *Independent* headed its editorial 'Thatcher Abandons Patten'.

The Greenpeace report, *Why Britain Remains The Dirty Man of Europe*, received especially high publicity because of Patten taking the unusual step of releasing a statement to the Press Association the night before its publication, denouncing it as 'the worst kind of political pollution' and full of 'exaggerations, distortions and worse'. Greenpeace and Media Natura never discovered what these, particularly the 'worse' might be, as press enquiries yielded only a series of blandishments and the DoE challenged none of the report's facts. Despite Patten's remark at the time that the Greenpeace document had been 'on his desk' all weekend, one of his civil servants finally stated in a letter to the author that the Secretary of State's outburst had been based on 'coverage drawn from the newspapers' (which was strange, as there hadn't been any).

Inadvertently, Chris Patten drew the attention of environmentalists and many of the press whose main concern up to then had been with domestic policies rather than with Britain's international role. Tom Burke of the *Green Alliance* wrote shortly afterwards that Britain had earned the title 'more in truth for our political than our environmental performance'.

The DoE claimed that the White Paper contained 350 policy commitments, although on closer examination many turned out to be existing policies (such as the 'campaign' to save 15% of the government's own energy bill). At the 1990 Conservative Party Conference which followed a few days later, the environment was hardly mentioned. The environment groups and the press had succeeded in torpedoing any attempt to use the White Paper as a green blind, and UK environment policy continued much as before.

Speaking a few weeks later at the Second World Climate Conference in Geneva, Margaret Thatcher declared that Britain's commitment to emit no more carbon dioxide in 2005 than in 1990 meant 'reversing a rising trend before that date'. In fact there was no 'rising trend' (emissions fell from 180mt in 1979 to 158mt in 1988), only the Energy Department's non-sensical forecast of growth, designed to make doing nothing look like doing a lot.

Shortly afterwards, Geoffrey Lean of the *Observer* reported that far from the 'increased' budget for the Energy Efficiency Office which the White Paper claimed, the level of funding was sustained only by transferring the Home Energy Efficiency Scheme from the Department of Employment. Once inflation was taken into account, the true budget had decreased by 10%.

Lean also revealed that despite the government's pledge to demonstrate its own 'commitment to energy efficiency', to set 'an example to other energy users', and persuade the public to buy 'energy efficient' cars, it had recently changed 570,000 civil servants from a flat rate, to a scale which gave more money to those using cars with bigger, less thrifty engines. The Government was thus acting directly against its own policy.

Magaret Thatcher's speech to the Climate Conference in Geneva was to be her last Prime Ministerial foray into global environmental politics. Days before, her Deputy Prime Minister Sir Geoffrey Howe had resigned, principally over Mrs Thatcher's attitude to Europe. Senior UK civil servants at the Climate Conference joked that Howe had resigned over Britain's insistence on a 2005 date for CO_2 stabilisation rather than a 2000 date favoured by the rest of Europe. There was at least an echo of truth in this. Thatcher's anti-European belligerence had helped make the UK an environmental laggard in practice and in attitude, and helped earn it the title 'Dirty Man of Europe'.

Howe's resignation triggered a tidal wave which resulted in a Conservative Party leadership election and Margaret Thatcher's replacement by John Major. Environmental issues were noticeably absent during the leadership contest, while the Green Party, lacking both MPs and a convincing public persona, disappeared from studio discussions.

At the end of the Thatcher era, the environmental movement has found itself with no clear agenda and, for the time being at least, disorientated. By waiting a year during which the White Paper was produced, and by spending two years adjusting to its own increased membership and hoping for Thatcherite recipes such as 'green consuming' to deliver results, the movement lost the initiative to the Government which then dumped the issue. Indeed, with the departure of Chris Patten from the Ministry of Environment, and of Mrs Thatcher from Government itself, even the major players had vanished from the stage.

It would be easy to portray this as part of a slide of interest in 'green issues' across the developed world. The Greens lost representation in the Bundestag following the elections in a reunified Germany. The US environment movement lost the 'Big Green' referendum in California, which, had it been won, would have forced readjustments to policies ranging from pesticides to fuel efficiency throughout the United States and the developed world. But the Germans were experiencing the unique dynamics of reunification, while the Californians were fed up with being asked to vote and vote again.

If there is one factor common to the slumping of the environment as an issue in all three countries, it is that when the environment ceases to be perceived as an acute, immediate problem, it gets to be pushed into the background by other, mainly economic concerns. In the UK, environmental issues are, together with 'education', consistently at or near the top of public concerns 'in the longer term'. From the heady days of 1989, when the green consumer looked ready to sweep conventional economics from the high street (it was in fact, something of a flop), and the Greens won 15% of the vote at the European election, the environment has sunk back to eighth or ninth place among the list of concerns uppermost in the public mind.

The same thing had occurred on a issue basis. Although acid rain has been displaced as *the* apocalypse issue by the climate change, there is still considerable concern. Nevertheless, it appears that the government will now exempt power stations - the major source of oxides of nitrogen (NOx) - from a schedule under the Environment Protection Act which would require NOx-removing technology to be fitted. The Government's motive was, as usual, to avoid spending money and also, in this case, to avoid jeopardising the eventual successful privatisation of electricity.

Similarly, there is widespread disatisfaction with the state of transport in the UK, but at the time of writing, no environmental group has succeeded in converting that into an acute political issue which demands the implementation of environmental solutions. At present, there are pitifully few votes in the environment, or, as the leader of the Liberal Democrats Paddy Ashdown put it, 'there are no environmental marginals'.

Government itself dithers, reflecting continuing uncertainty over how seriously to treat environmental issues. As this is written, Malcolm Rifkind has taken over from the car-loving Cecil Parkinson as the new Transport Secretary, but he is sending out conflicting signals over transport policy. Indeed, it seems that there is still no transport policy as such, only policies to cope with the railways, roads and so on, on a basis of crisis management and in response to lobbies such as the truck-owners. On the one hand, Rifkind is reported to be thinking about not privatising the railways, considering a possible increase in rail investment, and maybe putting public funds into a high speed link to the Channel Tunnel. On the other hand, he says the M25 should be widened to eight or ten lanes, even though this is a famous example of how putting more roadspace into a congested environment causes more traffic.

Unlike the rail-hating Margaret Thatcher, John Major while still a Treasury Minister, at least talked of 'looking at' investment in light rail mass-transit systems as an alternative to road schemes. It seems likely that his - indeed almost any UK government of the 1990s - will be less doctrinaire and less antagonistic towards 'the environment' than were the early Thatcher governments, whose antipathy had as much to do with the origin of these environmental ideas and their proponents, as with the ideas themselves.

While on the back-benches, Environment Secretary Michael Heseltine made a series of personal public commitments to environmental reforms strengthening the power of Her Majesty's Inspectorate of Pollution over hazardous wastes; committing more funds to international bodies; introducing a British ecolabelling scheme; removing the proposals to break up the Nature Conservancy Council from the Environmental Protection Bill (and then merging the NCC and the Countryside Commission), and, perhaps most important, cutting UK CO_2 emissions by 10-20% by 2005. At a press briefing given to environmental journalists within days of taking up his new role, it seemed that Mr Heseltine had forgotten, or chosen to forget, all of these commitments. Perhaps he will find time to recall them.

What progress there is on environmental issues depends very much on how hard environmentalists will work to achieve them, and how uncompromising they are prepared to be. Instant cures, such as the notion of the green consumer or green taxes are misleading novelties, tools which are mistaken for mechanisms that will achieve ends in themselves. Chris Patten's most lasting achievement may be the creation of a public list of 'green Ministers', one for each government department, who can be held to account on environmental matters. It is a list that 'green groups' should make use of.

That there is no alternative to concerted political action to change policies, is well illustrated by the case of the electricity industry. Mr Robert Malpas has resigned as chairman of the electricity supply company PowerGen and spoken out strongly in favour of energy conservation. He has pointed out that the average three-year payback on buying energy efficient technology is more than twice as profitable an investment than the norm for British industry. Yet even economic forces such as these are too weak to prevail over institutional inertia, financial short-termism, management lethargy, psychological barriers to desirable change and, most important of all, to overcome a price structure which is fixed so as to encourage the industry to generate and sell as much electricity as possible, rather than to sell the service of efficiency.

To achieve such changes requires intervention: practical government action. And to obtain that, there is no substitute other than the engaging of popular support to create political commitment. It remains the case that Britain could raise itself up to the level of the best environmental achievers among its 'competitor' countries by simple, widely-supported and economically-rational measures. This would rid the country of the label of 'Dirty Man of Europe'.

It is a small but necessary step to ease the way for much larger changes which must come if humanity is to repay its debts to Nature, and keep the planet a place worth living in.

References

Introduction

1 Paul Brown, 'Power station showers sewage dust on villages', *Guardian*, 23 October 1989.
2 In 1987, Drax power station emitted 321,000 tonnes of sulphur dioxide (by weight as SO_2) and in 1988 278,000; Sweden and Norway emit around 200,000 and 70,000 respectively. Christer Agren, pers. comm.
3 The CEGB's non-nuclear power stations are now run by Powergen and National Power.
4 Richard North, 'Ridley lays claim to "green credibility"', *Independent*, 1 March 1989.
5 'Common ground' (editorial), *New Scientist*, 20 May 1989.
6 John Ardill, 'Cost-conscious view of improving the ecology', *Guardian*, 3 March 1989.
7 Roger Highfield, 'The call to keep our lands green and clean', *Telegraph*, 16 November 1988.
8 Jonathon Porritt and Charles Secrett, *The Environment: The Government's Record*, FoE, 26–28 Underwood Street, London, N1.
9 Chris Patten, letter to Tom Burke as chairman of the EEB UK, 21 November 1989.

Part I
Introduction
Water: Pollution in our Seas, Rivers, Wells and Taps

1 James Cutler and Rob Edwards, *Britain's Nuclear Nightmare: The Shocking Truth Behind the Dangers of Nuclear Power*, Sphere Books, 1988.
2 John May, *The Greenpeace Book of the Nuclear Age: The Hidden History, The Human Cost*, Victor Gollancz, London, 1989.
3 A. Scott, *The Good Beach Guide*, Marine Conservation Society and Ebury Press, London, 1989.
4 Granada TV, 'How Green is our Valley?', *World in Action*, Broadcast May 1989, Reporter Mike Walsh.

Chapter 1
Out of Sight, Out of Mind

1 E. Pike and V. Cooper, 'Control of Pollution in Recreational Waters – The Way Forward', paper at Seminar, *Preventing Water Pollution – The Environmental Perspective*, Blackpool, 23 June 1987, Institute of Environmental Health Officers and 'Cleaning up the sewage business', *ENDS*, 182, March 1990.
2 D. Kinnersley, *Troubled Water: Rivers, Politics and Pollution*, Hilary Shipman, 1988, p.46.
3 M.J. Andrews, 'Thames Estuary: Pollution and Recovery', in P.J. Sheehan, D.R. Miller, G.C. Butler and Ph. Bourclean, Scope, *Effects of Pollutants at the Ecosystem level*, Wiley, 1984.
4 A. Wheeler, *The Tidal Thames: The History of a River and its Fishes*, Routledge Keagan & Paul, 1979.

5   n4 op.cit.
6   n4 op.cit.
7   n4 op.cit., pp.34-5, citing G. Thurlston, *The Great Thames Disaster,* Allen and Unwin, London, 1965.
8   n4 op.cit.
9   D.C. Renshaw, 'The EEC Directives and Water Quality, The Institute of Water Engineers and Scientists', Symposium on EEC Directives, London, 1980, cited by N. Haigh, *EEC Environmental Policy and Britain,* 2nd Edn, Longman, 1988.
10 N. Haigh, *EEC Environmental Policy and Britain,* 2nd Edn, Longman, 1988.
11 ibid.
12 ibid.
13 DoE papers, 'Bathing waters: possible European Court of Justice Proceedings concerning Blackpool', May 1986, leaked to Friends of the Earth.
14 Ken Collins, *Report on the Implementation of European Community Legislation relating to Water,* on behalf of the Committee on the Environment, Public Health and Consumer Protection, European Parliament 1987-8 Series A, Doc AA2-0298/87.
15 University of Surrey Water Investigation and Research Laboratory Service, 'The Public Health Implications of Sewage Pollution of Bathing Water', Guildford, *SWIRLS,* 1987, available from Greenpeace UK; cited in S.J. Eykyn, 'Health Hazard from British Beaches?', *British Medical Journal,* 296, 28 May 1988.
16 Nicholas Farrell and Ronald Gribben, 'Beach clean up will increase water charges', *Daily Telegraph,* 22 February 1989.
17 M. Souster, 'Sea sewage health probe planned', *The Times,* 5 May 1989.
18 T. Davenport, 'Come on in the water's disgusting', *Today,* 29 May 1989.
19 J. Davies, *Daily Express,* 29 May 1989.
20 Simon Hardeman, *ITV Oracle,* 'Buzz World', 10 June 1989.
21 Foreign currency earnings of UK tourist industry were put at over £7bn (ca £6.2 spending and £1.4bn on UK air carriers) in 1988. Report of the British Tourist Authority, p.42.
22 The hotel and catering trade, one part of the tourist industry, employed 1,136,000 people in 1989. *Monthly Digest of Statistics,* No. 523, Central Statistical Office, HMSO, June 1989.
23 See for example Lord Forte, 'The Lady at No 10 Means Business', in *The First Ten Years,* Conservative Party, 1989.
24 n20 op.cit.; and 'Beaches win blue flag awards for cleanliness', *Independent,* 6 June 1989.
25 n20 op.cit.
26 M. Linton, 'Ridley defends sewage dumping', *Guardian,* 23 March 1989.
27 n13 op.cit.
28 D. Brown, 'Fishermen fight sewage threat', *Sunday Telegraph,* 30 April 1989.
29 E. Pike and V. Cooper, 'Control of Pollution in Recreational Waters – The Way Forward', paper at Seminar *Preventing Water Pollution – The Environmental Health Perspective,* Blackpool, 23 June 1987, Institute of Environmental Health Officers.
30 n17 op.cit.
31 R.R. Colwell, 'Microbial Contaminants and Littoral Pollution', *International Conference on Environmental Protection of the North Sea,* 24-7 March 1987, IMO, London, WRc Environment, Henley Road, Medenham, PO Box 16, Marlow, Bucks. SL7 2HD.
32 K.A. Gourlay, *Poisoners of the Seas,* Zed Books, London & New Jersey, 1988.

33 Thames TV, *Thames Reports*, 5 June 1989.
34 World Health Organisation, *Correlation between Coastal Water quality and Health Effects*, Report issued jointly by UNEP and WHO: Long-term Programme for Pollution Monitoring and Research in the Mediterranean Sea (MED POL Phase II), Copenhagen, 1986.
35 Jennifer M. Brown, Elizabeth A. Campbell, Andrew D. Richards and David Wheeler, 'Sewage Pollution of Bathing Water', *The Lancet*, 21 November 1987.
36 n34 op.cit.
37 Medical Research Council, Memorandum submitted by the Medical Research Council to the House of Commons Select Committee on the Environment, Third Report, Session 1986-7, *Pollution of Rivers and Estuaries*, Vol.II, HC 183-11, 1987, p.403.
38 Public Health Laboratory Service 1987, Memorandum submitted by the PHLS to the House of Commons Select Committee on the Environment, Third Report, Session 1986-7, *Pollution of Rivers and Estuaries*, Vol.II, HC 183-11, 1987, p.410.
39 ibid.
40 ibid.
41 S 9 Shellfish, in *Water Quality Report: Anglian Water Authority*, 1986.
42 O. Bergh, K.Y. Borsheim, G. Bratbak and M. Heldal, 'High abundance of viruses found in aquatic environments', *Nature*, 340, 10 August 1989, pp.467-8.
43 E. Scherr, 'Aquatic viruses: And now, small is plentiful', in News and Views, *Nature*, 340, 10 August 1989.
44 Dr L. Barnard and Partners, *A Microbiology Report on Seawater samples from South Essex from 8 October 1987-31 August 1988*, Report from Dr L Barnard & Partners, 424 Victoria Avenue, Southend on Sea, Essex.
45 'Cleaning up the sewage business', *ENDS*, 182, March 1990.
46 *Review of Sewage Sludge Disposal at Sea*, Oslo Commission, London, 1989.
47 *Review of the Mersey Clean Up Campaign*, Greenpeace, 1985.
48 Dougg Stewart, 'Nothing goes to waste in Arcata's teeming marshes', *The Smithsonian*, April 1990.
49 Volkert Dethlefsen, 'Marine pollution mismanagement: towards a precautionary concept', *Marine Pollution Bulletin*, Vol.17, 2, 1986, pp.54-7.
50 ibid.
51 ibid.
52 n46 op.cit.
53 Michael McCarthy, '£1.7 bn to be spent on alternatives to dumping', *The Times*, 6 March 1990.
54 Stephen Castle, 'Thatcher put sewage dumping deal at risk', *Independent on Sunday*, 18 March 1990.
55 Mark Simmonds, Nicola Kemp, Yosuf Jarrah, P. Johnston and R. Stringer, *A Review of the Mersey Clean-up Campaign*, Greenpeace UK, 1985.
56 D. Vethaak, 'Fish diseases, signals for a diseased environment?', paper presented at the *2nd International North Sea Seminar*, Rotterdam, 1-3 October 1986.
57 T. Dybbro, WWF Denmark, in C. Rose, (ed) 'Call for a Ban on Wetland Drainage', in *EEC CAP and IMPs: Impacts and Reforms of the EEC Common Agricultural Policy and the Integrated Mediterranean Programmes*, WWF Intl, 1196 Gland, Switzerland, 1987, p.3.
58 D. MacKenzie, 'North Sea target to cut pollution cannot be met', *New Scientist*, 5 November 1988, p.22.

59 'The Pollution of the North Sea', *The Tide Must Turn,* Greenpeace UK, 1987, table p.17, and 'Calculated Annual Total Depositions from the Atmosphere to the North Sea (Area =572,000 km^2), in Iversen, Saltbones, Sadnes, Eliasen and Hov', EMEP *MSC-W Report* 2/89, Table 5.2.

60 C. Clover, 'North Sea or Dead Sea?', *Daily Telegraph Weekend Magazine,* 8 October 1988, pp.15-26.

61 n56 op.cit.

62 Evidence Submitted by Friends of the Earth to the House of Lords Select Committee on the European Communities Committee: Sub-Committee D (Agriculture and Food) enquiry into the European Commission Proposal for a Council Directive concerning the Protection of Fresh, Coastal and Marine Waters against Pollution caused by Nitrates from Diffuse Sources, COM (88) 708, p.19.

63 FoE n59 op.cit., citing Nitrate Coordination Group, 1986, para 5.12.

64 n58 op.cit.

65 R. Milne, 'North sea algae threaten British coasts', *New Scientist,* 10 June 1989.

66 n60 op.cit.

67 n58 op.cit., p.22.

68 Select Committee on the European Communities, 16th Report, *Nitrates in Water,* HoI, 1988-9, 73-1, Ev.p.63, cited by John Gibson, *The Implementation of the North Sea Declarations in the United Kingdom,* Greenpeace International North Sea Research Report 17.

69 Geoffrey Lean, 'Report reveals toxic algae plague off Britain's coast', *Observer,* 1 October 1989.

70 Charles Clover, 'North Sea pollution timetable is agreed', *Daily Telegraph,* 10 March 1990.

71 'Huge water treatment bill at stake as North Sea crisis deepens', *ENDS,* 163, August 1988, pp.4-5.

72 'Sweden takes a major stride in environmental protection', *ENDS,* 160, May 1988, pp.16-8.

73 'Germany to cut nutrient pollution of the North Sea', *New Scientist,* 30 June 1988, p.39.

74 ibid.

75 'The Pollution of the North Sea', *The Tide Must Turn,* Greenpeace UK, 1987, table p.17.

76 ibid.

77 'North Sea Conference, The Hague, 7 and 8 March 1990: 1990 Interim Report on the Quality Status of the North Sea', *Third International Conference on the Protection of the North Sea,* 1990.

78 calculated from tables in n75 op.cit.

79 A.M. Scheuhammer, 'The chronic toxicity of Aluminium, Cadmium, Mercury and Lead in Birds: A review', *Environmental Pollution,* 46, 1987, pp.263-95; cited in n53 op.cit.

80 n53 op.cit.

81 Tenth Annual Report: Paris Commission, London, 1989, p.105 *et seq.*

82 n79 op.cit., p.111 *et seq.*

83 'Dirtier water flushes under the bridge', *New Scientist,* 3 December 1988, p.26.

84 n53 op.cit.

85 n53 op.cit.

86 n53 op.cit.

87 n53 op.cit.

88 n53 op.cit.

89 n53 op.cit.

90 Greenpeace in Evidence to the House of Commons Select Committee on the Environment, Third Report Session 1986-7, *Pollution of Rivers and Estuaries,* Vol.II, HC 183-11, p.203.

91 R.R. Dickson and R.G.V. Boelens, 'The status of current knowledge on the anthropogenic influences in the Irish Sea', *International Council for the Exploration of the Sea,* Palaegrade 2-4, 1261 Copenhagen K, Denmark, Cooperative Research Programme Research Report 155, 1988, pp cited in n53 op.cit.

92 ibid.

93 A.J. Murray, 'Trace metals and organochlorine pesticide and PCB residues in mussels from England and Wales', *Chemistry in Ecology,* 1,1978, pp33-45.

94 n89 op.cit.

95 A.J. Murray and M.G. Norton, *Fisheries Technical Report No 69,* MAFF, 1982, 42 pp; cited in n53 op.cit.

96 n89 op.cit.

97 M.G. Norton, A. Franklin, S.M. Rowlatt, R.S. Nunny and M.S. Rolfe, *Fisheries Research Technical Report 76,* MAFF, 1984, 50 pp cited in n53 op.cit.

98 E.J. Perkins, J.R. Gilchrist and O.J. Abbott, 'Incidence of epidermal lesions in fish of the north-east Irish Sea area, 1971', *Nature,* 238, 1972, pp.101-3, cited in n53 op.cit.

99 n53 op.cit.

100 'The ever widening agenda for the North Sea environment', *ENDS,* 181, February 1990.

101 'North Sea waste dumping, discharge reports', *ENDS,* 156, January 1988, p.6.

102 'Ban the Burn', *Toxic Pollution Briefing,* Greenpeace, 1989.

103 n99 op.cit.

104 'Incineration ships poison North Sea's sediments', *New Scientist,* 29 September 1988.

105 n73 op.cit.

106 'Spills from North Sea rigs lead upturn in oil pollution incidents', *ENDS,* 163, August 1988, p.6; and *Monthly Digest of Statistics,* 523, Central Statistical Office, June 1989.

107 'Agreements on marine incineration, dumping', *ENDS,* 163, August 1988, p.26.

108 n104 op.cit.

109 n73 op.cit.

110 n73 op.cit.

111 n73 op.cit.

112 *Environment Digest,* 13 June 1988, p.8.

113 *ENDS,* 170, March 1989, p.7; *New Scientist,* 1 April 1989, p.18; and O. Bowcott, 'Hunt for pesticide ends', *Guardian,* 26 April 1989.

114 n105 op.cit.

115 Sheila Gunn, 'MP wants "dirty beach" signs to warn sea bathers', *The Times,* 22 March 1990.

116 Polly Ghazi, 'Legal attack on Britain's dirty beaches set to escalate', *Observer,* 3 June 1990.

Chapter 2
Pollution of Rivers and Fresh Water

1   D. Milward, 'Ridley unveils £1bn clean-up plan for rivers', *Daily Telegraph*, 5 November 1988.
2   Insight, 'Exposed: The men polluting Britain's rivers', *Sunday Times*, 26 February 1989.
3   Leader, 'Private water, public costs', *Financial Times*, 3 August 1989.
4   ibid.
5   D. Kinnersley, *Troubled Water: Rivers, Politics and Pollution*, Hilary Shipman, 1988, p.46.
6   T. Birch, *Poison in the System*, 2nd Edn, Greenpeace UK, London, 1989, p.11.
7   A. Wheeler, *The Tidal Thames, A History of the River and its Fishes*, Routledge & Kegan Paul, London, 1979.
8   n6 op.cit.
9   M.J. Andrews and D.G. Rickard, 'Rehabilitation of the Inner Thames Estuary', *Marine Pollution Bulletin*, Vol.II, 1980, pp.327–32.
10 M.J. Andrews, K.F.A. Aston, D.G. Rickard and J.E.C. Steel, 'The Macrofauna of the Thames Estuary', *The London Naturalist*, 61, 1982, pp.30 – 62
11 n9 op.cit.
12 Third Report: Session 1986–7, *Pollution of Rivers and Estuaries*, Vol.I, HoC Environment Committee HOC 183 – 1, HMSO, London.
13 n5 op.cit., p.89.
14 n5 op.cit., p.101.
15 J. Bowers, K. O'Donnell and S. Whatmore, *Liquid Assets: The Likely Effects of Privatisation of the Water Authorities on Wildlife Habitats and Landscape*, CPRE/RSPB, December 1988, p.10.
16 F. Pearce, Watershed: The Water Crisis in Britain, Penguin, London, 1982; cited by Birch in n6 op.cit.
17 n6 op.cit., p.18.
18 n6 op.cit., p.18.
19 n12 op.cit., p.xvi.
20 n12 op.cit.,
21 Memorandum Submitted by Friends of the Earth Ltd, pp.160–96, in Third Report: Session 1986–7, *Pollution of Rivers and Estuaries*, Vol.II, HoC Environment Committee HOC, 183 – 1, HMSO, London.
22 Memorandum Submitted by the Department of the Environment, pp.1–14, in Third Report: Session 1986–7, *Pollution of Rivers and Estuaries*, Vol.II, HoC, Environment Committee HOC, 183 – 1, HMSO, London.
23 cited in n21 op.cit.
24 cited in n21 op.cit.
25 Insight, 'The Water Rats', *Sunday Times*, 26 February 1989, p.A14.
26 *Your Water Authority has been Discharging Sub-Standard Sewage Effluent and that's Illegal*, Friends of the Earth booklet, 1989, para 22, citing *The Water Environment: Policies and Procedures for the Control of Water Authority Effluent Discharges*, DoE and Welsh Office, January 1985.
27 London Wildlife Trust (unpub) letter of objection sent to HMIP to TWA application to DoE for relaxation of consent at Mogden, 14 August 1989, and details of consent from TWA/NRA.
28 'Dirty water flushes under the bridge', *New Scientist*, 3 December 1988.
29 n12 op.cit., para 26, p.xvi.

30 n5 op.cit., p.123.
31 *ENDS*, 162, pp.18 – 9.
32 *ENDS*, 167, December 1988, p.14.
33 n32 op.cit., p.15.
34 n32 op.cit., p.14
35 n26 op.cit., p.6.
36 n26 op.cit., p.6
37 In conversation with the author.
38 G. Lyons, 'Water Pollution', in *Ground Truth: A Report on the Prime Minister's First Green Year*, Media Natura, 45 Shelton Street, London WC2, 1989.
39 ibid.
40 n66 op.cit., p.20.
41 J. Connolly, 'Water Authority escapes prosecution over sewage', *Independent*, 17 September 1989.
42 n38 op.cit.
43 n12 op.cit., note 58, para 25, p.xvi.
44 n12 op.cit., p.9.
45 NCC Evidence to the House of Commons Environment Committee, n12 op.cit., p.256.
46 n12 op.cit., p.258.
47 n12 op.cit., p.xii.
48 n26 op.cit., p.6.
49 cited in n21 op.cit.
50 n21 op.cit., p.170.
51 n21 op.cit., p.171.
52 n6 op.cit.
53 n6 op.cit., pp.19 – 20.
54 n6 op.cit., p.20.
55 n6 op.cit., p.21.
56 Birch citing *Northern Echo* interview with Nicholas Ridley, 14 November 1988, on p.16, n6 op.cit.
57 n6 op.cit., p.19.
58 n6 op.cit., p.19.
59 C.F. Mason, 'A Survey of Mercury, Lead and Cadmium in Muscle of British Freshwater Fish', *Chemosphere*, 16, 1987, pp.901 – 6.
60 n59 op.cit.
61 n59 op.cit.
62 n12 op.cit., note 58, p.xxv.
63 'Rising trend in water pollution incidents accelerates', *ENDS*, 163, August 1988, p.6.
64 n12 op.cit., pp.xxv – xxvii.
65 *Torridge Report*, p.52, cited n21 op.cit., p.175.
66 P. Vallely, 'A deadly harvest of the land', *The Times*, 16 May 1989, p.15.
67 n12 op.cit., p.xxv – xxvii.
68 *Water Pollution from Farm Waste*, from Water Authorities Association, St Peter's House, Hartshead, Sheffield, 1988; cited in 'Legal clamp down on farm pollution approaches as incidents increase again', *ENDS*, 171, April 1989, p.7.
69 n68, *ENDS*, 171, op.cit.
70 n12 op.cit., p.xxvi.
71 n66 op.cit.
72 n68 op.cit.

73 Birch citing *Water Pollution from Farm Waste*, report by WAA/MAFF, 1986, p.23 n66 op.cit.
74 'Huge increase in Scottish farm pollution', *ENDS*, 163, August 1989, p.6.
75 R. Palmer and J. Rowland, 'Leaked: a history of spills', *Sunday Times*, 27 August 1989, p.A7.
76 M. Porter, 'Mersey spill damage "was avoidable"', *Sunday Telegraph*, 10 September 1989.
77 'Oil pollutes rivers', *Independent*, 11 August 1989.
78 P. Vallely, 'Raider blamed as oil pollutes river', *The Times*, 17 May 1989.
79 n12 op.cit., p.xxxiv.
80 A. Raphael, 'Poll charts tidal wave of disapproval for H2Owners ads.', *Observer*, 24 September 1989.
81 n15 op.cit.
82 J. Bowers, K. O'Donnell, S. Jay and L. Murphy, *Liquid Costs: An Assessment of the Environmental Costs of the Water Industry*, WWF and Media Natura, 1989.
83 BBC 'Panorama', *Tories – Friends of the Earth?*, Broadcast 14 November 1989.
84 Editorial, *Daily Telegraph Weekend Magazine*, 24 June 1989.
85 *Regional Trends 1988*, Central Statistical Office, HMSO, 1988, Table 5.12.
86 'Sewage prosecution', *The Times*, 18 July 1989.
87 A. Morgan and C. Seton, 'Water board defends effluent plant', *The Times*, 24 June 1989.
88 S. Barwick, 'Fish die as pig slurry poisons river', *Independent*, 31 July 1989.
89 'Water bosses who let sewage pour into rivers', *Sunday Times*, 12 March 1989, p.1.
90 ibid.
91 n6 op.cit.
92 G. Coster, 'Up the filthy river', *Telegraph Weekend Magazine*, 24 June 1989.
93 ibid.
94 A. Morgan, 'A toxic swirl that is the country's dirtiest river', *Sunday Correspondent*, 13 May 1990.
95 P. Valley, 'The poisonous hand of man', *The Times*, 15 May 1989, Spectrum, p.14.
96 F. Turner, 'Mere or mine?', *Guardian*, 31 August 1989.
97 M. Linton, 'Ridley derided over clean rivers claim', *Guardian*, 5 January 1988.
98 Granada TV, 'World in Action', *How Green is our Valley*, Broadcast 14 August 1989.
99 ibid.
100 M.J. Andrews, 'Thames Estuary: Pollution and Recovery', in P.J. Sheehan, D.R. Miller, G.C. Butler and Ph. Bourclean, Scope, *Effects of Pollutants at the Ecosystem level*', Wiley, 1984.
101 J. Renton, 'Water: quantity v quality', *Observer*, 30 July 1988, p.55.
102 C. Clover, 'River polluters warned of all-out attack', *Daily Telegraph*, 2 September 1989.
103 Mark Souster, 'Dirty river prosecutions "blocked" before sell-off', *The Times*, 27 November 1989.
104 A. Morgan and A. Gliniecki, 'Parasite threat to water supplies', *Sunday Correspondent*, 24 September 1989.
105 Paul Brown, 'Water firms escape weekend scrutiny', *Guardian*, 15 March 1990.
106 Caroline Lees and Richard Palmer, 'Battle to clean up Britain's dirty rivers "is being lost"', *Sunday Times*, 15 April 1990.

107 N. Haigh, *EEC Environmental Policy and Britain*, 2nd edn.,Longman, London, 1987.
108 n26 op.cit., p.12.
109 n107 op.cit., p.70.
110 n107 op.cit., p.55
111 n107 op.cit., p.89.
112 n107 op.cit., p.90.

Chapter 3
Tap Water: Nitrates, Lead and Aluminium

1   H. O'Shaughnessy and G. Lean, 'Britain to face new charges on dirty water', *Observer*, 24 September 1989.
2   G. Lean and F. Pearce, 'Your tap water pure or poisoned', *Observer Magazine*, 6 August 1989.
3   'Farms will poison more tapwater', *New Scientist*, 15 September 1988.
4   'Background to Nitrate Directive', *Waste Management Today*, 2(4), April 1989.
5   D. Wheeler, 'Water pollution and public health: A time to act', *Environmental Health*, 94 (8), 1987, pp. 201 – 3.
6   N. Haigh, *EEC Environmental Policy and Britain*, 2nd edn, Longman, 1988, p.49.
7   N. Dudley, *Nitrates in Food and Water*, London Food Commission,1986, cited in n 5 op.cit.
8   n4 op.cit.
9   n5 op.cit.
10 Letter from Sir Donald Acheson, Chief Medical Officer Department of Health, to Department of the Environment, 26 August 1988, reproduced as Annex II in n35 op.cit.
11 n4 op.cit. citing *Hansard*, HoC, Written Answers, 4 December 1985.
12 National Farmers' Union, *NFU Insight*, December 1987, NFU, London.
13 *Reasoned Opinion Addressed to the United Kingdom Pursuant to Article 169 of the EEC Treaty about the Failure to Transpose and the Failure to Apply Correctly the Council Directive 80/778/EEC on the Quality of Drinking Water.*
14 'New curbs on nitrate in drinking water held back by stalemate on farm payments', *ENDS*, 156, January 1988.
15 Ripa di Meana, *Reasoned Opinion Addressed to the United Kingdom pursuant to Article 169 of the EEC Treaty about the Failure to Apply Correctly the Council Directive 80/778/EECC on the Quality of Drinking water*, September 1989.
16 n13 op.cit.
17 J. Renton and H. O'Shaughnessy, 'Water: Quality control row threatens sale', *Observer*, 25 June 1989.
18 S. Gunn and P. Guildford, 'Britain faces action over nitrates in water', *The Times*, 20 July 1989.
19 C. Coughlin, 'Is our water really worse than theirs?' *Daily Telegraph*, 20 July 1989.
20 P. Pryke, 'Minister warns EEC not to prosecute on water', *Daily Telegraph*, 20 July 1989.
21 P. Brown, 'Water experts gagged over nitrate costs', *Guardian*, 20 July 1989.
22 'Court action against UK on drinking water may not be the last', *ENDS*, 176, September 1989.

23 M. Binyon, 'Patten meets EC on water purity', *The Times*, 19 September 1989.
24 'Green water', *The Times*, 17 August 1989.
25 M. McCarthy, 'Reservoir sealed after discovery of algae' *The Times*, 9 September 1989.
26 Mary Fagan, 'Rivers facing threat from algae caused by pollution', *Independent*, 3 March 1990.
27 Richard Palmer, 'Water company admits 1m drank contaminated supply', *Sunday Times*, 29 April 1990.
28 *Nature Conservancy Council Evidence to the House of Lords European Communities Committee Subcommittee D on Nitrates in Water*, Proposals for a Community Directive Concerning the Protection of Fresh, Coastal and Marine Waters against Pollution Caused by Nitrate from Diffuse Sources.
29 ibid.
30 ibid.
31 Insight, 'A nightmare called nitrates', *Sunday Times*, 5 March 1989.
32 'UK set to oppose EEC plans to curb nitrate contamination', *ENDS*, 170, March 1989.
33 n12 op.cit.
34 n28 op.cit.
35 *Memorandum from the Department of the Environment and the Ministry of Agriculture, Fisheries and Food April 1989. Submitted to House of Lords European Communities Committee Sub-committee D (Agriculture and Food) Nitrates in Water* (4136/9).
36 ibid.
37 ibid., S4.9.
38 Halcrow & Partners, *Assessment of Groundwater Quality in England and Wales*, HMSO, 1988, cited in *ENDS*, 167, December 1988, p.6.
39 S4.8, n35 op.cit.
40 'The grass could grow greener where nitrates pose a risk', *New Scientist*, 8 October 1989.
41 S4.6 – 4.7, n35 op.cit.
42 S6.4, n35 op.cit.
43 Nitrate Sensitive Areas Scheme (MAFF) cited in 'Pilot plans to curb nitrate leaching breach "polluter pays" principle', *ENDS*, 172, May 1989.
44 J. Erlichman, 'Farm drive to clean up water "flawed"', *Guardian* , 2 August 1989.
45 C. Clover, 'Nitrate cuts plan "will be costly failure"', *Daily Telegraph*, 2 August 1989.
46 S4.15, n35 op.cit.
47 S5.3, n35 op.cit.
48 S5.5, n35 op.cit.
49 n40 op.cit.
50 *The General Public's Attitude to Environmental Issues and the European Election*, November 1988, Research Study by MORI Conducted for Friends of the Earth, the Council for the Protection of Rural England, WWF and the International Institute for Environment and Development.
51 *Memorandum from the Department of the Environment and the Ministry of Agriculture, Fisheries and Food*, April 1989. Submitted to House of Lords European Communities Committee Sub-committee D (Agriculture and Food) Nitrates in Water (4136/9).
52 n14 op.cit.

53 n14 op.cit.
54 *A Report by the Nitrate Coordination Group*, Pollution Paper No.26, DoE Central Directorate of Environmental Protection, HMSO, 1986.
55 n4 op.cit.
56 n14 op.cit.
57 'Key study on nitrate controls', *ENDS*, 167, December 1988.
58 n57 op.cit.
59 n57 op.cit.
60 R.K. Byers and E.E. Lord, 'Late effects of lead poisoning on mental development', *American Journal of Diseases in Childhood*, 66, 1943, pp.471 – 494; cited in B. Price, 'Lead Astray', in E. Goldsmith and N. Hildyard, *Green Britain or Industrial Wasteland?* Polity Press, 1986.
61 B. Price, 'Pollution the invisible violence', in D. Wilson, *The Environmental Crisis*, Heinemann Educational, 1984.
62 n60 op.cit.
63 Robin Russel-Jones, 'Lead and health now . . . with special focus on lead in water', *CLEAR Newspaper*, September 1989.
64 *Lead in Drinking Water*, Pollution Paper No. 12, Department of the Environment/HMSO, 1977; cited in n60 op.cit.
65 n2 op.cit.
66 M.E. Moore, *Proceedings of the Symposium on Toxic Effects of Environmental Lead*, Conservation Society, 1979; and D. G. Wibberly *et al.*, *Journal of Medical Genetics*, 14, 1977, p.339, cited in n68 below.
67 n63 op.cit.
68 F. Pearce, *Acid Rain: What is it and What is it Doing to us?* Penguin, 1987; citing *European Community Screening Programme for Lead*: United Kingdom Results, DoE.
69 n4 op.cit., p.47.
70 *Lead in Drinking Water*, Water Research Centre, 1983; cited in n71 op.cit.
71 n13 op.cit.
72 n6 op.cit., p.44.
73 Parliamentary Answer, cited in n2 op.cit.
74 Bow Group Statement.
75 n63 op.cit.
76 n68 op.cit.
77 C. Randall, 'Aluminium keeps water clear', *Daily Telegraph*, 14 January 1989.
78 P. Gillman, 'Something in the water', *Sunday Times Magazine*, 18 June 1989.
79 E. Pilkington, 'Toxicity on tap', *Guardian*, 14 June 1989.
80 ibid.
81 ibid.
82 n78 op.cit.
83 n79 op.cit.
84 ibid.
85 n78 op.cit.
86 n79 op.cit.
87 ibid.
88 ibid.
89 n78 op.cit.
90 n78 op.cit.
91 n79 op.cit.
92 n78 op.cit.

93   ibid.
94   N. Hodgkinson and P. Gillman, 'Aluminium found in poison water victim', *Sunday Times*, 18 June 1989.
95   P. Stokes, 'Acid water supply "ecological disaster"', *Daily Telegraph*, 15 November 1988.
96   Andrew Morgan, 'Water poison "stays in victims"', *Sunday Correspondent*, 14 January 1990.
97   n79 op.cit.
98   J. Joyce and R. Palmer, 'Camelford authority pollutes Devon river', *Sunday Times*, 21 May 1989.
99   Eamonn Mallie and Geoffrey Lean, 'Poison spilt in Ulster tap supply', *Observer*, 18 June 1989.
100 Mark Ellis and Richard Palmer, 'Contaminated water cover-up', *Sunday Times*, 27 August 1989.
101 n94 op.cit.
102 n2 op.cit.
103 n2 op.cit.
104 Geoffrey Lean, 'Cancer fear in tapwater for 500,000', *Observer*, 7 January 1990.
105 B. Price, 'Pollution on tap', in E. Goldsmith and N. Hildyard, *Green Britain or Industrial Wasteland?*, Polity Press, 1986.
106 C. Clover, 'Cancer danger detected in London drinking water', *Daily Telegraph*, 27 October 1988.
107 J. Craig, 'Warning given on tapwater', *Sunday Times*, 8 November 1988.
108 n2 op.cit.
109 n22 op.cit.
110 ibid.
111 P. Ghazi, H. O'Shaughnessy and G. Lean, 'Patten's water deals break EC laws', *Observer*, 22 October 1989.
112 n2 op.cit.
113 J. Renton, 'Tories face water price revolt', *Observer*, 23 July 1989.
114 J. Young, 'Clean-up of water may cost an extra £14.5bn', *The Times*, 7 August 1989.
115 Leader, 'Private water, public costs', *Financial Times*, 3 August 1989.
116 n3 op.cit.
117 Michael Hornsby, 'Farming's nitrate nightmare', *The Times*, 11 December 1989.
118 Christopher Joyce, 'Lead poisoning "lasts beyond childhood"', *New Scientist*, 13 January 1990.
119 Jeremy Warner, 'Government drops £1 bn plan to replace lead pipes', *Independent*, 23 June 1990.
120 n111 op.cit.

Part II
Introduction
Air Pollution: Exhalations of Industry, Power and Transport

1   'Acid rain' can just be defined as unnaturally acid rain. Many scientists use the term 'wet deposition' which includes acid snow, mist and so on. But the damage done by 'wet deposition' and the action needed to stop it cannot be separated from other pollution. In a wider and more useful sense, acid rain refers to rainfall quality, gases and dry fallout (dry deposition). 'Wet deposi-

tion' predominates at long distances (for example, over 1,000 km), whereas dry fallout is most significant close to the source.

Chapter 4
Acid Rain: Power Stations and Air Pollution

1 P. Bassett and D. MacIntyre, 'Victim of nuclear fallout', *Sunday Correspondent*, 12 November 1989.
2 M. Tolba, UNEP executive director, 5 June 1983.
3 Leader, 'Good sense about acid', *Daily Telegraph*, 26 June 1984.
4 S. Oden, *The Acidification of the Air and Precipitation and its Consequences on the Natural Environment*, Swedish National Science Research Council, Ecology Committee, 1968.
5 SNSF, *Acid Precipitation – Effects on Forest and Fish, Research Report 1980*, Norwegian Ministry of the Environment, Oslo, 1980.
6 C.I. Rose, *Acid Rain: It's Happening Here*, Greenpeace, London, 1988.
7 N. Haigh, *The Overall European Scene* Conference on Desulphurisation in Coal Combustion Systems, Institution of Chemical Engineers, Conference at University of Sheffield, 19–21 April 1990.
8 Ivor Owen, 'Waldegrave defends acid rain decision', *Financial Times*, 12 January 1985.
9 A. Wellburn, *Air Pollution and Acid Rain: The Biological Impact*, Longman, 1988.
10 UK Terrestrial Effects Review Group, *First Report: The Effects of Acid Deposition on the Terrestrial Environment in the United Kingdom*, Prepared at the request of the DoE, HMSO, 1988.
11 *Memorandum from the Natural Environment Research Council, 16 March 1988, The House of Commons Environment Committee Inquiry (First Report) on Air Pollution*, Vol.II, HMSO, 270 – II.
12 UK Review Group on Acid Rain, *Second Report: Acid Deposition in the United Kingdom, DoE/Warren Spring Laboratory*, HMSO, 1987.
13 M. Kruse, H.M. ApSimon and J.N.B. Bell, *An Emissions Inventory for Ammonia Arising from Agriculture in Great Britain*, Imperial College Centre for Environmental Technology, 1986, cited in n12 op.cit.
14 n10 op.cit., p.43.
15 Data calculated from M. Ashmore, in *Workshop on Effects of Photoxidants*, ILV, 1984, ed. P.Grenfelt (Gotheburg), and M. Ashmore, *et al.*, 'The distribution of phytotoxic ozone in the British Isles', *Environmental Pollution (Series B)*, 1, 1980, pp. 1955–216 to construct figure in C. Rose and M. Neville, *Tree Dieback Survey: The Final Report*, FoE, London, 1985.
16 *Memorandum of Evidence by Warren Spring Laboratory, 28 March 1988, to the House of Commons Environment Committee Inquiry (First Report) on Air Pollution*, V.II, HMSO, 270 – II.
17 ibid.
18 E. Buijsman, J.F.M. Maas and W.A.H. Asman, 'Ammonia emissions in Europe', University of Utrecht, IMOU Report, R – 85 – 2, 1985; also n13 op.cit.
19 Photo-oxidant Review Group, cited by FoE in *The House of Commons Environment Committee Inquiry (First Report) on Air Pollution*, V.II, HMSO, 270 – II, p.441
20 C. Rose and C. Holman, *Stop Acid Rain*, Briefing from Friends of the Earth, 1984

21 *Memorandum by the Department of the Environment, 20 January 1988*, submitted to House of Commons Select Committee on the Environment, *First Report: Air Pollution*, HMSO, 270 – II, 1988.

22 *Memorandum Submitted in Evidence by the Norwegian Ministry of the Environment, 10 February 1988, House of Commons Environment Committee First Report: Air Pollution*, Vol.II, HMSO, 270 – II, 1988.

23 Cross examination of witnesses, n21 op.cit., para 30.

24 R.G. Derwent, 'The nitrogen budget for the UK and NW Europe', ETSU, R37, 1985.

25 A.E. Dingle, 'The monster nuisance of all: Landowners, alkali manufacturers and air pollution, 1828 – 64', pp.529 – 48, in R.M. Macleod, 'The Alkali Acts administration: The emergence of a civil scientist', *Victorian Studies*, IX, 1965, p.93.

26 ibid.

27 E. Ashby, 'The politics of noxious vapours', *Glass Technology*, 16, 1975, pp.60–7.

28 cited in F. Pearce, *Acid Rain: What is it, and What is it Doing to Us?*, Penguin, 1987.

29 n9 op.cit.

30 n29 op.cit.

31 see, for example, S.1.1, para 2, in UK Terrestrial Effects Review Group, *First Report: The Effects of Acid Deposition on the Terrestrial Environment in the United Kingdom*, prepared at the request of the DoE, HMSO, 1988.

32 J.L. Longhurst, 'The British flue gas desulphurisation programme', *Acid Magazine*, 8 September 1989.

33 D. Dear and C. Laird, 'In pursuit of acid rain', *New Scientist*, 22 November 1984.

34 Meteorological Office, Appendix 3, p.327, in *The House of Commons Environment Committee Inquiry (First Report) on Air Pollution*, V.II, HMSO, 270 – II.

35 S.J. Ormerod, S.J. Tyler and J.M.S. Lewis, 'Is the breeding distribution of Dippers influenced by stream acidity?', *Bird Study*, 32, 1985, pp.32–9.

36 F. Pearce, 'The menace of acid rain', *New Scientist*, 95, no.1318, 1982, pp.419–24.

37 CEGB document dated 1983 released by Royal Society, in press release 17 (83), 5 September 1983.

38 Armin Rosenkranz, 'The Stockholm Conference 1982', *Acid News*, 1, 1983, pp.4–8.

39 A. Tomforde, 'Britain criticised for thwarting acid rain curbs', *Guardian*, 26 June 1984.

40 One result of the 1970s East-West 'Helsinki Process' was a decision to cooperate on the environment. The UN ECE Convention gave form to initiatives begun by the OECD, the Nordic states and others to stem transboundary air pollution. The UN ECE is the only working body including East and West Europe, North America and the western USSR.

41 'Control by convention', in C. Rose, (ed.), *Acid Rain*, WWF Special Report No. 2, 1987, WWF International, Gland, 1196, Switzerland.

42 Giles Shaw in the House of Commons, July 1982, cited by S. Elsworth, *Acid Rain*, Pluto, 1984, p.59.

43 n38 op.cit.

44 n41 op.cit.

45   n39 op.cit.
46   n7 op.cit.
47   n30 op.cit.
48   S. Elsworth, *Acid Rain*, Pluto, 1984.
49   n30 op.cit., p.137.
50   S. Elsworth, 'Britain is buying time', *Acid News*, 5 October 1983.
51   ibid.
52   NCB Press Release, 5 September 1983.
53   G. Rosie, *Sunday Times*, 19 September 1984.
54   T.H. Davies *et al.*, 'Black acidic snow in the remote Scottish Highlands', *Nature*, 312, 1984, pp.58 – 61.
55   n30 op.cit., p.27.
56   n30 op.cit., p.137.
57   ibid.
58   R.W. Battarbee, *Lake Acidification in the United Kingdom 1800–1986*, ENSIS, London, 1988.
59   R.J. Flower and R.W. Battarbee, 'Diatom evidence for recent acidification of two Scottish lochs', *Nature*, 20, 1983, pp.130–3.
60   n38 op.cit.
61   'The Acid Test', Central Television, , 21 October 1986.
62   Rose, C. and Holman, C. *Stop Acid Rain*, Briefing from Friends of the Earth, 1984.
63   B. Silcock, *Sunday Times*, 18 March 1984, and letter to Steve Elsworth, 19 April 1984.
64   n62 op.cit.
65   Ian Hargreaves, 'EEC increases pressure on acid rain', *Financial Times*, 31 January 1984; citing 1981 Alkali and Clean Air Inspectorate Annual Report.
66   *Memorandum by the Central Electricity Generating Board, 21 May 1984, to the House of Commons Environment Committee, Report on Acid Rain*, HMSO, September 1984, para.9.
67   ibid., para.10.
68   n4 op.cit.
69   *Memorandum from the Department of the Environment, 11 June 1984, to the House of Commons Environment Committee, Report on Acid Rain*, HMSO, September 1984, para.2, p.76.
70   J. McCormick, *Acid Earth: The Global Threat of Acid Pollution*, Earthscan, IIED, 1985.
71   n69 op.cit.
72   N. Haigh, 'The overall European scene', Keynote Address, *Conference on Desulphurisation in Coal Combustion Systems*, organised by the Institution of Chemical Engineers, University of Sheffield, 19–21 April 1989.
73   J. Young, 'Appalled MPs demand pollution control', *The Times*, 7 September 1984.
74   R. Boston, 'Acid rain policy attacked', *Guardian*, 25 June 1984.
75   n72 op.cit.
76   n14 op.cit.
77   N. Haigh, 'The overall European scene', Keynote Address, *Conference on Desulphurisation in Coal Combustion Systems*, organised by the Institution of Chemical Engineers, University of Sheffield, 19–21 April 1989.
78   *Verbal Evidence from the Central Electricity Generating Board, 27 January 1988, to the House of Commons Environment Committee, First Report Air*

Pollution, V.II, HMSO, 2270 – II.

79 *ENDS* table reproduced in n77 op.cit.
80 'Greenhouse effect may reduce benefits of acid rain curbs', *ENDS*, 181, February 1990, pp.6 – 7.
81 'Foul called over retreat on desulphurisation programme', *ENDS*, 181, February 1990, p.6.
82 House of Commons, *Hansard*, 20 February 1990, col. 803.
83 'Policy changes likely on sulphur emissions', *Financial Times*, 7 February 1990.
84 Letter from D. Aspinwall, Department of the Environment, to Andrew Tickle, Greenpeace, dated 20 March 1990.
85 David Thomas, 'Battered by green issues', *Financial Times*, 29 March 1990, Section III.
86 ibid.
87 Nigel Haigh, 'UK obligations to reduce acid rain'; letter to the *Independent*, 20 February 1990.
88 Nicholas Schoon, 'Thatcher warning over quick response to "green" problems, *Independent*, 23 March 1990.
89 Margaret Thatcher interviewed by Michael Buerk, BBC 2, 'Nature', 1 March 1989.
90 n21 op.cit.
91 J. Nilsson, *Critical Loads for Sulphur and Nitrogen*, Nordic Council, Oslo, 1986.
92 ibid.
93 *Memorandum of Evidence by the Nature Conservancy Council, to the House of Commons Environment Committee Inquiry (First Report) on Air Pollution*, Vol. II, HMSO, 270 – II 1988.
94 *Memorandum by the World Wide Fund for Nature (Formerly World Wildlife Fund), submitted to the House of Commons Select Committee on the Environment, First Report: Air Pollution*, HMSO, 270 – II, 1988.
95 Leif Hallbacken and C.O. Tamm, 'Changes in soil acidity from 1927 to 1982–4 in the forest area of southwest Sweden', *Scandinavian Journal of Forest Research*, 1, 1986, pp.219–32.
96 n22 op.cit.
97 *Memorandum of Evidence by the Nature Conservancy Council, to the House of Commons Environment Committee Inquiry, First Report: Air Pollution*, V.II, HMSO, 270 – II.
98 n94 op.cit.
99 *UK Terrestrial Effects Review Group, First Report: The Effects of Acid Deposition on the Terrestrial Environment in the United Kingdom*, prepared at the request of the DoE, HMSO, 1988.
100 *Verbal Evidence from the Swedish, Norwegian and West German Governments 10 February 1988, to the House of Commons Environment Committee, First Report: Air Pollution*, V.II, HMSO, 270 – II.
101 F. Pearce, 'Unravelling a century of acid pollution', *New Scientist*, 25 September 1986, pp.23–4.
102 n38 op.cit.
103 *UK Acid Waters Review Group Second Report: Acidity in United Kingdom Freshwaters*, DoE, HMSO, December 1988.
104 n97 op.cit.
105 N. Dudley, *Cause for Concern: An Analysis of Air Pollution Damage and Natural Habitats*, FoE, 1989.

106 *The Plantlife Report*, Plantlife with Media Natura, London, 1989.
107 C.I. Rose and D.L. Hawksworth, 'Lichens recolonize in London's cleaner air', *Nature*, 1981.
108 n6 op.cit.
109 ibid.
110 I. Renberg, 'Acid rain and the flora of the Netherlands', in A. Markham and L. Blundell, *The Effects of Acid Rain and Air Pollution in Northern Europe*, FoE, 1987.
111 n22 op.cit.
112 S. Bjorklund, 'West German coal and lignite power stations come clean', *Acid Magazine*, 8 September 1989.
113 Memorandum by the Government of Sweden, in the *House of Commons Environment Committee First Report: Air Pollution*, Vol. II, HMSO, HC270 – II, 1988.
114 Catherine Mitchell and Jim Sweet, *Response to the DoE Consultation Paper on the Implementation of the Large Combustion Plants Directive*, (Earth Resources Research for Greenpeace), Greenpeace, 1989.
115 n77 op.cit., para.67.
116 ibid., para.85.

Chapter 5
Forest Decline

1 Information from foresters in the Black Forest at 1987 UN ECE Forest Assessment Training Course, pers. comm.
2 P. Schutt *et al., So Stirbt Der Wald (How the Forests Die)*, 4th edn, BVL, Munich, Vienna, Zurich.
3 K.A. Ling and M.R. Ashmore, Acid Rain and Trees, *Focus on Nature Conservation*, 19, Nature Conservancy Council, 1987.
4 Tickle, pers. comm.
5 *World Resources 1986: An Assessment of the Resource Base that Supports The Global Economy*, World Resources Institute and International Institute for Environment and Development with Basic Books Inc, 1986, NY.
6 n2 op.cit.
7 n3 op.cit.
8 n3 op.cit.
9 F. Pearce, *Acid Rain: What Is It, And What Is It Doing To Us?*, Penguin, 1987.
10 See for example, *Forests for Britain: The BANC Report*, 1987, Packard Publishing, 16 Lynch Down, Funtington, Chichester, W.Sussex PO18 9LR.
11 W.O. Binns and D.B. Redfern, *Acid Rain and Forest Decline*, Forestry Commission R & D Paper 131, Forestry Commission, 1983.
12 R.G. Pawsey, *Ash Dieback Survey*, Commonwealth Forestry Institute Occasional Paper No. 24, 1983.
13 Letter from Dr J.N. Gibbs to Professor Bengt Nilghard of Lund University, 1985.
14 Tickle, pers. comm., based on report by John Gibbs of the Forestry Commission at 1988 UK Status of Tree Health Survey meeting between DoE, Greenpeace and others, 1 February 1989.
15 C. Rose, *When the Bough Breaks*, Greenpeace, 1988.
16 *Acid Rain: Report of the House of Commons Select Committee on the Environment*, HMSO, 1984, 446 – I.

17 W.O. Binns and discussion in *The Report: The Acid Rain Inquiry*, Scottish Wildlife Trust, 1984.

18 W.O. Binns, *Coal and Energy Quarterly*, Summer Issue, 1984.

19 *Command 9397*, HMSO, 1984.

20 C.I. Rose and M. Neville, *The Final Report: Tree Dieback Survey*, Friends of the Earth, 1985.

21 ibid.

22 Letters from R.G. Pawsey; A.J. Grayson and H.G. Miller, *New Scientist*, 5 December 1985, p.69.

23 *Forest Health and Air Pollution*, Forestry Commission R & D Paper 147, HMSO, 1986.

24 1986 Report and Forestry Commission Press Release 42/86.

25 S. Power, K. Ling and M. Ashmore, *Native Trees and Air Pollution*, Report for the Nature Conservancy Council and Forestry Commission, Contract No. HF3 – 03 – 326, 1989.

26 n24 op.cit.

27 D. Lonsdale, cited in n9 op.cit.

28 n9 op.cit.

29 *Bulletin 74*.

30 Examination of Witnesses, 17 February 1988, *House of Commons Select Committee First Report on Air Pollution*, V.II, HMSO, 1988, 270 – II, pp.106–18.

31 ibid.

32 *Memorandum of Evidence by C.I. Rose for Greenpeace UK*, pp.333–53, *House of Commons Select Committee First Report on Air Pollution*, V.II, HMSO, 1988, 270 – II.

33 J.L. Innes and R.C. Boswell, 'Monitoring of Forest Condition in the United Kingdom, *Forestry Commission Bulletin 88*, Forestry Commission, 1988.

34 J.L. Innes and R.C. Boswell, *Forest Condition in 1989: Preliminary Results of the Monitoring Programme*, Forestry Commission Research Note 163, 1989.

35 n25 op.cit.

36 n25 op.cit.

37 *Forestry Commission Memorandum to the House of Commons Select Committee, First Report on Air Pollution*, V.II, HMSO, 1988, 270 – II, p.105.

38 n33 op.cit., p.54.

39 A. Tickle, *A Tree Survey of Southern England*, Greenpeace, 1988.

40 Judy Warschauer, 'Bucks trees ravaged by air pollution', *Bucks Free Press*, 25 November 1988.

41 P. Gerosa, 'Air Pollution and Trees', *Tree News*, (Tree Council Newsletter), May 1989.

42 C.I. Rose, (ed), *Acid Rain: Special Report No. 2*, WWF Intl, 1987.

43 *Sanasilva Report 1987*, available from Eidgenossiche Anstalt für das forstliche Versuchswesen, Bibliotek, 8903, Bern, CH.

44 W. Fluckiger, 'Investigation of Forest Decline in Beech Stands of the Swiss Cantons of Basle–Country, Basle–City, Argovie, Soleure, Berne, Zurich and Zoug, *Swiss Journal of Forestry*, 137, No.11, 1986.

45 D. Lonsdale, I.T. Hickman, Mobbs and R.W. Matthews, 'Beech health: shoot growth analysis reveals a decline across pollution gradients in southern Britain', *Naturwissenschaften*, in press.

46 n30 op.cit., p.118.

47 G.Taylor, M.C. Dobson and P.H. Freer-Smith, *Proceedings of the INRA/IUFRO*

Symposium Tree Physiology, Nancy, France, 25–30 September 1988.
48 D. Fowler, letter to Andy Tickle, Greenpeace.
49 R. Milne, 'Corrosive clouds choke Britain's forests', *New Scientist*, 17 March 1988, p.27.
50 J.A. Emberlein, 'Sulphur hexafluoride tracer experiment from a tall stack over complex topography in coastal area of Southern England', *Atmospheric Environment*, 15, (9), 1981, pp. 1523–30.
51 J. Elrichman, 'Acid mist blamed for tree damage', *Guardian*, 12 October 1989.
52 I. Birrell and R. Palmer, 'Acid rain pollution blamed on Europe', *Sunday Times*, 22 October 1989.
53 B. Ulrich, 'Interaction of indirect and direct effects of air pollutants in forests, in Tryoyaanowsky', 1984; cited in Clement, ed, *Air Pollution and Plants Proceedings of the 2nd European Conference on Chemistry and the Environment*, 21–24 May, Lindau, FRG, Verlagsgessellschaft.
54 n44 op.cit.
55 E. Arnold, 'Veranderingen in de Paddenstolen (Mycoflora)', *Wetenschappelijke Mededlingen KNNV*, March 1985.
56 P. Spinks, 'Fungus protects trees against acid rain', *The Times*, Science Report, 14 April 1984.
57 L.E. Liljelund, 'Effects of acidification on the flora and fauna of Sweden', 1986; cited in *The Effects of Acid Rain and Air Pollution in Northern Europe*, Proceedings of a Scientific Seminar organised by Friends of the Earth, January 1987.
58 UK Terrestrial Effects Review Group, *The Effects of Acid Deposition on the Terrestrial Environment in the United Kingdom, First Report*, prepared at the request of the DoE, HMSO, 1988, p.52.
59 ibid.
60 UN ECE, *ECE Critical Levels Workshop*, Bad Harzburg, FRG, 14–18 March 1988, Final Draft Report.
61 M.L. Williams, D.H.F. Atkins, J.S. Bower, G.W. Campbell, J.G. Irwin and D. Simpson, *A Preliminary Assessment of the Air Pollution Climate of the UK*, Warren Spring Laboratory/HMSO, 1989.
62 A. Tickle, *Margaret's Favourite Places*, Greenpeace, 1989.
63 Letter to Peter Melchett at Greenpeace from Margaret Thatcher, Prime Minister, 30 October 1989.

Chapter 6
Pollution from Traffic

1 prediction of 50 m cars.
2 *Transport Statistics 1975–1985*, Department of Transport and others cited by Greenpeace briefing document *Air Pollution from Cars*, Greenpeace, 1988.
3 M. Ferguson, C. Holman and M. Barrett, *Atmospheric Emissions from the Use of Transport in the United Kingdom. Volume One: Estimation of Current and Future Emissions*, WWF/Earth Resources Research, 1989.
4 n2 op.cit.
5 M. Walsh, statement at the Eurasap/transport and Road Research Laboratory, *Review Seminar on Pollutants from Motor Vehicles and their Effects*, TRRL, 16 October 1986.
6 M. Barrett, *Transport and Air Pollution*, 1988, A Discussion Paper for World Wildlife Fund (unpublished).

7   ibid.
8   C. Holman, *Particulate Pollution from Diesel Vehicles*, FoE, 1989.
9   C. Holman, Air *Pollution from Diesel Vehicles: A Friends of the Earth Report*, FoE, 1987.
10 ibid.
11 A. Markham, *The Perils of Vehicle Emissions*, FoE, 1987.
12 C. Holman in Media Natura report for Greenpeace, in press.
13 *The Green Effect on Company Cars: The 1990 Hertz Report*, Hertz, 1989.
14 N. Haigh, *EEC Environmental Policy and Britain*, 2nd edn, Longman, 1987, p.205.
15 n13 op.cit.
16 n8 op.cit.
17 n8 op.cit.
18 n8 op.cit.
19 Department of Transport, *Roads for Prosperity*, Command 693, HMSO, 1989.
20 n3 op.cit.
21 C. Holman, *Air Pollution and Health*, FoE, 1989.
22 n12 op.cit.
23 n12 op.cit.
24 Photochemical Oxidants Review Group Interim Report, *Ozone in the United Kingdom*, February 1987. Prepared at the request of the Department of the Environment.
25 *Britain Breaching EC Air Pollution Directive, Claims FoE*, FoE Press Release, 6 November 1989.
26 Cathy Read, 'Dangerous to breathe', *Observer*, Section 5, August 1989.
27 n25 op.cit.
28 Department of Transport, *Roads for Prosperity*, Command 693, HMSO, 1989.
29 *Hansard*, 7 December 1989.
30 M.J.H. Mogridge, *Jam Yesterday, Jam Today and Jam Tomorrow?*, Lecture, UCL, 17 October 1985,UCL.
31 *Roads to Ruin*, Council for the Protection of Rural England, The Environmental Council, FoE, Greenpeace, Ramblers' Association, Royal Society for Nature Conservation, Transport 2000, WWF, Youth Hostels Association.
32 John G.U. Adams, *London's Green Spaces: What are they Worth?*, London Wildlife Trust/FoE, 1989.
33 Mick Hamer, 'A concreting of the contours', *Observer Magazine*, 1989.
34 John Adams, *Transport Planning: Vision and Practice*, RKP, 1981, p.136.
35 Jeremy Vanke, pers. comm.
36 T. Grifin, (ed), *Regional Trends 23*, 1988 edn, HMSO, London, 1988.
37 Stephen Joseph, pers. comm.
38 R. Harris, 'Free market off the rails', *Sunday Times*, 9 July 1989.
39 A. Raphael, 'Parkinson leads London up a traffic cul-de-sac', *Observer*, Open Space, 17 December 1989.
40 M. Hamer, *Wheels Within Wheels*, FoE, 1974.
41 Stephen Joseph, pers. comm.
42 Maurice Weaver, 'Driving Britain to distraction', *Daily Telegraph*, 20 April 1989 and, Roland Gribben, 'Parkinson bows to pressure on £2bn road plans', *Daily Telegraph* 28 March 1990.
43 Leader, 'Transport strategy in a jam', *Sunday Times*, 2 July 1989.
44 Angela Lambert, 'The double-edged appeal of the car', *Daily Telegraph*, 10 June 1989.

45 David Black, 'Road tolls "essential to ease jams"', *Independent*, 22 March 1990.

46 n25 op.cit.

47 Transport 2000, *Feet First*, leaflet, 1988.

48 News in Focus, 'Breakdown, why Britain is grinding to a halt', *Sunday Times*, 28 August 1989.

49 David Nicholson-Lord and Nicholas Comfort, 'Transport in London: Confusion breeds a capital jam', *Independent on Sunday*, 1 April 1990.

50 n31 op.cit.

51 Michael Harrison, 'Passengers bear the strain of BR costs', *Independent*, 14 July, 1989.

52 pers. comm.

53 David Black, 'Call for rail links across London', *Independent*, 20 March 1990.

54 n53 op.cit.

55 Michael Smith, 'Cash blow to Jubilee line', *Guardian*, 20 March 1990.

56 Colin Speakman, 'Transport', *Environment Now*, November 1989, p.26.

57 European Cyclists' Federation, *Policy and Provision for Cyclists in Europe*, IVU-GmbH, Budesallee 129, 1000 Berlin, FRG.

58 Dick Murray, 'Blitz the bus lane motorists', *Evening Standard*, 6 April 1990; citing 'About Turn' report by London Regional Passengers' Committee.

59 ibid.

60 Roland Rudd, 'Good intentions, bad politics on the road to hell', *Sunday Correspondent*, 1 April 1990; citing study by TEST.

61 'World View', *Observer Magazine*, 15 April 1990.

62 M. Durham, 'Hell on Wheels', *Observer*, Section, 5 August 1989.

63 TEST (Transport and Environment Studies), *The Company Car Factor*, London Amenity and Transport Association, Tress House, 3 Stamford Street, London, SE1.

64 C. Clover, 'Taxing the polluter in your tank', *Daily Telegraph*, 12 June 1989.

65 David Black, 'Road tolls "essential" to ease jams', *Independent*, 22 March 1990; citing Paying for Progress, the Chartered Institute of Transport.

66 n60 op.cit.

Part III
Chapter 7
Burying Toxic Waste

1 Geoffrey Lean and Polly Ghazi, 'Britain's buried poison', *Observer Magazine*, and 'Revealed: 1,350 poison dumps threaten water', *Sunday Observer*, 4 February 1990.

2 Memorandum by Clayton Bostock Hill and Rigby Ltd, *Contaminated Land*, Appendix 38; House of Commons Environment Committee, *Second Report Toxic Waste*, Vol.III, HMSO, 22–111, 1989.

3 n6 op.cit., p.xvii.

4 n2 op.cit.

5 'Lead in London Soils and Vegetables: A Further Case Study', Association of Chief Environmental Health Officers and Public Analysts, *London Environment Supplement*, No.16, Winter 1987/8.

6 *House of Commons Environment Committee, First Report Contaminated Land*, HMSO, Vol.1, HoC 170–1.

7 n6 op.cit., p.xix.

8 *Environment Committee: Second Report, Toxic Waste*, HMSO, Vol.1, 22 – 1,

   1989, p.xxix.
9   n6 op.cit.
10 Graham Searle, 'The great green disaster', *Mail on Sunday*, 20 August 1989.
11 P.A. Johnston and R.L. Stringer, Greenpeace QMC Technical Note, *Contaminants in Marine Mammals from Liverpool Bay*, Greenpeace.
12 P.A. Johnston and R.L. Stringer, Greenpeace QMC Technical Note:8, *Halogenated Hydrocarbons and Mercury in Sediments from the Weston Canal, Merseyside*, Greenpeace.
13 Theodora E. Colborn *et al* (eds), *Great Lakes: Great Legacy?*, The Conservation Foundation/The Institute for Research on Public Policy, 1990.
14 ibid, p.173.
15 *Memorandum* (and verbal evidence) *Submitted by Dames & Moore International in Environment Committee Second Report, Toxic Waste*, Vol.II, 22 – II.
16 n1 op.cit.
17 *Environment Digest*, 12 May 1988.
18 *Department of the Environment, verbal evidence to House of Commons Environment Committee Second Report: Toxic Waste*, Vol.II, 22 – II, HMSO, 1989, p.35.
19 n8 op.cit.
20 n8 op.cit., p.xxviii.
21 n1 op.cit.
22 n8 op.cit.. p.xxviii.
23 n1 op.cit.
24 DoE , *Assessment of Groundwater Quality in England and Wales*, 1988; cited in n8 op.cit., p.xxix.
25 Steve Connor, 'Why Britain plays dustbin to Europe's poisons', *Daily Telegraph*, 26 June 1989.
26 David Thomas, 'Call to ban imports of waste for tips', *Financial Times*, 29 March 1990.
27 'Public rush to recycle', *Greengauge*, 12 January 1989.
28 n8 op.cit.
29 Memorandum (and verbal evidence, 30 November 1988) Submitted by Dames and Moore International (Dr Robert Holmes and Dr Alistair Clark) in *Environment Committee Second Report, Toxic Waste*, Vol. II, 22–11.
30 n8 op.cit.
31 n8 op.cit., Table 2, p.lxvi.
32 Memorandum (and verbal evidence, 13 December 1988) Submitted by Aspinall & Co Ltd in *Environment Committee Second Report, Toxic Waste*, Vol. II, 22 – 11.
33 n8 op.cit.
34 n8 op.cit., p.xxviii.
35 Sarah Boseley, 'The waste watchers', *Guardian*, 6 October 1989.
36 Andrew Morgan, 'Britain to curb toxic cargoes', *Sunday Correspondent*, 1 October 1989.
37 C. Clover, 'Registers to be drawn up on chemical waste sites', *Daily Telegraph*, 2 November 1989; and C. Clover, 'Recycling to be statutory post', *Daily Telegraph*, 3 November 1989.
38 Nicola Tyrer, 'Now who will recycle it for me?', *Daily Telegraph*, 6 November 1989.
39 Mike Flood, 'A visit to Gothenburg's Waste-to-Energy Plant', *Warmer Bulletin*,

22, Autumn 1989.

40 *Warmer Bulletin*, 22, Autumn 1989, p.14.
41 Roger Highfield, 'Power out of trash', *Daily Telegraph*, 30 October 1989.
42 Keith Richards, 'All gas and garbage', *New Scientist*, 3 June 1989.
43 n6 op.cit.
44 Andreas Grunig, talk to The Peat Conference, 16 December 1989, British Association of Nature Conservationists.
45 n8 op.cit., p.xxvii.
46 n35 op.cit.
47 n8 op.cit., p.ix.
48 n8 op.cit., p.ix

Chapter 8
Litter

1   R. Bedlow, 'Tourist chief attacks dirty streets', *Daily Telegraph*, 1988.
2   The Tidy Britain Group, *Annual Report, 1988–9*.
3   The Tidy Britain Group, *Clean Nineties*, Summer 1989.
4   Simon Jenkins, 'A clean fight to beat Britain's litter', *Sunday Times*, 10 September 1989.
5   Charles Knevitt and Sheila Gunn, 'Thatcher warning on litter', *The Times*, 19 January 1989.
6   Francis Rafferty, 'Cleaning "gimmicks" under fire', *Sunday Times*, 10 September 1989.
7   *Feet First: Putting People at the Centre of Planning*, Transport 2000, Table 2.2, 1989.
8   Deirdre Fernand and Richard Palmer, 'Streetwise initiatives change face of a city', *Sunday Times*, 14 May 1989.
9   ibid.
10 Richard Caseby, 'Litter-lout tide overwhelms the street sweeper', *Sunday Times*, 20 August 1989.
11 The Tidy Britain Group, *Annual Report 1988–9*.
12 Simon Jenkins, 'A clean fight to beat Britain's litter', *Sunday Times*, 17 September 1989.
13 Nick Nuttall, 'Britain bottom in waste recycling league', *The Times*, 16 September 1989.
14 Ian Birrell and Richard Palmer, 'Britain throws away millions in the dustbin', *Sunday Times*, 19 February 1989.
15 Jonathon Porritt, 'Back pedalling on recycling', *Sunday Telegraph*, 5 August 1989; and *FoE Recycling Directories, Daily Telegraph*/FoE.
16 n14 op.cit.
17 Charles Clover, '£43 m glass saving is cast aside', *Daily Telegraph*, 31 May 1989.
18 James Erlichman, 'Britain's rubbish recycling policies the worst in Europe, says survey', *Guardian*, 20 July 1989.
19 ibid.
20 ibid.
21 Charles Clover, 'Paper makers stuck in a glut', *Daily Telegraph*, 14 August 1989.
22 Lee Rodwell, 'Environmentalists turn to the bottle', *The Times*, 22 May 1989.
23 Giles Whitwell, 'What to do with plastic that will not go away', *Daily*

Telegraph, 18 September 1989.
24 *Recycling Facilities in Britain: A National Picture*, Press Release and Pack from FoE/*Daily Telegraph*, 28 December 1989.
25 Statement by David Heathcote-Amory Esq, MP, Parliamentary Under Secretary of State at the Department of the Environment, 28 December 1989.
26 Nicholas Schoon, 'Recycling city finds a future in the growth of its rubbish', *Independent*, 27 September 1989.
27 H. Aldersey-Williams, 'Weighing up the contents of our dustbins', *Independent*, 11 September 1989.
28 see for example the Pearce Report.
29 Stephen Castle, 'Whitehall drive for "green" paper folds', *Independent on Sunday*, 4 February 1990.
30 Anne Chick, *Anticipatory Design*, 1988.
31 Tim Hunkin, 'Things people throw away', *New Scientist*, 24–31 December 1988.
32 Alastair Hey and Geoffrey Wright, *Once is not enough*, FoE, 1989.
33 Franny Moyle, 'A battery of charges against baby power stations', *Guardian*, 10 November 1989.
34 ibid.

Chapter 9
The Hottest Dustbin in the World

1   James Cutler and Rob Edwards, *Britain's Nuclear Nightmare: The Shocking Truth Behind The Dangers Of Nuclear Power*, Sphere Books, 1988.
2   *Atlas of the Seas around the British Isles*, Directorate of Fisheries Research, Ministry of Agriculture, Fisheries and Food, 1981.
3   W.C. Camplin and M. Broomfield, *Collective Dose To The European Community From Nuclear Industry Effluents Discharged In 1978*, National Radiological Protection Board, 1983, cited in C. Caufield, *Multiple Exposures: Chronicles Of The Radiation Age*, Secker and Warburg, 1989.
4   n1 op.cit.
5   *The Tide Must Turn: The Pollution Of The North Sea*, Greenpeace, 198, p.20.
6   Paul Watts and Patrick Green, *Unacceptable Levels: A Report By Friends Of The Earth's Radiation Monitoring Unit Of The Sellafield Contamination Of The River Esk, Cumbria*, Foe, 1989.
7   n1 op.cit., p.90.
8   'Sellafield milk most radioactive', *The Times*, 24 April 1990.
9   Alexander Artley, 'Going from rad to worse', *The Spectator*, 6 May 1989.
10 n1 op.cit.
11 Paper given by John Dunster to the 1958 United Nations Conference in Geneva on 'Peaceful uses of atomic energy', quoted in James Cutler and Rob Edwards, *Britain's Nuclear Nightmare*, Sphere, 1978, p.78.
12 Peter Taylor, *The Case for the Cessation of Magnox Reprocessing with respect to BNFL, Sellafield*, Greenpeace Submission to the Paris Commission, June 1987; Special Report SP – 12.
13 ibid.
14 Walter C. Patterson, *Going Critical: An Unauthorised History of British Nuclear Power*, Paladin, 1985.
15 n12 op.cit.
16 ibid.

17 ibid.

18 James Cutler and Rob Edwards, *Britain's Nuclear Nightmare*, Sphere, 1978, p.87.

19 n12 op.cit.

20 ibid.

21 ibid.

22 Douglas Black, 'New evidence on childhood leukaemia and nuclear establishments', *British Medical Journal*, 7 March 1987.

23 ibid.

24 Nicholas Timmins, 'Leukaemia linked to atomic weapons bases', *Independent*, 3 September 1987.

25 P.J. Cook-Mozaffari, S.C. Darby, R. Doll, *et al.*, 'Geographical variation in mortality from leukaemia and other cancers in England and Wales in relation to proximity to nuclear installations 1969–1978', *British Journal of Cancer*, 59, 1989, pp.476 – 85.

26 Environment Digest, 12 May 1988, p.5.

27 Martin J. Gardner, *et al*, 'Results of Case-control Study of Leukaemia and Lymphoma among young people near Sellafield Nuclear Plant', *British Medical Journal*, 6722, Vol. 300, 1990, pp.423 – 8.

28 Helen Slingsby, 'Cancer slur blights Sellafield', *PR Week*, 22 February 1990, p.1.

29 Gordon MacKerron, 'The decommissioning of nuclear plant: timing, cost and regulation', *Energy Policy*, No.2, Vol.17, 1989, pp.103–15.

30 Jane Bird, 'Britain seeks nuclear waste from abroad', *Sunday Times*, 14 May 1989.

31 Frans Berkhout, Sonja Boehmer-Christiansen and Jim Skea, 'Deposits and repositories: electricity wastes in the UK and West Germany', *Energy Policy*, April 1989, pp.105–15.

32 Gordon MacKerron, 'The decommissioning of nuclear plant: timing, cost and regulation', *Energy Policy*, Vol.17, No.2, 1989, pp.103–15.

33 'Radioactive waste disposal sites chosen', *ENDS*, 170, 1989, p.9.

34 Chris Frizelle, 'A million years in the life of a waste site', *New Scientist*, 15 October 1988, pp.43–7.

35 C. Caufield, *Multiple Exposures: Chronicles of the Radiation Age*, Secker and Warburg, 1989.

36 Department of the Environment, verbal evidence to House of Commons Environment Committee, *Second Report: Toxic Waste*, Vol.II, 22–11, HMSO, 1989, p.35.

37 n35 op.cit., p.203; and n8 op.cit., p.175, citing Geoffrey Lean, *Observer*.

38 A. Morgan, 'A Chernobyl fallout to last 150 years', *Sunday Correspondent*, 28 January 1990.

39 n8 op.cit., p.176.

40 *Tenth Annual Report*, Paris Commission (London 1989).

Chapter 10
Pesticides

1 John Home-Robertson, MP, *Hansard*, House of Commons, 18 December 1979.

2 V. Thorpe and N. Dudley, 'Pall of Poison: The Spray Drift Problem', *The Soil Association*, 1984.

3 *Report and Proceedings of the Committee: Agriculture Committee Second*

Special Report, The Effects of Pesticides on Human Health, Volume 1, 1987, 379 – I, para 108.

4   Andrew Watterson, *Pesticide User's Health and Safety Handbook,* Gower Publications Company Ltd.

5   n2 op.cit., para 168, p.xxix. The chairman of the Agriculture Select Committee, Sir Richard Body, drafted the report *The Effects of Pesticides On Human Health* but lack of parliamentary time prevented the Committee from reaching the usual consensus on a final draft. Rather than make no report, the Committee divided and both the *Report of the Proceedings* and the *Minutes of Evidence* are a valuable source of information. Here, either volume may be referred to as the Body Report or as the Select Committee Report.

6   C. Rose, 'Pesticides: An Industry Out Of Control', in E. Goldsmith and N. Hildyard, *Green Britain or Industrial Wasteland?,* Polity Press, 1986.

7   ibid.

8   J. Watts, *An Investigation into the Use and Effects of Pesticides in the United Kingdom,* FoE, London, 1985.

9   n2 op.cit.

10 *BAA Annual Report,* 1987/8.

11 B.L. Hardwood, A. Lees and D. Buffin, 'Chemical Trespass – Whose Turn Next?', *Friends of the Earth's Second Incident Report,* FoE, London, 1987.

12 ibid.

13 n2 op.cit.

14 ibid.

15 R.S. Nicholason, *Report of the Association of Public Analysts,* 1983.

16 n6 op.cit.

17 *Report Of The Working Party On Pesticide Residues (1982–1985) – The Sixteenth Report of the Steering Group on Food Surveillance,* Food Surveillance Paper 16, HMSO.

18 *Memorandum Submitted By P.J. Snell, The London Food Commission, 12 June 1986: Agriculture Committee Second Special Report, The Effects Of Pesticides On Human Health,* Vol II, Minutes of Evidence, HMSO, 379 – II, 1987.

19 ibid.

20 n8 op.cit.

21 Oral Evidence, *Agriculture Committee Second Special Report, The Effects Of Pesticides On Human Health,* Vol II, Minutes of Evidence, HMSO, 379 – II, 1987, p.255.

22 n17 op.cit.

23 n3 op.cit., para 147.

24 *Memorandum Submitted By Friends Of The Earth, 15 May 1984: Agriculture Committee Second Special Report, The Effects Of Pesticides On Human Health,* Vol II, Minutes of Evidence, HMSO, 379 – II, 1987.

25 n3 op.cit.

26 n24 op.cit.

27 n24 op.cit.

28 n11 op.cit., p.13.

29 *Pesticides: Implementing Part III of the Food and Environment Protection Act 1985: Second Consultative Document on Pesticide Residues,* MAFF/Welsh Office Agricultural Department/DHSS, April 1988.

30 *Pesticide Residues In Food Worry Government Experts: Consumers At Risk,* FoE Press Release, 3 August 1988.

31 Minutes leaked to FoE but subsequently published as the Ministry of

Agriculture's *Pesticides Residues Report*, (n32 below).

32 Papers from Kew Public Records Office, MAFF Files 130/61, 130/58, 43/142.

33 *Pesticides News*, May 1989.

34 J. Sheail, *Pesticides And Nature Conservation: The British Experience 1950 – 1975*, Clarendon Press, 1985.

35 n24 op.cit.

36 Comment: 'American Honesty Shames Britain', *Sunday Times*, 3 September 1989.

37 C. Rose, 'Pesticide Controls', in E. Goldsmith and N. Hildyard, *Green Britain or Industrial Wasteland?*, Polity Press, 1986.

38 ibid.

39 M. Frankel, 'Environmental Secrecy: The Government's Record', p.333, cited in E. Goldsmith and N. Hildyard, *Green Britain or Industrial Wasteland?*, Polity Press, 1986.

40 N. Haigh, *EEC Environmental Policy And Britain*, Second Edition, Longman, 1987.

41 n3 op.cit., para 167.

42 n3 op.cit., para 169.

43 n3 op.cit., para 181.

44 n3 op.cit., para 188.

45 n3 op.cit., p.xxxxvii.

46 *Pesticide News*, January 1989.

47 n24 op.cit., para 39.

48 J. Erlichman, 'Six Weedkillers May Be Health Hazards', *Guardian*, 25 June 1989.

49 n24 op.cit., para 37.

50 Agriculture Committee Second Special Report, *The Effects of Pesticides on Human Health*, Vol.II, Minutes of Evidence, HMSO 379 – II, 1987, Q714, p.383.

51 n3 op.cit., p.xlvi Annex.

52 C. Rose, ed, *The First Incidents Report*, FoE, London, 1985.

53 E.J. Tait, 'Pest Control Decision Making On Brassica Crops', *Applied Biology*, 8, 1983, p.174, cited in n2 op.cit.

54 n3 op.cit., para 32.

55 n3 op.cit., para 34.

56 n3 op.cit., para 48.

57 n11 op.cit.

58 ns52 op.cit. and n11 op.cit.

59 n6 op.cit.

60 S. Law, 'Pesticides team up to damage birds', *New Scientist*, 21 October 1989, p.36.

61 ibid.

62 n46 op.cit.

63 P.R.F. Chanin and D.J. Jeffries, 'The decline of the otter *Lutra lutra L.* in Britain: an analysis of hunting records and discussion of causes', *Biol. J. Linn. Soc.*, 10, 1978, pp.305–28; cited in C.F. Mason, T.C. Ford and N.I. Last, 'Organochlorine residues in British otters' *Bull. Environ. Contam. and Toxicol.*, 36, 1986, pp.656–61.

64 C.F. Mason, T.C. Ford and N.I. Last, 'Organochlorine residues in British otters', *Bull. Environ. Contam. and Toxicol.*, 36, 1986, pp.656–61.

65 ibid.

66 *Memorandum by the Royal Society for the Protection of Birds to the House of Lords Select Committee on the European Communities; Amended Proposal For A Council Directive Concerning Limit Values For Discharges Of Aldrin, Dieldrin and Endrin Into The Aquatic Environment.*

67 RSPB citing I. Newton and M.B. Haas, 1984, in *The return of the sparrowhawk*, n66 op.cit.

68 E. MacDonald, 'Major toxin leak threat to water supply', *Observer*, 19 February 1989.

69 Letter from Andrew Lees to Lord Belstead, Minister of State for the Environment, 3 July 1987.

70 David Nicholson-Lord, 'Shell criticised over poisoned Cornish land', *Independent on Sunday*, 8 April 1990.

71 n46 op.cit.

72 *Pesticide News*, September 1988.

73 A. Lees and K. McVeigh, *An Investigation Of Pesticide Pollution In Drinking Water In England And Wales*, FoE, 1988.

74 ibid., pp.1 & 8.

75 n73 op.cit., p.10.

76 B.T. Croll, 'The Effects of Agricultural Use Of Herbicides On Fresh Waters', cited in J.F. de L.G. Solbe, ed, *Effects of Land Use on Freshwaters*, Water Research Centre, 1988, pp.201–9, cited in n73 op.cit., p.45.

77 S.C. Warren, *Conclusions of the Seminar on the EEC Directive 80/778 on the Quality of Water Intended for Human Consumption: Pesticides, European Institute of Water, Como*, 5/6 May 1988, cited in n73 op.cit., p.45.

78 British Geological Survey, *The Pollution Threat From Agricultural Pesticides And Industrial Solvents: A Comparative Review In Relation To British Aquifers*, Hydrogeological Research, Hydrogeological Report 87/2, Natural Environment Council, 1987, cited in n73, op.cit., p.44.

79 n73 op.cit., p.37.

80 n73 op.cit., p.v.

81 n73 op.cit., p.41.

82 n73 op.cit., p.v.

83 n73 op.cit., p.33.

84 n73 op.cit., p.iv.

85 n73 op.cit., p.vi.

86 n73 op.cit., p.40.

87 n73 op.cit., p.41.

88 n73 op.cit., p.60.

89 n73 op.cit., p.33.

90 n73 op.cit., p.33.

91 n73 op.cit., p.57.

92 n73 op.cit., p.80.

93 n73 op.cit., p.59.

94 *Pesticides In Tap Water: European Commission Starts Legal Action Against UK*, FoE Press Release, 20 January 1989.

95 *Pesticides In The South-East's Water Supplies*, FoE Press Release, 14 April 1989.

96 n73 op.cit., p.80.

97 *Pollution Paper*, 21, HMSO, 1983, cited by MAFF in *Memorandum Submitted by the Ministry Of Agriculture, Fisheries and Food*, 27 February 1986: *Agriculture Committee Second Special Report, The Effects of Pesticides on*

Human Health, Vol. II, Minutes of Evidence, HMSO, 1987, 379 – II.
98 ibid.
99 n33 op.cit.
100 *Environmentalists and Agrochemicals Industry Join Forces To Urge Improved Pesticide Control*, BAA/others Press Release, 7 August 1989.
101 Gordon Conway addressing Institute of Biology, 18 March 1988, *Pesticides News*, June 1988.
102 *FoE Demand Immediate Suspension of 'Older Pesticides'*, FoE Press Release 16 May 1989.
103 Briefing Sheet. *Pesticides,* FOE.
104 n3 op.cit., para 84.
105 n73 op.cit., p.135.

Chapter 11
The Global Atmosphere: The Greenhouse Effect and Ozone Depletion

1 Steve Elsworth, pers. comm.
2 J.C. Farman, G. Gardiner and J.D. Shanklin, 'Large losses of total ozone in Antarctica reveal seasonal CLOx/NOx interaction', *Nature*, 315, May 1985, pp.207–10.
3 EPA cited by FoE, in *Memorandum of Evidence to House of Commons Environment Committee*, 2 March 1988, p.170, *First Report Air Pollution*, Vol II, 270 – II, HMSO.
4 J. Gribbin, *The Hole in the Sky: Man's Threat to the Ozone Layer*, Corgi, 1988.
5 F.S. Rowland and M.J. Molina, 'Stratospheric sink for chlorofluorocarbons – Chlorine catalysed destruction of ozone', *Nature*, 249, 1974, pp.810–12.
6 n4 op.cit., p.52.
7 BAMA (British Aerosol Manufacturer's Association), pers. comm.
8 N. Haigh, *EEC Environmental Policy and Britain*, 2nd edn, Longman, 1987.
9 Kathy Johnston, *Into the Void? A Report on CFCs and the Ozone Layer*, FoE, 1987.
10 *The Global 2000 Report to the President: Entering the Twenty-first Century*, Pelican, 1982.
11 n9 op.cit.
12 n2 op.cit.
13 n9 op.cit.
14 n4 op.cit.
15 n8 op.cit.
16 n9 op.cit.
17 n4 op.cit.
18 n9 op.cit.
19 Farman quoted in *Guardian*, 7 August 1987; cited by Gribbin in n4 op.cit.
20 n4 op.cit.
21 Fiona Weir, *The Montreal Protocol: A Critique*, FoE, 1989.
22 I. Anderson, 'Halons hit new high over Antarctica', *New Scientist*, 20 May 1989, p.24.
23 Joe Farman, 'What hope for the ozone layer now?', *New Scientist*, 12 November 1987.
24 *Ozone Trends Review Panel Report*, NASA/UNEP, 1988.
25 J. Hoffman, (ed). *Future Concentrations of Stratospheric Chlorine and Bromine*, EPA, Washington (EPA 400/1 – 88/005).

26 n21 op.cit.

27 D.J. Hofman, *et al.*, 'Stratospheric clouds and ozone depletion in the Arctic during January 1989', *Nature*, 340, 1989, pp.117–21.

28 F. Pearce, *Turning up the Heat*, Paladin, 1989.

29 cited in Irving Mintzer, *A Matter of Degrees: The Potential for Controlling the Greenhouse Effect*, WRI, 1987, p.4.

30 J. Jaeger, ed, *Developing Policies for Responding to Climatic Change*, WC1P – I WMO/TD, N.225, WMO/UNEP, 1988.

31 Gammon cited in n28 op.cit., p.3 .

32 P.M. Kelly and J.H.W. Karas, *The greenhouse effect: overview and implications*, Paper presented at the FoE Clean Coal Conference, London, June 1988.

33 J. Hansen, *The Greenhouse Effect: Impacts on Current Global Temperature and Regional Heatwaves*, statement to the US House of Representatives and Senate, 23 June and 7 July 1988.

34 n28 op.cit.

35 *Intergovernment Panel on Climate Change Report* cited in J. Sinclair, 'Rising sea levels could affect 300 million', *New Scientist*, 20 January 1990.

36 J. Hecht, 'America in peril from the sea', *New Scientist*, 9 June 1988.

37 R.L. Peters and J.D.S. Darling, 'The Greenhouse Effect and Nature Reserves', *Biosphere*, Vol.35 (11), 1985, pp.707–17.

38 n28 op.cit.

39 G. Marland, *The Prospect of Solving the CO_2 Problem through Global Reforestation (TRO39)*, DoE, Washington, DC.

40 D. Lashof *et al.*, *Policy Options for Stabilising Global Climate*, Report to Congress, EPA, 1989.

41 ETSU contribution by Dr Currie to Downing Street Seminar, 26 April 1989, cited by *Energy Select Committee 6th Report*, V. I, 1988 – 9, p.xxvi.

42 DoE, *Digest of Environmental Protection and Water Statistics*, HMSO, 1989. (Each 44 tonnes of carbon dioxide contains 32 tonnes of oxygen and 12 tonnes of carbon)

43 Letter from Mr A.J. Grayson, Forestry Commission, to Dr J.H. Fenton, 1989, citing yield class 10 for mixed spruce and pine.

44 E. Goldsmith, pers. comm.

45 Adam Markham, 'The climate challenge', in *Climate Change WWF Special Report*, WWF Intl 11996, Gland, Switzerland.

46 n29 op.cit.

47 Watson cited in 'China attacks "unfair" ozone protocol', *New Scientist*, 20 May 1989, p.24.

48 n40 op.cit.

49 W. Bach, F. Krause and J. Koomey, *Energy Policy in the Greenhouse*, Vol One: *From Warming Fate to Warming Limit*, IPSEP/EEB, 1989.

50 Stephen Schneider, 'Climate-change scenarios for impact assessment', presented at *The Consequences of the Greenhouse Effect for Biological Diversity*, Conference, Washington DC, 4 – 6 October 1988, WWF.

51 R. Mott, pers. comm.

52 n28 op.cit., p.95.

53 Speech, 27 September 1988, to Royal Society in *Ground Truth: A Report on the Prime Minister's First Green Year*, Media Natura and British Association of Nature Conservationists; Media Natura, 45 Shelton Street, London WC2H 9HJ.

54 DoE Oral Evidence, p.184, *House of Lords Select Committee on Science and Technology (Sub Committee II), 18 May 1989 , 6th Report: Greenhouse Effect,*

V.II, HL 88 – II.

55 Nicholas Schoon, 'Nuclear power decline forecast', *Independent*, 17 November 1989.

56 Tom Wilkie, 'Government may drop action on greenhouse effect', *Independent*, 1989.

57 Ronald Gribben, 'MP's call for curbs to fight greenhouse effect is rejected', *Daily Telegraph*, 1989.

58 T. Heslop, pers. comm.

59 Geoffrey Lean and Jan Sinclair, 'UK hinders moves to halt global warming', *Observer*, 5 November 1989.

60 Collier quoted in C. Clover, 'Market forces fear over power policy', *Daily Telegraph*, 13 April 1989.

61 Speech by Margaret Thatcher at the opening of the Hadley Centre for Climate Prediction and Research, Bracknell, 1990.

62 Greenpeace Briefing, *100% Now Cut CFCs*, 1989, 12 pp. refs available from Greenpeace, 30–31 Islington Green, London, NI.

63 ibid.

64 ibid.

65 Charles Clover, 'Offer to recycle fridge gases', *Daily Telegraph*, 29 January 1990.

66 Richard Palmer, 'UK blocking chemical ban', *Sunday Times*, 10 December 1989.

67 CO_2 per capita figures: this calculation is based on figures given in Table 23.3, *World Resources 1988–89. An Assessment of the Resource Base that supports the Global Economy*, WRI/IEED/Basic Books Inc, NY/London, 1988, p.336.

68 Memorandum 1, Submitted by Association for the Conservation of Energy to *House of Commons Energy Select Committee, Vol.II, Memoranda of Evidence Sixth Report*, 192 – II, 1988 – 9.

69 ibid.

70 *Solving the Greenhouse Dilemma: A Strategy for the UK*, ACE/WWF, 1989.

71 Bill Keepin and Gregory Katz, 'Greenhouse warming: comparative analysis of nuclear and efficiency as abatement strategies', *Energy Policy*, December 1988, pp.538 – 61.

72 ibid.

73 Andrew Warren, 'The global forecast: getting warmer', *Financial Times*, 1989.

74 Stewart Boyle, 'Energy Conservation', in *Ground Truth: A Report on the Prime Minister's First Green Year*, BANC/Media Natura, 1989.

75 ibid.

76 Robin Oakley, 'Nuclear power is "greener" says Thatcher', *The Times*, 26 October 1988.

77 Editorial, 'Nuking the greenhouse', *New Scientist*, 5 November 1988.

78 n76 op.cit.

79 T. Jackson and S. Roberts, *Getting out of the Greenhouse: An Agenda for UK Action on Energy Policy*, FoE, London, 1988.

80 ibid.

81 'Sorry, ducks', *New Scientist*, 14 April 1990.

82 R.A. Houghton, *The flux of carbon dioxide between atmosphere and land use as a result of deforestation from 1850 to 2100*. In press.

83 Geoffrey Lean, 'British aid to Third World at record low', *Observer*, 29 May 1988 (citing OECD).

84 G.E. Thomas *et al.*, 'Relation between increasing methane and the presence of

ice clouds at the mesopause', *Nature*, V. 338, 1989, pp 117 – 21.

85 Memorandum 9, Submitted by Greenpeace, to *House of Commons Energy Select Committee VII, Memoranda of Evidence Sixth Report*, 192 – II, 1988 – 9.

86 Fred Pearce, 'Methane: the hidden greenhouse gas', *New Scientist*, 6 May 1989.

87 'Getting to grips with greenhouse gas emissions', *ENDS*, 179, December 1989, citing DoE estimates.

88 n85 op.cit. and n54 op.cit.

89 K. Richards, 'All gas and garbage', *New Scientist*, 3 June 1989.

90 Tom Wilkie, 'Government may drop action on greenhouse effect', *Independent*, 25 November 1989, p.2.

91 Speech by Carlo Ripo di Meana to the Club de Bruxelles; cited in *The UK Government's CO$_2$ Projections: A Labour Party Analysis*, from the office of Bryan Gould, MP.

92 Intergovernmental Panel on Climate Change, *Policymaker's Summary of the Scientific Assessment of Climate Change,* Report to IPCC from Working Group 1 (Third Draft 2 May 1990), prepared by the IPCC Group at the Meteorological Office, Bracknell, UK.

93 Department of Energy, *An Evaluation of Energy-related Greenhouse Gas Emissions and Measures to Ameliorate them*, Energy Paper No. 58, HMSO, October 1989.

94 Stewart Boyle, pers. comm.

95 n93 op.cit.

96 ibid.

97 CBI Preliminary observations on the Department of Energy's Report to the Intergovernmental Panel on Climatic Change, *An Evaluation of Energy – related Greenhouse Gas Emissions and measures to ameliorate them*, CA 36 90, undated.

98 File note, CBI, 10 January 1990.

99 P.M. Kelly, *Halting Global Warming*, Greepeace UK, 1990.

100 n92 op.cit.

101 Michael McCarthy, '£120 billion energy savings possible in Britain in 15 years', *The Times*, 25 May 1990; citing Gerald Leach and Zygfryd Nowak, *Cutting Carbon Dioxide Emissions from Poland and the United Kingdom*, Stockholm Environment Institute, Jarntorget 84, 10314 – Stockholm, Sweden.

102 Amory B. Lovins, 'Abatement at negative cost', *Acid News*, 2 March 1990.

103 David Olivier, 'A cool solution to global warming', *New Scientist*, 12 May 1990.

Chapter 12
Conclusions

1 Paul Brown, 'Whitehall group "rejects curbs on private cars"', *Guardian*, 19 April 1990.

2 Richard North, 'Delaying tactics earn Britain its "dirty" tag', *Independent*, 8 May 1990.

3 'Scientists to discuss acid rain project', *Financial Times*, 2 February 1984.

4 Oral Evidence by the Royal Society to the House of Lords Select Committee on Science and Technology (Sub committee 11), 6th Report: *Greenhouse Effect*, Vol. 11, HL 88 – 11.

5 'Protests over "league table" of crimes', *Independent*, 8 May 1990, p.9.

6 'Officially "clean" beaches are still unhealthy', *Environmental Health News*, 9

February 1990.

7 Peter Guilford, 'Harsh penalties curb river polluters', *The Times*, 13 June 1989.

8 'Concern grows over sheep dipping', *The Environment Digest*, 31 January 1990.

9 David Pearce, Anil Markandya and Edward B. Barbier, *Blueprint for a Green Economy*, Earthscan, 1989.

10 OECD, *Economic Instruments for Environmental Protection*, HMSO, 1989, cited in 'Environmental charges and taxes: A key international issue for 1990', *ENDS*, 179, December 1989.

11 Ingemar Leksell, 'Road traffic: far from paying its way', *Acid News*, 1 January 1990.

12 n10 op.cit.

13 Nicholas Schoon, 'Chancellor likely to heed pressure for green Budget', *Independent*, 19 March 1990.

14 Kevin Eason, 'Tax incentive demanded to reduce car pollution', *The Times*, 9 January 1990.

15 n13 op.cit.

16 Ian Morton, 'Company cars for all', *Evening Standard*, 6 April 1990.

17 Michael McCarthy, 'Green lobby condemns "missed opportunity"', *The Times*, 21 March 1990.

18 'Patten calls on UK industry to meet pollution challenge', *The Times*, 28 March 1990.

19 n10 op.cit.

20 Professor Tim O'Riordan, BBC Radio 4 interview, May 1990.

21 John Adams, *London's Green Spaces: What Are They Worth?* London Wildlife Trust/FoE, 1989.

22 D. Pearce, *Cost-Benefit Analysis*, Macmillan, 1971, cited in n21 op.cit.

23 Robin Grove-White, 'Fall-out from the nuclear debacle', *Daily Telegraph*, 25 November 1989.

24 Fred Hirsch, *Social Limits to Growth*, Routledge & Kegan Paul, 1977.

25 Peter Brimblecombe, *The Big Smoke: A History of Air Pollution in London since Medieval Times*, Routledge, 1984.

26 n23 op.cit.

27 Paul Abrahams, 'Chemicals 6: level playing field is necessary', *Financial Times*, VI 1989.

28 Nick Nuttall, 'Hundreds submit plans for environment-friendly power stations', *The Times*, 11 December 1989.

29 Nicholas Schoon, 'Use PWR cash to "save billions"', *Independent*, 20 November 1989.

30 'Energy Department admits 60% cuts possible', *The Environment Digest*, no.31, January 1990.

31 Mike Flood, 'Why renewable energy deserves better', *Warmer Bulletin*, Winter 1989, p.23.

32 Charles Clover, 'Supermarkets are pressed to boost recycling', *Daily Telegraph*, 20 November 1989.

33 'Newsprint recycling market crashes but brighter future ahead', *ENDS*, 180, January 1990, p.9.

34 Nick Nuttall, 'British scientists unveil biodegradable plastic', *The Times*, 21 October 1989.

35 'BMW: preparing the ground for the recyclable car', *ENDS*, 180, January 1990, pp.15–16.

36 Charles Clover, 'Thatcher stuck in a traffic jam', *Daily Telegraph*, 20 May 1989.

37 'Newsnight' Report, BBC 2, 8 February 1990.
38 Steve Elsworth, pers. comm.
39 'Sir Clive runs into Peugot's baby', *Greengauge*, 12 January 1990.
40 Nicholas Webster and Nicholas Faith, 'Preparing to pay the price of peace', *Independent on Sunday*, 13 May 1990.
41 Jeremy Rifkind, 'Put the "green dividend" to work on tomorrow', *International Herald Tribune*, 9 May 1990.
42 Hugo Young, *One of Us*, Macmillan, 1989, p.147.
43 'Business schools slow to act', *Greengauge*, 12 January 1990.
44 Charles Clover, 'Taxing the polluter in your tank', *Daily Telegraph*, 12 June 1989.
45 Philip Johnston, Charles Clover, *et al.*, 'Thatcher fears for future of the planet', *Daily Telegraph*, 28 September 1988.
46 Peregrine Worsthorne, 'Green is for Danger', *Sunday Telegraph*, 18 September 1988.
47 C.I. Rose (ed), *Ground Truth: A Report on the Prime Minister's First Green Year*, BANC/Media Natura, 1989.
48 n42 op.cit., p.147.
49 John Kenneth Galbraith, *The Age of Uncertainty*, BBC/André Deutsch, 1977; he cites J.M. Keynes, *The General Theory of Employment Interest and Money*, Harcourt, Brace & Co, New York, 1935.
50 n23 op.cit.
51 James Cutler and Rob Edwards, *Britain's Nuclear Nightmare: The Shocking Truth behind the Dangers of Nuclear Power*, Sphere Books, 1988.
52 Anne Spackman, 'Walker scorns MPs censure over Sellafield', *Sunday Times*, 16 March 1986.
53 'Nuclear privatisation U – turn: A Special Report', *The Environment Digest*, No.31, January 1990.
54 'The electricity act: A special report', *The Environment Digest*, September 1989.
55 ibid.
56 n36 op.cit.
57 Sir Hugh Rossi, 'Why we need a guardian of the environment', 2 May 1989.
58 Tom Burke, 'Leaders forced to heed the worried', *The Times*, 21 December 1989.
59 William Wilkinson, 'The Union of Hands and Hearts', Speech to the RSNC Conference, Nottingham, 21 April 1990.

Postscript

In June 1990, 58 countries met in London and agreed to strengthen the Montreal Protocol, adopting a 50 per cent reduction in consumption of CFCs by 1995 (on 1987 levels), 85 per cent by 1997 and 100 per cent by 2000. Halons will be cut 50 per cent by 1995 and phased out by 2000, excepting the many 'essential' uses. Despite an ICI position that methyl chloroform should not be phased out until 'towards the middle of the next century', it was agreed to ban it from 2005 with a 70 per cent cut in 1989 consumption by 2000. The new agreement still allows atmospheric chlorine to rise 15 per cent by 2000.

At the same time a study for the Department of Trade and Industry showed that Britain could phase out CFCs by 1997 'at relatively low costs', although not without government intervention.

Index

Figures in **bold** type refer to chapters, or significant passages

Photochemical-Oxidant Review Group 121, 179
Pilkington, Edward 100, 101, 102
Pipeline Inspectorate 62
plants & acid rain 140–1, 142
plastic 212, 309
plutonium 3, 217, 219, 220, 222, 227
poliomyelitis 14, 18
pollution incidents **59–62, 241–46**
Pollution, Her Majesty's Inspectorate of (HMIP)
    52, 71, 142, 197, 205, 289
Porritt, Jonathon 6, 211, 312
Porter, Lady 210
Power, Sally 155, 158, 159
PowerGen 133, 134, 135
precautionary principle 25, 29, 35, 93, 281
Prince of Wales, HRH 5, 139, 271
privatisation of water 42, 52, 61, 64–5, 71, 84,
    107, 306
product design 213–15
propazine 107, 263
Public Health Laboratory Service (PHLS) 20, 21
public transport 308–10
Puhe, Dr Joachim 150

radioactive discharges 39, **216–228**
radon 227
railways 185, **188–90**
Ravenglass Estuary 217, 218, 222
Reagan, Ronald 269
recycling 211–13, 214, 308
refrigerators 213, 284, 286, 295
"relaxed consents" 49, 51, 52, 54, 65, 69
reservoirs 86–7
respiratory diseases 177, 179, 180
Rhine Action Plan 301
Richards, Keith 206, 288
Ridley, Nicholas 5, 17, 18, 28, 41, 42, 51, 52, 57,
    64, 69, 107, 173, 185, 186, 213, 287, 306
Riley, Peter 67, 68, 248
Ripo di Meana, Carlo 11, 40, 82, 83, 108
rivers **47–75**; River Authorities 47; solutions to
    pollution 92–5; river surveys 54–5
Rivers: Arrow 68; Avon **67–8**; Bourne 247;
    Clyde 24, 26; Cammdwr 123; Erewash
    198; Esk 123, 217; Forth 29, 33; Frome
    249; Great Eau 87; Humber 2, 26, 29; Lyd
    62; Mersey 22, 26, **33–5**, 42, 50, 57, 62, 307;
    Mole 248; Newlyn 251; Ouse 1, 2; Roding
    231; Rother **66–7**, 249; Severn 65, 308;
    Solway 123; Stour 65; Tamar 62; Tay 87;
    Tees 36; Thames 13, 22, 26, 29, 33, 41,
    43–4, **69–70**; Torridge 55–6, 60; Trent 2,
    62; Twyi 123; Tyne 29; Wey 249; Wye
    87
road policy **182–87**, 192
Robens Institute 16, 19, 71, 241
Roberts, Simon 214, 287
Roe, Dr F.J.C. 239
Rossi, Sir Hugh 40, 131, 156, 157, 165, 197, 207,
    319

Rowland, Sherry 267, 268
Royal Commission on Environmental Pollution
    19, 78, 96, 174, 225, 258
Royal Society 85, 126, 299
Royal Society for the Protection of Birds (RSPB)
    127, 140, 148, 236, 248, 249
Rugby sewage works 68

salmon 44, 69, 73, 123
salmonella 20
"Salter's Duck" 288, 308
Scandinavia *see* Denmark, Norway, Sweden
Schneider, Stephen 280
Schutt, Professor Peter 145, 151
Scotland 61, 96, 97, 127, 136; lochs 87, 139,
    140; Scottish River Purification Boards 62;
    Scottish Universities Reactor Centre 217;
    Scottish Wildlife Trust 127, 150
Scriven, Ron 127
sea: levels 276; pollution **12–40**; EC directives
    on 73; *see also* bathing beaches, Irish Sea,
    North Sea
Seaforth 36
Seascale 217, 222
secrecy *see* information, freedom of
Sellafield 3, 10, **216–28**, 316
sewage: in sea **12–40**, 298; in rivers 41–63
    passim, **49–50**, 65; on soil 197
Shaw, Giles 124
Sheffield 190, 203, 206, 210, 212
Shell Company 62, 251
shellfish 20, 221; Directive on 73
Shipley Europe Ltd 62
silage 60, 61
simazine 107, 252, 253, 254, 256, 263
Skeffington, Dr R.A. 150
Skelmersdale, Lord 250
sludge *see* sewage
slurry 61, 65
Smith, Angus 122
Snowdonia 139, 142, 152
Society of Motor Manufacturers and Traders
    (SMMT) 172, 173
Spain 77, 191, 257, 300
spillage: of oil 37; of chemicals 38–9
Stavely Chemicals 66
Sterling Organics 35, 36
Stockholm Conferences: on Acidification 124,
    148; on the Environment 117
straw burning 298
sulphur 1, 2; sulphur dioxide 118, 120, 123,
    129, 134–6, 159, 166, 170, 178, 296
Surface Water Acidification Project (SWAP) 126,
    299
Sweden 31, 102, 117–8, 124, 141, 142, 165, 182,
    206, 239; transport in 191, 192, 303
Switzerland 61, 182, 207, 212, 215, 257; forests
    145, 162, 165; transport 172, 191, 303, 305

tall stack policy 1, 113